THE GRIFTER'S RAZOR

THE GRIFTER'S RAZOR

NDUBICHI

Published in the United Kingdom by Red Sargon Publishing

ISBN: 978-1-7397724-0-6

Cover photo credit: Canva Inc
Cover art designer: Ndubichi Okezue

STAY UP TO DATE

If you would like to be notified when new novels are released, and interact with me on a personal basis, please follow: www.facebook.com/groups/ndubichi

To get exclusive content when they are made available, please kindly visit my blog and sign up to my **VIP mailing list** at https://ndubichi.blogspot.com

AUTHOR'S NOTE

The inspiration to pen this novel came to me in the early 2000s. At that time, one of the most interesting real-life crimes reported in the media was the gigantic Banco Noroeste scam in which a group of Nigerian con artists managed to deceive Nelson Sakaguchi, a São Paulo-based Japanese bank director, into investing hundreds of millions of dollars in a non-existent contract for a new international airport in the Nigerian capital city of Abuja.

The ringleader of the swindlers, impersonating the then Nigerian Central Bank Governor, Paul Ogwuma, had promised Sakaguchi a personal commission of $10 million in exchange for the investment. Authentic-looking false documents produced by the swindlers played a role in convincing the Japanese banker that the deal on offer was real.

So, between 1995 and 1998, Sakaguchi used his position as the Head of International Finance in Banco Noroeste to transfer $242 million of the Brazilian bank's money illegally to accounts in Switzerland and the Cayman Islands operated by the swindlers. The scam was discovered only after the Spanish-owned Banco Santander began to make moves to acquire the Brazilian bank. This discovery led to the arrest of Sakaguchi and the Nigerian fraudsters in 2002 and 2004, respectively. Sakaguchi would be tried and jailed in Switzerland while his swindler-associates would suffer the same fate in Nigeria.

After Nick Leeson's trading losses at Barings Bank, and the looting of the Iraqi Central Bank by Qusay Hussein (Saddam's son), the Banco Noreste scam has been rated as the third largest crime in banking history.

Interestingly, the Brazilian bank scam, and several others similar to it, occurred during Nigeria's pre-internet era. Before internet became widespread, in period between the mid-1980s and the late 1990s, Nigerian fraudsters had to make use of the fine technologies of the day— telex, fax, telephone and the conventional postal system— to communicate and organize face-to-face meetings with their potential foreign victims.

The plot of this crime novel is set in the early 1990s, when Nigeria was still under the yoke of military dictatorships and long before the advent of internet-based Nigerian scams. I hope you, my readers, will enjoy it, and leave an honest review on the website of the book retailer from which you purchased it.

DEDICATION

For the Okezue family

LAW ENFORCEMENT AGENCIES MENTIONED IN THE NOVEL

You may skip over this section of the book to read the novel without loss of enjoyment. Alternatively, you can use it as reference material, especially for Nigerian agencies. The choice is entirely yours.

FOREIGN AGENCIES:

Federal Bureau of Investigation (FBI):

The main federal law enforcement organ in the United States, combining the duties of a police force with that of a domestic (counter-espionage) intelligence service

London Metropolitan Police (a.k.a "Scotland Yard"):

The Metropolitan Police is the organization responsible for enforcing the law in 32 of the 33 districts that constitute Greater London in United Kingdom. Its headquarters is known as Scotland Yard.

Suffolk Constabulary:

The police organ for law enforcement within the English county of Suffolk in the United Kingdom

Royal Cayman Islands Police Service (RCIPS):

The police organ responsible for maintaining law and order on the Cayman Islands. In the novel, this organisation is referred to as the Royal Cayman Islands Police Force (RCIPF)

Jamaican Constabulary Force (JCF):

The national police force of Jamaica

NIGERIAN AGENCIES:

National Drug Law Enforcement Agency (NDLEA):

A Nigerian government agency charged with combating drug trafficking across the country. The NDLEA is distinct from the Nigerian Police Force.

Federal Road Safety Commission (FRSC):

A government agency charged with enforcing traffic laws on federal motorways across Nigeria. The FRSC is distinct from the Nigerian Police Force

Nigeria Police Force (a.k.a "The Force"):
Nigeria's largest law enforcement agency with a very complicated organogram. This highly centralized agency has branches called "State Police Commands" in all 36 states that make up the Nigerian Federation. Each State Police Command is led by a Commissioner of Police (CP). Overlaying the 36 State Police Commands are 12 Zonal Commands, each led by an Assistant Inspector-General of Police (AIG). A Zonal Command can be defined as a grouping of two or three adjacent State Police Commands. One example of a zonal command is *Police Zone Two*, which is mentioned in the novel.

Force Headquarters (located in North-Central Nigeria):
Officially known as **Louis Edet House**, Force Headquarters is a sprawling high-rise building in Abuja City, serving as the managerial and administrative centre of the Nigerian Police Force. The Inspector-General of Police (IG) and seven Deputy Inspector-Generals of Police (DIGs)—the senior management team of the Nigerian Police Force—operate out of the building.

Lagos State Police Command (located in Western Nigeria):
This branch of the Nigerian police enforces the law in Lagos. It is subdivided into 14 Area Commands. In total, the branch operates 107 police stations. The Lagos State Criminal Investigation Department (LSCID) comes under its authority. The fictional Lagos State Criminal Investigation Division (a.k.a "Ikeja CID") in the novel is based on the very much real LSCID.

Ogun State Police Command (located in Western Nigeria):
This Nigerian police branch handles law enforcement in Ogun State, which borders Lagos State to the south. Ogun State Criminal Investigation Department comes under its authority.

Police Zone Two (located in Western Nigeria):
This Zonal Command consists of Lagos and Ogun State Police Commands. It is led by an Assistant Inspector-General of Police (AIG) who exercises oversight over the activities of the Lagos State Police Commissioner and his/her counterpart in Ogun State.

Enugu State Police Command (located in Eastern Nigeria):
This branch of the Nigerian Police in Enugu State is subdivided into five Area Commands. The Enugu State Criminal Investigation Department comes under its authority.

Onitsha Area Command (located in Eastern Nigeria):
This is the main law enforcement entity in the bustling commercial city of Onitsha. It is the largest of the three Area Commands that constitute the Anambra State Police Command.

Onitsha Marine Police (located in Eastern Nigeria):
A branch of the Nigerian Police Force in-charge of patrolling the waterways of Onitsha city with speedboats. Onitsha Marine Police is organizationally separate from Anambra State Police Command. Nevertheless, its leadership reports to the head of the Anambra State Police Command (i.e. Anambra Commissioner of Police).

Federal Investigation and Intelligence Bureau (FIIB):
The FIIB was the intelligence arm of the Nigeria Police Force with branches across the country. It was headed by a Deputy-Inspector General of Police (DIG) based in the federal city of Abuja.

X-Squad:
A special investigative unit charged with combating corruption among police officers. The FIIB had oversight of all X-squad units scattered across the thirty-six states of the federation. The author of this novel invented the fictional Anti-Police Corruption Squad (APCS) to act as a foil to the very much real (and highly ineffective) X-squad.

Mobile Police (MOPOL):
MOPOL is the paramilitary arm of the Nigerian Police Force charged with putting down riots, insurrections and other incidents of civil disturbance across the country. They also perform guard duties for senior police officers, federal government officials, and foreign diplomats.

PROLOGUE

AUGUST 1975

EASTERN NIGERIA

It was a hot Saturday afternoon throughout the East Central State and even hotter in the semi-arid dusty swathe of land that formed the state's frontier with the neighbouring Benue-Plateau State.

Back in May 1967, in the run-up to the civil war, the dispute over status of the arid terrain was symbolic of the larger conflict between the national government and the then separatist Eastern Region.

To the Easterners, especially the ethnic Igbos, the frontier was the international border that demarcated their secessionist nation—the Republic of Biafra—from the Nigerian Federation. Their bid for self-determination following the massacre of their kith and kin resident in the northern part of the country had the sympathy of Charles de Gaulle's France, The Vatican, Portugal, Israel, Spain and a sprinkling of African and Caribbean countries.

To Nigeria's Northern-dominated federal military government, the frontier represented an internal boundary separating two administrative regions within the same "indivisible" country. The Biafrans were separatist rebels to be whipped back into line "within two weeks of police action". On their side were the United Kingdom, Soviet Union and many other countries in the world. The United States of America was too busy with the Vietnam War to develop a coherent policy over the brewing African conflict.

So, it was not surprising that the rugged area was the scene of the first shots that opened the civil war in July 1967. The war lasted almost three years and ended with the defeat and demise of Biafra. Over two million lives were lost. To ensure that the defunct Biafran Republic stayed that way forever, her vast territory was split into three smaller and weaker Nigerian provinces— the East Central, Southeast and Rivers States.

The cessation of hostilities on 15th January 1970 brought demilitarisation to the dusty frontier that once hosted two opposing armies during the thirty-month conflict.

But that Saturday afternoon in August 1975, something spectacular happened. For the first time since the war ended, two military vehicles— an olive-green open-air army jeep and a Bedford truck painted in camouflage livery — bowled into the dusty frontier. When the vehicles halted, ten soldiers dressed in desert fatigues disembarked from the truck's rear. Kalashnikov rifles dangled from straps slung over their shoulders. Five men in handcuffs were dragged out from the bed of the truck and propelled to wooden stakes erected twenty-feet away.

The door of the dusty army jeep flung open and a young man dressed in the starched khaki green uniform of a Nigerian Army captain emerged, carrying a swagger stick.

As three soldiers tied the handcuffed men to the wooden stakes, a Sergeant gestured to the remaining troops. They took several steps backwards before bunching together to form a firing squad twenty-five feet from the wooden stakes.

The Captain threw a careless glance at the dishevelled convicts. His lips twitched in amusement as he tucked the swagger stick under his left armpit.

After trussing up the convicts, the three soldiers tugged on the ropes to ensure that there were no slacks before withdrawing from firing range.

The Captain fished out a folded piece of paper from his breast pocket and pushed back the peaked cap perching tenaciously on his head. Turning to the men tied to the stakes, he unfolded the paper and started reading loudly from it. Calling their names one by one, he declared, 'you have been found guilty of one thousand seven hundred counts of armed robbery by the military tribunal and are hereby sentenced to be shot by firing squad. May God have mercy on your souls.'

He crumpled the piece of paper and dropped it on the dust. Surveying the ashen faces at the stakes, he laughed sadistically. 'You have three minutes left, any last words; maybe an apology to the families of your victims.'

One of the convicts burst into tears. 'I don't want to die!' he cried as his trousers rapidly soaked in the urine that was then seen streaming down slowly from his legs to the sand at the foot of the stake.

The other condemned convicts flinched in disgust before barking at him to stop bawling. They were terrified too, but also determined to maintain the façade of defiance in the face of death. It was better than squealing all the way to eternity.

The Captain stood there stunned in disbelief. These armed robbers were not as tough as the media had hyped, he thought. He stared at the puddle of urine for a couple of seconds and shifted his gaze to the face of the convict weeping. 'Ah, Mister Tunde Olukemi, you know what they say,' he began, removing the swagger stick from under his armpit. 'A coward dies several times before the real thing hits him.'

He moved closer to the firing squad and raised his swagger stick as he had done in previous executions. The soldiers cocked their rifles and aimed at the condemned men. More urine streamed down Tunde's legs, swelling the size of the puddle in the dust.

The Captain smiled and was about to give the order when an army Land Rover drove into the execution ground at break-neck speed. Its tyres screeched to a halt, throwing up a dust haze that temporarily blinded everyone outside the vehicle. As the haze cleared, the outline of a middle-aged man in the uniform of a Brigadier emerged.

The Captain recognized him and promptly threw his right hand up to his forehead in salutation. The left arm holding the swagger stick fell to his side. 'Sir,

I didn't know you were coming,' he said apologetically, sensing something ominous about the senior officer's visit.

'It's alright Captain. Read this,' the Brigadier replied impatiently, thrusting a piece of folded paper in his face.

The Captain gently received it and unfolded it with trepidation. This was the second time top military brass had interrupted the process of execution. He had no illusions about what the note contained. The white sheet in his hand had the letterhead of the federal military government on it. He scanned the typed contents of the note quickly and grimaced when he had finished. Turning to the men at the stakes, he read it aloud. 'Misters Eugene Igolo, John Nwosu, Tunde Olukemi, Moses Adrika and Adamu Esan,' he paused and observed the hopeful looks on their faces. No doubt, they were obviously expecting good news. His gaze reverted to the paper before him.

'The state governor has considered your pleas for clemency. Your death sentences have been commuted to fifteen years imprisonment each.'

Shaking his head despondently, the Captain folded the paper and returned it to the Brigadier. A couple of inches behind him, the Sergeant looked on glumly.

Shortly after the Brigadier departed in the Land Rover, the condemned men began to whoop with laughter.

The Captain watched them silently, angry thoughts crowding his mind. The homicidal bastards before him were on the brink of getting away with armed robbery. Fifteen years? Was that a bloody joke?

The Sergeant barked an order to members of the firing squad, and the Kalashnikovs fell to their sides instantly...

PART ONE

CHAPTER 1

LAGOS, WESTERN NIGERIA

The landing gear of the Boeing 747 British Airways plane touched down at Murtala Mohammed International Airport and taxied along the tarmac. At exactly 2.30 PM local time, it halted.

Among the jet-lagged passengers alighting from the plane was a grey-haired American dressed in a white safari suit with a beige Stetson hat to match. As he stepped onto the pavement from the mobile stairway, he pushed back the brim of his hat and the tropical sun hit his pale face. He smiled. The weather could not have been better for business.

Passing through passport control was a matter of minutes. Nigerian immigration officials did not fuss over American passports. Soon, he was in the arrivals concourse facing a man dressed in a brown safari suit carrying an A5-sized white cardboard paper with the name GARY LOGAN written boldly on it. The American approached the wiry, intensely dark-skinned man smiling. 'Hi, I'm Logan, pleased to meet you,' he said, extending his right arm for a handshake.

The man in safari suit smiled back and shook the proffered hand. 'My name is Stephen Obi. Welcome to Nigeria.'

Gary nodded slowly as the man took his travelling bag and headed for the exit. The car park hosted rows and columns of exquisite saloon cars. Stephen led the way through the rows, and then halted before a gleaming black Mercedes Benz 500 SEL. The rear passenger door opened and Logan got in as Stephen took the luggage to the boot of the car. The searing heat inside the car reminded the American of the summer climate of his West Texas childhood, one that was rural, unhappy and deprived. Flustered and sweating, he quickly removed his hat and wound down the glass window.

Stephen got behind the steering wheel and started the engine. The air conditioner instantly came alive in full blast. 'John sends his apologies for not being here to pick you up personally. He is busy arranging the big meeting for tonight.'

'No sweat,' Logan replied as the Mercedes bowled out of the airport car park and joined the main road. At cruise speed, the American stared out at the view of Ikeja—the capital of Lagos State— sliding past the rear car window. At first, he saw miles of grass verges, mahogany trees, a series of bungalows and duplex houses partly shielded by fencing on either side of the road, and a scant number of pedestrians trekking under the scorching afternoon sun. However, as the car approached the centre of the city, the scenery became denser and more colourful. Skyscrapers, mosques, churches, crowded open-air markets and palm tree-lined streets began to appear. There was also a tremendous increase in the volume of vehicular traffic on the road and pedestrians on the sidewalks. As the Mercedes passed over bridges, Logan could see barges, speedboats and canoes in the lagoon down below. Moments later, the car ran into a gridlock.

'It's like New York City here,' the American remarked, staring at the traffic chaos through the windscreen.

'Uh-huh,' replied Stephen in agreement, although he doubted his passenger's claim.

'Have you been?' Logan asked.

'No, I have never been to America,' Stephen replied.

'The traffic jam in New York City is similar,' Logan repeated.

Stephen did not reply.

In the rear-view mirror, Logan observed the driver's disbelieving eyes. He wanted to elaborate on his comment, but thought better of it. He wasn't saying that the traffic congestion here was *exactly* the same as that of New York City. For one thing, the bottleneck far ahead was caused by a cavernous pothole right in the middle of the two-lane road. The huge pothole had eaten into the tarmac of one lane, damaging and rendering a portion of it impassable. For another, he had never seen a pothole of that size on any road in New York City. He also thought it weird that such a major thoroughfare was devoid of traffic lights. In New York, all busy road intersections had the green-yellow-red signalling devices.

In the distance, a policeman dressed in a light orange uniform was standing on a small traffic island, struggling to manage the chaos. He raised the palm of one hand to indicate that a certain minibus should halt and using the other hand to beckon a saloon car to move forward in the opposite direction. The process devised by the traffic cop to unlock the gridlock was simple— whenever oncoming traffic was halted, vehicles bypassed the crater-sized pothole in front of them by crossing over to the opposite lane and rejoined their own lane where the tarmac was undamaged and pristine.

Several yards behind, in the long queue of vehicles, Stephen suppressed an exasperated sigh as he surveyed the road far ahead. The two-way traffic was flowing again. But it was torturously slow and intermittent as only one vehicle from either direction could pass through the bottleneck at any point in time.

Logan was not exasperated. He might be stuck in a noisy traffic jam under the African sun, but he was pleased and expectant. Inside the Mercedes, the oppressively hot humid air had since dissipated, supplanted by a sweet-scented cool breeze coming from the air conditioner vents in the dashboard. His eyes scanned the dashboard in front, but failed to find the hidden source of the sweet lavender scent wafting towards him. The American gave up the search. His attention soon turned to himself.

Using both hands, he slackened the knot of the brown paisley silk cravat around his neck. Feeling more relaxed, his gaze shifted from the car's centre console to the windscreen. Through the glass, he saw the distant orange-clad traffic policeman gesturing in his direction. Moments later, the long line of vehicles in front of the Mercedes Benz began to move in slow procession.

Stephen shifted the gear lever, released the clutch pedal and the car began to follow. Leaning forward in his seat, Logan observed the dense foot traffic on raised stone pavements flanking either side of the road. Crowds of pedestrians were going about their daily lives in the bustling commercial city under the sweltering heat.

As the scenery gradually slid past the rear windows of the moving car, Logan observed more people walking up and down the sidewalks; waiting patiently by the bus stop; moving in and out of big shopping malls; standing on street corners haggling over the price of fruits with hawkers or going through piles of audio cassettes displayed for sale in roadside kiosks painted in garish colours. White collar workers in business suits—bankers, managers, accountants, lawyers, secretaries, etc— were walking in and out of high-rise buildings.

The American watched some of the pedestrians veering into narrow off-road footpaths that led to boisterous open-air markets far beyond his line of sight. Being his first ever visit to the African continent, Logan felt something incongruous about what he was seeing. The sights and sounds around him did not conform to the images routinely painted by the American media. He was going to take lots of photographs, but only after the business that brought him from across the Atlantic.

Balanced on his laps was the only object he had not let out of his sight since he got off the plane: *his briefcase.* Earlier on, at the airport, he had politely refused Stephen's offer to carry it for him, allowing only his luggage to be taken. He had every reason to guard the briefcase jealously. It contained one million dollars in cash.

The traffic cop suddenly raised his palm and the procession of vehicles trundled to a halt. Stephen sighed as he disengaged the clutch and returned the gear lever to its neutral position. Frustrated motorists in the queue honked their horns and yelled abuses at the unperturbed policeman. Stephen turned to his rear seat passenger with an apologetic look on his face. 'Sorry about this, sir.'

Logan smiled, 'you haven't done anything wrong. I'm not worried at all about the traffic delay.'

Stephen smiled back. 'Your hotel in just fifteen minutes away. We will be there soon.'

Logan nodded. The noisy traffic outside did not worry him at all. Tapping gently on the lid of the briefcase, his mind wandered off to a soirée that he had attended five months earlier in Washington DC...

*****

He was one of several Americans who had been invited to a soirée at the Nigerian Embassy in Washington DC. On the advice of his financial consultants, he had honoured the invitation to party with the newly appointed ambassador. His consultants had told him that the late evening party was a possible avenue to warm his way into the fold of the unaccountable power brokers that controlled the vast oil fields in the petroleum-rich African nation. With a bit of luck, his ailing Texas-based company, Logan Star Oils, could become a proud owner of a number of those fields.

That fateful night, on 15th January 1990, his sleek black limousine glided to a halt in the driveway of the Embassy. The commissionaire opened the rear passenger door and flashed a salute. Logan alighted, dressed in black slacks and a matching shawl collar tuxedo over a cream shirt and a brown velvet bow tie.

The new ambassador, Emmanuel David Balogun, was on hand to receive him at the doorway. 'I am honoured to have you here, Mister Logan,' Balogun smiled and ushered him into a large room teeming with guests. Although the vast majority of the guests were Nigerians, there were several Europeans and Americans present. Among the American guests, Logan recognized US congressmen, State Department officials, and a few business rivals. In the large room, colourful Nigerian traditional robes mingled with black-tie dinner suits and evening gowns.

Mr. Balogun introduced Logan to a German couple and quickly disappeared. A waiter carrying a tray of wineglasses served him and the couple and then left. Logan introduced himself and learnt from the subsequent boring fifteen-minute conversation that the couple were members of an evangelical church in Nigeria that have won acclaim for their charity work, especially in orphanages over there. They were on holidays in the United States and felt honoured to be invited to the party. When they asked Logan if he was a believer, he smiled thinly and downed his glass of wine. They were not the sort he had in mind to meet when he decided to come to party.

He quickly excused himself and dashed off to the quadrangle bar tucked into a corner at the far end of the room. The barman fixed him another drink. He turned around and watched the guests standing in small groups as they chatted, feigned smiles and sipped their cocktails. Suddenly, his eye caught an image in the centre of the room.

A light-skinned black man with an Afro hair-do, mid-forties, dressed in a navy blue suit, was walking towards him. The man had an empty glass in his hand. He stepped in front of Logan and shot out his hand. 'I'm John Eze. Personal assistant to the Deputy Ambassador,' he smiled revealing a set of white teeth that somehow impressed the grey-haired American.

'I'm certain I haven't met the deputy ambassador. Is he here?' Logan asked smiling.

John gestured to the barman with his empty glass. The glass was promptly refilled. 'No, the deputy is not here. He is based in New York where he doubles as the Nigerian Consul-General.'

Logan nodded slowly, absorbing the explanation. 'Oh, I see, I see...by the way, I'm Gary Logan.'

'I know all about you, Mister Logan,' John replied and shook the hand the American had proffered.

The Texan oilman was surprised. 'You do?'

John nodded and told the American what he knew about him, including the financial problems facing his company. 'Mister Logan, in spite of these problems, I believe that you are an astute businessman. That is why I am here with an attractive business proposition.'

Excitement shook Logan like a hurricane. Was this the moment he had been waiting for? Was he getting carried away?

John led Logan to a quieter corner of the room and they settled into the armchairs there to chat.

'Well, my friend John, let's hear what you have in mind,' Logan said before sipping some wine.

'It is an oil deal,' John replied, pausing to read the American.

Logan's face lit up. He sat upright in the armchair, sloshing the contents of his wine glass.

John smiled and continued. 'Recently, the federal government opened some deepwater oil wells and is keen on leasing them out to foreign investors.'

The American dropped his wine glass on the side table and leaned forward as if to get a better view of the Nigerian's mouth.

'The lease is for forty years. These wells have a potential daily production rate of six hundred thousand barrels of sweet crude and forty million cubic feet of natural gas.'

Logan felt a lump form in his throat, which caused him to sip from his glass. The sensation of the champagne running down his throat seemed to relax the muscles down there.

'Officially, there is going to be a government board accepting tenders for the oil blocks from different bidding companies. But the petroleum minister is personally interested, if you know what I mean.' John paused and smiled.

Logan smiled back knowingly. His consultants had briefed him well. Corruption is the grease that lubricates the machinery of government business in Nigeria. He had no moral qualms about it. If bribing a bunch of third world bureaucrats was all it would take to pull his company from the steep slope to bankruptcy, then he was going to do it without hesitation. 'Yeah, I know what you mean,' the Texan replied with a mischievous grin.

'The minister, who is a personal friend, has asked me to find somebody, a foreigner, willing to play the game.'

The oilman nodded and gulped the last contents of his glass. 'So, I'm your man?'

'If you are interested,' John responded.

Logan beamed. 'Of course, I am interested,' he whispered excitedly as a tall brunette from the State Department walked past them on her way to the quadrangle bar.

'So what's the plan?'

'The plan is to receive tenders from various bidding companies, including yours. The Tenders Board will then go through the motions before deciding that your company has offered the right price. Then all the oil wells would be leased to Logan Star Oils for the next forty years,' John paused to observe Logan's reaction. It was what he had expected. The story continued. 'Obviously, we'll need to bribe members of the Tenders Board to get their cooperation.'

Logan set the empty wine glass down on a side table and asked, 'you say your minister is an interested party. Why not just use his powers to dictate a decision for the board?'

John shook his head gravely. 'The minister cannot be seen to be influencing the board in any way. In fact, he does not want anybody to know he is personally interested in the lease contract. Money meant for board members can never be traced back to him. That is why he needs an outsider, a foreigner investor, like you to supply external funding for this project.'

Logan nodded to indicate that he understood. 'What do you need me to do?' he asked.

John downed the remaining contents of his glass and smacked his lips. 'The board will start calling for tenders in three months time, I expect your company to apply as well. You can quote any price you like. It's a sealed bid. No bidding company will know what the other is offering until the board declares somebody the highest bidder—that would be you, obviously.'

Logan's attention span waned and he began to daydream about all the money he was going to make from the clandestine venture. The potential windfall would be enough to bail his company out of its financial mess; pay for the big divorce settlement to his third wife; buy a new yacht; and keep his personal bank account healthy.

'Mister Logan, are you with me?' John asked, nudging the absent-minded Texan out of his reverie.

'Yeah! I'm with you one hundred percent,' the startled oilman blurted out.

John smiled. It was easier than he had originally anticipated. He continued the story from where he had left off. 'One month before the board meets to decide the winning tender, I'll arrange a meeting between you and the board members in Nigeria. You will deliver one million dollars in cash to the chairman of the board. I'll get a cut, the minister too, and the rest will be shared among the board members. Then thirty days later, Logan Star Oils will clinch the contract'.

The part of the statement about clinching the oil contract electrified the American.

'Obviously, you stand to gain over a thousand times the amount you paid in the long run,' John said, rubbing his palms together.

'A hell more than that!' Logan interjected, laughing as if he had just won the jackpot.

Lowering his voice and sounding grave, John added, 'everything I have said here is confidential. So, I would appreciate….'

Logan interrupted him. 'Hell, I never met you and this conversation didn't take place.'

John nodded in satisfaction. At this point, the loud sound of ringing wine glasses filled the air. Logan and his new business associate observed that all the guests had stopped chatting and were now facing towards the front of the room. The glasses stopped ringing and the room fell silent.

Somewhere in front of the room, obscured by a crowd of standing guests, a female embassy official asked with a slight accent, 'can I have your attention please?'

John and Logan rose to their feet and faced forward. Outside their line of sight, the unseen female continued, 'please join me in toasting to the success of Emmanuel Balogun, our new Ambassador.'

Logan waved his empty glass at a passing stewardess bearing a tray of filled wine glasses. The stewardess approached the men and the empty glasses were swapped with filled ones. Both men walked across the room to where the other guests were standing. Over the shoulders of some guests in the small crowd, Logan gazed at the beaming ambassador in front of the room. Standing next to him was a young, fair-skinned black woman.

She raised her wine glass, prompting all the guests to do the same. 'To the health of the Ambassador!' she shouted.

At the back of the small crowd, John and his associate also had their wine glasses raised. But they were toasting to the success of their own nascent business venture...

*****

The Mercedes Benz decelerated as it neared Lagos Hilton Hotel. The driver, Stephen Obi, swerved the car towards the pole barrier gate barring the hotel's premises. The uniformed security men in front of the gate rose from their seats and eyed the car suspiciously. Upon recognising the number plates, both men saluted and lifted the pole barrier to let the car through.

Stephen drove up to the hotel's entrance. The commissionaire opened the rear passenger door for Logan to alight. Stephen disembarked and walked round to the rear of the car. He opened the boot to fetch the luggage. Moments later, the commissionaire got behind the steering wheel and Stephen offered him the car keys.

In the hotel lobby, Logan relaxed on a sofa while Stephen went to the reception desk to obtain the card key for his presidential suite. The climate inside the lobby was cool and pleasant, courtesy of the hotel's central air conditioning system. Minutes later, Stephen returned to Logan with the card key in his left hand. 'I'll show you to your room,' Stephen declared, picking up Logan's luggage. They walked across the lobby and got into an elevator. It whisked them to the third floor...

*****

At the same time Gary Logan was resting in his hotel suite in Ikeja town, something malignant and dark was happening in a rundown apartment, eleven miles away in Mushin— a district of Lagos known for its large industrial estate and congested residential areas.

Inside a poorly lit room in the shabby apartment, five men, all in their forties, all seated around a table, were busy putting finishing touches to an elaborate scheme to finagle one million dollars from the foreign visitor.

Present at the table were John Nwosu alias "John Eze", Eugene Igolo, Adamu Esan, Moses Adrika and Tunde Olukemi alias "Stephen Obi". Together, they reflected the multi-ethnic composition of the Nigerian Federation. John the gang leader and Moses were ethnic Igbos from Eastern Nigeria, which fought a separatist war with the rest of the country more twenty years earlier. Tunde was Yoruba from Western Nigeria. Adamu and Eugene both belonged to the Bini ethnic minority that dominate Midwestern Nigeria.

'Today is our day,' John said, surveying the grim faces around him. 'Everybody knows what to do. No screw-ups, please!'

The men nodded slowly.

'Eugene, you did well. The clothes are superb,' John remarked.

Eugene beamed with smiles. He had procured the clothing that the men would wear later that night. The impeccable three-piece suits he had obtained on the cheap from a high-end bespoke tailoring shop, using subterfuge, bore testimony to his ability to pull surprises despite his general reputation for not being resourceful. Such flickers of brilliance and ingenuity, John had noticed in him when they first met during the Nigeria-Biafra war, two decades earlier.

Eugene was not the only person in the gang that John found useful. There was the genius, Tunde, who had discovered Logan and planned the entire swindle operation down to the smallest detail. Tunde was the gang member that John trusted the most. He was the master strategist who plotted and executed all assignments efficiently, no matter how difficult and complex they were. Adamu and Moses were not exceptionally gifted in John's reckoning, but they were efficient and ruthless, and that was sufficient.

Two hours after it began, the nocturnal meeting came to an end. Every one of them was ready to play his part. Tonight, three of them were going to play honourable members of the Nigerian Federal Tenders Board receiving a businessman from the United States of America.

CHAPTER 2

Logan was reclining on the double bed watching *CNN International* when there was a gentle rap on the door. He turned down the volume of the TV audio with the remote control and made for the door. He grinned when he opened it and recognized the smiling face. 'Ah, John, good, good, good to see you,' he said effusively and stood aside to let his visitor in.

John apologised for not coming personally to pick him up from the airport. 'I was busy preparing the meeting with petroleum minister,' he added.

The American smiled. 'It's fine. Stephen, nice guy, took good care of me.'

John settled into one of the armchairs while Logan sat on the bed.

'How are you enjoying our country?' John asked.

Gary's face beamed with smiles. 'I like it here already. I saw those great buildings dominating the skyline. The weather is very good. I can't wait to take pictures.'

John smiled, 'wait until you see our beaches, especially Lagos Bar Beach. You will love it there.'

Logan took in the information and wondered if he brought enough film rolls for his camera.

John glanced at his watch and politely reminded the American that the meeting would be starting at 9.00 PM prompt. It was time they got moving.

Gary, wearing a white bathrobe, disappeared into the bathroom. He emerged few minutes later dressed in a blue dinner suit with a black bow tie round his neck. 'How do I look?' he asked spreading his arms.

'Oh, you look wonderful,' John replied with a wide grin. Moments later, he was leading the American to the Mercedes Benz in the hotel's car park.

When the Mercedes hit the road, it was plain sailing. The Lagos traffic jam, notorious for choking up streets, highways and bridges, had vanished for the night. The hot winds that blew in the afternoon were long gone, supplanted by a cool breeze.

Logan viewed the city from the moving car with the window fully wound down. Lagos at night was still abuzz with roadside traders displaying their wares; supermarkets still open; neon signboards flashing; young people going in and out of discotheques blasting local and western pop music at full volume.

The absence of traffic congestion on the Lagos-Ojoo expressway—which includes the 7⅓-mile-long Third Mainland Bridge— meant that the car journey from Ikeja to Victoria Island took 27 minutes rather than an hour or two.

When the Mercedes finally came to a rest in the driveway of a white mansion, Logan was ushered into a tastefully furnished sitting room already occupied by three men dressed in identical beige suits. They were sipping red wine and laughing when John arrived with the American. They slowly rose to their feet to greet their visitor.

'I have the pleasure of introducing Mister Gary Logan to you all,' John announced.

The suited men nodded in the direction of Logan. Addressing the Texas oilman, one of them said, 'in my capacity as the chairman of the Federal Tenders Board, I welcome you wholeheartedly to Nigeria. Please sit down.'

The men shook hands with the American and then sat down. Logan and John took their seats opposite the board members.

There was momentary silence. Then John realised what he had overlooked. Turning to Logan, he said, 'my apologies. I should have introduced the board members.'

The board members let out a short mocking laugher.

John feigned embarrassment. 'The chairman that spoke to you is Mallam Salihu Adikwu and next to him are David Likudu and Maxwell Kabiru...'

As John mentioned their names, each member leaned forward to shake hands again with the American across the coffee table. After the introductions, refreshments were served, and then they went down to business.

Mallam Adikwu picked up the attaché case next to his feet and balanced it on his laps as the others looked on. At the sound of a click, the lid of the case sprang open. Adikwu fished out some documents and handed them over to John. The documents were quickly passed on to Gary Logan.

The American dipped his hand into the interior pocket of his jacket and fetched his spectacles. He put them on and quickly went through the five sheets of paper stapled together. Each sheet had the official letterhead of the Nigerian Federal Ministry of Petroleum.

'This document,' Adikwu explained, 'contain the terms of agreement for our deal. You will need to sign it before we proceed any further.'

John gave Logan a fountain pen. The American appended his signature at the bottom right-hand corner of the last sheet of the five-page document.

'Congratulations! Mister Logan,' the chairman said, beaming with smiles. All three board members gave him a round of applause. John returned the documents to Adikwu. The chairman placed them inside the attaché case. Snapping the case shut, he leaned forward and said in a whisper, 'we believe that you have something for us.'

Logan was puzzled at first then it suddenly came to him. He smiled to signal that he understood. 'Ah yes, of course,' he responded and gave his briefcase to John who passed it to the chairman.

Eugene alias "Mallam Adikwu" opened the briefcase. The bribe was neatly arranged in stacks of crisp dollar bills. Adikwu nearly whistled in excitement, but he restrained himself in time. Maintaining his composure, he glanced at Logan and nodded in approval, and then passed the open briefcase to other board members. Each member took a glimpse, nodded in approval, and passed it to the next person.

Moses alias "David Likudu" picked up a bundle and flicked through the dollar bills. Putting the bundle back into the briefcase, he turned to the oilman and said, 'Mister Logan, the next time we meet, it will be to celebrate your leasehold on thirty of our nation's most lucrative oil wells.'

The word "lucrative" excited Logan. In a fleeting moment of giddiness, he pictured himself lying on a mattress covered in piles of dollar bills.

Board member, Maxwell Kabiru, suddenly stood up and crossed over to where John was sitting. He dropped on one knee and leaned towards John, who cocked his ear to one side.

The room fell silent while Maxwell whispered into his ear. John nodded and Adamu alias "Maxwell" rose to his feet and returned to his seat.

John stood up to address all of them. 'It gives me great pleasure to announce that we now have a deal. I'll like to thank all of you for attending this meeting.' Turning to the American sitting to his left, he said, 'only astute entrepreneurs like Mister Logan deserve to do business with our nation.'

The board members nodded in agreement. Logan beamed with pleasure.

'With the transaction concluded,' John continued, 'the distinguished members of the board would like to retire for the night.'

The beige-suited trio sprang to their feet.

Logan arched his eyebrows. 'Come on guys! Let's drink to the deal.'

Mallam Adikwu declined, saying that the board members had another appointment to keep. Moments later, the suited men walked over to Logan and shook hands with him. As they filed out of the room, Mallam Adikwu, carrying the briefcase of dollars, informed Logan that he would hear from them within thirty days. 'Just for the record, we have received your sealed bid proposal along with those of other companies as formality requires,' Adikwu said, standing by the door. 'Not that it matters anyway,' he added before walking away.

Logan smiled mischievously. Two and half months earlier, a DHL Express Envelope from Lagos had arrived at his office in Downtown Houston, Texas. Inside the large sturdy cardboard envelope was a Sealed Bid Proposal Form for him to complete and a cover letter signed by John. In that letter, Logan was instructed to enter a symbolic bid price of one hundred dollars in the proposal form.

Yes, a hundred dollars was paltry, the letter admitted, but there was nothing to worry about. The opacity of the sealed bidding process granted the Federal Tenders Board plenty of leeway to declare any company of its choice the "highest bidder". To clear up any doubts that Logan might harbour, the letter laid out in great details how the entire game worked.

Interested companies write what they are prepared to offer for the oil leases in the bid proposal forms and submit them in sealed envelopes to the Tenders Board. None of the bidding companies would ever know what its competitor was offering for the oil leases until auction day when the board chairman gets to open all "sealed" envelopes and declare a winner. The declared winner being the beneficiary of a sleight of hand—the secret amendment of a bid price in one of the "sealed" envelopes—sometime between the close of the tender submission process and the day before the actual auction date.

The cover letter concluded with an assurance. Provided Logan agreed to produce the requested one-million-dollar bribe beforehand, Logan Star Oils Incorporated would be declared the "winner" and "highest bidder" on auction day. If astonished rival bidders—representatives of the supermajor oil companies—insist on a close examination of his bid proposal form, they would find the paperwork to be in order.

Gary Logan had chuckled after reading the letter and then fed it to his shredder. With the cross-cutting paper shredder buzzing in the background, Logan had asked his secretary for coffee over the intercom. Moments later, Logan began to fill in the bid proposal form while sipping mocha from a blue mug. It took him twelve minutes to complete the form, seal it inside an A4-sized brown envelope, and hand over the entire package to his secretary with instructions. His secretary then drove to the FedEx Shipping Centre on Sam Houston Parkway West, where the brown envelope was placed inside a larger cardboard envelope for onward transmission to Lagos, Nigeria...

*****

When the chauffeur-driven limousine carrying the board members left the premises of the white mansion, John and Logan returned to the living room to drink to the deal. John served champagne.

'To the success of our venture,' Logan toasted. Glasses clinked followed by roaring laughter. It had been a great night. Stephen soon appeared to drive the American from Victoria Island back to Ikeja.

The next morning, John picked up Logan from his hotel suite for a guided tour of the city. As the American readied his camera, John explained that Lagos city—the metropolitan area of Lagos State— with its twelve million inhabitants, was one of the most densely populated urban centres on the African continent.

The lens of Logan's Fuji Camera captured several images, including the National Arts Theatre in Surulere district; the industrial estate of Mushin; the stilt houses and canoes in the floating slums of Makoko situated right under the Third Mainland Bridge; Tinubu Square and the tall buildings of the Central Business District on Lagos Island; the wealthy district of Ikoyi with its golf courses, upscale shops and modern high-rise luxury apartment buildings; and finally, Victoria Island—the palm-tree studded local equivalent of Manhattan—with its skyscrapers, posh mansions and beaches.

After exhausting three rolls of film, John took Logan to sunbathe in Lagos Bar Beach. At nightfall, they moved from one nightclub to another, before finally landing in a bar to get drunk.

At dawn, Tunde alias "Stephen Obi" arrived at the bar and piled the nearly comatose men into the back of his car. He took them back to his own apartment so that they could sleep off the effects of the alcohol.

In the mid hours of the morning, John and Logan woke up with a terrible hangover, which took three hours to subside. After taking breakfast prepared by

Tunde, the visibly embarrassed Logan requested a lift back to the hotel. 'I have a plane to catch in four hours,' he said. Tunde obliged.

At 2.00 PM, the American boarded his return flight to New York. As he reclined in his seat waiting for the airliner to take off, the dream of new wealth beyond his dreams came to his mind. The thought pleased him immensely.

CHAPTER 3

The five men who conned Gary Logan were brought together by a twist of fate on 16th January 1970, the day after the Biafran government surrendered unconditionally to the Nigerian Army besieging Owerri town, the last major population centre still fully controlled by the dying republic.

When soldiers of the rapidly disintegrating Biafran Army defending the town learnt about the surrender over *Radio Biafra*, many of them hurriedly swapped their army fatigues for plain clothes and melted into the civilian population. The victorious Nigerian Army was expected to march into the town at any moment.

However, inside Emmanuel College, the Biafran flag was still proudly fluttering on a pole in the courtyard. The commander of the 68th Battalion of the elite "S" Brigade was addressing his men amidst distant sporadic small arms fire, noise and chaos outside the school's walls. He was dressed in plain clothes, having just disposed of his uniform. He thanked his still uniformed men for their service to the fatherland. 'No one will say that we did not fight hard,' he said ruefully. 'History will remember the 68th Battalion as one of the best fighting units in Biafra.'

Turning to a small group of soldiers dressed in a slightly different combat uniform, he smiled. 'You R.O.B boys from Benin, Agbor and Asaba also fought well.'

He advised his audience to exchange their uniforms for civilian clothes, adding, 'the vandals will neither forgive nor forget how we humiliated them last year on the battlefield.' He saluted, prompting his men to do the same. And for the very last time, the Biafran Army Major bellowed, 'dismissed!'

A bugle sounded the call to retreat and the gathering broke up, the men dispersing in different directions. The sound of approaching machine gun fire grew louder.

Not all the Biafran soldiers were eager to scramble into the bush or just disappear into the civilian crowd to avoid the wrath of advancing Nigerian "vandals". Staff Sergeant John Nwosu, Sergeant Moses Adrika, and Corporals Eugene Igolo and Adamu Esan seized the unique opportunity created by the pandemonium following the collapse of civil authority in the town to break into the Bank of Biafra. Their aim was not to steal stacks of Biafran Pounds, worthless fiat currency bills that had just ceased to be legal tender. The target was the hundred thousand United States dollars stored in the steel vaults of the bank.

Penetrating the deserted duplex house that was the provisional headquarters of the central bank was no problem at all. It was getting past the locked vault that proved difficult. When efforts by Moses to pick the vault's combination lock failed, Adamu used a rocket-propelled grenade to blow a gaping hole through the lock. Shoving bundles of dollar bills into a Biafran Army-issued duffel bag took fewer than five minutes. When they stepped outside, an enemy soldier who had just entered the town ahead of a slowly advancing Nigerian Army division was waiting for them.

'Don't move!' that soldier barked, raising his Sterling submachine gun. The bank thieves froze in their tracks. They recognized the starched khaki green uniform of the lean man pointing his weapon at them.

Out of curiosity, the Nigerian soldier stepped forward to examine the men's tattered yellowish-green combat fatigues. Some battledresses had the military insignia of the "S"-Brigade, which he instantly recognized as the military unit that had inflicted heavy casualties on Nigerian troops in all their previous vain attempts to conquer the town. Others uniforms had shoulder patches with the letters "R.O.B" embroidered on them. The Nigerian soldier gazed at them with puzzlement. He was unfamiliar with the long defunct R.O.B Brigade— a paramilitary unit of Midwestern Nigerians with Biafran sympathies that had been utterly destroyed several months earlier in a different battlefield, and whose surviving elements had been reassigned to serve in the regular Biafran Army.

The expression of puzzlement on the Nigerian's face did not last long. The sleeves of the same shirts, bearing the unfamiliar shoulder patches, were also spotting the very familiar yellow-rising-sun emblem of the Biafran national flag. It confirmed that every single one of the bank thieves, regardless of insignia design, was an enemy of the Nigerian Army.

'You are rebels,' the Nigerian soldier said redundantly. Twenty minutes earlier, the soldier had broken away from his regiment, which had orders not to enter the enemy-held town without the protective cover of armoured vehicles, all of which were still in the rear, trundling through long stretches of muddy terrain to get to the frontline. Despite howls of disapproval from his fellow soldiers in the trenches, he had climbed out and walked straight into Owerri on his own. Half a mile inside enemy territory, he was surprised to find a war-ravaged town without any visible presence of "rebel soldiers". Every man he had seen was dressed in plain clothes and none seemed worried that a lone Nigerian soldier, an enemy of Biafra, was sauntering through the town. He had not felt threatened until he ran into the bank thieves, the first group of men he had seen in town dressed in "rebel" uniforms.

'What is that?' the soldier asked, eyeing the bloated duffel bag in John's right hand. The light-skinned thief smiled and pried the bag open for the Nigerian to see. The soldier's eyes widened in alarm as his brain registered the contents.

'Look, I'll make you a deal,' John said, closing the duffel bag. 'You put down that gun and we split the money five ways. What do you say?'

A lump grew in the Nigerian's throat. '*Oya! Oya!* Give me that bag or I shoot!' he barked, pushing the gun towards John's stomach as he reached out with his left hand for the bag. What happened next was a series of movements too quick for the Nigerian to follow. Suddenly, the gun was no longer in his possession, and then he felt himself falling down.

Adamu pointed the Sterling submachine gun menacingly at the Nigerian soldier lying on the ground.

'What is your name, my friend?' John asked, slinging the duffel bag over his shoulder.

The Nigerian sat up and replied, 'Regimental Sergeant-Major Tunde Olukemi, Nigeria Military Police.'

'Which unit will enter the town?'

'Third Marine Commando Division.'

John nodded, absorbing the information. In the earlier days of the war, he had been part of a defending military unit that thwarted attempts by Third Marine Commando to capture Aba, a commercial town in southern Biafra.

John surprised his men by helping the Nigerian soldier to his feet. 'Tunde, we need your help,' he said. His men frowned, but said nothing.

Addressing the disapproving faces, John said, 'the Nigerian Army is about to enter the town. I am sure they have sealing up all the exits out of Owerri. If we stay here, we will be caught.'

Turning back to Tunde, he continued, 'help us sneak out and you get an equal cut. The hundred thousand dollars here is enough for everybody.

Tunde eyed the gun poised menacingly at him and agreed. 'Okay. But you need to get out of those clothes. My commander issued an order to every soldier to shoot anyone dressed in rebel uniform. They will enter the town as soon as armoured protection is available.'

Adamu lowered the gun. Moments later, the Biafran soldiers started stripping to their underpants while Tunde wandered off to abandoned residential houses to search for plain clothes.

'Sir, are you sure this is the right course of action?' Moses asked, worried that Tunde would return with a detachment of Nigerian soldiers instead of plain clothes.

John was about to speak when an army jeep drove in at top speed and screeched to a halt three feet from the scantily dressed men.

Four Nigerian soldiers clad in olive-green uniforms jumped out of the vehicle, aiming their rifles at the men. 'Put your hands into the air!' one of them barked. Another one who appeared to be their leader stepped forward, his eyes focused on the pile of yellowish-green clothes on the ground. He bent over and picked one of them. 'Rebels!' he cried, waving a ragged leopard-pattern camouflage shirt at his men. Guns were quickly cocked.

'Please, don't shoot!' Adamu shouted, stepping forward.

The lead soldier pulled out his service pistol. Just then, a staccato burst of gunfire erupted from behind the army jeep. The Nigerian soldiers swung round with their guns, but it was too late. They fell under a deadly hail of bullets.

Tunde dropped the submachine gun, whipped out a pistol, and stepped forward. 'Let's go!' he hissed at the stunned Biafrans, throwing at them the plain clothes he had brought with him.

All the men, except John, started struggling into the clothes quickly. 'You are now a traitor,' John smirked, staring in disbelief at the crumpled bodies at his feet.

The growling noise of approaching armoured vehicles came within earshot. Tunde panicked. 'Guys, hurry up!' he hissed again.

John quickly jumped into the workman's tunic provided.

They piled into the army jeep. Tunde turned the key in the ignition and the engine roared to life. He checked the fuel gauge in the dashboard. It indicated that the fuel tank was full. Following John's directions, Tunde drove through clearings in forests and dirt tracks, avoiding major roads until it became impossible to do so.

At Nigerian Army checkpoints in Ikot-Ekpene town, Tunde flashed his military police ID. 'These men are suspected rebels. I am driving them to military intelligence near the border,' he said to inquisitive troops manning the barricades at each checkpoint.

At dusk, the five men reached Bakassi Town, near the border and ditched the jeep. Under the cover of darkness and heavy machine gunfire, they successfully crossed the international border into Cameroon with the stolen money.

In Yaoundé city, they lived life on the fast lane, spending the money on alcohol, women and gambling. Fifteen months later, most of the money was gone.

Faced with a life of penury in Cameroon, they quietly sneaked back across the border into Nigeria with their guns. They burst into First Bank in Calabar city, guns blazing, and made off with 70,000 Nigerian Pounds, launching a four-year reign of terror as ruthless armed robbers. The media portrayed them as invincible, sensationalised their deadly exploits, and chronicled the police's failed attempts to apprehend them.

In the fourth and final year of their criminal impunity, the soldiers-turned-robbers carried out their most spectacular operation—the attempted hijacking of an armoured security van transporting cash money to a bank in Rivers State.

The robbery operation had begun very well with the detonation of an improvised TNT explosive on the side of the road in which the van was travelling. The blast wave picked up the vehicle and hurled on its side. Hot shrapnel cratered the tarmacked road surface and shattered the van's bulletproof glass windscreen without breaking it. Before the robbers could close in on the disabled vehicle, several police estate cars, sirens wailing, were spotted in the distance speeding towards the scene. The armed robbers had no choice than to abort the operation and scurry away.

Owing to its armoured plating, none of four security guards in the van was hurt and the plentiful stacks of naira bills—Nigeria's then new currency— in the vehicle's rear remained intact.

Despite this happy ending, governmental authorities across the southern states of Nigeria were frightened. It was the first time, they had heard of common criminals using a powerful roadside bomb in the course of an armed robbery. They appealed to the federal military government for help and a small team of well-equipped, battle-hardened soldiers was made to join the multitude of poorly equipped policemen in a reinvigorated manhunt for the outlaws. The mixed team of soldiers and policemen tracked the movement of the armed robbers across state lines, catching up with them five months later.

It was one poorly executed bank robbery in the commercial city of Aba that finally did them in. They had been in such a haste that they failed to secure the back door and do the usual head count. So, no one noticed when a female bank clerk slipped out through the back. Minutes later, the team of policemen and soldiers stormed the bank.

Five of the twenty-five hostages had been injured in the crossfire before all the robbers were apprehended. At the time of their arrest on 5th August 1975, the thieves had robbed 1,400 banks and engaged in 300 carjacking operations on highways across the southern part of Nigeria.

The trial by an ad hoc military tribunal was speedy. It took only seven days for the military judge, an army colonel with a law degree, to find them guilty of armed robbery. They were sentenced to death by firing squad. Appeal was denied. Their civilian lawyer pleaded for clemency, but that was also swiftly denied by the ad hoc tribunal.

A week later, the men were brought out of prison to be executed, even as their lawyer was still pursuing the case for clemency with the governor of the East Central State. The robbers were twenty minutes away from execution when the governor finally acceded to their lawyer's request for clemency. The convicts were lucky that Brigadier Malik Ahmed, the State Commissioner for Justice, had arrived seconds before their execution.

The death sentences had been commuted to fifteen years imprisonment with hard labour. It was a long period to spend incarcerated, but enough for the ex-soldiers to think of the kind of business they wanted to engage in when they finished serving their sentences. Going back to the crimes that nearly got them executed was out of the question.

They considered smuggling, pimping and racketeering before finally settling for the easiest of them all: *Advance Fee Fraud.*

The idea came to them in the late 1980s, at a time when criminals convicted of multi-million-dollar scams were beginning to swell the prison population at Kirikiri Maximum. Imprisoned fraudsters beat their chests as they boasted of their exploits before the law finally caught up with them.

Three weeks before their early release in July 1989, John and his men sat in the prison courtyard and listened to one of such fraudsters relate the story of how he became a millionaire from monetary donations to his bogus non-governmental organization. The foreign donors had been fooled into thinking that the money was contributing towards the provision of homes for street children in Lagos.

'Well, lucky you!' John had said, clapping. 'When you get out of this shit-hole, you can live like a king!'

The man shook his head gravely. 'The government recovered the money.'

John shouted, 'no way!'

    With sadness in his eyes, the imprisoned fraudster recounted how soldiers and policemen had taken turns to whip him until he disclosed the deposit account details of all eight Nigerian banks holding the ill-gotten money.

    John rubbed his chin and turned to his men. 'Well chaps, we have to learn from mistakes,' he said, thinking of Swiss bank accounts far from the reach of the Nigerian federal government.

CHAPTER 4

DECEMBER 1990

SOUTHEAST TEXAS, USA

Four days before Christmas, Gary Logan was in his office in Downtown Houston. He was not in a festive mood. He was standing nervously next to his oak desk, the phone handset pressed against his right ear, listening impatiently to the voice at the other end of the line. Something he heard caused him to groan in despair. The handset fell from his right hand and clattered down onto the desk. Having lost interest in what the caller had to say, he moved across the room to the floor-to-ceiling plate glass window and stared gloomily at the thirty-five-storey Entex Building standing across the street from his own building—the thirty-storey green glass skyscraper that served as the headquarters of Logan Star Oils Incorporated.

Gary watched the intermittent kaleidoscopic flashing of LED lights festooning a giant Christmas tree erected near the entrance of the Entex Building. Utterly alone, with his melancholy thoughts for company, Gary suddenly smiled wrily. There was something funny and yet profoundly sad— and perhaps, karmic— about receiving the worst news of his life on his birthday.

The Chief Finance Officer (CFO) had not called to serenade him with a birthday song or wish him a merry Christmas. The CFO had phoned to update him on the unfolding calamity, which started a week earlier when Logan Star Oils filed for bankruptcy. In the course of that phone conversation, in which the CFO did most of the talking, Gary learnt that angry shareholders were thinking of filing a $10 billion lawsuit against him; the FBI and the IRS were snooping around; and more worryingly, there were persistent rumours that a secret grand jury had been convened to indict him for securities fraud. Upon hearing about the grand jury rumour, Gary lost the fortitude to carry on. There was no point continuing the telephone conversation. *All was lost.*

Five months had elapsed since he discovered that the entire oil deal in Nigeria was one big swindle. Following his return from an eventful Lagos trip, he had eagerly awaited the official announcement that his beleaguered Logan Star Oils had been awarded a forty-year leasehold on thirty new deepwater oil wells located 90 miles from Nigeria's southern coastline. He was stunned when his press officer presented him with the banner headline of *The Daily Times of Nigeria* declaring that a European petroleum company had been awarded the oil leases. While still in the throes of shock and panic, it occurred to him that the front-page article in the Nigerian newspaper might be untrue. After all, yellow journalism was not the exclusive preserve of the American press. He experienced a fleeting moment of hope. In a state of frenzy, he tried unsuccessfully, for three hours, to phone his business partner, Mr. John Eze, to ascertain whether there had been a mix-up somewhere. Maybe during the press conference called to announce the successful bidder, the Nigerian petroleum minister had gotten confused and mentioned the European company in error.

Logan's adrenaline soared as each vain attempt to make the international call returned a recorded female voice on the phone line repeating the message: *"the number you have dialled does not exist. Please dial the correct number"*.

The next day, 23rd July 1990, he flew from Houston to Arlington, Virginia. From there, he made his way to the Nigerian Embassy in Washington DC to see Ambassador Emmanuel Balogun. The diplomat was stunned when he heard the American's plight, but he was unsympathetic. The ambassador berated Logan for not seeking information directly from the Trade and Investments Desk of the Nigerian Embassy. He blasted the American for his willingness to pay bribes and work with shady characters claiming to be Nigerian government officials. 'Your greed and eagerness to defraud the Nigerian Federal State,' the ambassador growled, 'has cost you your money. I do not know the men who defrauded you, including the one you claimed to have met at my party.'

Out of desperation and disbelief, Logan hopped into another aeroplane bound for West Africa and stepped on Nigerian soil for the second time. Perhaps, he could meet personally with John Eze and members of the Federal Tenders Board to settle this matter, but that was not to be. What he discovered in Lagos deepened his sense of shock and indignation.

The Victoria Island mansion—the venue for the nocturnal meeting between him and the fraudsters—was not a Nigerian federal government building as he had been led to believe, but rather the private residence of a deceased timber magnate. The empty mansion had been on sale at the time of Logan's first visit to the country. Further enquiries made at the Federal Ministry of Petroleum revealed that the authentic call for submission of tenders had closed a month before he met "John Eze" at the soirée in Washington DC. The "board members" he had met were imposters unknown to any of the federal parastatals operating under the jurisdiction of the petroleum ministry.

The Nigerian Police Force was brought in to investigate the scam. Its detectives did not have any leads, but promised to keep hunting for the elusive fraudsters.

Logan returned to the United States empty-handed and despondent. It wasn't about the one million dollars he had lost to the scammers. He had already gotten over that miniscule personal loss. It was about the loss of a dream. He had lost his last chance to make things right. There were serious accounting irregularities on the financial books of Logan Star Oils, which he had hoped to "correct" as soon as money started rolling in from the West African oil fields. There were debts that he had hoped to pay off as soon as Logan Star Oils reaped windfall profits. There were the investors he had convinced to buy company shares with promises of riches beyond their wildest dreams. None of them believed his hard-luck story about being conned by a bunch of Africans. All of them wanted their money back. But that matter was not the worst of his problems.

Upon his return to Houston, he was greeted with a menacing-looking writ from the U.S. District Court for the Southern District of Texas. When the document was unfolded and read, Logan learnt that the court was permitting the expropriation of his company's assets by the consortium of banks he was owing millions of dollars in loans.

Finally, the day he had feared might come arrived with the phone call from his Chief Financial Officer. The class action lawsuit by irate shareholders wasn't the scariest problem he was facing. It wasn't even the fact that the very building he was occupying was up for grabs by vengeful bankers who had taken almost everything from him and were still baying for more blood. What had terrified and sent shivers down his spine was talk of a secret grand jury and stories of snooping FBI and IRS agents.

At 65 years of age, Logan didn't believe he could cope in federal prison. He wasn't even sure he could survive the stress of a long drawn out court trial for securities fraud, money laundering, wire fraud, making false statements to banks and auditors, etc.

He felt a tremor in his clammy hands as he lit the Marlboro cigarette with his favourite gold-plated lighter. He inhaled deeply and blew smoke rings against the plate glass window overlooking the city of Houston. With the cigarette still wedged between his lips, he slouched back across the room and fell into the padded swivel chair behind the oak desk. He stubbed out the half-smoked cigarette in an ashtray and grabbed the crystal decanter of brandy sitting on the desk next to the telephone. He poured a generous amount of liquor into a tumbler. With trembling hands, he raised the glass to his mouth, gulped down its contents in one swig, and smacked his lips in satisfaction.

For a moment, his face froze in fear as he contemplated his next line of action. Then his face turned crimson as his right hand reached down to the bottom drawer of the desk. He pulled it out and grabbed an old Japanese-made pistol, the same Nambu semi-automatic that he had pulled from the hand of a dead Vietcong fighter back in the jungles of South Vietnam in 1968. He rested its cold muzzle on his temple at an angle. Suddenly, an old army tune his troops had whistled on their way to fight in the Tet Offensive started ringing in his head. Then he experienced a brief flashback in which he was younger, fitter and dressed in the starched uniform of a US Army Colonel.

It was a memory from April 1972. The Lockheed C-141 Starlifter carrying Logan and his men had just landed on the asphalt-paved runway at Fort Campbell— the army base straddling Kentucky and Tennessee— to the blaring music of a military band and cheering sounds of overjoyed families and friends happy to see their loved ones returning from the lost war in Southeast Asia.

The memory made Logan smile wistfully. It was a simpler and nicer time back then. In those days, all he had to do to get a decent pay cheque was to take and execute orders from his superiors. For heroism on the battlefield, he got his medals, ribbon bars, and promotions. Back then, the purely civilian stress of how to start and keep a business afloat was still in the distant future, and so were the tax-dodging schemes that would eventually attract the attention of prosecutors and a secret grand jury.

The memory also recalled a moment in time when random strangers in restaurants, in bars and on the streets of America would stop to admire his army uniform before thanking him for his military service. But that was then. Now, nobody smiled appreciatively at him. His estranged children from his three ex-wives wouldn't talk to him; his friends were no longer taking his calls; his erstwhile business associates were preparing to sue him into oblivion; arrest and prosecution were looming in his future. Logan's world, which had enjoyed a promising start, was now finishing as a bleak and barren moor.

'I should never have left the army,' he murmured to himself and finally squeezed the trigger.

In the anteroom, the secretary was busy working behind a desktop computer, composing a letter that her boss had asked her to prepare for the Internal Revenue Service (IRS). She was doing a final spelling check when there was loud blast inside the office behind her. Startled by the sound, the secretary shifted reflexively and fell out of her swivel chair. She quickly picked herself up and rushed into Logan's office. Inside the office, there was blood, cerebro-spinal fluid and brain matter splattered on the desk, the telephone, the crystal decanter, the chair, and on the walls. She screamed.

*****

On the same day in Lagos State, Eugene Igolo killed the engine of his 505 Peugeot saloon car in the driveway of his gang's favourite bar and restaurant, DePauls. It used to be a daily hangout where the swindlers socialized and planned future gang operations until Moses Adrika screwed up. Now, it was just a place visited intermittently to enjoy delicious meals while keeping a low profile.

One week earlier, Moses Adrika had visited DePauls alone and hit the bar. Heavily drunk, he had boasted to fellow drinkers about defrauding a rich American of his "entire life savings". The police received a tip-off and the drunk was promptly arrested that night. A few hours later, before detectives could question him, the inebriated fraudster vanished from detention along with the two police constables assigned to guard his holding cell.

Eugene walked into the bar and made for the gang's favourite spot— a table positioned inside an alcove. As he sank into the chair behind the table, a waitress scurried towards him armed with a notepad. 'What would you like sir?' she asked, her pen poised over the notepad.

Eugene looked up from the table. 'Get me a bottle of Star Beer. That's all I want.'

The woman nodded and walked away.

Thirty minutes later, Eugene had nearly finished the bottle of beer and still no sign of the man he was supposed to meet. He cursed under his breath, struggling to understand how a man who had no respect for punctuality ended up a detective in the Lagos State Criminal Investigation Division. He fixed his eyes at the entrance, watching customers come and go as he downed the last contents of the green bottle.

Forty-five minutes in, there was still no sign of the man who had made it possible for Moses to vanish from police custody. Eugene was now visibly angry. He held his face in his hand and shook it in frustration. He was staring down at the Formica surface of the table when he felt a presence nearby.

'Hello my friend,' a voice suddenly whispered close to his ears.

He looked up and frowned, 'you are late Mister!'

Detective-Inspector Michael Otunba shrugged and apologised for the lateness, claiming traffic hold-up as the culprit. Eugene waved him to a chair opposite him. The young waitress reappeared with a winning smile on her face.

'Please, get us two bottles of Star Beer. Chilled, Okay?' Eugene requested.

The waitress promised to be back in a jiffy and sped off.

Otunba surveyed the walls of the alcove partially hiding their table from view. Nodding in approval, he said, 'carefully chosen spot, I would say.'

Eugene ignored the comment and asked frostily, 'shall we get down to business?'

'Sure. You got the dough?'

Eugene stared at the face of the dark-skinned man in his early forties. It was his first physical contact with him. He had spoken to the detective over the phone on the night Moses was taken into custody. Fifteen minutes on the phone with the rogue cop, a deal was struck. Mike Otunba would receive ₦1000 down payment that night and ₦5000 extra when the job was done. The crooked policeman gave his home address. An hour after the phone conversation, the down payment was delivered in a fat envelope by Tunde Olukemi. Just before dawn, the prisoner disappeared in mysterious circumstances.

'This is the dough for a job well done,' Eugene said, dropping a new fat envelope on the table.

Mike's face lit up. He grabbed the envelope with both hands. It was heavier than the previous one. 'This is five thousand?' he asked smiling.

'You could always check,' Eugene replied, turning his head to see if any other person was watching. There was none as most of the customers in the bar and restaurant had left. The time was 11.45 PM.

'Nah, there is no need. I trust you. If you say it is five thousand, then it is,' the policeman replied sonorously as he stuffed the envelope into an extra large bum bag.

'Well, suit yourself,' Eugene said drily as the detective zipped up the bag. The waitress returned with the tray of drinks. She laid out the chilled bottles on the table with tumblers and left.

The swindler used an opener on the table to uncap the beer bottles. 'There you are,' he said, pushing a bottle towards the bent cop. 'Look, my man,' he began, swigging beer directly from the bottle. 'We are ready to offer a decent stipend if you agree to report on State CID whenever we ask.'

Otunba shook his head slowly as he poured beer into his tumbler. 'Can't be done. There is an ongoing investigation into the disappearance of your friend and the two policemen detailed to guard him. One of the investigators suspects me'

'Any chance they will find out?' the fraudster asked, concerned about what would happen if Mike Otunba was caught and he confessed.

Shaking his head, the detective replied, 'I don't think so. Most of the investigators have already concluded that the missing guards acted alone after the detainee bribed them heavily, but...' he trailed off.

Eugene leaned forward on his elbows. 'But what?' he asked anxiously, his mind was already plotting a course of action should the rogue cop be apprehended. He was also beginning to think that the detective was downplaying the seriousness of the internal police investigation.

Mike sipped beer from his tumbler. 'Well, there is this bastard, Chief Inspector Nduka Ikwunne from APCS on the investigative panel. He is not convinced that I am not involved. Every other investigator thinks I am not involved. Nevertheless, I don't think we need to worry too much about him. I am confident that I will be exonerated by the panel, eventually.'

Eugene cracked his knuckles. The detective's glibness was starting to irritate him.

'What the Chief Inspector thinks doesn't matter. Everyone in CID hates him because they see him as a witch hunter looking for crooked cops where there are none,' Mike added in between gulps of beer.

'So there is no problem?' Eugene asked somewhat relieved. He knew that many ordinary policemen hated anti-police corruption squad (APCS) officers with a passion.

Mike responded to his interlocutor's question with a wide grin.

'Good,' Eugene said and then drank from the bottle. 'Now, where are the mugshots?' he asked smacking his lips.

Mike's face creased. 'None were taken when your friend was brought in.'

Eugene stared at him in disbelief.

The policeman continued, 'your friend was brought in drunk. He couldn't even stand on his own feet. The mugshots were going to be taken in the morning, but he escaped before we had a chance to photograph him. We don't even have a description of him.'

Eugene was now smiling. It was all music to his ears. 'What if we pay you five thousand naira every month so that you can keep us informed.'

Otunba's countenance changed. He rubbed his chin in silent contemplation while Eugene swigged from the bottle.

'What do you say?' Eugene prodded impatiently.

The detective snapped out of his reverie, smiling broadly. 'For six thousand, I can take the risk,' he said, scratching the surface of his beer bottle with the nail of his forefinger.

'It's a deal then,' Eugene replied, extending his right arm across the table. The policeman shook the fraudster's outstretched hand.

'Mister Igolo, I have to run. It is now midnight,' Mike declared, rising to his feet, prompting the other man to do the same. They shook hands again.

The policeman turned to leave and suddenly remembered something. 'Because of the risks involved, I think it's better for us not to meet again, unless in exceptional circumstances...'

'Yeah, like when it is time to hand over another fat envelope,' Eugene interjected.

Mike ignored the sarcasm and continued, 'I'll call you whenever there is information to pass on. Under no circumstance should you call my home telephone or office telephone. That bastard, Ikwunne, might bug them.'

Eugene shook his head vehemently. 'No, that will not do for my people. There will be times when we will need to contact you. You have to do better than that.'

Mike smiled wrily and then rubbed his chin thoughtfully. 'Okay, I will set up a secure phone line in the basement of my house, but it will take a while. I don't think you will run deficit on information. I'll be in touch every fortnight. You and your friends don't have to worry about that. And you can call me whenever you want once the new phone line has been installed.'

Eugene nodded in satisfaction and sank into his chair as Mike made for the doorway. The swindler watched the detective walk past the entrance of DePauls and into the driveway. The policeman stopped beside a black Mazda sedan, parked next to the Peugeot 505, and unstrapped the bum bag round his waist.

As the Mazda pulled out of the driveway, someone touched Eugene's right shoulder. He turned and saw the waitress smiling apologetically.

'Sir, its ten minutes past midnight. Its late and we have to close,' she said.

Eugene smiled back. He placed some naira notes into the palm of her right hand and rose slowly from his seat. 'You can keep the change,' he said and staggering to the exit, slightly dazed by the alcohol in his system.

CHAPTER 5

JANUARY 1991

IBADAN, WESTERN NIGERIA

Ibadan, one of the oldest cities on the continent, started out as a small nondescript settlement at the edge of the Oyo Empire— a powerful ancient West African sovereign state occupying the land between the River Volta in the west and River Niger in the east. The vast empire, established by ethnic Yorubas in the 12th century, was presided over by an *Alaafin* (emperor). Below the *Alaafin* were homage-paying *Obas* (kings). Some *Obas* were governors of the empire's autonomous provinces while others were semi-independent rulers of the empire's tributary states.

Through the control of all trade on their territories, especially with European merchants, the *Obas* prospered. The enormous wealth generated from trading activities in the provinces and tributary states allowed the empire to maintain a trained infantry and a strike cavalry force, both of which allowed it to engage in continuous territorial expansion and consolidation through relentless conquest. However as the wealth increased, so did the political ambitions of the *Obas* who began to consider themselves rivals to the *Alaafin*.

By 1789, the provincial rulers were in open rebellion against imperial authority. Civil war ushered in the era of the empire's decline as it gradually shrunk in influence and territory. The rebel province of Ilorin declared independence from Oyo Empire in 1817 and subsequently became part of the neighbouring Sokoto Caliphate—a confederation of Sunni Muslim principalities.

Dahomey Kingdom— a semi-independent tributary state of Oyo Empire— rose in rebellion; defeated the *Alaafin*'s army; and became a full-fledged independent nation in 1823. It would later lose this hard-won sovereignty to the French colonial empire.

Meanwhile, the civil war between the rump Oyo Empire and its rebellious provinces continued, forcing many war refugees to flee to the relative safety of Ibadan. With rapid population growth and expansion of living quarters, Ibadan began to move away from its previous status as a small, irrelevant, nondescript settlement at the edge of a tottering empire.

By 1829, Ibadan had completed its transformation into a sprawling urban centre, one of the few cities in pre-colonial Africa. As the Oyo Empire continued to disintegrate, the Ibadan city-state prospered and grew stronger militarily, defeating all attempts by the Muslim rulers of the Sokoto Caliphate to subjugate and commit it to annexation.

Having established a foothold along the Atlantic coast through the 1861 takeover and colonization of the Kingdom of Lagos, colonial officers of the

British Empire decided in 1886 that it was time to advance into the hinterlands. In 1888, the plodding British colonizers finally made it to the *Alaafin*'s royal court, almost two hundred miles northwest of their coastal stronghold. They and the *Alaafin* concluded a treaty, which reduced him from a de jure sovereign to a vassal of Her Majesty, Queen Victoria. The treaty also stipulated that all territories that once belonged to the Oyo Empire would be submitted to the authority of Her Majesty's Government.

As the British would later discover, the treaty was barely worth the paper it was written on. The *Alaafin* was already a powerless figure long before the British arrived at his royal court. He was in no position to handover any meaningful territory to the British colonial overlords because the Oyo Empire of 1888 existed in name only. The de jure territories of the empire had become de facto independent statelets fighting amongst themselves. While rejecting the right of the *Alaafin* to rule over them, some of those warring statelets had continued, nevertheless, to respect his moral authority.

It would take the British colonials a lot of time and effort to seize the huge swathes of land promised them by the 1888 treaty. Through persuasion, military aggression or both, the Yoruba statelets submitted, one by one, to the advancing British colonial regime. For instance, the independence of the powerful Ibadan city-state came to a peaceful end following a separate treaty signed in 1893 by its ruler and Sir George Denton, the British colonial governor of Lagos. But not all statelets were willing to follow Ibadan's example. Places such as Oyo-Atiba and Ilorin rejected peaceful surrender and annexation-by-treaty, forcing the British to use artillery bombardment to "pacify the unruly natives". By 1897, all former territories of the defunct Oyo Empire—except French-controlled Dahomey—were under firm British control.

Under British colonial rule, Ibadan modernized. In 1959, the city made history as the site of the first ever terrestrial television station established anywhere on the entire African continent. Meanwhile, the local population continued to grow, allowing Ibadan to maintain its old reputation as one of the largest cities in Africa.

On the morning of 12th January 1991, this same historic city was agog with final preparations for the hosting of an evangelical rally by famous American Pentecostal preacher Michael Grams. Posters announcing the imminent event were plastered all over the walls of the city. Pastors of local Pentecostal churches were busy patting themselves on the back, having invested lots of time and money in organizing the event. Amongst them was Pastor Richard Ibeh of Evergreen Glory of God Ministries Incorporated. Unlike the other celebrating pastors, he was not a local. He had travelled all the way from Onitsha city in Eastern Nigeria.

Four weeks earlier, he had turned up uninvited to a nighttime prayer gathering of twenty-five local pastors, inside a hotel in Ibadan, where heated discussions were being held on how to pool meagre resources to ensure the successful hosting of the American evangelist. Richard's sudden appearance had unnerved the pastors who wondered if their decision to cut security arrangements from their budget was wise.

Richard Ibeh had introduced himself calmly to the perplexed pastors of Ibadan. He was a pastor based in Onitsha and would be honoured to be included in the committee organizing the hosting of the American preacher. He had prayed hard about it and God had willed him to shuttle regularly between the Eastern and Western halves of the country to lend a helping hand to the pastors. More importantly, he was also offering to underwrite a huge chunk of the cost of the expensive venture. Though the local pastors, mostly Yorubas, had their doubts about this bizzare Igbo interloper from the East, they were short on cash. So when they heard the staggering amount of money the stranger was willing to contribute, they beamed with delight and promptly co-opted him into the gathering.

But Pastor Richard Ibeh could still see the doubt in their eyes as he addressed them. His money may have bought him a place in their midst, but the pastors had never heard of him before that night and so didn't fully trust him. Richard had anticipated this and had come fully prepared to win them over.

At the end of the prayer meeting in the hotel conference room, the side door opened and a male hotel steward wheeled in a shiny stainless steel trolley containing a TV and a video cassette recorder. The pastors of Ibadan watched in bemusement as the steward pushed a VHS tape cassette into the video machine. Seconds later, video footage of Richard preaching and performing miracles before a teeming congregation filled the TV screen.

On the television set, a crippled man in a wheel chair jumped to his feet when Pastor Richard on video touched his back. A blind man with a walking stick had Richard's saliva rubbed in his closed eyes and they opened instantly. By the time the twenty-minute video clip ended, the local pastors were loudly praising God. All doubts about Richard's pastoral calling disappeared. Shortly after, the local pastors left the hotel for their respective homes, but Richard stayed behind to tip the hotel steward handsomely. And for the entire four weeks preceding 12th January 1991, Richard travelled back and forth between Ibadan and his true base of operations, providing copious amounts of money requested by local pastors preparing the Western Nigerian city for the visit of the famous American preacher...

The afternoon of 12th January was very sunny, hotter than the previous days. Liberty Stadium was packed to the rafters with people seeking God and solutions to their worldly problems. When Reverend Pastor Michael Grams mounted the podium with the hosting pastors, the crowd erupted in a frenzy of singing and dancing. The Louisiana-based preacher took the microphone. He opened with a prayer for the crowd, that God may solve their plethora of problems— illness, poverty, unemployment, childlessness, etc.

Eight hours later, the evangelistic rally in the packed stadium came to an end and Michael was whisked to a five-star hotel at the edge of the city. After dinner in the hotel restaurant with all twenty-six pastors who had organised the great event, the American retired to his room with Richard who had requested a private audience. In the large room, Richard sat on the only armchair available and the American sat opposite him on the bed.

'Woah! Those huge crowds seeking the face of God! It was such a beautiful day. You guys are such superb organizers,' Michael said gleefully for the umpteenth time since the rally ended. It irritated Richard, but he smiled diffidently, and again thanked the American for the compliment.

'Next year, I look forward to carrying the good news up North.' The American was referring to the next evangelistic crusade scheduled for Kano city in Northern Nigeria.

'The lord will make it a success,' Richard said, although he didn't believe it. The last time an evangelist organized a huge proselytizing rally in Kano, Muslim street urchins, known as the *Almajiri,* went on the rampage. When the smoke of the fires they had started cleared, many churches and businesses owned by non-Muslims were in ruins. Ninety Christians lost their lives too.

Michael was aware of the tragedy. Back in 1989, he had read about it in *The New York Times*, which had a journalist in Northern Nigeria reporting from the scene of the riot. The newspaper had published pictures of the carnage in its centre-spread. Accompanying the pictures were reports of the US State Department, US Congress and President George Herbert Bush condemning the violence; the Nigerian Federal Military Government's announcement of an investigation into the riot; and the Kano State governor's condolence messages to victims and their families. A delegation of the Christian Association of Nigeria (CAN) and a representative of the World Council of Churches (WCC) had met separately with the Kano State Commissioner for Religious Affairs. On both occasions, the affable state commissioner, a Sunni Muslim, assured his interlocutors that future Christian rallies would be provided with a well-armed security detail for protection.

Michael had taken those assurances to heart because in a follow-up article in the weekly *New York Times Magazine*, the WCC representative—an East Tennessean— had said that the Kano State Government, deeply embarrassed by the deadly riot, was determined to prevent such violence from occurring again.

Richard was in Lagos when the religious riots broke out in the North. He also heard the apologies and assurances of the Kano State Government back then. In a radio interview broadcast in November 1989, a month after the deadly riot, the Kano State governor had reiterated his pledge to deploy mixed teams of policemen and soldiers across the state capital—Kano city— to protect all future Christian rallies. Richard had reacted to what he heard on the radio with mirthless laughter and utter disbelief.

And fourteen months later, inside the hotel room in Ibadan, those same feelings of skepticism and pessimism came back to him as he watched Pastor Michael Grams talk excitedly about the Kano rally planned for the first quarter of 1992. He toyed fleetingly with the idea of telling the American some home truths—trusting the assurances of any government official was terribly naive;

holding huge Christian revivalist rallies in the middle of a predominantly Muslim city was just asking for trouble.

Suppressing his true feelings behind a facade of wide smiles, Richard nodded at intervals to signal agreement with what Michael was saying. He was not there to disabuse the mind of the American. His mission was to maintain a companionable atmosphere and wait for an opportune moment in the conversation to segue into what he was really there to talk about. To keep the dialogue moving smoothly, Richard even volunteered a comment to the effect that God had preordained the American to bring the word of God to the people of Kano. The Louisana-based preacher was delighted to hear the comment. He rose from the bed. Raising both arms towards the ceiling, a few inches from the blades of the fan spinning above, he exclaimed, 'Praise Jesus!'

'Amen!' Richard replied, his smile unfaltering. Then the conversation was interrupted by a knock on the door. Michael opened it and accepted a silver tray of drinks and tumblers from room service personnel. 'Do you take cognac or coca-cola?' he asked, settling the tray on the glass coffee table between the armchair and the bed. Richard requested for the soft drink. Michael poured himself a generous amount of liquor.

'Down in Eastern Nigeria, my ministry in Onitsha city runs an orphanage and a reformatory for young juveniles,' Richard said before pausing to sip his drink. The American sat up on the bed to listen to the interesting story. Richard produced glossy photographs of thin children smiling in front of a dilapidated four-storey building with a wooden signboard hanging above the doorway with the words: YOUNG SAINTS ORPHANAGE.

'For the past three years,' Richard continued, 'we have been having financial difficulties, which is threatening to roll back many years of hard work...'

The American preacher, without taking his eyes off the pictures, interrupted Richard. 'The good Lord will not allow that to happen. The orphanage and the reformatory are his evangelical instruments,' he said, shaking his head. A moment of companionable silence fell as the American continued to go through the 8-inch by 6-inch photos. Then he looked at the Nigerian and broke his silence. 'I am willing to help,' he said and shifted his gaze back to the photographs between his hands.

Richard smiled, raising his eyes to heaven to thank God for providing manna for the poor orphans under his care. Another brief moment of silence followed.

'Can I keep these?' the American asked, already reaching for the black attaché case at the foot of the bed. Richard replied in the affirmative and watched silently as the American slotted the thin stack of photographs into one of the internal sleeve pockets inside the now open attaché case. The Nigerian also caught a glimpse of a King James Version Bible and a leather-bound diary lying on the navy blue, velvet-lined, padded interior of the attaché case just before Michael snapped its lid shut.

'Work out how much it will cost...what you need to settle the financial problems and send it to me in the States. I will sit with my church council and consider how we can best assist your ministry,' the American said as he handed the Nigerian a business card with a Baton Rouge postal address and telephone number.

Pastor Richard was overjoyed. He thanked God and the American profusely. And before he left the hotel, he joined hands with the American and prayed.

CHAPTER **6**

LAGOS, WESTERN NIGERIA

The champagne bottle made a "pop" sound as John Nwosu uncorked it. His men laughed and clapped as he wiped away the foam oozing from the bottle. He poured a generous amount of the wine into his glass before passing the bottle to his men.

'Cheers!' he exclaimed raising his glass, prompting the rest of the gang to do the same. The men were celebrating their windfall— a whopping $80,000 (₦1,360,000) and counting— from a single operation, still running smoothly after twenty months.

Initially, John had been skeptical of the plan for the operation when Tunde first approached him with it. 'These white guys will fall for anything, I tell you,' the gangster assured John who was wary of wasting money on high-risk schemes. Tunde's scheme required a huge budget— ₦150,000— most of which was earmarked as a lump sum donation to a bunch of Pentecostal preachers to buy goodwill. The rest of the budget was to be spent on actors hired to shoot a twenty-minute faith healing video and renting different cars for frequent travel to Ibadan through accident-prone expressways full of potholes.

Tunde's scheme also required John to reacquaint himself with the Bible, which he had not touched since his teenage years. When Tunde first mentioned that prerequisite, John had laughed hard and then dismissed the entire scheme as complex, protracted, risky and too expensive. But Tunde persisted. 'Have I ever failed to deliver?' he asked his boss.

The boss, John, knew the answer. Tunde, a highly meticulous man, always delivered the goods with his well-thought out plans. 'You are our genius!' the gang leader replied heartily and asked for more time to think about the proposal.

The following day, he approved the scheme despite his misgivings about the hefty budget involved. An excited Tunde reassured his skeptical boss that the plan would work like a charm.

A fortnight after the revivalist rallies in Ibadan ended, and Michael Grams returned home to USA, John had reason to be glad that he had placed his trust in Tunde Olukemi.

The American preacher had been true to his word, sending a cheque for an initial sum of $4000 to Nigeria to help fund an orphanage and reformatory that did not exist.

John Nwosu alias "Pastor Richard Ibeh" made sure to send monthly letters of gratitude—along with pictures of well-fed orphans and reformed teenage juveniles reading the Bible— to Michael. The con artist had no need for doctored pictures when real ones could suffice. He simply visited real government-owned orphanages and reformatories across Lagos State, every four weeks, and donated second-hand clothes and some sacks of rice at low cost to himself. The grateful authorities of these poorly funded orphanages were always happy to take pictures of him smiling with the overjoyed children. In the reformatories, amiable head wardens allowed the best-behaved juveniles, reading bibles in their chaplaincies, to pose for photographs.

For John, the process of cherry-picking which pictures will accompany the letters going overseas was an earnest exercise in curatorship. Photographs showing only the orphans and the juveniles, standing next to donated clothes, sacks of rice, crates of soft drinks and other goodies, went to the American preacher. Photographs showing "Richard" posing next to the children were destroyed. It was a terrible waste of 35 mm film, but it could not be helped. Always wary of being photographed, John found himself being cajoled into posing for group pictures during his visits. Every month, he cooked up an excuse to avoid appearing in group photographs, and every time, those persistent kids in the orphanages, with their wide innocent smiles, managed to coax him into wasting half a roll of good film.

The monthly letters and pictures sent to Baton Rouge turned what was originally meant to be a one-off monetary assistance into a monthly stipend of $4000. Every letter sent to the American preacher expressed gratitude in the first two paragraphs and then catalogued a plethora of new problems facing the phantom orphanage and reformatory. There was always the threat of imminent financial collapse if the money wasn't sent quickly enough.

Michael Grams noticed, but did not make much of the fact, that envelopes bearing Richard's monthly letters were always postmarked in Lagos, although the return address on each of them was in Onitsha city. He simply read the contents of each letter earnestly and wrote a reply as soon as he was done, enclosing a cheque for $4000 in a personalized envelope, before driving down to the Baton Rouge FedEx Shipping Centre on Coursey Boulevard, three miles from his church.

Afterwards, Eugene had the task of driving 300 miles from Lagos to Onitsha, along vast stretches of poorly maintained roads, to reach the doorstep of a specific house, where he was to wait for a FedEx courier to deliver Pastor Gram's package for the month. Sometimes, city traffic in Onitsha delayed Eugene's arrival at the address. But that was nothing to worry about; the cheerful courier always waited patiently by the house doorstep, knowing Eugene was one of a few FedEx package receivers who bothered to offer a tip, and the only one whose generosity in tipping increased with each contact.

Five months into the scam, John and his men started laundering their ill-gotten gains through two front enterprises. They had established the companies in 1990, shortly after the suicide of Gary Logan, to launder the one million dollars they had swindled from him. The fronts were Dixon Job Agency and ELAJ Enterprises, a vehicle spare parts dealership.

Unlike Dixon Job Agency, ELAJ Enterprises had beaten all expectations to become their only lucrative legitimate business. The inexpensive spare parts offered by ELAJ had become the favourites of distributors who poured into the company's warehouses to order loads of them. At the end of the first year, the company's turnover was staggering enough for the swindlers to regard it as more than a front.

The fraudsters, basking in their new multi-millionaire status, moved from their single-room apartments in Mushin to mansions in the affluent Victoria Island. They started wearing designer suits and drove in flashy cars. To their neighbours and anyone concerned, they were all respectable members of society, self-made entrepreneurs who went to work early in the morning and returned home late at night, on a daily basis.

On the night that marked the twentieth month since the first $4000 was received, the men decided to meet in a room in the basement of John's mansion. The room, dubbed "the situation room", was a place where the men met to discuss new ideas and plan better ways of finagling money out of rich westerners.

Tunde was responsible for seeking out gullible businessmen in the Western world. This was usually achieved by going through British and US financial newspapers and attending business conferences hosted by the Nigerian Chamber of Commerce to identify key European and North American delegates. Sometimes, he went abroad for advanced information gathering. At the end of it all, he was expected to prepare a dossier on the targeted individual, which will then be discussed in the "situation room" down in John's basement.

The economic strengths and weaknesses of the individual played a big role in determining whether the swindle operation would go ahead. Usually, the gang tended to approve only operations against wealthy individuals who had gotten themselves into financial trouble. Experience had taught the gangsters that such individuals were the most gullible. Financial problems had blinded a desperate Logan to the swindle that unfolded before his very eyes.

As the leader of the gang, John was in charge of co-coordinating all swindle operations. He also handled American businessmen personally since he could also affect a decent General American accent when necessary. He had acquired the trained accent by spending the last five years of his prison sentence listening and pronouncing words broadcast by *Voice of America*. He also used tapes mailed to him by the Education Services Division of the United States Information Service (USIS) in Lagos.

Everyone in the "situation room" listened to John with rapt attention as he spoke. 'I received a letter from Mike Grams. The photos pleased and convinced him. He has pledged to continue sending us money. The money, of course, will be used judiciously to improve my orphanage.'

The men chuckled at the obvious joke.

'But there is a little problem,' John announced gravely.

The laughter ceased and silence fell.

'For the fifth time in a row, Reverend Grams have requested a visit to see the progress we are making with his money. He wants to come to Nigeria next year. I am beginning to run out of excuses to stop him,' John paused, his eyes searching the faces staring at him for suggestions.

'Well sir, we all knew it wasn't going to last forever,' Adamu reasoned with a smug smile on his face. 'So let's enjoy it while it lasts. If we are lucky, he will keep sending money for the next twelve months before he realises the scam.'

Everyone nodded in agreement, although they all thought that twelve months was too optimistic. They gave Pastor Michael Grams another six months, at the most, to uncover the fraud and cut off the money tap. Another six months would make them $24,000 richer, they all thought.

John left the floor and returned to his seat. Tunde distributed yellow manila folders to each of the seated men and then took the floor.

'I have made progress on the European front,' he announced, flipping open an identical copy of the folder. The seated men promptly flipped their own folders open.

'If you study the documents inside, you will notice that this is the best dossier I have ever produced,' Tunde remarked with a smile. The rest of the gang, except John, grunted derisively at the boast.

'The target is this man, Roy Seed.' A poster-sized picture of a smiling young white man was held up for all the fraudsters to see. 'This man is from the UK. He is heir to a multi-million pound chain of stores built by his late grandfather, Lord Lindsay Seed, a British Peer, who passed away seven years ago. Roy's father, Lord Hugh Seed, who previously ran the sportswear division of the chain, took over the reins of the whole company after Lindsay died. But his control over the company is now slipping away. Last year, Hugh was diagnosed with stage-four lung cancer. Effective day-to-day running of the business has been entrusted to the inexperienced Roy who has a penchant for gambling away money in the casinos...'

'An obvious weak point,' John interjected, knowing where the narration was heading.

Tunde smiled. 'Yes, exactly. I managed to track our man, Roy, down at his favourite hangout, a pub in South London, and introduced myself as Tony Oke, a low-level Nigerian government official willing to do business with the right person. He became interested and I told him the story of the oil tanker floating in the Atlantic Ocean.'

The audience chuckled. Tunde paused to let the laughter subside before continuing the story. 'I told him that the petroleum minister had diverted five hundred thousand barrels of crude oil into a privately owned barge concealed somewhere in the Atlantic. The minister lacks money to finance the transfer of the oil illegally to apartheid South Africa. Roy asked me how it was possible for a minister in charge of the ministry's coffers not to have money to finance the operation. I had to explain to him that the minister could not just appropriate government money. He would require the cooperation of other government officials. Ministry accountants would have to sign cheques and and federal permanent secretaries would have to sign authorization documents. The minister would rather avoid such a situation because the paper trail would eventually lead to his exposure and imprisonment. Therefore, the plan is to get an interested foreign investor to provide external funding. Roy has expressed an interest in getting involved provided the return on investment was good. We had a few beers and I promised to get back to him with the details after consultations with the minister.'

John was so elated that he started clapping, prompting the others to join in. When the applause subsided, Tunde, feigning diffidence, added, 'thank you guys, but I don't have all the answers. I'll let the boss explain our general strategy in dealing with this delicate target.'

He walked back to his seat and the gang leader retook the floor. 'We are con-artists, experts in creating our own reality,' John began like a preacher exhorting his flock to keep the faith. 'We will make Roy feel at home when he comes to visit us, because I'm sure he will request it, just like the others before him. We shall mesmerize him with artifacts of our trade. The meeting environment, the documents, the photographs, and the promises shall be more than enough to persuade him to part with a hundred thousand pounds or even more. I am still working on some minor details of the plan with Tunde. When we meet here again in a week's time, I'll present the finished product,' he paused to let the message sink. 'We will get nothing less than hundred thousand pounds from Mister Roy Seed.'

The men rose from their chairs and gave their leader a standing ovation...

CHAPTER 7

Among the suburbs of Baton Rouge city, Oak Hills Place was by no means the biggest. With a population of 5,480, it was no match for denser suburbs such as Merrydale and Shenandoah. But, as one of the most affluent places just outside the city limits of Baton Rouge, Oak Hills Place had its advantages. It had nice public parks, respectable residents, decent houses and well-groomed lawns; an ideal place to live in and commute to work in Baton Rouge proper.

Tucked into the northwest corner of Oak Hills Place was Don Budge Avenue— an avenue lined on both sides with detached houses, each one with its own trimmed grass lawn, each one separated from the other by concrete walkways.

Pastor Michael Grams and his wife lived in a five-bedroom detached house at one end of that avenue, next to a grove of trees. The elegant atmosphere of serenity made it the ideal place to raise children, read and reflect quietly on the scriptures, and commute into the rather lively centre of Baton Rouge city where his Pentecostal church was located. That was why Mrs Sarah Grams insisted on purchasing the house four years earlier.

Four years earlier, Pastor Grams had been hesitant to buy the house—the asking price was prohibitive; five bedrooms was too extravagant and unnecessary, considering that the good Lord had not yet blessed him and his wife with any children. Besides, he reckoned that there was nothing wrong with their rented apartment in Baton Rouge, just a stone's throw away from their church.

Mrs Grams, who had always wanted to live in the quiet suburbs, had pushed back strongly when he shared his feelings on the matter with her. Then aged thirty-seven, she told him that it was not too late for them to have kids. And for her, a spacious house in a decent neighbourhood was a prerequisite for raising the plenty children that the good Lord was going to bestow upon them in the near future. When Michael showed signs of demurring, she berated him. Did he not have faith that the Lord would give them children soon? Had he forgotten that her own mum—his mother-in-law—was in her late thirties when she gave birth to her? Did he not understand that no price was too high for a decent home for their future kids? Did he not see the benefits of moving away from the hustle and bustle of city life?

The evangelical preacher was so taken aback by the ferocity of his wife's pushback that he wondered if something dark had taken possession of his normally pleasant wife. He deeply resented the fusillade of rhetorical questions she had barked at him. Of course, he had faith in God. If God willed it then they would have children, many of them. His instinctive reluctance to spend large sums of money on vanity was influenced both by scriptures and by the frugality he had imbibed from his deprived childhood in the Appalachian Mountains of East Tennessee.

For obvious reasons, Michael did not say any of this to his wife. He did not want to risk the ire of his wife by calling the house purchase a "vanity project". He simply nodded after his wife finished barking at him and then placed a call to the realtor who had earlier shown them around a lightly wooded residential area called Don Budge Avenue. A few days later, they received the keys and title deeds to the house, and thus, became owners of a property in Oak Hills Place.

One of the happiest days in Sarah's life was 6th April 1989, the day she and her husband finally moved into their suburban home. Michael compelled himself to be happy for her sake. He had prayed about it and believed it was God's wish that he support his wife. Nevertheless, as much as he tried, he could not the shake off the feeling that money spent on the house could have been better spent as donations to the multiple religious charities that he and his wife supported. Although, they regularly donated to several charities helping poor families and orphaned kids in the Greater Baton Rouge area, they could still do more to help. After all, the Bible says, *to whom much is given, much is expected.*

However, over a long period, as the population of Baton Rouge city soared and crime rose, Michael came to appreciate the necessity of living outside the city limits. He was glad that he had listened to his wife. She had been right about buying a suburban home, but not for the main reasons she had given. The good Lord had still not seen fit to grant them their own children. They had already been to several fertility doctors, and each one had assured them that there was nothing medically wrong with them. They just had to keep trying to conceive a child; although some doctors did warn in December 1991 that time was running out as his wife edged closer to the age of menopause.

Michael and his wife doubled up on their prayers and charity work among the orphaned and the poor, which drew a lot of praise from all communities in Baton Rouge, particularly from the Black American community, where poverty rates were disproportionately higher. Michael also began to undertake frequent trips to various poorer countries in Eastern Europe, Asia, Africa and Latin America, where he held Christian revivalist rallies and donated generously to local religious charities. And for years, he never doubted that the largesse he had been extending to those foreign charities in third world countries was being used for anything other than God's work. That was, until the start of 1993...

On 13th February 1993, eight days after his 43rd birthday, Michael Grams undertook an early morning stroll around the premises of his residence to clear his head. He walked out of the front door; sauntered across the carpet grass lawn in front of his house; and manoeuvred around the side of the building to get to the backyard. In the rear of the house, he stopped briefly to admire the brightly coloured flowers in his wife's beautiful garden before carrying on. The stroll did nothing to combat his anxiety. He remained deeply troubled by what he had been thinking about since January that year.

When he got to the grove of trees abutting the garden, he turned back and re-entered the house through the back door. The back door led into the kitchen where he stopped briefly and examined the wooden flooring and the exquisite kitchen decor. He suddenly became aware of the fact the granite tabletop and lacquered wooden kitchen cabinets had no scuff marks on them despite the great passage of time. A remarkable testament to the furniture company which had outfitted the kitchen several years earlier, he surmised as he opened the sliding glass patio doors that separated the kitchen from the living room.

He walked across the Persian rug to the built-in Art Deco-style bar in the far corner of the tastefully furnished living room. There, he fixed himself a small amount of bourbon whiskey and started towards the other end of the room. He stopped in front of the fireplace decorated with a mantelpiece made of bronze-gilded marble and sipped bourbon from his glass tumbler. The burning sensation he felt as the alcohol slipped down into his gullet somewhat calmed him a little bit. His eyes shifted to gaze at three large framed pictures hanging high up on the wall above the mantelpiece. One was a portrait painting inside a wooden neo-Baroque frame. The other two were black-and-white photographs encased in glass-fronted metal frames. Each depicted a young man dressed in a military uniform.

The portrait painting was of his great-grandfather, Seymour David Grams— a third generation member of a Scots-Irish family that immigrated to the United States in the 17th century. Born in May 1842, Seymour was raised in the Appalachian Mountains of East Tennessee, a poverty-stricken area where suspicion and resentment ran high for the wealthy slave-owning planter aristocracy that dominated political, social and economic life throughout the Southern United States. Seymour was nineteen when the State of Tennessee joined the Confederacy on 2nd July 1861, despite fierce resistance from many East Tennesseans who remained loyal to the United States. In the civil war that ensued, he was among the very large numbers of East Tennessean men who enlisted and fought on the Union side. After the civil war, he married and became a sharecropper. Together with his wife, he sired five boys, three of whom survived to adulthood.

Hanging next to the painting in the overmantel was the framed black-and-white photograph of Michael's grandfather, Sheldon Davis Grams. Sheldon was born in 1869, eight years before the end of the Reconstruction Era. As the youngest of his three surviving sons, Seymour dotted on Sheldon and borrowed heavily to ensure that he had a decent education. When young Sheldon turned seventeen, he joined the United States Army and soon found himself fighting in various conflicts—Geronimo's War (1886) within US territory; Spanish-American War (1898) on the territory of Cuba; the Battles of Veracruz (1914) and Parral (1916) on Mexican territory; and finally, the First World War (1917-1918) on the territory of France.

After the First World War, Sheldon retired from the army, moved to New York, and invested his savings and pension in the stock markets. For a while, he prospered until the Wall Street Crash of 1929 wiped him clean. Impoverished, he returned with his wife and only son to East Tennessee. That only son, Thomas Davis Grams, was the other framed photograph hanging in the overmantel of Michael's living room, next to Sheldon's picture.

Following the family tradition, Thomas had joined the army in 1933 at the age of nineteen. He would see combat action in the Second World War and Korean War before resigning his commission, after 20 years of service, to return to civilian life. Like his father, his success as a businessman was short-lived. His fall from grace was preceded by a series of bad investments, which eviscerated all his business concerns in the city of Nashville. And, like his father, he returned penniless to the Appalachian Mountains of East Tennessee with his wife and son, Michael. There, he began to eke out a living by selling firewood on street corners.

Michael was eighteen when he received his military draft papers in March 1968. Soon he was fighting in the dense jungles of South Vietnam, dodging bullets and deadly booby traps of Vietcong guerrillas, and artillery barrages of the conventional North Vietnamese army. He saw young men his age, brothers-in-arms, dying all around him in firefights and ambushes. It was a tough life in the jungles of Southeast Asia, but it was okay because he was fighting the Reds, the Commies. If conscription had not come sooner, he reckoned he would have volunteered.

But alas, his war against the Commies was short-lived. It ended early for him on 5th January 1970 when a soldier in his reconnaissance platoon stepped on a taut thin wire, hidden in the undergrowth, while traversing a forest clearing. The thin wire snapped, causing a buried improvised explosive device—an oil drum filled with nails, ball bearings, trinitrotoluene and gelignite—to blow up, spraying hot shrapnel in all directions. Ten soldiers, including the one that stepped on the tripwire, died on the spot. Thirty soldiers were wounded, their injuries ranging from minor to life-threatening. Michael's injury was neither minor nor life-threatening, but it was serious. His lower torso had caught some ball bearings and nails scything through the air. Just before losing consciousness, he had seen the gleam of blood oozing from his abdomen, and felt a burning sensation mixed with excruciating pain in his gut.

When he regained consciousness on a hospital bed, it was twenty-four hours later, and he was no longer in Vietnam. As the bleariness of general anaesthesia wore off, he found a beautiful eighteen-year-old nursing assistant bending over him, cleaning the wound on his torso with cotton wool soaked in silver nitrate. He flinched in pain, prompting her to apologise. He asked her where he was and she told him. He was on an air base operated by the United States Airforce in northeast Thailand. He asked the nursing assistant her name and she told him, and then gave him a shot of sedative. Looking at her dreamily, he said, 'Sarah Bonnet, you are pretty lady,' and then fell asleep. She looked upon his sleeping face with an appreciative smile.

Two months later, fully healed, he was redeployed to Fort Hood Army Base in Texas, where he served until honourable discharge in May 1973. Throughout his deployment in Texas, he kept corresponding with Miss Sarah Bonnet who remained in Thailand until July 1973.

She reunited with Michael upon her return to United States, and within a year, they were married. With the then newly minted Mrs Sarah Grams, he moved to the city of New Orleans to start a new life in the summer of 1974. His generous father-in-law provided a loan, which he put to good use. He started a whiskey distillery, and soon became the first member of the Grams family to break the jinx, the first to become wealthy and stay wealthy. He did not allow it to get to his head. He never forgot about his East Tennessean childhood, the rustic one-room timber shack, where he lived with his parents, where he listened to them bicker about how best to ration their limited resources, and bemoan the dire financial straits they were trapped in. He also remembered the time before that, the happier period of his childhood in Nashville, living in relative luxury, before his father lost everything. It taught him a lot about life. Wealth was a gift from God, one that should be shared. So he spent generously on charities, especially those devoted to poor families and orphaned children.

His survival of a ghastly car accident in the winter of 1984 shook him immensely; made him increasingly religious, and he soon became a lay Presbyterian Church preacher. By 1986, he had sold his distillery, moved to Baton Rouge city, and founded his own evangelical ministry in the form of The Louisiana Church of Jesus Christ. From there, he preached the scriptures, helped the poor materially and spiritually. He also ignored advice from those who warned him to be careful about splashing vast sums of money on unaccountable foreign charities claiming to help orphaned children in poor countries. He felt justified in his refusal to heed such advice, because he had visited various countries—Romania, Moldova, Panama, Cambodia, Laos, Nicaragua, Haiti, Ghana, Gambia, Kenya and Tanzania—and had seen with his own eyes how his money have been used to improve the lives of poor families and orphaned kids. He had never had any cause for alarm, no reason to distrust the foreign religious charities that solicited and accepted his cheques regularly. That was until he met Pastor Richard Ibeh and began sending money to Nigeria...

Michael sipped more bourbon while staring at the pictures of his forebears on the wall. He wondered what his late father would have made of the matter troubling him. His father probably would have smiled sardonically, and said, 'I told you so.' Before passing away two winters earlier, the old man was one of those who had cautioned Michael about his "excessive" generosity and willingness to trust without verification. The late Thomas Grams had not approved of many of his son's life choices, especially the decision to sell the distillery and become a full-time evangelical preacher.

Michael gulped down the remaining contents of the tumbler and placed it on the mantel shelf next to a copy of the King James Version Bible. Then he sank into an armchair positioned three feet from the fireplace. Reclining on the chair, he was soon lost in deep contemplation. Something was not right. He just couldn't understand why Richard was strongly against his desire to visit Nigeria to see for himself how his money— $100,000 donated over a period of twenty-five months— was being used to improve the lives of those poor children he had only seen in photographs. Each time he wrote or phoned to inform Richard of a plan to visit, there was always a dissuading excuse given. It was either that the country was on the brink of civil strife or that Onitsha city was unsafe for foreigners. The first time Richard proffered the excuse, Michael had wholeheartedly believed it.

He believed Richard's excuse because the events of 4th March 1992 were still fresh on his mind. On that fateful day, he had woken up in his hotel room in New York City and prayed, commending his impending visit to West Africa into the hands of God. Then he grabbed his luggage and checked out of the hotel. He was still en route to JFK International Airport, when news arrived from Nigeria that the Kano State government had cancelled his evangelistic rally for Kano city following anti-Christian riots spearheaded by *Almajiris*, who were on the rampage following unfounded rumours that a Christian woman had shredded a copy of the Koran. After his return to Louisiana from New York, Michael participated in a telephone conference call with the Nigerian pastors who had organized the cancelled rally. The Kano-based pastors were full of apologies and promised to go ahead with the rally as soon as peace returned to their city. Michael agreed to visit Kano upon the receipt of a fresh invitation from the pastors, even though he suspected that such an invitation might never come; that the pastors might not want to risk another round of social unrest by hosting the event in the volatile city.

Because of the tragedy in Kano city, Michael was not bothered when Richard turned down his first request for a visit in April 1992. Although, he found it a bit odd that Richard would declare Onitsha unsafe for a visit. Onitsha city was inhabited almost exclusively by Christians. Moreover, it was located in Eastern Nigeria, hundreds of miles away from the troubled Northern city of Kano. Back in January 1991, during his visit to Ibadan, Mike had met many local Christians who told him that both Western and Eastern regions of Nigeria were generally safe. The problem was always in the relatively poorer Northern region where Muslims were predominant...

In a corner of the living room, the grandfather clock began to chime loudly, jarring Michael out of his thoughts. He glanced briefly at his watch. The time was 12 noon. He rose from the sofa, picked up the empty tumbler from the mantel shelf, and headed towards the built-in bar. A few inches from the bar, he changed his mind.

Orange juice is better, he thought as he walked through the open patio door to the kitchen. From the humming refrigerator, he fetched himself a 200 ml carton of chilled orange juice. Then he settled on a high stool behind the large granite topped table, facing the electric kitchen stove. He was sucking the orange juice through a plastic straw when he began to hear the sounds of footsteps in the upstairs bedroom directly above the kitchen. The footsteps clicked down the wooden staircase and across the terrazzo-tiled floor.

The glass patio door opened and Sarah entered the kitchen. She walked straight up to him. 'There you are,' she smiled, handing him an A4-sized plain white paper and a pen. Then she picked up the orange juice carton and sucked on the straw.

Michael sighed heavily. His wife had been urging him not to think the worst, to write to Richard since the night before. He had been too depressed to think clearly. Placing the paper on the granite tabletop, he started writing his final letter to Nigeria, as Sarah worked the electric stove.

For two years, Michael had believed the excuses of Richard whom he considered a man of God. Doubts started emerging in January 1993 when skeptical members of his church elders' council finally wrote to the Pentecostal Fellowship of Nigeria (PFN) — the umbrella organisation of evangelical churches in Nigeria— to make enquires about the authenticity of Richard's ministry. The PFN wrote back saying that Richard's church was not a member of their organisation, but made it clear that there were many genuine evangelists who were not members.

Based on information supplied by PFN, the Elders' Council of The Louisiana Church of Jesus Christ called a meeting chaired by Michael Grams. In the gathering, Michael defended himself before the church elders and called for Richard to be given the benefit of doubt, refusing to contemplate the possibility that the Nigerian pastor was actually a fraudster. The council ignored his pleas and forbade him from sending more money to Nigeria until he was allowed to see for himself what the $96,000 donated so far had been used for. As the most senior church elder pointed out to Michael, 'it is not a matter of giving the benefit of the doubt. It is the fact that a man who has received a lot of money from us is refusing accountability. Stalling your plans to visit the country is reasonable grounds for suspicion.'

On 12th January 1993, two days after the meeting of his church's elders, Michael made his seventh request to Richard for a visit to Onitsha city. Over the phone, he told Richard that the church elders were tired of the excuses. Funding was going to be suspended if the request for a visit was denied again. To Michael's surprise, Richard readily agreed, but requested for money and a full month "to set things right" for the visitation. An elated Michael Grams quickly agreed. Over the next seven days, the American preacher lobbied the church elders individually and collectively, and succeeded in cajoling them into sending what was to become the final $4000 to Nigeria to help Richard "set things right" for a visitation.

The full month requested by Richard elapsed on the afternoon of 12th February 1993, and Michael decided it was time to call Nigeria to fix a date for his international trip. He called the telephone number on which he had conversed so many times with the Nigerian pastor. To his utmost surprise, a recorded female voice announced that the phone number he had dialled did not exist. He double-checked the Nigerian telephone number. It was correct. He tried not to panic as he dialled the number again. The same soft female voice repeated the recorded message: *"the number you have dialled does not exist. Please dial the correct number"*. Upon hearing that again, Michael felt himself plunged into sadness of incomprehensible depths. He had been suckered. He had persuaded skeptical church elders to act against their better judgement and authorize more money to be sent to a conman.

Over dinner with his wife that night, he told her what had happened. She was equally appalled that a man her husband had described as a man of God would do a thing like that. But being an optimist, she counselled her husband. 'Maybe, there is a good reason for what happened. The phone could be out of order...'

Michael began to shake his head, saying that he doubted that possibility.

'At least, give him the benefit of doubt,' she insisted. 'Write him a letter; you never know.'

Michael was not in the state of mind for an argument so he agreed to write a letter the following day even though he believed it to be a waste of time. He did not sleep a wink that night. In the morning, as he dawdled poignantly around the environs of his house, he decided not to bother to write Richard. But Sarah was a persistent woman...

She placed a mug of steaming coffee on the granite tabletop as Michael was finishing the first draft of the letter. When he was done, he picked up the coffee mug while his wife picked up the handwritten letter. She read the spidery text on the paper.

In the draft letter, Michael told Richard that his credibility as a man of God was at stake. Some church elders already considered him a charlatan. Michael made it clear that he still believed Richard to be genuine, but this could quickly change if no reply was received within a month of posting the letter to Nigeria. In the final paragraph of the letter, Michael vowed to come to Nigeria and personally hunt Richard down if it was discovered that he and his church had been duped out of $100,000.

Sarah frowned at the belligerent tone of that paragraph and crossed it out with her pen. 'That's now better,' she said. 'Your handwriting is not that great. Mine is clearer and neater.'

Michael watched silently as she produced a blank sheet of paper and began to write into it in her own exquisite handwriting, faithfully copying his letter, skipping only the last paragraph, which she had earlier struck out. She also added a few sentences of her own, which included a few biblical quotations drawn from the New Testament, appealing to the conscience of Pastor Richard Ibeh.

Michael read his wife's version of the letter carefully and approved it. Soon it was folded and placed inside a personalized envelope bearing the logo and name of his church.

An hour later, he emerged from the Baton Rouge FedEx Shipping Centre on Coursey Boulevard—where he had just deposited the letter for onward delivery to Onitsha city— looking quite glum and filled with ominous foreboding that there would be no response from the Nigerian end.

CHAPTER 8

MARCH 1993

KENSINGTON, WEST LONDON, UK

The black taxicab waited patiently as the gates parted automatically. John was excited. It's showtime, he thought to himself, reclining on the rear passenger seat. His impeccable three-piece suit and the trained General American accent were there to make a good impression on the Englishman waiting to meet him.

Six months had elapsed since Roy Seed was presented as a target in the "situation room". John had not anticipated such a long delay. The day after the situation room meeting, he had taken time off from his other engagements to refine Tunde's original plan. He completed the task within a week, condensing the entire plan running into several pages into a two-page document, which he duplicated and and distributed to his men. Shortly after, the operation kicked off with Tunde alias "Tony Oke" making phone calls to London, introducing "Alex" as his associate and a date was fixed for a meeting with Roy.

John applied for a UK visa. Then everything ground to a halt. The British High Commission had taken its time, slow-walking the visa application process. John worried that embassy staff had discovered some issues with the Nigerian passport that he had submitted. But the Nigerian Immigration Service (NIS) officer, whom he had bribed for the new green passport, assured him that it was perfect. It was an authentic travel document issued by the NIS. Yes, the passport was bearing a fake name and a false date of birth, but the Brits had no way of knowing that. Whatever was causing the delay in issuing the UK visa, the NIS officer opined, had nothing to do with the passport.

With the visa application process seemingly stalled, Tunde had no choice but to phone Roy Seed in London to cancel the meeting, citing unforseen circumstances. The plan to swindle Roy was shelved indefinitely and the gang moved onto other matters. Then one day, six months later, John found a letter from the British High Commission in a P.O. Box that he was renting at Ikeja Post Office. The letter informed him that his visa had finally been issued. It invited him to the High Commission to collect his passport in person. No explanation was offered for the long delay.

When the passport containing the UK visa came into John's possession, the dormant swindle operation whirred back into life. "Tony Oke" phoned Roy once more and a new date was fixed for a London meeting between "Alex" and the young Englishman...

The black taxicab wheeled past the open gates and into the driveway of a large detached house in Kensington, West London.

A young blond man emerged from the front door of the house carrying a glass of lemonade. Despite the cold weather, he was sporting a yellow T-shirt and khaki brown shorts.

John murmured a short prayer as the cab pulled up beside the house owner. He paid his fare and got out of the cab.

Roy was smiling as the cab driver made a three point U-turn on the driveway. 'You are welcome to my humble abode' he said, pumping the hand of his guest.

'Thank you. I'm Alex Karidi. It's a pleasure to meet you, Roy.'

The gates swung shut as soon as the cab passed through them and Roy led his visitor towards the front door. John's eyes surveyed the premises quickly. 'Nice pad you have got down here,' he remarked.

Roy smiled, 'Thank you. It is well above the reach of the average property buyer.'

John nodded and asked, 'how much is it worth?'

Roy held his chin as if in deep thought for a while and then he shrugged, 'well, I guess only Bill Gates can afford it'. They both laughed.

'Please come with me,' Roy asked and led the way into the big house.

Inside the well-furnished sitting room, John made himself comfortable in an armchair. Roy excused himself and disappeared through a side door.

John alias "Alex Karidi" rose from his seat to survey the glass-framed pictures hanging on the walls. There was a picture of Roy as a teenager riding a horse. Another teenage picture of him with a couple that John assumed to be his parents.

John walked across the room to take a closer look at a large framed picture of an old man with piercing blue eyes and bushy eyebrows. The grin on the old man's face appeared to be mocking John's plans. The Nigerian guessed that the old man in a black suit and bowler hat was none other than the late Sir Lindsay Seed, the founder of Seed Stores— one of the largest chain of stores in the UK.

'That's my late grand dad,' remarked a voice behind him. John spurn round. Roy was now dressed in a blue denim jacket with matching jeans trousers.

For the first time since they met, John gazed at his host in order to size him up. The Englishman was of average build, immensely handsome, blond and couldn't be more than twenty-seven years old. The Nigerian had no doubt that the ladies would be falling over themselves to get him.

'Here you are, mate,' Roy said, handing his visitor a can of Stella Artois beer. He fell into an armchair with a beer can in his right hand. With his left arm, he waved John to the armchair opposite him.

John sipped his drink in silence, waiting for his host to open the conversation for which he had come all the way from Nigeria.

Roy stared at him for several seconds, probably sizing him up too, and then spoke. 'First trip to the UK, I presume?'

The Nigerian shook his head. 'No, I have been here several times on business.' He lied without thinking and then regretted it. Had Roy asked him to mention and describe which parts of the country he had been to, he would not have had the slightest idea of what to say. Luckily, Roy did not go that far. The Englishman asked him what line of business he was in, and his relationship with "Tony Oke".

'Well, I specialise in importing computers and other electronic gadgets like videocassette recorders, radios, TV sets, record players and so on, from Japan, UK and continental Europe,' John paused and sipped beer.

'Pretty lucrative, isn't it?' Roy remarked.

The fraudster nodded as he smacked his lips, and the lying continued. 'Tony Oke is an ex-colleague of mine. I used to work in the Nigerian Federal Ministry of Petroleum as a civil servant before I left to start my own business...'

Roy nodded slowly with a smile on his face. He liked a man who was prepared to take his destiny into his hands and become his own boss.

'... I also know the Petroleum Minister personally because I served under him several years ago. He wasn't a minister back then, but rather a middle-level civil servant, two levels above me. He became a federal minister two years ago. And being a shrewd businessman, who knows his onions, he is currently looking for foreign partners to work with. He sent a message, through Tony, asking for my help. I agreed to do it for a ten percent cut from the proposed deal. He accepted and here I am representing his interests.' John paused to sip his beer. His enthralled host urged him to continue with the interesting story.

'I am sure Tony has briefed you on the business proposal. There are five hundred thousand barrels of diverted crude oil in a barge floating on the Atlantic Ocean, forty miles from Nigeria's maritime boundaries. The oil is destined for South Africa, which, as you know, has no diplomatic ties with my country and is under an international regime of economic sanctions. Our problem is the money for logistics. We need to pay bribes to coastguards as the barge passes through the maritime boundaries of several African countries en route to South Africa. Without the money, we have no means of moving the barge. I'm sure Tony told you why the minister does not want to invest his personal money or dip into the petroleum ministry's coffers to fund the illicit project. We are his proxies as far as this deal is concerned.'

Roy nodded. 'Your mate told me that he is scared of being caught by the President of your country.'

John smiled wrily, taking mental note of the sneer in his host's voice. Obviously, Roy's interest in the deal did not necessarily mean that he respected his prospective business associate— the minister about to rip-off his own country.

Scratching his blond hair, Roy asked where he fitted into the clandestine picture John was painting.

'I was coming to that,' the fraudster replied, his mind working quickly on what to say and how to say it. 'We need a foreign investor who will put up money for the logistics, as Tony suggested to you. We will give you forty percent of the proceeds when the apartheid regime pays for the oil and the barge.'

Roy shook his head in disagreement. 'I want sixty percent.'

John smiled. 'We will offer fifty-five percent, nothing more.'

Roy frowned and remained silent for a moment. In theory, it was a good deal. But he had mixed feelings about the nature of the business. It was either a money-spinner or a scam. Not totally convinced, he decided to ask a few more questions to enable him decide whether to draw back or dive straight into it with all the attendant risks. One thing he had learnt from gambling was that money should only be bet if the odds of winning were very high and risks low. In this case, he was undecided on the risks, but the potential gains were quite high, if everything was on the level.

He drained his can of beer and asked, 'why did you and your mate, Tony, come to me? Why me?'

John hesitated before replying, 'we were looking for a foreign investor with the balls to take risks and you happened to fit the bill.'

The Londoner took that in and probed further. 'How did you guys find me?'

Although John remained outwardly calm, his adrenaline levels rose as he racked his brain for a quick answer. 'Well, my friend, Tony, is quite gifted in spotting people with business acumen. When he ran into you in the pub, and both of you had a conversation, he realised that you were the man we have been looking for.'

Roy's anxious face relaxed. He seemed satisfied with the answer. 'Yeah, I guess your mate is right. How much is this deal worth?'

John promptly replied, 'we expect to make twenty million pounds.'

Roy's eyes widened in alarm as his brain worked out his fifty-five percent share of the money— £11 million!

The conman noticed this and smiled. The operation was back on track and moving smoothly according to plan. Then suddenly, it looked like the operation was about to derail again. Roy's face had lost all its excitement and in its place appeared graveness. This worried John.

'One other thing,' Roy said, wagging his finger at his unsettled guest, 'I still have my doubts about this. You need to convince me that this is for real. I want to meet the minister in person, if that's okay.'

John brightened up. He had a ready answer. 'Certainly,' he said rubbing his chin thoughtfully, 'I will speak to the minister… see if a nocturnal meeting can be arranged.'

Roy frowned.

John noticed this and added, 'the meeting can only take place at night. You do understand that the minister has to be discreet, right?'

Roy nodded and gulped the last contents of his Stella Artois can. John adjusted the tie on his neck.

'How much do you need for logistics?'

'Two hundred thousand pounds.'

Roy thought about it for a few seconds. 'It's a deal,' he beamed, extending his arm to his pleased visitor for a handshake.

'I will discuss the plan for a meeting with the minister; see how soon we can set a date,' John explained as he felt a mixture of relief and elation. He was delighted at the prospect of gaining £200,000 for his gang.

Roy was also pleased. This was a once-in-a-lifetime opportunity to earn a huge amount of money without much of an effort. His ailing father would admit, for once, that the son, whom he had written off as a "good-for-nothing" gambler, had the astuteness required to run the family chain of stores.

Roy sprang to his feet, fumbling in his trouser pockets for the car keys. 'Do you fancy a ride down to my favourite boozer to celebrate?'

John quickly drained the contents of his beer can. 'Of course,' he replied as he rose to his feet.

Roy led him through the side door to the kitchen. The kitchen was spacious and looked like it had been outfitted by IKEA. There was a stainless steel door at one end. Roy pulled it open with considerable effort and stepped through it into a dimly lit garage containing a red Lamborghini convertible. The fluorescent light tubes attached to the ceiling suddenly brightened up.

'This is my babe,' Roy declared proudly as he slid behind the steering wheel. The car gleamed under the bright white fluorescent lights.

The Nigerian was awed. 'Your babe is beautiful,' the fraudster remarked archly, walking over to the front passenger door. Roy leaned over and opened the door for him. John sank into the passenger seat as the garage door slid noisily into a side wall, allowing daylight to flood the interior of the garage.

Roy started the car, revved it for a few seconds, and then put on his seatbelt, prompting his passenger to do the same. He shifted the gear lever. The car rolled down a concrete ramp in front of the garage before wheeling into the driveway. The entrance gates parted slowly while John and Roy waited in the idling car.

As the car cruised on the narrow roads of London, John regretted his request for £200,000. A man rich enough to drive such a flashy car could certainly afford to pay more.

CHAPTER 9

MARCH 1993

LAGOS, WESTERN NIGERIA

At Murtala Mohammed International Airport, Pastor Michael Grams went through passport control, picked up his luggage from baggage reclaim, walked through the customs area and ended up in the arrivals concourse.

A very dark-skinned man walked up to him and shot out his hand for a handshake. 'Welcome to Lagos. I'm Trevor, your driver. I was sent by Detective-Inspector Mike Otunba, the police officer assigned to your case,' he explained, smiling.

Michael Grams was surprised. He had been expecting a driver attached to the US embassy not one from the Nigerian Police Force. He shook Trevor's hand. 'Thank you Trev, I am Michael Grams from the State of Louisiana. I thought the American Embassy was sending somebody.'

The driver smiled apologetically and replied, 'the embassy car broke down in the middle of the road. We are doing the embassy a favour.'

The American nodded, satisfied with the answer.

Trevor was not wholly lying when he said that the embassy car broke down en route to the airport. Forty-five minutes earlier, on the dual carriageway leading to the airport, a Mercedes Benz L-911 lorry had left its lane and rammed into a Peugeot 504 saloon car travelling in the opposite direction. Surprisingly, the Peugeot driver emerged unscathed from the severely wrecked saloon car with American diplomatic number plates. The equally uninjured lorry driver emerged from the dented Mercedes Benz L-911 and knelt down before the furious saloon car driver. A grovelling apology began.

A small crowd gathered at the scene of the accident. Other vehicles on the carriageway slowed down and began to manoeuvre around the scene to avoid the gathering crowds, the shards of glass, plastic and metal pieces strewn across the road.

The US embassy driver—a Nigerian—was still barking at the kneeling lorry driver making a grovelling apology, when a sleek black BMW sedan driven by Trevor trundled past the chaotic scene en route to the airport...

'I will take your bags,' Trevor said, taking Michael Gram's luggage.

'Oh, mighty kind of you,' the American preacher replied, as he followed Trevor into the car park.

In the rear seat of the BMW, Mike felt a bit at ease. He wound down the rear car windows for ventilation whilst Trevor was dumping his bags into the boot at the back. Moments later, Trevor got behind the steering wheel and started the car.

It was a hot sunny afternoon in Ikeja, the capital of Lagos State. Michael felt the searing heat despite the open windows. He slackened his necktie and peeled off his jacket as the BMW bowled out of the parking lot.

The past month had been a sad one for him. He had discovered that the man he regarded as a fellow man of God was nothing but a common criminal who had conned his church out of $100,000. As feared, no response was received to the strongly worded letter he had sent to "Richard". That confirmed, once and for all, that he had been a sucker for the last two years.

In a state of great distress, he had flown from Baton Rouge to Atlanta to visit the Nigerian Consulate. The Consul-General was sympathetic to his story, although he still berated the American preacher for his naivety. 'Before sending any money, you should have done background checks on this "Richard" through the Pentecostal Fellowship of Nigeria or through our Embassy in Washington,' the Nigerian diplomat told him. At the end of the visit, the Consul-General promised to get the Nigerian Police on the case.

Two weeks later, in Baton Rouge, Michael Grams received a phone call from Atlanta. The Nigerian Consul-General told him that the local police in Onitsha city had checked out the addresses for the reformatory and orphanage and confirmed that they did not exist. The police could not locate any Pastor Richard Evans Ibeh of Evergreen Glory of God Ministries Incorporated. By law, all Pentecostal churches in Nigeria had to register with the Corporate Affairs Commission (CAC). Richard's church was not on the list of registered churches held by CAC. Therefore, it did not exist. The "church address" provided by Richard to Michael, for the purpose of correspondence, turned out to be the actual address of an old abandoned house slated for demolition by Onitsha city authorities. Pictures of smiling orphans sent to Michael were real. They were taken by a mysterious philanthropist who frequented various government-run orphanages in Lagos. The philanthropist fit the sketchy physical description of the fraudster provided by the American preacher. That meant "Richard" was most likely based in Lagos and not three hundred miles away in Onitsha. Lagos State Police Command would be grateful if the American preacher could visit the country to give a statement in person and help police investigators fill in some of the blanks.

These revelations made Michael feel dizzy with anger. He struggled to maintain his composure as he spoke to the Consul-General on the phone. He expressed his gratitude to the Nigerian Police Force for taking his case seriously and expressed willingness to help in any way possible. A week later, he was on a Nigerian Airways flight bound for Lagos...

As the black BMW gained speed on the expressway, cool breeze wafted in through the open car windows. Michael Grams relaxed to read a Christian newsletter. Trevor turned on the car radio, and gentle classical music, Handel's *Alleluia*, pervaded the car from concealed loudspeakers.

'Do you like classical music?' Michael asked the driver.

Trevor hesitated before replying that he liked the music genre. It was a lie. He couldn't stand classical music and wondered why *Radio Lagos* played it all the time at the expense of good local music.

The American launched into a tedious story about how he had grown to like classical music while attending high school on scholarship. His high school in Chattanooga city was one of the best in East Tennessee, he said.

Trevor nodded impatiently, willing the American to change the topic, or keep quiet.

'Handel, Chopin, Mozart, Beethoven. Who amongst them is the most talented in your own opinion?' Michael asked obliviously.

Silence followed. The BMW decelerated as it approached the entry point of a side road. 'There is heavy traffic ahead. We shall make a detour here,' Trevor explained and swerved the car from the thoroughfare into the narrow side road.

Michael took the driver's brusque tone as a sign that his attempt at conversation was not well received. So he gave up and returned to reading his newsletter.

The car gained speed on the asphalted road lined on both sides by picturesque palm trees. Then suddenly, the car swung off the road, bowled past the road verge, and bounced violently into a dirt track hemmed in by trees and tall grasses.

Michael looked up from his newsletter. 'Where are we?' he asked anxiously, his eyes darting around the strange-looking forest clearing through which the BMW sedan was now travelling bumpily.

'This is a shortcut,' was the curt reply.

The answer was not convincing. Mike mumbled something to himself about the area being creepy. Trevor remained silent. The BMW gained speed. The American reverted to reading his newsletter.

The car suddenly screeched to a halt, throwing up a haze of ochre dust from the dirt track, and causing Michael to jerk forward, dropping his newsletter. He was about to ask the driver what had just happened when he saw two fierce-looking men dressed in identical white singlets and khaki grey shorts emerge from the bushes on either side of the dirt road. The one who emerged from thickets abutting the left-hand side of the dirt road was armed with what Michael thought was a sawn-off pump-action shotgun. The other, who came from the grove of trees on the opposite side, had what seemed to be an assault rifle. Both gunmen met up in the middle of the dirt road, a few yards from the stationary BMW, and began to walk abreast, the soles of their sandals clicking and squelching against the laterite ground as they advanced towards the car.

Michael was gripped by fear. Trevor gazed silently at the road ahead.

'What the hell is going on? They have guns!' Michael shouted at Trevor.

The driver did not respond. His expressionless eyes remained focussed on the road ahead.

'Are you sleeping? Don't you see those bandits!' the American cried as he leaned forward from the rear passenger seat to tug at the driver's shirt.

At first, those nonchalant eyes remained focussed on the road, and the man to whom they belonged did not flinch even as his shirt was being tugged at. Then suddenly, as if he had just woken up from a trance, the man, Trevor, turned sharply and brushed away the hand gripping his shirt near the waist.

Michael saw the glare in the driver's eyes and finally understood. 'You know those men? Who are you?' he asked, scared of what he was suspecting. There was a sharp click and the driver's door suddenly opened.

'Sweet Jesus! What are you doing? What is happening? Trevor! Answer me!'

Ignoring the yelling behind him, Tunde Olukemi alias "Trevor" got out of the car and walked into the bush. He barely acknowledged the presence of the armed men silently approaching the BMW.

Michael Grams reached for the door lever and pulled it, but the rear passenger door did not open. Fear paralyzed him. Suddenly, he felt a strong urge to defecate.

The armed men halted three and a half feet from the bonnet of the car. By then, Michael was holding back tears and praying loudly. Both men trained their guns on the BMW, unperturbed by loud voice of its lone occupant.

One of the assassins made eye contact with the nervous preacher and grinned sadistically. Then he opened fire on the car, prompting the other to join in. Chains of flying bullets and steel shots tore into the BMW. The windscreen disintegrated and blood splattered all over the car's interior.

The assassins backed twenty paces away from the car and then paused to reload. Red cartridges went into the shotgun; an empty magazine was ejected from the assault rifle and a fresh one slammed into place. Soon the guns were blazing again. The rear screen and all the windows exploded into smithereens. All four tyres deflated. Paint peeled from the bullet-riddled metal chassis. A steel shot hit the fuel tank, starting a fire. The killers turned around and retreated into the bushes. Seconds later, there was a deafening explosion that could be heard for miles.

*****

Detective-Inspector (DI) Michael Otunba entered the tastefully furnished office. A middle-aged man, dressed in a crisp black uniform and sitting behind a mahogany desk, waved the detective to a seat opposite him.

As indicated by the shiny brass nameplate in a corner of the desk, the uniformed man was named Cyrus Udeh. He held the rank of a Chief Superintendent of Police (CSP), which meant that he was Michael's superior by rank. Several officers within the Lagos State Police Command also bore the rank of a CSP. But unlike them, Cyrus Udeh was the chief of all detectives within the state by virtue of his command position as the Divisional Police Officer (DPO) in charge of Lagos State Criminal Investigation Division, also known variously as State CID, Lagos CID, and Ikeja CID because it was headquartered in Ikeja town.

Cyrus Udeh waited for the plain-clothes detective to sit down before he started spitting fire. 'I am disappointed with your handling of the Logan case! And the case of Reverend Grams! It has been two weeks since the murder of that poor man and you have nothing. No clues! No leads! I have the Police Commissioner and the Americans breathing down my neck. I can't believe that a man we had invited to our country to help with a fraud investigation was intercepted and killed just like that...'

Otunba couldn't hold back any longer. He interrupted his superior. 'Sir, my squad is doing everything in their power to get these murderers. It's quite difficult to get clues from the wreckage of that car. Nothing of forensic value survived the fire and the explosion.'

The DPO nodded grudgingly. 'Okay, but what about Mister Gary Logan's case? What is your excuse for not solving it? Anyways, we will talk about that old case, later. My main concern for now is this recent murder. The embassy driver detailed to pick up Pastor Grams reported the accident with the lorry driver on the day of the murder. Have you apprehended the lorry driver?'

Mike Otunba shook his head, pulled a small notepad from his breast pocket, and flipped through it. 'Well sir, as you already know, we believe that the lorry driver may be connected to Pastor Gram's murder. The lorry driver prevented the US embassy driver from reaching the airport on time, paving the way for the criminals to get to Pastor Grams first.' Mike paused to turn a page on the notepad.

Cyrus nodded impatiently. This was not what he wanted to hear. Otunba was repeating the same story from a week ago. The DPO wanted to hear that progress had been made— the lorry driver had been caught or at least a description of him has been obtained for the police artist to sketch.

'Mike, I know that part of the story. Quit stalling and answer my question '

'No sir, we have not apprehended the lorry driver since he left the accident scene,' the detective stated poignantly. 'But we have got a detailed description of the lorry driver from the driver attached to the American embassy. My men ran the number plate of the lorry and discovered that it had been stolen from the garage of a cement manufacturing company. The stolen vehicle was part of a fleet of lorries used to deliver cement bags and concrete blocks to building sites. We recovered video tapes from the company's vandalized security camera system. The tapes showed that cameras stopped working around five o'clock in the morning of that fateful day. The company's drivers was alerted around ten o'clock that morning when they entered the garage to get the lorries ready for the day's deliveries. The company reported the robbery to Alausa Police Station. The desk sergeant there was still filing the case when the American Embassy rang to report Pastor Grams missing from the airport. The embassy driver worked with our police artist,' Mike paused and watched Cyrus open a folder lying on the desk. Then he added, 'sketches of the suspect are being readied for distribution as we speak.'

Cyrus seemed not to be listening. He was scribbling something into the folder. This carried on for a few minutes while Mike Otunba silently waited for a response with trepidation. Normally, the DPO was not a man given to outward displays of emotion. Nevertheless, he was known to vent his frustrations on certain occasions, and when that happened, his temper could be fiery.

Striking a conciliatory tone that surprised the Detective-Inspector, Cyrus said, 'Mike, I know you are already working hard, but you must work harder. The Inspector-General of Police is personally interested in this case. So are the Americans, obviously.' Averting his gaze from the face of the detective, he added, 'if no further progress is made before the month runs out, I'll have no other choice than to replace you with someone else.'

Mike Otunba's countenance changed from pleasant surprise to fear. He had just learnt that his career was hanging by a thread, and could only be saved if he cracked the case. Suddenly, the sordid ordeal of a recently sacked Detective-Suprintendent came back to him. The Detective-Suprintendent, the former head of the homicide squad, had been forced out of Ikeja CID for his failure to track down assassins who had murdered a Lagos State government official. When the disgraced senior detective refused to accept his demotion to a desk job at traffic division headquarters, he was promptly fired from the Nigerian Police Force. And with that sack, came the loss of a police pension for a man who had devoted twenty-three years of his life to detective work.

The thought of suffering the same fate horrified Michael Otunba. He had no plans of letting himself go down for the sake of a bunch of criminals who were paying him a fraction of his annual salary.

The DPO turned back to the folder before him and wrote something else down. 'That will be all for now, detective,' he said without looking up from the folder.

Mike closed his small notepad, pushed it into his breast pocket, and rose to his feet. He walked out of the room and closed the door behind him. Moments later, inside his own office, four doors down the corridor, he sat in his swivel chair, contemplating the events of the past several weeks.

Three weeks earlier, he had been in the same office reviewing contents of a criminal case file at the request of Lagos Directorate of Public Prosecutions, when a police constable came to announce that the DPO wanted to see him. His adrenaline had soared, as he recalled that not too long ago, Cyrus had berated him for lack of progress in the Logan case. He was apprehensive about meeting the DPO because he had nothing new to report. The excuse he had planned to give Cyrus was simple. The two-week internal investigation conducted to find out whether he (Mike Otunba) was involved in the jailbreak of a suspected fraudster had distracted his anti-scam squad from pursing hot leads that could have resulted in the capture of those who swindled Logan. The leads were now cold, making it more difficult to track down the criminals. He was still revising the excuse in his head even as he knocked on the door with great trepidation.

From behind the closed door, the unmistakable baritone voice of Cyrus asked him in. He had settled uncomfortably in the seat opposite his superior. Cyrus did not ask for an update on the Logan case. Instead, he spoke of a new criminal case involving an American preacher.

According to Cyrus, the Nigerian Consul-General in Atlanta had phoned the Inspector-General of Police (IG) in Abuja city to discuss Michael Gram's case. After the Consul-General hung up, the Inspector-General rang the Zonal Assistant Inspector General of Police (AIG) in Lagos to issue some orders. Shortly after, the AIG phoned the Lagos State Police Commissioner to give orders of his own. The Commissioner relayed those orders to Cyrus at Ikeja CID.

'Pastor Grams is coming to Lagos to help with your investigation,' Cyrus told Michael Otunba.

The detective frowned and promptly voiced his objection. 'His presence is unnecessary. He can write his statement in America and send it to us by fax. His presence here is going to constitute a nuisance.'

The DPO had nodded his agreement with the Detective-Inspector. But the matter was out of his hands. His superiors in the police hierarchy all felt that the presence of the Pastor would spur on the investigation. A sentiment the DPO had attributed to the strong lobbying efforts of Nigeria's top diplomat in Atlanta.

Before dismissing an unhappy Mike Otunba from his presence, the DPO had said, 'prepare to receive Reverend Grams in seven days. When he arrives, I'll make sure that he stays out of your way and only help when you ask for it.'

Hours after leaving the DPO's office, Mike Otunba suddenly "stumbled on new leads" and his squad officers swung into action. Several small-time crooks—counterfeiters, burglars, and even prostitutes alleged to be the fraudsters' girlfriends—were arrested. Meanwhile, John Nwosu and his gang were tipped off about Michael Grams' impending visit.

The frivolous arrests had their intended effect. For a time, they caused the DPO and the Lagos State Commissioner of Police to believe that progress was being made on the case despite the fact that all the suspects were released within days due to lack of evidence.

The night before Grams boarded his final trans-atlantic flight, the telephone in the basement of Otunba's bungalow began to ring. Yinka, the detective's wife, had wanted to go down there and answer the call, but thought better of it. Mike had warned her never to venture into the basement for any reason, not even when the telephone down there was ringing in his absence.

Yinka had always thought it strange that the telephone in the basement ran on a landline separate from their regular residential phone line. She had asked her husband about it when it was first installed by technicians from NITEL (Nigerian Telecommunications Limited). Mike had been quite circumspect in his reply. He told her it was a secure, bug-proof landline for "police business". She had pushed for further details, but he refused to say more, only warning her never to venture into the basement.

On the fifth ring of the phone, she got up from the sofa in the living room where she was watching TV and went into the bathroom. She called out to her husband in the shower and returned to the living room.

With a towel wrapped round his waist, Mike ran down the wooden staircase into the basement to answer the ringing phone. He already knew who the caller was. Only five people had the number of the special telephone in his basement. Minutes after picking up the handset, he learnt what the gangsters wanted to do about the visiting American preacher.

He was told that Mike Grams would be abducted and "persuaded" to drop the case. Otunba was promised that no harm would come to the American. Just a little shake-up to scare the preacher, to convince him to return home to his religious flock in Louisiana. But events that unfolded the day after the phone call showed the corrupt policeman that his paymasters had misled him about their true intentions.

On the morning of that fateful day, the US embassy had phoned to report the bashing of their official car on Apapa-Oshodi expressway and the subsequent disappearance of the American preacher from the airport. Embarrassed by the incident, the Lagos State Commissioner of Police had ordered a statewide search for the missing foreigner. Two hours later, Detective-Inspector Mike Otunba, leading the police search party, received an anonymous tip about the whereabouts of the missing man. He and his men were horrified when they discovered the burnt-out and bullet-riddled wreckage of a BMW saloon car containing the charred remains of an unidentified human being. A partially burnt American passport found on the floor of the wrecked car confirmed the identity of the human remains as Michael Grams.

That night, the Detective-Inspector phoned John Nwosu, furious at the cold-blooded murder. He angrily accused the swindlers of betraying their promise not to harm the American preacher. He cited the problems their "excesses" were creating for him every time he had to cover up their crimes. He told the fraudsters about the kind of pressure the DPO was exerting on him. He was also sure that it was only a matter of time before somebody suspected him of sabotaging CID investigations. He was beginning to think it was a bad idea to continue working for the swindlers because it was not worth the risk of losing his police career and ending up in Kirikiri Maximum Prison.

John had listened patiently—while the bent cop ranted and raved—before responding. In a soothing voice, he told the detective that he understood that the monthly six-thousand-naira bribe was not good enough. For that reason, the gang was now willing to pay ten thousand naira monthly if the policeman agreed to continue working for them.

The pay rise had excited the rogue detective and he agreed to continue spying. But following his last meeting with the DPO in which he was threatened with the sack if no progress was made in Pastor Grams' murder, he was faced with two stark choices— carry on as normal on the gangsters' payroll and ruin his career or turn them in and keep his beloved job; even earn a promotion. He chose the latter option.

*****

In the situation room, down in the basement of John's residence, a single light bulb was glowing overhead. There were two topics on the agenda of the meeting. The first was how to "entertain" their next victim, Roy Seed, who was due to visit the country within a month. The second was what to do with Detective-Inspector Mike Otunba. The discussion of both topics was preceded by a brief conversation about the successful elimination of a problem; the gruesome murder of a man who had done the discussants no wrong.

'I will like to thank Eugene for a job well done. The elimination was neat. No evidence was left behind…' John was still speaking when Moses, Adamu and Tunde interrupted with a round of applause.

Eugene beamed with smiles and shook hands with his admiring colleagues. He had planned the murder of the American preacher down to minute details. It was he who had stolen the lorry from the cement company. It was he who had rammed the stolen vehicle into the US embassy car to prevent it from reaching the airport where Michael Grams was.

Eugene had no reason to fear police sketches of the heavily bearded and dishevelled lorry driver circulating all over Lagos State. His disguise was so perfect that the posters on the streets and the pictures on television bore no physical resemblance whatsoever to his natural forty-six-year-old self.

When the applause subsided, John resumed speaking. 'Tunde, are we ready to receive our boy from London next month?' he asked archly, drawing chuckles from some of the men.

'Yes sir, everything is ready. No problems.' Tunde replied, tapping a red folder on the table before him. 'The plan is laid out here in stages. You can go through it.'

John nodded and asked him whether the clothes, cars and other props required for the elaborate deception were ready.

Tunde held up the folder and replied, 'everything is here, including the costs of acquiring these things; even the white paint needed to mark the cars as federal government property.'

John smiled, 'very well then.' He rubbed his eyes and moved on to the other important issue at hand. 'I have told you guys about the phone call from Mike Otunba,' he said and paused to survey the grim faces staring back at him. 'From the tone of his voice, I get this strong feeling that the man wants to sell us out to save his own skin.'

There were mumbling in the room as John spoke indignantly. 'We spent a lot of money to cultivate that man. Now, it's all a waste. He has become a loose end.'

Eugene cleared his throat and John paused instantly. All eyes turned to Eugene. 'I believe this is a problem that can be tackled quickly,' he remarked with a grin on his face. 'When do you want it done sir?'

'As soon as possible'

'Consider it done, sir.'

On that note, the meeting in the basement ended and the men went above ground for drinks.

CHAPTER 10

LAGOS, WESTERN NIGERIA

On the night of April Fools' Day, most of Ikeja town was in darkness due to a power outage. None of the town's inhabitants was surprised. The national electric power company, better known as NEPA, has always been unreliable. Across the country, those who could afford it simply relied on their own standby power generator sets. Those who could not afford generator sets resorted to candles and kerosene lanterns to illuminate their homes until NEPA engineers restored electric power supply to their district.

Three minutes after the power outage in the capital of Lagos State, a huge diesel electric power generator at the backyard of Ikeja CID complex roared to life, vibrating noisily as its exhaust pipe belched a stream of thick, oily, black smoke. In one office on the topmost floor of the five-storey complex, two ceiling-mounted fluorescent tubes flickered and came on.

Under those bright lights, Detective-Inspector Mike Otunba was hunched over a typewriter, labouring to produce yet another report on the Logan case, which he had been "investigating" for almost two years without making any significant progress. Writing such progress reports was now a chore he would rather not undertake because they revealed nothing new about the crime under investigation, but he had no choice. The State Commissioner of Police had personally requested the fortnightly reports. Otunba had no doubt in his mind that what he was typing would enrage the man who was both the head of the State Police Command and the second most senior police officer in Lagos after the Zonal AIG. Again, he recalled the sordid fate of the Detective-Superintendent who had failed to solve a high-profile homicide and concluded that his own position in Ikeja CID would eventually come under review unless he cracked the Logan case and showed some progress on Gram's murder investigation.

Tapping furiously on the typewriter keys, he vowed that this was the last time he would saddle his superiors with bad news on the Logan case. In a fortnight, he planned to redeem himself and save his career. He would stop protecting the gang responsible for his extra source of income. He was going to lead a nocturnal police raid on the Victoria Island home of John Nwosu, rounding up the entire gang as they emerge from the basement of the sprawling mansion. The police chiefs in Lagos and Abuja would be thrilled. Mike Otunba was sure that a commendation and a promotion would follow shortly. But, for now, he would have to bide his time. He would wait patiently for the gang of swindlers to pay him his monthly fee before pouncing on them like the wily cheetah in those folktales that his late grandfather used to tell him as a child.

The detective's thoughts were interrupted when the ringing telephone startled him. Cursing under his breath, he answered the call. The caller identified himself and that angered the rogue cop. 'I thought I told you not to ring this phone. It might be bugged. You know some people here are suspicious.'

The voice at the other line laughed and told Otunba the purpose of his late night call. The detective's mood softened.

John Nwosu was calling to set up a meeting near the Seme border with Bénin Republic (formerly Dahomey). The gang leader's voice on the phone was soothing and what he was saying sounded like music to the ears of the policeman. Otunba was glad to hear that the swindlers understood the grave risks he was taking on their behalf and the pressure he was under. The gang wanted to show their appreciation by handing him a hundred-thousand-naira bonus in addition to his standard monthly fee of ten thousand naira. They hoped that the gesture would strengthen his loyalty to them. More importantly, the swindlers wanted to bring forward the date of the meeting.

'When are we now supposed to meet?' the excited detective asked.

'Next week on Friday,' came the reply.

Mike could scarcely believe his luck. He was going to earn ₦110,000 before his treachery, and he did not even have to wait two weeks to rendezvous for the cash.

After the phone call ended, he reclined on his seat, deep in thought. Why would these criminals pay him three times his annual police salary? He pondered for a few minutes and then shrugged. Who cares? Perhaps, the swindlers valued him more than he valued them.

The phone call had changed everything. A police raid on John Nwosu's mansion on a Saturday night was not likely to snare the entire gang in one fell swoop, the detective reasoned. He knew that the gang did not meet in the mansion on Saturdays. He wasn't going to arrest one swindler and risk alerting the others still at large. He did not like long drawn-out manhunts. He wanted the entire gang in one location.

Otunba revised his plan accordingly. He would collect the hefty bribe from the gang on Friday night. Then he would lead a Saturday morning raid on ELAJ Enterprises and Dixon Job Agency, both located on the same street in Mushin. The gangsters, who turned up daily for work in those front companies, would not survive the raid. They would all die in a hail of bullets while "resisting arrest". That way, the detective would be rid of the spectre of exposure as a crooked cop.

It was a marvellous plan, Otunba thought with a devious smile as he tapped the keys on his electric typewriter. One more sentence was needed to conclude the police report.

*****

Roy Seed entered the arrivals concourse of Murtala Mohammed International Airport. It was filled with people milling around, waiting to receive family and friends arriving from different parts of the world. He surveyed the area for familiar faces. There was none. He dropped his rucksack on the shiny polished floor and gazed at his watch. It was exactly 12 noon. He suddenly felt a presence in front of him and his gaze shifted from his watch to the two individuals standing before him.

'Welcome to Nigeria,' both individuals chorused.

Roy smiled. 'Oh, thank you. You are Alex Karidi, right?'

John's lips twitched and he replied, 'don't tell me you have already forgotten our names.'

'No I haven't. You are definitely Alex,' Roy stated defensively, 'and your mate is Tony Oke.'

'You haven't forgotten. Our surnames, you even got the pronunciations right,' Tunde remarked.

'I have a sharp memory. Never forget stuff like that.'

'I must confess that I am impressed.'

They laughed and shook hands. A few minutes of banter followed before John glanced at his watch and announced that it was time to hit the road. Tunde heaved Roy's rucksack onto his back. John led the way out of the concourse. Roy slackened the knot of his tie and peeled off his coat. The afternoon sun was unbelievably hot.

Outside, they crossed the strip of road separating the sprawling airport complex from the entrance of the car park. Upon entry, they weaved through several rows and columns of parked vehicles until they reached a sleek black Mercedes Benz 500 SEL.

John Nwosu got into the rear passenger seat with the exhausted Englishman while Tunde took the steering wheel. Moments later, the black Mercedes was cruising down the main road towards Ikeja Airport Hotel.

'The minister will be pleased to meet you Roy,' John said, drawing a nod from his jet-lagged guest. 'We will soon be at the hotel,' he announced, glancing at his watch. 'We have booked a suite so that you can freshen up and relax.'

The additional information drew another weary nod from Roy.

'At ten o'clock tonight, Tony will pick you up and bring you to the federal government lodge where the petroleum minister will be waiting anxiously to meet you.'

Roy smiled, elated by the feeling of being important. Wow, a high-ranking government official could not wait to meet him, he thought to himself. Back in the UK, the closest he ever got to a senior cabinet minister of Her Majesty's government was when he stood silently behind his father and watched him exchange banters with the Home Secretary at a Tory party conference. Roy was seventeen years old at the time.

The car pulled up in the driveway of the multi-storey hotel. The glass door at the entrance automatically slid into the side of a wall and a porter walked through it to attend to the new arrivals. He collected the room keys from the front desk and took the guests to the presidential suite on the third floor. As John tipped the porter, Roy fell onto the soft double bed and kicked off his shoes.

'While the porter is still here, would you like something to eat?' John asked, standing next to the porter at the doorway.

Roy rolled over on the bed to face the door. 'Yes sir, I'll like a bottle of champagne and any nice food to go with it.'

John turned and issued instructions to the porter and tipped him again. The porter grinned and promised to compel room service personnel to deliver the order on the double. When the door closed behind the porter, John shook his head and sank into the sofa opposite the bed. 'Once you give these porters some money, they promise you the moon.'

Roy sat up on the bed, nodding in agreement. It didn't take long for the food and wine to arrive. The porter meant what he had said.

*****

At exactly 8.30 PM, six hours after John left Roy's hotel room in Ikeja, Detective-Inspector Michael Otunba was driving through Badagry, a coastal town in Lagos State famous for its historic role as a major outpost for trans-atlantic slave trading.

Another twenty minutes on the seaboard expressway, he reached the rendezvous at the edge of Seme town, half a mile from the international frontier with the neighbouring Bénin Republic. He decelerated and applied the brakes, bringing the cream Volvo 244DL sedan to a gradual stop. He killed the engine and doused the headlamps. He remained in the car, observing the empty road ahead bathed in moonlight.

Minutes later, as he had expected, two silhouettes approached from a distance with torchlights.

'Put on your headlamps, the batteries of our torches wouldn't hold out for long,' one of the silhouettes called out loudly. The headlamps switched on. The light beams turned the silhouettes into Adamu and Eugene.

Mike pushed his Smith & Wesson revolver into the gun holster strapped over his shoulders and pulled his denim jacket over it. He opened the door and alighted. 'Shall we proceed?' he asked impatiently, walking briskly towards the men standing in front of the car.

Adamu nodded and lifted a light blue attaché case onto the bonnet. He manipulated the combination locks and the lid of the case sprang open. Eugene stepped forward and lifted the lid, revealing its contents— neatly packed stacks of mint fifty-naira notes in bundles.

'That is hundred and ten thousand naira, cash,' Eugene declared.

Otunba whistled and started laughing. It was a lot of money; three times his annual salary. The excited detective edged both men aside and ran his fingers on the surface of the stacked currency bills as if checking to see that they were really there. Adamu and Eugene watched in bemusement. The policeman slammed the lid shut and grabbed the handle of the case.

69

'There is more where that came from, if you remain loyal,' Adamu told the rogue cop.

With the attaché case in the firm grip of his left hand, the smiling detective stretched out his right arm and shook the hands of his paymasters, saying, 'I'll keep in touch.' He turned around and took two steps towards the car door. Then two gunshots in quick succession pierced the silent night.

The attaché case fell to the ground. Michael swung around to face the fraudsters with an expression of shock and fear on his face. He touched his burning stomach and his hands were covered with blood.

Eugene fired his Browning pistol again and the detective crumpled to the ground. The gangster came closer to the inert body lying on the ground and pumped another bullet into it.

*****

At 9.55 PM, the Mercedes Benz 500 SEL pulled up in the driveway of Ikeja Airport Hotel. Roy Seed emerged from the hotel, dressed in a black three-piece suit. The commissionaire opened the rear passenger door of the car for him.

Tunde turned his head, smiling, 'hope you rested well. Was everything in the suite to your taste?'

Roy got into the rear passenger seat and the commissionaire shut the door. Placing his briefcase on his laps, the Englishman responded to Tunde's remark. 'Tony, the suite is superb and I did catch some sleep. Thanks for asking.'

Tunde nodded and turned to face the steering wheel. He started the car and engaged the transmission gears. The uniformed guards swung the gates open, allowing the car to wheel out onto the main road.

Like Logan two years earlier, Roy was fascinated by the nightlife in Lagos— streetside traders working below streetlights, blazing florescent lights of supermarkets still open for business, young people milling about under the neon signboards of nightclubs blaring disco music. In fact, the city was kept alight by glowing street lamps.

When the car made it past the dual carriageway of Allen Avenue, Roy's mind turned to the issue at hand. He was nervous about meeting the minister in charge of the world's sixth largest petroleum producing sector. He would have to be on his best behaviour in the presence of this important government official. He would keep his acerbic sense of humour to a minimum. He wanted more than ever to clinch the oil deal.

The car pulled up inside the premises of John's residence in Victoria Island, which as far as Roy Seed knew, was the "federal government lodge"— a place for Abuja-based government ministers to stay whenever they popped into Lagos.

Roy alighted from the Mercedes with his briefcase and looked around. A few yards away, Nigeria's green-white-green tricolour, hoisted on an iron flagpole, was fluttering in the cool breeze beside the imposing cream-coloured mansion. Tucked away at corner of the driveway, under the glare of bright halogen floodlights, was a fleet of black Peugeot 504 saloon cars with the phrase FEDERAL GOVERNMENT OF NIGERIA stencilled on their sides with white paint.

As he was led towards the entrance of the house, Roy couldn't help but be impressed by the high quality of the landscaping—the beautifully trimmed green hedges, the water fountain and the rows of dwarf coconut trees lining the edges of the tarmacked driveway. The mahogany door of the mansion opened as he and Tunde reached the portico.

John, dressed in a fawn coloured suit, emerged smiling. 'You are welcome to the government lodge,' he intoned shaking Roy's hand. 'The minister is anxious to meet you,' he said as he ushered the guest into the spacious foyer of the large house.

A glass-fronted sliding door at the far end of the foyer suddenly opened and another man appeared. Unlike John who was fair-skinned and tall, this man was dark and of average-build. He was dressed in a blue *babaringa* robe with a brimless cap of the same colour to match. Beaming with smiles, he strode across the marble floor to Roy to shake hands. John introduced the man as the Federal Minister for Petroleum Resources.

'You must be the famous Roy,' the minister remarked archly. 'My aides have told me a lot about you. I'm Alhaji Mustapha Alkai.'

'It's a pleasure to meet you,' Roy replied as the minister led him through the glass sliding door into the sitting room. The Englishman quickly surveyed the room. The floor was covered in Persian rugs. On them were cream coloured armchairs arranged in a semi circle around a glass coffee table. A large TV and VCR set was in a corner of the room. Framed pictures of smiling federal government officials along with surrealist paintings were arranged in rows on the walls. A huge gold-plated chandelier hung from the ceiling.

'Wow! Nice place you've got here,' Roy remarked, sinking into a sofa facing the minister.

Mustapha smiled, 'the federal government always aim to please.'

John, who had been standing in the doorway of the sitting room, disappeared. Moments later, he reappeared carrying a silver tray containing a bottle of brandy and some cans of beer.

'Roy, what would you like?' Mustapha asked as John placed the tray gingerly on the glass table. The Englishman pointed at a can. John handed him the chilled beer can and turned enquiringly to the minister.

'I'll have the same,' Mustapha answered and got a chilled can as well. The minister and his visitor lifted the ring-pull of the cans in unison. There was a pop sound followed by frothing from the open cans. Both men quickly directed the frothing beer to their mouths.

Smacking his lips, seconds later, the minister said, 'I trust Alex have already told you everything you need to know about the deal.'

Roy nodded slowly as he withdrew the beer can from his lips.

'The crude oil barge will set sail for South Africa within a fortnight if the deal is sealed tonight,' Mustapha announced as he placed his beer can on the glass coffee table. 'Alex, if you please,' he requested, extending his right arm sideways to John alias "Alex Karidi". A light blue attaché case was quickly handed over. Mustapha placed it on his laps and started manipulating the combination locks on the case. The lid sprang open and he lifted the cover revealing a stack of documents.

'I will show you the barge,' he said, flipping through the documents. Suddenly he stopped and extracted an enlarged colour photograph. He leaned over the table as Roy sat up to collect the item.

The Englishman studied the picture. It was a huge black boat in the middle of what looked like an ocean. 'I will sign the deal for a sixty percent cut,' Roy announced placing the photo on the glass table. Then he braced himself for a pushback from the minister. He had agreed to a fifty-five percent cut when Alex met him in London, but he had since changed his mind. The minister would have to offer him a bigger slice of the cut in exchange for his cooperation.

Mustapha grinned and turned to John. 'You were right, Alex. Our friend here is a tough businessman.'

John laughed uncomfortably.

'Okay, Roy,' Mustapha smiled, 'I accept. Since you are the only one providing money for logistics, it is only fair that we split the profits in that manner. My associates and I will take forty percent.'

Roy was pleasantly surprised by this response. The minister was such a fair-minded man. The sort of person he could do business with, he thought, quickly overriding the uneasiness that he always felt when something was too good to be true. He was a gambling man and the odds of winning here were phenomenally high. He had made a demand and the minister had folded without a fight. He was in control of the situation. These Nigerian chaps were no smarter than he was.

'That's excellent. I'm already in love with this deal,' Roy replied as he picked up the photograph again from the table.

The minister reached into the attaché case and extracted two documents. 'Roy, could you sign these for me? That will formalise our business deal.'

Roy laid the photograph and the beer can down on the table. Then he took the documents from the minister's outstretched hand and squinted at them. Each document had the genuine letterhead of the Federal Ministry of Petroleum Resources.

'Read them carefully. If you are happy, please append your signature at the bottom right-hand corner of each document,' Mustapha instructed and sipped beer.

Roy studied them for a few minutes and then placed the two paper sheets on top of the picture on the table. He appended his signature at the space provided at the bottom right-hand corner of each sheet.

Alhaji Mustapha Alkai transferred the open attaché case from his laps to the glass table. 'You got the money?' he asked, raising his eyebrows anxiously.

Roy smiled reassuringly. Not long after, he passed the signed documents and the briefcase containing the desired £200,000 to the excited government official.

Eugene alias "Mustapha Alkai" opened the briefcase on his laps and was overjoyed to see bundles of £50 notes, arranged in neat stacks. He picked up a bundle and flipped through it, restraining himself from kissing it. Salivating openly over a few hundred thousand pounds would not fit the comportment of a federal minister who oversaw the collection of millions of pounds in oil and gas taxes. In the presence of a foreign visitor, it was important to keep up appearances.

With a countenance expressing seriousness, Mustapha snapped the briefcase shut and handed it to John, saying, 'the deal is done.' He scooped up the photograph and the documents from the table. He appended his signature next to that of Roy in each document.

'I'll keep the duplicate copy. Yours is the original,' he explained as he gave one of the signed documents back to the Englishman. The photograph and the other document went inside the open attaché case on the glass table.

'Okay, mates! Let us drink to deal,' Roy proposed, raising his can of beer. John placed the briefcase on the Persian rug and quickly took a can from the tray in the middle of the table.

Mustapha snapped the lid of the attaché case shut and raised his half-empty beer can. 'Yes, let's toast to our deal. May it signal the beginning of a wonderful business relationship between us,' he said. The men laughed as their cans clinked.

The meeting ended at 11.00 PM and Roy was whisked back to his hotel in the Mercedes. Later that night, Roy dreamt that he had visited his cancer-stricken father in hospital carrying a rucksack filled with stacks of bank notes worth 12 million pounds from the Nigerian deal. Though in a lot of pain, Lord Hugh Seed had laughed heartily and admitted that his earlier perception of his son as a "never-do-well" gambler was wrong.

When Roy woke up the next morning, he smiled. The next two days was spent on a guided tour of the Lagos city-state. At Lagos Bar Beach, he enjoyed nightly drink and dance parties by the sandy edge of the Atlantic Ocean.

On the third day, in the departures concourse of Murtala Mohammed International Airport, John and Tunde presented Roy with a beige-coloured *danshiki* tailored to his lean size. Roy expressed his sincere gratitude for the gift as he shook their hands vigorously. Four hours later, he boarded the British Airways flight to London Heathrow.

CHAPTER 11

Detective-Inspector (DI) Ikenna Kodilinye sat down opposite the uniformed man poring over some documents on the mahogany desk. 'How do you feel about this assignment?' the man asked without looking up from the documents.

The question caught the detective off guard. He had not expected it; at least not as the first question. 'Eh…I guess sir, em…I mean it is challenging,' was his hesitant reply.

Chief Superintendent of Police (CSP) Cyrus Udeh froze momentarily, dropping the papers in the process. He gradually lifted his head to face the detective. 'I did not ask you whether it is challenging or not. Do you think you can do it…produce results?' The Chief Superintendent literarily spat the words at the detective.

'Yes sir. I can produce results,' DI Ikenna Kodilinye replied. There was momentary silence in the room. A part of Ikenna regretted what he had just said. He knew that he would be held to those words.

Cyrus' countenance changed. In a conciliatory tone, he said, 'Look Ikenna, I know it is a little bit outside your comfort zone. This is obviously not the same as taking down druggies and their dealers, but I am sure you will quickly adjust to your new role outside narcotics. My hope for this case is riding on you. I have taken angry phone calls from the State Police Commissioner, the Zonal Assistant Inspector-General, and the Inspector-General, himself. They all ask why I should carry on as the Divisional Police Officer if I can't catch those murderous swindlers. We didn't get them when they killed the American. Now, they have gone a step further and killed a policeman.'

Ikenna shifted on his seat and interjected, 'crooked policeman, sir.'

Cyrus nodded, taking mental note of the colourful adjective contributed by his subordinate. The adjective explained, in retrospect, why the police had not been able to apprehend the gang of swindlers. It could plausibly explain how a suspected member of the gang was able to escape from police custody. Finally, the pieces of the jigsaw puzzle were beginning to fall into place, almost three years late.

Twenty-one days earlier, the decomposing corpse of DI Michael Otunba, head of the anti-scam squad, was found by a tramp pitching a tent nearby. The sheer brazenness of the murder had shocked and outraged every police officer in Lagos State Police Command.

In the suburban district of Agege, a Police Superintendent expressed his outrage by shooting all pickpockets and burglars in the holding cells of his police station. The petty criminals were just days away from arraignment in Orile Agege Magistrate Court before their cold-blooded murder.

When a crowd of incredulous journalists descended on Eleresun Police Station in Agege to check if those extrajudicial killings had indeed occurred as rumours would have it, they found the Superintendent in a combative mood. He bellowed into the cluster of microphones and tape recorders that all criminals were the same and deserved to die. The press reporters took note of the roundabout admission of guilt. Dozens of camera flashes intermittently lit up the Superintendent's face as he continued to rant and rave. The next day, all newspapers in Lagos State carried his words as banner headlines along with pictures of his snarling face. Highly embarrassed and disgusted, the State Commissioner of Police, Stanislaus Zikora, promptly sacked the Superintendent and got him charged with homicide— an unusual step for an organization notorious for protecting its trigger-happy members from justice.

Meanwhile, back in Ikeja CID, a joint investigation by homicide squad and anti-police corruption squad (APCS) into Mike Otunba's bank account revealed a huge amount of money, way above the means of an ordinary detective. Probing further, the investigators were surprised to learn that monthly deposits into the bank account had begun just days after an earlier ad hoc police panel had (wrongly) absolved the deceased detective of any involvement in the December 1990 escape of one swindler from police custody. There weren't any money trails to follow since the deposits to the bank account were made in cash.

After the ad hoc team of homicide and APCS detectives wrapped their preliminary investigation, Cyrus decided it was time to fill the vacant leadership position of the anti-scam squad, also known as the "419 squad" because it deals with crimes that fall under *Section 419* of the Nigerian Penal Code on Advance Fee Fraud.

Determined not to risk another bent cop taking charge of the anti-scam squad, Cyrus refused to promote Mike Otunba's former deputy from acting to substantive squad leader. Although this acting squad leader had a good service record, was cleared of any involvement in Otunba's crooked ventures, Cyrus wanted someone else for the substantive leadership role. Cyrus asked Ikenna Kodilinye, the narcotics squad leader, to assume control of the anti-scam squad with an expanded mandate to investigate not just scams, but also homicides linked to them. To help fulfil the expanded mandate, Cyrus reassigned a few homicide squad detectives to the anti-scam "419" squad on an ad hoc basis.

'What have you got for me?' Cyrus asked reclining on his chair, staring intently at his subordinate.

Ikenna cleared his throat. There wasn't much to report. He had just been appointed leader of the anti-scam squad the week before. 'I had all my men checked out. APCS has declared them clean,' Ikenna replied, referring to the vetting of all anti-scam squad members by the much-hated APCS leader, Chief Inspector Nduka Ikwunne.

Cyrus nodded slowly. 'Anything else?' he asked as he arranged the pile of documents on the table.

'Yes sir, I have applied for a search warrant for Mike Otunba's house. I will like to turn it over for clues.'

The Chief Superintendent frowned, 'homicide squad have already done that. And they didn't use a search warrant.'

Ikenna shook his head. 'I want to go through the house again with my own team.'

Cyrus shrugged, 'okay, I'll ask the magistrate to issue the warrant on the double. But there could still be a delay. I don't manage the magistrate's time. You know you could always skip the red tape. Nobody would mind if you took the shortcut.'

But Ikenna wasn't one to take the shortcut. He had always disapproved of the widespread practice of executing police searches without court order. The look on Ikenna's face confirmed to Cyrus that the detective wanted to play it by the book.

The DPO smiled knowingly at the high-minded detective sitting across the desk from him. 'As you wish, the warrant will be approved first thing tomorrow morning. I will lean on the magistrate tonight. Apart from this house search, is there anything else you would like to talk about?'

'No, sir... that is all I have at the moment.'

Cyrus nodded silently. He lifted the stack of papers on his desk and dropped them into the OUT tray close to the edge of his desk. 'That would be all, Ikenna. Go out there and get me results,' Cyrus said, dismissing the detective.

Ikenna rose and walked out of the office without saying a word. The Chief Superintendent watched the door snap shut. He smiled. He had always admired the straightforward style of the detective he had mentored. Ikenna Kodilinye had been a star cop who had put away many drug dealers in his role as the leader of the narcotics squad. Perhaps, if Ikenna had replaced Mike Otunba sooner, Ikeja CID would have already caught the murderous swindlers, Cyrus thought.

The telephone on his desk started ringing. He promptly picked up the handset. It was the Lagos State Commissioner of Police on the line.

*****

There was pin-drop silence when John entered the situation room to speak to the men sitting on wooden chairs positioned on one side of a glass-topped table. 'Adamu, how far have you gone with your assignment?' he asked, breaking the silence.

Adamu scratched his head saying 'Not much progress yet. I am still working on it. It will probably take some time.'

John sighed, 'Look man! You are wasting time. Without our own guy on the inside, our work will become dangerous.'

Adamu rubbed his chin; something he always did when he was nervous. He understood how important it was to act fast. The gang needed to fill the information gap, which the demise of Mike Otunba had opened up. They needed another highly placed policeman inside Ikeja CID to be their eyes and ears. In that way, they would always be a step ahead of all police investigations targeted at them.

'Boss, it is not easy. What you are asking for is a high-level source. I am still studying the characters of the detectives that work there.'

There was momentary silence then John asked, 'what about that chap, Detective-Inspector Ikenna Kodilinye?'

'I checked him out. Too honest. There is no way he would agree to work for us. He would rather arrest us on sight,' Adamu replied.

'What about the other man, Gbolahan?'

Adamu shook his head.

'The Divisional Police Officer...the Ikeja CID chief...what's his name again?'

'Chief Superintendent Cyrus Udeh.'

'Yes, that's it! Can't we get him?'

'Sorry boss. I don't think so.'

'Come on Adamu! Surely there is a policeman over there willing to play ball for the right price.'

'There are lots of policemen who will take our money. But we need a specific kind of policeman, an officer in a position of authority within Ikeja CID.'

'Well, that is pretty obvious, isn't it? So when are you going to find that such an officer?'

'Sir, I am working hard on it. Give me two more weeks.'

'Okay Adamu. You have two weeks or I'll reassign the task to someone else.' John said, casting an admiring glance at Tunde.

Adamu did not like that. He cursed under his breath. He would have to double down on his efforts to deliver the task assigned to him. Tunde was not going to upstage him, yet again.

'Roy will be expecting good news about our deal in a week's time,' John announced, changing the topic. 'So what is our plan, Tunde?'

All eyes focussed on Tunde as he opened the manila folder lying on the glass tabletop in a histrionic manner. 'Boss, we are going for the obituary plot,' he replied finally.

'Okay, when are you sending out the poster?' John asked.

Tunde said it would be mailed to London the following day. He expected Roy Seed to get it within a fortnight. John nodded.

'Sir, how is your new project coming along?' Eugene asked the gang leader. A few weeks earlier, John had boasted about a new "American operation" he was working on. A brand new green passport had been procured from Nigerian Immigration Service (NIS) under his new alias. The usual NIS officer on the payroll had fast-tracked the passport application process. The US Embassy had just approved a business visa for him. Despite entreaties from the excited men, John had refused to disclose details of the plan, saying that all would be revealed at the right time. Eugene was betting that the time was right, that John would be receptive to his probing question.

John smiled broadly and the anxious men sat upright in their chairs to hear what he had to say. 'I'll be going on a working holiday to New York,' he blurted out.

The men were intrigued.

'I'm going to meet our new target. He is a successful millionaire businessman...well, he used to be successful.' John paused and picked up a small plastic bottle of water from the table. 'A series of bad investments and some serious tax issues, which he is trying to iron out with the IRS, have landed him in a mess. To cut a long story short, he is in financial straits right now; an ideal candidate for what I have in mind.' He paused and drank water from the bottle. Then he surveyed the excited faces before him before resuming the narration. 'For the past six months, I have been following the news about our target in American newspapers. My impression is that he is in a desperate situation. He will part with a lot of money if we can persuade him.'

John raised a spiral-bound notebook above his head. 'The plan is in black and white here. I will make photocopies for each of you, tomorrow.' He paused again, dropped the notebook on the table, and drank from the bottle.

The usually taciturn Adamu cleared his throat and asked a question. 'What is the name of our man?'

John removed the bottle from his mouth and wiped his lips with the back of his hand. Capping the bottle, he replied, 'David Steinberg.'

*****

At seven o'clock in the morning, in a quiet neighbourhood of Ikeja, there was a loud knock on the front door of a bungalow. Mrs Yinka Otunba drew the curtain to one side, surprised at the number of police estate cars in the driveway of her home. She opened the glass door and stepped back to study the search warrant that her late husband's friend was showing her from the doorstep.

'What is the meaning of this?' she asked trepidatiously.

'Yinka, it is a warrant to search your house' Ikenna replied calmly, avoiding her eyes.

'Why? My husband did nothing wrong. He was the victim. You should be out there looking for his murderers. I thought you were his friend,' she said, tears rolling down her eyes.

Ikenna shook his head slowly, sad at what he was about to tell the widow, sorry that he no longer considered himself a friend of her late husband. He was no friend of crooked policemen.

'I am sorry, madam,' he began in a formal tone of voice. 'But we have good reason to believe that your husband worked with the men who subsequently killed him. The same men had defrauded two Americans, one of whom was murdered here in Lagos. Your husband sabotaged a police investigation to protect these men. That was until they finally turned on him.'

'No! No! You are lying. It is not true!' Yinka cried, shaking her head in denial. Ikenna pushed past her into the foyer, followed by a team of plain-clothes detectives and uniformed policemen. The only other female present on the scene— a uniformed policewoman who had not barged into the house with her male colleagues—finally walked through the doorway to the foyer. She put her arm around the shoulder of the sobbing Yinka and led her into the kitchen while the other cops fanned out across the house to search it for evidence tying the deceased detective to the fraudsters.

Inside of an hour, the policemen succeeded in turning the house upside down. A diary recovered from the bedroom contained phone numbers. A quick check in the phone directory revealed nothing out of the ordinary. The phone numbers belonged to mechanic workshops, restaurants, cultural clubs and other mundane places patronized by the deceased detective during his lifetime.

The discovery of the basement under the street-level floor of his study room failed to turn out anything interesting. What the police searchers would never know was that Michael Otunba—having decided that he no longer needed to telecommunicate with the criminal patrons he was about to double-cross— had disconnected and disposed of his specialised basement phone. The policemen checking the underground room did not even find a telephone socket or landline. All they found was a desk bedecked with dusty books written in Yoruba language and a couple of old police journals. The search was over.

The policemen spent forty-five minutes putting everything they had previously scattered back in their original positions. Ikenna apologised to Yinka for the intrusion and thanked her for cooperation. Moments later, all the policemen returned to their cars and vanished from the driveway.

Sergeant Temitope Maria Akinjide—the policewoman— spent another hour comforting the bereaved woman in the living room before leaving for Ikeja CID in her Peugeot 505 sedan. She would later report to Ikenna that her two-hour conversation with Yinka had not yielded any useful information. In fact, in her own considered opinion, the grieving widow was oblivious of what her perfidious husband had been up to.

*****

In a leafy neighbourhood in Kensington, London, Roy Seed was woken up by the alarm of his digital clock. He sat up in his bed, bleary-eyed. He rubbed his eyes with the back of his hands and turned to the clock on the bedside table. Its LCD screen indicated that the time and date were 10.00 AM and 5th May 1993, respectively. He jumped out of bed and wrestled into a beige-coloured house robe.

While stirring a cup of hot tea in the kitchen, he heard the clatter of the door letterbox. He walked to the foyer and spotted a brown A4-sized envelope lying on the rug next to the foot of the front door. He bent over and retrieved it. He took it back to the kitchen as he sipped tea. He studied the Nigerian stamps on the envelope before ripping it open. He extracted a poster folded in half. His face turned crimson, when the word OBITUARY leapt out at him from the unfolded poster. Under the caption was a colour picture of "Alex" smiling back at him. The text below the picture read:

We the family of Alexander Callistus Karidi regret to announce the untimely death of our son, brother and cousin in ghastly motor accident. This tragedy, which also claimed the life of his best friend, Mr Tony Oke, occurred on 10 April 1993. Funeral rites would be announced by the family soon...

Roy stopped reading and fell into a chair, shocked. He felt a dizzying attack of vertigo, imagining himself spiralling downwards into an abyss. He sipped his tea quietly as he tried to make sense of what he had just seen and read. He grabbed the brown envelope. Perhaps, there was something else in the envelope that would help him make sense of it all.

He dipped his hand into the envelope, fumbled around, and retrieved a small piece of white paper, the size of business card. The handwritten message on it informed him that due to the unforseen deaths of Alex and Tony, and the increasing vigilance of the Nigerian government, the oil tanker deal was off. The unsigned piece of paper concluded by warning him of the consequences of pursuing the matter any further:

Who we are doesn't matter, but be rest assured that we would do anything to protect the reputation of our honourable petroleum minister from any scandal. Do not try to pursue this matter any further. Foreigners who don't know when to quit have turned up dead in our country. Don't risk your life over two hundred thousand pounds. Think of your ailing father.

Roy thought of his dad. He knew the dying old man could easily stop him from assuming full control of the company. Already, there were rumours in company headquarters that Sir Hugh Seed was thinking of appointing the regional manager in charge of Seed Stores in Northeast England as substantive Chief Executive Officer (CEO) for the entire chain of stores across UK. Sir Hugh had denied the rumour from his hospital bed, but refused to promise Roy that he would eventually be promoted from his current role as acting company head to the substantive CEO.

Nine months after lung cancer forced his father to grant him temporary control of the entire chain of stores, Roy was still struggling to turn around his image as the reckless "never-do-well" son in the eyes of the old man. He knew what would happen if news of the botched oil smuggling deal reached his father's sick bed. The old man would certainly make good on the threat he had made years earlier in a fit of anger. One more false move and Roy would have to contend with the prospect of being written out of the old man's will. In the face of his father's wrath, he would be lucky to retain a job at Seed Stores, not to mention becoming its CEO.

Pursuing the money, the two hundred thousand pounds, was useless. Roy did not even know how to go about trying to recover it. And there was the explicit threat in the unsigned note, the unacceptable risk of death at the hands of government thugs in a third-world country.

Screaming in frustration, the young Englishman picked up the teacup and smashed it against the stainless steel kitchen sink.

CHAPTER 12

NEW YORK CITY, USA

The yellow cab pulled up outside the Manhattan coffee shop. John pulled a tweed coat over his cream turtleneck sweater and overpaid the cab driver. Alighting from the car, he asked the driver to keep the change. The driver grinned and sped off.

John walked through the double glass doors into the shop teeming with customers. The thick smell of coffee latte hit his nose. He quickly surveyed the place in search of a person fitting the description of the man he was supposed to meet. His eyes caught a fat white man dressed in a grey suit, sitting alone on a round table. The man fit the description— dark-haired, grim face, sloe-eyed, prominent nose and a square jaw. Studying the grim face sipping coffee and reading a folded copy of the *Wall Street Journal* convinced John that his assignment was going to be onerous.

He walked up to the man and smiled, 'hello sir, I am Johnson Ezeka'. Stretching out his arm for a handshake, he added, 'and you must be David Steinberg.'

The big man's face lit up immediately. He rose to his feet and shook the hand of the fair-skinned black man. 'You sounded younger on the phone,' he remarked as they sat down. 'Black coffee?' he asked, raising the porcelain coffee pot on the table.

John nodded and the American poured a generous amount into the empty cup before him.

'Oh, by the way, nice American accent. Where did you pick that from?' David asked curiously, as he pushed the cup gently across the table to his prospective business partner.

John stirred the steaming coffee with a spoon. 'I went to a secondary school ran by an American evangelical mission in Lagos.'

David nodded and remarked that the school had done a good job. An elderly white couple nodded at the big man as they walked past his table. David winked at them and turned back to John. 'I always see them here whenever I come in for my afternoon coffee. For the past three years, they come in daily at about this hour.Never missed a single day.'

John nodded impatiently. He wanted to get on with his business proposal. The American noticed this and changed to the subject of the meeting— a weird African deal in which he stood to make at least forty-five million US dollars.

'Tell me more about this deal,' he said, holding his face in his hands and staring expectantly into John's face.

The Nigerian sipped coffee then spoke. 'Seven years ago, the former Nigerian Minister for Transport and Works awarded a multi-million dollar contract for the building of a two hundred and fifty mile rail track to connect the western and the eastern parts of the country.' John paused surveyed the face of his client; what he observed was encouraging and he continued. 'The contract was awarded to a local contractor that lacked the necessary experience needed to execute the sort of capital project the minister was proposing. For five years, the company laid inferior tracks made of cast iron and aluminium rather than steel. After laying two-thirds of the total distance of the rail tracks required, the federal government, smelling a rat, insisted on running a test train.' John paused to sip coffee.

David urged him to continue, completely enthralled by the story. A few feet behind him, the old white couple finished their coffee on their table. Moments later, they walked past the fat American again, nodding as they went. Distracted by the engaging story, David ignored them.

'Under the hot weather conditions, the rail tracks buckled and the test train derailed. There was uproar within the federal government. The transport minister was sacked, arrested and charged with corruption. The contractors were sued for doing a shoddy job and a presidential inquiry committee was commissioned to investigate the contract awarding process.'

David sipped his coffee and asked his business associate to continue.

By this time, even before the business proposal had been pitched, John knew that he had Steinberg where he wanted him. This excited him inwardly. 'The committee was made up of buddies of the Finance Minister. I was a member of the committee in my capacity as a permanent secretary in the Federal Ministry of Transport and Works. Three months of investigation revealed a web of corruption involving the sacked minister, his cronies, and of course, the contractor. The investigating committee found that the project's real value was at fifty million dollars and yet it had been awarded for two hundred million dollars.'

David's eyes widened in alarm. He adjusted himself on his chair and sipped his coffee.

John lowered his voice and leaned forward on his elbows. With his face inches from that of Steinberg, he whispered, 'the committee and its chairman, the Finance Minister, recovered all the money split and hidden in five banks in Nigeria. The committee said that it had only recovered fifty million dollars and swiftly arranged for it to be returned to the coffers of the federal government. They claimed that the remainder was lost, could not be recovered, but that is not true. The committee members intend keep the remaining one hundred and fifty million dollars for themselves.' John reclined on his seat, smiling mischievously at the astonished American. 'But they need to hide the money abroad. So they need a foreigner they can trust.'

David removed his hands from his head and sat up, his mouth twitching at the sides. 'You think I am that trustworthy foreigner, eh?' he asked with a wide smile.

'Yes I believe so. I would not want to deposit a hundred and fifty million dollars into your bank account if I didn't think so,' John replied confidently.

David took his cup, his hand trembling with excitement, and downed the remaining contents.

John grabbed the coffee pot and refilled the American's cup.

'How did you find me?' the American asked.

John drank from his cup, wiped coffee on his lips with a napkin and spoke truthfully for the first time. 'I got your contact number from the Nigerian–American Chamber of Commerce. You are a smart businessman, one ready to take reasonable risks to secure a lucrative transaction'— then the lies resumed and continued apace—'I am acting for the interests of my boss, the Finance Minister. If you help us to stash the money in your account, we will give you thirty percent of the money when we move it to another bank account, our own bank account in the Cayman Islands.'

David raised his eyes to the ceiling as though he was trying to gather his thoughts.

John watched him intently, waiting for the anticipated reaction.

It arrived seconds later in the form of a double-barrelled question. 'When do we set the ball rolling and for how long will it be staying in my bank acccount.'

John answered the questions in a long-winded way. 'I will need to get back to my minister. Only he will say when the process of transfer should happen. It is going to be a drawn-out process because we need to protect ourselves. The money has been distributed and hidden in twelve Nigerian private bank accounts under assumed names. Over the space of five weeks, we plan a piecemeal withdrawal of the money from those bank accounts in the form of hard cash. Each chunk of withdrawn cash money will be ferried by private helicopter to banks in the Republic of Togo. Once all the money is safely lodged in fifteen Togolese bank accounts, then we shall start the electronic process of transferring the money piecemeal to your bank accounts. You will obviously need multiple accounts, preferably in different American banks, to receive each large chunk of money we transfer.' John paused and sipped his tea.

'And there was I thinking you guys are crazy enough to contemplate a single transfer of the entire one hundred and fifty million dollars,' David remarked with a mirthless laugh.

'Nope, we are good at what we do,' John smiled. 'Like I was saying, the timing of the electronic transfer from Togo to United States will be determined by the finance minister. I would imagine that each chunk of money we send you will stay in your bank account for three months before it goes to the Cayman Islands.' John paused and then delivered the next line with bated breath. 'But first we need the name of your current bank, your account number, and other important details.'

David's countenance changed. He squirmed on his seat. Eyeing his prospective business associate suspiciously, he asked, 'you need my bank details, right now?'

John noticed this and he moved fast to disabuse the American's mind. 'Well, we do, for a couple of reasons. First reason is that my minister would see it as a sign of good faith, a sign of your commitment to the deal on offer. The second reason is that we need to know whether the bank is one we would want to place our money in.'

David relaxed smiling. The explanation satisfied him. 'I maintain an account with Manhattan Chase Bank. The bank account number is…wait a minute...' he paused, dipped his fat hand into the breast pocket of his coat, and removed his business card. He turned the card over, wrote the bank account number on its blank side, and gave it to John.

The fraudster studied it for a while before pocketing it, remarking, 'Manhattan Chase Bank is okay for our business.'

David cleared his throat and John froze in trepidation. Was the American having second thoughts?

'Look man, if you put that money in my account it could come back to haunt me. The IRS may come after my ass. You know what I mean?'

John knew exactly what he meant, but he knew how to squelch his friend's skepticism. 'Obviously, we are only using your Manhattan Chase bank account for our initial business. I have already said you will need to open multiple accounts in other banks other than Manhattan Chase.'

The American shook his head, 'Too risky!'

John ignored the histrionics. He knew David Steinberg was already committed to the deal and willing to take on the risks. 'You will have to be careful,' John advised. 'I'm sure you can figure out a way to conceal our business from the financial authorities of your country. I have also been given the discretion to raise your share of the money to thirty-five percent. That is fifty-two-point-five million dollars for your troubles.' John paused and sipped his coffee.

David rubbed his chin. He desperately needed that kind of money to reinvigorate his dying business concerns. It took him seconds to decide that he was going ahead with the unscrupulous transaction. He plunged his hand into his jacket and felt around for his small bottle of whisky. 'We have to drink to this,' he said pouring a generous quantity of the spirit into the empty cup that once held his coffee.

John quickly drank up and presented his own empty cup eagerly to the American.

David filled it with whisky. 'To the success of this fantastic deal,' he proposed and they drank to the deal.

*****

More than seven thousand miles away, in Lagos, a prominent policeman sat behind his desk rethinking his decision to take up the offer of spying for the fraudsters who have already shown their ruthless side by killing two people, one of which was a fellow cop. Though the money the homicidal fraudsters were offering was mouth-watering—almost twice his annual salary—he was still reluctant to work for them for the simple reason that they could also kill him whenever they thought he was no longer useful. He rose from his desk in Ikeja CID complex and walked to the window overlooking the busy city.

Three storeys down, on the street level, a silver-coloured Toyota Land Cruiser slowed to a stop at the roadside kerb and a fat man dressed in beige *babaringa* alighted. He crossed the road in the flowing wide-sleeved robes and strutted into a seven-storey glass building where scores of lawyers, real estate agents, independent auditors and insurance brokers maintained offices.

The policeman bit his lips in envy from his window. The Toyota owner was obviously rich and didn't shy away from showing it off. Although relatively well paid, the prominent policeman craved for the kind of wealth that could embolden him to leave the Force and do something better with his life. A man without wealth had no respect even in his home village, he thought, recalling an incident that occurred decades earlier, when he was 17 years old, long before he joined the police force.

The teenager's poor dad had died living him a large plot of farmland. A wealthy native of the village, who had made it big in the oil-rich city of Port Harcourt, returned home seeking to buy land. He had approached the teenager's family with an offer to buy their farmland. When the family refused to sell, the rich man expropriated the land by force with the aid of hired thugs, claiming falsely that his ancestors originally owned the land.

The family went to court. The rich man bribed the local magistrate and the traditional ruler of the village. Both supported the argument of the rich man that the land once belonged to his ancestors and that the teenager's family were illegal squatters who should be evicted.

The magistrate ruled that the poor family, the rightful owners of the land, should vacate the farmland within two weeks, taking with them all the plants they were growing on it. The court also ordered them to pay the legal costs of the rich man.

The teenager and his widowed mum ended up selling their own home to pay the costs. Luckily, their lawyer took pity on them and did not demand payment. The injustice would change the teenager's life forever. Within days of his nineteenth birthday, he had joined the Nigeria Police Force hoping to make a difference; to ensure that everyone was treated equally under the law, to guarantee that no one's rights were violated on account of their socio-economic status.

Thirty years down the line, naïve idealism had given way to the depressing cold reality. Money still ruled the world and the law only worked for people who had lots of it stuffed into laundry bags and briefcases, ready to be delivered at short notice to politicians, judges and law enforcement officers.

The policeman returned to his desk, nodding to himself. He had made his decision. He wanted to have lots of money like the owner of that Toyota Land Cruiser. Yes, he was going to spy on other police officers in Ikeja CID. In his eyes, the money offered for his services was worth the risk of being caught by his police colleagues or getting himself killed by his paranoid criminal associates.

PART TWO

CHAPTER 13

JUNE 1993

LAGOS, WESTERN NIGERIA

Alhaji Mahmoud Gamji stepped on the accelerator pedal and the silver-coloured Toyota Land Cruiser gained speed on the highway. He switched on the car air conditioner to combat the heat inside the vehicle. Shortly after, the Land cruiser ran into the scene of a traffic jam and came to a halt behind a long queue of vehicles held up by a semi-trailer truck negotiating a turn.

A policeman, dressed in a light orange uniform, stood on a traffic island directing the slow-moving trailer truck.

Bus drivers honked their horns and bellowed, 'Come on! *Oga Yellow Fever!* Get that truck out of the way quickly!'

The policeman turned and smiled at the queue of motorcycles, saloon cars, SUVs, and battered commuter buses. He turned back to the semi-trailer truck as its driver successfully completed the three-point U-turn.

'*Oga Yellow Fever!* Thank you,' the trucker said, amidst the honking and shouting. Stretching out his hand, he offered a fifty-naira note. '*Make you carry dis wan drink beer,*' he said to the traffic cop in Pidgin English.

At this stage, other motorists were going berserk. 'What is wrong with that mad truck driver? Please stop chatting! This is not your living room! Move this bloody truck out of the way! *Oga Yellow Fever,* do your job! Stop taking bribes!'

The traffic policeman ignored the irate motorists and calmly thanked the truck driver as he slid the crisp banknote into his trouser pocket.

The truck moved on. The road unblocked and traffic flow resumed. The white gloves covering the cop's hands shimmered in the sunlight as he swiftly waved the vehicles on.

Mahmoud Gamji slowed down next to the traffic policeman, threw a couple of folded fifty-naira notes out of the window, and drove on. From the side mirror, he could see the grateful cop clutching the money in one hand and waving at him with the other. Mahmoud smiled. He liked it when the lower classes paid obeisance to him. It made him feel very important and indispensable. It always reminded him of how far he had come from his childhood days when eating three square meals a day was a huge challenge. He shook his head and exclaimed, '*Kai! Wallahi!* Poverty is a curse!'

Born in penury in Zaria, Kaduna State, he had gained riches beyond his wildest dreams. With the help of his friends—the army generals ruling the country—the fertilizer business he started with a paltry sum of money from his uncle in the late 1970s was now a multi-million naira business.

His company, FERTILCO, was the military regime's sole distributor of subsidised fertilizer to farmers across the whole country. He had made millions of naira by hoarding fertilizer in order to create an artificial scarcity of the product in the regular markets. Desperate farmers ended up buying the same fertilizer bags in the black market at prices almost ten times the subsidized rate.

His wealth was a standing guarantee that no member of his family would ever experience hardship in the way he had so many years earlier. Alhaji Gamji had great plans for his eldest son, Tunji, who was studying engineering in the United States. He had recently established another company, which had grown rapidly and was now handling forty percent of contracts awarded for road maintenance across the country—thanks to the Alhaji's top-level links to the federal military government. That thirteen-month-old company would be his gift to his son after graduation from Stanford University.

The Land Cruiser swerved into a side street named after its driver: *Gamji Street*. As soon as they spotted the approaching vehicle, two security guards dressed in immaculate white uniforms scrambled to open the gates of a posh residence.

Mahmoud Gamji drove past the open gates into a large compound. He circled a concrete roundabout, which doubled as a fountain spouting water dyed blue and finally stopped under a canopy erected at the left-hand corner of the forecourt of his sprawling mansion.

One of the uniformed guards named Adamkus Suleh hurried over to open the vehicle door for the boss to alight.

Mahmoud disembarked smiling. In accordance with his tradition, he rewarded this quick display of servility by tipping the guard with ₦100. 'Good man, Adam,' the rich man said, patting the guard in the back. With a sneer on his face, he turned to the other guard and said, 'James, you must learn to run like Adam or he will make more money than you.'

Standing behind the delighted Adamkus, a sombre James mumbled an apology, blaming his slow legs for his latest misfortune. He earned a decent salary working for the Alhaji, but tips and bonuses were still nice things to receive. He eyed Adamkus with envy for a few moments before returning to his post inside the security booth next to the wrought iron grill gates.

The front door of the mansion suddenly swung open and a fair-skinned plump lady emerged smiling. '*Rankadede Alhaji*,' she greeted in Hausa language with a heavy Igbo accent and took his briefcase.

The husband, Mamhoud, kissed her on the cheeks. He put his right arm over her shoulder as they walked into the house.

Closing the door behind her, the wife asked in Pidgin English, '*Alhaji how now? Dis one wey you dey quiet...abi sometin' happen?*'

Mahmoud smiled wearily. 'I am fine, just tired after a hard day's work. Onyi, could you get me a glass of cold water?'

He settled into an armchair in the living room while Onyinye went into the kitchen to get him chilled water. Within few minutes of sitting down, he began to sweat. With a weary sigh, he heaved his large body frame up from the chair and walked across the room to switch on the central air conditioning system.

'It's so hot here,' he remarked to his wife who was standing beside his armchair with the glass of cold water in her hand. 'Don't you feel it?' Mahmoud asked, wiping sweat beads from his forehead with a white handkerchief. The overhead air conditioner humming began pumping cold air into the spacious room.

His wife smiled, 'Well I have been in the kitchen, bedroom and the study room. The atmosphere in those rooms isn't hot at all.'

The husband accepted the cold water and drank it. 'Maybe it's because this part of the house is facing the sunlight,' he postulated.

Onyinye nodded in agreement. Mahmoud drank all the water and requested for more. His wife went into the kitchen and came back with a large bottle of cold water. She filled up his glass.

He consumed the water and held out his glass for more. His wife laughed as she refilled his glass. '*Haba Alhaji!* I didn't know that you now drink like a fish.'

Mahmoud smiled. Onyinye still looked radiant and beautiful even at the age of forty-three. So far, he had no regrets for breaking his family's ethnic Hausa Muslim tradition to marry an Igbo Christian woman. He had encountered stiff opposition from his devout parents who were opposed to his bid to marry a non-Muslim who had refused to convert to Islam, and from the Onyinye's parents who threatened to disown their daughter if she went ahead with the marriage to the Hausa man.

Unlike Mahmoud's parents, the opposition of Onyinye's parents were based mainly on Gamji's ethnic nationality rather than his religion. Having lost seven members of his family to the anti-Igbo pogroms of 1966, Onyinye's father was horrified at the prospect of he and his wife becoming in-laws to people from the ethnic group that he held responsible for the massacres. As a colonel in the defunct Biafran Army, he had fought Nigerian military forces dominated by that same ethnic group for almost three years.

Despite the opposition, Mahmoud and Onyinye got married on 7th July 1974 in a local registrary in Lagos Island. The difference in religion had made it impossible to wed in the mosque or the Catholic Church. No single member of his or her family was present at their marriage ceremony.

Nineteen years on, their marriage had been a success blessed with four children. The eldest son Tunji was a university student in USA while his younger siblings were in boarding schools in different parts of Nigeria. With all the children away, the Alhaji, his wife, and their live-in houseboy, Zaky Ideh, were the only occupants of the twelve-room mansion situated in the affluent district of Ikoyi.

Mahmoud Gamji drained the glass. 'Thank you, Onyi,' he said, handing her the empty glass.

A dark-skinned short, stocky man emerged from the kitchen. Onyinye passed the glass to him and asked him whether the food was ready. The servant answered in the affirmative.

'Okay, bring it to the dining table for Alhaji. He is very hungry,' Onyinye instructed. Zaky nodded and quicky disappeared back into the kitchen.

The phone on a stool next to an empty sofa started ringing. The Alhaji frowned. He was in no mood to answer phone calls. While in the office, he had received and made enough phone calls to make his right ear ache from the pressure of the plastic receiver pressed against it.

His wife picked up the handset of the phone and spoke into its mouthpiece. After listening for a few minutes, she held it out for her husband, saying, 'it is for you, Alhaji.'

Mahmoud leaned forward and accepted the curved plastic from his sprawled position on the armchair. 'Hello?' he quivered into the mouthpiece.

'Are you Alhaji Mahmoud Gamji?' a voice at the other end asked.

'Yes and who are you?' the Alhaji asked in an impatient tone.

The voice at the other end softened. 'I am Dikibo, your son's friend at Stanford.'

Mahmoud's face lit up and he sat up on his seat. He had heard a lot about Dikibo.

Twelve months earlier, his son had returned to Lagos for summer holidays with an interesting story to tell. According to Tunji, when he first arrived in Stanford University, he had felt isolated with virtually no friends in a country whose culture he wasn't familiar with. By the end of the first semester of his first year, he was feeling homesick and depressed. All this changed when he became friends with Dikibo, a Nigerian student who had transferred to Stanford from University of California, Los Angeles. The outgoing Dikibo introduced shy Tunji to clubs and eateries frequented by other Nigerians living in the locality. A much happier Tunji would later tell his parents that before he met Dikibo, he was so consumed by misery that he once came close to jumping off from the top floor of his apartment building.

Mahmoud and Onyinye were horrified to learn that their son had once felt suicidal and yet never disclosed it to them. They were grateful for the fellow who had unwittingly saved their son's life and wanted to meet him. Under the assumption that Dikibo was spending his holidays in Nigeria as well, Mahmoud had asked his son to invite his friend to dinner. Tunji disabused his father's mind. Dikibo had elected to remain in California over the holiday season. At the end of the three-month holiday, as Tunji prepared to return to United States, the Alhaji had given his son a Rolex watch to present to Dikibo as a token of his appreciation....

Mahmoud adjusted his posture on the armchair. Cupping the mouthpiece, he turned to his wife excitedly and whispered that it was her son's best friend on the line from America. His wife smiled and he turned his attention back to the phone.

'Hello, Dikibo. How is my son? He is okay, I presume?' He asked as he straightened out the beige *babaringa*, which had become entangled in his groin area.

There was ominous silence at the other end for some seconds then a strained voice replied, 'eh...sir...things are not fine at all.'

Mahmoud's smile vanished. Tiny cold sweat beads began to appear on his forehead despite the air conditioner humming overhead. The Alhaji felt his heart thumping so fast that he feared for a brief moment that he was going into cardiac arrest. 'Is my son, Tunji safe?' he asked with trepidation as he stretched out his legs on the rugged floor.

Onyinye observing the change in his countenance drew closer to him.

'Eh, that is why I called you, Alhaji,' the voice responded guardedly.

Mahmoud bit his lips and shouted into the receiver. 'What is the matter? Tell me boy!'

There was momentary silence at the other end then the voice spoke again. 'Tunji and I were smoking dope in a club in L.A. when the police burst in.'

The Alhaji frowned. 'Dope? What the hell is that?'

The voice on the other end of the phone line grew more strained. 'It is cannabis, marijuana, sir.'

'What?'

'I'm so sorry, sir. It was my fault and now the police have us'

'Dikibo! You devil! My son is in trouble because of you!' Mahmoud yelled. Turning to his wife, he said, 'that devil, Dikibo, gave drugs to our son and now he is in police custody in Los Angeles.' Onyinye fell on the floor sobbing.

Zaky emerged from the kitchen to announce that lunch was ready for serving. He was surprised to find his usually tough madam on the floor wailing and the Alhaji screaming into a phone. He attempted to intervene, but stopped himself. It wasn't his business. Quietly, he retreated back to the kitchen with a mischievous grin on his face. The lunch on the silver tray was ready for conveyance to the master dining table, but it remained on the kitchen table. His boss and her husband were in no mood to eat just yet.

'I am so sorry, sir' the remorseful voice on the telephone apologised for the umpteenth time.

This made Mahmoud Gamji angrier than ever. By this point, he felt like jumping into the receiver and travelling through the phone line to give the sonofabitch a sound beating. 'Look here, boy, stop whining. Just tell me what I can do to save my son!'

There was momentary silence and then the voice spoke again. 'Sir, the police want money.'

Mahmoud relaxed at this revelation. Giving bribes was something he was very much at home with, but it sounded odd that LAPD cops were trying to extort him. Bribe-taking Nigerian policemen, he understood, because they were poorly paid. But an American cop?

'How much do they want?'

'Two hundred thousand dollars, sir.'

'Shit! What kind of police is that?' he asked, stunned at the amount of money the American cops were demanding.

He had never bribed anybody with such a huge sum of money—at least, not since he handed over several laundry bags of cash to the Federal Minister of Agriculture, Major-General David Craig-Tzadok, for turning a blind eye to the hoarding of fertilizer. The resulting scarcity of NPK fertilizer from regular markets disproportionately affected ethnic Tiv farmers of Benue State, the minister's own home state.

'Can I speak to the policemen?' Mahmoud asked, struggling to contain his anger and fear.

The voice hesitated and then said, 'No you can't. They only released me temporarily to give you the message. If you fail to pay, they will charge us to court with drug offences. I am here because Tunji convinced them that you, his father, will pay them anything they wanted if they let us off the hook. The cops waited until it was around four o'clock in the morning before they released me from their holding cell to make this phone call.'

'Why did they choose to use you for this call? Why not my own son?' the Hausa man asked skeptically.

'I'm sorry, sir. I have no idea why they did that. One LAPD cop just came to our holding cell, woke me up and asked me to make the phone call.'

Mahmoud nodded with the handset pressed against his right ear. He was not really interested in an explanation. All he could think about was how to liberate his eldest son from jail. He wiped sweat beads from his forehead with the back of his clammy left hand. He glanced at his wife sitting on the floor, wiping her reddened eyes with a handkerchief.

'Boy,' the Alhaji began, fishing out a handkerchief from the pocket of his *babaringa*. 'How do I deliver the money to the policemen?'

There was yet another annoying silence at the other end.

'Are you deaf? Boy, speak up! I don't have all day,' the exasperated tycoon barked into the mouthpiece of the handset.

The other end of the line remained quiet.

'Hello? Are you still there Dikibo?' the Alhaji asked calmly, worried that the young man was about to hang up.

The voice finally replied in the affirmative and reported that one of the LAPD cops was now standing next to him on the payphone stand.

'Give him the phone immediately!' the Alhaji thundered down the line.

The Nigerian fertilizer magnate heard crackling noise at the other end of the line for a few seconds before an American-accented voice took over. 'Look here sir, we don't wanna make trouble, but your kid is in a mess. It will cost you two hundred grand to make that mess go away.'

The tone of the American policeman was peremptory, but Mahmoud remained calm. He was now getting ready to haggle over the price of his son's freedom. For the benefit of the foreigner, he spoke slowly to mitigate the thickness of his Hausa accent. 'Mister Policeman, I will be more than happy to pay the princely sum of fifty thousand dollars.'

He interpreted the silence at the other end of the line as a sign that the cop was thinking about his offer. Fingers crossed, the American will drop the outrageous demand for two hundred thousand dollars and accept the offer, which the Alhaji considered a fair price.

The American did not accept the offer. 'Sir, the gravity of your son's offence is high. You will have to do better than that. A hundred and eighty thousand US dollars and we forget that this ever happened. Take it or leave it.'

There was an awkward silence on both ends of the phone line, then the American-accented voice boomed, 'you know what? I think this whole thing was a bad idea. Your son and his friend will need a lawyer in the morning. We are handing the case to the district attorney...'

The Alhaji panicked. 'Okay, okay, sir. I'll pay. Just release my son!' cried Mahmoud, surprised at his own behaviour. It was the first time the flamboyant tycoon had ever referred to anyone he considered beneath his status as "sir". But the situation at hand was desperate. He didn't mind ingratiating himself to a "riff-raff" American cop if that would get his son off the hook.

Just in case Mahmoud was thinking of changing his mind, the American accented voice added, 'one hundred and eighty grande is reasonable. If you disagree then this phone call is over. Your son's rat ass would stay in jail.'

Mahmoud sighed heavily. 'It's a deal, sir. How should I deliver the money to you?'

'Wire the money to the bank account number I am going to name. Do you have a pen?'

Mahmoud scrabbled for a pen on the coffee table with his free left hand. The other hand kept the receiver of the handset pressed firmly against his ear lobe, which was beginning to ache.

Onyinye flipped open an old diary lying on edge of the table and pushed it towards her husband.

Poised with a fountain pen, the Alhaji asked the American cop to call out the account number and the name of the bank.

The voice obliged, adding that the money had to be paid into the named bank account without delay. 'I will check if the money is there in three hours time. If it aint there, your boy is off to jail.'

On that note of warning, the phone line went dead just as Mahmoud was about to make a final appeal for his son to be treated well.

The Alhaji jumped to his feet, prompting his wife to do the same. For Onyinye, there were too many unanswered questions. She demanded that her husband fill her in on the details of the phone conversation. Mahmoud shot his wife a puzzled look and loudly called out Zaky's name several times.

When the servant finally appeared, the Alhaji issued an order. 'Tell Adamkus to prepare the car!' Zaky nodded and vanished. Turning to his wife, he said, 'I have to leave for my bank immediately. I have to pay for our son's freedom.'

Onyinye persisted with her questions. Mahmoud sighed and quickly gave her a summary of the phone conversation.

She broke down in tears again. The Alhaji cuddled her, assuring her that everything was going to be fine. 'Once the money is paid,' he said, 'they will release him. They will not harm him.'

At that point, Adamkus appeared in the living room and announced that the Cadillac was ready.

*****

At an open-air bar in the Surulere district of Lagos, Moses Adrika was reclining in a wooden chair skimming through *The Vanguard*. There was nothing particularly interesting in the newspaper, only mundane stuff— the military governor of Lagos was commissioning a newly constructed dual carriageway; the Lagos State Police Command was making the usual noises about being tough on crime; the trade unions were demanding higher wages for workers. There was no news report about the police's effort to solve the murders of DI Mike Otunba and Pastor Michael Grams.

Moses shook his head, folded the paper, and tossed it into the nearby waste paper bin. Sitting beside him at the table were John, Adamu, Tunde and Eugene, playing a game of poker.

'*Na wah-ooo!*' Tunde exclaimed. 'You just bought that paper and now you are throwing it away without reading it,' he expostulated, staring at the folded newspaper jutting out of the waste paper bin.

Moses frowned, 'not much in the paper, only the usual rubbish.'

'You have money to waste,' Tunde remarked, shaking his head in disapproval before turning his attention back to the game of poker.

A smiling Zaky Ideh sauntered into the nearly empty bar. He stood a few inches from the entrance and watched John dropped his cards on the table and let out a throaty laugh while the other poker players gazed at the aces on the table in disbelief.

'Hi guys,' Zaky said, sitting on an empty rattan chair next to Moses.

Everyone nodded in acknowledgment except John. The gang leader was busy scooping the pile of banknotes on the table into a satchel. 'I am the poker champion for all time!' he boasted, raising clenched fists above his head. Then he suddenly noticed Zaky in the fold. 'Oh, hello Mister Ideh, welcome to the den,' he said as he put away the bag.

Moses looked enquiringly at John.

'Give him the dough,' John ordered.

Moses pulled out a fat brown envelope from the pocket of his jeans trousers and gave it to Zaky.

The valet from Alhaji Mahmoud Gamji's household ripped the envelope open excitedly like a kid who had just received a Christmas present.

'Man, take it easy!' Moses hissed at Zaky, drawing chuckles from his comrades.

Unperturbed, Zaky counted the bundles of green crisp twenty naira notes meticulously while his paymasters looked on. The entire bundle of currency bills amounted to a total sum of ₦6000. Zaky was miffed. The agreement was for ₦10,000.

'Satisfied?' John asked smiling.

Zaky glared at him.

John had read the valet's mind. 'Hey! Six thousand naira is fair for a guy who did not contribute significantly to the successful execution of the operation.'

Zaky lost his temper. 'What do you mean by that? Without the information on Alhaji's son, you won't be here celebrating your success!'

The smiles on the faces of the criminals vanished. Moses lunged at Zaky. He gripped the terrified valet by the scruff of his shirt. 'Shut up, boy!' the gangster growled. 'You have no idea what we are capable of doing to you if you challenge us. You only supplied valuable information while we planned and executed the job successfully. What we have given you is much more than you actually deserve, considering your minor contribution.'

Apart from disputing the notion that he was a "boy" at the age of thirty-nine, Zaky strongly disagreed with the assertion that the sum of money given to him was his fair share. At the prevailing foreign exchange rate, he knew the $180,000 that Mahmoud Gamji had paid out roughly translated to ₦3,000,000. It pained him that the gang made such a huge killing from the scam, and yet they refuse to pay the modest ₦10,000 he was requesting. They were greedy, double-crossing bastards, he thought. But he had to be careful. He knew their type—cold-blooded murderers. Moses was not bluffing. One false move and he could end up dead at the bottom of the Atlantic Ocean. Never to be seen or heard of again by his family, friends and the Gamji household who were unaware of his treachery.

He swallowed hard and nodded. In a strained voice, he apologized to Moses and the rest of the gang for his "insolence".

'Take the money and piss off!' Moses snarled as he released the valet from his grip.

Zaky quickly shoved the bundles of cash back into the envelope with violently shaking hands. His heart was beating so fast that he thought it would explode. He jumped out of his chair. 'Look guys, thank you for the money. I must be on my way now,' he blurted out as he backed away slowly from the grim-faced gangsters. As soon as he made it past the bar entrance, he turned around and broke into a run, clutching the envelope close to his chest as he ran.

The grim faces creased and then broke into a prolonged round of laughter. 'What a bloody fool!' Eugene remarked when the laughter subsided. Tunde called the barmaid and asked her to get chilled bottles of beer. It was time for celebration, she was told.

The men were celebrating the successful transfer of Mahmoud Gamji's money from Seychelles to The Cayman Islands. The money was scheduled to move again in a few hours to its final destination where it was safer and more difficult to trace.

*****

Three weeks before the extortion of Mahmoud Gamji, the fraudsters had been at the same open-air bar in Surulere celebrating the conclusion of the Roy Seed operation. The "obituary plot" had worked. There was no sign that Roy was keen on pursuing his money, which the gang had exfiltrated to a numbered bank account in Zurich, Switzerland.

The gangsters drank beer and argued loudly about who had contributed the most to the unbelievable windfall they have reaped since they were released from Kirikiri Maximum Prison.

Moses did not participate in the heated debate. He found the whole exercise boring. Of course, everybody contributed equally to the success of the gang, he thought. He sipped his beer quietly and surveyed his surroundings. Soon he got interested in a dark-skinned short, stocky man sitting on the adjacent table nursing a bottle of Golden Guinea Beer. The man was appeared worried and talked to himself at intervals.

Without warning, Moses rose from his table with his glass of beer and walked over to the table of the nervous man. He placed his glass of beer on the table and sat on an empty chair opposite the nervous stranger. 'Hello. My name is Moses,' he said smiling and extending his hand to the man.

The man looked up from his beer and shot the smiling fraudster a wary look.

'You look miserable. What is eating you?' Moses asked.

The man smiled sheepishly and shook the fraudster's hand.

'C'mon, tell me what is eating you,' Moses persisted.

By this time, the rest of the gang had stopped arguing amongst themselves and were watching Moses talking to the stocky man on the adjacent table.

John instructed the barman to deliver another cold bottle of Golden Guinea Beer to the stocky man's table.

The man smiled and thanked John for his generosity. He introduced himself as "Zaky". When he saw the puzzled looks on the faces of his interlocutors, he quickly added that his full name was Zakariah Ideh.

Sensing that the man's story would be interesting, John, Adamu, Tunde and Eugene picked up their chairs and joined Moses on Zaky's table. The barman delivered the bottle minutes later and Zaky started pouring his heart out.

Five minutes into the story, Tunde pulled out a notepad from his cargo trousers and started jotting down important points that would eventually form the basis for the first scam his gang had ever pulled off on a fellow Nigerian.

According to Zaky Ideh, he had been working for one rich man called Alhaji Mahmoud Gamji for the past ten years. Despite having served him loyally, the rich man has refused to give him a pay rise, which he had been requesting for the past four years. He had explained to Mahmoud that he needed more money to fund the education of his children back in his hometown in the Eastern Nigeria, but the Alhaji wouldn't budge. The fertilizer tycoon accused Zaky of lying to elicit sympathy.

The servant tried to appeal to the ethnic sensibilities of Onyinye, the Alhaji's wife— she was Igbo like him—but she refused to intercede on his behalf, saying that her husband had exercised the right judgement over the issue.

Zaky paused to sip his beer.

The captivated fraudsters urged him to continue.

'I received a letter from my son,' Zaky recounted smacking his lips. 'He said that he had been expelled from school for not paying his fees. I took the letter to the Alhaji, but he screamed at me, claiming that the letter was a forgery.' Zaky paused to wipe tears from his eyes. 'So here I am, trying to drink away my sorrows.'

Moses clicked his fingers as he said, 'your master is a wicked man.'

John was so moved by the sad story that he gave Zaky all the money in his pocket— about three hundred naira, cash.

Tunde was more interested in figuring out how to punish the Alhaji and make money from it. He asked Zaky several questions about the Alhaji's background, personality and family.

After thirty-five minutes of questioning, Tunde learned pretty much everything he wanted to know about Mahmoud and his household. Of all information he had received, the one that interested him the most was the story of Tunji Gamji, the Alhaji's eldest son who was studying Engineering at Stanford University in the United States.

During his last visit to Nigeria, Tunji had told his parents about his Stanford classmate and best friend, Dikibo Alagoa. An ethnic Ijaw from Delta State, Dikibo Alagoa was from a family of wealthy timber merchants based in Sapele Town, Midwestern Nigeria.

Zaky learnt all of this by eavesdropping from behind the kitchen door. Later on, when his parents were out of earshot, the loquacious Tunji told Zaky in confidence that Dikibo was a bit of a partygoer and cannabis smoker. When Zaky asked him if he had ever smoked cannabis, Tunji denied ever doing that, saying he would never disgrace his family in that way. Yet Tunji spoke so admiringly of Dikibo's fearlessness and willingness to break all social rules and moral boundaries. Somehow, that made Zaky doubt Tunji's claim that he had never smoked cannabis with his Ijaw friend in America.

Tunde meticulously jotted down the nuggets of information supplied by Zaky Ideh in his flip notepad. Over his last glass of cold beer, Zaky expressed doubts about the value of the information he had supplied. Tunde smiled and assured him that all scraps of information were useful.

John weighed in, declaring that Tunde was the greatest genius he had ever met. The gang leader predicted that Mahmoud Gamji was going to part with a lot of his money in the coming weeks. He promised Zaky the sum of ₦10,000 or even more, depending on how much money his gang was able to wrench from the tight-fisted Alhaji.

Before finally putting the notepad away, Tunde scribbled down the address and telephone number of Mahmoud Gamji's residence in Ikoyi district. As the servant emptied the contents of his glass, John and his men rose in unison. 'We will be in touch,' he said.

Zaky, dazed by the effects of the alcohol, simply nodded. Moments later, the fraudsters walked out of the bar and melted into the darkness. The time was 7.00 PM.

Four days later, Zakariah Ideh was alone in the mansion, vacuum cleaning the living room when the telephone began to ring. Madam Onyinye Gamji who would have picked up the handset was away shopping.

The phone rang seven times before Zaky reluctantly answered the call. He had expected the caller to be one of those odious friends of Madam Onyinye— wives of other rich men— who called almost everyday to gossip about other people.

He was about to bellow into the handset of the phone that his madam was away, when he heard a familiar male voice. At first, he could not place it. Then, in a flash, the events of the open-air bar came back to him. He smiled. The caller was one of the guys who had paid for his beer and given him some money.

The phone call lasted three minutes only. John did not say much. He reiterated what he had said earlier— that the Alhaji would pay the price for refusing to help his loyal servant.

Despite Zaky's entreaties over the phone, John had refused to reveal how his gang was going to "punish" the Alhaji. 'Just wait and see,' the gang leader had said enigmatically before the phone receiver went cold.

A few hours later, the Alhaji returned from work and was relaxing in the living room when the telephone began to ring again. Zaky did not know the exact details of what had occurred at the time. But he observed that the phone call had caused Madam Onyinye to cry hysterically and sent the Alhaji scrambling to the bank to release money to the fraudsters.

Later on, the servant would learn what had actually transpired. The phone call had been an elaborately staged hoax. John had dusted his General American accent and used it to play the brusque LAPD cop while Eugene Igolo with his calm, soft voice played Dikibo. Tunde's well-executed plan had fooled Alhaji Mahmoud Gamji into transferring $180,000 into the gang's offshore bank acount in Seychelles.

It took the Alhaji seven days to realise that he had been duped, that everything that happened throughout the forty-five-minute phone call was a complete charade.

Shortly after transferring the money to Seychelles, he had repeatedly attempted to call his son, but he always got the answering machine. His mind began to conjure frightening images, none of which persuaded him that his son was safe and well in the United States.

By the time his son returned the phone calls a week later, Alhaji Gamji was already in the process of obtaining a visa from the American Embassy.

Tunji apologised for the late response, explaining that he was not in California when his father phoned. He had been on a short visit to New York to commiserate with Dikibo's uncle who had just lost his wife to cancer.

Mahmoud had reacted angrily. 'Boy, don't lie to me! I have just spent millions of naira to bail you out of trouble!'

Puzzled by the outburst, Tunji had asked, 'What trouble?'

The Alhaji sighed and angrily recounted what had happened. 'Son, I can forgive you,' Mahmoud said calmly, 'but not if you continue playing with my intelligence.'

Tunji vehemently denied that the Los Angeles Police Department (LAPD) had ever held him in custody. He restated that he and Dikibo were not even in the west coast of the United States when the hoax phone call was made.

Only then did it finally dawn on the fertilizer tycoon that he had been scammed. An enraged Mahmoud enlisted the help his friends in the top echelons of the Nigerian Police Force in an effort to track down the fraudsters and retrieve his money.

The cops swung into action and made some progress. Phone records from the national telephone company— NITEL— indicated that the phone call that Mahmoud Gamji had received did not originate in the United States. The fraudsters had made the call from a phone booth in Surulere, Lagos.

The bank in Seychelles refused to cooperate, citing certain strict banking laws. Even if the bank had agreed to help, the Nigerian police investigators would not have found anything. The money was transferred out of the Seychellois bank a few hours after the Alhaji deposited it. The money had passed through The Cayman Islands before finally landing in Zurich, Switzerland—the place with one of the most confidential and secretive banking systems in the world.

CHAPTER 14

JULY 1993

NEW YORK CITY, USA

David Steinberg wiped the sweat beads away from his face with the back of his fat hand. He pulled out the bottom drawer of his oak desk and fished out a bottle of brandy. It has been a harrowing year for all his business enterprises. His multi-million dollar conglomerate STRAADL had virtually collapsed under the weight of mismanagement. Shareholders, who have been deceived about the state of the company for years with falsified balance sheets, were calling for his head. The Internal Revenue Service (IRS) was after him because of the money he had stashed away in tax havens of the Caribbean.

David shook his head as he unscrewed the cap of the bottle. He took a swig of the spirit. The mild burning sensation of the liquor down his gullet was just subsiding when there was a knock on the door. The flustered man slammed the bottle of brandy on the desk and rolled his red eyes to the offending door.

'Who is it? Sandy, I thought I said "no disturbance",' he growled as he screwed the cap back on the bottle.

'Sir, it's important,' replied a female voice from behind the closed door. 'You have a letter marked "urgent". Should I come back later?'

'No, just come in,' said David as he quickly put the brandy bottle back into the bottom desk drawer. The door opened and a young ginger-haired woman stepped into the room with a white envelope that appeared somewhat familiar.

David stiffened. 'Is that from the IRS?' he gasped.

The secretary smiled wryly and shook her head. Her boss heaved a sigh of relief. The secretary held out the envelope timidly to him. He accepted it with his left sweaty hand and dismissed her. The envelope did not have the IRS logo that he thought he had seen earlier. Was his indulgence of the bottle making him see things that weren't there? he wondered as he watched Miss Sandy Neuberger walk back towards the door.

Once she was out of the office, the bottom drawer of the desk reopened and the brandy bottle came out again. After two swigs of the liquor, he opened the envelope with a silver-plated letter opener. He reclined on his upholstered swivel chair and began to read the letter from Nigeria.

> *Dear Dave,*
> *It is your friend, Johnson Ezekah, the permanent secretary in the Federal Ministry of Transport and Works. Six weeks ago, we met in Manhattan. Remember? I am sorry I haven't been able to keep in touch. It was due to circumstances beyond my control. The finance*

minister and other members of the presidential commitee have spent a lot of time drawing up plans to cover our tracks because what we are proposing is illegal and could land us all in jail for decades, if not managed carefully.

We have procured and readied the helicopters for flights to Togo. However, we hit an unexpected snag. The Accountant-General of the Nigerian Federation accidentally discovered our plans. Now, he wants $1,000,000 cash to keep his mouth shut. We tried to co-opt him into our deal, but he doesn't trust us. He wants cash upfront. The minister and the Presidential Committee members are livid, but they can't do anything about it. We want you to pay the one-million-dollar bribe. In return, we are willing to increase your stake in this venture. For your troubles, we are now offering you 40 percent cut. In case, you were wondering, that translates to 60 million US dollars. Think about that!! We look forward to your reply and...

At this point, David rolled his eyes at what he was reading and paused. 'Mr. Johnson must take me for a fool. One million dollars! He must be out of his fucking mind.'

He crumpled the letter into a ball and tossed it across the room into the plastic waste paper bin. He raised the bottle to his mouth to swig the brandy and then froze.

Rising instinctively from his swivel chair, he took two steps towards the waste paper bin to retrieve the crumpled paper and then halted. Was he throwing away his chance to make sixty million dollars? What if it was actually a clever trick, a con job?

Shaking his head, he swung around and returned to his desk, confused and not sure what to do next. For a few minutes, he stood next to his chair, staring up at the ceiling with brooding eyes. An idea suddenly flashed through his mind. He bent over his desk and searched the top drawer for his leather-bound diary.

He sank into the chair and began to flip through the diary. He stopped at the entry that contained Johnson Ezeka's phone number. Tapping the desk interminably with the fingers of his left hand, he contemplated whether to make the phone call. Finally, he resolved to hear Johnson out. If the Nigerian couldn't give a convincing reason for demanding money from him then he would simply pull the plug on the deal. David picked up the handset of the telephone and dialled Lagos, which was five hours ahead of New York.

On the African side of the world, John Nwosu was already in bed when the phone started ringing. The small clock on the nightstand indicated 9.00 PM. Bleary-eyed, the swindler reluctantly picked up the handset without checking the provenance of the call on the telephone's LCD screen.

'Hello, this is John Nwosu on the line,' he said, still feeling drowsy.

'Hi, I'm David Steinberg from New York. Can I speak to Mister Johnson Ezeka?' the American voice requested.

John's eyes widened in alarm— he had inadvertently introduced himself by his real name, and spoken English in his normal speaking voice.

'Hello, hello, do I have the right phone number?' Dave enquired when his request to speak to his Nigerian associate was met with silence.

'Yeah, this is the right number. Johnson is my cousin,' John replied. 'Wait a moment while I fetch Johnson.'

Smiling, he held the handset away from his ear. After four minutes, he pressed it against his ear and began to speak with an affected General American accent. 'Hello Dave! This is Johnson speaking. Sorry, I was in the shower when you rang. So what's up? You got my letter?'

'Yeah I got it alright. You must take me for a fool...one million dollars... you gotta be kidding!'

John's countenance changed. 'Look Dave, without the money, the accountant-general wouldn't play ball. We need to bribe him to secure his cooperation.'

Unconvinced, Steinberg retorted, 'then I suggest you pay the man! Hell, your minister can pay him!'

The Nigerian laughed dryly and then explained to David why that was impossible. 'All federal ministers are being watched by independent anti-corruption agencies. The minister would rather call off the deal than risk getting caught.'

John paused to let his explanation sink in. He had deployed this same excuse several times successfully. He was sure David would eventually buy the explanation and hand over the money requested.

David hesitated and said softly 'Look man, I don't know if I should do this. One part of me says go for it and the other part says be careful.'

What John heard over the phone pleased him. It meant that— like several others before him— David was ready to be led down the garden path paved with false promises and the allure of unearned riches. The American only needed a coax and a nudge to start moving.

'Listen Dave,' the swindler began in an arch tone. 'What is one million dollars compared to the sixty million dollars you stand to make? C'mon, man, this opportunity comes only once in a lifetime!'

David Steinberg knew that "Johnson" was right. One million in exchange for sixty million was a bargain. With all the financial problems threatening to engulf him, he certainly needed that kind of money. 'Okay, I will do it,' David said, though some doubts lingered in his mind.

'Good! You are a wise man, Dave, and an astute businessman.'

'What's next? What is the next step?'

'Well my friend, you will be meeting the federal minister here in Nigeria. We will book you into a five-star hotel, all expenses paid. Bring the one million bucks with you. We want cash not cheque.'

'Why?' David asked, worried about walking the streets of Africa carrying a briefcase filled with cash.

'Well my friend, we have to avoid the paper trail. No one can easily trace the cash, but cheques leave a paper trail behind.'

David nodded in agreement. Of course, he thought. But his interlocutor had not addressed his main concern. 'You think it is safe to do that? Carry that much cash around in a box?'

'Don't worry my good friend. It is going to be a safe transaction.'

'When do we meet in Nigeria?' David asked, flipping the pages of his diary.

'We meet in four weeks. The federal minister is already making the necessary arrangements. Because he is being watched by anti-corruption agencies, we cannot meet in the capital city of Abuja. Our plan is to...'

'What about Lagos?' the American interjected. 'I know it is one of the greatest cities in Africa.' The moment after blurting out that remark, David realized that he sounded facetious even though he really meant what he had said. The month before, he had read a feature article in the *Wall Street Journal* about Lagos city— the metropolitan area of Lagos State—being one of the most populous urban centres in Africa. David was both surprised and impressed to learn that despite the deficit in infrastructure, chaotic road traffic, frequent power outages and subpar governance, the city was still one of the continent's major financial hubs with an economy larger than those of several African countries put together. The city was also home to one of the largest and busiest seaports on the continent. If David had to choose a venue for the meeting in Nigeria, it would be somewhere in the intriguing city of Lagos.

'Yes, Lagos is nice,' John replied, 'however, we must act discreetly and far away from watchful eyes. Our meeting will take place in the eastern part of the country. The minister will be there under the pretext of visiting his ailing grandfather. Once we are ready, I will fax you all the information you will need.'

There was awkward silence on the phone, which led John to believe that David was disappointed by his answer. Under normal circumstances, he would have gladly held the meeting in Lagos State, probably in Ikeja or Victoria Island, but that was not an option now. The Lagos State Police Command still had active case files on the murders of Pastor Michael Grams and Detective-Inspector Michael Otunba. John had consulted the police spy within Ikeja CID who told him that detectives of the anti-scam squad were redoubling their efforts. Plain-clothes cops were being deployed to airports, the lobbies of five-star hotels and to upscale restaurants to observe Nigerian men of a certain age bracket interacting with foreigners, particularly those from Europe and America. Declaring Lagos a "hot zone", the police spy advised John to implement all future swindle operations outside the state. It was safer that way.

David broke the awkward silence on the phone line. 'Hey, I'm gonna need a date for the meeting, even if it is tentative.'

John pondered the request for a while before replying, 'okay, my good man. It's going to be sometime between the tenth and seventeenth day of August.'

David picked up a fountain pen and scribbled into his diary rapidly. Then he asked another question: 'when do I get the fax?'

'Expect it tomorrow or next'

'You have my fax number?'

'Yeah, I do. Are we good now?'

'Oh yes, thank you, man. I guess it is already night over there in Nigeria.'

'Yes it is,' John responded impatiently. He wanted the call to end so that he could go back to sleep.

'Okay then. Good night and bye-bye,' David replied.

John thanked him for the call and put down the handset. He jumped back into his double bed, but then he found it difficult to sleep. All he could think about was the new scam that was going to yield a million dollars for his gang. It excited him.

*****

On the second floor of the Ikeja CID complex, Detective-Inspector Ikenna Kodilinye was going through some documents in a ring binder folder in his office when there was a gentle rap on the door. He closed the folder. 'Come in!' he bellowed.

The door swung open and two uniformed police constables stepped into the room, each bearing an open carton labelled "Mike Otunba" with a blue marker. They silently deposited them on the detective's desk. One constable perfunctorily whipped out a clipboard from one of the open boxes. 'Sir, you will have to sign for them.'

Ikenna accepted the proffered clipboard and scrutinized the yellow sheet attached to it. It was an inventory of the items inside the boxes. It was everything cleared out from the office of his late predecessor. He pulled a pen from the breast pocket of his denim jacket and quickly appended his signature at the bottom right-hand corner of the sheet.

'You can come back for the items in four hours, say five o'clock this evening,' he said, giving the clipboard back to the constable.

'Yes sir,' said the constable with the clipboard. Both uniforms saluted and left the office to return to their posts in the records department down on the first floor.

Ikenna rose from his seat. He lifted the lighter box from his desk and placed it on the floor next to the base of his chair. He sat down again and pulled the heavier box on the desk closer to himself. He poured all the contents of the carton onto the desk and began to examine them one by one. There were mundane items such as sunglasses; police identity cards; a framed university degree certificate; passport photographs of the deceased cop; and old mugshots of long dead criminals from dusty files.

None of those was of any interest to Ikenna. The items that attracted his attention were the flip notepads and the diaries, both of which were vital in the

108

search for clues linking the deceased to the criminal underworld. However, one mundane item did attract his attention— a framed, glass-fronted picture showing the deceased cop, his wife and Ikenna grinning with their half-filled glasses of beer raised in salutation at a social event, four years earlier. In the picture, both Ikenna and Mike were dressed in their red-and-black ceremonial police uniforms.

Ikenna smiled and placed the framed photo back inside the box along with the other mundane items. It reminded him of the past, a moment in time when he still thought of the deceased detective as a man of integrity, an honest cop. He and Michael had joined the Nigerian Police Force on the same day— a part of the new generation of educated men eagerly recruited to bolster the ethnic diversity and intellectual capacity within the foremost law enforcement institution in the country. Michael Otunba was recruited upon completion of his law degree at Lagos State University (LASU). Ikenna Kodilinye joined the police towards the end of his final year as a psychology student at the University of Lagos (UNILAG).

Despite coming from different ethnic and socio-economic backgrounds, both men became close friends while training at the Police College in Ikeja. Ikenna had been the best man in the 1987 wedding of Michael to his childhood sweetheart, Yinka. The career progressions of both men over the years were quite similar. Both were uniformed cops on patrol for three years before receiving additional training that allowed them to become junior detectives. Both rose to the rank of detective-inspector at the same time. The two detectives became leaders of different CID squads within weeks of each other. Ikenna led the narcotics squad while Michael took charge of the anti-scam squad.

Their rise to prominence within Lagos State CID (i.e. Ikeja CID) would cause them to drift apart as the sheer workload left little time to socialise. For years, after the assumption of squad leadership positions, both men barely saw each other despite the fact they operated out of the same high-rise building, albeit on different floors. There were, of course, the odd chance meetings along the long dimly lit corridor where quick pleasantries were exchanged as one man exited the office of the DPO and the other entered it.

When Mike Otunba went missing, it was to Ikenna that Yinka turned for help. Ikenna would lead the team of homicide and narcotics detectives in the statewide search for the missing cop. And when the rotting corpse of the missing cop turned up in Seme Town, near the international border with Bénin Republic, it was Ikenna who had the difficult task of informing the widow of the tragedy.

However, it did not take long for Ikenna to get over the initial sorrow he had felt for his fallen friend. Days after the corpse was recovered, the Detective-Inspector was disgusted to learn that his deceased friend was a corrupt cop apparently killed by his criminal associates to cover their tracks.

He was pleased when Cyrus Udeh appointed him head of the anti-scam squad for two reasons. First, it presented an excellent opportunity to personally track down and capture Mike's killers who were also suspects in the defrauding of Gary Logan and Mike Grams, the latter murdered for his troubles. Secondly, it offered a great occasion to leave behind the twin headaches of running the narcotics squad and fighting a four-year-old turf war with the National Drug Law Enforcement Agency (NDLEA).

The police force had vehemently opposed to the creation of the NDLEA in 1989 as a parallel organization tasked with fighting drug trafficking. For obvious reasons, the police did not like the idea of having some of its law enforcement roles usurped by a rival institution. That ignited a turf war.

The turf war reached its climax in 1992 when the Director of the NDLEA— an army brigadier who spent most of his time playing politics rather than enforcing drug laws—began to campaign for the abolishment of all narcotics squads within the police. The one-star general argued that the police was better off channelling its limited resources to fighting other crimes like homicide, scams and armed robbery, and leaving drug law enforcement entirely to the NDLEA.

The police countered with an untrue allegation that the vast majority of NDLEA officers were inexperienced and couldn't tell talcum powder from cocaine. Despite his best efforts, Ikenna had to watch helplessly as the politically well-connected brigadier gradually undermined the power and authority of all police narcotics squads across the country including his own.

Ikenna had lost count of the number of times his squad had been forced to hand over a wealthy drug trafficking suspect to the Lagos branch of the NDLEA. Only for said suspect to be released for "lack of evidence". A number of "less influential" drug suspects handed over by the police ended up dead in NDLEA detention facilities without ever revealing the structure of the vast drug networks to which they belonged or the names of powerful crime bosses who run them.

And yet, for all the corruption rife in the agency, NDLEA did manage to burst and roll up the operations of several small-time drug traffickers. Drug traffickers were successfully tried, convicted, and jailed at a rate that convinced the Nigerian military junta of the agency's effectiveness. Ikenna was willing to bet his annual salary that the end of all police narcotics squads in the country was close at hand. There was no evidence to back up his fears, just a strong feeling based on the political headwinds blowing against the police force. His reassignment was a source of relief to him because it meant he wouldn't be presiding over the narcotics squad when it eventually gets the axe.

*****

Ikenna went through the small heap of items on his desk, separating out mundane stuff and placing them back into the box. When he was done with the cherry-picking process, only flip notepads, diaries and a few manilla files remained on the desk. He selected a paperback diary and started going through it in the hope of finding out what Mike Otunba was up to in the final days of his life.

He flipped through several blank pages until he arrived at one with an interesting entry written with a pencil. The handwritten notes on the page were either too faint to read or had faded off. Ikenna switched on his desk lamp. For

110

several minutes, he studied the diary entry under the white glow of the light bulb, struggling to fill in gaps created by missing words. In the end, only one phrase made sense to him in the entry: *Da Silva at 1850 hours*. The rest of the entry was riddled with incomplete and incoherent sentences. He noted that the entry was made weeks before Mike Otunba's death.

He pondered over what *Da Silva* actually meant. Was it a codeword, a person's name, or a place? He toyed briefly with the idea of asking his boss, CSP Cyrus Udeh, to deploy a detachment of policemen to search Lagos State for a person or place bearing the name, but he knew better. The DPO would dismiss Ikenna's request as a sheer waste of time and refuse to commit limited police resources to it. Thousands of people in the state, particularly those of Afro-Brazilian slave descent, had "Da Silva" as surnames. Numerous business enterprises bore names that, to varying degrees, had "Da Silva" in them.

Ikenna knew that Cyrus could not afford to let his detectives go on a wild goose chase. He would need to find out what the Portuguese phrase meant if he wanted the DPO to authorize any statewide search that would cost a lot in terms of money and manpower.

The detective went through the remaining pages of the paperback diary. They were all blank. Frustrated, he slapped the desk with his left palm and tossed the diary into the box alongside the mundane items. He picked up a dog-eared flip notepad and went through all the pages. The pages were all blank save for deep impressions created on them by writing on leaves torn out of the pad. Ikenna placed the notepad on the table. Suddenly, there was a knock on the door. 'Come in,' he bellowed, feeling flustered.

The door swung open and a young, baby-faced constable dressed in a new police uniform walked in carrying a silver tray containing a teacup, a sachet of powdered milk and a small jar of granulated sugar with a teaspoon inside. 'Your tea, sir,' the constable said as he approaching the desk.

Ikenna nodded as the constable placed the tray on the untidy desk. Ikenna pushed aside a jotting pad and a manila file, both of which he had not yet examined and pulled the tray closer to himself. He leaned forward and lifted the steamy teacup out of the tray and onto the table. He took the spoon out of the sugar jar to stir the tea.

'Sugar, milk, sir,' the constable prompted shyly when the detective started drinking the tea without adding sugar and milk.

'It's alright, Chibuzor. I take my tea without the rest. Thank you,' Ikenna replied, smiling. Chibuzor saluted and then picked up the tray containing the untouched sugar and milk, and quickly left the room.

Sipping his tea, Ikenna smiled at the closed door. The young man's uneasiness was typical of new constables fresh out of Police College. The newbies always struggled to adjust to the fast-paced work in State CID, one of the police force's foremost divisions. A good number of them tended to be nervous around superior police officers who could potentially help or break their careers.

Ikenna was glad that the nervous constable had served him his tea without incident. A year earlier, a different young constable named Edet had spilled a lot of coffee while attempting to deliver a mug with trembling hands. Ikenna had quickly jumped away from the scalding coffee spreading rapidly in all directions on the surface of the mahogany desk to save himself from second-degree burns. Unfortunately, the narcotics police report he was working on at the time could not be saved. It was soaked and ruined. The appalled detective forgave the remorseful Edet. However, not every senior officer in Ikeja CID was so forgiving of such sloppiness. A month later, Edet spilled coffee again while serving CSP Cyrus Udeh. For that, he was promptly banished from the city, redeployed to a rundown police station in a remote backwater town at the edge of Lagos State.

As Ikenna sipped his tea, an idea came to him. He smacked his lips and grabbed the dog-eared flip notepad. With a HB pencil, he started shading over the impressions on the notepad. Slowly, the deep impressions started turning into sentences. He repeated this action on all the pages. To his dismay, only the first page yielded anything of meaning. That page contained jottings that seemed sensible under the HB graphite coating, but there was a snag— it was written in Yoruba language, which Ikenna could neither read nor comprehend. He pressed a button on his intercom and asked the newbie constable, Chibuzor, to send for Kehinde Keyamo, an ethnic Yoruba detective in his squad.

One floor below, in an open-plan office, the constable, speaking into the telephone-intercom, asked Ikenna to wait and left to search for Keyamo.

Several minutes later, while Ikenna was rummaging through the second box on the ground, Chibuzor's voice returned to the intercom's speakers. 'Sir, I have checked. Detective-Sergeant Keyamo is not in his office.'

Ikenna instructed the constable to keep an eye out for Keyamo and to inform him as soon as the detective-sergeant showed up. The constable promised to do so. Ikenna pressed another button on the intercom and turned his attention back to the second carton on the floor. In his rummage through the box, he found glass-framed academic certificates, blank exercise books, a measuring tape, a torch, a pair of eyeglasses, deodorant sprays, unopened packets of biscuits, etc. It took Ikenna three minutes to realize that there was nothing else of interest in the second carton.

He turned his attention back to the interesting items he had obtained from the first carton, which were on the desk. He put aside the dog-eared flip notepad, which had already examined and focussed on the jotting pad, a leather-bound diary and three manilla files.

Finding nothing of interest in the diary, jotting pad and two manilla files, he returned them to the first box sitting on the edge of the desk. Then he turned to the only remaining item yet to be examined— a dusty manilla file. He felt the fine ochre dust on his fingers when he touched it.

Picking up a damp rag on the floor of his office, he wiped the dirt from the surface of the file. When he was done, he flipped open the file and removed the binder clip attaching a sheaf of papers to it. He separated the thin stack of papers from the file and began to study them.

The single sheet of paper turned out to be a document faxed by the Nigerian Consulate in Atlanta, USA, to Michael Otunba's office some weeks before Pastor Gram's murder. It gave a brief description of who the American Preacher was. Ikenna put the faxed document back into the file and began to go through a stapled nine-page document titled: *Swindling Mr. Michael Grams: A Preliminary Police Report.* Under that title, Michael Otunba was credited as the author of the report.

Ikenna flipped past the title page and began to read the executive summary on the third page. He had barely read three sentences from the first paragraph when the intercom started buzzing. The detective instinctively pressed a button and asked 'Chibuzor, is Keyamo back?'

'No, sir, but the chief wants to speak to you in his office,' Chibuzo replied. The "chief" was Chief Superintendent of Police (CSP) Cyrus Udeh.

Ikenna sighed. He was not ready yet to meet the increasingly impatient DPO. There had been no progress in the hunt for the murderers of Michael Grams and Michael Otunba.

'Tell him I will be there in five minutes. Okay?'

'Certainly, sir'

Ikenna pressed another button on the intercom and turned his attention back to the stapled sheets of paper on his desk. The preliminary report was not an easy read for it was littered with blacked-out words, phrases and sentences. Ikenna was puzzled. Apparently, Mike Otunba had drafted a report of his investigation and then went on to redact large portions of it. But for what reason? None of it made any sense to Ikenna. Maybe the deceased cop was merely carrying out the orders of his criminal patrons, Ikenna thought as he began to parse the nine-page document.

In the executive summary of the report, Mike Otunba reported that Pastor Michael Grams had been conned out of $100,000 over a period of twenty-five months. The US embassy was an interested party in both the Logan and Grams fraud cases, and had arranged Reverend Grams' visit to Nigeria to help with the police investigation. Mike had expressed reservations about the American preacher coming to the country—his argument being that Pastor Grams would actually get in the way of the investigation and hinder its progress.

Ikenna spent ten minutes poring over the heavily redacted document and, to his great disappointment, failed to recover new information that could help his investigation. In fact, once the myriad of unreadable words, phrases and sentences—blotted out with lines of black ink— had been excluded, the rest of the document essentially read like the last official report that Mike had filed with police records before his demise. Ikenna had seen two identical copies of that official report— one copy handed directly to CSP Cyrus Udeh and the other filed with police records department.

Ikenna bit his lips as various thoughts ran through into his mind. The official report was merely a sanitized version of the redacted document, which in turn was a censored version of an unknown original report. The redacted copy of the preliminary report had been recovered whilst clearing out the deceased's office. So where was the unredacted original? Was it still in existence? Did Mike destroy it?

Ikenna thought the latter to be true. After all, the police had searched the deceased's office and private residence twice and failed to find anything that remotely resembled the original of the preliminary report.

With nothing else to examine for clues, Ikenna picked up the flip notepad and the manilla file containing the redacted document, and walked across the office to a steel safe leaning against a wall in the corner. Stooping in front of the safe, he curled his fingers around the knob of the combination lock and began to rotate it clockwise and anti-clockwise in quick, short steps. The safe unlocked with an audible click. Ikenna pulled the door handle. The door of the safe swung open effortlessly, revealing the three equidistant shelves. The top shelf contained a small metal cashbox. The intermediate shelf bore a stack of ring binder folders of various colours and an old pistol, a MAB PA-15 semi-automatic. The bottom shelf was empty.

Ikenna dropped on one knee and placed the notepad and the manilla folder on the bottom shelf. He rose to his feet, closed the safe door and was about to relock it when the intercom started buzzing again. He dashed across to his desk and pressed a button on the machine, hoping that it was Chibuzo with the news that Keyamo was now available to translate the Yoruba words in the notepad, but he was wrong. It was not Chibuzo on the line.

'Detective, why have you kept me waiting for the past fifteen minutes? I might take that to be insubordination!' It was the unmistakable baritone voice of Cyrus Udeh growling down the line. Ikenna apologised and left hastily for the meeting with his superior, locking neither the safe nor the office door.

An hour later, he returned to his office with sweat beads on his forehead. The chest area of the blue shirt he was wearing under his denim jacket was dampened by sweat. He had expected a one-on-one meeting with the DPO. Instead, to the detective's great surprise, Cyrus had two other men with him for the meeting. They were Lagos State Police Commissioner Stanislaus Zikora and a diplomat from the United States Embassy called Mark Nichols. The meeting had been a grilling session for Ikenna with several uncomfortable questions thrown at him, in turns, by all three men. Throughout the meeting, Ikenna felt intimidated by the Police Commissioner who expressed displeasure at the pace of the investigation and repeatedly made it clear to the Detective-Inspector that the Logan–Grams–Otunba cases could either make or break his career. Apart from a few tough questions, the American diplomat mostly limited himself to voicing the dismay of the US government at the lack of progress in solving the cases. By the time the meeting ended, the detective was sweating despite the air conditioner in Cyrus' office running at full blast mode.

Back in his own office, Ikenna stalked straight to his desk and fell into his upholstered chair, clearly exhausted by his encounter. Reclining on his seat, he caught sight of something that caused his eyes to widen in alarm and his mouth to drop open— the door of the safe was wide open and the bottom shelf was empty. The manilla file and the flip notepad had disappeared!

CHAPTER **15**

AUGUST 1993

ENUGU CITY, EASTERN NIGERIA

It was late in the night when the light blue Mercedes Benz W140 saloon car finally pulled out of the hotel. In the rear passenger seat was a white man dressed in a two-piece grey suit. The buttoned suit jacket was ill-fitting, too tight for its obese wearer.

By contrast, the Nigerian chauffeur was dressed in a proper-fitting white uniform with a peaked cap to match. From the driver's seat, his eyes shifted intermittently between the rearview mirror and the laterite road ahead. In the rearview mirror, he observed the creasing in the grey suit jacket where it wrapped around the torso of his passenger and predicted that it was only a matter of time before the buttons popped off. More worryingly, the passenger appeared to be uncomfortable. Perhaps, it was the unusual warm nighttime weather, he thought as he turned the knob for the air conditioner to its maximum setting. As the Mercedes approached a bump on the laterite road, the chauffeur adjusted the peaked cap on his head and turned to his passenger. 'You are okay, sir?' he asked, concerned that David Steinberg was squirming on his seat.

'I'm fine...just...a bit nervous...nothing to worry about,' the American replied in staccato bursts.

The chauffeur turned his gaze back to the road. After a few minutes of silence, he finally said, 'don't worry, sir. The minister is a nice host.'

Blowing his nose with a handkerchief, David managed to muffle out a reply. 'I certainly hope so.' Uneasy silence reigned for a moment before it was broken again. 'Are most the roads in the city like this?' David asked, studying the ochre-coloured, laterite-surfaced road, under the glare of moonlight, from the moving car window.

'A good number are properly tarmacked with asphalt, but laterite roads are also quite common in this city,' the chauffeur explained. David nodded silently.

There were no further comments from either man for the rest of the journey. The chauffeur concentrated on his job. The passenger tapped rhythmically on the surface of the brown attaché case on his laps, recalling the gruelling schedule of journeys he had to endure to get from his New York City home to Enugu.

David had taken an eleven-hour overnight direct flight from New York to Lagos. Already severely exhausted upon landing at the international airport in Lagos, he craved a hotel room to relax and unwind. But he was on a travel schedule dictated by the instructions faxed to him by his business associate, Johnson Ezeka. Soon, he was on a domestic flight from Lagos to Enugu— an aerial journey that took forty-five minutes to cover the 435-mile road distance between the two cities.

By the time he got to the arrivals terminal of Enugu airport, he was tottering from the effects of jet lag and the sweltering afternoon heat. He was rescued by a tall dark-skinned man dressed in a chauffeur's uniform.

'You are David Steinberg. Aren't you?' the dark-skinned man had asked, approaching the American.

'Yeah, how did you know?' David was both worried and surprised. He held tightly to his luggage and attaché case.

'Johnson gave me your description,' the man replied. 'I'm your chauffeur for the day. You can call me Adam.'

David smiled and extended his arm for a handshake. Moments later, David Steinberg was in the back seat of a Mercedes heading towards the five-star hotel where a room had already been booked for him.

In the hotel lobby, Johnson Ezeka was waiting. He greeted the American visitor and fixed him a drink from the lobby quadrangle bar while the porters took the luggage to the room reserved on the third floor. Eyeing the attaché case under the firm grip of the American, Johnson said that the federal minister had flown in from Abuja and was resting in the government lodge. The minister was looking forward to the meeting, scheduled to start in the middle of the night, five and half hours from then. The American stared at the clock hanging on the wall above the bar. The time was 5.45 PM.

Inside the hotel's narrow elevator, on the way to the third floor, Johnson told David to make the best out of the five hours. 'A decent nap and you will be as good as new,' the Nigerian had quipped as patted the fatigued American on the back.

Later on, while alone in his hotel room, David opened his holdall and fished out a digital alarm clock, which he set to wake him up at ten o'clock at night. At the set time, the clock sounded. David took thirty minutes to shower, shave and dress up. Downstairs in the hotel lobby, a smiling Adam, resplendent in his immaculate white uniform, was waiting to take the American to the meeting...

The Mercedes Benz W140 saloon car slowed down and made a right turn. Suddenly, the vehicle's tyres were no longer treading on moonlit laterite roads but on a smooth asphalted tarmac illuminated by bright streetlights. Soon, the car was gliding through the tree-lined, well-paved streets of Independence Layout, an affluent neighbourhood where the wealthy upper classes lived side by side with upper-middle-class professionals.

David Steinberg was genuinely surprised to see rows upon rows of huge detached houses separated from each other by high concrete fences. 'Are all these government owned?' he asked as the car passed a mansion with a forecourt covered in carpetgrass.

The chauffeur shook his head. 'No, they are all privately owned. The federal government lodge is at the end of the street.'

The Mercedes slowed down and halted in front of a pair of giant gates. Adam honked the car horns twice, an old man wearing an azure uniform with a name tag appeared, and pushed the solid iron gates apart, revealing a sprawling mansion set inside a large compound with trimmed hedges lining the driveway. The car wheeled in as David sat up to admire the aesthetic beauty of the premises lit up by florescent tubes attached to two lamp posts at opposite ends of the fence.

Adam stopped the car near the marble steps leading to the smoked, glass-fronted door at the mansion's entrance. He slid out of the car and opened the rear passenger door for the guest to alight.

The smoked glass door opened. A delighted Johnson, in a T-shirt and denim trousers, ran down the marble steps to meet his bulky visitor standing beside the car.

'Welcome to Enugu city and to the federal government lodge,' Johnson beamed as he shook the hand of the American.

David smiled back and thanked his host for his hospitality so far. The American's initial nervousness was by now a distant memory, displaced by excitement, which had been welling up inside him ever since his eyes began to take in the exquisite scenery of Independence Layout. Something about the area reminded him of his own upscale neighbourhood back in New York City. The familiarity both reassured and relaxed him.

'The minister is eagerly waiting to meet you,' Johnson said as he escorted David into to the large house.

The American made himself comfortable in one of the armchairs set inside the tastefully furnished living room.

Johnson excused himself and disappeared through a sliding glass door at the corner of the room.

David gazed at an enlarged picture of the Nigerian military dictator, General Ibrahim Babangida, hanging on the wall at the opposite end of the room. The caramel-skinned army general in the picture frame gazed back with a gap-toothed smile. The American was still gazing at the photo when the glass door behind him slid open. David rose from the armchair and turned around.

Standing on the red Persian rug in front of the glass door was a fair-skinned man of average height. He was dressed in the native garb of ethnic Igbos— the traditional *Isiagu* attire with a matching red brimless cap called *"Okpu Mmee"*. The man strutted to the centre of the room and gave David a bear hug. 'Welcome to Nigeria, my brother,' he said softly as if David was a close friend.

Mildly surprised by this behaviour, David said, 'oh, thank you!' and patted the back of the man hugging him.

The man unlocked from the embrace and introduced himself. 'I'm George Madubuko, the federal minister for finance. I'm pleased to meet you.'

Touching the minister's *Isiagu* clothing in admiration, David said, 'nice suit you have got here.'

George smiled. 'Thank you, I can arrange for one of my talented tailors to make one for you on the double.'

David politely declined. He liked the attire, but it wasn't made for somebody like him. He was certain that he would appear clumsy in such an outfit.

The minister strutted to an empty armchair opposite the American and sank into it. 'Please, sit down my brother,' he said, gesturing at David.

David set his attaché case on the Persian rug at the foot of armchair and sat down. The minister removed his cap and dropped it on a glass side stool.

'How are you finding our weather?' George asked his guest, eyeing the attaché case lustfully.

'Fine, fine, I love it...kinda like California,' the American replied.

The glass door slid into the side of a wall and Johnson stepped into the living room with a silver tray containing drinks. He served the American a bottle of Budweiser Beer. The federal minister requested for a bottle of Coca-cola. After serving the drinks, Johnson exited the room via the sliding glass door.

Getting down to business, George stated, 'I am sure Mister Johnson Ezeka has briefed you on the business deal.'

David nodded in between gulps of cold beer.

'And its clandestine nature,' George intoned with a mischievous smile.

The American's bushy eyebrows arched as he lowered the bottle. Smacking his lips, he replied, 'Johnson told me everything, including the improved cut of forty percent.'

The minister smiled apologetically. 'It was the least we could do since we are asking you to invest one million dollars in this venture. Mister Omorodion, our accountant-general, is a difficult man. He will scupper the deal if he is not paid upfront.'

David rubbed his chin briefly and lifted the attaché case from the rug. 'Yeah, like I said earlier, Johnson told me everything. In my briefcase, there is a million bucks. The money you need.'

The minister's face lit up in excitement and his smile broadened.

'But there is one condition,' the American stated ominously, tapping the attaché case across his laps.

The smile vanished from the minister's face. 'Yes? What is the condition?' George asked, a little worried.

'You have to promise to take the money, use it judiciously, and never ask me again for more money.'

The minister nodded in agreement, totally relieved. He happily accepted the condition. After all, neither he nor his associates had any further plans to wheedle more money out of David.

'My word is my bond,' George declared histrionically with his palm pressed against his chest. Both men laughed heartily and the conversation moved on.

In a theatrical move that occurred whenever a foreign visitor was present, John Nwosu alias "Johnson Ezeka" reappeared with a light blue briefcase and handed it to the "finance minister". A stapled two-page document was removed from the briefcase and handed to the American.

'You will have to sign it, now,' George said.

David ignored him and began to scrutinize the pages of the document, carefully. The letterhead on the first page contained an image of the Nigerian Coat-of-Arms with a bold phrase printed underneath, reading: OFFICE OF THE FEDERAL MINISTER OF FINANCE. Below that phrase was the main body of the document, the text announcing the award of sixty million dollars to David Allan Steinberg for *consultancy work resulting in the elimination of financial waste, hence shoring up the federation account.*

Flipping to the second page, the puzzled American saw a dotted line, on the left-hand corner, above which was an empty space for his signature. The blank space above the other dotted line, on the right-hand corner, was for the signature of the "Honourable Minister of Finance, George Madubuko".

David glanced at George with a quizzical look on his face. 'Consultancy work? Federation account? What does these actually...?'

George quickly interjected. 'The federation account is the national treasury. As the finance minister and national treasurer, it is my job to hire external consultants to do various things for the federal government. The things that external consultants do for us range from supervising our local auditors to lobbying the World Bank, the IMF and foreign countries to which we are indebted. As far as this document is concerned, I hired you to do some "consulting work" for the federal government. You have concluded the work. The government is satisfied and now paying your fee of sixty million dollars.'

David looked more confused than ever. Both Nigerians could see that David did not understand the explanation and laughed mirthlessly as the puzzled American placed the Budweiser bottle on the glass table in front of his armchair.

'If this is an official document, how are you gonna square this with...' David began as he pulled a fountain pen from the breast pocket of his coat.

John interrupted him. 'Hey Dave, we are good at what we do. This document is a symbol of our strong partnership. There is nothing to worry about.'

A moment of awkward silence followed.

'Okay, then. If you say so,' David said skeptically as he placed the document on top of the attaché case on his laps. As he scribbled his signature in a corner of the second page, he fired off a few rhetorical questions. 'Is this whole thing now official? I mean... this, here, is a legal document. Should we be leaving behind a paper trail by signing this?'

George was by now struggling to control his irritation. 'Our deal with you is illegal under Nigerian federal law, hence its clandestine nature. This confidential document is merely an expression of good faith, a symbol of our great partnership.'

David said nothing in response. He merely handed over the document to John, who was standing next to him.

'Can we have the money now?' the minister demanded in a polite, but firm, tone of voice.

'Yeah, sure man,' David responded in a subdued voice and lifted the attaché case from his laps. The attaché case was passed to John and then to the minister.

The minister opened the case. The sight of neatly stacked bundles of dollar bills delighted him.

'Good! We are now in business,' he announced excitedly. The attaché case quickly snapped shut and returned to John's custody.

David picked up the Budweiser bottle and gulped down its remaining contents as the finance minister rose to his feet. David rose to his feet, yawning and feeling suddenly dizzy.

'Dave, it's getting late,' the minister said, sticking out his hand, 'it has being a pleasure doing business with you. Now, all you need is a good night sleep. My driver, Adam Tolbert, will take you back to the hotel.'

'The pleasure is all mine,' the American said as he shook the minister's hand. Accompanying the dizziness was a mild headache. The minister noticed the American tottering as he tried to walk and moved to help him.

'I will walk you back to the car,' George said as he put his hand under David's armpit. With the support of the minister, the American was propelled slowly out of the living room, past the foyer, out of the entrance door, down the marble steps and into the driveway. Some yards away, the silhouette of the Mercedes stood in the moonlight. Its headlamps suddenly lit up and the engine roared to life.

David and the minister waited patiently by the bottom of the marble steps for the car approaching slowly. The Mercedes pulled up inches from them, prompting the men to step back instinctively. Adamu Esan alias "Adam Tolbert" alighted from the car. He adjusted the peaked cap on his head and walked round to open the rear door.

'Have a good night sleep my friend,' the minister said, propping and propelling the sick American to the rear door of the car. 'Tomorrow, I'll meet you at the hotel lobby before you fly home,' he added.

David grunted and literarily fell into the back seat. The headache and dizziness seemed to be growing worse.

Adamu promptly slammed the rear passenger door shut and walked back to the driver's side. He winked at George standing on the marble step and slid behind the steering wheel. The car engine roared back to life. Adamu revved the engine for a few minutes and then held down the clutch pedal with his left foot. He wound down the car window as John Nwosu ran down the marble steps to join Moses Adrika—alias "Minister of Finance, George Madubuko"—on the driveway.

Both men waved at Adamu as he shifted the gear lever from the neutral position to the first gear. The elderly security man opened the gates for the car to pass through. John waited for the red taillights of the Mercedes to disapppear from view before he remarked, 'that was one hell of a performance, my good man. I guess you should be nominated for the Oscar movie awards.'

Moses grinned. 'Boss, that white chauffeur's uniform is great. Adamu was right and I was wrong.'

John responded dismissively, 'nah, it was not just you. We all thought it was a waste of money, but he was right. The uniform looks marvellous on him.'

The men turned around and began to slouch back towards the marble steps. 'Boss, I was really surprised with that man,' Moses said, slapping a mosquito that landed on his forearm.

'Yes, I know!' John exclaimed.

'That drug only just affected him. I wonder why?'

'Who knows? Maybe the beer diluted the sedative. He is an obese guy. Perhaps, the dosage was too low for somebody of that size.'

Moses ran up the marble steps, reached the entrance, and swung open the smoked glass-fronted door. Just before he walked through the door, he remarked, 'as I walked him to the car, I sensed that the drug was just beginning to take a hold of him. Maybe the sedative only works slowly.'

'It doesn't matter now. We have the money. The rest is now up to the boys.' John entered the mansion and slammed the door shut. The time was 12.45 PM.

*****

The Mercedes Benz W140 slowed down on the nearly empty main road and swerved into a side road hemmed on both sides by a dense screen of forest shrubs. The American suddenly became alert. 'Where are we going?' he asked, staring out of the window at the bushes.

The silent driver squeezed the accelerator pedal to the floor mat with his foot, causing the saloon car to lurch forward. The vehicle sped down the moonlit strip of dirt road, ran over a metal rod, and then jumped onto the rusty rail tracks of an abandoned train station. Adamu applied the brakes. The car screeched to a halt, jerking violently as it did. David Steinberg hit his head on the back of the driver's seat.

'What the hell!' the American barked and then froze when he saw the muzzle of the Makarov semi-automatic pistol pointing at his nose.

'Get out! Run for your life,' Adamu growled, emphatically swinging the gun sideways from David's nose towards the rear passenger door.

'Oh, my God!' the American cried as he scrabbled for the door lever with both hands. 'Please don't kill me! I gave you guys all the money,' he begged still fiddling violently with the stiff lever.

Adamu sighed, lowered the gun, and climbed out of the car. He walked over to the rear passenger door and pulled it open with his gloved hand.

David fell out of the car onto the dirt ground, crying and trembling. He looked up at the hostile face standing over him and asked, 'why? What did I do to you?'

Adamu threw his head backwards and laughed sadistically. 'You want to know why?' he asked tauntingly. 'I'll tell you why,' Adamu said, poking David's head with the muzzle of the gun. 'It is because you are a fucking dickhead!' he snarled, grabbing the hapless American by the scruff of his neck. Pulling David to his feet, he bellowed, 'now run for your life!'

David stood there frozen in fear.

'C'mon! Move your fat arse!' Adamu barked, giving David a shove.

The American staggered, fell, and then began to scream. 'Help! Help! Help!'

Adamu laughed at the prostrate man in the dirt. 'It is one'o clock in the morning in this god-forsaken place. Nobody comes here. Nobody will hear you.'

David stopped screaming and sat up. 'You don't have to this man. I gave you guys the money you asked for. What else do you want from me?'

Adamu lifted his arm into the air and fired a shot in the sky. 'For goodness sake! Just go! Run! Now!' he barked.

The obese man jumped to his feet and then took to his heels for the first time since he left the athletics team of Syracuse University, twenty-eight years earlier. He ran along the disused rail tracks partially covered in weeds and grass. Panting, he sped past the decrepit building that used to be a train station, two rusty railway carriages, and a gigantic stack of rail chairs.

Adamu pushed the Makarov into a waist gun holster hidden underneath the jacket of his chauffeur's uniform and walked quickly towards the boot of the car.

David stopped for a moment to catch his breath and then took off again. He ran a few more yards along the disused rail tracks before there were two loud bangs accompanied by bright yellow flashes. The impact of the shots fired from a pump-action shotgun lifted David from the ground and threw him a few inches down the rusty tracks.

Moments later, the screen of forest shrubs to the left side of the tracks rustled, and Tunde and Eugene emerged. They were dressed in identical black shorts and white singlets soiled by mud and sweat.

'The grave is ready,' Tunde called out as he set his shovel on the ground. 'It is in the middle of the forest. Nobody will ever find it.'

'Good!' Adamu called back, from nineteen feet away, as he returned the shotgun to the boot of the Mercedes.

'We heard the shots. Where is he?' Eugene asked, surveying the moonlit environment.

Adamu snapped the car boot shut and pointed to the silhouette of a small heap partly obscured by tall grasses and shrubs a few yards away from Tunde and Eugene.

Tunde switched on his torch and flashed it in the direction of the heap. The heap turned into the belly of a corpse lying on its back in a pool of blood. Tunde turned to Eugene and said, 'let's go to work.'

Adamu wedged a Cuban cigar between his lips as Eugene laid his shovel on the ground next to that of Tunde. He fished out a silver-plated lighter from the breast pocket of his jacket and lit the cigar. Puffing smoke rings into the air, he watched in mild amusement as the men in singlets and shorts struggled to lift the heavy corpse, pleased that he did not have to get his hands dirty. His immaculate white uniform was not going to be soiled.

CHAPTER 16

AUGUST 1993

LAGOS, WESTERN NIGERIA

Ikenna Kodilinye shifted uneasily on the chair as his superior, sitting opposite him, wrote silently on a sheet of paper inside an open manilla folder. 'You really think there is a mole here?'Cyrus asked incredulously, dropping the folder into the OUT tray next to the desk intercom.

'Yes, I think somebody may be trying to sabotage the investigation,' Ikenna replied. Although twenty-eight days had elapsed since the burglary of the detective's office, CSP Cyrus Udeh's awareness of the incident and its implications was less than twenty-four hours old.

In the evening of the previous day, Ikenna had surprised the Divisional Police Officer (DPO) with the belated news in the car park as the latter was unlocking the door of his Peugeot 504 saloon car.

'I'm sorry sir,' Ikenna had begun apologetically. 'I wanted to talk to you outside the building. You never know who might be eavesdropping.'

Cyrus was intrigued. He temporarily forgot his longing to return home to his wife's cooking. He listened in shock and indignation as Ikenna told him what he should have known four weeks earlier. After a ten-minute tirade over Ikenna's decision to keep him in dark until then, Cyrus got into his Peugeot 504 in a huff. As he drove away, he asked the detective to report to the office the following morning to explain himself under the pain of suspension from duty.

Ikenna had dreaded the meeting. CSP Cyrus Udeh was famous for his stoicism, but occasionally when he snapped, his temper could be volcanic. When the meeting finally started that morning, the detective had expected the DPO to begin with an excoriation. To his pleasant surprise, Cyrus calmly asked for an explanation. Ikenna apologized profusely, explaining that he had wanted to investigate the incident quietly given its sensitive and potentially explosive implications. He wanted to obtain tangible proof before coming forward with allegations of police spies in the service of a criminal gang.

Cyrus had taken the explanation well, only mildly criticising the failure to follow standard police procedures. Ikenna had detected what seemed like a flash of fear on the face of the DPO. It was fleeting, but he had seen it. Ikenna had never seen anything like that before in the face of the man in-charge of all Lagos detectives, except those assigned to APCS.

After listening to what Ikenna had just told him, Cyrus reclined on his seat and sighed heavily. That piece of information would surely drive Police Commissioner Stanislaus Zikora crazy if it ever reached him.

Five months had elapsed since Detective-Inspector (DI) Ikenna Kodilinye took charge of the anti-scam squad. There had been no break-throughs in the Logan–Grams–Otunba cases. Police top brass in Lagos and Abuja were already frustrated and under pressure from the US Embassy to apprehend the criminals who had murdered an American citizen.

An official investigation to uncover the mole within Ikeja CID was the last thing Cyrus wanted. His superiors will certainly hit the roof if they became aware of the situation at hand. The DPO had it on good authority that Zikora was already toying with the idea of sacking him as head of Ikeja CID— a move that will ultimately force him to retire early from the police force. His heart palpitated at the thought of such a dreadful and humiliating scenario. He wanted to be remembered as a tough cop who sent criminals to jail, not the policeman sacked for ineptitude.

He sat up straight and gazed straight into the eyes of the detective sitting before him. Wagging his finger, he said, 'I don't care what it takes, just find the damn mole, but it has to be very low key. I don't want to excite the Commissioner and the press.'

Ikenna nodded slowly. It seemed like the storm had passed; the chief of detectives was not going to dwell on the egregious offence of having information withheld from him by a trusted subordinate. In fact, the chief was now brainstorming with that subordinate on how to identify the rogue police officer acting as a mole for the swindlers.

'Okay, any ideas on how this mole can be smoke out?' the DPO asked, staring intently at the detective.

'Just to refresh your mind on what happened that fateful afternoon,' Ikenna began. 'I had discovered a flip notepad among Otunba's stuff. There were notes written in Yoruba. So I sent for Keyamo, but he wasn't in the office. He had gone to give evidence in court. I put the pad and the manilla file containing preliminary report on Pastor Grams in the safe and went to see you. When I returned, the notepad was gone, stolen by someone that works in this building. And that person is certainly not part of the cleaning staff. They only work in the small hours of the morning.'

Cyrus nodded impatiently. 'Yes, I already know all of that. You told me that story yesterday. What is your plan for catching the mole?'

Unperturbed, Ikenna continued his recapitulation of what his boss already knew. 'I had one of the forensic people dust the office door handle and the safe for fingerprints. The only fresh fingerprints were mine. This means the mole certainly wore gloves. I have a list of people present in the building at the time of theft. It's a very long one.' Ikenna paused and handed a sheet of paper to his boss.

Cyrus squinted at the unfamiliar document and frowned. 'Excluding you, Nduka, Daoud and myself, I see here on the list twenty-one names— ten civilian employees, the desk sergent, four constables, three corporals and three CID detectives.'

'One of the detectives on the list is in my squad. The other two are in the narcotics squad. They had just finished filing their reports and were awaiting fresh instructions from Gbolahan who was out on a lunch break that afternoon. My squad detective was in his office working, but he could be the culprit.'

'You suspect him?' the DPO asked, raising his eyebrows as he reclined on his seat again.

'I don't know; could have been any of the people on the list. I called in some favours at FIIB. Two FIIB officers quietly placed the desk sergeant, constables and corporals under the microscope. There was no funny activity in the bank accounts of the suspects. Weeks of surveillance did not yield anything unusual. We checked out all the people we saw these suspects meeting. They turned out to be clean; most of them were their friends and families.'

The DPO grimaced. He had not heard this part of the story before. Not only had Ikenna kept his boss in the dark about the burglary, he had involved the Federal Investigation and Intelligence Bureau (FIIB) without seeking proper clearance. The amount of rule infractions committed by the detective was too much for Cyrus to bear and he finally snapped.

'All this happened right under my nose? I cannot believe you kept these things from me. If you weren't good at what you do, I would have had you suspended!'

Ikenna apologised once again. His earlier assessment was wrong. The storm had not passed when he thought it had. Cyrus' fury had just been burning below the surface, building up pressure necessary for an eruption.

Cyrus calmed down again and gestured for his chastened subordinate to continue the briefing. The Detective-Inspector told the DPO that all eight uniformed personnel under surveillance had been eliminated as suspects.

'What about the detectives and the civilians?' the DPO asked.

'We have not investigated them yet. My belief is that these murderous fraudsters will certainly prefer to hire a police officer to act as their spy. So for this reason, we are not going to waste time investigating our civilian employees.'

'These civilians are the secretaries in our typing pool. They handle our documents and files all the time. They are certainly capable of stealing and passing them on to criminals. So, why not investigate them too?'

The detective shook his head. 'Sir, I don't think any of our secretaries is responsible for the theft. The person who tampered with my safe certainly wore gloves. He did not want to leave fingerprints behind. That rules out the civilian staff. They don't know forensics.'

Cyrus agreed with him. The civilian staff working in Ikeja CID complex wouldn't be of much use to criminals seeking real-time information on CID investigations.

In a grave voice, Ikenna continued. 'Given levels of seniority involved, I wasn't going to start the investigation of the detectives without your permission.'

'Permission granted,' Cyrus snapped. 'But tell me how you are going to do it. And please, I don't want to hear about the involvement of FIIB officers. This matter would be handled internally; only Ikeja CID officers would be involved in whatever you plan to do.'

'I was not going to involve the FIIB any further. I only called in a one-time favour. That was all. As for my plan, well, I intend to circulate a false case report within Ikeja CID. I will make sure it gets to the suspected detectives. If any of them is our mole, he will try to make contact with his criminal patrons to reveal the contents of the fake report, and hence lead us, unwittingly, to the swindlers. Upon dissemination of the report, we will start a twenty-four-hour surveillance on all three of them. Phone taps will happen and their bank accounts would be checked out. You may not like it, sir, but Chief Inspector Nduka Ikwune is best placed to lead the molehunt.'

The DPO nodded in agreement although he despised the policeman nominated by Ikenna to lead the operation. The idea of bringing in that pompous arse revolted him, but the APCS leader had the men and the skills required to run an internal molehunt smoothly and quietly. For the chief of detectives, the stakes were too high to let his personal feelings get in the way of serious police work. Until the saboteur police officer leaking information was apprehended, no progress could be made in finding the gangsters behind the scams and the cold-blooded murders.

As the meeting wrapped up, Cyrus pressed a button on his intercom and instructed his unseen police orderly, Constable Dixon Nkwamkpa, to provide coffee and biscuits.

*****

Later that night in Victoria Island, close to Lagos Bar Beach, Tunde killed the engine of the car and doused the headlamps, plunging the isolated area into darkness. He wound down the car window to let in mild breeze coming from the Atlantic Ocean nearby and began to wait.

Thirty minutes later, a silhouette of a man wearing a mackintosh coat and hat appeared in the horizon. The silhouette started towards the saloon car, dropping a broadsheet newspaper, folded in half, on the bonnet as he walked by. Tunde wound down the car window and threw a fat envelope out of it.

Without saying a word to Tunde, the silhouette bent over, picked up the envelope from the grassy verge abutting the tiled sidewalk, and stuffed it into his coat. He straightened up and, silently, continued down the chain of stone tiles.

When the silhouette was out of sight, Tunde got out of the car and collected the folded newspaper on the bonnet. Back in the car, under the glare of interior courtesy lights, he unfolded the broadsheet and began to flick through it. Lying between the middle pages of the newspaper was a buff manilla file and a flip notepad. He extricated both from the newspaper and placed them on the front passenger's seat. He refolded the newspaper and lobbed it out of the window. Soon the car was bowling down the smooth, tarmacked road towards a certain address on the affluent island.

Ten minutes later, Tunde reached that address. It took him another three minutes to steer the car past the automatic gates and into the driveway of John's sprawling residence. Killing the engine, he alighted from the car hurriedly and began to walk briskly towards the entrance of the mansion. He was already late for the nocturnal meeting in the situation room. In his mind, he could picture the others waiting impatiently in the basement of John's house, wondering what was holding him up.

'You are late!' John barked as Tunde took his seat next to Eugene.

'Don't blame me. Our friend was quite late, thirty minutes late,' Tunde responded defensively. John caught a glimpse of the items in Tunde's left hand. 'What have you got there?'

Tunde silently handed over the flip notepad and the manilla file to the inquisitive gang leader.

'This is useless. It did not merit the risk our informant took,' John remarked after examining the contents of the file at length. He tossed the folder onto Eugene's lap and turned his attention to the flip notepad. He squinted at one of its pages coated in pencil graphite and frowned. Through the graphite coating, he could clearly make out the indented outlines of Yoruba sentences, but all were incomprehensible to him for he neither spoke nor understood the language. Only one person in the situation room could read and write in Yoruba.

'I read the note,' Tunde said helpfully. 'It looks like the draft of a speech Mike Otunba was preparing for an unnamed cultural organisation of which he was patron— most likely, an organization in Ijebuland.'

John asked his subordinate how he knew the organization was in Ijebuland. Tunde smiled smugly and said rather cagily that it was his job to know. Tunde had investigated Mike Otunba's background before approaching him with a pecuniary offer to become an informant for the gang.

'In other words, this notepad is also useless. Our new man on the inside is taking too much risk. Can you imagine burgling the office of a top detective for this junk?' John asked incredulously as he tossed the notepad onto the tabletop. Eugene picked up the flip notepad and the file and passed them to Tunde for destruction.

A sudden thought came to John. 'Are you sure our new friend in Ikeja CID is not playing games with us? Supplying useless or outrightly false information?' he asked, looking at Tunde— the man with all the answers.

'No, he wouldn't dare. He knows what we are capable of. He knows what we did to Mike Otunba who tried to betray us. Besides, we pay him very well.'

John was not convinced. As far as he was concerned, bent cops were two-faced bastards, always ready to double-cross whenever it was expedient. However, he concurred with Tunde on one thing. The gang had spent a fortune to regain access to privileged State CID information lost when Otunba was dispatched. For that reason alone, John grudgingly agreed to give the new police informant the benefit of the doubt. Besides, in the past, the new police spy had provided some good information.

At the time of hiring the bent cop, the gang leader was dying to know more about the man who had replaced Otunba as the leader of the anti-scam squad and how his investigation was coming along. The rogue cop did not disappoint. He told his criminal patrons that Detective-Inspector Ikenna Kodilinye was an honest no-nonsense cop who could not be bought. Since Ikenna took over the investigation of the Logan, Otunba and Grams cases, no progress has been made. Mike Otunba had left little or nothing for his successor to work with. Official police reports filed by the deceased cop contained only vague descriptions of the gang. There was no information on the number of swindlers in the gang, no physical description of any of the swindlers on record.

According to the new police spy, this was not always the case. Once upon a time, there was a written statement provided by the late Pastor Michael Grams, which contained a physical description of a suspected swindler using the alias of "Pastor Richard Ibeh". But the case file containing that statement was no longer in the police records department. Apparently, Mike Otunba had removed it a few months before he was murdered, and all subsequent attempts to locate it after his death had failed. The police spy concluded by saying that apart from himself, nobody else in Ikeja CID had any idea who the swindlers were or what they actually looked like.

This revelation had been a great source of comfort to the gang of swindlers. Nevertheless, their leader, John, was a realist. Unlike his optimistic subordinates, his head was not in the clouds. He was not under any illusion that the gang's caravan of unbelievable good luck would go on forever. It was his firm belief that their caravan would eventually hit a huge pothole on the road and flip over. It would occur with the eventual unmasking of their identities and police warrants for their arrest. The execution of such arrest warrants would be easy since they were hiding in plain sight as respectable businessmen living in one of the swankiest corners of Lagos city. For the gang leader, it was only a matter of time before the shit hit the fan. His grand strategy was to delay the inevitable long enough to further enrich his gang and then disappear before the long arm of the law reached them. The key to the success of such strategy was a constant stream of privileged information from Ikeja CID. For that reason, John had demanded premium performance from the bent cop, but did not feel he was getting his money's worth.

Pacified by Tunde's persuasive argument that the new police informant be given the benefit of doubt, John moved on to the next agenda on the meeting. He announced to the rest of the gang that Moses Adrika had an important story to tell.

Moses rose from his seat with an A4-sized buff envelope in his right hand. He cleared his throat and began to speak. 'I was reading a copy of the *Times of London*, two days ago. The cover story was about a British businessman called Harel Suzmann.'

He paused, opened the envelope, and removed a newspaper cutting containing a passport photograph of a smiling 45-year-old white man. He circulated it among his colleagues. He allowed them few minutes to read the article beneath the photograph before resuming his narration. 'Until last year, he was among the richest people in the UK, but he fell on bad times last year. Poor judgement and his dishonest business associates ruined him, leaving a trail of debts, which he had to pay off by selling off most of his business concerns. To make matters worse, his wife filed for divorce and made him pay two million pounds as settlement.'

Tunde smiled, 'seems the man you are targeting is pretty dry already. I wonder how we can make a lot of money from him.'

Moses smiled back, noting the sarcastic tone of the remark. He suspected that Tunde was jealous because he was not the one who discovered the new target. 'Well, I think we will make a lot of money from him actually,' he said, staring at Tunde with mocking eyes. 'The man may be terrible at keeping his business concerns from becoming insolvent, but he still has property assets worth at least three million pounds. It is in the news article in your hand, if you care to read it thoroughly.'

John, Eugene and Adamu laughed while an embarassed Tunde quickly read through the newspaper clipping.

'I think we can offer him an attractive deal he cannot possibly refuse,' Moses concluded and returned to his seat.

John retook the floor. 'Tunde's expertise would be useful here. Moses, you will need to work with our genius on a plan of action.'

Tunde's heart swelled with pride as he watched John speak. *Everybody knows that I am the smartest when it came to planning operations*, Tunde thought to himself.

Although he relished his key role in the gang, the genius always felt under-appreciated, and deeply resented the fact that he got exactly the same share of the gang's ill-gotten proceeds as Moses, Eugene and Adamu. Another source of resentment was the gang leader getting most of the booty— each gang member's share of the proceeds was just a quarter of John's. Tunde steadfastly believed that he deserved the lion share of the money because without him, the gang was nothing. It was an unshakeable thought that popped to mind whenever he was asked to plan an operation for the group.

'I will have the plan in two weeks, piece of cake,' Tunde boasted.

'Very well, we will hold you to that' John replied, certain that his genius would deliver on the promise. Nevertheless, he was not going to cut Moses out from the planning phase of the operation.

'Tunde, I know you like to plan alone,' John began archly. 'But Moses discovered this man, Harel Suzmann, and proposed him as a viable target. So you must work with him closely on this one.'

Tunde smiled at Moses and said, 'Sure, boss. No problem at all. I'll work with anyone who wants to work with me.'

Tunde's smile did not seem sincere to Moses. And he wasn't the only one in the room who noticed the lack of mirth in that smile.

*****

The intercom rang for the third time and Cyrus sighed and picked up the handset. 'Dixon, I thought I made it clear. I wish not to be disturbed!' he thundered down the phone line.

'I'm sorry, sir,' the soft voice of the police orderly responded, 'it's the commissioner on hold.' Cyrus calmed down and asked Dixon to pass the call to him.

The other end of the phone line crackled briefly before the Police Commissioner's voice took over. 'Hello, CY, its being a while. How are those cases moving along?'

Cyrus was blunt. 'Not very well, sir. No break-throughs yet. But the new guy, Ikenna, needs more time to crack it.'

'Time is what we don't have. The Inspector-General is breathing down my neck. Anyway, I have more bad news for you. Something big has just come to my attention.'

Cyrus sipped his coffee, trying to reassure himself that the ominous tone of his superior did not mean that a bombshell was about to be dropped. Was Commissioner Stanislaus Zikora alluding to another scam/murder case committed by the same criminals behind the still unsolved Logan–Grams–Otunba cases? Has Zikora somehow found out that there was yet another police mole lurking around in Ikeja CID so soon after the Mike Otunba scandal?

Cyrus felt a deep sense of forboding. His future was looking bleaker than before. Perhaps, he would not even get the benefit of a dignified early retirement. He pictured himself standing next to Zikora at Force Headquarters in Abuja city, both of them chastened by the withering reprimand of a grim-faced Inspector-General of Police. He imagined the Abuja meeting ending with the Inspector-General barking that his days as a policeman was over and that he should submit his sidearm at the reception counter.

'...CY, CY... Are you still there?' Zikora asked again, wondering what was going on at the other end of the phone line.

Cyrus snapped out of his trance. 'Yes sir, I am still there,' he replied, 'you said something big is up.'

Cyrus always liked it when Zikora referred to him as "CY". The informality was reassuring— a sign that the Commissioner had come in peace. Nevertheless, he was worried. He just could not help it. Zikora may be about to drop a bombshell.

'Oh, yes,' the Commissioner began as Cyrus drank more coffee, attempting to wash down the trepidation gripping him. 'The Enugu State Commissioner of Police called me two days ago. Apparently, an American in the state on business has been missing for the past three weeks. The management of the hotel in Enugu where the American was staying had reported the disappearance to the police. A Nigerian, claiming to be a close friend of the missing white man, had made the reservation for the hotel room in advance. Few hours after the American arrived and checked in, the same Nigerian who reserved the room came back and took him away. This was the last time any member of the hotel staff ever saw the missing man to date. The hotel manager personally checked the American's room, all his personal effects were still in the room— bags, clothes, camera and so on. Four days later, the hotel called the police.'

Cyrus was puzzled by what he had just heard. He did not understand what the case of a missing person in another state, three hundred and sixty miles away, had to do with him. 'Sir, it is tragic that this American is missing in Enugu, but what has it got to do with Lagos State Police Command?'

But Stanislaus Zikora was not going to be rushed. His voice resonated with calmness down the phone line. 'Be patient, my good man. I am getting there... the Enugu State Police Command searched for the American for two weeks. They went through hospital wards, morgues and even dispatched divers to reservoirs, lakes and rivers. No sign of the American. Working on the theory that the Nigerian who lured him away from the hotel may have kidnapped and taken him outside the state, the neighbouring Anambra State Police Command was alerted. The American still failed to turn up there either. Meanwhile, back in Enugu, a hotel staffer— who said that she could not recall the face of the man who lured the American away— suddenly changed her story. She helped the police artist with a sketch of the man. It matches the physical description of the man who defrauded Pastor Michael Grams.'

Cyrus was staggered by the statement. 'I don't understand,' he blurted out. 'We don't have any physical description of that suspect in the police records. Not since Otunba sabotaged the investigations.'

There was momentary silence before the Police Commissioner's voice boomed down the line. 'It is you guys in Lagos CID that lost that critical information! Luckily for us, the American Embassy still has a copy of Pastor Grams' statement describing the fraudster who conned him out of a hundred thousand dollars.'

Cyrus closed his eyes and reclined on his swivel chair. His adrenaline level soared. Ikeja CID detectives had scoured the police records, Mike Otunba' office and home, and were confident that Pastor Gram's statement had been lost forever. Cyrus had passed on that bad news to Commissioner Stanislaus Zikora.

Cyrus' bewilderment turned to anger. The American diplomats sat on a critical piece of information that could have done a lot to advance the investigation of the Logan–Grams–Otunba cases. The livid DPO voiced his displeasure to his superior.

Zikora sighed and responded, 'you know these Americans. Who knows what goes on in their heads? Perhaps, they were worried that we cannot be trusted with their own copy of Pastor Gram's statement. The criminal actions of Mike Otunba certainly did not do CID any favours.'

Cyrus was going to interject with a disagreement, but thought better of it. He allowed Zikora to speak uninterrupted.

'Enugu State Police Command contacted Force Headquaters in Abuja who in turn alerted the American Embassy about their missing citizen. The Americans demanded and got a copy of the case file from police in Enugu. Two days later, embassy officials informed Force Headquarters that the police sketch in the case file matched the physical description in their copy of Pastor Gram's statement.' Zikora paused and then continued in a poignant tone. 'Force Headquarters is not happy at all with Lagos State Police Command. This missing guy is the third American victim of those fraudsters, and we are no closer to apprehending them. The US Ambassador is breathing down the neck of Inspector-General of Police.' Zikora paused again and then added, 'you know where all this is heading.'

Cyrus knew very well. His future as a policeman was bleaker than ever, would remain so until those murderous fraudsters were caught.

'The missing man has been identified as David Steinberg. His family in New York has been informed of the situation. According to our interlocutors in the American Embassy, Mister Steinberg told his family very little about his business trip to Nigeria. In any case, David's brother told the American FBI that he thought David was lying about his Nigerian trip. The brother believed that if David was going to flee USA then he would choose Brazil where he owned houses.'

Cyrus sat up in his chair. His right ear lobe ached from where it was pressed against the receiver of the handset. 'The missing man was fleeing America?'

'Yes,' Zikora explained, 'our missing American, David Steinberg, is under investigation for tax evasion. Criminal investigators of the Internal Revenue Service in New York were planning an arrest just before Mister Steinberg left the country. His family simply assumed that he was on the run. I would have assumed the same had it not been for the police sketch from Enugu connecting our missing American to the Logan–Grams–Otunba cases. The IG has ordered Police Commissioners in Enugu, Imo and Anambra states to deploy their RRARS teams in the search for Mister Steinberg. FIIB officers will monitor the situation from Abuja and keep the IG informed.'

Cyrus thought that the course of action taken by the Inspector-General (IG) was wrong. It was one thing to ask the Federal Investigation and Intelligence Bureau (FIIB) — the special intelligence wing of the Nigeria Police Force— to play a role in finding the missing American. It was another to authorize the Rapid Response Anti-Robbery Squad (RRARS) to lead the search. An elite CID squad devoted to combating armed robbers had no business with a missing person's case. Yet, Cyrus understood the pressure the Inspector-General (IG) was under. The IG and the entire police brass were anxious and desperately trying to mollify American diplomats frustrated and seething from the failure of Ikeja CID to solve any of the cases of fraud and homicide perpetrated against their citizens. It was obvious to Cyrus that the deployment of RRARS teams in three states were gestures being made to show the US Embassy that the Nigeria Police Force was doing all it could to find the missing David Steinberg.

'...well, CY, you have all the information. These cases are connected. I think DI Ikenna Kodilinye should collaborate with Enugu.'

Cyrus drained the contents of his cup, dismayed that he had one more unsolved case, involving an American and those faceless swindlers, to worry about. The stakes could rise drastically, if the missing foreigner turned up dead. Although the crime had occurred far away from his jurisdiction, Cyrus knew he would get the blame since the the perpetrators were the same Lagos-based criminals that had eluded him for the past three years. Police brass would hold him responsible for failing to stop the swindlers who now seem to be extending their impunity to other parts of the country. As Cyrus listened to the voice of his superior coming through the receiver, he felt his hope of leaving an excellent legacy slipping away from him.

'Lest I forget, when IRS Criminal investigators did get around to raiding Mister Steinberg's house in New York City, they found scraps of information from our missing man's diary about his Nigerian trip. There was an entry about a Johnson Ezeka, probably an alias, offering a lucrative deal which would fetch forty percent for Mister Steinberg.'

'Forty percent, sir?' Cyrus frowned, his sweaty grip on the handset tightening. He was beginning to feel irritated by the Commissioner's dawdling style. He held back the urge to tell his superior to get to the point.

'Yes, forty percent, that's what the IRS people in New York found in Mister Steinberg's diary. Seems to be forty percent of whatever dodgy deal the fraudsters were proposing. The diary suggested that our man wanted to spend two nights in Nigeria and then return home. He had plans to even sell his big house and move into a cheaper and smaller one...' the Commissioner's voice trailed off and a long pause followed, leaving an expectant Cyrus more irritated. He disliked histrionics.

'Sir, is that all?'

'Yes, that all the information I have. I don't have to remind you that your inability to make any headway in all these fraud-homicide cases is of great concern to me, the Zonal AIG and the IG.'

A dull pain welled in the Cyrus' lower abdomen. A mental picture of him being stripped of his position as Divisional Police Officer (DPO) flashed through his mind. If that ever happened, he would be lucky not to get demoted one rank below Chief Superintendent of Police (CSP) prior to compulsory retirement.

'Yes sir, I know. We are working daily, round the clock, to crack this case. Eventually we get those criminals. You can count that, sir.' Cyrus hoped that Commissioner Zikora did not notice the strain in his voice, the fear racking through him. He heard a heavy sigh on the other end of the line.

'Well, you simply can't afford to let us down any longer,' Zikora responded in a calm voice. 'The stakes are rising with these fraudsters targeting another American and expanding their operations to Eastern Nigeria.'

The DPO bit his lips and then reiterated that Ikeja CID would double their efforts to solve the case.

'I hope so, my dear CY. I want you to bear in mind that the patience of Force Headquarters is not limitless. Good bye for now.' With that icy response, the Commissioner hung up.

The dialling tone from the receiver filled Cyrus' ear as he pondered if he had done the right thing. Seconds later, he placed the handset back on its cradle. After much contemplation, he finally decided that he had made the right choice. There was no need to tell the Commissioner that there might be another mole lurking in the corridors of Ikeja CID. Such a bombshell will send sonic booms of anger sweeping through the senior ranks— the Commissioner, the Zonal Assistant Inspector-General (AIG), the Deputy Inspector-Generals (DIGs) and finally, the Inspector-General (IG).

'No! I won't let it happen,' Cyrus swore to himself. He would handle this problem internally and surreptitiously. Catching a mole was all about exploiting the element of surprise. He pressed a button on the telephone-intercom. Three floors below, the intercom on DI Ikenna Kodilinye's office desk began to ring.

CHAPTER **17**

SEPTEMBER 1993

LAGOS, WESTERN NIGERIA

The morning of 10th September was busier than usual for the civilian staff of Ikeja CID complex. Inside the concrete and glass edifice, built in the modernist style, most were engaged in the humdrum tasks of cleaning, handling in-coming and out-going mail, procuring stationaries, and slotting documents into the pigeonholes of squad detectives. Outside, a few were standing on step ladders, putting finishing touches to a huge cloth banner hanging elegantly above the entrance. The banner read: POLICE IS YOUR FRIEND. WE ARE HERE TO SERVE YOU.

Detective-Inspector Gbolahan Akinola arrived at the entrance of the sprawling police station as the male civilian workers were climbing down from the ladders. He stood there for a few seconds, silently admiring the banner.

'Good morning, sir!' the workers greeted in unison. The detective forced a smile, waving at the men as he walked through the double doors into the tumultuous atmosphere of uniformed police officers, plain-clothes detectives, civilian employees and visitors crisscrossing the foyer. He stopped to banter with some female secretaries on their way to the typing pool. One of them asked him about his son in the hospital.

'He seems to be slowly recovering,' he replied and thanked her for asking. With sympathetic looks on their faces, the other secretaries chimed in with their best wishes for the recovery of his son.

'Have courage, sir. After all, your son's name is *Oludare*,' one secretary noted, reminding everyone of the literal meaning of the Yoruba name— *God has not forsaken.*

The women, all ethnic Yorubas, nodded in agreement. They were sure that God would not forsake the ailing boy.

Gbolahan certainly hoped so. He was not a religious man by any stretch of the imagination. He smiled weakly and waved as the ladies began to walk across the cavernous foyer towards the hallway that would lead them to the open-plan office containing their tables and typewriters. As the women disappeared from view, the detective turned around and began to head in the opposite direction towards a huge bank of wooden pigeonholes fixed to the wall at far end of the foyer. The pigeonholes were adjacent to the quadrangle-shaped reception desk manned by a pot-bellied policeman. Three red chevron stripes sewn into the short sleeves of his uniform shirt indicated the rank of a sergeant.

'Good morning, sir,' the portly man greeted with a salute. Gbolahan returned the desk sergeant's salute and quickly removed a yellow folder jutting out of his pigeonhole. Across the folder's cover, the word IMPORTANT was boldly written in red marker. Gbolahan squinted at the word, a little intrigued, but did not bother to open the folder. He simply placed it inside the leather satchel slung over his right shoulder and moved on. Seconds later, he was climbing the long staircase leading to his office on the fifth floor. He would have preferred to use the elevator, but it had been out of order for the past five months. A repair order sent out was still awaiting approval, trapped in a bureaucratic red tape nightmare in the offices of the Lagos Police Equipment Fund.

As the detective titanically ascended the flight of stairs, all he could think about was his son in Lagos University Teaching Hospital (LUTH). The fourteen-year old was lying on a hospital bed with both legs cast in plaster-of-paris and suspended in the air by cloth ropes. The consultant surgeon, Professor Stella Adenaike, had invited him earlier that morning to her office to update him on his son's progress.

The boy, Oludare Akinola, had been somewhat lucky. The vehicle that knocked him down, two nights earlier, did not damage any vital organs despite leaving him with serious injuries. Since his arrival at LUTH, his condition had improved, going from critical to stable state—thanks to a trephination of the skull to drain blood and relieve pressure on the brain, and a blood transfusion delivered intravenously through the arm. The consultant surgeon had showed Gbolahan radiographs of his son's lower limbs. The boy had suffered complex fractures to both fibulas and would have to spend three months in hospital with both legs hanging in the air. The doctor also gave the detective a list of extra medicines he would have to purchase himself for Oludare, apologising for their unavailability in the hospital. Before rushing off to the pharmacy, the detective had thanked her for everything she was doing to help his son recover...

On the fifth-floor landing of the staircase, Gbolahan felt as exhausted as a mountaineer who had just reached the mountaintop. He leaned against a wall to relieve his thirty-nine-year-old aching back, cursing under his breath. He wanted to be in hospital by Oludare's bedside. He knew that the DPO would grant him leave from work if he asked, but an important meeting with all narcotics squad members had already been scheduled for the afternoon. And as the leader of that squad, he felt obliged to attend. Gbolahan reckoned that he could sit through the first hour of the three-hour meeting before leaving everything in the capable hands of his top lieutenants, Detective-Sergeants Martin Okoye and Christopher Igiebor. And finally, go to be with his son.

Gbolahan opened the door of his office at the end of a dimly lit corridor, seven doors away from that of the DPO. He unslung the satchel and lobbed it across the room. The bag landed in the centre of the office desk. Gbolahan quickly shut the door and switched on the fluorescent lights on the ceiling above. Upon reaching the desk, he retrieved the yellow folder before placing the satchel on the floor next to the base of his swivel chair. As he sat down, his eyes focussed on the intriguing word—IMPORTANT— written across the folder's cover. The Detective-Inspector opened it.

The first page bore the title: *The FIIB Report on the Disappearance of David Steinberg and the Drug Menace in Lagos State.* He quickly flipped over to the next page and started reading a typewritten report. The document revealed that Federal Investigation and Intelligence Bureau (FIIB) had obtained a diary belonging to David Steinberg from one of its officers working with Enugu State CID during a search of the missing American's hotel room. The report said that the diary contained names of Nigerians whom the American last had contact with before he went missing. Some of the names were linked to drug dealers and fraudsters in Lagos State.

Flipping to the next page of the report, Gbolahan learnt that the FIIB had discovered the identities of the criminals who were suspected of murdering the American preacher, Reverend Michael Grams. The report said that a secret operation to locate and sweep up the criminals was underway. A handwritten note signed by the Lagos State Police Commissioner called on CSP Cyrus Udeh to keep all his detectives in the narcotics, homicide and anti-scam squads on standby in case they were needed on short notice to conduct raids and arrests.

Halfway through the contents of the folder, Gbolahan was no longer thinking about his ailing son. He had only questions about the provenance of the bizarre police report. It lacked a police case file number, which was mandatory for reference purposes. There was also no indication of who authored and compiled it. He began to wonder who dropped the folder into his pigeonhole. Was it one of his squad detectives? Martin? Chris? Daniel?

The narcotics squad leader was so engrossed in the report that he did not realize that the telephone-intercom had been ringing. He finally heard it on the seventh ring and reluctantly picked up the handset. 'Hello, Gbolahan speaking.'

The unmistakable baritone hit the detective's ear. 'It's the DPO. You have read the report, haven't you?'

Gbolahan was relieved. He had just discovered the origin of the dossier. Now he knew who held the answers to all the questions nagging him. 'Yes sir, I have read large portions of it,' he replied, closing the folder.

'That's good. Now, come to my office. And bring the report as well.'

There was an audible click and the phone's receiver went cold, prompting Gbolahan to return the handset to its cradle. He scooped up the folder and rose from his desk. With a mind full of expectations, he walked out of his office and back into the dimly lit corridor. He halted at the door situated a few inches from where the fifth-floor landing abuts the start of the corridor and knocked twice. A muffled voice behind the door invited him in.

Gbolahan opened the door and a surge of cool air hit his face. The artificial breeze was coming from the wall-mounted BOSCH air conditioning unit humming in a corner of the office. Gbolahan quickly closed the door and threw up his hand in salutation.

CSP Cyrus Udeh was sitting calmly behind his neatly arranged desk, dressed in his trademark crisp black police uniform, complete with a matching beret. A fairly dark-skinned man about the same age as Gbolahan was seated across the desk from the DPO. The man was not in police uniform. Just like Gbolahan, he was dressed in plain street clothes, as expected of all CID detectives on the job. Gbolahan recognized the man as DI Ikenna Kodilinye, his former leader in the narcotics squad. Gbolahan was promoted to the leadership position when Ikenna left narcotics to take control of the anti-scam squad.

Cyrus waved the detective to an empty chair next to Ikenna. As Gbolahan sat down, he took note of another empty chair on the other side of Ikenna. He wondered who else was expected to join their small party.

Ikenna extended his arm out for a handshake, asking, 'how is your son doing?'

Gbolahan shook the hand with a smile. 'I went to see him this morning. The doctor says he is recovering slowly.'

'Thank God,' Ikenna said, sighing in relief. He had feared for the worst when he heard of the boy's head injury. The doctor had called it an epidural haematoma, undoubtedly fatal if emergency surgery is not performed. The police was still looking for the hit-and-run driver and his blue van, but no success yet.

The DPO cleared his throat and welcomed Gbolahan to the gathering before adding, 'after this meeting, you will take the rest of the day off. Your son needs you.'

Gbolahan told the DPO about the narcotics squad meeting he was going to chair later in the day.

Cyrus shook his head vehemently. 'You'll have to postpone it. You are taking the day off. And it's an order.'

Gbolahan did not respond. Cyrus scribbled something into a folder open before him and then tossed it into the OUT tray.

The DPO harboured reservations about including Gbolahan in the sensitive gathering. It had nothing to do with fears that the detective's personal problems would interfere with the sting operation being planned to snare corrupt policemen in league with the elusive swindlers. In fact, the role planned for Gbolahan in the sting operation would be minimal, not enough to stop the man from spending quality time with his ailing son in the hospital. Cyrus' problem with Gbolahan had to do with trust. Could the narcotics detective be trusted?

Ikenna had argued in favour of his ex-deputy, insisting to the DPO that Gbolahan was an honest man. Besides, Ikenna's preliminary investigation had established that Gbolahan was not in Ikeja CID when the office burglary occurred. After weighing Ikenna's considered opinion, Cyrus had agreed to include Gbolahan in his plans, reasoning that the narcotics detective's cooperation could prove crucial to the success of the mole-baiting exercise.

'Looks like the AC is not doing its job properly,' Cyrus remarked to no one in particular as he scooped up two folders from the IN tray. Although the climate within his office was quite cool, he felt beads of sweat trickling down his back. Later on, as he moved to toss one folder into the OUT tray, he felt a sticky sensation when his shirt rubbed against his sweaty back. 'Please, can you turn the AC to maximum blast?' he asked Gbolahan.

Gbolahan and Ikenna exchanged puzzled looks. Then the narcotics detective got up from his chair, walked up to the air-conditioning unit, and rotated a big black knob on it. The machine hum grew louder. The detective felt a stronger blast of cold breeze hit his face from the front grills of the air-conditioner.

Ikenna asked, 'are you alright, sir?'

Without looking up from the second folder and the attached document, which he was annotating, the DPO replied, 'I'm okay. Just bear with me. I need to address this.'

Cyrus was not okay. Ten tumultuous days had passed since his immediate superior, Police Commissioner Stanislaus Zikora, informed him that yet another American—the missing David Steinberg—was most likely a victim of the murderous fraudsters. Although that crime had occurred outside his Lagos jurisdiction in faraway Enugu, Cyrus was still feeling the heat from the police top brass and the American Embassy. After all, the criminals were known to be based in Lagos even if some of their crimes were committed outside the state. It was his responsibility to apprehend them and so far, he had failed to do so.

Zikora had been pushing for DI Ikenna Kodilinye to be sent to Enugu city to assist with the David Steinberg investigation, but Cyrus had been stalling. Ikenna was needed in Lagos to assist in solving a big problem, which the DPO had been hiding from top brass—the emergence of another mole, just like the late Mike Otunba, operating out of Ikeja CID complex. Cyrus desperately wanted to resolve the scandal before news of it got out to Zikora or even worse, Zikora's direct superior, Zonal Assistant Inspector-General (AIG) Stanley Idoko.

The DPO was hopeful. So far, the desk sergeant and all other uniformed officers, present at the time of the burglary, had been quietly investigated and eliminated as suspects. The civilian secretaries were ruled out because they barely ventured beyond the first (ground) floor of the five-storey building. Moreover, they knew little or nothing about forensics. The person who burgled Ikenna's second floor office wore gloves to avoid leaving any fingerprints behind.

Chief Inspector Nduka Ikwunne and his second-in-command, Inspector Daoud Mamman had claimed that they were in a three-hour teleconference with one of the Deputy Inspector-Generals of Police based in Force Headquarters, Abuja. Ikenna had confirmed that such a teleconference did indeed take place within the time frame of the burglary.

With Nduka and Daoud excluded, the list of viable suspects narrowed down to three plain-clothes cops, namely Detective-Sergeants Martin Okoye, Christopher Igiebor and Akpan Uko-Effiong. Worryingly, all three detectives were on the second floor on the day of the burglary at the time Ikenna was on the fifth floor attending a meeting in the DPO's office. Meaning that any of them could have been responsible for theft of evidence from Ikenna's safe.

None of the suspected detectives had any blemishes on their service records. Cyrus checked. But then Mike Otunba had no blemishes on his service record too, and yet he turned out to be a crook, the DPO had thought after going through the police service files of the suspects.

Compelled by the exigencies of the moment, Cyrus was forced to accept Ikenna's recommendation to call upon the much-hated anti-police corruption squad (APCS) to lead the surreptitious molehunt. Cyrus considered the APCS leader Chief Inspector Nduka Ikwunne to be a personal enemy. The arrogance, the insubordination, and the pomposity of the Chief Inspector sickened the DPO.

Nduka had strongly supported Ikenna's push for DI Gbolahan Akinola to be included in the molehunting operation; an idea that Cyrus was initially reluctant to take onboard. After all, out of three detectives under suspicion, two were members of Gbolahan's narcotics squad. However, there were points of disagreements between Nduka and Ikenna.

The latter wanted Gbolahan to play a major role in the molehunting exercise while the former wanted the opposite. Nduka rejected the idea of including Gbolahan in the planning stages of a sting operation. Still harbouring reservations about involving Gbolahan in the operation, Cyrus readily endorsed Nduka's strategy. Gbolahan would not be made aware of the operation until it was all set up and ready to go. In fact, the role of the narcotics squad leader would be passive, mostly limited to playing along with the ruse that Nduka had created with manilla folders, all identically yellow—his favourite colour. Each yellow folder contained official-looking documents filled with disinformation and forged signatures of senior FIIB officers in Force Headquarters, Abuja. After the folders were disseminated to the three suspects, Nduka boasted to the DPO that the fake documents would smoke out the crooked cop at the shortest possible time. However, in order to avoid arousing the suspicion of the suspects, the cooperation of their immediate superiors was crucial.

Ikenna was required to tell his second-in-command in the anti-scam squad, Detective-Sergeant Akpan Uko-Effiong, that the yellow folder had come from FIIB officers based at Alagbon Close in Ikoyi, a highly affluent district of Lagos city. The mid-level FIIB officers of Alagbon Close had in turn obtained the folder from senior FIIB officers in Force Headquarters, Abuja.

Gbolahan's case was dicey, as he had been kept in the dark about the entire sting operation. In addition to the official-looking documents purportedly signed by FIIB officials, Nduka had included a note of instruction with the forged signature of Gbolahan in the yellow folders sent to narcotic squad detectives Christopher Igiebor and Martin Okoye. Nduka was going to send to Gbolahan an identical dossier ahead of the meeting where all will be revealed to the narcotics squad leader, but Cyrus had stopped him. Gbolahan would hit the roof if he saw the fake note of instruction with his forged signature on it, Cyrus had told Nduka. Any fuss made over the forged signature could alert the suspects, jeopardizing the sting operation. Nduka had removed the fake note from the folder before placing it in Gbolahan's pigeonhole.

It would be better for the narcotics squad leader to learn everything during the meeting, the Chief Inspector thought. It would be better for Gbolahan to kick up a fuss about the forging of his signature within the confines of the DPO's office before receiving an order to lie to his squad detectives, to claim that he was the author of the forged note of instruction. Nduka knew that Gbolahan would protest, but in the end, he would have to comply with Cyrus' order. Knowing Gbolahan's hatred of him was visceral, the Chief inspector revelled in the knowledge that the narcotics squad leader would be compelled to work with him. Full and unfettered cooperation with the APCS was part of a series of orders that Cyrus would be imposing on DI Gbolahan Akinola to ensure the smooth operation of the mole-baiting exercise...

*****

Cyrus mopped his sweaty face with a handkerchief. The air conditioning unit at maximum power was not helping. The DPO knew he was nervous. Cold sweat was always a sign of that. A tumultuous multitude of thoughts had crowded his mind. What if the mole-baiting exercise fails to uncover the mole? What would happen if his superiors found out that a new mole, in the style of the deceased Mike Otunba, was lurking around in Ikeja CID? Would this nightmare ever be resolved? Would this issue be the one that finally destroys his twenty-three-year career?

Cyrus did not have any faith in the abilities of Chief Inspector Nduka Ikwunne. The man was good in throwing his weight around and making boastful statements, but his track record of catching corrupt police officers was abysmal. In fact, the APCS leader had sent down far more innocent cops than he had the corrupt ones.

Cyrus sighed. The humming of the air conditioning unit was now irritating him. He rose instinctively from his desk and strode across the room. 'It's getting chilly in here,' he remarked as he switched off the air-conditioner. Of course, Ikenna thought, relieved that the machine had finally been turned off. He was beginning to feel his insides freeze.

'About the dossier, I will let DI Ikenna Kodilinye do the talking,' CSP Cyrus Udeh declared, stuffing the folded handkerchief into his breast pocket. Gbolahan Akinola turned to his former squad leader. Ikenna flashed an apologetic smile. Gbolahan did not deserve to be shocked by what he was about to say, he thought to himself. The narcotics squad leader should have known about the sting operation from the very start.

With a rueful facial expression, Ikenna blurted out, 'we are conducting a molehunt. Your cooperation is required.'

Gbolahan's eyes widened in alarm and his heart skipped a beat. He thought he had heard the term "witch-hunt". The last time a "witch-hunt" was carried out, Ikeja CID lost two star cops, and the allegations of police corruption proved to be false. Gbolahan gazed at the empty chair next to Ikenna and realized who was expected to occupy it. The chair was being reserved for Chief Inspector Nduka Omenuko Ikwunne, the in-house "witch-hunter". The infuriated narcotics detective was about to protest when there was a gentle rap on the door. All eyes turned to the door. The DPO sighed and bellowed, 'come in!' As the door handle turned,

Cyrus mumbled something about the entrant being a perpetual latecomer to meetings.

The door finally swung open and a middle-aged man of fair complexion stepped on to the Persian rugged floor. He smiled wrily at the exasperated face of the DPO before shutting the door behind him. Cyrus saw the smile as a sign of disrespect, but restrained himself from jumping across the table to strangle the uniformed Chief Inspector.

'I am sorry for being late,' Nduka began. 'It was due to unforeseen circumstances beyond my...'

'Shut up and sit down!' Cyrus barked, waving him to the empty chair next to Ikenna. 'I don't have time for your antics.'

The smile on Chief Inspector's face vanished. He adjusted the collar of his starched uniform shirt and silently took his seat next to Ikenna. The set was now complete. Nduka, Ikenna and Gbolahan —in that order— were seated in a horseshoe formation around the mahogany desk and across from the DPO.

'Akin, you know Chief Inspector Ikwunne. He is leading this operation,' Cyrus said, addressing Gbolahan by an abbreviated version of his surname.

Gbolahan Akinola glared at the man sitting next to him. Of course, he knew the Chief Inspector of Police, the leader of the so-called anti-police corruption squad (APCS), which had the entire third floor of the building to itself. Cyrus Udeh—the most senior police officer inside that building—once remarked that Nduka's personal office was thrice as large as his own.

The Chief Inspector always made the point that he deserved the space of an entire floor because the work carried out by his squad was much greater than those of other CID squads in the building. Of course, this was patently untrue. Homicide, narcotics and rapid response anti-robbery (RRARS) squads had far greater workload than APCS. But that did not stop the flamboyant APCS leader from repeating those brazen claims in various press conferences. Because his assertions went unchallenged, with the passage of time, Nduka became a media star. The Lagos press manufactured a legendary hero with a stellar reputation for bursting pervasive police corruption.

The media's adulation of the star cop did not really bother Cyrus. What concerned the DPO greatly were the autonomous powers bestowed on the APCS by Abuja-based politicians, which had rendered the Chief Inspector unanswerable to his immediate superiors in Lagos. Nduka reported directly to federal politicians in Abuja. Cyrus hated that because it disrupted the regular chain of command, and in his opinion, promoted insubordination and indiscipline.

*****

Before APCS ever existed, the Nigerian Police Force had the X-squad, which was supposed to fight internal corruption among police officers. However, the X-squad—a creature of Force Headquarters—proved to be largely ineffective. In fact, many members of the X-squad were themselves caught engaging in bribery, extortion and other forms of corruption. After years of public outrage over police collusion with criminals, the federal military government decided to impose a solution on the Nigerian Police Force. Over the objections of police top brass at Force Headquarters, the military junta created an anti-police corruption squad (APCS) for each of the State Police Commands across the country. To the dismay of Force Headquarters, these ad hoc APCS units would operate autonomously and mostly outside the police chain of command.

Although these APCS units varied in size and composition from one State Police Command to another, each unit had, at the very least, 15 plain-clothes detectives led by a mid-level, uniformed police officer. That officer was directly answerable to an Abuja-based Federal Police Committee consisting of seven civilians and a token senior policeman with the rank of a Deputy Inspector-General (DIG). All APCS leaders were required to have an unblemished service record and a grasp of public relations.

The rank-and-file of the Nigeria Police Force deeply resented their exclusion from the process that ultimately led to the formation of the APCS. Right from the start, the high-powered consultative panel of civilians raised by the federal military government was determined not to seek the input of any police officer on the question of how to combat rampant corruption within the Force.

Every serving police officer had an explanation for why the Nigeria Police Force was institutionally corrupt. Every single one vehemently disagreed with the widely accepted notion that dishonesty was programmed into the genes of the average police officer. They all argued that poor renumeration that often left cops and their families feeding from hand-to-mouth, antiquated police equipment, inadequate training, and low police recruitment rates were giant obstacles to effective policing in the country and the reason for unbridled corruption in the Force.

None of these contrarian views featured in the deliberations of the high-powered consultative panel because the police was not represented on it. Efforts by the Inspector-General to get police input into the consultative panel were met with a stern warning from the ruling military regime— back off or be fired. The Inspector-General heeded the warning, determined not to end up like that bold Police Superintendent who was sacked back in 1987 for using his position as the official spokesman of the Lagos State Police Command to talk to the media and the public about the military junta's refusal to provide adequate funding and equipment for the Nigerian Police Force.

The high-powered panel wrapped up after two months of deliberation. It recommended the formation of APCS units to be funded and operated outside the control of Force Headquarters. Understandably, there was uproar at Force Headquarters when the panel's recommendations were made public. Police top brass railed against the financial and operational autonomy bestowed on APCS units—consisting of junior and mid-ranking cops— arguing that it would encourage insubordination against senior officers. Eager to maintain high approval ratings from a public tired of soaring crime rates, the ruling military junta intervened again to silence Force Headquarters.

Like their counterparts across the nation, officers of the Lagos State Police Command felt that they had enough problems on their hands pursuing criminals with meagre resources and simply did not need the zealous interference of gadflies like Nduka Ikwunne who saw their politically ordained roles as vehicles to rise to the top. This anti-APCS sentiment was strongest amongst the squad detectives and uniformed personnel of the Lagos State Criminal Investigation Division (Ikeja CID) in whose headquarters Nduka and his men were based.

No policeman in the entirety of Lagos State hated the flamboyant cop as much as Cyrus Udeh did. It did not seem that this would be the case when the then Inspector Nduka Ikwunne first arrived in March 1989 to take up his position as the top investigator of corruption among the police personnel in Ikeja CID. Being a fellow ethnic Igbo from Enugu who grew up under similar socio-economic circumstances, Cyrus had welcomed Nduka warmly into the fold and did not oppose the inspector's insistence that he and his APCS detectives have an entire floor of the building to themselves.

However, within a month, it became clear to Cyrus that Nduka's concept of "fighting corruption" did not match his own. While Cyrus believed that corruption was a cancer that should be rooted out wherever it was found, Nduka believed that every policeman was corrupt until proven otherwise. In the APCS leader's opinion, the only way to combat corruption was to carry out regular "random sweeps"—select a random segment of the police personnel in Ikeja CID or in the wider Lagos State Police Command, accuse the selected cops of corruption and force them to prove their innocence. To Cyrus and the others, these "random sweeps" were crazy witch-hunting exercises staged for the benefit of the media and ordinary citizens fed up with pervasive police corruption and desperate to believe that Nduka's sham exercises were a genuine panacea.

By September 1989, the feud between Cyrus and Nduka reached a crescendo when the latter rudely barged into the former's office. In a tone no other middle-level police officer would ever use against a policeman of superior rank, Nduka claimed that the CID complex was crawling with dirty cops and that he had started investigating allegations of corruption against five detectives in the RRARS. The DPO attempted protest, but Nduka rudely cut him off, telling him that the days of condoning and covering up corruption was over.

To show the DPO that he meant business, Nduka used the sweeping autonomous powers bestowed upon him by federal decree of the military junta to suspend all RRARS personnel. Among those suspended from duty were twenty unaccused detectives and uniformed police officers on the verge of bursting an armed robbery gang that had been terrorizing the Lagos Island—a commercial district within Lagos city— for many years.

Cyrus made vain attempts to rescue the five accused detectives whom he believed to be innocent, but was blocked by the Federal Police Committee seating hundreds of miles away in Abuja. The civilian commitee members stated their reason—full confidence in Nduka's judgement—for blocking the reversal of the suspension of the entire RRARS, including the five accused plain-clothes officers. The DPO's argument that the removal of the detectives from active duty and the temporary shutdown of the RRARS had hampered efforts to combat a particular dangerous gang was dismissed out of hand as the excuses senior policemen often made to shield their own from the microscope of accountability. The lone policeman on the committee— the Deputy Inspector-General of Police (DIG)— was sympathetic to Cyrus' cause, but had no power to act, his membership of the committee being largely ornamental.

For the entire four-month duration of the APCS investigation of the five accused detectives, armed robberies in Lagos rose to an all time high. Finally realizing the mess he had created, Nduka reactivated those RRARS personnel who had never been accused of any offence, but had been suspended for months. His belated lifting of the suspension did nothing to cheer up the demoralized RRARS team who then tried and failed to stem the rising tide of violent crimes sweeping the entire state.

Catching wind of a new police attempt to destroy them, the Lagos Island gang mounted one last daredevil bank robbery operation. Fifteen people were killed, including two policemen guarding the bank. The robbers escaped to neighbouring Bénin Republic with the five million naira they had stolen.

The day after the devastating bank robbery, Nduka and his APCS detectives ruled that allegations levelled by their anonymous "confidential informants" had been found to be untrue. Accordingly, the five accused RRARS detectives had been absolved of any wrongdoing. Out of the five RRARS detectives, two refused to return to work, submitting their resignation letters saying they couldn't work for a police that put politics above law enforcement.

Cyrus campaigned quietly, but tirelessly to get the APCS boss removed on grounds of abusing his position. In a letter to the Federal Police Committee, also copied to the Inspector General of Police (IG), he accused Nduka of using his powers to conduct sham investigations to give the gullible public the impression that APCS was tackling police corruption. He called for Nduka to be sacked and for all APCS personnel in the state to be brought under the direct control of the Lagos State Police Commissioner.

The powerful civilians of the Abuja-based committee, deeply cynical about senior police officers, responded by publicly issuing a statement, broadcast by many TV channels within and outside Lagos, commending Nduka for a "job well done despite resistance from detractors". With the abstention of the lone policeman on the committee, the civilians passed a resolution recommending Nduka for rapid promotion. Anxious not to offend the power brokers in Abuja, the IG ordered Lagos State Commissioner Stanislaus Zikora personally to change the cloth on the shoulder epaulettes of Inspector Nduka Ikwunne's uniform to reflect the brand new rank of Chief Inspector. A telegram from the IG reprimanded Cyrus Udeh and forbade him from interfering with the APCS leader's campaign to rid the police of corruption. There was also an implied threat that the Chief

Superintendent of Police (CSP) could lose his Divisional Police Officer (DPO) position if he continued to "obstruct" Nduka.

CSP Cyrus Udeh complied with the directive of the IG. However, the daily sight of the arrogant APCS boss was rankling to him. Cyrus found it hard to accept that a policeman junior to him in rank, occupying the entire third floor of his building, would snub fortnightly meetings of all CID squad leaders, which he chaired in his capacity as the DPO. He took this up with Commissioner Stanislaus Zikora.

Zikora rationalized the APCS leader's behaviour. Since those meetings were held to keep the DPO abreast of the current activities of all seven squads under his direct control, Nduka had no obligation to attend. The Commissioner reminded the DPO that while the APCS nominally constituted the eighth squad of Ikeja CID, it was autonomous from the regular police chain of command and its leader reported directly to a committee in Abuja.

Of course, Cyrus knew all of this, but was still taken aback by what seemed to be a blithe acceptance of insubordination on the part of the Commissioner. Mr. Zikora asserted that APCS was a political instrument and, as such, would have a life span as short as public memory.

'Don't worry we will deal with that bastard,' he told Cyrus, 'but wait until that so-called "police committee" is dissolved and their contraption, the APCS, is dismantled nationwide. There is no point losing your job over that insolent man.'

Cyrus took Zikora's advice to heart. He knew only too well that ad hoc bodies borne out of populism such as the APCS rarely lasted in Nigeria. They always tended to disappear quietly once the general public turned its attention to something else. For four years and counting, he had tolerated the excesses of the Chief Inspector, waiting patiently for the day the APCS would be scrapped, and Nduka Ikwunne transferred back to regular police duties commensurate with his rank. Then and only then, the DPO thought, would he teach the insolent Nduka not to mess with his real superiors...

*****

The DPO removed his spectacles as Nduka shot out his arm in an apparent attempt to shake the hand of Gbolahan. The glowering narcotics detective ignored the gesture and the hand withdrew to the side of the clearly embarrassed Chief Inspector. A mischevious smile flashed across the DPO's lips.

'Yes, as I was saying before Nduka came in,' Ikenna began, turning to Gbolahan. 'We are conducting a molehunt. We believe that someone working in Ikeja CID is supplying information to the fraudsters that murdered Otunba and Grams.'

The narcotics detective's heart sank. In a strained voice, he reminded Ikenna of how a false allegation against five RRARS detectives adversely affected the crime-fighting ability of the police. Glaring at the amused Chief Inspector, Gbolahan added, 'don't give this man another excuse to destroy the CID.'

Ikenna shook his head. 'You have got it wrong. Evidence connected to the Otunba and Grams murder cases was stolen from my unlocked safe when I left my office for an hour to see the boss; most likely perpetrated by somebody who wants to pass them on to the killers.'

Gbolahan turned to the boss, CSP Cyrus Udeh, who nodded to confirm Ikenna's story. 'Anyone could have entered your office. Could even be civilian visitors to the building,' Gbolahan responded, skeptical about the presence any mole.

Ikenna suppressed a sigh. 'I checked with the desk sergeant, no visitors came into the building in the period before the theft and after the theft. Only three detectives, eight uniformed police officers and all ten secretaries were in the building within the time frame. None of the contract employees— I mean the cleaners— was in the building at the time as they are only present in the early hours of the morning. The burglary happened in the afternoon. We ruled out the secretaries as suspects because whoever stole from my safe knows forensics. The perpetrator wore gloves. We checked out the uniformed officers. They are clean; that leaves the detectives present at the time.'

Gbolahan looked apprehensively at Ikenna, then at the APCS leader. 'We?' he asked incredulously.

Ikenna nodded. 'Nduka and I investigated and cleared the uniformed personnel. Now, we are moving on to the plain-clothes guys.'

With bated breath, Gbolahan asked, 'which detectives are you planning to investigate?'

Ikenna called out the names of the three detectives to be placed under watch.

Gbolahan panicked. Two of them were his most productive detectives. The third was not a member of his narcotics team.

'My men are not rogues!' he barked, focussing his blistering gaze on the silent APCS leader who was struggling to suppress a grin.

The DPO weighed in to allay Gbolahan's fear. 'Don't worry Akin, Mister Nduka Ikwunne'— Cyrus said, glancing at the Chief Inspector—'is not going to suspend your men. He understands that it would be detrimental to the continued running of the narcotics squad. This is a covert operation under my control.'

Gbolahan Akinola heaved a sigh of relief. The DPO's words reassured him that his squad will remain intact, and that the Chief Inspector was not in overall control of whatever the hell was going on. The last thing Gbolahan wanted was for "Nduka the witch hunter" to wreak havoc on the narcotics squad. He did not believe that his men were moles spying for murderous underworld figures. As far as he was concerned, DPO and Ikenna were misguided souls unwittingly giving ammunition to a demon in human form who claimed to be fighting corruption within the police.

Ikenna added to what his uniformed boss had said. 'I'm not saying your men are crooked. At the moment, there is no proof of that. I am saying that it is reasonable to suspect them because they were present in the building when evidence disappeared from my office. My own deputy was present too when the theft occurred and is now being watched.'

Gbolahan Akinola stared at his former squad leader in dismay. Many thoughts flooded into his mind. One particular thought stood out and kept nagging at Gbolahan's mind: *if Ikenna does not trust his current deputy now, did he ever trust me when I was his second-in-command?*

Cyrus broke his silence again. 'Look Akin, we are not taking chances. This is not a time to be sentimental. After all, who knew that Mike Otunba would turn out to be a rogue?'

Gbolahan sighed, grudgingly accepting that the DPO was right. 'Okay sir,' he replied wearily, 'what do you want me to do?'

The DPO opened his top drawer and fished out a yellow folder identical to the one the narcotics detective was bearing. He passed the folder to a bemused Gbolahan. The detective quickly went through it. The contents of the folder were similar to the one in his possession. While going through the sheaf of documents attached to the DPO's folder, Gbolahan also noticed an item that was absent in his own folder. The item was a handwritten instruction to narcotics detectives scribbled in green ink on a sheet of paper with his signature on it.

'I did not write this,' he said stentoriously, pushing the folder across the table towards Cyrus.

The DPO smiled mischievously, 'I wrote it in your handwriting and forged your signature. Your men got that version of the report not the one that was sent to your pigeonhole.'

Gbolahan felt like telling off his superior, but thought better of it. If he had not been consumed by seething anger at what Cyrus had just said, if he had been more observant, he would have noticed the flash of suprise across Nduka's face, which was quickly replaced by a disdainful smile on the lips.

The APCS leader had not expected Cyrus to lie about who wrote and signed the fake note of instruction. Why would the DPO do that? he asked himself before it suddenly dawned on him. He finally understood why Cyrus had to take credit for the forgery of the note and the signature. The old fox wanted to pre-empt the fulmination that would have surely erupted if Gbolahan knew the truth. It was one thing for CSP Cyrus Udeh— the chief of all Lagos detectives— to forge the signature of a detective for a good cause and another thing for the universally hated Nduka to do the same, whatever the reason might be. Gbolahan would swallow his anger if he thought the DPO had faked his signature, but not if he knew Nduka was the actual forger. The narcotics detective would never have given the benefit of doubt to a man notorious for smearing innocent cops as corrupt. Nduka knew this and smiled at Cyrus' quick thinking. Such craftiness, Nduka secretly admired in the DPO. He also admired Cyrus' level-headedness and stoicism, even in face of daily provocations by insubordinate APCS personnel.

'Akin, I know you don't like this, but it was for a good cause,' Cyrus said as he collected the yellow folder that Gbolahan had brought with him and dropped it inside the bottom desk drawer. 'Read my own version. It is identical to the one sent to your men,' DPO ordered, pushing the other yellow folder containing the forged note of instruction back across the table. 'You have to be well versed in its contents in case your men raise any questions, especially about the forged note. The men must believe that the instructions came from you; that it passed from your office to theirs. Understand?'

Gbolahan nodded impatiently, irritated by the DPO's haranguing tone. He disliked having to deceive men fiercely loyal to him, but he had no choice other than to obey his superior. His glaring eyes fixed on Nduka's face again.

'Sir, why is it that none of his men are under surveillance?' he asked Cyrus without taking his eyes off the Chief Inspector's face.

'All detectives and uniformed officers of the APCS were on field assignments on that day,' Nduka countered, finding his voice. 'They were busy investigating corruption cases in Mushin, Agege, Surulere, Ikorodu and Lagos Island. Daoud and I were inside the building, on a three-hour-long teleconference, when the burglary happened.'

Gbolahan turned to Ikenna for confirmation. The anti-scam squad leader nodded to signal agreement with what the Chief Inspector had said.

'Akin, as I said before, I know you are not pleased, but this must be done'— Cyrus said toying with a fountain pen— 'we cannot surveil all eighty-three people that work in this building. Good thing that only twenty-one individuals were present in the time frame under investigation. Good thing, we have eliminated eighteen of the twenty-one individuals as suspects.'

Dropping the fountain pen on the table, the DPO added, 'imagine the investigatory resources we would have needed to deploy if most of the cops on field assignment had been in the building at the time of the burglary. Thank God.'

Chief Inspector Nduka Ikwunne nodded in agreement. APCS personnel were stretched to the limit investigating various police corruption cases across Lagos State. *Thank God indeed*, he thought. The molehunt was focussed on just three suspects, which made things easier and manageable. If the sting operation uncovered a mole, it would be a huge surprise. But, at least, he would claim joint credit with the DPO. If the operation ended in a fiasco, without revealing a mole, as he was anticipating, then the DPO will take all the blame. After all, the DPO had overall command of the molehunt. The APCS was there to provide assistance not to take the lead. As far as Nduka was concerned, there were no downsides for him and his men.

'What happens now? What is the next step?' Gbolahan asked Cyrus, averting his gaze from the mocking eyes of Chief Inspector Nduka Ikwunne.

'We wait for the suspects' reaction to the contents of the yellow folders. Watch out for any suspicious behaviour… I will hand over to Mister Ikwunne to provide insight into our operational strategy,' the DPO replied, sneering at the uniformed man sitting across the table.

Nduka Ikwunne was used to Cyrus' contempt. It never bothered him. What bothered him was being addressed disdainfully as "mister". He firmly believed that he had earned the right to be addressed by his rank; that the DPO's behaviour was irregular and unprofessional. He could have protested, but he let it pass. He wasn't in the mood to get into a fight with the Ikeja CID boss over an issue would seem trivial to many people.

'Yes, my men have already started monitoring the movements of our three suspects. We have phone taps, mail intercepts and twenty-four-hour watch.' Nduka paused, turned to Gbolahan, and continued, 'of course, your men and the other guy in Ikenna's squad are free to continue working unhindered. But my detectives will be hovering in the shadows, watching their every move.'

Nduka turned to face Cyrus who was toying with his fountain pen again, pretending not to be listening, and said, 'Chief, if any of them make any attempt to contact the swindlers, we will pick that person up quickly.'

The Chief Superintendent of Police, still toying with his pen, nodded listlessly, blurting out: 'yes...yes...impressive...very impressive, Mister Ikwunne.'

Gbolahan Akinola was unimpressed and did not pretend. 'And if the men are found to be innocent, then what?'

The room grew quiet, not even the boastful anti-corruption czar had an immediate answer to Gbolahan's question. The narcotics squad detective firmly believed that none of his interlocutors in the room had stopped to consider possibility that all three detectives may turn out to be innocent. He also believed that none of his interlocutors had considered the sheer waste of time and money if the molehunt turned out to be useless.

In reality, his assessment of the situation had only been partially correct. Ikenna and Cyrus had indeed not contemplated the possibility that all three men could be innocent. On the other hand, Nduka had thought deeply about it. The Chief Inspector knew that the whole operation would end in a fiasco. For that reason, he had not attempted to wrest control of the mole-baiting exercise from the DPO, even though the task of investigating corrupt cops was the exclusive preserve of the APCS.

'Well, if they are innocent, then we are back to square one,' Ikenna replied, breaking the thick silence in the room.

Gbolahan glanced at Cyrus who seemed to be trying to gather his thoughts together. The DPO nodded his agreement with what Ikenna had said. He had nothing to add to what had been said because he had not thought of that scenario. Although the DPO remained outwardly calm, thinking of that scenario scared him: *If none of the trio is the mole, then who is? For how long would such a mole remain hidden? How would the Commissioner react to existence of this mole? Would my career survive the ensuing scandal?*

The APCS leader cleared his throat and spoke. 'I'm sure we will apprehend the mole very soon. Definitely, one of the three guys is the culprit. There is no doubt in my mind.'

No one else in that room felt reassured by Nduka's bold remark, given his long track record of targeting cops who turned out to be innocent of wrongdoing.

On that note, the DPO declared the meeting over. Nduka left immediately for the third floor where his anti-police corruption squad (APCS) of fifteen detectives and five uniformed officers were waiting to either brief him about ongoing investigations or be assigned new corruption cases for investigation.

A little over an hour after Nduka left the DPO's office, four APCS detectives were in place, watching every move of their three quarries. The sting operation had officially kicked off.

CHAPTER **18**

HAMPSTEAD, NORTHWEST LONDON, UK

The postman pushed a Royal Mail delivery trolley loaded with letters and parcels up an inclined, concrete sidewalk, which together with the exquisite detached houses lining both sides of the long stretch of road constituted Maresfield Gardens, a quiet street in the affluent district of Hampstead.

Upon reaching the junction where Maresfield Gardens intersected with Nutley Terrace, he paused and straightened up, uncrumpling the navy-blue jacket of his postal uniform. He waited patiently for the oncoming vehicle to pass. The speeding Vauxhall Nova saloon car swept past the junction and continued along Nutley Terrace.

The postman gripped the handles of the trolley, crossed the road, and continued up the sidewalk. He stopped in front of the gates of 1200 Maresfield Gardens. Beyond the grill gates stood a big detached house. Hunched over his trolley, the besuited postman rummaged through the envelopes and wrapped parcels looking for a particular item. Seconds later, he found and extricated a white A4-sized envelope bearing the name "Harel Suzmann" and the above-mentioned address. The envelope had South African stamps affixed to them.

Armed with the white envelope, his pale blue eyes searched for a letterbox, the metal container with a slit usually attached to the gates of detached houses. He frowned. There was none available at the address. Why can't this rich numpty get a box like other residents? he thought to himself. Just as the exasperated postman was about to press the bell switch mounted on one of the gateposts, the front door of the large red brick house swung open. A clean-shaven man in his mid-forties, almost six feet tall, emerged, smiling. He scratched his dark coarse hair, and then walked briskly towards the postman holding out an envelope through the vertical bars of the grill gates.

'Sorry about the absence of a letter box,' the tall man apologised as he received the mail. 'I will install one as soon as possible.'

'Cheers mate,' replied the postman. The tall man disappeared back into his house while the postman carried on, propelling his trolley up the sloped sidewalk to continue his early morning rounds.

Back inside the house, the tall man, Harel Shimmle Suzmann, fell into a chair inside his study room and threw his feet onto the smooth, shiny mica surface of his desk. He used a letter opener to slit the envelope open. Soon he was staring at the letter. On its letterhead was the bold heading: HEINTZ & SHARMANN LAW FIRM. Beneath the heading was a motto written in italics: *To serve clients honestly.*

From the letterhead, he learnt that the Johannesburg-based law firm had two senior partners—James Heintz and Eli Sharmann—two junior partners and five associates. Bemused, Harel reclined on his seat. His eyes quickly ran over the rest of the letter and then returned to the body text, which read:

Dear Mr. H. Suzmann,
My partner and I are pleased to inform you that there is over 25 million pounds here in South Africa for you to inherit!!! I know this may come as a great surprise to you, but this is for real!

Our late client, Robert Suzmann, a South African businessman was the original beneficiary of the windfall, a fruit of his investment in a diamond mining company called Volkstar Diamond Ltd.

Harel stopped reading and removed his feet from the table. He pondered over the name as his bare feet felt the cold terrazzo floor. He could not recall any member of his family named Robert. Although, he did vaguely recall his late father saying that a section of the Suzmann family had immigrated to South Africa in the late 1940s. He thought of whom to contact in the UK for more information, but no one came to mind. Both parents were dead and most of his extended family immigrated to Israel a long time ago. Twenty-five million pounds was a lot, he thought, imagining a hundred and one things he could do with that kind of money.

'I will bounce back, if that money came my way!' he exclaimed, picturing a brand new yacht, a new car and a reinvigorated business. He laughed and continued to read:

To put our story in context, I will give you a brief history of the inheritance. In 1981, Volkstar Diamond— a company founded in 1909 by some Afrikaner veterans of the Boer war— was on the verge of bankruptcy due to crippling UN sanctions imposed on apartheid South Africa. The company launched a direct appeal to prominent businessmen to invest in it to avoid the looming collapse. Many South African businessmen, including our client Mr. Robert Suzmann, responded to the call of the ailing company with a collective investment of £5,000,000.

By 1991, the sanctions regime was beginning to slacken due to the gradual reversal of apartheid policies by the government of President F.W. De Klerk, and Volkstar was back in international business making an annual turnover of £100 million. Our client made a profit of £25.5 million from his investment. Unfortunately, he died intestate at the age of 61 on 1ˢᵗ June 1993. We have tried to locate the next of kin of our unmarried and childless client, but to no avail. We hired a private investigator to try to find any member of his family in the Diaspora. He checked with the immigration records office in Pretoria and recovered documents proving that your family in England is related to the Suzmann family that settled in South Africa many decades ago.

If you are interested in receiving this money, we can make a strong claim on your behalf. All we need is a photocopy of your birth certificate and passport details. You can post them to the return address on the letterhead. Contact us via the phone number in the letterhead to let us know that you have posted the documents or if you have any questions.

Good luck Mr. Suzmann. My partner and I look forward to hearing from you.

Yours faithfully,
James Heintz (Esq)

Harel whistled to himself and walked to the window of his study. As he stared out at the trees outside his house, he contemplated what to do. In his head, he could hear two voices. One voice was optimistic, telling him that he should not miss that once-in-a-lifetime opportunity, a second chance to rebuild his life and shame those bastards—including his ex-wife—who had written him off. The other voice was more skeptical. It warned him not to go ahead with the deal. This could be a monumental fraud in the making, the skeptical voice argued. The optimistic voice in his head countered with the argument that the South African lawyers were not demanding any money from him. They were merely trying to help him secure a family inheritance.

After several minutes of pondering, the optimistic voice won the debate raging in Harel's mind. Nevertheless, he was determined to verify whether there had ever been a man called Robert in his family tree who was South African and wealthy.

Harel peeled himself away from the window. Back behind his desk, he produced a bottle of Scotch whisky from the bottom drawer. He uncapped the bottle and swigged the small quantity of the spirit left in it. Pushing the bottle aside, he opened the top desk drawer and grabbed his black leather-bound diary. He flipped through the leaves quickly until he arrived at the particular page he was looking for. Then he turned to the telephone. Lifting up the handset with one hand, he began to use the other to punch buttons corresponding to numbers highlighted in his diary.

Moments later, a telephone rang in another part of the world— the Middle East. When a voice answered at the opposite end of the phone line, Harel dropped into flawless Hebrew.

*****

Over in Lagos State, a brand new digital clock was sitting on a large mahogany desk in an office on the topmost floor of Ikeja CID complex. The clock's LCD screen indicated the time and date as 10.00 AM and 11th October 1993, respectively.

On one side of the desk sat three men: Detective-Inspector Ikenna Kodilinye, Chief Inspector Nduka Ikwunne and Detective-Inspector Gbolahan Akinola. Seated on the other side of the table was Chief Superintendent Cyrus Udeh, the DPO and host of the meeting.

'Do you like it?' Cyrus asked, smiling giddily while caressing the top of the digital clock. 'It is an anniversary gift from my wife. She gave it to me yesterday.'

Ikenna and Gbolahan both glanced at the garish pink object on the desk and smiled awkwardly. Ikenna praised the DPO's unseen wife for her good taste in gifts. Gbolahan nodded perceptively. Nduka Ikwunne said nothing. He seemed rather aloof, totally detached from his immediate environment and the two detectives pretending to admire a timepiece that they did not really like.

'Okay, let's get down to business,' Cyrus said, his countenance instantly assuming an aspect of seriousness. 'Nduka, bring us up to speed.'

The Chief Inspector suddenly burst into life, cleared his throat and began to speak. The anti-corruption czar began by recapping what had happened over the last thirty-one days. The three suspects had read the fabricated contents of their yellow folders and asked their immediate superiors—Gbolahan or Ikenna—some questions about them. As previously planned, the three suspects learnt from their respective superiors that the contents of the yellow folders were confidential and no photocopies of them should ever be made lest they fall into the wrong hands. The suspects were also instructed to remain on standby, ready to help in any future FIIB raid to apprehend the drug traffickers and scammers suspected of being behind the disappearance of American businessman, David Steinberg.

The Chief Inspector told his small audience that the first phase of the mole-baiting exercise had been a great success as all three suspects now believed the fake story of an FIIB investigation into the activities of the scammers who were being portrayed as drug-dealers as well. With the aid of forged documents in the folders, the suspects had also been led to believe that they could be called upon, in the future, to assist FIIB officers in conducting raids and arrests. For most detectives, a chance to work with officers of the highly esteemed FIIB, even on a temporary basis, would be considered a great honour. For a rogue detective on the payroll of scammers in the crosshairs of the premier intelligence agency of the Nigerian Police Force, there was a lot to be fearful about. Nduka had hoped that such fear and panic would cause the mole in Ikeja CID to expose himself, unwittingly.

The DPO nodded contently as he listened to the recapitulation of what he already knew. However, when the Chief Inspector's briefing segued into the less familiar second phase of the exercise, a dark gloom suddenly began to spread over

156

the DPO's countenance. Nduka explained to Cyrus that his APCS detectives had spent four weeks and three days watching the suspected moles around the clock without a single break in continuity. This was achieved with a rotating shift work schedule that saw different groups of APCS detectives taking turns to monitor every step taken by the suspects, day and night. After a full month of surveillance, the APCS detectives had not observed any suspicious activity among the suspects.

'I am afraid the men are innocent,' the APCS leader told the DPO, 'we checked everything...bank accounts; their lifestyles; ownership of property and other assets; their acquaintances, friends and families. They were all clean. There were no clandestine meetings in the dead of the night. They left their yellow folders in their offices; no photocopies were ever made. Residential and office phone taps did not reveal anything out of the ordinary.'

The silent DPO turned gloomily to Ikenna, signalling that he wanted to hear the Detective-Inspector's perspective on the matter. Ikenna said that he concurred with the APCS leader.

'I agree with the Chief Inspector. A month is enough to know whether they are guilty. If these men were moles, they would have attempted to warn their paymasters about an upcoming FIIB swoop. We don't have any of them on the phone doing anything suspicious. We don't see them trying to pass copies of our fake dossier to the scammers. Sir, it is your call, but my opinion is that we should wrap up this operation. Of course, I am not saying that we should totally abandon the search for the mole. On the contrary, we must continue to be on the lookout. However, we need to conserve our limited resources by shifting from a proactive disposition to a passive one. Just like we do on cold cases.'

When Ikenna finished speaking, a period of uneasy silence followed. The DPO turned unexpectedly to his digital clock and started stroking it again in admiration while his subordinates looked on silently with bemusement.

'So this has been a wild goose chase,' the DPO remarked softly, finally breaking his silence.

'I'm afraid, sir. It is so. I agree with Ikenna. It is no use wasting limited police resources on this matter. The operation should be stepped down,' Gbolahan said, relieved that the subterranean "witch hunt" against two members of his narcotics team was finally coming to an end.

Cyrus breathed heavily and reclined on his chair. He grabbed the pink clock with both hands and began to toy with it. Ikenna looked on, concerned. He knew that the DPO was struggling to remain outwardly calm. The old fox always toyed with objects whenever he was feeling nervous.

'If it isn't any of the three detectives, then who is the mole in my building?' the DPO suddenly asked in exasperation.

The question was addressed to Chief Inspector Nduka Ikwunne, but Ikenna weighed in, 'Sir, we'll just have to keep our eyes open.'

Nduka nodded in agreement.

Another period of uneasy silence followed. Then the telephone-intercom began to ring. Cyrus quickly placed the digital clock on the table and picked up the handset. 'Hello? Who am I speaking to?' he asked and then listened silently. Minutes later, he thanked the caller and placed the handset back on its cradle. His eyes fixed on Ikenna's face.

'Okay guys, I have heard what you have to say. I am suspending the molehunt until new evidence comes to light or we get some fresh leads,' he said, suppressing a sigh.

'My men and I will keep an eye out for those leads. It is only a matter of time. We will get the mole eventually,' Nduka replied with a level of confidence that none in the room reposed in him.

Nevertheless, a morose Cyrus nodded along to the Chief Inspector's bombastic rhetoric. Then he remembered something that made him brighten up. With an enigmatic smile on his face, he said, 'by the way, that was Anambra Police Commissioner on the phone. He says that he has something of interest to me. So, if you don't mind, gentlemen, I will like to attend to that matter now. This meeting is over. You may return to your offices... Ikenna, you may stay.'

Gbolahan got up immediately and made for the door as if he had been waiting for the opportunity to get away. Nduka Ikwunne remained in his seat, intrigued by the sudden twist in events— their meeting was ending a little earlier than scheduled because of a phone call from Eastern Nigeria. *What was that all about? What was going on in Anambra State*, he thought with his backside firmly planted on his seat.

'Mister Ikwunne, the meeting is over,' the DPO repeated sternly. The Chief Inspector opened his mouth to say something, but the scowl on Cyrus' face changed his mind. He got up quickly and walked out of the office. Gbolahan, hitherto standing by the doorway, walked out, and closed the door behind him. The DPO waited until Gbolahan's footsteps had faded before he started speaking to Ikenna.

'Anambra police pulled out a light blue Mercedes Benz W140 saloon car from River Niger in Onitsha city. A bunch of fishermen found it when their dragnet was entangled in the car. They alerted the Onitsha Marine Police. A wallet and a pair of cufflinks with the initials "DS" were recovered from the car. The wallet contained a ten-dollar bill, one thousand naira, cash, and the photo of a woman we have confirmed as the ex-wife of the missing David Steinberg.'

With elbows resting on the desk, Ikenna leaned forward. 'Sir, with your permission, I'll like to go down there. It could be the lucky break we have been waiting for.'

The DPO nodded. 'No problem, but I want you to stop by Enugu Central Police Station first before proceeding to Onitsha. You leave tomorrow.' Lowering his voice, the DPO added, 'do not tell anyone where you are going. Can't trust anyone these days.'

Ikenna stood up, turned around, and was already walking towards the door when he heard the DPO behind him say, 'Oh, I almost forgot... there was an American Express card in the wallet.'

Ikenna nodded to indicate he had made a mental note of his superior's remark. He left the office, closing the door behind him. Alone in the office, the DPO resumed his interest in the digital clock.

*****

Moses Adrika brought in the last carton and heaved it onto the floor of his garage. His back ached from the strenuous exertions of moving three large cartons. Each box contained ten tins of paint thinner, the type normally used by carpenters to dilute oil-based wood paint.

Two hours earlier, Moses had walked into the Ikeja branch of Leventis Stores—one of the largest chain of stores in Nigeria—and made straight for the carpentry section. He went through multiple racks of upholstery fabric, wooden planks, steel nails, wood glues, spray paint and polyurethane varnishes before finally locating the desired paint thinner.

The lone store assistant was pleasantly surprised when Moses requested thirty tins of paint thinner. Sales in the carpentry section have been slow all week. Carpenters always got what they needed at cheaper prices in the large open-air markets of Ebute Metta, a lively rundown district of Lagos city.

As the store assistant merrily packed the jumbo-sized tins into big cartons, Moses told him that he was a carpenter who had just landed a huge contract to supply the offices of a Lagos municipal authority with furniture. He had been in the middle of spray-painting some chair frames when he noticed that he was running low on paint thinner. The store assistant nodded, smiling. He helped Moses load the three cartons into the back of his hired panel van out in the parking lot.

Back inside the store, at the checkout terminal, Moses overpaid. The store assistant rifled through the trays of the cash register, but the coins and bank notes in them were not enough to complete the transaction. He was fumbling histrionically in his trouser pockets for some extra cash when Moses asked him to keep the change.

The assistant smiled. 'Sir, we have quality spray paint here. If you buy ten tins, then you'll get…'

'Nah, I don't need them,' Moses interjected and left the store. The nineteen-mile-drive back to his residence in Victoria Island took almost two hours, courtesy of a long bridge choked with traffic.

After securing the cartons of thinners next to a high-density polyethylene jerrycan containing a mixture of nitric and sulphuric acids, Moses pulled down the retractable steel door, shutting his front garage. As he slouched back towards the doorway of his mansion, his mind wandered back to the night the decision was made to kill Detective-Inspector (DI) Ikenna Kodilinye.

*****

The decision to kill Ikenna Kodilinye was taken in an atmosphere of conviviality down in the basement of John Nwosu's mansion, the week before Moses visited Leventis Stores. The nocturnal meeting in the situation room had begun with the usual exchange of banter over a newly installed marble table crowded with perspiring bottles of chilled beers spotting various brand labels: Guinness, Golden Guinea, Star, Gulder, Premier, Budweiser, Heineken, etc.

The financial health of the gang's two front companies was discussed at length. Struggling to turn a legitimate profit, Dixon Job Agency was sustained by laundering part of the gang's ill-gotten gains through it. By contrast, ELAJ Enterprises— their vehicle spare parts dealership— was raking in millions of naira annually, and there was talk of expanding the highly profitable business beyond Lagos State. John put his brilliant acolyte, Tunde Olukemi, in charge of creating new branches for ELAJ Enterprises across the country.

Having just returned from his first ever trip to South Africa, John told the gang that the first phase of their newest swindle operation had been activated. With that declaration, the gang moved on to the main item of the agenda—a discussion of what to do with DI Ikenna Kodilinye.

The rogue policeman at Ikeja CID had told his handler, Tunde, about the mole-hunting operation when it kicked off. Throughout the thirty-one-day duration of that sting operation, John kept fretting despite repeated reassurances from the corrupt policeman that there was no cause for alarm.

John had always believed that his gang's "gamesmanship" against the police could not last forever. For him, it was only a matter of time before the police reached a breakthrough in their investigation; the identities of he and his men would inevitably be unmasked, at which point a statewide manhunt would follow.

The rest of the gang did not share John's firm convictions, which they regarded as pessimism verging on fatalism. Nevertheless, they agreed with him that they needed a getaway plan, just in case.

John wanted another eighteen months— free of police interference—to further enrich himself and his men before leaving the country for good to spend the money in peace. So the revelation of a secret molehunt within Ikeja CID came as an unpleasant surprise. It was too soon, the gang leader thought to himself when Tunde relayed the message from their police spy.

By the time, the spy brought the good news that the mole hunt had subsequently ended in failure, John was at the end of his tether. The nerve-racked gang leader wanted DI Ikenna Kodilinye dead as soon as it was possible.

In between swigs of dark beer, John told his men that the assassination of Ikenna would be a huge psychological blow to Ikeja CID—yet another murder of a squad detective. The Lagos State Commissioner of Police would blame the disaster on CID incompetence, and then sack Chief Superintendent Cyrus Udeh. John reckoned the gang could buy more time from the disruption, confusion and demoralization that will engulf Ikeja CID following the death of a well-regarded detective and the subsequent sacking of a popular DPO.

'So what do you guys think?' John asked, putting down his bottle of Guinness Stout. There was uneasy silence.

'Killing another policeman,' Tunde said, breaking his silence, 'it is problematic, boss.'

Picking up his bottle of stout again, John asked his acolyte to elaborate. Tunde demurred.

'He is worried that we are painting a fresh target on our backs,' Eugene chimed in.

'Okay, I get where Tunde is coming from. What is your own opinion?' John asked Eugene who was nursing his second Heinken bottle.

Eugene blurted out the reply. 'I say kill the bastard. There is nobody else in Lagos CID that is as good as he is. His death would be a massive blow to their morale. It would be ages before the other CID guys recover their balance. Such disruption within the ranks of the police can only benefit us.

Adamu and Moses clinked together their bottles of Star Beer before drinking to Eugene's remark. But the killjoy in their midst interposed with a pushback.

'This is could backfire,' Tunde hissed, his elbow almost toppling a bottle of Gulder Beer on the grey marble tabletop. 'The outrage of such a killing could motivate the police to work harder.'

Addressing Tunde, John said, 'well, it is been months since Mike Otunba died. And yet, we haven't seen the police work any harder to solve his case.'

Tunde was about to interpose a comment, but John cut him off. 'Yes, I know Otunba was an embarrassment to State CID, but he was still a policeman, a detective-inspector. There is no doubt in my mind that CID pulled out all the stops to investigate his death. But the truth of the matter is that, like the rest of the sclerotic police force, the CID boys are slow and inefficient. We just need to slow them down much further by throwing a big spanner into the works.'

Tunde wanted to speak, but thought better of it. He dawned on him that John had come to the meeting with his mind already made up. The gang leader just wanted to hear his men affirm his point of view.

John gulped down the remaining stout, placed the Guinness bottle on the table, and then asked his men to vote by a show of hands. All the gang members—except Tunde— raised their hands to ratify their leader's decision. They all agreed that DI Ikenna Kodilinye should die. Tunde reluctantly accepted the decision, and the meeting moved on to the question of how and who would carry out the assassination.

John already knew the answer. He informed the group that Moses Adrika would carry out the hit. Turning to Tunde who was already frowning at the decision, the gang leader smiled. 'Moses is an excellent bomb-maker. The best I have seen. This is not your area of expertise. I'm sorry, Tunde.'

The gang leader's arch remark elicited laughter from Adamu, Eugene and Moses, and a morose expression from Tunde.

Moses had accepted the assignment wholeheartedly, thrilled to be free to work alone without Tunde and his condescending "know-it-all" attitude. As he celebrated, Moses was mindful of his rusty technical skills. He would have to delve deep into the inner recesses of his memory in order to summon old knowledge, which he had not used in a very long time. The assignment would require what he had learnt twenty-four years earlier, during his stint in the workshops of the Research and Production Directorate (RAP)—a military engineering outfit charged with producing weapons to augment meagre overseas supplies trickling into the Republic of Biafra through narrow gaps in the land, sea and air blockade imposed by Nigeria.

At the start of June 1968, Sergeant Moses Adrika, then a Biafran Army sapper, had only served a few days in his new place of posting at 68th Battalion of the elite "S"-Brigade, when he began to hear from other soldiers about the impending visit of the RAP scientists. The scientists, highly respected across Biafra, were mostly a collection of civilian industrial engineers and former university professors in the sciences who gathered and melted down scrap metal to built rockets, bombs, guns and howitzers. They also salvaged electronic components from household gadgets and used them in the construction of radio equipment for the Biafran military.

Moses was excited. In previous military postings to other theatres of the war, he had heard vaguely about the great things the geniuses of RAP had been doing for the secessionist republic. He knew they had designed the famous makeshift Uli Airport, which had been built hastily to compensate for the loss of two international airports after the Biafran cities hosting them fell to advancing Nigerian forces.

The makeshift airport—dubbed one of the world's busiest at night by the international mass media of the time— had captured the popular imagination within Biafra. And it wasn't just because the aerodrome served as a major lifeline for the besieged secessionist republic in the last two years of the war. The existence of the airport was a physical manifestation of Biafra's defiance in the face of the Nigerian military juggernaut, overrunning everything in its path.

Under non-stop artillery and anti-aircraft gunfire from the Nigerians, the makeshift airport continued to receive over fifty flights per night from international relief agencies supplying Biafran war refugees with badly needed food. The airport's configuration allowed an endless stream of relief planes, which had successfully evaded missiles in the air, to land on the runway and taxi straight into an ingeniously designed underground hanger, a gigantic bunker, to avoid being destroyed by explosive shells raining down on the tarmac, which had to be resurfaced regularly to eliminate potholes and shell craters. Without that feat of civil engineering, mass starvation in the Biafra, during the final stages of the war, would have been much worse.

A week after Moses arrived at the military camp of the 68th Battalion, the anticipated visitation of the RAP scientists occurred. Before the assembled troops, there was a test demonstration of the *Biafran Red Devils*—the clunky, beetle-shaped, armoured tanks that the scientists had improvised by adding armoured plates to heavily modified chassis of civilian bulldozers.

While the army sapper appreciated the level of ingenuity that went in the creation of those war machines, the things that really impressed him were the tubular micro-refineries—portable crude oil processing facilities— that the scientists had fabricated and were then distributing to every Biafran military formation. This was being done to compensate for Nigeria's capture and destruction of all industrial-scale oil refineries that had hitherto supplied the national fuel needs of the secessionist republic. As Moses was to remember, and reflect on, two decades after the cessation of hostilities, if not for that particular technological feat in modular petroleum processing, the beleaguered Biafran Armed Forces would have collapsed sooner, instead of having the wherewithal to keep their electricity generators, light propeller aircraft and military vehicles operating up until the very moment the Biafran government officially surrendered to Nigeria in January 1970.

But that sunny afternoon in June 1968, the brutal civil war was still far from over, and like every other soldier in that military camp, Moses was ready to sacrifice his life in the fight for the survival of Biafra as a sovereign state. When the visitors from RAP announced to the assembled troops that they were also on a recruitment drive to replace technicians killed in a laboratory accident, Moses promptly volunteered to be seconded from his military unit to work with the legendary Biafran scientists. He was not in the least deterred by the head scientist's pro forma statement about the potential risks that all volunteers faced, working in accident-prone machine workshops and mobile test laboratories, all hastily built, without the proper safety protocols, due to the exigencies of war.

Until the termination of the secondment, a month before the war ended, Sergeant Moses Adrika worked under the coruscating tutelage of the RAP scientists. From them, he learnt multiple ways of producing high explosives from readily available household chemicals...

*****

Moses lay across the sofa to relieve the painful cramps he was feeling on his waist and lower back. He knew he should been more careful when he lifted those heavy cartons. He knew he should have purchased a wheelbarrow for the job. 'Wheelbarrows aren't that expensive,' he groaned in regret as he adjusted his head on the upholstered armrest of the sofa.

Lying face up across the long cushioned seat, with his eyes fixed on a spot on the ceiling of the room, he tried to gather his thoughts together. He wasn't going to allow the pain get in the way of his first solo project in years, his best chance to prove his worth to John. He noticed the pain recede somewhat as an exhilarating feeling washed over him at the thought of working on his own time and initiative without that haughty bastard, Tunde, hovering in the shadows, waiting to steal his thunder.

No amount of pain was going to take away the thrilling fact that he was free to make decisions without consultation. He was free to make any type of explosive he wanted. Money was no object. John had made generous budgetary allowances. The night after that fateful situation room meeting, Moses had pondered the sort of explosive needed for the job and which household items to use in its production. He could buy glycerine—which millions of Nigerian ladies applied to their skins—and subject it to nitration, but the resulting nitroglycerine would be highly unstable and sensitive to shock. The risk of an accidental detonation during or after the production of that kind of explosive was unacceptably high.

He also considered the possibility of producing a Triacetone Triperoxide (TATP) bomb from acetone-based nail polish removers. Since nail polish removers were sold in small plastic bottles, Moses considered this option to be the least attractive. To obtain anything near the quantity of acetone required to make his bomb, he would have to raid the feminine beauty sections of several Lagos shops and buy every single bottle of nail polish remover on sale. More importantly, TATP require refrigeration facilities to maintain stability and prevent premature decomposition. Moses considered other kinds of high explosives before settling on the relatively stable Trinitrotoulene (TNT).

Acetone, naptha, turpentine and toluene were among chemicals found in household paint thinner. Moses was only interested in toluene, which constituted about twenty-five percent of the liquid volume of the thinner. To compensate for the low percentage of toluene, Moses bought thirty large tins of thinner. These were more than enough to extract the quantity of pure toluene needed for his assignment.

He planned to wait a few hours after nightfall before putting together a metal workbench in his garage. He had already acquired a gas mask and protective gloves in readiness for the time when he would need to pour the mixture of nitric and sulphuric acids into his improvised TNT production apparatus.

The apparatus was quite crude, and yet sturdy enough for use in the nitration of the pure toluene extract. Nevertheless, Moses was nervous. He knew there was still the risk of an accidental explosion from the release of large amounts of heat and nitrogen oxides during the three-step nitration process. The former army sapper was only too aware that if the exothermic reactions rumbling inside the apparatus ever got out of control then Lagos firefighters would need a few hours to recover all his body parts strewn across the concrete rubble of what used to be his mansion. He flinched at the possibility of such a rude end to his existence. Lying on the sofa, he made a mental note to check the deep freezer to see if the aluminium buckets of water had frozen—lots of ice would be required to keep the exothermic reactions under control. He reassured himself again that he just had to get through the nitration process and all would be well. The pale yellow flakes of solid TNT synthesized from that process were safe to handle and store in the house until ready to use.

One great advantage TNT had over TATP and nitroglycerin was its insensitivity to shock, which meant that the risk of an accidental detonation were extremely low. Therefore, TNT was safe for the bumpy, three-hundred-mile drive from Lagos to Onitsha along poorly maintained expressways strewn with large potholes. A domestic flight from one city to the other was out of the question. He was never going to risk being caught smuggling an explosive on board an aeroplane.

As he began to fall asleep on the sofa, it just occurred to him that that he had forgotten to buy some other chemical and extra items needed to make an explosive booster. Without an explosive booster, the TNT bomb was useless. Too late now, he thought. He would have to buy it the next day. Before he drifted off to sleep, he set the alarm on his watch to wake him up in five hours, 9.00 PM to be exact.

CHAPTER 19

OCTOBER 1993

ENUGU CITY, EASTERN NIGERIA

The Dryax Airlines plane touched down on the runway of Enugu Airport. It taxied on the tarmacked surface for a few minutes and then came to a stop. The aircraft stairs were put in place and the passengers started disembarking. Among them was a relieved DI Ikenna Kodilinye.

The flight from Lagos to Enugu had taken just forty-five minutes, but those were forty-five harrowing minutes for man afflicted with aviophobia.Throughout the flight, he did not, even once, look out of the cloudy window next to his seat. Whenever the aeroplane gained altitude or underwent rapid descent, his heart skipped a beat. Increasing his sense of unease during the flight was the knowledge that planes operated by domestic airlines were not properly maintained and over thirty years old.

While boarding the Boeing 707 plane in Lagos, he had noticed a steel data plate riveted to the door jamb with engraved markings indicating the aircraft was manufactured in 1960. So, he was quite pleased and relieved when the air hostess—who had been rude to passengers all through the flight— announced that the plane was due to touch down in Enugu city in a matter of minutes. 'Please fasten your seat belts!' she had barked at the passengers. Ikenna, like the other passengers, had complied, fastening the frayed seat belt round his waist. He closed his eyes seconds before the plane started its descent and opened them again when the plane was safely on the ground, taxiing along the tarmac.

Climbing down the aircraft stairs, he felt the searing heat of the afternoon sun on his skin, making him regret his choice of clothes: a black two-piece suit. Once on the tarmac, he joined a small crowd of passengers walking towards the double glassdoors of the airport building.

Inside the Arrivals hall, a fairly dark-skinned voluptuous lady in her early thirties, dressed in denim, approached him with a smile on her face. She greeted him in Igbo language. Ikenna acknowledged the greeting, mildly surprised. The lady read his mind and explained in English. 'Your boss in Lagos gave my boss your physical description. I was selected to pick you up.'

She shot out her hand. 'I am Detective-Sergeant Ngozi Oduche, Enugu State CID.'

Ikenna shook her hand. 'I haven't met a lady detective in a while,' he remarked smiling.

Ngozi smiled back. 'I will take that,' she said, taking Ikenna's small holdall. She led him into the car park. They walked through several rows and columns of saloons cars until they got to a dark blue Peugeot 504 SR saloon car with ENUGU

STATE POLICE COMMAND stencilled on both of its sides. She dumped his bag on the lukewarm bonnet, brought out the car keys from her jeans trouser pocket, and walked over to the driver's door.

Ikenna stood near the bonnet on the other side of the car, silently admiring her beauty as she unlocked the door. He figured that she was about his height—five feet and eight inches. Her demeanour was pleasant and radiated a striking personal confidence; the sort exhibited by a woman unintimidated by her tough work environment, which was overwhelmingly masculine.

She adjusted the multi-coloured Alice band perching tenaciously across the shoulder length strands of corkscrew hair curls and waved Ikenna to the front passenger door. She opened the car door and slid in behind the steering wheel. She heaved the holdall into the rear seat of the car and pressed a button near the gear lever. The centrally locked doors unlocked instantly with a click.

Ikenna opened the front passenger door and slid in beside her. The searing heat inside the car caused him to sweat.

'Its very hot today,' Ngozi said, winding down the windows. She peeled off her denim jacket revealing a loose white sleeveless blouse, damp at the chest area. 'I hope you don't mind. It's damn hot.'

Ikenna smiled and wound down his window.

'I think you should do the same. That coat will kill you,' she advised him.

Ikenna peeled off the jacket of his two-piece suit. The white shirt he was wearing beneath the jacket showed small spots of dampness. He slackened the brown leather gun holster strapped over his shoulder and pulled out his pistol.

Ngozi turned the key in the ignition and the car engine roared to life. Ikenna switched on the safety lock on the handgun before placing into the glove compartment in the dashboard.

The Enugu CID detective pushed the lever into the first gear and relieved the clutch pedal.

Ikenna dumped his jacket next to his bag in the rear passenger seat as the car pulled out of the park. Cool breeze wafting in from outside displaced the hot air in the car's interior.

'How is Lagos?' she asked.

Ikenna grinned, 'it's a tough place...like always.'

Soon they were driving through the centre of Enugu city. The Lagos CID detective felt a wave of nostalgia as he took in the sights and sounds of the city's hilly geography. Although, he was born in Enugu, he hadn't visited since he and his father moved to Lagos in March 1970—two months after the civil war ended.

*****

As the oldest city in the Igbo-speaking part of Nigeria, Enugu had a long history, complicated by the constantly changing nature of its politico-administrative status. Long before any European set foot on West African soil, the place that will eventually form the nucleus of the city comprised ten villages set atop a series of hills. For centuries, life in these Igbo villages followed a simple format—everyday, upon hearing colourful roosters crowing, village men descended to the valleys under the dim light of dawn to tend to their farms while the women prepared to engage in a variety of activities, namely nurturing children, pottery-making, weaving baskets, petty trading and tending to various farm animals. At sunset, after the men had retired to the huts for the night, old women gathered the children under the moonlight to regale them with Igbo folk tales while groups of young women gathered in cliques to engage in tittle-tattle.

From 1903 onwards, this uncomplicated, slow-paced, semi-isolated rural life began to be punctuated with visits from the pale-skinned khaki-clad men of the British colonial administration. During the first visit, the colonial authorities—with the aid of dark-skinned interpreters who spoke a strangely accented Igbo—carried out a census and informed the locals that they would have to start paying taxes to His Majesty's Government in London. This caused uproar, but soon enough, the villagers acquiesced. They had little choice in the matter. Subsequent visits of the colonial officers and their interpreters involved not just tax collection, but prospecting for solid minerals.

In 1909, the colonial administration finally caught a break. Deposits of coal had been discovered, under village farmlands, in the valleys. Once the bituminous coal deposits were determined to exist in commercially viable quantities, the colonial authorities initiated talks to buy the farmlands from the villagers.

By 1915, a colliery had been developed to exploit the coal deposits, the largest in West Africa. Life in the ten villages radically changed. The farmers metamorphosed into colliery employees, many of them working in the deep underground mines, hewing away at seams of black coal.

Over the next twenty years, the hilly villages and its environs slowly transformed into a vibrant urban centre as rural men from nearby and far-flung corners of Igboland began to arrive in search of coal mining jobs. Shops began to open to sell luxury goods to the wives of the coal miners. Christian missionaries established schools to educate their children. Modern infrastructure—concrete buildings, roads, portable water, electricity, railways—began to appear everywhere.

The establishment of the railways and electric power stations, both fuelled by burning coal, accelerated the migration of rural Igbos into the hilly urban centre, which by then, had been recognized as the city of Enugu by the colonial authorities.

In 1939, the city was declared the capital of the Eastern Provinces of Nigeria. As a consequence of that declaration, the ethnic composition of the people migrating to Enugu acquired a heterogeneous tinge. While migrants continued to be predominantly ethnic Igbos, people from smaller ethnic groups native to faraway southeastern villages dotting the coastline of the Atlantic Ocean began to come to Enugu in significant numbers in search of jobs in the colonial civil service, schools, railways, electric power plants, factories and coal mines. They spoke native languages that were unintelligible to the Igbo inhabitants of the city.

Over a period of three decades, city's population experienced almost a twenty-fold increase from 3,170 people in 1921 to 62,000 in 1952.

In 1954, as independence from colonial rule neared, the British authorities abolished the Eastern Provinces. In its place, Eastern Region of Nigeria, with Enugu as its capital city, was created to widen the participation of Eastern Nigerians in local governance. The influx of people into Enugu continued to grow so that by 1960, the year of Nigeria's independence from the British, the city had 93,000 residents.

In the days and weeks following the September 1966 pogroms directed against ethnic Igbos resident in Northern Nigeria, the city experienced an influx of a few thousand refugees from the sum total of 300,000 surviving Igbos who had fled to the East.

During the brutal civil war that followed, Enugu city served as the official capital of the secessionist Republic of Biafra. When that war ended in January 1970, Enugu reverted to its previous status as a Nigerian city, serving as the administrative capital of a newly created province named East Central State until its dissolution in 1976.

Enugu city would later undergo its fourth iteration as the administrative centre of yet another short-lived province before finally arriving at its current status as Enugu State's largest metropolitan area and capital city. By 1993, Enugu city's population was estimated to be slightly below 500,000 residents.

*****

As the Peugeot 504 SR saloon car turned into the dual carriageway named Ogui road, Ikenna heard the familiar tolling bell of a railway level crossing. It reminded him of the colonial era railway corporation that his late father worked for. The same one that the British colonial regime had built to move coal from Enugu mines to the seaport of Port Harcourt for onward shipment to UK.

The Peugeot 504 joined a queue of cars, lorries and motorcycles at the level crossing as the red-and-white striped pole barrier came down to discourage any vehicular intrusion onto the railway line running across the road.

'Wow, a train is coming through this place. Quite rare,' Ngozi said, pulling up the hand brake of her idling car. A loud siren sounded and a hundred-car diesel cargo train appeared.

Ikenna stared as each train car sped across the road, his mind wondering off into the distant past bearing traumatic memories of his wartime childhood.

After what seemed like an eternity, the final car of the diesel cargo train hurtled across the road, clearing the railway level crossing. The warning bell tolled again as the red-and-white striped pole barrier rose skyward. When the pole barrier was fully raised, the bell stopped ringing, and the queued vehicles began to traverse the rail crossing one after another.

Detective Sergeant Ngozi Oduche put down the handbrake, stepped on the clutch pedal, and then shifted the gear lever. The Peugeot 504 SR became mobile

169

again. Ngozi noticed that her companion was lost in a world of his own. She smiled and nudged him.

Detective-Inspector Ikenna Kodilinye snapped out of his thoughts, returning to 1993 from 1967 in a split second.

'What were you thinking about?' she asked.

Ikenna did not answer. He looked out of the window. His gaze capturing the parked saloon cars, shops, fax and photocopy kiosks, restaurants and several high-rise buildings lining the street. A plethora of colourful wooden and neon signboards hung under the sills of several glass windows, giving the tall buildings a garish appearance.

When the Peugeot 504 SR slowed down due to heavy traffic, Ikenna' eyes surveyed the business signage on one cream-coloured high-rise building. There were vehicle spare parts dealerships and photographic film processing laboratories sharing the first floor, different barristers' chambers on the second floor, independent auditors-for-hire and real estate agents sharing the third floor, and an architectural firm on the fourth floor.

Ngozi noticed Ikenna gazing at the buildings intently. 'You have never seen a high-rise before?' she asked archly. 'Are you sure you came from Lagos?'

Ikenna ignored her teasing comments, his gaze fixed on the city beyond the car window. After a few minutes of uneasy silence, during which Ngozi wondered if she had offended him, Ikenna finally turned to her and responded. 'I haven't visited since the war ended. The last time I was here, there was nothing, but a heap of smouldering rubble. None of these buildings were here.'

Ngozi whistled. 'You mean you haven't been to Enugu since 1970?'

'Yes,' Ikenna replied and turned to stare out of the window. The car slowed down and halted some distance away from a truck executing a three-point U-turn.

'My father works over there,' the Enugu detective said, pointing to a window on a four-storey office complex.

'Your father is a lawyer,' he remarked coolly, gazing at the signboard hanging below the sill of the window, which read:

C.C. ODUCHE & ASSOCIATES,
SOLICITORS & ADVOCATES.

The truck concluded its manoeuvres and drove past the patrol car. Ngozi released the brake pedal. 'You sound like you disapprove,' she said, slowing down to avoid hitting a feral dog crossing the road.

'No, no,' Ikenna responded before Ngozi interrupted him.

'It's alright. Many people don't like lawyers. My dad is different. He is a human rights activist and a criminal barrister specializing in death row cases. He is against the death penalty,' she added as she shifted the gear lever.

Ikenna nodded slowly to indicate his perceptiveness. He did not like or dislike lawyers. For him, lawyers were simply a necessity in much the same way as judges and policemen. The conversation was already boring him, but something that Ngozi had said had intrigued him. Nigerians generally did not oppose capital punishment. So it was always interesting to hear about the minority that did oppose it.

'Your father's opinion of the death penalty is quite unique.' Ikenna remarked circumspectly.

'I know! Strange, isn't it? My father studied abroad. That's were those liberal views come from.'

'Seems like you don't agree with his views on the death penalty,' Ikenna said probingly.

'When you do the kind of work we do, you meet criminals doing all sorts of abominable things that deserve the death penalty,' she replied as the car cruised past the imposing British Council building. 'C'mon! Nobody can convince me that a child killer does not deserve to be hanged!' she added.

Ikenna did not respond. He was staring at large numbers of well-dressed passers-by boldly moving up and down the sidewalk. They were nothing like the dishevelled and terrified crowd of people fleeing the city back in October 1967 under Nigerian artillery and aerial bombardment. Ikenna recalled with a slight shudder how his mother and several others were killed in the outskirts of the city during an airstrike conducted by a Nigerian jet bomber. He and his father never identified her among the multitude of burnt body parts strewn across the road. Despite the great passage of time, Ikenna still felt nauseated as he recalled seeing a grotesquely disfigured torso that looked more like a large jelly of blood, tissue and smashed bones. Ikenna adjusted his posture on the car seat and realized that he would never win the struggle to bury those wartime memories somewhere deep and inaccessible in his mind. Those traumatic memories would always co-exist, unrepressed, alongside the happier pre-war memories of his childhood.

The car sped past the Enugu Stadium, a Roman Catholic cathedral, a crowded open-air market before slowing down at a junction. Ngozi turned the steering wheel, swinging the car into Okpara Avenue. A big signboard in the median dividing the dual carriageway read: WELCOME TO ENUGU—THE COAL CITY-STATE.

She slowed down again when the red taillights of a panel van ahead suddenly switched on. The van moved into a lay-by and pulled up. Ngozi's car wheeled past quickly. As the Peugeot 504 SR passed by the gates of the Enugu Campus of the University of Nigeria, Ikenna remarked, 'Chudi, my brother, was a student there before the war.'

Ngozi accelerated and changed gears. 'Oh, where is he now?'

'He didn't make it. The war took him,' Ikenna replied.

'My brother was a law student there too. He served in the Biafran Airforce. Nigerian anti-aircraft guns brought down his helicopter.'

There was momentary silence.

'I guess we were luckier than many others,' Ngozi laughed awkwardly, 'at least, my brother's body was recovered by the airforce people. We had a closed coffin funeral. I think it was in early 1968. I don't remember the exact date. I was a kid back then.'

There was another momentary silence before she added, 'It was a long time ago. I have gotten over it.'

Ikenna silently watched her as she rubbed her eyes with the back of her left hand. He thought he saw tears, but he wasn't sure.

'Its usually hotter here than in Lagos,' Ikenna remarked, changing the subject.

'Yes, definitely...I will take you to see my boss in CPS then from there I'll take you to the police guest house.'

'What about Onitsha?' Ikenna asked, thinking there was some kind of mistake. The plan was that he would see the Enugu police chief for a briefing about the investigation into Steinberg's disappearance and then quickly proceed to Onitsha city to see the local police chief about the Mercedes Benz W140 fished out of River Niger.

'There is no point going to Onitsha today because the main police officer in control of the investigation down there is away in Kano State. He will return tomorrow morning. I'll drive you there tomorrow.'

The Peugeot 504 SR swung into a narrow street lined on both sides by colonial era Georgian buildings. Ikenna recognised it as the Government Reserved Area (GRA), once the "Europeans Only" quarters of the British colonial administration. The car drove past a cluster of brick and concrete buildings—collectively known as the Enugu State Secretariat—which house the civil servants running the Enugu State bureaucracy and a number of municipal workers employed by Enugu city authorities.

The Peugeot 504 meandered through narrow laterite roads before turning into a large compound dominated by a large dilapidated building. Ikenna noticed that the paint was peeling off the cracked walls of its facade, and the wooden signboard reading CENTRAL POLICE STATION was fading.

'Well, this is CPS,' Ngozi said as she pulled into a driveway half-filled with Peugeot cars of various models and a few Toyota pickup trucks. Every vehicle parked on the driveway had ENUGU STATE POLICE COMMAND stencilled on their sides with white paint.

Ngozi expertly manoeuvred the Peugeot 504 SR into the rectangular space between two black Peugeot 505 GLX saloon cars and pulled up. She killed the engine and opened the car door, prompting Ikenna to do the same.

They walked across the driveway and quickly ran up the concrete steps leading to the arched doorway of the Central Police Station (CPS). A man dressed in a shabby police uniform was at the entrance to welcome them. Ikenna observed that his faded black uniform was frayed, especially at the knee area of the trousers. The name tag hanging from his breast read, DAVID AGU.

'This is Sergeant Agu,' Ngozi said, introducing the man to Ikenna. The man threw up his hand in salutation.

Ikenna did not return the salute. Instead, he extended his arm for a handshake.

The man shook the hand, mildly surprised. He wasn't accustomed to shaking hands with superior officers. 'Sir, welcome to our station,' he smiled.

'Take Detective-Inspector Kodilinye to the boss,' Ngozi ordered.

David nodded and saluted her.

Turning to Ikenna, she said, 'I have to collect my niece from school. I will be back in a few hours. Sarge, will take you to my superior.'

Ngozi walked back down to the driveway while David Agu led Ikenna into the huge building. They walked past a typing pool filled with middle-aged female secretaries tapping furiously at the keys of their mechanical typewriters. Then they climbed two flights of stairs, walked past several offices and a narrow corridor before finally halting in front of an old mahogany door. The police sergeant knocked and waited. A deep voice behind the door asked him in. David opened the door and stepped aside for Ikenna to enter first.

The cool air of the air-conditioned room was the first thing that hit the detective's nerve endings. Ikenna welcomed it as a great improvement on the hot outdoor weather. As the Lagos detective entered the room, he could not help but notice the stark contrast between the shabby exterior of the Enugu CPS building and the tastefully furnished office of the police chief.

David stepped behind Ikenna at the doorway and saluted the police chief sitting behind a shiny mica desk half a yard away from them.

The fairly dark bald man glanced up from the paperwork on his desk. 'That will be all for now, Sarge. Thank you,' he said peremptorily.

Sergeant David Agu saluted again, stepped outside, and closed the door behind him.

Ikenna walked up to the uniformed man sitting down and saluted.

'Welcome Kodilinye. Please, sit down,' the middle-aged bald man said, gesturing at an empty upholstered chair.

DI Ikenna Kodilinye took the seat across the desk from Chief Superintendent (CSP) Peter Ikedife. 'I have been expecting you. *Dede* C.Y. Udeh informed me a few days ago.'

Ikenna raised his eyebrows. The man had referred to the Lagos CID boss, Cyrus Udeh, as *dede*, which meant "brother" in Igbo language.

As if he was reading Ikenna's thoughts, Peter Ikedife added, 'Cyrus and I went to secondary school together, College of the Immaculate Conception. You know it?'

'Yes sir,' Ikenna replied. He knew the Roman Catholic school. It was one of the best secondary schools in Eastern Nigeria, and his late brother, Chudi, was an alumnus.

The Chief Superintendent swept all the documents on his desk into a box file and shifted it to a corner of his table. He pulled a red manilla folder from his OUT tray and handed it to Ikenna. 'This is what we have so far. It also contains information supplied by Anambra State Police Command.'

Ikenna opened the folder and started going through its contents.

'The number plate of the Mercedes fished out of River Niger was checked by the Onitsha Traffic Division,' Peter continued. 'It belongs to Dike Car Rentals, a vehicle hiring service here in Enugu.'

Ikenna stopped flipping through the documents and enlarged crime scene photographs, and glanced up at the Enugu CPS boss.

'My men checked out the Dike Car Rentals people. The owner, Mister Obinna Dike, was not pleased at all. He had reported the Mercedes as stolen after the man who hired it failed to return it several days after it was due. At our request, he also checked his log book for the customer services assistant who was on duty when the car was rented out. The assistant's name was a young woman named Chidinma Ede. She had not reported for work since the day after the car was rented out. We got her address and raided her apartment in Zik Avenue. Her decomposing body was found seating in front of the television in her living room. She had been shot twice. One bullet in her left leg and the other one hit her in the forehead.' Peter stopped to let Ikenna digest the information.

'Did she live alone? What about the neighbours?' the Lagos detective asked.

'She lived alone and the neighbours all claimed that they saw and heard nothing.' Peter paused and then added, 'Of course, they may be lying. Personally, I can't believe that no one heard two gunshots unless if the bullets were fired through a sound suppressor. My men promised full witness protection, but no one came forward. They all stuck to their story that they saw and heard nothing.'

Ikenna closed the red manilla folder.

'Our forensics people told me that she died around nine o'clock, the same night that the car was rented out. Seems the killers wanted to tie all loose ends. She was the only one who would have been in a good position to give us a physical description of the guy who hired the Mercedes...' Peter broke away from his story and asked Ikenna if he wanted something to drink.

Ikenna declined.

'She was only nineteen years old, an only child. I feel sorry for her parents,' Peter continued with a sorrowful countenance, 'I had to send somebody to Nsukka to inform them of their daughter's death. It is terrible to lose an only child. I understand that. I am a parent too.'

While studying a crime scene photograph, Ikenna asked whether a murder weapon was recovered.

CSP Peter Ikedife shook his head. 'The gun used to commit the homicide was not recovered. But our doctor extracted the bullets lodged in her head and the left leg. He was sure they came from a Browning pistol. It is all in the report. You can read all about it.'

'Can I keep this?' Ikenna asked, tapping the folder.

The police chief smiled. 'Of course, that is your copy of the report. I have mine. DS Ngozi Oduche will take you to Onitsha tomorrow morning...'

'Yes, she told me, sir,' Ikenna interjected.

Peter Ikedife glanced at his watch and said, 'it's already half past two. Detective Oduche would be here soon…I heard you haven't being to the East since the war ended. You had better go on a tour with Ngozi. You will find that a lot has changed in the city since nineteen-seventy.'

Ikenna was surprised.

Ikedife noticed this and chuckled, 'I am sure you understand what *Dede* means.'

Ikenna smiled uneasily. He perfectly understood. Cyrus Udeh probably did not keep any secrets from Peter Ikedife.

'Why haven't you visited since then?' Peter asked.

'When I was much younger, my father wouldn't let me come down from Lagos. Enugu reminded him of my mother's death. If he were alive today, he would have disapproved of this visit.'

'Even if you are a policeman handling an important investigation?' the Enugu police chief asked in disbelief.

The Lagos detective nodded. It wasn't strictly true and both men knew it.

'I heard your father passed away some time ago. When did that happen?'

'Three years ago. Prostrate cancer.'

Peter Ikedife expressed his belated condolences to Ikenna. The Ikeja CID detective thanked him. There was a long pause before Ikedife rose to his feet. Ikenna stood up as well and they shook hands. Then, there was a knock on the door, and Peter bellowed, 'come in!'

The door swung open and Detective-Sergeant (DS) Ngozi Oduche walked in. she stopped inches from the desk and saluted her superior.

'Ngozi, please take Ikenna to the guest house,' Peter ordered, 'if he wants to see the city, then be his guide.'

Ikenna wanted to say that he didn't need anybody to guide him around a city where he spent his childhood, but he thought better of it.

'Yes sir,' Ngozi said, smiling.

'Okay, Ikenna. Have a nice day,' the bald man said, sitting down. 'We will meet again when you return from Onitsha.'

Ikenna walked ahead of Ngozi towards the exit. He opened the door and stepped outside with Ngozi following closely.

When the door closed behind them, Peter grinned. He had seen the excitement in Ngozi's eyes as soon as he instructed her to be Ikenna's guide for the day. With women, you never know, he thought, shaking his head. His attention returned to the box file he had pushed aside earlier. The Enugu State Police Commissioner was scheduled to visit the Central Police Station (CPS) in seven days time, and the building required a few electrical repairs, some plumbing work, and an extensive paint job. All these were pending tasks that had to be executed before the visit of the man who was in charge of the entire State Police Command. Enugu CPS could not afford to make a bad impression on the visiting Commissioner for that could make the difference between securing or not securing more funding for the upkeep of the police station.

Peter Ikedife opened the box file, fished out a purchase requisition form listing all the items needed for the renovation work, and began to scrutinize the estimated prices on it. This had to be done before any order approving the release of funds could be signed.

*****

That same afternoon back in Lagos, the rogue policeman—the elusive mole in Ikeja CID —made a phone call from his office. He was not afraid of being caught because no one suspected him. In fact, he was confident that he was above suspicion. This made him smile smugly whenever his criminal patrons expressed concern about his cavalier attitude to security, especially his habit of making phone calls from the office during working hours.

His criminal patrons, especially John Nwosu, have warned him several times that his office phone could be bugged. Each time, the mole laughed it off, saying it was impossible. No one would ever think of doing that to a police officer of his calibre. Nevertheless, he swept his phone line for bugs regularly with a Scanlock ECM receiver in order to ease the minds of his criminal associates.

The highly placed rogue policeman knew that DI Ikenna Kodilinye was travelling from Enugu to Onitsha city and it was his job to keep his handler, Tunde Olukemi, informed. He dialled a number on his office telephone and waited. When a voice answered at the other end of the phone line, the rogue cop spoke in flawless Yoruba.

Tunde was impressed by the policeman's fluency in the language. It was the first time that they had not communicated in English. He listened patiently and then responded in Yoruba. He thanked the crooked policeman for the information, and revealed that Moses Adrika was already on his way to Onitsha. Then, he told the policeman that he would be awarded a bonus on top of his regular pay in a fortnight. The rogue cop thanked him profusely and hung up.

CHAPTER 20

OCTOBER 1993

ONITSHA CITY, EASTERN NIGERIA

After an hour-long drive along the pothole-strewn Onitsha-Enugu expressway, the 504 Peugeot SR, finally entered Onitsha city— the unofficial commercial capital of Igbo-speaking Eastern Nigeria, the largest metropolitan area within Anambra State, and one of the country's major centres for commerce, industry and education.

It was Ikenna's first visit to the riverine city in twenty-three years. The last time he was there, it was March 1970. The war had ended two months earlier, and he and his father were on their way to a new life in Lagos, hundreds of miles away from the scene and ruins of armed conflict.

As much as he had tried over the years, Ikenna could not forget the horror he had seen as a dishevelled teenage refugee travelling with his father in the back of a lorry through war-devastated Onitsha en route to their new life. Seared indelibly into his memory were the sprawling scenes of catastrophic damage that stretched for miles, in all directions, across the riverine city—the burnt-out office complexes, excavated roads, blown-up flyovers, bomb-cratered streets, bullet-riddled houses with caved-in roofs, endless columns of grotesquely twisted vehicle carcasses, and the rubble of what used to be schools and churches. Ikenna recalled his father, standing beside him in the bed of the slow-moving lorry, saying repeatedly that Eastern Nigerians were resilient people and would definitely rebuild themselves and their damaged cities. But he had doubted his father's words. The gargantuan scale of the devastation in Onitsha and many other places in the defunct Biafran Republic made reconstruction seem insurmountable in the eyes of teenage Ikenna.

But now, in October 1993, sitting next to Ngozi in the Peugeot 504 SR saloon car, Ikenna realized that his late father was right. Staring out of the car window at the scenery sliding past, Ikenna marvelled at the miracle of post-war recovery. Onitsha had become a bustling metropolis with a population approaching half a million, old familiar landmarks had been restored, several new tall buildings dotted the landscape, and lively traffic flowed through new dual-carriage roads. In fact, Onitsha looked like it had never experienced the devastating effects of a war.

'We are here finally!' Ngozi exclaimed, suddenly applying the brakes. The tyres screeched as the car swung into the sprawling forecourt of the Onitsha Central Police Station. On the tarmacked driveway, she slowed the car down and steered it gently towards the parking lot in the left corner of the forecourt. As the Peugeot 504 SR was pulling up next to a row of patrol cars, twelve policemen, totting antiquated Mark IV bolt-action rifles, suddenly emerged from the run-down three-storey building serving as the central police station. They jumped down the concrete steps in front of the building and ran towards the Peugeot 504 SR saloon car, rifles poised menacingly at Ngozi and Ikenna. The hostile faces surrounding the saloon car evinced a mixture of fear and anger. And they had every right to feel that way.

Seven days earlier, in broad daylight, a gang of armed robbers driving a black pick-up truck, with the blue-yellow-green tricolour of the Nigerian Police Force painted on its sides, had stormed Onitsha Central Police Station with Uzi submachine guns. They sprayed bullets at a group of unsuspecting policemen standing in the forecourt before running into the police station. Inside the station, on the first floor, the armed robbers gunned down the policemen guarding the holding cells and released all fifteen of their comrades awaiting court trial. Some brave policemen came down from the second and third floors of the building to resist, but were quickly cut down by submachine gunfire. Without further resistance, the armed raiders and their freed comrades escaped, leaving behind the bodies of thirteen policemen strewn across the forecourt and ground floor of the police station. A hunt for the criminals was still underway, but the daring savage attack had left all policemen in the building quite jumpy. So when the Onitsha city policemen heard the screeching tyres of Ngozi's car, they thought the daredevil robbers were back to deal more death and destruction. The police officers had boldly emerged from their station, knowing that their obsolete weapons were no match for the criminals' superior firepower, knowing the risk of their rusty bolt-action rifles jamming in mid-fire, and yet they were determined to make a last stand, to die fighting for their lives.

In a semi-circle formation, the policemen moved slowly towards the Peugeot 504 SR. Clearly visible to all were the stencilled words ENUGU STATE POLICE COMMAND on the side panels of the saloon car. But that did not dissuade the policemen—the armed robbers who raided their station, a week earlier, wore the standard-issue black police uniforms and came in a fake police pick-up truck. The only things not standard-issue were the Uzi submachine guns the criminals had brought with them.

The door on the driver's side of the Peugeot opened and Ngozi emerged. 'Hi guys, calm down. I'm Detective-Sergeant Ngozi Oduche, Enugu CID,' she smiled, holding up a plastic ID card to the nervous cops. The policemen squinted at the card for a few seconds and then heaved a collective sigh of relief and lowered their guns.

'Sorry ma'am …eh, our station was attacked by armed robbers a week ago,' one policeman explained. The stripes on his faded police uniform indicated the rank of a corporal.

'I can see that,' Ngozi replied, staring at the pockmarked facade of the police station where the armed robbers had discharged fifty rounds of ammunition during the early stages of their raid. DI Ikenna Kodilinye emerged from the car.

He glanced at the bullet holes on the walls, and then at the obsolete guns the policemen were carrying. He felt sorry for them.

The era of military dictatorships in the country brought the Nigeria Police Force to a sorry pass. Fearing that the police could stage a coup d'etat against them, successive federal military governments, over the decades, had systematically damaged the police force, denying it badly needed funding, stripping it of all its modern equipment and leaving them with obsolete ones. As implausible as it might have seemed, the paranoid military dictators believed that modern police equipment such as anti-riot water cannon tanks could be converted to fire artillery shells if the police force ever decided to topple their regimes. Police were also denied helicopters and tactical armoured personnel carriers for the same reasons. Senior policemen who complained loudly about the deprivation of modern equipment were quickly sacked, causing the rest of the top brass to be cowed into silence. Under their silent watch, the Nigeria Police Force declined precipitously.

Lagos State Criminal Investigation Division was luckier than its counterparts in other parts of the country. Successive Zonal Assistant Inspector-Generals had successfully lobbied for some modern police equipment to contain runaway crime in Lagos city, the country's largest metropolitan area with more residents than the combined population of several African countries. The federal military regime had grudgingly furnished Lagos State Police Command with some of the necessary crime-fighting gadgets. Because of that, Lagos State CID was one of a few state criminal investigation divisions in the country that had relatively modern police tools at their disposal, albeit still inadequate.

After apologising for their behaviour, the Onitsha city policemen led Ngozi and Ikenna into the foyer of the Central Police Station (CPS). Inside, a pot-bellied desk sergeant welcomed them with a salute and took them upstairs to meet Assistant Commissioner of Police (ACP) Musa Abdul— a lean, dark-skinned Hausa man from Northern Nigeria— who enforced the law throughout the commercial city in his capacity as the Onitsha Area Commander.

'Come in,' Musa said, gesturing to the figures standing in the doorway of his office. 'Have a seat, please,' the Area Commander added with a strong Hausa accent.

The detectives walked in and sat down opposite the Hausa man. Ikenna stared at the dark-skinned oblong face with tribal marks running down both cheeks, and guessed that Hausa man was in his early forties.

'Detective-Inspector Koliene, you are highly welcome,' Musa smiled, revealing his nicotine-stained teeth.

'Thank you. It's Kodilinye, sir,' the Lagos detective corrected in a polite tone. Musa nodded, his smile remained unfaltering. His eyes shifted inquisitively to the policewoman.

'Sir, I am DS Ngozi Oduche from Enugu CID.'

Musa Abdul nodded again in acknowledgement and returned his gaze to Ikenna. Like some conservative Northern Muslims, he was not a great fan of women getting involved in the business of law enforcement. Throughout his police career in various northwestern states of Nigeria, he had never had to deal with a female police officer. He only began to encounter policewomen when he was posted to the southern states.

To his profound distaste, he had worked alongside a few female coppers while at Ondo State Police Command. As if that was not enough, he was obliged to do a stint in the neighbouring Ogun State Police Command where he had to report to a female boss—an experience that nearly drove him insane and made him curse police top brass for promoting women to the upper echelons of the Force. After that sordid experience in Ondo State, Musa Abdul requested a transfer to Katsina State Police Command in northwest Nigeria. He had worked previously in various parts of Katsina State, but particularly loved Katsina city—the state capital—for its serenity and dry weather. Moreover, there were no female police officers there to bother him.

His hopes of returning to Northwest Nigeria were dashed when the authorities rejected his request and sent him further south to Anambra State Police Command. Initially, he was not happy with his posting to Onitsha. But, over time, he grew fond of the commercial city and the conterminous Onitsha Area Command, which he administered. He admired the bravery of the policemen serving under him. These were underpaid men who were trying their best to solve crimes without the necessary equipment needed for modern policing. While there were certainly many policewomen in Anambra State Police Command, ACP Musa Abdul did not have to contend with any of them for long. Through a variety of cunning schemes, he rid himself of all female officers who were in place at the time of his arrival in Onitsha Central Police Station, and then made sure no further female officers would ever be posted to the wider Onitsha Area Command under his jurisdiction.

Seeing DS Ngozi Oduche seating across his table, wanting to participate in the "masculine business" of crime detection, was rankling to him, but he could do nothing about it. She was from a different State Police Command. More importantly, he could never display overt hostility to her or any female police officer of similar rank or higher because it could cost him his post as Area Commander if a discrimination complaint was filed against him. He had successfully fought a few of such complaints in the past, but he knew that he was not a cat with nine lives. There was no guarantee that he would survive yet another sex discrimination complaint, especially now that the police top brass in Abuja were increasingly becoming sensitive to allegations of human right violations within and outside the Force.

After a few seconds of contemplation, while half-listening to Ikenna, the Onitsha Area Commander decided to play it safe—no harsh words will come from his lips, but he will certainly cut *that woman* from the conversation by ignoring her input. 'Sorry about the pronounciation…Kodilinye,' he apologised, putting on his spectacles.

Ikenna chuckled and told him that many non-Igbos have gotten the pronunciation wrong on their first attempt. The Hausa man nodded and reached for a dog-eared manilla folder lying on the desk. He opened it in front of him and squinted at the words written on the attached paperwork.

'At three-thirty in the afternoon, five days ago, some local fishermen stumbled upon a detached bumper from a Mercedes Benz. They alerted the Marine Police Division in the area, which is next to the Onitsha Main Market.'

ACP Musa Abdul was referring to the vast open-air market set on the east bank of the River Niger, which was famous for being West Africa's largest marketplace in terms of geographical size and volume of traded goods and services.

'I called up our divers and they found the complete car at the bottom of the river. We pulled the vehicle out. I personally checked its interior once it was brought onto land. I found cufflinks and a wallet containing some items'— the Hausa man paused and handed Ikenna a sheet of paper before resuming his narration—'as listed in the sheet, inside the wallet, we found one thousand naira, a ten-dollar bill, a credit card in Mister Steinberg's name, and the picture of a white woman. We faxed the picture to Enugu State Police Command and the US Embassy. The embassy identified the woman as the former wife of the missing man. Or shall I say, deceased man? I'm assuming he is dead since Enugu Police have spent months searching without success.'

Ngozi cleared her throat and Musa paused and glanced at her quizzically. 'With all due respect sir, it is still an ongoing missing person's investigation at Enugu CID,' she began. 'For all we know, the American may still be alive and is being held against his will for the past two months.'

Without looking in her direction, the Onitsha Area Commander smiled thinly and continued his narration. 'The wallet was in the back seat of the car. Most likely, Mister Steinberg was chauffeur-driven. My men turned the car inside out. They checked the glove compartment. Nothing turned up. Not surprising for smart criminals, but then they forgot to dispose of the wallet and cufflinks.' Musa paused to allow his male visitor to respond, but Ngozi spoke instead.

'Sir, the detective and I would like to see the car,' she requested. The Hausa man glared at her and turned back to Ikenna.

'Yes sir, we will like to see the Mercedes,' Ikenna concurred, wondering why the policeman was hostile to Ngozi.

Musa responded by pressing a button under his desk. Moments later, the door swung open. The pot-bellied desk sergeant walked in and saluted the Area Commander. 'You sent for me, sir?'

'Yes, Sarge, Detective-Inspector Kodilinye and the woman want to see the car. Take them to our impound garage. If they want anything, give it to them...'

Musa Abdul dished out further instructions while the sergeant nodded repeatedly like a programmed android. After he was done with the instructions, Musa smiled at Ikenna, revealing the brownish-yellow teeth again. Then he rose to his feet, prompting Ngozi and Ikenna stand up as well. Musa shook hands with Ikenna and sat down again.

The pot-bellied sergeant ushered the detectives out of the office. Ngozi and Ikenna were expecting the sergeant to lead them back to the same staircase that they had used when they first arrived. Like the layout of several police stations across the country, they thought that ingress to and egress from the building was only in one direction. So they were surprised and intrigued when the sergeant led them in a different direction into a long narrow corridor illuminated by the bright lights of fluorescent tubes fixed to the ceiling.

As they walked through the eerily quiet narrow corridor, Ngozi and Ikenna began to observe open office doors, revealing empty rooms with walls and furniture riddled with bullet holes, shards of glass from broken windows littered the floors of those rooms, and there was dried blood splatter on the walls. More disturbing for the detectives were the large reddish-brown strains on every room floor—the dessicated remains of what were once pools of fresh blood.

As they walked further down the corridor, the trio came across a much larger room, which Ikenna and Ngozi guessed was a squad briefing room. Like the smaller offices, they had seen earlier, the squad room was equally wrecked—overturned tables; broken chairs; dried bloodstains on the floor; and walls with bullet holes and dried blood splatter. The image of the ruins reminded Ikenna of similar scenes at his school, the day after the invading Nigerian Army repeatedly shelled Enugu city back in October 1967.

The detectives paused when they heard voices inside the wrecked squad room. They walked towards the open entrance for a closer look. Inside the large room, amidst the ruins, three uniformed police constables were busy. One constable was adjusting a camera resting on a tripod stand in order to snap the crime scene. The others had yellow rolls of cordon tape to preserve the scene after the photographer had done his job.

'I hope you guys catch the bastards who did this,' Ngozi remarked as the trio walked past the ruined squad briefing room.

The sergeant, who was leading the way, halted and turned to face the detectives walking behind him. 'Thirteen lives were wasted,' he recounted bitterly. 'We will catch the criminals who perpetrated this great evil. It doesn't matter how long it takes. So far they live on planet earth, we will get them.'

Ikenna nodded sympathetically, but said nothing. He doubted Onitsha Area Command had the wherewithal to apprehend a bunch of heavily armed criminals who had already demonstrated their excellent organizational skills in the manner in which they successfully executed the jailbreak. *Besides, wasn't it a tad late to be photographing and combing a week-old crime scene for evidence?*

The sergeant turned around and continued leading the visiting cops down the narrow corridor. 'That Hausa man is a misogynist,' Ngozi remarked in Igbo language. Ikenna raised his eyebrows in alarm, his eyes darting furtively to the back of the sergeant walking ahead of them.

The pot-bellied policeman stopped and turned around. 'Sorry, I don't understand Igbo. I'm from Edo State.' The sergeant had assumed that Ngozi was talking to him.

Ikenna smiled, 'It's alright, Sarge. She was speaking to me.'

The police guide smiled back, embarrassed.

Ngozi Oduche was smiling too, but hers was mischevious. She knew that the sergeant wouldn't comprehend what she had just said. Earlier on, she had seen the name tag hanging from his breast pocket. It indicated that his name was Alexander Osaze Idemudia, which meant that he belonged to the Bini ethnic nationality of Edo State.

There was a staircase at the end of the narrow corridor. Alexander, Ngozi and Ikenna descended it and soon found themselves outdoors in the backyard of the Onitsha Central Police Station. There was another car park there, but much smaller than the one situated in front of the police station. Alexander led them to a black Peugeot 505 GR estate car.

'The police impound garage is not far from here. A ten-minute drive and we will be there,' he explained, opening the car door on the driver's side. He got behind the steering wheel, leaned over to the side, and opened the front passenger door for Ngozi. Then he leaned backwards, reached for the rear passenger door behind him, and unlocked it.

When Ikenna heard the clicking sound of the latch, he promptly opened the door. He was about to board when he felt a dull sensation in the groin area. He informed the driver that he needed to pay a quick visit to the toilet.

At that moment, a black Peugeot 504 pickup truck wheeled in and pulled up behind the Peugeot 505 GR estate car. On each side of the pickup, a painted strip of the blue-yellow-green police tricolour ran horizontally from the front fender through the outer door panels to the rear fender. The words stencilled in white paint over the bonnet of the black pickup truck read:

ONITSHA AREA COMMAND
ANAMBRA STATE POLICE COMMAND
NIGERIA POLICE FORCE

Ikenna watched the pickup truck's door open and a dark-skinned hefty man dressed in the uniform of a police sergeant alighted. The hefty sergeant smiled and approached the estate car.

Alexander and the hefty man were exchanging banters when Ikenna interrupted them. The hefty man chuckled at Ikenna's request and said, 'sure sir, I will show you where the toilet is.'

The hefty sergeant led the Detective-Inspector back into the police station, up the stairs and into the narrow corridor. They walked past the wrecked squad briefing room, past the series of ruined offices, past the mahogany door of ACP Abdul's office, turned a corner, and then stopped. Pointing to a door tucked away in that corner, the hefty man said, 'there it is, sir. Should I wait for you, sir?'

'Not necessary. I know my way around, thank you.' Ikenna replied and rushed towards the knob of the toilet door.

But the hefty man did not leave. He stood outside the door, glancing intermittently at his watch, confident that Ikenna would finish his business inside the toilet and come out in no time. Four minutes in, the hefty man became a little bit worried and began pacing around. Surely, it did not take that long to urinate unless the Lagos detective was having prostrate problems, he thought. When, four minutes turned into seven minutes, the hefty man cursed under his breath and bit his lips. He hung around for a few more minutes, glanced at his watch again, and gave up on Ikenna. He ran down the staircase and then exited the police station. Back in the backyard, he walked briskly to the car park, smiling at the occupants of the Peugeot 505 GR estate car.

'Benji, where is the detective?' Alexander asked.

The hefty man—Benji—smiled. 'He is still in the toilet. I'm guessing he didn't go there just to urinate. Maybe he is taking a dump as well.'

Alexander and Ngozi laughed.

'Okay, guys, I'm leaving now. See ya later,' Benji said and began to walk away from the estate car. He did not return to the Peugeot 504 pickup truck that he had arrived in earlier. Instead, he scurried across the car park to an isolated brown Mazda 626 Capella sedan parked under a mango tree, several yards away.

Ngozi thought it odd that the unmarked saloon car was parked so far away when there was plenty of space in the car park. But there was nothing unusual about Benji parking his personal Mazda under the mango tree. He had been doing it for years, and every policeman who worked at the central police station had accepted it as one of his many idiosyncrasies.

A few years back, when ACP Musa Abdul was still new to the job as Onitsha Area Commander, he had asked Benji why he parked his personal car far from the car park. The answer that Musa got from the hefty sergeant had sounded quite reasonable.

Benji had offered two explanations— the car park was directly exposed to sunlight, which meant that the interior of the car got hot quickly in the searing afternoon heat. Parking his car under the shade of the mango tree kept the interior of the car from getting hot. Secondly, the tree faced the gates, making it easier and faster for him to drive in and out of the police station.

From his distant position under the tree, Benji waved at Alexander and Ngozi before he slid behind the steering wheel of the Mazda. He turned the key in the ignition and the car engine roared to life. He shifted the gear lever and relieved the clutch pedal; the Mazda wheeled out of the premises. Outside the gates, he waited patiently for an approaching car to zoom past before swinging his car into the main road. Seconds later, the Mazda was hurtling along Court Road. It sped past the Onitsha Magistrate Court, past the police barracks, past a series of small retail shops and vehicle repair garages, only decelerating when it reached a portion of the road strewn with potholes. Benji shifted the gear lever and began to manoeuvre the car slowly around the potholes on the tarmac.

Back in the car park, inside the Peugeot 505 GR estate car, Ngozi was beginning to worry about Ikenna. Was he suffering from diarrhoea? What was delaying him? she wondered. Sergeant Alexander Idemudia did not seem perturbed by the delay. He was busy solving crossword puzzles on a folded copy of *The Vanguard* propped against the steering wheel.

Ngozi tapped him lightly in the shoulder. 'Sarge, please go and check on Detective-Inspector Kodilinye. Maybe he is stuck in the toilet.'

Alexander laughed heartily and put away the folded newspaper. Just as he was about to open the door, the Peugeot 504 pickup, parked behind his estate car, exploded. The blast wave shook the ground, crushed a dozen cars in the car park, sent hot shrapnel flying in all directions, and shattered all the windows in the central police station. The pickup was completely obliterated and in its place was a gigantic crater, large enough to swallow a small car.

Back in the police station, Ikenna regained consciousness on the toilet floor, covered in a mixture of water, concrete debris, and small pieces of glass. He sat up dazed, confused and wondering what had happened. As the clouds of confusion receded from his mind, he began to recall the previous moments before hell broke loose. He recalled being relieved that his fifteen-minute marathon atop the toilet bowl were finally over. Urination had been easy. Defecation over the objections of his constipated bowels had been a herculean task. He recalled standing over the sink, rubbing liquid soap between the palms of his hands under the running water tap. He remembered the floor below his feet shaking and the deafening explosion that slammed him against the toilet door. Then total blackout.

While still seated on the floor, Ikenna quickly surveyed his surroundings. The blast had caused small pieces of concrete debris and broken glass to rain down from damaged walls and shattered windows. He checked himself for any signs of injury before wiping moist debris and pieces of broken glass from his clothes and body. Rising to his feet, the first thought that came to his mind was that the police station had suffered an accidental gas explosion. Somebody, probably a junior officer, had stowed a cylinder of liquefied petroleum gas inside the building. The sort used in the kitchens of roadside eateries run by the wives of police constables.

Ikenna opened the toilet door and ran into a tumultuous multitude of policemen and civilians stampeding out of the three-storey building through the still brightly lit narrow corridor—the fluorescent tubes had survived the blast wave.

Outside, in the spacious backyard of the police station, a group of shabbily dressed police officers were pushing back a large crowd of civilian onlookers and attempting to cordon off the devastated car park with a yellow barrier tape. Some in the crowd were pedestrians passing by the station when the explosion rang out; some were people living in nearby houses; and the rest were curious motorists who had abandoned their cars in the middle of the road to see for themselves the horrific scenes in the police station.

Once he was out of the building, Ikenna realized what had actually happened. It wasn't an accidental gas explosion— the car park had borne the brunt of the powerful blast while the station itself suffered only minor damage. Surveying the devastated landscape strewn with twisted metal, broken glass, human body parts and a cavernous crater, Ikenna felt shock that he had not experienced since he was a boy growing up in a time of war. He walked briskly to the group of policemen instructing the teeming crowd to stand back from the yellow barrier tape in front of them. He flashed his plastic ID card. The policemen promptly saluted and lifted a section of the stretched yellow barrier tape encompassing the wrecked car park. Ikenna ducked underneath the tape, crossing the police cordon.

On his way to the centre of the bomb explosion, Ikenna meandered around a plethora of obstacles—piles of damaged vehicle carcasses, chunks of twisted metal, shards of glass, pieces of broken plastic and a severed human foot. When he reached the centre of the blast, he walked carefully around the circumference of the cavernous crater, side-stepped more broken glass and chunks of twisted vehicle chassis, before finally joining a small group of policemen standing beside the wrecked Peugeot 505 GR estate car.

Ikenna observed the scene. The roof of the estate car was caved in and its sides knocked inwards. The windscreen, the rear window, and all four side windows were destroyed in the explosion. The bonnet was missing and the boot was a crushed metallic mess. The stunned policemen made way for Ikenna to move closer to the wreckage. On the driver's seat was a bloodied corpse slumped, face down, over the steering wheel. Ikenna recognized corpse as Sergeant Alexander Idemudia. The Detective-Inspector edged even closer to the grisly scene. The back of Alexander's head was open, oozing a mixture of blood, cerebro-spinal fluid and brain matter. Then he suddenly remembered the policewoman who had driven him to Onitsha. In his shock, he had forgotten all about her. His gaze shifted fearfully from the dead driver to the bloodied figure in the front passenger seat. He scrambled over to the ruined front passenger door.

Ngozi's face was a mask of blood with shards of glass sticking out of her head, arms and torso. She was leaning back on her seat. The newspaper she had picked up, just before the blast, was still in her right hand, soaked in her blood.

Ikenna grabbed the twisted passenger door separating him from her. He tugged at the door, and to his surprise, it came away completely, without any resistance. He heaved the detached car door to the ground and quickly felt Ngozi's neck for a pulse. There was really no need because she was breathing, though it was laboured. He reached inside the car, lifted the comatose policewoman out of the destroyed car and laid her gingerly onto the grass. He glared at the stunned police constables standing a few inches behind him. 'Don't just stand here! Go and get an ambulance!'

The policemen unfroze and scrambled for their walkie-talkies.

ACP Musa Abdul emerged from the police station, carrying a revolver in his right hand. When he first heard the blast, he thought that the same armed robbers, who had attacked his police station seven days earlier, were back. The sight of twisted metal and debris everywhere quickly disabused his mind. Local criminals, even those with excellent guns, wouldn't have access to military-grade explosives, he thought. In Musa's reckoning, the bomb attack was the work of an individual—perhaps, a rogue soldier— with access to the armoury of the Nigerian Army. What he could not figure out was a motive. *Why would such an individual attack his station with a bomb?*

Upon reaching the epicentre of the blast, Musa got emotional when he saw his men pulling the bloodied remains of Sergeant Alexander Idemudia out of the wreckage of the estate car. Twenty-three minutes earlier, that corpse was a living man, a loyal subordinate, taking orders from him.

Next to the wrecked Peugeot 505 GR estate car, Ikenna was crouching next to another bloodied figure lying on a patch of carpet grass. Musa Abdul recognized the comatose figure as the policewoman from Enugu State Police Command. A policewoman whose name he could not recall.

'How is she?' he asked, stooping down beside Ikenna. The detective did not respond. He was busy propping up Ngozi's head with his arms. Musa extended his arm and touched Ngozi's neck with his fingertips for a few seconds, and then retracted it. The woman was still alive, but she was dying, he thought as he quickly rose to his feet.

He turned around and barked orders at a group of constables inspecting debris from the blast. He asked for his staff car. The group informed him that the car was two streets away being serviced by auto-mechanics. He snatched a walkie-talkie from the nearest constable and radioed his orderly, Shehu Shinkafi—a fellow Hausa man— who was overseeing the repair of the Peugeot 504 SR sedan in the auto-mechanic garage.

Owing to the long distance between the police station and the auto-mechanic garage, the signal reception of the walkie-talkie was poor. Musa Abdul struggled to hear the faint voice of his police orderly over the static noise. Nevertheless, he managed to hear Corporal Shehu Shinkafi say that the servicing of the staff car was nearly done, that the auto-mechanics needed fifteen minutes more to finish the wheel balancing. ACP Musa Abdul yelled into the walkie-talkie. 'I don't care! If you don't bring that car back now, you will be in trouble!'

Five minutes later, the staff car appeared— with slightly wobbly wheels— and pulled up at the kerb across the police station. Musa motioned to two police constables. They bent over and scooped up the critically injured policewoman. They carried her across the road, leaving a trail of blood dripping behind them. Following far behind, ACP Musa Abdul ducked below the yellow barrier tape, squeezing through the teeming crowd of onlookers, which had grown in size to include several local news reporters bearing television cameras, still image cameras, portable audio cassette recorders and microphones.

Upon sighting the Area Commander, the journalists began to approach, shouting questions at him. Musa ignored their queries and violently pushed aside those standing in his way. When he saw Ikenna struggling to squeeze through the crowd, he yelled at the onlookers to give way to the detective, warning that those who failed to heed his order would be arrested for obstructing police work. 'I am the police chief around here! I have the authority to act on my threat!' he exclaimed and the noisy crowd began to disperse slowly.

Ikenna walked through the dissipating crowd and then crossed the road to join the constables struggling to place Ngozi inside the staff car.

Musa ordered the policemen standing in front of the yellow barrier tape to close the stretch of road facing the backyard of the station. He also ordered the expansion of the police cordon to keep the journalists and other onlookers at bay. Then he crossed the road and got into the front passenger seat of his staff car beside Corporal Shehu Shinkafi. The comatose policewoman was lying on the back seat with Ikenna squeezed between her feet and the rear passenger door.

Musa Abdul was surprised to see Ikenna sobbing quietly behind him. It was the first time he had ever seen a grown man cry over a woman. Under normal circumstances, he would have chided the Lagos CID detective for that *disgraceful attitude*, but he let it pass. After all, this was the South. The people down here did not share the Northern mentality, did not understand what stoicism and manliness was all about, he thought.

He turned back to the driver and spoke rapidly in Hausa language. Shehu nodded and started the engine of the iron-grey Peugeot 504 SR. Eight minutes later, the staff car pulled up on the driveway of Onitsha General Hospital. Three male hospital orderlies removed Ngozi from the sedan and placed her on a gurney, and then quickly propelled her into the Accidents & Emergencies Wing of the hospital. Ikenna, Musa and Shehu followed behind.

An hour later, a grim-faced doctor, dressed in a light green surgical gown, emerged from the operating theatre of the Accident & Emergencies and walked down the entire length of a long corridor, which brought him to the hospital reception area.

Ikenna, Musa and Shehu were sitting in a corner. Upon seeing the approaching surgeon, they sprang to their feet in anticipation.

The surgeon shook his head and announced the demise of Detective-Sergeant Miriam Ngozi Oduche. She was thirty-one years old at the time of her death.

CHAPTER 21

Nine hours after Ngozi died, the hefty policeman parked his Mazda 626 Capella sedan at the agreed rendezvous—a clearing in a forest very close to the Onitsha–Owerri expressway that connected Anambra and Imo States. He put on the courtesy lights inside the car and glanced at his watch. It was one o'clock in the morning, but it was still dark. He stared into the distance, observing the road ahead illuminated by moonlight. There was nothing on the dual carriage road—not surprising for that hour of the day. He switched off the interior courtesy lights and switched on the headlamps instead. Then he got out of the car and sat on the bonnet, waiting impatiently for his business associate to show up with the rest of the promised money.

The extraordinary sequence of events that would ultimately lead the hefty policeman to plant a TNT-laden pickup truck in the backyard of his own police station began twenty-four hours before the bombing. It all kicked off when he concluded a busy work shift that fateful night and left the station to go home. He was at the bus stop waiting for the night bus when a Volkswagen Santana sedan suddenly pulled up in front of him. Its unfamiliar driver had offered him a lift home, which he quickly accepted.

Once the car started moving, the driver turned on the interior lights and introduced himself as Mr. Chinedu.

The hefty policeman said his name was Sergeant Bernard Akpovorie, but everybody down at Onitsha Central Police Station referred to him as "Benji".

Mr. Chinedu laughed and told the cop that he once owned a dog that answered to that nickname. Besides, wouldn't the nickname be more befitting of a person named Benjamin?

Bernard felt offended by the remark, but he smiled politely and told the motorist that he liked the nickname. A brief silence elapsed before the conversation shifted to other mundane issues. The driver mentioned the poor state of certain roads and the inefficiency of public transportation services in Anambra State.

The police sergeant told him of the daily frustration of waiting for public buses that were never on time and how that frustration had forced him to buy his first personal car, five years earlier.

Mr. Chinedu then asked the cop what he was doing at the bus stop if he already had a car. The policeman explained that his Mazda was in the capable hands of his auto-mechanic and would be ready for collection the following day.

'Good for you,' Mr. Chinedu had replied, 'you wouldn't have to wait at bus stops any longer.'

The cop nodded in agreement. Then Mr. Chinedu changed the topic. He asked his sole passenger if he would be interested in doing a "small job" worth a hundred thousand naira. The policeman turned to Chinedu with an alarmed look on his face. The money on offer was ten times his monthly police salary.

'It is chump change to me,' Mr. Chinedu boasted, dropping onto the policeman's lap the five bundles of crisp naira notes he had just retrieved from the car's armrest storage box. 'What I have given you is twenty-five thousand naira, cash advance. If you do what I want, then you will get the remaining seventy-five thousand naira.'

Bernard smiled giddily at the neatly stacked cash bundles and told the driver that he was interested. Mr. Chinedu then stopped the Volkswagen Santana, alighted, and led the policeman by torchlight to the boot of the car where he showed him three rectangular metal boxes, each the size of a six-bottle-wine case, each with a plastic keypad attached. He showed Bernard how to use the keypads to activate and program the timing device for the TNT bombs concealed within each sealed metal box.

Back inside the car, the policeman began to show signs of dithering. Mr. Chinedu noticed this and responded by dropping another cash bundle worth ₦5000, promising to give his passenger the remaining ₦70,000 upon completion of the job. The policeman accepted the offer without further hesitation. For the rest of the journey to Benji's home that night, Mr. Chinedu carefully instructed the policeman on how to position the bomb for maximum effect and a shared a picture of the individual targeted for assasination.

The next morning, Benji came to work as usual in his refurbished Mazda. He parked it under the mango tree in the backyard of the police station and borrowed an official police pickup truck from the nearby car park, and then drove to Onitsha High Court.

In the presence of a phlegmatic judge in black robes and a long cream wig, he spent an hour testifying, showing evidence, and getting cross-examined at the trial of three ransom kidnappers that he had helped apprehend a month earlier. When he was finished with the court, he drove back to his house.

From his garage, he transferred all three metal boxes laden with TNT to the bed of the pickup truck. After that, he covered the bed and its contents with a tarpaulin stretched tight over the top railing and finally fixed in position with clips on the side panels of the truck.

Arriving back at the police station, he pulled up at the main car park tucked into the left corner of the forecourt. Ngozi's Peugeot 504 SR was packed there. Just as Mr. Chinedu had said, the saloon car had markings on both sides indicating that it was a property of the Enugu State Police Command. But the car was unexpectedly empty.

Where were they? he wondered as a feeling of panic washed over him. Moments later, he got his answer. A passing policeman informed him that Ngozi and Ikenna were at the other car park at the back of the police station. The visiting detectives were about to leave in another vehicle, an estate car, for the police impound garage. The hefty cop would have to hurry over to the rear of the station if he wanted to catch up with them.

After thanking the passing policeman, Benji quickly executed a U-turn in the forecourt and drove out of the premises of the station. He stopped at a secluded spot on the side of the main road and alighted. He went round to the rear of the pickup truck and released the clips holding the tarpaulin in place. He scanned the road ahead to see if any motorist or pedestrian were approaching. Satisfied that no one else was within sight, he quickly unrolled the tarpaulin. With the tips of his finger, he tapped buttons on the keypad fixed to each metal box. By the time he was done, the timing device for each of the three bombs had been activated.

After restoring the tarpaulin cover to its previous position, he hurried back to the driver's seat. He drove through the remaining length of the asphalted main road before making a right turn into the adjoining street. He trundled slowly along the bumpy laterite road until he reached the open gates leading to the backyard of the central police station.

When he pulled up behind the black Peugeot 505 GR estate car, he was relieved to see the prime target—Ikenna Kodilinye—standing beside it. However, he was not happy to see his colleague, Sergeant Alexander Idemudia, sitting behind the steering wheel of the doomed car. As he bantered with the colleague his bombs were going to tear apart, Benji felt a sudden twinge of guilt and self-loathing. He had always liked the jovial, pot-bellied desk sergeant, not only because they were both from Midwestern Nigeria—albeit of different ethnicities—but because the man was a decent policeman who had done nothing to deserve a horrific death.

Just when he thought things couldn't get any worse, Ikenna suddenly requested the use of a toilet. Benji found himself leading the prime target of the bomb attack away from his appointment with death. Later on, as Ikenna battled constipation atop the toilet bowl, Benji stood outside the toilet door, vacillating on whether to return to the pickup truck and reset the time bombs. In the end, he decided not to tamper any further with the explosives. After all, it was not clear to him how long the detective was going to spend inside the toilet. Moreover, the idea of fiddling with bombs, already primed to explode, did not appeal to him.

Afterwards, as he sped away from the police station in his Mazda, he felt the pangs of guilt about what he had done to his own place of work. However, he was consoled by the fact that he was getting ₦100,000 out of that sordid business. It was worth it, he thought to himself as he manoeuvred the car around some potholes on the road. He was already two streets away when he felt the mild tremor generated by the exploding bombs.

He went into hiding immmediately for he knew it was only a matter of time before it became apparent to police investigators that he was the perpetrator. He did not plan to hang around in Onitsha or in any other part of the country for much longer. His plan was to meet Mr. Chinedu at the agreed rendezvous, collect the outstanding payment of ₦70,000 and flee the country through the Nigeria–Cameroon border within twenty-four hours...

*****

After waiting for a long time, with chirping bush crickets for company, Bernard "Benji" Akpovorie spotted a silhouette approaching from a distance under the glare of the moonlight. The approaching silhouette was too far away, beyond the luminous range of the bright headlamps of his Mazda. So Bernard had no way of telling whether the silhouette was friendly or not. He thought of going for the Smith & Wesson revolver in the Mazda's glove compartment, but decided against it. There was no need to overreact, he thought to himself. Within minutes, the silhouette came within the luminous range of the headlamps and transformed into the long awaited Mr. Chinedu.

Bernard felt a strange mixture of relief and anger. He was glad that his paymaster had arrived and yet furious that he was late. Jumping down from the bonnet of his Mazda, he glanced at his watch histrionically. It was 2.30AM. Mr. Chinedu was late by one hour and thirty minutes.

Benji began to rant in Pidgin English with a rapid-fire accent peculiar to ethnic Urhobos of Midwestern Nigeria. '*Nawa for you! Wetin dey keep you? Abi you know I dey cut out dis night! Abeg bring di money make I waka!*'

Mr. Chinedu said nothing. He crossed the empty expressway, walked silently into the forest, and stopped in the clearing about three feet from the Mazda. He reached into his trench coat and pulled out a Browning pistol.

The Urhobo man pulled back in horror. '*Ha! Igbo man, wetin be dis now? We agree say you go give me money. Now you dey pull gun.*'

'You don't get it. Do you?' Mr. Chinedu said, pointing the semi-automatic pistol at the policeman.

Bernard gazed at the stony face of his erstwhile criminal associate, then at the muzzle of the gun pointing menacingly at his head, and finally realized the gravity of the situation. Without further thinking, he swung around and made a run for it. But it was already too late. Three gunshots rang out in quick succession. Benji screamed and fell on top of the car bonnet.

Mr. Chinedu wrapped the smoking pistol in a white cloth and threw it into the back seat of the Mazda. He pulled Benji's bloodied corpse off the bonnet, dragged it further into the forest and left it concealed behind a screen of thick shrubs. Then, he pushed the Mazda away from the clearing and deeper into the bush. After that, he surveyed his surroundings to check if he had left anything behind at the crime scene. It was not necessary, as he had taken adequate precautions.

He had made sure to park his car very far away from the scene to avoid leaving tyre tracks that could be useful to the cops. He was not carrying any item on him to avert the risk of something falling out of his pockets. He wore leather gloves to ensure that no trace of his fingerprints could be found on anything he had touched. His shoes were marked for destruction as soon as it was convenient.

Afterwards, as he embarked on his seven-hour road journey back to Lagos, Mr. Chinedu congratulated himself on a job well done. Everything had gone according to plan. Two hours before he arrived at the moonlit rendezvous to meet

Bernard, he had been in his hotel room in Awka town— the capital of Anambra State—watching the local TV news report. On television, a female reporter at the scene of the bomb blast said that two police officers—a man and a woman— in a Peugeot 505 GR estate car had been killed in the explosion. The female reporter did not identify any of the dead police officers by name. But Moses Adrika alias "Mr. Chinedu" had no doubt in his mind that the deceased cops were Detective-Inspector Ikenna Kodilinye and Detective-Sergeant Ngozi Oduche.

CHAPTER 22

OCTOBER 1993

TEL AVIV, STATE OF ISRAEL

Inside the cafeteria of Tel Aviv University, a history professor was sitting quietly by the window, reading his copy of *Ha'aretz* newspaper and sipping tea. After draining the last contents of the teacup, the professor rose from his table. He pushed the folded newspaper into his brown leather satchel and buckled it. Five minutes later, he was walking down a well-lit corridor lined with doors.

He stopped in front of a door with a nameplate reading: PROF. GREGORY BERNSTEIN. He was about to fumble in his trouser pockets for the keys when he suddenly recalled something. He dipped his hands into the right-hand flap pocket of his tweed jacket and fished out a small diary. He adjusted his spectacles and flipped through the pages of the journal until he arrived at the entry for 12th October 1993, a date in the future. He studied it and frowned. He nearly forgot— in seventy-two hours, he was due to give a talk to the student wing of the Israel-Palestine Friendship Organisation (IPFO). He was a patron of the leftwing activist organisation committed to a fair and peaceful resolution of the most fissile conflict in the Middle East, which has its roots in the formation of the State of Israel in 1948.

The 53-year-old grey-haired historian had no illusions that his old friends from the Shin Bet, the Israeli domestic intelligence agency, would be attending the talk alongside two hundred Arab and Jewish student members of the IPFO. It wouldn't be the first time his events have been attended by *Shabak* officers displeased with his fiery activism and his forays into the "disputed" territories to fraternize with "Arab radicals".

After several warnings to curb his "extracurricular" activities were ignored, the agency tried and failed to get his tenure at the university revoked. To the chagrin of the Shin Bet, the frequency of his forays into the "disputed" territories dramatically increased. After one quick visit to the West Bank to express his solidarity with the "radicals" of Hebron University resisting the presence of *Tzahal* on their premises, *Shabak* officers conducted a search of his house and office. Finding nothing incriminating there, the Shin Bet had no choice than to withdraw all threats of bringing him up on charges of "aiding and abetting terrorists".

Despite that setback, the agency never gave up on its "mission" for it was blessed with resilient officers who believed that activist academics like Gregory could still be "persuaded" to change their ways for the "good of the country".

For Gregory, no amount of intimidation— subtle or plain— could sway him from his passion for a fair and peaceful settlement of the Levantine conflict.

Regardless of how the agency felt, he would keep talking about the Jewish State's treatment of Palestinians. The focus of the upcoming talk would be on Israel's control of aquifers in the Gaza Strip. He was going to argue that state expropriation of water for the benefit of Israeli citizens, at the expense of the Gazans, was an inhuman act. He also planned to attack the discriminatory policies of Israel towards its Arab minority citizens. He knew that the talk would spark outrage in large sections of the Israeli society, but he did not care. His views were already well known, and it had won him few friends inside the country.

He was not on speaking terms with his own parents, siblings and some members of his own university faculty. Most of his friends were Israeli-Arabs, Palestinian academics, leftwing Jewish academics and some socialist parliamentarians in the Knesset, as well as a galaxy of well-wishers from Europe and America who wanted a peaceful and just settlement of the conflict.

His involvement in peace activism began in 1963 when he was twenty-three years old. He had received a special deferment from *Tzahal* in 1960, which allowed him to attend university. Three years later, upon completing his studies, he refused to report to army camp, citing "conscientious reasons". As a result, he spent a year in the gaol for "desertion" before regaining his freedom. Shortly after release, his orthodox Jewish family disowned him. Rightwing newspapers denounced him as a "coward" and "traitor".

Undeterred, he returned to university for his postgraduate studies and took an active part in a small Arab-Jewish activist group that staged several demonstrations in the country to protest about the ill-treatment of Palestinians in the occupied territories. Jail soon became his second home as he was frequently confined for participating in peaceful demonstrations that often turned violent when rightwing activists were allowed to hold counter-protests close by. The police were always lenient with the rightwing rioters, but the peaceniks were beaten with batons before being hauled into dingy cells for the night. The boisterous street-level activism, the police baton charges and temporary arrests would last until he made the transition from student to academic life.

Early in his academic career, Gregory decided that his peace activism was better served giving speeches, writing books and newspaper articles, and visiting the occupied territories to highlight the plight of the Palestinians. Abandoning street protests did spare him the indignity of having to endure baton charges and spend time in police custody, but it did not spare him from the Shin Bet. In other words, his change in tactics merely caused the pattern of his mistreatment by the state to change form.

Professor Gregory Bernstein popped the small diary back into the flap pocket of his jacket and produced the keys to his office from his trousers. He unlocked the door and stepped into the cramped office overflowing with hardback textbooks, some of which he had authored himself. He quickly peeled off his jacket and draped it round his swivel chair. He quickly surveyed the room. Everything seemed to be in the order he had left them— the books and research papers were still on the shelves hanging from the wall above his head, the cork noticeboard still had the plethora of newspaper cuttings and other important notices stuck to it. Nothing appeared to have been moved in his absence. He tried not to be paranoid, but it wasn't easy. The Shin Bet had bugged him before. It will have no difficulty doing so again. He pulled the window blinds aside to let in daylight. He shrugged and murmured something about not having anything to hide. As soon as he settled on his chair, the phone stated ringing. He picked up the handset and spoke in Hebrew.

The voice at the other end of the phone line replied in the same language with a British accent. Gregory was surprised and excited to hear from his maternal cousin in London. Two years had elapsed since he spoke to any member of his family. The last time he did was when he rang his much younger sister to congratulate her on the birth of her third child. The phone conversation with his sibling had been so awkward, frigid and tense that he regretted making the call.

After the initial exchange of banter, Harel Suzmann told his cousin why he phoned. The Londoner wanted the Israeli history professor to investigate whether Robert Suzmann or any branch of the Suzmann family had immigrated to South Africa between 1939 and 1960.

Gregory asked his cousin why he needed the information. Harel told him that he was just curious. The historian did not believe his cousin, but agreed to help. He asked his British relative to call back in five hours' time. He placed the handset back on its cradle and rose from his desk. He knew where to obtain the information— the Beth Hatefutsoth Museum of The Jewish Diaspora.

The late Nahum Goldman, President and founder of the World Jewish Congress, first suggested the museum in the 1950s. The institution, which opened its doors in 1978, was located inside Tel Aviv University and maintained a huge electronic database containing the history of three thousand Jewish communities in the diaspora and their migration patterns.

Thirty minutes after he spoke to his cousin, Gregory was at a computer workstation inside the museum searching the electronic archives for immigration to South Africa, starting with Jews fleeing Nazi Germany in the 1930s to ones that moved there in the 1950s and 1960s for economic reasons. It took him an hour to get the information, which he printed off before logging out of the computer terminal.

Six hours later, the Briton called his cousin's office at Tel Aviv University again. Professor Gregory Bernstein confirmed that a part of the extended Suzmann family, originally from Hamburg, had indeed immigrated to South Africa following the end of the Second World War while the rest remained in Europe, electing to either go back to post-war Germany or stay in the UK.

Harel thanked his cousin effusively for the information and hung up when the inquisitive Israeli asked him again why he really needed information.

Gregory stared at the receiver emitting a dial tone for a while and shook his head. He placed the handset back on its cradle and turned his attention back to the blank sheet of paper and fountain pen on his desk. He still needed to write the keynote speech he was going to give at the Tenth Conference of the Israel-Palestine Friendship Organisation.

CHAPTER 23

OCTOBER 1993

HAMPSTEAD, NORTHWEST LONDON, UK

On the afternoon of 16th October 1993, Harel Suzmann was getting ready to contact Heintz & Sharmann, the South African law firm that had written him about the £25.5 million inheritance.

Seven days earlier, he had asked for help from his maternal cousin, the much-hated "black sheep" of the family, Professor Gregory Bernstein. The Israeli historian had not disappointed him. He had provided good information on the Suzmanns who had immigrated to South Africa. Nevertheless, Harel was not satisfied with verbal information read out over the phone. He wanted more details. So he called his Israeli cousin again and asked him to fax the printouts he had obtained from the museum in Tel Aviv University.

Professor Bernstein gladly obliged without bothering to ask any more probing questions. Even if he had asked, his cousin would not have told him anything.

Harel had no plans to share the Robert Suzmann inheritance with any family member. He wanted all the money for himself. With £25.5 million in his possession, the possibilities were endless. He could reinvigorate his failing business and expand into real estate development. He was certain his sudden comeback would surprise all those bastards who had written him off when most of his businesses collapsed years ago. His new success would prove to all and sundry that he was a true son of the late Hapel Suzmann.

Hapel, a diamond magnate from Hamburg, had all his businesses expropriated from him and only avoided death in a concentration camp by agreeing to cut and polish diamonds for the Nazis. Despite his best efforts, he could not save his pregnant wife. She perished in Buchenwald. After the war, Hapel, virtually penniless, had moved to London where he remarried and rebuilt his businesses from scratch. By the early 1960s, he was one of the richest men in Britain, and remained so until his death in 1990.

To his pleasant surprise, Harel got more than he had requested from his Tel Aviv-based cousin. The reams of paper that emerged from his fax machine contained far more information than was originally drawn from the Beth Hatefutsoth Museum. It also included photocopies of selected newspaper cuttings of South African dailies covering the period from 1960 to 1980. Professor Bernstein had spent some hours in the electronic archives of the university library to impress his maternal cousin— the only family member who had bothered to keep in touch, albeit tepidly.

From the faxed documents, Harel learnt that Robert Wolfgang Suzmann was born in 1932 to a man called Zeev Suzmann in the German city of Hamburg. With the aid of a diagrammatic illustration of the Suzmann family tree faxed over from Tel Aviv University, Harel learnt that Zeev was his father's younger half-brother—the illegitimate product of an adulterous affair in the late 1890s between Harel's grandfather and a female employee that worked in the family diamond polishing shop.

Harel was surprised that his father had gone to the grave without ever disclosing the existence of Zeev and his son, Robert. He pondered briefly over revelation and decided that it must have been too embarrassing for the devoutly Orthodox Hapel to admit that Yitzhak— Harel's grandfather —had an illegitimate child. Thinking about it, Harel recalled that his father barely spoke about Yitzhak. The only thing that Hapel had ever said about Yitzhak was that he was decent man who died in agony from stomach cancer in 1925. Harel, born in 1948, never saw any pictures of his grandfather. None had survived the destruction of many homes in Altona during the allied bombing of Hamburg in July 1943.

On his study desk, Harel set aside the sheet of paper containing the diagram of his family tree and concentrated on the pile of documents bearing some details of Robert's life up until 1980.

Robert was just 11 months-old when the Nazis came to power in Germany. Within two years of the Third Reich, his father, Zeev, began to suffer harassment at the hands of the *Hitlerjugend*. At first, the pro-Nazi teenagers spray-painted threats and anti-Semitic graffiti on storefront windows of his bookshop, which a defiant Zeev wiped clean as soon as the youths had gone. Then the harassment progressed to smashing the windows, which were quickly replaced. An arson attack followed, damaging books and other valuables worth thousands of Deutsche Marks. Zeev went out of business, but not for long. The Altona Orthodox Jewish community, including his estranged half-brother Hapel, raised the money for the restoration of the shop. On seeing the restored bookshop, the teenage boys of *Hitlerjugend* decided to ramp up the terror. Zeev's house was firebombed when he and his family were away. The next day, a stone smashed through the glass storefront of his bookshop. Attached to the stone was a folded piece of paper with a message informing the bookshop owner that next time the Molotov cocktails would not miss his family.

Zeev moved to a different house and continued to persevere in face of oppression until the militarized thugs of the *Sturmabteilung* initiated *Kristallnacht* on 9th November 1938. This time Zeev did not resist. He fled to Poland with his wife and six-year-old son, Robert. Less than a year later, on 7th September 1939, the family was on the run again because of the German occupation of Poland. He and his family entered the UK through France. In May 1940, the UK government began to round up German citizens resident in the country to detain them in internment camps under the suspicion that they might be used as spies. Being a German citizen, Zeev was also detained as an "enemy alien"— his Jewish origin notwithstanding.

In 1942, Zeev escaped from his detention camp and ended up hidden by sympathetic British Jews in the London district of East Finchley. He was later smuggled to Southern England. From there, he crossed the English Channel with his wife and son, and then began the long perilous journey from Nazi-occupied France to neutral Switzerland using various forged documents. Zeev and his family resettled in serene Geneva until the war ended.

In August 1946, the entire extended family of the Suzmanns met for the first time outside a synagogue in Hackney, East London. They shared what was left of the family assets before going their separate ways. Some members of the family opted to go back to post-war Hamburg and revive the family business. Hapel Suzmann, who was detained inside Nazi Germany throughout the war, decided to stay in London with his new spouse. There, he revived his old diamond business and thrived.

Zeev moved with his wife and fourteen-year-old Robert to the Union of South Africa. Settling in Cape Town, the hard-working German Jew opened a bookshop. It prospered well enough for Zeev to expand his enterprise to include a jewelry shop. His son, Robert, became a successful man in his own right. After acquiring a master's degree in Economics from the University of Witswaterstrand in 1960, the then twenty-eight-year-old Robert founded an investment company.

According to the faxed documents in Harel's hand, the company founded by Robert prospered despite the encumbrances of international sanctions placed on apartheid South Africa.

Beyond January 1979, Harel found that the faxed documents had no further information on Robert and his parents, save for a South African newspaper clipping from February 1980 announcing the death of the millionaire Zeev Suzmann at the ripe age of 84.

Harel wanted corroboration of the claims in the letter he had received from James Heintz (esq.). He wanted to know more about Robert Suzmann's investment in Volkstar Diamond Limited back in 1981. He did some quick research and got the contact details of the South African mining company.

The company spokesman in Pretoria answered Harel's phone call. When he heard what Harel was requesting, he laughed and told the Briton not to make any more prank calls and hung up.

At first, Harel was puzzled and then disgusted by the unprofessional behaviour of the company representative. All he had asked for was a simple confirmation that the late Robert had been a shareholder and investor in the company.

The Briton's anger soon gave way to a growing fear, a vague suspicion that some unseen person or group of people within Volkstar Diamond Limited were trying to block enquiries about Robert to ensure that the inheritance money never left the company's coffers. For obvious reasons, Harel was never going to tolerate such shenanigans. Nobody was going to keep him away from his just entitlement.

He dialled the Johannesburg telephone number printed on the letterhead of the letter he had received from James Heintz. An American-accented voice answered at the South African end of the phone line. Harel sat up in his chair and smiled. It was showtime.

'Hi, my name is Harel Suzmann,' he said calmly, though his heart was racing.

'Hello! Mister Suzmann. My name is Eli Sharmann. I am glad you got the letter sent by my colleague.' The voice was friendly, confident, and promising.

Harel relaxed a bit. 'So am I, Mister Sharmann. By the way, I have posted copies of my birth certificate and passport details as requested.'

Eli congratulated him for taking the first step in the long process to acquire his inheritance. Then Harel told him about the previous phone call to the diamond mining company and the spokeman's rude reaction to his query.

'Volkstar Diamond wants to keep all the money,' Eli replied curtly. 'The company have refused to discuss the possibility of awarding any money to anyone not listed in a written will. They do this in the full knowledge that our client had died intestate.'

'What are you going to do?' the Briton asked. There was momentary silence on the other end.

'Eli, are you still there?'

'Yes…sorry…we will have to drag them to the law courts if they continue stonewalling us.'

Finally, Harel asked about something that had intrigued him since the phone conversation started. 'You have an american accent. I don't mean to be rude. You are South African Jew, right?'

There was an ominous silence on the other end of the line. Harel began to regret asking the question as various thoughts whizzed through his mind. Was his unseen interlocutor offended? But why? Was it wise to raise doubts about the identity of somebody trying to help him gain money he never worked for?

Harel was about to blurt out an apology when Eli finally replied. 'Yes, I am South African, but I went to high school and university in the United States. Yes, you are right about the ethnicity part. I hope that isn't a problem for you.'

'No problem at all. On the contrary, it's all good.' Suzmann was elated. The storm had passed. It all made sense now. He was glad the law firm handling his claim to inheritance was Jewish-owned.

'What is the next step now that I have sent out the requested docs?' he asked, buoyed by the calmness of the American accented voice.

'As soon as your documents reach us, we will make a formal inheritance claim on your behalf.'

Harel wanted to know more. Eli Sharmann told him that his law firm would wait for the mining company's reaction to the claim. If the company agree to settle, Harel could get all the money within a few months. If the company refuses to play ball then legal action would commence.

'You said if all goes well, it will take some months. Well, how…'

'Yes, it will take a while to receive the money,' Eli interjected.

'How long?' Harel asked. There was a moment of silence on the line before the voice responded.

'It could take four months, a year or even longer, depending on whether the company decide to settle or fight a legal battle that they are likely to lose in the end.'

'You mean this could drag for years?' Harel asked with trepidation.

'Like I said before, it all depends on the route taken by the company. My own feeling is that the company would want to settle rather than go through a lengthy legal battle, which they would surely lose. You have nothing to worry about.'

'So, all I have to do is wait?'

'At the moment, the answer is "yes" .We are still in the early stages of this process. Be prepared for there is going to be a lot of paperwork, some might require your signature. We will keep you informed and up to date about everything. There is nothing to worry about.'

'You want me to come down to South Africa?' Harel asked, rubbed his chin with his left hand.

On the South African end of the phone line, Eli laughed enigmatically and said, 'well, you could do that, but it would add nothing of value. Best thing would be to let us handle this end of the transaction. A few weeks from now, a junior partner in our law firm will travel to The Netherlands to attend to some of our overseas clients. If there are any documents that need your signature, he will bring them to you in London. If there is any other thing we need from you, he will tell you.'

'What is the name of your go-between and when is he arriving?'

'About the exact timing, we cannot be certain, Mr. Suzmann. We still have a few travel plan issues to iron out over here. But, definitely, our man will be in Europe in a few weeks. We will let you know as soon as possible. We will be sending Matthew Molozi, our African junior partner, a very talented young man.' Eli paused to allow the Londoner take in the message.

Harel looked glumly at the plastic housing of the telephone on his desk. 'This is serious business. I will like to deal with a more experienced person in your firm,' he hissed into the mouthpiece of the handset.

'Our man, Matthew, may be young, but he is quite good. You have nothing to worry about, Mr. Suzmann,' replied Eli Sharmann, but his reassuring American-accented voice did not persuade the man on the other end.

'No, I really think you ought to send somebody else,' Harel insisted, his sweaty grip on the handset tightening. A thick moment of silence followed, leaving the Londoner wondering if he had gone too far. His fear of offending his South African interlocutor returned.

'Mr. Suzmann,' Eli began in a calm, but firm voice. 'Right from the founding of our law firm in nineteen-sixty-four, my father and Mister Heintz's uncle, the founding partners, have always articled Africans. It may not have won our law firm lots of friends, but we are proud of it. Our offer to help you with this inheritance claim will be withdrawn if you refuse to deal with our African partner.'

Harel's adrenaline shot up. He gasped and began to babble apologetically, claiming to have many black friends in London. The calm voice on the other end cut him short.

'Apology accepted, Mister Suzmann. Once we get your documents, we will get to work...by the way, when did you post them?'

'Two days ago.'

'Okay. We should get it in a week or slightly longer. Like I said before, once we receive those particulars, we will set the ball in motion. Mister Heintz or I will let you know when Mister Molozi is coming over. For most of his time in Europe, he will be our man on the ground feeding you with real-time updates on what is happening down here in Johannesburg as regards to this matter. If there is any paperwork for you, he will bring them to London and provide guidance on how fill them correctly in a manner that is legally compliant.'

'If you don't mind me asking, what is in it for you and Mister Heintz?' Harel asked.

There was momentary silence on the other end, which suggested that Mr. Eli Sharmann was trying to gather his thoughts together. When the American accented voice returned, it answered with care and measured words.

'Robert Suzmann was a friend and a great client. We feel honoured to be fighting for one of his relatives to inherit his fortune. So we will not charge for this transaction, but you may have to reimburse the law firm for costs accrued if we were to take legal action against Volkstar Diamond. Compared to the money you stand to inherit, these costs would be peanuts.'

Harel was surprised by the answer and yet pleased. Nevertheless, he said, 'I insist on you guys getting a cut.'

Eli laughed and replied, 'when the transaction is done, you can come down to South Africa and buy me and my partner a drink. Yes?'

'I will do that certainly.'

'Okay, Mister Suzmann, I will be in touch. Good bye.'

Seconds later, Harel put down the handset of the telephone. Visions of a new yacht and a new holiday beach house in the Caribbean flashed through his mind. The gush of mesmerizing optimism shooting through his body had overruled and pushed aside that part of him that once nursed reservations about the "too-good-to-be-true" scheme.

He quickly pulled out the bottom drawer of his study desk and reached for the bottle of Scotch. Things were beginning to look good for him. All things being equal, he reckoned, his financial troubles would be gone within a year or two. He drank to that prospect. Soon his idiotic ex-business associates who had written him off a long time ago would be back, begging him to invest in their enterprises. He could not wait to see the look on his ex-wife's face when she learned that he was back on the groove.

*****

In another continent, Africa to be precise, another man was happy too. Like Harel Suzmann in London, he was drinking to the success of the same transaction. His real name was John Nwosu, but as far as Harel was concerned, he was the American-educated, South African Jewish lawyer Eli Sharmann, one of two senior partners in Heintz & Sharmann. Seating in a Johannesburg café, he was confident that Harel would part with his money when asked. He had dealt with desperate men before. John could tell from the tone of the Briton's voice that he was so desperate for the inheritance scheme to be real that he had forgotten to use his brain properly.

As he poured another glass of beer, he could not help, but praise the brilliant, well-researched efforts of his genius, Tunde Olukemi. Without him, the latest operation would not have made it past the drawing board. Out of respect for Moses Adrika—who had discovered Harel Suzmann while reading the *Times of London* and proposed him as a potential target— John had ordered Tunde to take a back seat and let Moses lead in the development of a plan. John knew that Tunde preferred to work alone, but he still insisted that both men work together. He also pretended not to notice that Tunde resented his position as a mere assistant to a man whom he felt immensely superior to.

However, new events emerged and got in the way, forcing John to reassign Moses to a role where his talents could be best applied— the eradication of a growing danger called Ikenna Kodilinye. An overjoyed Tunde was then left to work alone on an operational plan for the Suzmann swindle. And he did not disappoint.

For three weeks, Tunde visited newspaper kiosks in Lagos almost daily, buying only British newspapers, which surprised the vendors who were used to seeing European and American expatriates—rather than Nigerians—buying their foreign dailies. At the end of the third week of poring through the pages of *Financial Times, Times of London, Daily Telegraph, The Sun* and *Daily Mail*, Tunde collected enough information about Harel Suzmann and his fractious marital and business life to develop a good plan to ensnare him in a scam.

As he set about planning the operation, he stumbled upon an article in a South African business newspaper about an entrepreneur called Robert Wolfgang Suzmann, who had died of a heart attack on 1st June 1993. The news article reported that the late entrepreneur had died while on the cusp of reaping the rewards of a risky investment he had made in 1981, one that many South African investors had shied away from at the time.

As he read the paper, Tunde took note of two remarkable coincidences. Robert had expired in a Johannesburg hospital whilst the swindlers were busy, in Lagos, shaking down the fertilizer magnate, Mahmoud Gamji. More importantly, the late South African businessman, a member of a wealthy family in Cape Town, also happened to share the same surname as Harel. The news article had made

204

passing reference to the deceased's German Jewish origins, which got Tunde interested in exploring the possibility that Robert and Harel were related.

When Tunde broached John with the proposal, the gang leader scoffed at the idea of pouring extra money on a wild goose chase. The possibility that both men were related was just too far-fetched to be taken seriously, the gang boss had thought.

'You cannot say people on different parts of the planet are related just because they happen to have the same surname,' John had argued. 'Suzmann, I think, is not an uncommon name. But good luck, if you still want to go ahead and do the research.'

In a grave voice, the gang leader issued a warning to his brilliant underling. 'I won't increase your budget. If you fritter away the money provided for this operation, you will have to pay out of your own pocket.'

Undeterred, Tunde plodded on. After reading one dusty volume of an old edition of the *Encyclopaedia Judaica* he had found in Lagos State Library, he hit upon an idea. He placed a phone call to Dr. Cain Sharak, Director of the Beth Hatefutsoth Museum of the Jewish Diaspora in Tel Aviv. When the director answered the phone, the fraudster claimed to be a research student interested in Jewish migratory patterns, especially immigrations to South Africa.

Dr. Sharak was pleasantly surprised that a Nigerian student was interested in that aspect of history. He asked a few probing questions and Tunde responded with well-rehearsed answers.

'Yes, I am studying the history of African Jews. I am researching Ethiopian Jews and German Jewish settlers in South Africa... but currently I need your help with a particular family that immigrated to South Africa after the Second World War.'

The director, anxious to help, asked for the name of the family he had in mind. Tunde told him. The director took his fax number and promised to fax all relevant information to Nigeria. A few hours later, the fax machine at ELAJ Enterprises in Mushin, Lagos, was buzzing and spitting out reams of printed papers. After the machine had gone silent, the nearby telephone rang and Dr. Cain Sharak told a grateful Tunde that if he ever wanted to come to Tel Aviv University for further research studies, he would be more than willing to help.

It took eleven days for Tunde to develop a plan based on information he had pieced together from documents faxed from Israel and reports from South African newspapers. The greatest boon to the plan was certain aspects of Robert's life history—the South African had been an only child, had never married, died intestate, and was indeed Harel's blood relative. The deceased had indeed invested heavily in large and medium-sized South African companies that specialized in coal, diamond and gold extraction, but none of them bore the name, Volkstar Diamond Limited. In fact, it would never have occurred to Robert to invest in a family-owned company like Volkstar Diamond for it was such a small player in the field of South African mining.

As he weaved into his grand plan the false narrative of a Robert heavily invested in Volkstar, Tunde never feared that Harel would uncover the truth because he understood the psychology of the gullible and the greedy. In Tunde's estimation, the prospect of gaining unearned millions of pounds would dazzle and distract the Briton from taking any serious steps towards due diligence— a common error of judgement among victims of fraud.

Six weeks after Moses first proposed Harel Suzmann as a target, Tunde presented a complete operational plan to the gang. It was the most ambitious plan that John Nwosu had ever seen. A radical departure from the gang's usual modus operandi, and more worryingly, at least for the gang leader, the plan required huge financial resources to be staked on a risky venture that had no absolute guarantee of success. And yet, despite his misgivings, his fear that Harel might be too smart to take the bait, John approved the plan because, above all, he trusted Tunde's judgement. After all, he had a history of feeling trepidatious when approving Tunde's high-risk strategies and elated when those plans yielded incredible successes.

Tunde's operational plan for the Harel Suzmann swindle was complicated. It required one gang member to be in South Africa and another to take up temporary residence in a European country close to the UK. Tunde had France, Belgium or The Netherlands down as options.

Eventually, John elected to go to South Africa where he was to use make good use of his American accent since he could not affect a convincing South African accent.

Eugene Igolo was to fly to Amsterdam on a multiple visa. There, he would play the role of "Matthew Molozi", a black South African lawyer of ethnic Ndebele origin.

From his hotel room in Johannesburg, John Nwosu invented Heintz & Sharmann, the imaginary law firm retained by the deceased Robert Suzmann. He designed the letterhead of the phantom law firm. Then he paid a local print shop to superimpose the letterhead on a large stack of blank office papers. Thereafter, he bought an old second-hand mechanical typewriter, which he subsequently used to type the letter that Harel received two weeks later by post...

*****

John finished his beer and started reading the *Mail & Guardian* that he had brought with him to the Johannesburg café. Under newspaper's banner headline was the front-page article about the negotiations between the African National Congress (ANC) and the apartheid government. The October 1993 negotiations, the newspaper reported, was tough and yet promising in its aspirations for the smooth transition of the apartheid state into a multiracial democracy.

John read that the F.W. de Klerk administration was stalling because it feared that a "one man and one vote" democracy would produce a black-dominated government that would repress the white minority. In spite of that, the newspaper praised President de Klerk's gradual removal of the pillars of segregation and state oppression.

A few more lines of the article read and John became bored. He had never bothered himself with politics unless it served his objectives. He folded the newspaper and rose to his feet. He looked around him and suddenly became aware of something. He was the only black person in the café teeming with white customers. That would have been inconceivable not that long ago. South Africa was indeed changing, he thought as he stepped out of the café and into the busy street.

CHAPTER 24

OCTOBER 1993

ONITSHA CITY, EASTERN NIGERIA

Assistant Commissioner of Police (ACP) Musa Abdul was not smiling. In fact, the Onitsha Area Commander was angry and frustrated at the inability of his men to uncover the mastermind of the bombing that resulted in the death of two police officers, the destruction of more than a dozen staff vehicles, and some damage to infrastructure on the premises of Onitsha Central Police Station.

His written request for funds to repair the ruined car park at the rear of the station and replace the ruined vehicles and the shattered windows inside his building was still weaving its way slowly through the Kafkaesque maze of bureaucratic red tape in the Office of the Anambra State Commissioner of Police.

The frustrated Area Commander glared at the uniformed Inspector briefing him on the little progress made in the investigation of the explosion. 'Mister Inspector, you haven't made much progress. So why are you here?' he asked in his trademark acerbic tone.

The Inspector standing before the Hausa man did not respond to the question. His hands trembled with the dog-eared file from which he had been reading. Musa glanced across the desk at those trembling hands, then reclined on his swivel chair, shaking his head slowly as he let out an audible sigh.

Eighteen days had passed since the bombing and the police investigators had still not traced the origin of the bomb and its maker. But they knew who carried out the bombing— Sergeant Bernard "Benji" Akpovorie. He was the suspect. It was the official police pickup truck that he borrowed that exploded minutes after he returned it to the car park. The investigators believed that Benji was just a hired gun. Nothing in his background suggested that he could have made or procured the military-grade bomb on his own. Someone else had put Benji up to that outrageous act and the investigators were ready to beat a confession out of him, if they had to. The only problem was finding and arresting Sergeant Akpovorie on one count of wanton destruction of police property and two counts of capital murder.

The manhunt for Benji began with a raid on his residence in Fegge Town, a rundown district in the southern part of Onitsha city. The suspected bomber was not at home. The police investigators ransacked the interior of concrete bungalow. Kitchen cupboards were yanked open; bookshelves emptied of its contents; desk drawers pulled out; sofas and mattresses overturned; and the garage run through with a fine-tooth comb. Forty-five minutes later, the disappointed investigators ended the search after failing to find anything of importance.

But key evidence, hidden ten feet above the floor, was missed because the eyes of the police investigators never shifted towards the ceiling. If the investigators had bothered to climb a ladder and poke at the square ceiling tiles above their heads, they would have discovered a loose tile. Uncovering that loose tile and shining a torchlight into the dark void between the ceiling and the roof would have led to the discovery of an oblong metal box containing an old colt revolver and bundles of naira notes, each strapped with a rubber band, all of which amounted to ₦ 30,000 cash.

Having failed to find Benji, the Anambra State Police Command asked their colleagues in neighbouring Delta State to be on the lookout for the suspected bomber in case he turned up in Warri, the oil-producing port city where he was born and raised.

Officers of the Delta State Police Command acted immediately. They raided Benji's family home in Warri, but the suspect was not there. His relatives claimed not have seen him in years. Despite the promise of a handsome reward, no member of the public came forward to claim that he or she had seen the suspect anywhere in Delta State.

Back in Anambra State, on the tenth day of the manhunt, three passers-by, walking along the hard shoulder of the Onitsha-Owerri expressway, perceived a pungent odour coming from behind the screen of shrubs that formed the verge of the road. The unpleasant smell had been hanging in the air for at least the five days, but no one had bothered to investigate. Motorists on the expressway simply zoomed past in their vehicles barely noticing anything was amiss. Pedestrians merely covered their nose and walked faster until they were too far ahead to perceive the foul odour. Most assumed it was the cadaverous stench of some poor animal knocked dead into the vast forest beyond the road verge. It happened all the time to small animals that chose the wrong moment to attempt to cross the expressway.

The three passers-by did not make the same assumptions. The overpowering nature of the stench convinced them that it was not a small wild creature that met its demise while scurrying across the expressway. It was something much bigger. The trio stepped off the hard shoulder, walking through the verge into the sloped footpath leading into the clearing of the forest.

Down there, they pushed through a screen of tall grasses and a concentrated waft of putrid smell nearly suffocated them. They reeled backwards in shock. They had expected to find the dead carcass of a large animal rotting away behind the shrubs not the badly decomposed body of an unidentified man half-eaten by vultures and infested by hundreds of maggots.

The trio promptly called the police from a public phone kiosk, a few miles away. When the desk sergeant on duty at Onitsha Central Police Station asked for their names, the passer-by speaking into the handset on behalf of the trio hung up immediately. They had done their civic duty and did not want to have any further interaction with the police. The last thing they wanted was to be accused, by the cops, of being responsible for the same homicide they had just reported.

Police chicanery always followed the same format—the good citizen, who had done his civic duty of reporting a crime, would be invited to the police station to make a witness statement. On getting there, the citizen is ambushed with accusations of being an accessory to the crime before detention in a holding cell until he or she is ready to pay a bribe to regain his or her freedom.

While the fears of the passers-by were understandable—given the pervasiveness of police corruption across the country— they really had nothing to fear from ACP Musa Abdul. The Onitsha Area Commander was many things, but corruption was not one of them. He simply wanted to apprehend everybody connected to the bombing of his police station.

An hour after the tip-off, uniformed Onitsha city policemen cordoned off portions of the expressway adjacent the forest. Several homicide detectives in plain clothes held their nose as they hovered over the rotting corpse swarming with a thousand buzzing blowflies. Identification of the corpse by visual examination was out of the question. Its face was missing, eaten by vultures. Nevertheless, the men were sure the putrefying body dressed in plain clothes was Sergeant Bernard "Benji" Akpovorie. They had discovered and recognized the brown Mazda 626 Capella hidden deep in the bush.

A detective, wearing green surgical gloves, swatted at the blowflies and reached into the deceased's trouser pockets. He fished out car keys and a wallet drenched in gooey cadaverine. He fought off the buzzing flies and wriggling maggots feeding on the foul-smelling yellowish slime covering the surface of the leather wallet as he extricated a plastic ID card with the logo of the Nigeria Police Force. The passport photo and full name on the ID card confirmed Benji as the deceased.

Upon identification of the corpse, the homicide detectives fanned out across the forest, combing the area around the crime scene for clues. The murder weapon, a Browning pistol, was recovered. It did not provide any useful leads for it was clear of trace evidence and fingerprints. Using graphite powder, the police team dusted the Mazda's interior for fingerprints. To the dismay of the detectives, several unusable smudged fingerprints were found inside the car. Moments later, one detective announced the discovery of three fingerprints in pristine condition, eliciting cheers from other detectives. Those were the first set of of useful evidence recovered by investigators still mourning the loss of the only suspect directly connected to the bombing.

Out of the three fingerprints, two were identified as belonging to the deceased policeman, which made sense as both were found on the steering wheel. Photographs of the remaining unidentified fingerprint— the one found on the interior surface of the Mazda's glove compartment— were sent to Enugu and Delta State Police Commands. Detectives in Enugu city had no suspects, but kept the fingerprint on file just in case. The filing soon turned out to be unnecessary as the owner of the fingerprint was identified the next day in a different part of the country.

Delta State police detectives travelled to Warri city and were able to match that fingerprint to Benji's 78-year-old mother who had visited her son in Onitsha three weeks before the bombing. For obvious reasons, nobody believed that the old woman—a retired fishmonger— was in any way involved in her son's crime.

*****

'Mister Inspector, why are you here, then?' Musa Abdul repeated, glowering at the uniformed Inspector of Police who remained silent and kept his eyes focussed on the terrazzo floor. Musa leaned forward in his chair and demanded for the case file. The Inspector quickly handed over the dog-eared manilla file and was relieved when Musa raised his hand to dismiss him.

When the office door snapped shut behind the uniformed Inspector, ACP Musa Abdul turned to the absent-minded cop in plain clothes sitting across the desk. It was obvious that the death of Miriam Ngozi Oduche had deeply affected DI Ikenna Kodilinye on an emotional level, and that surprised the Onitsha Area Commander.

It was sad that *the woman* had lost her life, but violent death comes with the job, Musa thought, recalling numerous cops who had sacrificed their lives in the line of duty. The Hausa man firmly believed that law enforcement work was the exclusive preserve of men. It was sad, but *the woman* should never have been in the Force in the first place. Her death was the will of Allah. Such was the fate of women who refused to confine themselves to their God-given roles of staying home and making babies.

When ACP Musa Abdul first arrived in Onitsha city, he was introduced to the policewoman that would act as his orderly. He reacted with disgust and rejected her offhand, telling the Deputy Commissioner of Police (DCP) — who was not just his superior, but also the third most senior officer in the Anambra State Police Command—that he wanted a male secretary. The easy-going DCP was taken aback by the rudeness of his subordinate, but he quickly acceded to the request. He knew better than to court trouble with Musa who was rumoured to have a powerful cousin higher up in the echelons of the Force, one who held the rank of a Deputy Inspector-General (DIG) in the Federal Investigation and Intelligence Bureau (FIIB).

The rumour had been a concoction, one of several cunning schemes Musa had devised to allow him choose his own staff, free of his superior's meddling. After consolidating his control over the Onitsha Area Command, Musa reassigned the only female detective in Onitsha CID to desk duties. She promptly put in for a transfer to the neighbouring Imo State Police Command, which was granted by the DCP. Musa was pleased to be rid of her entirely. Other police jurisdictions could have as many female CID detectives as they liked, but his would be the exception.

Over time, the remaining policewomen—thirty of them, all uniformed personnel—in the Onitsha Area Command were transferred, one by one, out of

211

Onitsha city to various towns and villages in Anambra State. By the third month of Musa Abdul's assumption of the role of Onitsha Area Commander, not a single policewoman was present anywhere in the city. That reality did not make the city any safer from crooks, but it pleased the police chief.

'Detective, I think you should have this,' ACP Musa Abdul said, holding out the dog-eared case file. 'As you can see so far, my boys haven't made much progress on this case.' Musa paused and waited for a reaction.

Ikenna Kodilinye accepted the proffered folder without saying a word.

'I am sorry that you did not find anything of value in our impound garage. Like I said earlier, before you and *the woman* arrived, my men and I went through the Mercedes with a fine-tooth comb,' the Onitsha Area Commander continued. 'There is nothing of value there in terms of evidence. The car had been in the river too long. For what it is worth, I think your American, Mister David Steinberg, is probably already dead and buried somewhere in Enugu. If my thinking is correct, then the resulting murder case should be the problem of police in Enugu not Lagos or Anambra.'

Ikenna nodded. He was seething with anger. The misogynist smiling at him was still being disrespectful to a brave detective who had laid down her life in the line of duty. For a fleeting moment, he fantasized about leaping across the desk and knocking out the Area Commander.

'Thank you sir,' Ikenna smiled back through gritted teeth as he placed the dog-eared case file inside his satchel.

'Oh, before I forget,' Musa began, pulling out the bottom drawer of his desk, 'you should have these as well.' The Area Commander handed over a cream-coloured plastic box resembling a small food storage container.

Ikenna opened the box and found a wallet; cufflinks; a thin stack of dried, water-damaged fifty-naira notes amounting to a thousand naira; a ten-dollar note; an American Express card; and the picture of a middle-aged white woman. They were all items recovered from the Mercedes Benz W140 shortly after it was winched out of River Niger.

'Thank you, sir,' Ikenna smiled to Musa. 'Like I said earlier, I have a suspicion that the bombing here may be connected to our fraud-cum-murder cases back in Lagos. Of course, it could be unrelated. I doubt it though. Most likely it is all connected.'

The Hausa cop stared glumly as the Lagos city detective spoke.

'While your men work the case from this end, I'll return to Lagos CID to continue my investigation from there. I want this to be a joint investigation between Onitsha and Ikeja.'

The Hausa cop nodded grimly and said nothing. It had been eighteen days since the bombing of the Onitsha Central Police Station, and eight days since Benji's corpse showed up inside a bush. Although upset that his men had failed to apprehend Benji alive, ACP Musa Abdul was relieved that Ikenna was finally returning to Lagos. With Ikenna gone, there was nothing stopping the Onitsha Area Commander from redirecting all his meagre police resources back into tackling local crimes while pretending to keep the bomb investigation open. The Hausa cop knew he would not be able to pull it off while Ikenna was present in Onitsha.

As soon as Ikenna revealed that the same ruthless and faceless swindlers, based primarily in Lagos, could be behind the bombing, Musa began to detach himself mentally from his initial commitment to throw every resource at his disposal into solving the case. The initial burning desire that seized him following the outrageous bombing of his police station was doused. Long before Ikenna shared his suspicions of who might have been behind the bombing, Musa had begun to sense that he and his men were out of their depth in their drive to apprehend the ultimate masterminds of the bombing.

Explosive experts from the Onitsha Military Cantonment—home to the 302nd Artillery Regiment of the Nigerian Army— had disabused ACP Musa Abdul of the notion that the bomb had come from the army's armoury. The soldiers, who pieced together the bomb fragments, reported that it was homemade. The intricate design of its detonator indicated the bomb-maker was exceptionally skilled.

After the briefing at the Military Cantonment, Musa had driven the four miles back to the Central Police Station in a daze, wondering why anybody would go through the trouble of making a military-grade bomb to attack his building. His fears heightened when Ikenna shared his suspicion that the swindlers might have followed him to Onitsha in order to assassinate him. Musa Abdul had thought of his two wives and eleven children back in Northern Nigeria. Who would have taken care of them if he had died in the deadly bombing? Not the Force and their meagre compensatory payouts to families of fallen policemen, he thought.

As Ikenna spoke of the need for a joint investigation, the Onitsha Area Commander nodded in feigned agreement, but deep down, he had already decided not pursue the bombing case any further. The day after the bombing, he had given Ikenna the case file containing all the information about the Mercedes W140 winched out of the river. Now, he had just handed over the personal effects of David Steinberg, recovered from the back seat of the car, and the dog-eared folder— another case file—reporting a cursory investigation of the bombing. Therefore, in his mind, Musa had concluded his dealings with Lagos State Police Command.

Being a polite man, the Area Commander had resolved to sit patiently behind his desk and listen to the Lagos detective's exhortations, but not a single unit of the scanty resources available to Onitsha Area Command would be wasted investigating a spillover crime from distant Lagos State. A terrorist spillover crime that would not have occurred in the first place if Ikenna had not come to Onitsha, Musa thought.

He smiled broadly, revealing his nicotine stained teeth, before rising to his feet, forcing Ikenna to do the same. The men shook hands across the desk, promising to keep in touch. Ikenna left immediately for Enugu city in a patrol car sent by Chief Superintendent Peter Ikedife.

Observing the patrol car from Enugu State Police Command leaving the forecourt of the Onitsha Central Police Station, Musa Abdul heaved a sigh of relief and pulled down the shutters of his office window. He was glad that Ikenna had finally gone. Returning to his desk, he picked up the handset of his desk phone, dialled a number, and waited. When the Onitsha CID detective leading the investigation answered, Musa ordered him to wrap up the manhunt for the mastermind of the bombing.

'Why sir?' the puzzled voice of the Onitsha city detective came down the phone line.

'Detective, I am in charge here. You have to stop now. We don't have resources to waste on this case. It is now the responsibility of Lagos. You are to instruct your men to return to their previous assignments with immediate effect.'

'I don't understand sir.'

'What don't you understand, Donatus? Onitsha Area Command is not equipped to combat terrorist bombers. We cannot fight people wielding military-grade bombs with Mark-Four bolt-action rifles. Besides, how are we going to apprehend those common criminals who came to our police station and gunned down thirteen of our men if you keep wasting time on this spillover crime from Lagos?'

There was silence, which suggested to Musa that Detective-Sergeant Donatus Ikegwuonwu was thinking about what he had just said.

'Sir, I get what you are saying, but remember that we lost a good man in that bombing, Sergeant Alexander Idemudia, and the detective from Enugu, DS Ngozi Oduche.'

'Donatus, the masterminds of the bombing came from Lagos. They are probably not in Onitsha anymore. This terrorist crime is now the problem of Lagos State Police Command. The Ikeja CID people should deal with it. They have the resources. We don't.'

'Sir, we have already promised to cooperate with Lagos on this case. We cannot just shut it down.'

'Of course, it won't be shut down. This case will officially remain open, but our efforts and resources will revert to combating local crimes. Our counterparts in Ikeja have the resources; they have the Lagos Police Equipment Fund. We have nothing like that.'

'Sir, are you saying we should do nothing about this brazen bomb attack on our station?'

'Yes, that is exactly what I am saying. Please, instruct your men to return to their previous duties, and stop questioning my order.'

'I will communicate your order to my men,' the subdued voice of Donatus came down the phone line.

'Good, detective. You should do that,' Musa responded and slammed down the handset. Now his men could return to the simpler and more productive task of combating local crimes in the city. The most urgent task being the capture—dead or alive— of the local criminals who raided his police station three and half weeks earlier and murdered thirteen policemen in the process.

Two hours later, Ikenna Kodilinye arrived in Enugu city in time for a lunch meeting with Chief Superintendent Peter Ikedife. After that, he visited Barrister Cornelius Oduche and his wife—the grieving parents of DS Ngozi Oduche—to offer his belated condolences before boarding an evening flight back to Lagos.

CHAPTER **25**

OCTOBER 1993

LAGOS, WESTERN NIGERIA

The digital clock sitting on the mahogany desk indicated the time and date as 5.30 PM and 31st October 1993, respectively. Chief Superintendent Cyrus Udeh stared at it gloomily for a few seconds. Then he instinctively rose from his swivel chair and began to pace up and down his office, rubbing his jaw at intervals as he always did when he was extremely upset.

Seven months had passed and the Logan–Grams–Otunba cases were no closer to being solved than the day they were opened. Any doubts he may have had about the connection of those cases to the disappearance of David Steinberg in Eastern Nigeria were disabused by the attempted assassination of DI Ikenna Kodilinye in Onitsha city.

Over the telephone, the Lagos State Police Commissioner Stanislaus Zikora has been raising hell since the story of the Onitsha bombing broke in the press. Zikora was outraged that the Onitsha trip, meant to be a secret known only to himself, Cyrus, Ikenna and relevant senior police officers in Enugu and Onitsha, had somehow leaked to the murderous swindlers.

At that point, Cyrus felt he had no choice than to finally reveal the information he had tried to conceal from the Commissioner. Without missing any detail, the DPO told his superior about the existence of a mole within Ikeja CID. When he mentioned the sting operation that failed to uncover the spy, Zikora snapped and shouted some obscenities down the phone line before demanding a full report on everything about the incident.

'Make sure nothing is left out!' the Commissioner had barked seconds before Cyrus heard a sharp thud followed by a dialling tone. Zikora had just slammed down the handset of his telephone.

The Ikeja CID boss recalled the conversation he had two months earlier with the Police Commissioner about the waning patience of top brass in Force Headquarters, Abuja. The Inspector-General of Police (IG)—the overall head of the Nigerian Police—was personally interested in the Logan–Grams–Otunba cases because of their international dimension, because the American diplomats in Abuja were breathing down the necks of federal government officials, who were in turn applying pressure on Force Headquarters.

For the umpteenth time, Cyrus envisioned himself standing before a surly IG being told that he had been fired from the Force for ineptitude. He shuddered at the thought of such an undignified end to his police career. He feared for the security of his pension. He could lose it entirely or it could be slashed down, far below what he was entitled to as a Chief Superintendent of Police. That is, if he was allowed to keep the rank at the point of forced retirement.

Throughout his twenty-two years in the Force, Cyrus had never come across crimes as unique and as intractable as those involving the faceless Lagos swindlers. The luring of foreigners into the country to be fleeced and then murdered was certainly new to him. It was nothing like the local homicides, armed robberies, kidnappings, burglaries and other sundry crimes he was used to seeing. The gang of swindlers seemed sophisticated and well organized. They left no paper trails, no fingerprints, all known witnesses were dead and more troubling was the reality that their spies had penetrated the police. The faceless criminals had no qualms about killing cops. They had already killed four and tried unsuccessfully to kill another. Without knowing who the swindlers were, the dismayed DPO knew that his detectives, in essence, were chasing phantoms. There was no hope of ever solving any of the fraud-homicide cases unless the mole inside Ikeja CID was caught or the swindlers slipped up, revealing their identities unwittingly.

Cyrus was still pacing back and forth, deep in thought, when the intercom started buzzing. He reluctantly walked to his desk and depressed a button. 'Dixon, what is it?' he growled.

The voice on the intercom, replied, 'sorry to disturb you, sir. DI Ikenna Kodilinye has arrived from Enugu and...'

'Send him up, thank you,' the DPO interjected and pressed another button on the intercom.

*****

In the rundown district of Ebute Metta, fourteen miles south of Ikeja, Chief Inspector Nduka Ikwunne sat up in his bed in the darkness. He wiped sweat beads from his forehead and leaned over the side of the double bed, groping around for the pen torch lying on the nightstand.

As he stepped gingerly out of the bedroom door in his full pyjamas, he halted for a brief moment, turned around, and beamed the torchlight on his wife under the bedsheets. She was sleeping, undisturbed by the noise of the creaking door. Satisfied, Nduka shone the torchlight on the dial of his Seiko wristwatch and sighed. It was one o'clock on the morning of 2nd November 1993.

Moments later, he was downstairs in the moonlit kitchen, downing the remaining contents of a cognac bottle that was quarter-full when he first retrieved it from the cupboard. On realizing that the bottle was empty, the dismayed policeman groaned. He was not an alcoholic. But in times of great anxiety, he tended to indulge the bottle more than usual. It was his favoured form of escapism.

He rose from the foldable kitchen table with the empty bottle in his left hand and walked towards the glass-fronted windows. He gazed at the moonlit street outside. But for the unseen crickets chirping excitedly, the neighbourhood was

217

quiet. He pulled a cord, causing the linen blinds to descend and cover the windows, plunging the kitchen into darkness.

Guided by the narrow beam of his pen torch, he walked across the room and dropped the empty cognac bottle into the open dustbin next to a humming refrigerator. The cognac bottle made a clinking sound as it landed on top of the empty palm oil bottle his wife had dumped in the bin, six hours earlier.

Nduka was not surprised to hear quick footsteps descending the stairs. The clinking sound of glass must have awakened his wife. He pressed the wall switch adjacent to the refrigerator and the fluorescent lights on the ceiling illuminated the kitchen just as his wife opened the door.

'*Nkem, kedu ihe I na-eme?* Nkem, what are you doing?' his wife asked softly in Igbo language.

Nduka shook his head and smiled. She usually called him by his first name. This was the first time in a long time that she had referred to him as *Nkem*— a term of endearment, which literally translates as "my own".

Nduka was pleased and reciprocated. '*Ola m,* my pearl,' he smiled, 'nothing to worry about. I'm just thinking about an important matter.'

The wife left the doorway and moved closer to her husband. She threw her arms over his neck. '*Nkem*, tell me what is bothering you.'

Nduka averted his gaze as he gently extricated himself from her. Once he was free, he turned away. He did not want her to see the fear in his eyes. 'Chiamaka, you know I cannot discuss police work. I need to think about it alone. Go to bed. I'll join later.'

His wife wanted to press him, but Nduka summoned up a facade of defiance and swung to face her. The look on his face convinced her not to push any further. With a countenance expressing defeat and disappointment, she said quietly, 'okay then, but don't be long.' She turned around and walked out of the kitchen. Nduka waited for her footsteps to fade away before he returned to the foldable kitchen table. He sat there thinking about the source of his sleepless nights, which emerged two days before. One thought ran back and forth within Nduka's mind. How did Detective-Inspector Kodilinye survive? How did he escape unscathed from the bomb blast?

The rogue policeman's thoughts drifted to the events of 14th October, nineteen days earlier...

*****

When the news of the bombing in Onitsha city broke on 14th October 1993, everybody in Ikeja CID complex—from civilian cleaners to senior police officers—was shocked and disgusted by the heinous act. The identities of the bomb victims were not immediately clear to the people in Ikeja CID. The local press in Lagos had reported the death of a two unnamed cops—a male and a female—in the Onitsha Central Police bombing. Apart from the DPO and one other detective, nobody was supposed to know that Ikenna had travelled to Eastern Nigeria, not to mention Onitsha city.

Nduka was one of those not supposed to know about Ikenna's trip to the East. He was in the Ikeja CID complex when the news of the Onitsha bombing began to filter in. He did not share the widespread sentiments of horror within the complex. Rather than disgust, he smiled smugly when he overheard police officers, huddled in groups, discussing the news of the blast, which had occurred twenty-four hours earlier. He was smug because he knew something that they did not. Contrary to widespread speculations, he knew that the blast was not an attempt by local Onitsha drug lords to assassinate officers of the Onitsha Area Command.

The Lagos press did not identify the two cops who had died in the blast, but that did not matter to Nduka. He was certain about the identity of the unnamed male victim of the blast because Tunde had called the previous night to deliver the "good news". The female Enugu CID detective who had died along with him was an unavoidable collateral damage.

For all the gloom on the faces of people working at Ikeja CID, on the morning of 2nd November, almost nobody there thought that the well-liked Ikenna had been anywhere near the scene of the bombing, which was three hundred miles away from Lagos. But Nduka knew better and revelled in the knowledge that Ikenna would never return to Ikeja from his supposedly secret trip to Onitsha.

For a few morbid moments, the Chief Inspector tried to imagine the state of Ikenna's corpse. *Did the bomb tear off the limbs of the bastard or did it destroy his organs while keeping his body intact?* He could not decide on which scenario was likely. It all depended on how close *the bastard* was to the bomb when it detonated. Nduka made a mental note to ask Tunde about Ikenna's position relative to the explosive, and then changed his mind. It did not matter, the most important thing was that the bastard detective was dead, the Chief Inspector thought as a strange feeling of exhilaration washed over him.

Walking down a dimly lit corridor on the fifth floor of Ikeja CID complex, in high spirits, whistling a tune to himself, he nearly collided with Detective-Inspector Gbolahan Akinola approaching in the opposite direction.

Flustered, the narcotics detective paused to adjust his grip on the bundle of manilla files in his hand.

'Hello detective,' Nduka greeted cheerfully.

Gbolahan grunted, 'hello' and quickly walked past the man he loathed.

The Chief Inspector permitted himself a mischievous grin, then he swung around on his heel and started trailing the detective.

Gbolahan descended four flights of stairs, walked past the reception area in the foyer, exited the building through the double doors, and was standing next to his Toyota Crown in the forecourt when he felt a presence behind him. He placed the stack of manilla folders carefully on the roof of the car and fumbled in his trouser pockets for the car key. Upon slotting the key into the lock of the car door, he turned around.

'What do you want?' he asked gruffly, wondering why the Chief Inspector was in such a convival mood given the backdrop of information filtering out of Onitsha.

Nduka looked unsure of what to say next. Gbolahan shook his head slowly and then turned around. He unlocked the car door, threw the manilla folders into the front passenger seat, and was about slide into the driver's seat when Nduka suddenly called out, 'hey, detective, I'm really sorry about the death of your former squad leader.'

Gbolahan froze. He turned slowly and gazed across a distance of ten feet at the light-skinned man in full uniform. The narcotics detective took note of the mocking eyes and the thin smile on the face of the APCS leader.

Nduka continued, 'I'm sure you were not told. But the DPO sent Ikenna on a quiet mission to Enugu and Onitsha. He was at the Onitsha Central Police Station when the bomb went off.'

Gbolahan came away from the saloon car and began to approach the uniformed police officer.

Nduka added with feigned concern, 'I know he was a close friend of yours. If there is something I can do...' his voice trailed off when the Gbolahan's grim face stopped a few inches from his nose.

A few menacing seconds passed in silence as the men stood face to face. Suddenly, Gbolahan backed up, smiling and shaking his head. 'Yes, I was fully aware of Detective Kodilinye's itinerary. The boss told me everything. He is not dead. He was indeed there when the bombing took place. Sorry to disappoint you, Chief Inspector, but he was not hurt. As we speak, he is currently helping Onitsha Area Command with their investigations.'

At first, Nduka was dismissive, frowning at what he was hearing. But that rapidly turned to consternation when he observed the calm confidence and authority with which Gbolahan spoke. The narcotics detective was seriously contesting the information Tunde had transmitted to the rogue cop.

'That cannot be true,' Nduka blurted out incredulously. 'My source told me that Detective-Inspector Kodilinye died in the blast.'

Gbolahan stopped smiling. The odd statement intrigued him. 'What do you mean by your sources?' he asked eyeballing the Chief Inspector.

Nduka realised that he had committed a Freudian slip, one that could potentially land him in trouble.

'By the way, who told you that Ikenna had travelled to the East? Only the DPO and I knew that information. How did you know he had travelled to Onitsha? And who are these sources that told you that Ikenna had died in the blast?'

Nduka silently searched his mind for a cogent response and found none. Any substantive answer he gave would incriminate not exculpate him. He averted his gaze from the narcotic detective's face. 'Nothing, absolutely nothing, I guess was wrong,' he mumbled. Then he turned around immediately and scurried away from the suspicious detective.

Gbolahan stared at the back of the departing policeman for some seconds then shrugged and returned to his Toyota Crown sedan.

As he headed back into the building, Nduka's heart thumped so hard that he thought it was going to burst out of his chest. He was not in a state of panic because he had learnt that Ikenna Kodilinye was still alive and kicking. He was panicking because he had just created room for suspicion by opening his big mouth. Ascending the stairs to his office on the third floor, he asked himself several times what Gbolahan was going to do about the Freudian slip. Was the narcotics squad detective going to dismiss the blunder as the barbed words of a man deluded by his hate for a star cop who had survived an assassination attempt or was the detective going to take it seriously and report to the DPO?

If the latter scenario happened, Nduka was certain that Cyrus Udeh would start an investigation as a way of settling scores with him. These thoughts were still raging in his mind when a wiry constable dressed in a starched uniform came to his office to inform him that Cyrus wanted to see him.

In the DPO's office, the APCS leader was surprised to receive an apology from his archenemy, Cyrus, about being kept in the dark about Ikenna's secret trip to Onitsha.

'At the time, I found it prudent to keep the number of people who knew about the trip to a minimum, but in light of the terrible incident at Onitsha Central Police Station, I think it is about time you know that DI Ikenna Kodilinye was there when the bomb went off,' the DPO explained.

Nduka smiled in relief. It was obvious to him that Cyrus had no idea that he already knew about Ikenna's Onitsha trip long before the bomb attack occurred. He listened to the DPO's version of the events leading up to the bombing incident. The DPO's story checked out with Tunde Olukemi's account of what happened except that neither of the two cops killed in the bombing was the intended target. The intended target, Ikenna, had survived because he was nowhere near the car when the bomb went off. Tunde and his fellow swindlers had mistaken the Onitsha city policeman killed in the blast for Ikenna.

Just before the meeting ended, Cyrus told the Chief Inspector that Ikenna would remain behind in Onitsha to help local cops with their investigation of the bombing.

As he drove home from work later, Nduka, still deeply troubled about the Freudian slip, briefly toyed with the idea of killing Gbolahan Akinola. But he quickly purged the thought from his mind. For one thing, he felt it was an unnecessary overreaction. For another, murdering a fellow cop was a risky move.

At home, the APCS leader phoned Tunde Olukemi and poured all the invectives he could remember down the phone line in Yoruba, the third language he spoke fluently after English and his native Igbo.

Tunde apologised to the angry Chief Inspector for erroneously informing him that Ikenna had died in the blast and accepted that he was partly to blame for the corrupt policeman's predicament.

Although he thought it unnecessary, Nduka still broached the idea of solving that predicament by eliminating Gbolahan. The Yoruba swindler at the other end of the telephone line laughed before rejecting Nduka's suggestion.

'Do you what your real problem is?' Tunde asked before providing the answer. 'Your actual problem is paranoia. I'll gladly bet all my money that this detective, Gbolahan, has already forgotten about your Freudian slip. Notwithstanding the fact that you obviously dislike Ikenna, I doubt Gbolalahan seriously thinks that you were involved in the assassination attempt. My advice to you is to calm down and stop fretting about a non-existent problem.'

Nduka accepted Tunde's assessment of the situation. 'Of course, you are right. I was already thinking in that direction,' he said, signalling his agreement with the swindler.

When the phone call was over, the rogue cop headed to the dining room to eat the dinner prepared by his wife, Chiamaka. That night, he went to bed feeling much better.

Eighteen days later, on the morning of 1st November 1993, Chief Inspector Nduka Ikwunne looked out of the window of his third-floor office and spotted Ikenna down below, at street level, walking briskly along the adjoining road towards the forecourt of Ikeja CID complex. The anti-scam detective had finally returned to Lagos from Onitsha.

Seeing Ikenna unhurt, in the flesh, left Nduka distraught. Old fears of what Gbolahan might do with the Freudian slip resurfaced and refused to go away. He fleetingly envisioned a secret meeting of Cyrus, Ikenna and Gbolahan during which a decision was reached to investigate him.

Settling down behind his desk, Nduka berated himself for being paranoid. Reassured that Gbolahan must have forgotten about the slip-up, the Chief Inspector got on with the day's job of reading crime situation reports filled by detectives of his anti-police corruption squad (APCS). After that, he placed phone calls to some of his detectives to ask for clarification about something he had read in their situation reports. Later on, he held an hour-long teleconference with one of the Deputy Inspector-Generals (DIGs) based in Force Headquarters, Abuja. The DIG happened to be the token police officer in the civilian-dominated Federal Police Committee, which exercised direct oversight over all APCS units scattered across the country.

At the end of the teleconference, Nduka was pleased with himself. The DIG had commended him for job he was doing fighting sprawling corruption in the Lagos State Police Command. Several hours later, when it was time to go home for the day, he rose triumphantly from his desk, slung his leather satchel across his shoulder, and walked out of his office. On the landing of the second floor, he bumped into DI Gbolahan Akinola.

The narcotics detective looked him straight in the eye and said, 'you still haven't told me who told you that Ikenna had travelled to Onitsha.'

Nduka knew that Gbolahan had noticed the fear and alarm in his eyes. He smiled weakly and quickly walked past the detective. He was already descending the flight of stairs when he heard the narcotics detective behind him shout, 'hey! I'll be watching you from now on!'

The Chief Inspector reacted by quickening his pace down the staircase. The brio with which he had initially breezed out of his office had evaporated and in its place was just plain fear.

Later that night, he lay next to his snoring wife, unable to sleep. He got up and headed to the kitchen to fetch his favourite drink, *Rémy Martin* cognac...

*****

Outside the unpainted bungalow in Ebute Metta, a rooster began to crow. The fowl's shrill call of the morning jarred Nduka out of his thoughts. He glanced at his wristwatch and sighed. An hour and half had passed since his wife left him in the kitchen to return to bed. Nduka rose from the foldable kitchen table and switched off the fluorescent lights. At 2.45 AM, it was still too early to start preparing for work. The policeman resolved to catch a few more hours of sleep before rising to shave and bathe.

As he walked out the kitchen, the bent cop realised something that alleviated his fear. To mount an effective investigation of his activities, the DPO would require experienced detectives and sophisticated gadgetry. In Nduka's reckoning, that would mean Cyrus having to rely on the surveillance equipment and expert personnel of the APCS. Nduka knew that the detectives and uniformed policemen of the APCS were fiercely loyal to him and would gladly tip him off if the DPO ever ordered them to move against him.

As he joined his sleeping wife in bed, the Chief Inspector resolved to suspend regular contact with his paymasters—the gang of swindlers—until he could ascertain whether he was under surveillance. As he covered himself in bedsheets, he recalled something. He would need to replace the blown fuse in the Scanlock ECM receiver so that he could resume sweeping the telephone in his office for covert listening devices.

CHAPTER 26

NOVEMBER 1993

HAMPSTEAD, NORTHWEST LONDON, UK

On the afternoon of 10th November, Harel Suzmann was sitting glumly behind a round shiny metallic table in front of an outdoor café, watching the light two-way traffic flowing up and down Hampstead High Street. He had being waiting for an hour for the South African lawyer, Matthew Molozi. He sipped coffee, glanced at his wristwatch again, and sighed. He hated everything about his current situation. He abhorred meetings called at short notice, and above that, he abhorred lateness. For those reasons, he harboured a strong feeling that he might not like his prospective South African interlocutor.

The day before, he had been in his study room, reading an interesting book, when the telephone on his desk began to ring for the second time in seven minutes. Clearly flustered, he had quickly placed the leather bookmarker between the pages of the book and picked up the handset. 'Hello, who is it?' he had asked irritated. The caller at the opposite end of the phone line introduced himself as Matthew Molozi, a junior law partner in Heintz & Sharmann.

Harel heaved a sigh of relief. He had assumed that it was the damned electric company again trying to convince him to switch to one of their latest Energy & Money saving schemes. The company had the peculiar habit of lowering rates for customers who sign up to their numerous savings schemes for a few months before gradually raising the rates again. Newly increased rates were usually 15% higher than the pre-savings rates. After falling for that fraud twice, Harel realized that the purpose of the "energy savings" scheme had less to do with helping customers and more to do with luring them away from rival electric companies.

Moments before Matthew called, Harel had angrily slammed the handset of the telephone back onto its cradle when he recognized the cheerful voice of the usual company canvasser. She was already reciting the boilerplate statement about how pleased she was to introduce yet another energy savings scheme to their prized customer, but Harel was simply not having it and ended call. When the phone rang for the second time, he had planned to shout down the line if the caller had turned out to be same company canvasser. To his great relief, the second caller was not from the company.

'Hello, Mister Molozi, how do you do?' Harel asked cheerfully as he adjusted his grip on the handset.

'I am fine, sir,' the voice replied with a thick accent, 'I'm sure my boss told you some weeks ago that I'll be in Europe to attend to our law firm's overseas clients. Well, I'm now in Europe and I think we need to meet as soon as possible, tomorrow to be precise.'

Harel was surprised by the abruptness of his interlocutor. 'You are calling from where? The Netherlands?'

'Yes,' the heavily accented voice responded curtly.

The clipped response unnerved Harel, causing him to wonder if he was going to get along with the South African. 'Where in Netherlands?' he prodded.

'I'm in Amsterdam now. Before that, I was in Eindhoven, Rotterdam and The Hague dealing with overseas clients of Heintz and Sharmann. My schedule for the past eight days has been pretty hectic,' the voice responded.

The Briton was not pleased to hear that from his African interlocutor. 'You should have called me as soon as you arrived in Netherlands to schedule the meeting. I like to have plenty of time to prepare. I don't like impromptu meetings.' When Harel finished speaking, awkward silence descended. 'Are you still there?' he asked irritated, his right ear picking up from the receiver of the handset what appeared to be the sound of papers being shuffled.

'My apologies, Mister Suzmann,' the voice replied airily, 'but we do need to meet. Time is of the essence.'

'Okay. How do we do it? You want me to come to Amsterdam?' Harel prompted, frustrated by the dawdling style of his interlocutor, the clipped responses, the reluctance to speak comprehensively.

Another moment of silence followed, during which the Briton heard the sound of shuffling papers again.

'No, I will come to you in London,' the voice answered.

'What time of the day?' Harel asked.

There was no response from the other end of the phone line.

'One o'clock in the afternoon?' Harel suggested helpfully in case Matthew was having a hard time in making up his mind.

'That sounds good,' the voice responded, followed by the sound of shuffling papers. 'Where shall we meet sir?' the voice asked.

Harel thought about it quickly before replying, 'Hampstead High Street. It is in northwest London.' Then he spent the next fifteen minutes explaining to Matthew how to get the outdoor café in Hampstead High Street from Heathrow Airport.

The South African asked a few questions on the directions and Harel answered them clearly and patiently, advising Matthew to buy the *London Street Atlas* at the airport.

'You will have no problems, finding your way around London with that collection of street maps,' the Briton added, his ears picking up the annoying sound of shuffling papers for the umpteenth time.

'Sounds like you are quite busy over there,' Harel remarked, 'I'll leave you alone to get on with whatever you are doing.'

The voice on the other end replied, 'oh, thank you. I look forward to meeting you tomorrow.'

Both men exchanged goodbyes. It could have been worse, Harel thought as he returned the handset to its cradle. Although he disliked the impromptu nature of the meeting, he tried to be sanguine about it. After all, he stood to gain £25.5 million in the end.

The following day, at 12.30 PM, he sat himself behind the table of the open terrace café, gazing at the traffic while munching croissants and sipping coffee at intervals. He was dismayed when Matthew Molozi failed to turn up at 1.00 PM as agreed. For the next two hours, he watched customers come and go from the café.

At 3.00PM, he noticed that nearly all the tables and chairs in front of the café facing the road were now occupied. The customers ranged from couples to big families. At the table adjacent his, a young couple were busy snogging each other and giggling. Harel stared at them for a while and snorted, but they barely noticed. The young woman being caressed by her Romeo reminded him of his own ex-wife. He felt like telling the Romeo that women were bad news. They are there for you when money was available. Once that evaporates, they would leave you taking whatever is left. In short, women were nothing short of parasites, sucking you until you were dry.

Harel was so engrossed by the couple that he failed to notice the black taxicab halting next to the kerb, forty inches from where he was sitting.

Eugene Igolo alias "Matthew Molozi" alighted from the taxi. He thanked the driver for being extremely helpful in locating the café and thrust some money into the hand hanging out of the cabbie's window.

The taxi driver withdrew his hand from the window to examine the bank notes in his hand. He thought there was a mistake. The passenger had paid more than three times the actual fare. But Eugene smiled and asked him not to bother looking for change.

The cabbie was pleasantly surprised. In his ten years on the job, that was the largest tip he had ever received. The sight of £300 had transformed him from a sullen driver silently bemoaning being saddled with a clueless foreign passenger into a cheery driver grateful to have been selected by his cab company to pick up the well-dressed, polite African who spoke excellent English with an unfamiliar thick accent.

Earlier that day, at precisely 11.45 AM, the faux South African had stopped next to a pay phone and dialled a cab company office listed in the tourist guidebook he had bought from a kiosk tucked in a corner of the arrivals concourse at Heathrow Airport.

Around the same time, a taxi driver with the cab company named Mark Gordon was driving through the centre of Hounslow Town when the car phone suddenly crackled to life. He received a verbal instruction to go to the airport and pick up a foreigner who had just flown in from The Netherlands.

Fifteen minutes later, he pulled up outside the Terminal 2 building of Heathrow Airport. A slim black man, dressed in a blue three-piece suit, carrying a briefcase approached the kerb. He identified himself to the pale, freckled-faced, twenty-six-year-old cab driver as the prospective passenger. Mark smiled politely and asked the African to hop in.

On the road, the driver asked the passenger where he wanted to go. Eugene told him that the place was in northwest London, but he could not recall the name.

The cabbie frowned and turned off the taximeter. He steered the vehicle into a lay-by and pulled up. He killed the engine and turned to face Eugene. 'Okay mate, how do you hope to get to your destination if you don't know where it is?'

Eugene Igolo did not catch everything the sneering Mark Gordon had said—the driver's cockney dialect was miles away from the Standard English he had learnt in school back in Nigeria—but he understood that he had screwed up in a manner that would elicit dismay from his boss, John Nwosu, and mocking laughter from *that pompous arse*, Tunde.

Tunde had been John's first choice to play the role of "Matthew Molozi" because he was brilliant and the most travelled of his men. John reasoned that Tunde knew his way around UK, having been there multiple times, but Eugene lobbied relentlessly for the role. In the end, John gave in to the pressure, handing the delicate role of "a black South African law partner in Heintz & Sharmann" to Eugene who had never travelled outside Nigeria, had no experience of developing rapport with people marked as targets for the gang's scams.

'I'm not from around here. You see I'm not used to names of unfamiliar places,' Eugene smiled apologetically at the taxi driver. The swindler's adrenaline soared with the growing realisation that he was out of his depth. He suddenly discovered within himself a new appreciation for the outsized role that Tunde played within the gang. Between the freckled crimson face of the cabbie glaring at him and the prospect of missing his appointment with the gang's latest target, he wished Tunde would materialize in his place and take expert control of the situation.

Mark Gordon sighed and turned away from the passenger. Facing the road ahead glumly, he contemplated what to do next. Fleetingly, he thought of abandoning the clueless passenger at the side of the motorway.

In the back seat of the cab, Eugene tried hard, willed himself to remember the venue of the meeting. He regretted not writing down the venue on paper as Tunde or any other person would have done. He had been overconfident, had invested too much trust in his memory, which was now failing him in his hour of need. He thought of fetching the *London Street Atlas* in his briefcase. Perhaps, the street names listed in its index pages could help jog his memory. He had just finished manipulating the combination locks on the briefcase when he observed the taxi driver sigh and suddenly lean towards the glove compartment opposite the front passenger seat.

Mark Gordon retrieved a fold-out map from the glove compartment and then slammed it shut. He opened the door and emerged from the vehicle. 'Okay mate...out of the car,' he said calmly.

Eugene emerged, intrigued and smiling sheepishly. The cab driver walked round to the bonnet with his passenger tagging along. Mark unfolded the large map and then spread it over the bonnet.

Using his forefinger, the cabbie ran an imaginary circle around a portion of the map. 'Okay mate, this is northwest London. That ought to jog your memory.'

Eugene bent over the bonnet and squinted at the names of places on the portion of the map pointed out by Mark. After what seemed like an eternity, Eugene spotted two similar-sounding street names on the map that reminded him of Harel Suzmann's directives over the phone.

Mark Gordon had his back to Eugene, smoking a Benson & Hedges cigarette while gazing at passing vehicles on the motorway. He puffed smoke through his nose. 'Just my luck,' he murmured before sticking the smouldering cigarette back between his lips.

'I have found it, sir!' Eugene cried excitedly.

The taxi driver blew smoke rings into the air and swung round. He dropped the cigarette on the asphalted pavement and crushed it under his shoe. 'Are you sure? Where?' he asked, hunching over the large map.

'I'm certain of it,' Eugene replied confidently, pointing at a street name on the map with his forefinger.

Mark squinted at it momentarily and straightened up. 'Oh, that is Hampstead High Street...where are you dropping off?'

'It's a café. I am supposed to meet someone there by one o'clock.'

The driver glanced at his wristwatch. The time was 12.35 PM. 'Well, we won't make it on time for your meeting,' he announced with a frown on his face. 'So what is the name of the café?' he asked, carefully folding the large map.

Eugene smiled awkwardly and said that he could not recall the name of café, but he was sure it was on Hampstead High Street.

The driver laughed scornfully. 'I suppose you don't remember the name of the person you are meeting,' he remarked sarcastically, opening the driver's door.

Eugene laughed off the cabbie's barb as he got back into the rear passenger seat.

Mark slid behind the steering wheel and put on his seat belt. The engine of the taxicab roared to life. 'Let us go and find your café,' he declared, switching the taximeter back on.

The taxicab returned to the M4 motorway. From Hounslow to Chiswick, it was plain sailing for traffic was light. A short distance from Chiswick Roundabout on the North Circular Road, the cab ran into an eight-mile long traffic queue of vehicles. Mark glanced at his wristwatch again and shook his head.

In the thick silence of the taxicab, Eugene's mind began to generate various troubling mental images. He pictured Harel storming out of the café after spending hours waiting for him. He visualized furious members of his own gang hurling abuses at him for ruining their latest swindling operation—*their perfect operation devised by the equally perfect Tunde Olukemi*. Eugene recoiled at the thought of such a humiliation. Harel will wait patiently, he assured himself. After all, there was the promise of a £25.5 million inheritance. Observing his taxicab and other vehicles in the long queue moving intermittently in a slow and steady procession, he reassured himself that all was going to be well. His taxi would eventually get to Hampstead, and Harel would still be there in the café.

It took two hours for the taxicab to get through the traffic bottleneck caused by the presence of police patrol cars and the wreckage of two saloon cars that had been in a head-on collision. At 2.35 PM, the taxicab entered northwest London via Marylebone Road.

On Hampstead High Street, Mark decelerated. 'Mate, we are now on the high street. Where is your café?'

Eugene scanned the road ahead anxiously. Suddenly, he recalled Harel's remark about the meeting venue being opposite a commercial bank whose name he could not recall.

'There are four of them here, pick one,' Mark said, gesturing with his arm.

Eugene's eyes followed the taxi driver's left arm sweeping the air between the front passenger seat and windscreen before shifting to gaze at the road ahead. In the distance, he saw four outdoor cafés spread several yards apart from each other. As the cab trundled towards the first one, Eugene spotted a Barclays Bank building on the opposite side of the road. 'This is the place,' he said.

Mark slowed down and turned briefly to Eugene with a skeptical look on his face. 'The first one? You sure about that?'

Eugene answered in the affirmative and the taxi driver accelerated. Moments later, the black cab pulled up in front of the café opposite Barclays Bank.

Even before he got out of the taxicab, Eugene recognized the dark-haired white man sitting among other customers in the terrace of the café. Harel looked slightly older than the passport photograph in the clipping of the *Times of London* newspaper that Moses Adrika had shown Eugene and other gang members, two months earlier.

Eugene opened the rear door of the cab and alighted.

The relieved cab driver thrust his hand out of the cab window expecting to receive £90 determined as the fare by the taximeter. He got £300 instead. Initially, he frowned at the bank notes in his hand, thinking that his passenger had misheard him. Eugene disabused him of the notion.

Delighted and grateful, Mark Gordon produced a business card from the breast pocket of his shirt. 'This is my personal complimentary card,' he said, offering the card to Eugene, 'call me any time you need a taxi ride in London. Anytime, I mean it.'

Eugene laughed and accepted the proffered business card. When the taxicab had gone, the swindler adjusted his necktie and his grip on the briefcase. Then he surveyed the area. Beyond the narrow footpath abutting the kerb, most customers in the terrace of the café were seated in wicker chairs behind single round aluminium tables set under a blue retractable awning. In a few cases, five tables were joined together so that a family of four or five could sit round them.

Eugene's eyes fixed on the middle-aged white man sitting alone behind one of the tables furthest from the footpath. The swindler smiled as he observed the man gawking at the young couple fondling each other at the next table.

Harel was still lost in the world of misogyny when someone nudged his shoulder gently. He snapped out of his thoughts and looked up at the black man standing over him. The Briton quickly recalled why he was in the café. He smiled politely, but did not shake the hand proffered by Eugene.

'I'm Matthew Molozi. Sorry for being late.'

'Well, you are here now,' Harel replied drily, waving the faux South African to an empty wicker chair across his table.

Eugene retracted his right hand and walked awkwardly to the chair while Harel watched silently. The swindler settled into the chair and placed the briefcase on the ground beside his right foot.

'Ah, where are my manners,' the Briton said histrionically. 'I'm Harel Suzmann. Pleased to finally meet you,' he added extending his right arm for a handshake.

The faux South African smiled and shook the Briton's hand.

'Matthew, do you take tea or coffee?' Harel asked. The time was 3.05 PM

*****

That same afternoon in Lagos, Gbolahan was sitting across the desk from CSP Cyrus Udeh who was wearing a blank expression. There was a knock on the door and the DPO unclasped his hands. 'Come in!' he bellowed.

The door swung open and a man of average height, fairly dark in complexion, walked into the office. He was dressed in a blue, long sleeve shirt with khaki brown trousers to match.

'Ikenna, close the door and have a seat,' Cyrus said, gesturing to the empty chair next to Gbolahan Akinola.

The man quickly closed the door and walked across the room. He glanced inquiringly at Gbolahan as he sat down.

Cyrus cleared his throat and in an ominously calm voice, he said, 'Gbolahan, tell him what you told me.'

Gbolahan turned to Ikenna and told him about his encounter with Chief Inspector Nduka Ikwunne, a few weeks earlier. He emphasized the fear in Nduka's eyes when he realised that Ikenna had not died in the bombing. 'I have been observing him since that day. He gets jumpy whenever he sees me. When I confronted him with what he had said, he ran away, literally.'

The DPO interposed with a question. 'So what are you inferring, detective?'

A thick moment of silence, pregnant with accusatory implications, descended. Ikenna and the DPO already knew where Gbolahan's narrative was going. They just wanted him to be explicit.

'I think he was involved in the assassination attempt. I think he is connected to the Onitsha bombing,' Gbolahan blurted out, relieved that he had finally revealed what he should have reported twenty-seven days earlier.

Ikenna did not react.

Cyrus smiled smugly. 'I know, I know, I know,' he said repeatedly, grinning.

At first, Gbolahan was happy to hear this response. It was one thing to taunt Chief Inspector Nduka Ikwunne about his Freudian slip during a brief private encounter by the staircase, and another to make an official accusation without supporting evidence. Gbolahan knew that accusing an individual as powerful as the Chief Inspector, one who had the ear of federal politicians in Abuja, held serious implications, *career-ending implications*. Chief Superintendent Cyrus Udeh's support would be crucial in protecting him from any potential backlash. After all, the DPO was technically superior in rank to the highly autonomous Chief Inspector who operated his anti-police corruption squad (APCS) outside the regular police chain of command.

'Look detective, I know you don't like Nduka. No one does, especially me,' Cyrus said, jabbing his broad chest repeatedly with his left forefinger. 'But it is simply not possible that he was involved. As for the suspicious behaviour, you noticed... come on... the bastard is embarrassed that he said Ikenna was dead when he clearly wasn't. He is jumpy because he probably thinks you are going to tell Ikenna about it. If I said something that stupid, I would be uncomfortable too.'

With those words, Cyrus Udeh dashed Gbolahan's hope. The DPO believed that Nduka was too well paid to be involved in such lowly activities. Spying for common criminals was what poorly paid, cash-strapped junior police officers did. Some middle-level police officers on regular pay— such as the late Mike Otunba—may be tempted to involve themselves in such lowly activities, but not a cop on a special salary package such as Nduka Ikwunne.

As with all APCS personnel scattered across the country, Nduka did not receive his monthly pay from the Budget Department of the Nigerian Police Force. He received his generous special salary from the civilian-dominated Federal Police Committee, which exercised direct oversight over APCS units attached to State Police Commands across the country. The reasoning behind this state of affairs being that police officers in charge of investigating corruption within the Force ought to get a salary boost to make them invulnerable to bribery. The Budget Department of the Nigerian Police vehemently disagreed. The idea of paying salaries meant for mid-level police officers to junior police officers attached to APCS units was anathema. The notion of paying salaries normally reserved for senior police officers to mid-level police officers who led APCS units was just plain crazy.

Following the Budget Department's refusal to participate in the bastardization of the standard police salary structure, the responsibility for remunerating all police officers assigned to APCS units passed from the Nigerian Police Force to the Federal Police Committee, a creature of the military junta ruling the country.

Perhaps, in a bid to stick it to the recalcitrant leadership of the Nigerian Police Force, the civilians running the ad hoc police committee approved special salary packages for APCS officers that were far more generous than what the Budget Department had refused to pay.

In Lagos State, Chief Inspector Nduka Ikwunne and his second-in-command, Inspector Daoud Mamman—both from the uniformed division—had the committee to thank for earning more than any police officer on regular pay whose rank was below that of an Assistant Commissioner of Police (ACP).

Chief Superintendent Cyrus Udeh was sure that Nduka's habit of strutting around Ikeja CID in a cloud of self-importance had something to do with that distorted reality; the reality that Nduka earned twice as much as Cyrus despite the latter outranking the former.

Daoud Mamman was a polite and self-effacing professional, and Cyrus found him likeable. However, the DPO did not fail to note that the deputy APCS leader, who was four ranks below him in the police hierarchy, enjoyed a salary that was one and a half times as much as his own.

Below Nduka and Daoud, all subordinate APCS personnel—uniformed officers and plain-clothes detectives—attached to Lagos State Police Command out-earned their counterparts in other CID squads. This made them the subject of intense jealousy and resentment in an environment where the average policeman hated the very idea of other policemen looking over his shoulders in the name of fighting corruption.

'I don't think the Chief Inspector would have done a thing like that. I know that he is a bastard, but accusing him of collaborating with criminals is taking it too far,' said Ikenna, echoing the DPO's sentiments.

Gbolahan looked glum. Nobody in the room took his allegation seriously. Not even the man who had survived the assassination attempt. 'Sir, we can raise a discreet team to investigate. If he is innocent then good, if not....' the narcotics detective's voice trailed off as the DPO began to shake his head slowly.

'Detective-Inspector,' Cyrus began, suppressing a sigh. 'Just stop there. These allegations should cease henceforth. I will not tolerate a rumour mill. The last thing we need is the *wahala* of the people in Abuja.'

The two detectives in the room knew what the DPO meant. The powerful Abuja-based backers of Nduka Ikwunne would not be too pleased to hear unsubstantiated rumours about their star cop in Lagos.

What the two detectives might not have appreciated was the depth of their superior's fear of those Abuja-based power brokers. Cyrus did not consider it above the well-connected civilians in control of the Federal Police Committee to accuse him of planting a rumour to smear and damage the standing of their beloved Nduka— the man who could do no wrong in their eyes, the cop who regularly impressed them with reams of tractor-feed paper. Continuous form paper, with perforated edges, containing several bar charts that claimed corruption within Lagos State Police Command was going down slowly, week by week, thanks to the efforts of the APCS.

Cyrus had always wondered how anyone with an ounce of common sense could be dazzled and wowed by reams of statistical gobbledygook. Maybe the civilian committee members were impressed by the graphic quality of the charts on the lengthy computer printout—always neatly stacked and delivered in large padded envelopes to their offices in distant Abuja every month. Maybe Nduka fascinated the committee because he was so unlike APCS leaders in other parts of the country. He was the only head of an APCS unit, anywhere in the country, who bothered to submit large amounts of statistical data when a simple written report could have done.

Cyrus was not impressed. Nduka was nothing more than a cunning showboat. Cyrus knew that the lone policeman in the committee— a Deputy Inspector-General of Police (DIG)—could easily disabuse those barely numerate civilians of their foolish notions about the usefulness of those bar charts. But the DPO was not holding his breath.

Long sidelined and excluded from decision-making, the token cop on the committee had grown embarrassingly obsequious to his more powerful civilian colleagues who knew little about actual police work.

Cyrus reckoned that the DIG just wanted to preserve a successful police career, which was already approaching its twilight years after more than three decades of service. After all, the worst thing that could ever happen to any policeman so close to retirement is getting the sack and then losing a lifetime of pension.

Despite his disgust at the senior policeman's toadyish behaviour and failure to stand up for the Nigerian Police Force in that ghastly committee, Cyrus could understand the DIG's dilemma. After all, he too wanted to eventually retire with dignity and draw his pension peacefully. The last thing he wanted was for those phoneys on the committee to ruin his own career, already hanging in the balance because of his inability to apprehend the murderous swindlers who had just added yet another American and three more police officers to their death tally.

'Nothing said here leaves this room,' Cyrus said calmly, but firmly.

Ikenna assured the DPO that he and Gbolahan would abide by his directive, nothing discussed would leave the room, and none of them would discuss the matter any further or share their suspicions with anyone else.

Gbolahan squirmed in his seat. Ikenna was definitely speaking for himself. 'Excuse me sir,' the narcotics detective began. 'My own thinking is different from that of Ikenna. I believe we should...'

'No! Just let it go. That is an order,' the DPO interjected. A despondent Gbolahan closed his mouth.

'Come on, Gbolahan,' Ikenna waded in. The narcotics detective shot him a bristling look.

'Okay, my boys,' Cyrus said airily as if the detectives were schoolchildren, 'I have a meeting with the Commissioner in an hour. I have to prepare.'

Gbolahan and Ikenna rose from their seats, swung around and headed for the door.

'One thing before you leave!' the DPO called out. The detectives halted and turned to face their superior.

'I don't want to hear that any of you confronted Nduka about this matter. I don't want any trouble with those bastards in the police committee,' the DPO warned, wagging his finger at them. 'Please, act responsibly.'

'Yes sir,' Ikenna responded. Gbolahan silently opened the office door and stood aside for Ikenna to pass through it. Then he exited the office, closing the door behind him. He walked off, ignoring Ikenna who was waiting to talk to him in the corridor.

Back in his own office, Gbolahan sank into the swivel chair behind his desk. As he toyed with a fountain pen, his countenance assuming an aspect of the deepest gloom. He did not intend to obey the order issued by his direct superior. He would have to investigate Nduka himself, without the imprimatur of the DPO, and it would have to be done surreptitiously. But how was he going to do it without Ikenna and Cyrus noticing until he had found proof of Nduka's perfidy? he wondered.

After spending what seemed like an eternity to him in deep contemplation, a brilliant idea came to him. It was not too complicated, did not require so much manpower, and could generate enough evidence to convince Ikenna and the DPO to treat his allegations with the seriousness it deserves.

PART THREE

CHAPTER 27

Martin Tochukwu Okoye was seven years old when the war broke out in June 1967. Apart from the loud sounds of barking rifles, roaring howitzers, exploding artillery shells, the deafening thunderclaps of aerial bombs falling on civilian spaces and the bloodcurdling screams of the maimed and dying, most of the war between Nigeria and Biafra was a blur to him. The few memories that remained vivid in his mind, such as his life in various refugee camps, were often fragmented and episodic. But there was one exception; one that remained clear, unforgettable and had stayed with him all these years. It was the memory of the last time he ever saw his parents alive.

Although many details of that fateful day were firmly implanted in his mind, he could never recall the face of the Biafran Army officer who had found him unhurt and splattered with blood that wasn't his. The man, in khaki uniform and a peaked cap, who had scooped him up from the ground— the scene of the carnage, the gory aftermath of a Nigerian airstrike on a busy open-air market one hot afternoon in April 1968.

Martin could still recall people fleeing in all directions, making for the cover of the trees, running past road verges into the safety of the dense foliage of adjacent forests as soon as the ominous buzzing sounds of low-flying Ilyushin Il-28 jet bombers—piloted by Egyptian airmen on Nigeria's behalf—rented the skies above. Martin remembered his father pulling him by the hand as they ran behind his mother towards the forest. They almost made it.

They were on the asphalt tarmac, a few inches from the road verge separating them from the deep forest, when the strafing and aerial bombardment began. Men, women and children were torn apart as they ran. It was all over in ten minutes. By the time the planes circling overhead finally departed, the road surface surrounding Martin was strewn with burnt human corpses, blood, body parts, bone fragments and something white and soft, which he would learn was brain matter many years later.

Crying, calling for his parents, the seven-year-old looked around, but could not find them. All the charcoal black corpses on the road looked indistinguishable from each other. Nobody came to help him. None of the frightened survivors in the adjoining forest wanted to emerge in case the jet bombers returned. So Martin remained there until a passing convoy of Biafran Army jeeps and trucks halted by the side of the road, fifteen minutes later.

Vehicle doors opened and several men clad in khaki uniforms ran towards the scene of the carnage. Only then did a steady trickle of civilians begin to emerge from the forest. The faceless army officer lifted Martin from the ground, wiped blood splatter from his face, and asked him about the whereabouts of his parents. Martin did not know. He cried and cried. The army officer surveyed the landscape, shook his head, and carried Martin away from the scene.

Moments later, Martin was on the laps of the army officer inside an open-air jeep at the head of the convoy. The officer said some soothing words to him and then gave him a packet of biscuit— something Martin had not seen or tasted since the war broke out the year before. He was still eating the biscuit when the convoy, headed by the jeep in camouflage livery, stopped beside an abandoned primary school being used as a makeshift hospital. A doctor examined the boy and declared him slightly malnourished, but otherwise fine. He was fed and bathed by nurses in the backyard of the school, and then the search for next of kin began.

The army officer had asked Martin some questions while they were still in the jeep en route to the makeshift hospital. The name of the woman mentioned by Martin sounded familiar to the officer. So the army officer conferred with his soldiers while Martin was being bathed. One of the soldiers said something that finally jogged the officer's memory. He certainly knew the old woman very well. She was one of several hundred women contracted by Army High Command to supply sleeping mats to various military formations across Biafran territory still free and uncaptured by the Nigerian "vandals".

The army officer walked up to an olive-green land rover in the middle of the long convoy. He conferred with the five soldiers in it. The sergeant sitting in the front passenger seat pored over a topographic map, nodding as the army officer spoke. Moments later, the land rover's engine roared to life. The olive-green vehicle moved backwards briefly and then veered out of the column of stationary vehicles. It made a U-turn in the middle of the asphalt tarmac and sped off in a direction opposite to that of the stationary military convoy.

Martin was playing with the golden stars on the slide epaulette on the left shoulder of the army officer carrying him when the olive-green land rover returned. The sergeant and the old woman alighted from the vehicle. Her eyes were red and watery as if she had been crying. As soon as the officer gently lowered him onto the ground, Martin ran into warm embrace of the sixty-two-year old woman crouching on the ground. When the woman rose to her feet, the army officer began to ask the old woman some probing questions to confirm her relationship to the child.

The old woman frowned and snapped, 'Captain, I'm Ugoyemma Ogidi, also known as "Mama Ugoye". I am an army contractor. You have seen my face before. I supplied sleeping mats to you and your men two weeks ago.' Turning to Martin standing beside her, she continued, 'he is my grandson. His mother was my daughter.'

Satisfied with her answer, the army officer's countenance changed. He commiserated with her on the death of her daughter and son-in-law.

'I have seen too many deaths, within and outside my family, since this war started,' she said, steely-eyed. 'I insisted on being taken to the marketplace by your sergeant.The only thing that broke my heart was that I could not identify any recognizable remains to bury.'

Taken aback by her cold response, the officer awkwardly offered his condolences again. She waved him off.

'Thank you for taking care of my grandson. I don't want to keep you any longer. You and your men have a shooting war to win and I have a child to look after. Go and may God be with you.'

The officer smiled ruefully, dropped on one knee, and gave Martin another packet of biscuit. Minutes later, the military convoy was on the move again. Martin and Mama Ugoye watched until it disappeared down the road.

'You are now both my son and grandson,' she said, smiling at Martin as they embarked on a thirty-mile-long trek to her village, avoiding main roads, mostly walking through footpaths in dense woodlands, listening for the buzzing sounds of jet engines overheard. They heard nothing, but chirping crickets and birds that evening. They arrived at the village at nightfall.

As the Nigerian Army advanced slowly under the cover of unremitting and indiscriminate aerial bombardment, more and more Biafrans became refugees, crowding into an ever-shrinking Biafran-controlled territory. After the food-producing areas were overrun, mass starvation began to wreak havoc on the Biafran population, killing thousands of people.

By late 1968, Mama Ugoye's wartime business was already in a state of disarray. Many of the women she employed to weave the sleeping mats were dead or had become refugees running from one locality to another as Nigeria's military campaign made progress. The rapid decline in Biafran Army purchase orders for sleeping mats and the increasing worthlessness of fiat currency —the Biafran Pound— finally convinced Mama Ugoye that it was time to throw in the towel.

For the next thirteen months, she devoted her time to her grandson and the management of a special refugee camp for orphaned children with the help of the Catholic relief agency, CARITAS International.

When the war ended at the beginning of 1970 with the defeat and demise of Biafra, and the reintegration of its territory into Nigeria, Martin was ten and relieved to hear that he did not need to run into the nearest bush whenever the buzzing sounds of the evil airborne monsters rented the air.

For Mama Ugoye, it was not so straightforward. The end of the war left her with a dense jungle of emotions to explore. On one level, the war had ended with the clear defeat of her side, the Biafran side. She had lost her husband, her only daughter, her son-in-law, her only living sister and other relatives—all sacrificed in the noble struggle for freedom, which had resulted in millions dead and vanquishment. On another level, she was relieved it was all over. Now she could get on with raising her only living relative, her grandson, the boy, Martin.

In the months and years following the end of the war, the victorious Nigerian Federal Government had promoted the conciliatory mantra, *No Victor, No Vanquished*. However, Mama Ugoye and millions of former Biafran citizens did not believe it. In fact, they thought the mantra and the government policies that underpinned it were janiform in character.

Yes, the Nigerian Armed Forces had absorbed many soldiers, airmen and naval personnel—with punitive reductions in rank— who had fought for the defeated Biafran Republic. Yes, the Nigerian Civil Service had welcomed back their staff who had defected to the defunct Biafran State Civil Service. The problem was that these conciliatory gestures only benefited a few thousand people. What affected several more thousands of ex-Biafrans—mostly ethnic Igbos— was the contemporaneous struggle for the reversal of the "Abandoned Properties" policy of the Nigerian government.

Igbos attempting to move away from the war-ravaged territory of defunct Biafra, in order to resume their pre-war residency in northern and western Nigerian cities, found that they could no longer reclaim the houses and bank accounts they were compelled to leave behind as they fled the pogroms of 1966. Unbeknownst to them, while they were in their eastern homeland—soon to become a breakaway republic and the theatre of the ensuing war—the Nigerian government had declared their assets "abandoned properties" before expropriating them for redistribution to "loyal Nigerians".

The post-war struggle for the restoration of those bank accounts and landed property failed, leaving thousands of Igbos bereft and bitter. Mama Ugoye was one of them. She could not recover ownership of the duplex she had shared with her late husband in Lagos before the civil war and the single-storey building, which had housed her pre-war business enterprise. The "loyal Nigerians" occupying both properties had seized them in September 1966, soon after Ugoyemma and her then-living husband fled to the east, and even before the Nigerian military government passed decrees that gave its imprimatur to such expropriations. In similar vein, the pre-war Nigerian bank accounts of Mama Ugoye and her deceased spouse were also no longer accessible.

Taking the injustice in her stride, she resettled in Enugu city with her grandson to begin life afresh at age 64. With the help of Catholic charities, the grandmother obtained enough money to re-establish her pre-war business— wholesaling bales of dried tobacco leaves imported from Switzerland to local retailers who ground them down to the powdery form suitable for snuffboxes. The proceeds made from the business sent Martin to a good primary school, a top secondary school and a renowned polytechnic, all in Enugu city.

Halfway through his electronics engineering studies at the polytechnic, Martin joined the Nigerian Army, which subsequently took over the payment of his tuition from his grandmother. Upon graduation with a Higher National Diploma (HND) in 1982, he secured a position in the Corps of Nigerian Army Electrical and Mechanical Engineers (NAEME), the branch of the army tasked with maintaining and repairing its electrical, mechanical, electronic, optical and electro-medical equipment.

Four years later, aged 26, he was a captain in charge of a company of one hundred and fifty NAEME soldiers stationed at Bonny Military Cantonment in Victoria Island, Lagos.

Having successfully passed three officer promotion exams and rapidly progressed up the ranks, it all seemed that the spinning wheels of fate had destined Martin for greatness, preparing to propel him all the way to the rank of an army general, some day, in the distant future. Then a single incident caused things to rapidly fall apart.

It all began at the tail end of the second quarter of 1986. The Lebanese civil war—originally triggered by the presence of "interloping" Palestinian refugees, turbocharged by the military interventions of Israel and Syria— was in its eleventh year with no end in sight. The United Nations (UN) had managed to broker yet another ceasefire between the combatants and was looking to expand its existing 5,668-strong peacekeeping force in the war-torn Levantine country.

The UN secretary-general made some international phone calls and the pledges began to roll in. Fiji pledged to send 10 more soldiers to join its contingent already in Lebanon. France pledged an extra 100 troops. Ireland agreed to increase its contingent by 70 troops. Sweden threw its hat into the ring with an extra 200 troops. Italy promised to contribute three extra army helicopter units. Ghana, which already had 870 troops in Lebanon, pledged another 50 soldiers.

Being the regional hegemon and largest nation in West Africa, Nigeria was not going to let the much smaller Ghana outshine her. The Nigerian federal military government pledged 600 troops, of which 150 would come from NAEME. Out of the various NAEME formations across the country, Captain Martin Okoye's entire company in Victoria Island was selected to be part of the peacekeeping force scheduled for deployment in South Lebanon within a month.

There was great excitement when the news arrived at Bonny Military Cantonment. Deployments abroad were popular because they were lucrative assignments. Whether deployed to other African nations to serve as military advisors and trainers, or sent to far-flung parts of the world to serve as UN peacekeepers, Nigerian soldiers abroad were entitled to bonus pay on top of their regular salaries. For those lucky enough to be selected for blue-beret peacekeeping operations, a uniquely generous bonus awaited, in the form of a large dollar-denominated pay packet, courtesy of the UN.

Three weeks before deployment to the Middle East, a rumour spread that the UN had transferred the funds for the 600-strong peacekeeping contingent to the Federal Ministry of Defence, which in turn had passed the money on to the Nigerian Army.

Within days of the rumour, the money began to reach the men in batches. All 320 soldiers in the infantry component of the peacekeeping mission were the first to receive their cheques, followed by the 130 sappers of the Nigeria Army Corp of Engineers (NAE) selected to deploy alongside the infantry. Then everything suddenly ground to a halt.

At first, the 150 soldiers of the NAEME component of the peacekeeping force were not worried, believing that there was a minor delay in the disbursement of their entitlements. As far as they were concerned, the pay cheques were still weaving their way through some bureaucratic maze in the finance department of the Nigeria Army.

Two weeks came and went without the anticipated pay. Another week rolled by, and still no sign that anybody in the upper echelons of the army was concerned that some soldiers in Bonny Military Cantonment had not received their entitlement. Five days to overseas deployment, the patience of the NAEME soldiers snapped.

The most senior non-commissioned officer (NCO) in their midst—a Staff Sergeant—requested a meeting with Captain Martin Okoye to discuss the men's grievance. At that meeting, the Staff Sergeant told Martin that the men were indignant, distressed, and restless about the lack of payment. Everybody about to deploy had received the UN peacekeeping pay cheque except NAEME soldiers. What was going on?

Martin promised to look into the matter, but issued a stern order to the Staff Sergeant to maintain discipline in the barracks. 'Anybody who causes trouble goes straight to the guardroom. Ask military police to help, if necessary,' he said and dismissed the NCO.

Moments later, Martin rang his immediate superior, a Lieutenant Colonel, to complain. The Lieutenant Colonel listened carefully over the phone and promised to get the issue resolved within 48 hours. Two days rolled by and none of the NAEME boys got their pay, and the Lieutenant Colonel did not get back to Martin.

Smelling a rat, Martin phoned an acquaintance in Army Finance Department to find out what was happening. The acquaintance—a captain who worked in the office of the Director of Army Finance—was sympathetic to the plight of the unpaid soldiers and divulged some sensitive information over the phone. It was a very risky act with career-ending implications, and yet the acquaintance did it because of the disgust he felt about the state of affairs in the place where he worked. He extracted a promise from Martin never to reveal him as the source of the information. Martin thanked the army officer and hung up, barely able to suppress the anger and indignation at what he had just heard.

The mutiny occurred on the day the Nigerian Army contingent was due to leave for Lebanon. It began at 7.00AM, exactly three hours before the 280 soldiers belonging to NAE and NAEME were supposed to gather in front of Bonny Military Cantonment with their deployment gear and enter the military trucks that would transport them from Victoria Island to the airport in Ikeja where they were to wait for their flight to Lebanon.

Of course, none of the 150 NAEME soldiers intended to go anywhere unless their grievances were addressed. In fact, none of them had assembled their deployment gear in preparation for the 10.00 AM rendezvous at the cantonment's entrance gates. Their mutiny was presaged by a loud knock, at dawn, on an apartment door in the officers' quarters of the cantonment.

Martin opened that door in his pyjamas, his jaw still partly covered in the white creamy foam. Before he was rudely interrupted by the knock, the captain had been shaving in preparation for deployment. On his doorstep were the Staff

Sergeant and a Sergeant, both men under his command. They were in full olive-green uniforms, looking glum, and none saluted.

Martin glanced at the digital watch on his right wrist. The time was 5.45 AM. He opened his mouth to ask the non-commissioned officers (NCOs) if everything was fine, if there was a problem with their preparations to ship out, but he was cut off before his vocal cords could generate the words.

'Sir, the boys are not happy,' the Staff Sergeant said grimly. The Sergeant standing next to him nodded gravely. 'They are not ready to deploy until the matter of their allowances is settled.'

Uneasy silence followed, interrupted intermittently by chirping crickets and crowing roosters, both unseen. Martin stared at the bulge in the pockets of their trousers, and then at the handgrips of the Berreta automatic pistols jutting out of their waistbands. For a moment, he wondered if they were carrying grenades in those pockets.

'What should we do, sir?' the Sergeant asked, speaking for the first time. It did not seem to Martin that these men were at his doorstep to take his orders. It looked like they were there to sound him out.

'The boys have decided to protest this injustice'—the Staff Sergeant chimed in—'and I think they are right to do that, sir.'

At that point, Martin was supposed to rebuke the men for what they were suggesting, remind them that mutiny was a grave offence, and then order the NCOs back to their quarters with a message instructing all 150 men to prepare for the upcoming overseas deployment under the pain of a court-martial. If the NCOs then showed signs of recalcitrance, the military police would be brought in to disarm and arrest them along with any other NAEME soldier refusing to obey orders.

But Martin did not do any of that. He ignored the laid out guidelines on how to handle mutinous soldiers. Feeling a flush of anger at what he had learned from his contact at Army Finance Department earlier, Martin shrugged. 'I have no orders for you. You know the consequences of your actions. Do what you have to do at your own risk,' he told the NCOs.

Smiling, the olive-green uniforms stood at attention and saluted their superior. When they left, Martin retreated into his apartment and waited for the brewing shitstorm to kick off. He knew that it was going to scandalize and embarrass the Army High Command, and generate a lot of well-deserved negative publicity. By the time, Martin returned to the bathroom to pick up his shaving stick, it was sunrise.

At 7.05 AM, Martin Okoye—clean-shaven and in full uniform—headed to the Officers' Mess for breakfast. On his way, he sighted his men in the distance, close to the entrance of the military cantonment. The NAEME soldiers were marching in a single file with the Staff Sergeant in the lead. Martin watched the men clad in olive-green uniforms halt in front of the closed wrought iron gates while the Staff Sergeant and Sergeant entered the adjacent security guard booth. Moments later, both men emerged from the booth followed by two army privates on security duty. The privates opened the gates and saluted. The Staff Sergeant and Sergeant returned the salute and joined the NAEME soldiers marching past the open gates.

Martin shook his head. He had lost control of his men. There were going to be grim consequences, but he was not worried. He entered the dining hall of the mess, collected some food on a silver tray and settled down on a table to eat. Minutes later, two captains with food trays joined him. The one who sat on his right was the commander of the NAE sappers selected to go to Lebanon while the other was a staff officer in army administration.

Like all the 130 soldiers under his command, the NAE Captain had been received his UN-recommended bonus pay and could not fathom why his counterpart in NAEME and his men hadn't received theirs. 'Hey Martin, have you raised the matter with the Colonel?' he asked.

Martin answered in the affirmative. 'Yes, he said he would look into the matter. Not heard back from him.'

The staff officer scoffed. 'A month has passed since the money was released to Army Finance. There is no excuse for the delay. Something fishy is going on somewhere higher up on the food chain.'

Martin nodded, but said nothing.

'*Money don miss road*,' the NAE commander remarked sonorously in Pidgin English.

Martin did not respond. The UN pay cheques had indeed missed their way to him and his men, and he knew why. He was not really in the mood for chit-chat, but he nodded politely to whatever the army officers flanking him were saying. He drank his tea quietly, wondering what his men were up to, wondering how long it was going to take for the officers sitting beside him at the table, the Commandant of the Cantonment and the Army High Command to realize that a mutiny was underway; a brewing shitstorm that he had done absolutely nothing to stop.

The shitstorm kicked off at 8.45 AM. Martin knew this because he had heard loud excited voices and the sound of a military truck wafting in through the window of his office. He walked across the room and stared through the glass louvres of the open jalousie window at the patch of carpet grass located equidistantly between his low-rise concrete office building and the wrought iron gates of the cantonment.

Trampling the grass were the polished black boots of dozens of green-uniformed men with armbands emblazoned with the acronym "MP" and bright-red berets on their heads. They were military policemen. The one who appeared to be their leader was barking orders as the men were climbing into the rear of the truck. When all the military policemen were inside the truck, its six-cylinder diesel engine roared to life.

At the entrance of the cantonment, the privates from the security guard booth quickly opened the iron gates and saluted as the military truck zoomed past.

Martin walked back across the office. He had barely sat down behind his desk when there was loud banging on the door. Before he could speak, the door opened and an intensely dark-skinned tall man entered. The gold pips on the shoulder boards of his camouflage uniform indicated the rank of a Lieutenant Colonel. Martin rose from his chair and saluted. The furious visitor ignored it.

'I just received a call from the Commandant. Your men are blocking traffic on Third Mainland Bridge. What is going on?'

'They are protesting the non-payment of their peace-keeping allowance. NAE and Infantry soldiers were paid a month ago. My men won't deploy overseas unless this matter is settled now,' Martin replied in a steely voice.

'But I told you that I was addressing the issue with Army Finance!' barked the Lieutenant Colonel indignantly.

'The men will not deploy overseas until this matter is resolved,' Martin repeated. 'And they have my unalloyed support.'

The superior officer's eyes flashed with anger. 'Your men not only blocked the bridge, they also beat up traffic policemen doing their jobs. They are an embarrassment to the army, and so are you.'

'My men are not an embarrassment,' Martin responded, raising his voice. 'They are professionals who have been robbed of their allowances by the shenanigans of the Director of Army Finance and others protecting him. Those corrupt thugs are the real embarrassment to the army!'

The Lieutenant Colonel was taken aback, both by what he had heard, and by the venomous tone in which it was communicated. The insubordination! He banged a clenched fist on Martin's desk. 'Doesn't matter if what you allege is true. Mutiny is an offence. You will regret this soon enough!' he shouted and then stormed out of the office.

Twenty minutes later, the door to Martin's office burst open. He stood up and raised his hands as six red-bereted, grim-faced military policemen entered the room with Beretta pistols pointing in his direction.

'Captain, I arrest you for conspiring to commit mutiny,' declared their leader, a lieutenant by rank. Two lance corporals behind the lieutenant began to move. They walked past him, strode across the room, walked around the big office desk, and stopped beside Martin.

With a mocking smile on his face, Martin lowered his arms to the level of his chest and extended them towards the military policemen. One lance corporal slammed metal handcuffs on the extended wrists. The lieutenant and three red berets standing near the open door turned around and filed out of the office, followed by the lance corporals flanking the army captain under arrest.

'There is no need to drag me. I am not resisting,' Martin remonstrated as he was led outside into the veranda.

The red berets, on either side of him, did not react to his remark, did not slacken their tight grip on his upper arms. They kept propelling him forward, slowly, and silently, at the rear of the procession of military policemen led by the lieutenant.

A few feet from the veranda, Martin observed that the military truck that had gone out earlier was now back. Sitting on the patch of the carpet grass, beside the truck that brought them back, was a large group of men clad in olive-green uniforms, the insignia of NAEME clearly visible on their shoulder patches. Standing over the hapless soldiers on the grass were a dozen military policemen totting Kalashnikov rifles.

Martin recognized the seated soldiers with their wrists bound together with black plastic zip ties. He did not count, but he was sure that it was all 150 of his men under arrest, awaiting a closed-door court-martial for "conspiracy to commit mutiny". He could not see most of their faces as many were looking downwards at the grass as if in shame or embarrassment. Martin did notice a few defiant faces among the men seated on the grass.

Among those with their chins up were the ringleaders of the mutiny—the NCOs who had visited him at the crack of dawn. Martin saw the Sergeant staring straight ahead impassively. Sitting next to him on the grass was the Staff Sergeant who did not seem fazed by the fact that the muzzle of an AK-47 assault rifle was aiming downwards, a few inches from his head. He locked eyes with Martin and smiled ruefully. Martin nodded and turned to face forward, struggling to keep up with the quickened pace of the military policemen pulling him along.

As he was being hauled into the guardroom behind the expansive dining hall of the Officers' Mess, Martin felt a pang of guilt. Perhaps, he should have stopped the mutiny. That would have spared his men from the humiliation of being cashiered and imprisoned. But perhaps, nothing could have prevented the revolt, short of him ordering a mass arrest of all his men. After all, the NCOs had visited in the wee hours of the morning with their minds already made up. Martin was quite sure that the Staff Sergeant and Sergeant would not have led the mutiny without the consent and voluntary cooperation of the troops.

Martin had expected a swift closed-door court-martial for himself and his men, but that was not to be. The fallout of the mutiny was a public relations disaster for Army High Command and, by extension, the military junta running the country.

The mutineers had chosen the perfect location for their noisy, disruptive and illegal protest. Thousands of motorists, pedestrians—and more importantly, journalists—had witnessed the blocking of the Third Mainland Bridge, a major artery in the traffic-heavy road network of Lagos. They also witnessed the mutineers fight, beat up and subdue traffic policemen trying to arrest them. Journalists had taken photographs of the mutineers with improvised placards denouncing the non-payment of their entitlements. The protesting soldiers had granted on-the-spot press interviews, articulating their grievances into scores of tape recorders and microphones shoved in their faces.

While that impromptu interview was still going on, traffic policemen, bruised and battered, had taken the chance to retreat to the nearest police kiosk. From there, they phoned their superior—a senior traffic policeman— and gave him the situation report. That senior policeman then placed an angry phone call to the office of the Commandant of the Bonny Military Cantonment in Victoria Island.

The Commandant, shocked and furious, ordered the cantonment's military police to go out and apprehend the mutineers. No sooner had he returned to his office than the phone rang. He picked up the handset and was surprised to learn that he was speaking to the first secretary of the British High Commission—one of several embassies in Victoria Island that were a stone's throw away from the cantonment.

Apparently, the British High Commissioner, Sir Horace Granville-Jones, had witnessed some of the ruckus while stuck in traffic on the Third Mainland Bridge, and had used the carphone to call the embassy to request that the first secretary find out what was going on.

A clearly embarrassed Commandant waffled apologetically and assured the diplomatic officer on the phone that the situation was being dealt with. No, it was not a military coup d'etat in progress—just a bunch of unruly drunken soldiers misbehaving. When the phone call was over, the Commandant, who held the rank of a Brigadier-General, undid the top button of his barrack dress shirt to prevent himself from suffocating on the anger and the panic racking his body. The phone call from the first secretary had added a minor international dimension to the shitstorm.

When the Lieutenant Colonel responsible for the entire NAEME regiment inside the military cantonment appeared in the Commandant's Office to answer his summons, the Brigadier-General exploded in anger, growling and screaming.

The Lieutenant Colonel professed his innocence and ignorance of the revolt, narrowly avoiding arrest for "conspiracy to aid and abet a mutiny". Having pacified the Commandant, the same Lieutenant Colonel then proceeded to storm the office of Martin Okoye to demand an explanation for the mutiny before ordering the military police to arrest the insubordinate NAEME Captain.

While Martin and his men were incarcerated in separate guardrooms, the 130 sappers of the NAE departed for the airport in military trucks as originally scheduled. However, the trucks took a rather circuitous route to bypass the Third Mainland Bridge— still the scene of traffic chaos, even hours after it had been cleared of the mutineers.

Arriving forty minutes late to the airport, the sappers started jumping down from the rear of the military trucks, their shiny black boots hitting the tarmacked runway. With their deployment gear strapped firmly to their backs, the NAE sappers marched in a single file towards the Lockheed C-130H Hercules plane, already bearing the 320 infantry soldiers it had picked up at its first stop in the northern city of Kaduna. Climbing onboard, the sappers smiled and nodded amiably at their infantry counterparts already seated, and then began to occupy empty seats inside the plane. The aeroplane engines roared to life.

As the huge transport plane began to taxi on the runway, some of the sappers gazed sadly at the empty seats around them—the ones meant for their rebellious NAEME comrades detained back in the cantonment. Like their infantry colleagues, the sappers had been received their UN allowances and could not fathom why the NAEME guys had been denied theirs.

The C-130H Hercules turboprop had barely cleared Nigerian airspace, en route to the Middle East, when army top brass held an emergency meeting. The army generals were all of the view that the mutiny should be dealt with quickly and ruthlessly. They had already appointed a Major-General assisted by two Brigadier-Generals to preside over the impending court-martial. What had caused the meeting to last forty minutes were deliberations on whether the army should seek the death penalty for each of the men or settle for the more lenient 10-year-jail sentence followed by dishonourable discharge. There were heated debates before all agreed on the lenient sentence. The generals had scheduled the trial for the enlisted men and NCOs to start four days after the mutiny and that of the commissioned officer, Captain Martin Okoye, to start the week after.

The incarcerated NAEME soldiers were duly informed and advised to choose their defence counsels from the large pool of military lawyers in the Army Directorate of Legal Services (ADLS). Martin and his men rejected that advice and indicated their intention to seek civilian lawyers whom they could trust.

The day before the trial was to start, five different newspapers, with similar banner headlines, appeared on newsstands and in the arms of teenage newspaper hawkers. The headlines topped stories exposing massive corruption in the Army Finance Department. One of the newspapers, a tabloid, published a double-page news feature, which included pictures of the mutineers with their placards along with the transcript of their roadside interviews explaining the reason for their revolt.

Army top brass were alarmed by those newspaper headlines. More worryingly, dozens of human rights lawyers— civilians who could not be intimidated and stymied like military lawyers of the ADLS— were offering to represent the court-martialled soldiers on *pro bono* basis.

News of the sleaze in Army Finance Department soon reached the ears of the UN Secretary-General who then summoned Nigeria's UN Permanent Representative for a dress down. Later on, from his office in New York, that chastened Nigerian UN diplomat phoned his foreign minister in Abuja to pass on the angry message from the secretary-general. That civilian foreign minister then briefed members of the ruling military junta. The military junta, in turn, passed the buck to Army Headquarters with a firm order to clean up the terrible mess quickly.

With a huge public relations disaster on their hands, army top brass entered "damage control" mode. To mollify the UN secretary-general, soldiers from a different NAEME regiment based in Kaduna city were selected, paid their overseas deployment allowances, and sent to Lebanon in the place of the ones facing court-martial in Lagos.

The Director of Army Finance and his two deputies were fired and then court-martialled. The usual closed-door format of the court-martial proceedings was jettisoned and journalists were invited to observe and record the proceedings.

The court-martial returned a guilty verdict within seventy-two hours and the disgraced erstwhile Director and his two deputies earned a five-year prison sentence to be followed by dishonourable discharge.

By inviting the TV and print media to witness the humiliation of two senior army officers, top brass wanted to demonstrate their intolerance for corruption in the hope that journalists—especially the muckrakers among them—would not delve any deeper into the affairs of the military lest they stumble upon larger closets of sleaze.

But the print media did not let up. The newspapers campaigned for the release of the detained NAEME soldiers and carried transcripts of interviews with human rights lawyers who were complaining that the army was preventing them from meeting their prospective clients—the one hundred and fifty mutineers and their young commander.

The day before the court-martial of the enlisted NAEME soldiers, another emergency meeting took place at Army Headquarters. During that meeting, the four-star generals agreed the trial would turn into a media circus and damage the reputation of the army badly. Mutiny was abhorrent, but the wider civil populace did not care for military law. The court of public opinion, shaped by the media, would see any form of punishment as a persecution of soldiers protesting the unjust denial of their entitlements. To head off the public relations disaster, it was agreed that the enlisted men would be pardoned and released to return to their normal duties. The non-commissioned officers (NCOs)—the staff sergeant and the sergeant—would also be pardoned, but each would suffer a reduction in rank as mild punishment for leading the mutiny. The commissioned officer, Captain Martin Okoye, would get the most severe punishment for failing to stop the mutiny. The captain would no longer face a court-martial. Instead, he would be subject to some administrative disciplinary proceedings, which would result in a dishonourable discharge from the army.

When the news from Army Headquarters reached the enlisted NAEME soldiers, they were ecstatic. They celebrated, cried and hugged each other. The loss of their chance to serve as UN peacekeepers, and the bonus pay that comes with that assignment, was furthest from their mind.

The staff sergeant and sergeant accepted their fates with equanimity, glad that their military careers had survived the grave offence of mutiny.

The only person who loudly rejected the diktat from Army Headquarters was Martin Okoye. He wrote an angry letter to the Chief of Army Staff (COAS) swearing to fight the army in civilian courts to block attempts to cashier him. His flamboyant civilian lawyer followed up with a press conference in which he alleged that the reason for the continued detention of Martin was his possession of evidence of corruption higher up the ranks in Army Headquarters.

The lawyer's allegation was disingenuous. The order for the release of the NAEME Captain from the detention had already been issued the day before the press conference, but was only implemented an hour after that lawyer concluded the briefing session with the journalists. The lawyer's deceit was merely a pressure tactic to compel the Army Headquarters to change their mind about the harsh punishment they had imposed on his client.

Freed from incarceration, pending the completion of admin proceedings aimed at drumming him out of the army, Martin caused his firebrand lawyer to write another letter to the COAS threatening to grant media interviews that would claim that corruption ran deeper in the upper echelons of the army, far beyond the Army Finance Department.

As it had done with the first missive, the office of the COAS passed the second letter to the Department of Army Administration (DOAA). The four-star generals running DOAA binned that letter without bothering to read it. They had read the first insulting letter and already knew what the second one was going to say. They unanimously agreed that Martin's threat of exposing further corruption in the army was just a bluff. A lowly company commander in NAEME was in no position to know the shenanigans going on within the upper echelons of the army, was too remote to observe the inner workings of the army's highly politicized bureaucracy where corruption lived and flourished.

Nevertheless, the generals feared Martin's intention to sully them in the media. The press was sensationalist and unscrupulous, and would have no qualms about publishing any unsubstantiated allegations as if they were proven facts.

Like any other soldier with common sense, Martin perceived the stench of corruption emanating from senior officers controlling the finances needed to feed, equip and pay soldiers, as well as maintain army infrastructure all over the country. He just had no way of definitively proving this perceived corruption because, as a field officer, he was an order of magnitude removed from the murky world of army administration. But then, the absence of hard evidence had never stopped any media outlet from printing stories of corruption in high places. In a country where bribery, extortion, graft and embezzlement was pervasive, it did not take much to convince the general public, the consumers of print and broadcast media products.

Martin was optimistic that Army Headquarters, which had been ignoring his letters, would eventually come around to him with a decent proposal that did not include a disgraceful exit from the army. He was sure that the generals understood the implications of his threats; the fact that any allegations of sleaze levelled against them in the press would automatically be accepted as gospel truth, both by journalists and by the court of public opinion.

Martin did not have to wait so long. During yet another late night meeting in Army Headquarters, the generals discussed Martin's case at length. They reaffirmed their belief that most of the bold statements in the first letter were mere bluff and bluster. Martin could not expose their dirty laundry for all to see because he did not have access to the laundry room. But then, any allegation of impropriety, unproven as it might be, would further damage the already flagging reputation of the army. So the officials of DOAA made a decision. The media circus, which kicked off with the altercation on Third Mainland Bridge, must be brought to an end. On behalf of the army, the generals agreed to present Martin with a parting settlement package on a *take-it-or-leave-it* basis. They hoped he would take it and end their public relations nightmare.

When the letter bearing the proposed settlement reached Martin's lawyer, he took it to his client. Both men were surprised by the generous terms of the settlement—the army would halt all disciplinary proceedings against Martin; he would be honourably discharged; would retain his current rank; and receive a lump sum equivalent to his annual salary as a final pay-off. In exchange, Martin would have to agree, in writing, not to approach the press or publicly make any statement besmirching the reputation of the army and its leadership. If the settlement package on offer were rejected then the army would simply carry on with the disciplinary proceedings aimed at cashiering Martin.

At the urging of his lawyer, Martin accepted the offer and wrote to Army Headquarters to communicate his decision.

The generals were relieved to learn that he had accepted their offer without a fuss. Upon receiving Martin's written undertaking not to disparage the army, DOAA authorized the payment of the lump sum money; the dispatch of a letter of commendation for "meritorious service to the fatherland" accompanied by a Nigeria Star Medal; and an open invitation to attend the Armed Forces Remembrance Day annually, in full uniform, like any other military veteran.

With the offered settlement package accepted, and a non-disparagement letter received, the generals considered the matter closed and moved on to other issues.

For Martin, the end of the saga just opened up a new chapter in his life, one filled with uncertainties. With his military career gone, Martin was bereft. After checking his bank account at First Bank Plc to see that the money was all there, he got into the army-issued Peugeot 504 sedan, which DOAA had graciously allowed him to keep as a parting gift, and embarked on the 435-mile road journey from Lagos to Enugu, his home city.

Mama Ugoye was pleased to have her grandson back in Enugu, living with her once again. Although she had never approved of Martin joining the army, she felt his sadness at having lost his beloved career. 'You will get something better,' she said, seeking to cheer him up.

He would spend the next four weeks assisting his aged, but still spry, grandmother in the management of her tobacco business—doing the book-keeping, supervising the transfer of imported tobacco bales from delivery trucks to the warehouse and processing orders placed for those bales by retailers. In between helping out with his grandma's business, he scoured the vacancies section of local city newspapers for engineering jobs.

Within a month of arriving in Enugu, he had landed a job with Union Bank, which was in the middle of computerizing certain sectors of its banking operations, and keen to recruit brilliant engineers to help achieve that. He would go on to work for that bank for the next fifteen months, helping it to automate its cheque processing system before leaving to join the Nigerian Police Force.

The decision to join the police in July 1987 came as a surprise to everybody— his colleagues and superiors in the bank, and his grandmother. It was surprising because no one could understand the rationale behind leaving a well-paying job in favour of becoming a poorly paid policeman.

For his grandmother, it was pure madness. Like many in the civil populace, she had scant respect for the police because there was no institution that embodied corruption in the country more than the Nigerian Police Force. It was one thing to join the military, and another to join the gun-totting, corrupt wretches referred to as police officers.

She spent three days trying to talk Martin out of the decision, but his mind was made up. The Police Force was certainly corrupt, he reasoned, but it was not irredeemable. Moreover, a country bedevilled by high levels of crime could not do without a law enforcement organ, even one that was as flawed and corrupt as the Nigerian Police Force. If people like him, who were not personally corrupt, shied away from joining that institution then there was no hope of effecting a change from within.

Seeing that she had failed to convince him to alter his decision, Mama Ugoye grudgingly gave her blessing to her grandson's new career path.

Martin's journey into a career in law enforcement kicked off with an admission into the Police Training College in Oji River, a quiet town located thirty-one miles from the city of Enugu. Performing at the top of his class there, he was among the graduands selected to return to the city to undergo further training at the Police Detective College. After two years of training, Martin began to work as a detective in Imo State Police Command in June 1989.

Meanwhile, hundreds of miles away, in Lagos State, Chief Superintendent of Police (CSP) Cyrus Udeh was going through various options available to keep Ikeja CID running. Having repeatedly failed to secure money from the Lagos Police Equipment Fund for the purchase of ready-made surveillance equipment from abroad, the Ikeja CID boss had made the fateful decision to have the necessary gadgets fabricated in-house. Civilian engineers were hired for the job. Using semi-conductors available in local electronics stores, the engineers managed the feat. However, the quality of their gadgetry was not top-notch. The gadgets were prone to frequent breakdowns. And the exorbitant fees charged by the engineers to fix them proved an unacceptable drain on the budget of Ikeja CID.

A couple of months later, a highly frustrated Cyrus assembled a few CID squad leaders to brainstorm alternative solutions. Long before he summoned those senior detectives, he had thought of appealing to the lavishly equipped anti-police corruption squad (APCS) to donate some of their older radio equipment to other CID squads. But he could not bring himself to beg a junior police officer for anything; not even one that had been empowered by a federal government committee to ride roughshod on the police chain of command. He was never going to appeal to the insolent and insubordinate APCS leader, Chief Inspector

Nduka Ikwunne. Cyrus' brainstorming session was taking place in September 1989 when the feud between he and Nduka was at its peak.

The session had gone on for thirty minutes before somebody said that he had heard of police officers who had studied either electrical or electronics engineering before joining the Force. Perhaps, a handful of such police officers, wherever in the country they might be based, could be seconded to Ikeja CID.

Cyrus sat up. The anger building up within him began to dissipate as his mind shifted from the ghastly Nduka back to the meeting he was chairing. He smiled and then pondered over the suggestion. It was going to be tough, he thought to himself. The vast majority of police officers in the country were individuals whose formal education had terminated at the conclusion of primary or secondary school. Although, there were a growing number of polytechnic and university graduates joining the Force, they were still a small minority in the 1980s, and those who had studied engineering were bound to be a tiny fraction of that minority, if at all they existed.

But then Cyrus was not one to shy away from a challenge. If there was only one or two of such policemen in the country, he was going to poach them for Ikeja CID. Three days later, he got the Lagos State Police Commissioner to circulate a note to all State Police Commands across the country requesting for police personnel with electronics engineering qualifications.

Ogun State Police Command had three policemen who fit the criteria and was willing to release one to Lagos State Police Command to join Ikeja CID. Cross River State Police Command had two such policemen and was happy for one to transfer to Lagos. Imo State Police Command had just one and was not willing to let him go. Cyrus Udeh welcomed the two police transferees from Ogun and Cross River States, but they were hardly enough.

Two months later, while drinking his early morning cup of tea in his office, the police orderly, Constable Dixon Nkwamkpa, brought in a letter in a brown envelope. After the orderly left, Cyrus gazed at the envelope from the corner of his eye, as he sipped his tea. His name and address in the front of the envelope were handwritten. The postmark suggested that the letter had come from faraway Imo State. His curiosity was piqued. He was used to getting circulars and memos in white envelopes embossed with the police logo, which had his name and address neatly typed in front. Those official documents always came to him from police bodies within Lagos or from Force Headquarters in Abuja. He had never received any from Imo State, certainly not in a creased brown envelope with his name handwritten.

He hastily gulped down the remaining contents of his teacup and returned it to the saucer. Then he slit the envelope with an ornate brass letter opener and extricated the folded sheet of paper within. His eyes quickly ran through the handwritten sentences. What he had read surprised him in a way that he had not anticipated. The letter was not from a civilian. It was from an Imo State detective who had heard that Ikeja CID was looking for policemen with an electronics engineering background. The detective's name sounded vaguely familiar to

Cyrus, but he could not place where he had heard it. It was not until his reading eyes reached the middle of the letter where the detective was talking about his prior experience as an army engineer that it finally hit the Ikeja CID boss.

Of course, the author of the letter was the army officer who had been at the centre of a mutiny of soldiers based in Bonny Military Cantonment, three years earlier. Cyrus recalled reading all about it in the newspapers, hearing about it on radio, and seeing video footage of some of the mutineers on television. It was big news back then, and not just in the media. It was a big deal in the police force too. Every police officer in Lagos—from the commissioner to the lowly constable— was outraged by the news that the mutineers had beaten up traffic policemen who tried to arrest them for blocking the Third Mainland Bridge.

'But how and when did this young army officer become a policeman?' Cyrus asked the room, which was devoid of any other human being. A surreal feeling washed over him as he slowly re-read the letter to make sure he had caught the gist of Detective-Constable Martin Okoye's request. The army officer-turned-detective wanted to join Ikeja CID despite opposition from his superiors in Imo State. He wanted Cyrus to pull some strings to get him to Lagos, but understood if the Ikeja CID boss would rather not anger the Imo State Police Command by trying to poach one of their detectives.

Cyrus couldn't care less what the higher-ups in Imo State Police Command thought about poaching. In fact, he was actually ready to poach a man of Martin Okoye's calibre— an alumnus of the well-regarded Institute of Management and Technology in Enugu city, a detective who was once a commander of a military unit of 150 soldiers, a skilled person who had actually put his engineering knowledge to good use while in the army.

Only one thing stopped Cyrus from getting on the phone to the Lagos State Commissioner straightaway. He was wary of any man who had once rebelled against authority. Martin had been at the centre of a mutiny. Cyrus already had the ghastly APCS leader Nduka Ikwunne to contend with and was not keen on having any more troublemakers under the roof of Ikeja CID complex.

Cyrus set Martin's letter to one side and carried on with his duties. It would take another seven days of rumination before he came to conclusion that he definitely wanted Martin on his CID team. But first, he had to make some discreet enquiries about the temperament of the detective he was about to poach from Imo State Police.

He summoned the civilian lawyer who had represented Martin during his incarceration on mutiny charges. The civilian lawyer had only nice things to say about his former client and expressed some surprise that the former army officer—whom he had not been in contact for some years—had decided to join the police force. Next, Cyrus picked up the phone and called the head of the Police Training College in Oji River and the head of the Police Detective College in Enugu city. They also had only praise for Martin who was among their best graduates.

Cyrus thought of contacting his counterparts in the Imo State Police Command to ask questions about Martin, but quickly decided against it. Those senior police officers in Imo would quickly figure out that he was planning to poach one of their detectives, and perhaps make moves to block it.

Satisfied with answers he had gotten from the civilian lawyer and heads of two police colleges, Cyrus made his decision. He spoke to the Lagos Police Commissioner who in turn spoke to the Zonal Assistant Inspector-General (AIG)—the most senior police officer in Lagos State— who then lodged a request at Force Headquarters, Abuja, for Martin Okoye to be transferred to Ikeja CID over the objections of Imo State Police Command.

Martin's immediate superiors in Owerri town were both surprised and furious when the transfer order came down from Abuja, but nothing could be done about it beyond vituperative outbursts. The Imo State Police Commissioner, although equally displeased, ensured that the order was obeyed and that Martin's transfer to Lagos was smooth and without a hitch.

By November 1989, Martin Okoye was a fully integrated member of the narcotics squad operating out of the Ikeja CID complex. With the help of his electronic skills, the squad had been able to monitor the telecommunications of notorious drug dealers, intercepting their drug shipments and rolling up their entire trafficking operations. In recognition of his work, he was promoted to Detective-Sergeant (DS) and made third-in-command after DI Ikenna Kodilinye and DI Gbolahan Akinola.

When Ikenna became head of the anti-scam squad in April 1993, the position he left behind in narcotics was filled by Gbolahan, and Martin moved up to become second-in-command. Just as happened while he was in the army, Martin had risen quickly through the ranks of the police, propelled head and shoulders above his peers by his zeal and dedication to work.

CHAPTER 28

NOVEMBER 1993

LAGOS, WESTERN NIGERIA

Drug trafficking is a global phenomenon. Many countries across the world have had to deal with the menace of hardened criminals well practiced in the art of concealing and then distributing narcotics to addicted segments of the civil populace. Nigeria was one of such countries. Like many other nations, the West African country had not only witnessed the growth of drug trafficking, it had also seen its deleterious effects on a part of the citizenry, mainly the youths, who habitually consume the trafficked products.

Nigeria's drug trafficking problem began in the immediate aftermath of the Second World War, when young Nigerian men, who had served in colonial detachments of the British Army, began to return home from their military stations in Burma and India, bringing with them "Indian hemp", or more accurately, the seeds of the *Cannabis Sativa* plant. The demobilized military veterans planted the seeds on home soil, and under the favourable African sun, the alien plant germinated, spread all over and quickly became part of the landscape.

Sporadic and half-hearted enforcement of laws against drug trafficking, by government authorities of the day, encouraged criminal gangs who ran the cannabis trade to expand their repertoire to include cocaine, heroin and methamphetamines. With that expansion, came the rising tide of mental illnesses, robberies and homicides. Then, to the alarm of the federal authorities, Nigerian drug traffickers went international and began to appear in the detention facilities of countries across the world, notably in Thailand, Vietnam, Indonesia, India, Malaysia and Singapore.

In December 1983, a new military junta supplanted the democratically elected Nigerian federal government. The military dictatorship set about toughening existing penal laws and enacting new ones by decree. Drug trafficking suddenly became a death penalty offence. After a public outcry, the junta rescinded the harsh anti-narcotic trafficking law and replaced it with another that imposed sentences of between two years and life imprisonment, depending to the severity of the offence. The Nigerian Custom Service stepped up its efforts to tackle cross-border drug smuggling. The Nigerian Police Force vigorously patrolled seedy districts in various cities across the country, catching some drug dealers and causing several others to go into hiding.

But none of these measures had the desired impact that the federal military government had anticipated. For one thing, the Nigerian Federation has very long borders, which were extremely porous and not easy to patrol in certain places. The federation shares its international frontiers with Bénin Republic, Cameroon, Chad and Niger Republic, all transit routes through which narcotics were trafficked in. For another, Nigeria has vast unpoliced spaces within its own borders, where narcotics could be locally produced, where those smuggled in from abroad could be hidden for later distribution.

Unsatisfied with the performance of the Nigerian Police Force, the ruling military junta decided that a brand new organization was needed to combat drug trafficking. In December 1989, over the objections of the police, the National Drug Law Enforcement Agency (NDLEA) was born.

With better resources than the police, the NDLEA scored some significant victories in the interdiction of narcotics. Hectares upon hectares of secret cannabis plantations, hidden deep in the forests, were found and destroyed; several drug packages concealed inside innocuous-looking objects were seized across the nation's land, air and sea ports. Even a couple of persons carrying potentially deadly packages of narcotics in their stomachs were arrested at certain airports in the country. While not entirely free of the scourge of corruption scandals, the NDLEA was judged to be successful in its designated mission by a federal military government, clearly impressed with the record number of drug dealers, albeit small-timers, who had been prosecuted for their crimes.

Riding on the waves of their successes, NDLEA bosses began to lobby the federal military government to remove the police force entirely from the business of drug law enforcement, arguing that police officers was better off concentrating on other crimes such as homicides, scams and armed robbery. But the police top brass had no plans to cede ground to their turf rivals in the NDLEA.

To propitiate the military junta and head off any incipient plans to implement the recommendation of the NDLEA, the senior police officers in Force Headquarters began to rejuvenate narcotic squads scattered in State Police Commands across the country.

Because of limited resources, priority was given to Police Commands in states where drug trafficking was at its worst. Lagos State Police Command was among a lucky handful that received substantially higher financial support from Force Headquarters in Abuja.

CSP Cyrus Udeh, the divisional police officer (DPO) in charge of Lagos State CID, did not perceive himself to be that lucky. As far as he was concerned, the increased financial support from Abuja was feeble. It fell short of what was needed to combat drug trafficking in the bustling Lagos metropolis. Nevertheless, he was somewhat grateful for support from Force Headquarters, which was coming on the heels of his failure to secure money from the Lagos Police Equipment Fund— an organization already straining under the burden of supporting a hundred and seven police stations across the densely populated state.

With meagre funds from Abuja, Cyrus bought whatever materials—provided they were cheap enough— needed by Martin Okoye to build and maintain radio surveillance equipment, which had enabled conversations between drug kingpins and their underlings to be intercepted and recorded. The DPO also managed to acquire a couple of second-hand Nikon cameras and telephoto lens for the narcotics squad. These were put to good use, capturing still photographs of those big drug barons often overlooked by NDLEA, which seemed to be good only in apprehending small-timers in the Lagos narcotics trade.

On 25th August 1993, Ikeja CID made its largest drug bust, one that surprised the Lagos branch of the NDLEA for they had never achieved anything of that magnitude. Gbolahan and his right-hand man, Martin, had led a large team of policemen to the historic town of Badagry in a daylight raid of what appeared to be a cavernous warehouse filled to the rafters with piles of timber.

Ten drug traffickers found at the site were promptly placed under arrest while uniformed police constables unloaded the warehouse. Hundreds of wooden planks were brought out and laid out on the huge forecourt in front of the warehouse. Plain-clothes detectives wielding axes went to work, breaking apart each plank. Every single plank, split in half, revealed a hollow interior packed with several plastic bags containing various kinds of hard drugs.

After several hours on the site, Gbolahan phoned Cyrus at Ikeja CID to tell him what had been recovered from the police raid— thirty tonnes of cannabis, ten tonnes of cocaine, four tonnes of heroin and fifty thousand methamphetamine pills.

Under interrogation, the gang of ten, confessed to charges of narcotics trafficking and revealed that many of the drugs were destined for export to other countries in the West African sub-region. They also gave up the name of their boss, the drug baron, who presided over the underworld racket. Gbolahan and Martin raided the baron's swanky mansion in the upscale district of Ikoyi, but they were too late. The drug lord had already fled the country, never to return.

The NDLEA offered to assist in tracking down the fugitive using their extensive international contacts. Cyrus agreed in principle, but wanted assurances that the NDLEA would turn over the runaway drug lord to the police for prosecution. To his greatest surprise, the Lagos NDLEA Commander pledged not contest the police's right to prosecute the fugitive when he was eventually caught. With the hatchet of turf rivalry buried, Cyrus turned his attention back to the gang of ten in police custody. They had to be prosecuted to the fullest extent of the law.

Gbolahan and Martin produced a charge sheet against the suspects, which passed under the approving eyes of Cyrus Udeh, before it landed on the desk of the Investigating Police Officer (IPO). Using the charging sheet, Sergeant Temitope Maria Akinjide—the IPO— then prepared the case file, which again passed under the approving eyes of Cyrus Udeh, before ending up with the Lagos Directorate of Public Prosecutions (DPP). There, the case file got entangled in bureaucratic red tape, just like many others before it.

And Cyrus failed to do what he had always done in the past when a case file was trapped in the bureaucratic maze— hurrying along the ponderous lawyers of the DPP. He had failed to prod the DPP officials because a rapid chain of unforeseen events had intervened and diverted his attention away from the prosecution of the drug traffickers.

The first of these events was the burglary in DI Ikenna Kodilinye's office, which Cyrus did not learn about until days after the drug bust. That was quickly followed up by another event—the phone call from Commissioner Stanislaus Zikora informing him about the missing David Steinberg and berating him for his failure to apprehend the murderous swindlers. Then there was the molehunt, which had targeted a couple of innocent detectives, including Martin Okoye. Quickly following in the heels of the failed molehunt was the bomb blast, which killed two police officers, but ultimately failed to eliminate its primary target, Ikenna Kodilinye.

By the time Cyrus' mind circled back to the drug trafficking case file stuck in the DPP, the gang of ten had spent eighty miserable nights in Kirikiri Maximum Prison awaiting a trial that had never been scheduled. Finally, on 12th November, the Ikeja CID boss applied his customary pressure on the DPP, and the bureaucratic red tape holding up the case file was broken.

In the Directorate of Public Prosecutions, the Chief State Counsel dusted the case file and began to review it, finding it wanting in certain areas. To guarantee success in the prosecution of the gang of ten, the contents of case file would have to be revised to ensure that every evidentiary point within it was airtight.

He picked up the handset of his desk telephone and called the IPO whose office was in a sprawling building on the other side of Ikeja.

Sergeant Temitope Maria Akinjide drove across town to answer the summons. While seated across the desk from the Chief State Counsel, she received an earful about the sloppiness of the case file.

'I have marked all the problematic areas in the file,' he told her. 'These changes must be addressed before we can even think of presenting our case to the magistrate. I want our prosecution of the traffickers to be rock solid.'

Temitope nodded as she flipped through the documents in the case file, noting the many words, phrases and sentences that the state prosecutor had underlined or struck out with a red pen. She promised to do her best and then drove back to Ikeja CID.

Back in her office, she spent thirty minutes scrutinizing the case file before forwarding it to DI Gbolahan Akinola. Busy with other drug trafficking cases, the narcotics squad leader sent the case file back to her office with a handwritten note referring her to his deputy, Martin Okoye. Upon reading the note, Temitope hesitated, but was later relieved to hear from a colleague that Martin had travelled to Enugu to see his ailing grandmother.

When Martin returned from the East, five days later, he found a case file on his desk with a typed note from Temitope. He suppressed a sigh and pressed a button on the intercom. Seconds later, a female voice came through the speakers.

'Hello, Martin. How is your granny?' the female voice asked.

Martin replied that Mama Ugoye was doing well. She had been sick with a mild form of pneumonia, but was gradually recovering.

'Would you like to come over and review the case file with me?' he asked.

There was momentary silence on line and then she answered, 'I would like to, but I am going out now. By the way, you don't really need me. Just annotate the pages or make a note of what I am missing...what I need to know and send the whole thing back to my pigeonhole.'

Martin smiled wistfully at the intercom. He knew better than to persist. 'Okay, Temi, I will do that, bye for now.'

'Bye, say hello to your granny for me,' Temitope responded.

The intercom went cold before Martin could respond. He laughed ruefully. She was avoiding him again. It had been going on for at least a month. They used to have a great working relationship. He was the crack detective and crime-buster who arrested the drug dealers. She was the Investigating Police Officer, the liaison between Ikeja CID and the Directorate of Public Prosecutions (DPP), the woman who worked closely with the state prosecutors to ensure that the drug traffickers were successfully tried, convicted and sentenced to jail time by the magistrate courts.

From the moment he met her, worked alongside her, Martin had fallen heads over heels for Temitope— or Temi, as he preferred to call her. At first, he tried not to show it because it distracted from the work at hand. But with further contact, the love within his heart began to grow exponentially with such frightening intensity that he thought it might choke him if he did not vent those tender feelings. And so he did. She turned him down without explanation, although she was clearly fond of him too.

She had to do it because there was no use dwelling on what could never be. Her conservative Yoruba parents would never approve of her relationship with an Igbo man. Of course, she never mentioned this to Martin because she expected him to grasp the reason without her having to spell it out to him. His quiet persistence, after she had turned him down, both charmed and annoyed her. Was his love so blissful that he didn't want to understand why she couldn't go out with him? It wasn't like many Igbo fathers and mothers would roll out drums in celebration if their children brought back a non-Igbo fiancé or fiancée.

Temitope had met Mama Ugoye once while she was visiting her grandson at Ikeja CID. The old woman had been cheerful and very friendly, but then Temitope often wondered how Mama Ugoye would react if her grandson had said he was thinking of going out with a Yoruba woman. Temi was genuinely curious. She could have asked Martin, but she didn't, because she was wary of doing anything to encourage his persistence, because she did not want to raise any false hopes.

If she had asked Martin that question, he would have shrugged and told her. The old woman, Mama Ugoye, would have expressed her disappointment, but she would not have put up a fight. She would have grudgingly accepted their relationship because she was his granny and was invested in his happiness. Martin would have told Temi that her beauty and kindness would have worked wonders on his disapproving granny within a short time.

Martin gazed broodingly at the intercom for a while and then decided to put his personal issues aside and focus on work. Between fighting criminals in the streets and a comprehensive review of the case file on his desk, the detective had a very tight schedule. Time was not a luxury he could ill afford. He grabbed a pen and began to go through the fifty-page indictment attached to the case file folder. He went through the pages as quickly as he could, only slowing down to examine groups of text underlined or circled by the Chief State Counsel, before scribbling short notes at the page margins. He was still engrossed in the annotation of the document, when the intercom began to ring.

'Yes, what is it?' he asked impatiently after pressing a button on the intercom.

'Sir, you asked me to call you as soon as information on the funeral service for Samson was out,' replied the voice coming through the intercom's speaker.

Martin sighed. Of course, that was true. He had asked one of the police constables attached to the narcotics squad to get the information for he wanted to pay his respects to the family of Corporal Samson Adegbite, who had died in the line of duty, one week earlier.

Martin closed the case folder and shifted it to a corner of the desk. He pulled the intercom closer to himself. 'So when is the funeral?' he asked.

There was a momentary silence before the voice responded, 'It's on Sunday, sir. Twelve noon, sir.'

'Okay, constable. Thanks for letting me know.'

'No problem, sir.'

'Is there anything else I should know?'

'Eh... no, sir...nothing else, sir'

'Okay then, thank you,' Martin replied and pressed another button on the intercom. He pushed the intercom back to its previous position and grabbed the case folder. He was about to resume the review of Temi's case folder when he suddenly remembered something.

He had almost forgotten the pledge he made to the pregnant Mrs Adegbite when she came around to Ikeja CID to clear her late husband's police locker, two days after his death. Martin had promised the weeping widow that he would do everything in his power to fast-rack the payment of her late husband's gratuity. He would not allow bureaucratic red tape to hold up her husband's entitlement.

The widow did not seem concerned by that. She gazed at him with eyes reddened by tears and asked the question that no other policeman she had asked previously was willing to answer— did her husband suffer before death or did he go quickly? She had seen his bullet-riddled body, but could not tell from the corpse what the last moments of his life were like.

Martin had averted his gaze from the grieving face in front of him. He clearly recalled the events that led to the demise of Mrs Adegbite's husband.

On that fateful afternoon, in Ikeja CID, a call had gone out to the narcotics squad about an ongoing drug transaction in Festac Town, a gigantic housing estate in Lagos. Minutes later, Martin was leading a detachment of uniformed policemen and plain-clothes detectives towards the estate. Owing to horrendous traffic delays, Martin and his team arrived after the drug traffickers had concluded their business and were about to leave the crime scene.

A gun battle ensued as the doomed criminals attempted to shoot their way out of the surrounding police cars. The exchange of automatic rifle fire lasted thirty minutes. When the shooting stopped, the drug dealers, all fourteen of them, lay dead. One uniformed policeman and two plain-clothes detectives were injured. The injured uniformed policeman, Corporal Samson Adegbite, was hit multiple times in the abdomen and in the lungs. He was lying on his back on the ground, still conscious, struggling to breathe. Blood spurting out of bullet wounds in his stomach soaked his uniform. Tears were rolling down his cheeks and mingling with blood oozing from a corner of his mouth. The man knew he was dying.

Martin was kneeling next to Samson trying to staunch the bleeding with both hands. For a moment, he shifted his gaze away from the injured man to observe the narcotics squad members a few feet away.

The uniformed personnel were piling the limp bodies of the drug traffickers into the bed of a police pick-up truck while the plain-clothes detectives were crouching next to their injured colleagues—one was bleeding from his right arm and the other from both legs. To everyone's frustration, none of the ambulances summoned earlier had arrived at the scene. Lagos traffic was at its heaviest in the morning and afternoon hours.

Martin returned his attention to Samson whose face had taken on a pallid complexion and called out an order for the injured to be evacuated in patrol cars. Then there was a rasp, a forced gasping breath, and Samson died, his eyes staring up blankly at the sky. Martin remembered those blank eyes as he stood next to Mrs Adegbite who wanted to know about her husband's last moments.

'Your husband served his state and country bravely. I would do everything in my power to make sure his gratuity is paid in full without delay,' Martin had replied. Mrs Adegbite smiled wrily and silently walked away...

The prolonged ringing of the intercom snapped Martin out of his thoughts. Flustered, he dropped the pen he had been using to annotate the case file and pressed a button on the intercom.

'Hello, who is this?'

'Oh, it's just me.'

Martin recognised the voice as that of his direct superior, Detective-Inspector Gbolahan Akinola.

'Sir, I still reviewing the case file from Temi. I will be done with it by...'

'That can wait,' Gbolahan interjected, 'come to my office right away. We need to talk.'

The intercom went cold. Intrigued, Martin rose from his desk and made for the door.

CHAPTER 29

Detective-Inspector Gbolahan Akinola closed the folder in front of him and put it away. He watched his second-in-command settle into the chair across his desk. The ceiling fan above them rattled and wobbled as it spurn at high speed.

'How is Oludare doing?' Martin asked, staring at the framed picture of a smiling fourteen-year-old boy hanging on the wall behind Gbolahan.

'Well,' the narcotics squad leader began. 'After a couple of surgeries, the doctors are now saying that he is on the road to full recovery. The fractured legs are healing well. Hopefully, he would be discharged at the beginning of next month.'

'Oludare is a strong boy, I'm sure he will soon be out and about in no time,' Martin said, trying to cheer up his boss.

Gbolahan responded with a weak smile, 'thanks. I am sure you are correct.' A thick moment of silence descended, except for the ceiling fan rattling over their heads.

Martin broke the silence. 'Sir, you wanted us to talk about something.'

'Oh yes,' the absent-minded Gbolahan replied, recovering his composure. 'I want you to do something for me. Some surveillance work,' he said in a tone that sounded ominous.

'Sir, which drug dealer are we targeting,' Martin asked, leaning forward on his chair, half-expecting Gbolahan to pull out a manilla folder containing the photograph and the name of a drug trafficker.

But Gbolahan did nothing of the sort. He smiled mischievously and said, 'no, this task is outside the scope of narcotics. It is unofficial and rather delicate.'

'Okay, sir, let me hear what you want me to do,' Martin said in a cautious tone.

Gbolahan spent twenty minutes telling Martin what he wanted him to do and why. When he was done explaining the mission, he added, 'I know this is a lot to ask, may be you should go home, sleep on it and then decide. But it would be big favour for me and for the entire Force, if we manage to tackle this problem headlong.'

Martin was apprehensive. Planting eavesdropping bugs in offices, cars, warehouses and homes of suspected drug peddlers was his bread and butter. But he had never before targeted somebody who was not a known criminal suspect, least of all, the individual that Gbolahan was asking him to bug. It was all confusing for Martin to take in. Granted, he disliked the police officer he was being asked to bug, but Gbolahan had not presented any proof of wrongdoing. Moreover, he would be risking his police career if he went forward with Gbolahan's request.

'I know it is a big request. Perhaps, you should think on it when you go home. This is not an order. So, you can always decline, if you think it is too unsavoury for you,' Gbolahan said as he studied the anxious Detective-Sergeant in front of him.

'No, If I am going to do it, I will have to decide here and now before I leave,' Martin responded firmly.

'Okay, then,' Gbolahan said and reclined on his chair. Another brief period of silence followed.

'What if you are wrong...then what? Martin asked. 'Sir, if I am caught planting the bug...you know what that means for my career... and this has nothing to do with our work in narcotics'

'You will not be caught and even if you were, I will take all the blame,' Gbolahan stated. 'As you already know, there has been no progress in solving those fraud cases since the days of Mike Otunba as the principal investigator. Ever since these faceless fraudsters burst onto the scene, we have had a suicide, four confirmed homicides, one attempted homicide, and a missing person's case, which might as well count as another case of homicide. With each passing day, the impunity of these international scammers grows worse. The police have no clue what these killers look like, and they always seem to be a step ahead of our detectives. Why is that? It is obvious that these criminals know all our moves in advance.'

Gbolahan paused to allow his subordinate digest what he had said. Martin looked on glumly, seemingly unpersuaded by what his superior was telling him. Gbolahan pressed on with his pitch.

'Let us not kid ourselves. Ikeja CID is a single body. The failures of the anti-scam squad are also the failures of the narcotics squad. Until Ikenna's team is able to apprehend those murderous scammers, the reputation of Ikeja CID as a whole will continue to suffer. To apprehend the scammers, we must first identify the traitor in our midst, the one who is helping the criminals stay ahead of the law. I have no proof that the man I am asking you to target is the traitor, but my suspicions are well founded and reasonable. Based on the information that I spent twenty minutes breaking down for you, I think you'll agree that this man needs to come under scrutiny, covertly, of course.'

Martin nodded to indicate that he understood. If his superior's suspicions were right then that traitorous police officer on the payroll of murderers would have to be exposed for the good of Ikeja CID.

Martin was favourably disposed towards Gbolahan's proposition, but he was worried about the code-of-conduct violations that he would incur for acting without the approval of Cyrus Udeh, the only man who had the proper authority to approve an operation to bug the police officer alleged to be colluding with criminals. To violate the rules at the behest of Gbolahan, Martin would require a shield against the blowback that would inevitably follow if things went south.

'Okay, I will do it, but I am going to hold you to your word... that you will protect me from any fallout, if this whole thing ends in a fiasco.'

Gbolahan reiterated his pledge to take all the blame. 'You know me very well. I will lay down my life for all my men, including you.'

Satisfied with the answer, the Detective Sergeant asked his superior when he wanted the listening devices planted.

Gbolahan grimaced and remained silent as if gathering his thoughts. He picked a pen from his desk and started scrutinizing it. Without looking up, he replied, 'as soon as possible.'

Moments later, the meeting ended. The narcotics squad leader turned his attention back to the folder he had earlier put aside while his second-in-command left the room.

Back at the desk in his own office, Martin closed the case file he had been examining before he was summoned to the meeting and placed it into a tray marked PENDING. He walked briskly across the office to a small safe leaning against the wall. He opened the safe door and retrieved a small plastic box.

Back at his desk, he lifted the lid of the box and retrieved two miniature microphones about the diameter of a six-inch nail head. He also fished out a 2.5cm × 2.5cm square circuit board with three integrated circuit (IC) chips soldered on it. The small square board also had several colour-coded PVC wires sticking out. He connected the leads of one microphone to two wires, one red and the other black. The remaining wires jutting from the circuit board would serve as the antenna or as the conduit for the direct current (DC) power supply. The circuit board was an original mini-transmitter designed and built by Martin Okoye. It was a far cry from the very sophisticated eavesdropping gadgets imported from Germany and Yugoslavia for the exclusive use of the APCS.

Under normal circumstances, the surveillance task that Gbolahan had entrusted to Martin would rightly go to the APCS detectives, the plain-clothes police officers specially trained and officially tasked with investigating corruption within the Force. But enlisting APCS men in Ikeja CID to investigate their own squad leader for corruption was simply out of the question, even if the surveillance task had been officially sanctioned by Cyrus.

Despite its relative crudity, Martin was confident that his mini-transmitter would function well. At the beginning of his career as a Lagos narcotics detective, he had designed less capable listening devices, all of which performed satisfactorily when deployed to intercept and record incriminating conversations between drug dealers. The only thing that could potentially stop the detective's newest electronic contraption from working properly was faulty components. But Martin was a very meticulous man. He had made sure to purchase the semiconductor components used to make the transmitter from reputable electronic dealers in Idumota Market. And just in case, the components were individually tested with a multimeter to make sure they were genuine not duds.

*****

At 10.00 PM, seven hours after Martin's meeting with Gbolahan, the desk sergeant on reception duty in the cavernous foyer of Ikeja CID complex was on his second bottle of beer. He froze when he heard a sound outside, just beyond the double doors at the entrance. What he had heard was not the sound of vehicles wheezing past on the busy road outside; neither was it the annoyingly noisy crickets chirping away in hidden corners both inside and outside the building.

Failing to identify what had made the sound, the sergeant—the sole occupant in the building that night—carried on drinking until he heard it again. He stopped and listened. To his horror, what he was hearing were footsteps outside, just beyond the double doors positioned at the opposite end of the foyer.

Quickly, he hid the bottle under the reception counter as the wooden double doors creaked open. He rose to greet the man that emerged from behind the double doors. 'Good evening, sir!' he barked, his right hand next to his head in salutation.

The detective perceived the whiff of alcohol in the air. It was illegal for a police officer on duty to drink, but the detective let it pass; he had a far more important mission at hand.

'Hello sarge, I forgot something in my office. I am going upstairs to get it,' he said, adjusting the shoulder strap of cowhide satchel he was wearing.

'Yes sir, can I help?' the sergeant asked.

The detective smiled and declined. 'No, you hold the fort down here as before.'

With that remark, the plain-clothes cop made for the staircase while the sergeant settled back down on the high stool behind the quadrangle-shaped counter. As soon as the detective disappeared up the staircase, the booze resurfaced. The pot-bellied sergeant downed the entire contents of the bottle and belched. Sated, he gently placed the bottle on the floor, next to one of the legs of the stool, and turned back to the police radio equipment on the left-hand corner of the mahogany countertop. With a smile on his face, he reached out to switch the equipment back on, and then froze. His countenance assumed an aspect of deep caution. He gazed intently at the staircase at the opposite end of the vast foyer. From his sitting position, he could clearly see the lower section of the staircase— the newel posts, the handrails, the balusters and the upward run of marble stairs disappearing out of sight. But that was not enough. Before making his next move, he had to be sure nobody upstairs was observing him. He wanted to see the upper sections of the staircase. So he rose instinctively from his stool and quietly leaned across the countertop, pressing his belly on the glossy lacquered finish of the wooden surface. He craned his head upwards to get a better look. His eyes caught a glimpse of the first-floor landing of the staircase. There did not seem to be any movements up there. He also listened for footsteps and heard nothing.

Satisfied that no one was watching, he lifted his bulky frame from the countertop and straightened up. Moments later, he was tiptoeing out of the building. Outside, his crisp black police uniform merged seamlessly with the moonlit landscape. Walking down the sidewalk, he searched frantically for a public waste bin. There was none close by. 'Damn,' he hissed and was about to lob the beer bottle into the screen of shrubs behind the road verge when he spotted the outline of something better in the distance.

He sprinted to the yellow skip provided by the Lagos Sanitation & Environmental Agency, dumped the empty bottle and sprinted back to his building, gasping all the way. At the entrance, he pushed the double doors inwards and stopped at the doorway to catch his breath before walking back across the marble floor to his reception post. Resuming his position behind the quadrangle counter, he switched on the radio-communications equipment in the left-hand corner and pretended to be busy monitoring radio dispatches from patrol cars keeping the peace in the inner parts of Lagos city.

Upstairs, on the third floor, Detective-Sergeant Martin Okoye stopped in front of the door with a plastic nameplate reading N.O. IKWUNNE. He put on his leather gloves and fumbled in his pocket for the spare office key he had stolen from the racks in the cleaners' storage room on the second floor.

The cleaners were required to sweep the offices between 4.30 AM and 6.30 AM, five days a week, and therefore, had spare keys to all rooms in the building except that of CSP Cyrus Udeh. Notwithstanding the special vetting process that all the cleaners had undergone, Cyrus did not trust any of them. For that reason, his office was the only room in the building cleaned during working hours and while he was present.

In the last two weeks, Martin had suddenly become aware of the habitual carelessness of the cleaners who often forgot to lock the door to the storage room after stowing their cleaning equipment. Any intruder, interested in something more valuable than cleaning tools, could easily waltz into that storage room and have full access to an entire array of spare office keys hanging from several levels of wall-mounted, wooden racks. Horrified by the security risk posed by the cavalier attitude of the cleaners, Martin had planned to complain to Cyrus, but somehow always forgot to raise the issue each time he met up with the Ikeja CID boss. After his meeting with Gbolahan earlier that day, he suddenly remembered what he had forgotten, but instead of going straight to Cyrus to complain, he smiled and thanked God that he had not managed to see the Ikeja CID boss about the issue of stricter control over access to the spare keys. If he had, he would not be holding in his hand the spare key to the office of Chief Inspector Nduka Omenuko Ikwunne.

He unlocked the door with the stolen spare key and entered the dark office. He halted in front of the desk, set down the satchel and unzipped it. From the bag, he retrieved a pen-sized halogen torch, switched it on, and wedged it between his teeth. With the narrow beam of penlight focussed on the telephone, the detective picked up the handset with gloved hands and started to unscrew the perforated plastic cover concealing the mouthpiece. He fixed the bug— a micro-transmitter circuit board with a single IC chip—in place with a ball of plasticized chewing gum. He spliced the wires from the bug together with wires leading into the mouthpiece and screwed on the plastic cover again. The first listening device had just been planted inside Nduka's telephone.

Reaching into the satchel again, he extracted a bigger circuit board with three IC chips—the mini-transmitter—and checked it over. In the darkened room, the narrow beam of penlight went over the 2.5cm × 2.5cm surface area of the circuit board and found that the miniature microphone on it had been properly soldered into place. The focus of the penlight moved on to the adjacent item on the board—the small, disc-shaped lithium battery that supplied three volts of electricity to the IC chips and microphone. The battery was brand new and, therefore, guaranteed to perform optimally as the power source for the second listening device.

To plant the second device, Martin got on his knees and crawled all on fours under the Chief Inspector's desk, with the pen-sized halogen torch still wedged between his teeth. While there, he fixed a big ball of plasticized chewing gum on the back of his mini-transmitter circuit board and stuck the whole thing on the underside of the desk. He inspected it to make sure that it would not come away in the next three weeks. Satisfied, he crawled out and rose to his feet. Mission accomplished. Two separate bugs—one to capture phone conversations and the other to capture room chatter— had been successfully planted in Nduka's office.

The narcotics detective removed the pen torch from his mouth and was about to switch it off when he caught sight of something that gave him reason to pause. The bottom drawer of the desk was slightly open and something within it glinted when hit with halogen penlight. Martin pulled out the drawer by its knob, revealing a box-shaped, bright blue metal object that resembled an oscilloscope. Intrigued, the detective put the pen torch aside and lifted the metallic gadget out of the drawer. Placing it on top of the desk, Martin picked up the pen torch and began to examine the gadget's front panel—the knobs of various sizes; the yellow and red push buttons; the LCD display; and female radio frequency (RF) coaxial connectors. He moved the narrow beam of the penlight back and forth on the gadget and began to develop a vague feeling that he had seen it somewhere. Then it came to him. He whistled slowly and smiled.

Back in June 1986, while still an army officer in good standing, his superiors in the Corps of Nigerian Army Electrical and Mechanical Engineers (NAEME) had arranged for him to travel to Kaduna city for a seminar on military radio communications. After that seminar, he had visited the electronic repairs workshop of the newly established Defence Intelligence Agency where he was shown various signal intelligence gadgets. One of the gadgets exhibited was a Scanlock 2000 receiver used to detect listening devices hidden inside telephones, behind office walls, under desks, etc...

The box-shaped object under examination in Nduka's office, on the night of 12th November 1993, was definitely not a Scanlock 2000 receiver, but there was close resemblance. Martin had confirmed it by penlight. In his reckoning, the unknown gadget was a bug detector, probably more advanced than Scanlock 2000.

'You devil!' the detective hissed in the near darkness of the office. Several thoughts rushed through his mind at the same time. Why would the APCS leader have a sophisticated bug detector in his office? What terrible secret was the paranoid git trying to hide from eavesdroppers? Was this man really working with the swindlers, the murderers of Michael Otunba?

If Martin had any lingering doubts about the probable guilt of Nduka, it evaporated at that point. Even after agreeing to bug the office, at the behest of Gbolahan, the Detective-Sergeant had always maintained an open mind on the question of whether the Chief Inspector was guilty of colluding with criminals, but now he was sorry that he ever doubted the APCS leader's culpability. There was no excuse for Nduka's behaviour. Poor renumeration—the common cause of police corruption—could not be blamed here. The Chief Inspector's take-home salary was an order of magnitude higher than that of other police officers of identical rank not fortunate enough to be attached to an APCS unit. Nduka Ikwunne was even paid higher than Cyrus Udeh despite being his junior by rank!

Martin suppressed the anger welling up in him and pondered the next step. He could not leave the office without doing something about the blue metallic gadget on the desk. With that bug detector in good working order, it was only a matter of time before Nduka discovered the listening devices. Martin knew that the equipment would have to be sabotaged. He wanted to render the gadget useless without the APCS leader ever realising it. A machine that could not be switched on, that was obviously damaged, could easily be replaced with another. A man of Nduka Ikwunne's clout could quickly arrange for new equipment to be imported from overseas, if there wasn't a spare one already in the storage vaults of the APCS. The only way to forestall that scenario was to make Nduka believe that the bug detector currently in use was working fine. This would mean tampering with the machine in a way that won't interfere with its ability to switch on, perform an electronic sweep of a room, and produce a frequency-readout on its front panel indicating that all is well— no bugs detected.

After three and half minutes in deep thought, Martin figured out a way to achieve that. During his visit to Kaduna city, seven years earlier, he had observed a Scanlock 2000 receiver being disassembled. The metallic object glinting in the penlight may not be a Scanlock 2000, but it was functionally similar.

Martin directed the narrow beam of light at the base of the gadget and noted the Philips screws used to fasten the bright blue metal casing to its box frame. He reached into his satchel and produced a set of screwdrivers and a small plier. Moments later, the metal casing was separated from the gadget's box frame, revealing the motherboard inside.

Working by penlight, Martin scanned the motherboard filled with a multitude of semiconductor devices. Using the small plier, he damaged a ceramic disc capacitor, two transistors, an electrolytic capacitor and one axial resistor. After he was done, he placed the metal casing back on the box frame and fastened the Philips screws with the screwdriver. His work was done. Nduka Ikwunne would still be able to switch on the machine and operate it as usual, but the frequency reports from it would be wildly inaccurate. The Chief Inspector would never know that his bug detector, while apparently functional, has lost its ability to detect any listening devices hidden in and around his office.

Martin returned the small plier and the set of screwdrivers to the cowhide satchel. He restored the now sabotaged gadget to its initial position in the bottom drawer of the desk. After that, he switched off his pen torch, dropped it into the satchel and pulled the zipper. Two minutes later, he was in his own office, two floors above the transmitting bugs. He was there to set up the receiving end of the eavesdropping operation. From the satchel, he produced an old tape recorder, which he had modified by reconstructing its motherboard to include a receiver and a transistor-controlled timer. The receiver caught radio signals sent out only by the bug transmitting from underneath Nduka's desk. The electronic timer activated and deactivated the recorder at appropriate times of the day in order to save on battery power. The duration of recording sessions could be altered by means of a variable resistor on the circuitry of the timer.

Martin opened the cassette compartment of the recorder and slotted in a ninety-minute TDK audiotape. He rotated the knob of the variable resistor so that the recorder would switch on at 7.30 AM and switch off at 8.30 PM. That was thirty minutes before office hours and one hour after detective offices close officially for the day. He produced another modified tape recorder, identical to the first one, except that it was designed to activate whenever the handset is lifted out of the cradle of the telephone. The radio receiver circuit inside the second tape recorder only caught signals transmitted by the bugged phone. Into that tape recorder, Martin slotted in a SONY cassette. Then he pushed the "record" button on both tape recorders. Moments later, he placed both machines inside the middle drawer of his desk and locked it. He made a mental note to buy a box of empty audiotapes to replenish the recorders every ninety minutes.

Later on, as he descended the staircase from the topmost floor, he thought about the sabotaged bug detector in Nduka's office. What was that machine called? Perhaps, he could phone one of the friendly acquaintances that he knew in the Defence Intelligence Agency to find out.

Downstairs, on the ground floor, Martin found the desk sergeant asleep. The pot-bellied man was breathing stertorously, his head leaning against hairy arms resting on the lacquered countertop, next to the police radio. The detective watched the scene with disgust before lumbering around the sides of the quadrangle counter to reach the man sleeping behind it. There, he kicked the high stool supporting the bulk frame of the snoring policeman. The sergeant jumped to his feet instantly, throwing his hand to his forehead in a clumsy show of salutation. The plain-clothes detective glared at the bleary-eyed face and then at his creased uniform.

'Sarge, this is disgraceful. If you don't feel up to the job, then put in for early retirement,' Martin said evenly.

'Sir, sorry ooo,' the sergeant said softly, his countenance was grave and contrite. He knew he was in deep trouble if the detective reported his behaviour. He could face tough disciplinary procedures.

'You want to get into serious *wahala*?' Martin asked, adjusting the strap of his satchel.

'No, no, sir…sorry sir…sorry sir,' the sergeant spluttered.

Martin shook his head and smiled. 'It's alright, Sarge. I will not report this to your superior…just don't sleep again! Just do your job. Monitor the dispatches. If I catch you next time sleeping or drinking on duty, I'll report you, understand?'

The sergeant gasped when he heard the detective referring to his drinking problem.

'Oh yes, I know,' Martin said, guessing what was on the mind of the uniformed policeman.

A foolish grin appeared on the sergeant's remorseful face. He pledged never to sleep again, never to drink again, even when he was off duty.

Martin nodded impatiently. He knew chronic alcoholics were also chronic liars. He bid the portly policeman good night and started walking away. The sergeant heaped effusive praise on Martin, expressing his gratitude to the detective for the decision not to have him punished.

With both hands, Martin pulled the double doors inwards. A wave of cool night breeze wafted in. The detective stepped into street as the doors slowly closed behind him, cutting off the loud, babbling voice of the sergeant inside the building.

He reconsidered his decision to call an acquaintance at the Defence Intelligence Agency (DIA) to learn more about Nduka's bug detector. On second thought, it was not such a good idea. He would have to explain why he wanted such information. It was not worth the hassle, he reasoned as he ambled along the sidewalk, towards the next street where his car was parked.

If he had bothered to call his contact in the DIA, he would have learnt that Nduka's British-made gadget was a Scanlock ECM receiver, a direct descendant of the Scanlock 2000 model.

CHAPTER **30**

NOVEMBER 1993

SANDTON, SOUTH AFRICA

On the afternoon of 12th November 1993, while Gbolahan was trying to convince Martin of the necessity of eavesdropping on the hated Chief Inspector Ikwunne, John Nwosu was inside a hotel lobby, in the Greater Johannesburg area, nearly four thousand miles south of Lagos. The hotel was rather small compared to its much bigger five-star rivals—Southern Sun, Hilton, Radisson and Protea hotels—all of which were nearby. John Nwosu had the money and could have gone to any of those, but he chose the relatively cheaper Sandton Traveller Hotel.

In the cheap, three-star hotel, there was no 24-hour room service, no commissionaire at the entrance, and John was fine with that. He had never fancied himself as a king. He was perfectly happy to forgo breakfast in bed in favour of going downstairs to the hotel restaurant for food, and he had no need for the services of a uniformed attendant to open the double glass doors at the entrance.

Earlier in the day, he had been out and about, sightseeing, marvelling at the beauty and cleanliness of Sandton, a highly affluent locale just outside the city limits of Johannesburg proper. He had chosen to base himself in Sandton, for the time being, because of his role as a "senior partner" in the fictional boutique law firm, Heintz & Sharmann, because a discerning person like Harel Suzmann would expect the law firm trying to retrieve his inheritance to operate out of an office in an upmarket area. Sandton was in the correct postcode and had the desired telephone area code. Besides, many business corporations, law firms and other institutions in the heart of the boisterous city of Johannesburg were beginning to relocate their headquarters, further north, to the quieter suburban Sandton.

Like any other foreigner visiting South Africa, John Nwosu did not fail to notice the effects of the longstanding apartheid system, which was now beginning to collapse. Whites almost exclusively inhabited Sandton. The nearest residential area where blacks were permitted to live was the Alexandra Township, a poverty-stricken slum filled with shanty houses, a few reasonably built houses, and poor hygiene. The penurious black township was separated from the extremely wealthy white Sandton by the M1 motorway.

John had seen the township up close while travelling in a taxicab on the motorway. The squalid settlement reminded him of Ajegunle slum back in Lagos. But that was, in his own opinion, where the similarities ended. There were no government laws forcing Nigerians to live in slums, only poverty did that. Nigerian slum dwellers lucky enough to secure gainful employment, or find sudden fame and fortune, could always move to cleaner environments. In fact, Ajegunle slum boasts of many former inhabitants, who upon hitting the big time as entertainers, footballers and musicians, had moved to swankier corners of Lagos such as Victoria Island, Lekki and Ikoyi.

Long before the arrival of affluence, the posh cars and the big mansions, John recalled that even he and his men had once lived in rundown parts of Lagos, surrounded by squalor and the pungent smells of open sewers. The period between their release from Kirikiri Maximum Prison and the finagling of the late Gary Logan had been quite tough, but they overcame it.

Staring out at the squalid scenery sliding past his car window on the M1 motorway, John passed his judgement— those black South Africans, the poor sods living in Alexandra Township, had no chance of ever overcoming their circumstances; the apartheid regime had seen to that.

As the taxicab neared Sandton, its black driver, an ethnic Swazi, could not stop vocalizing his surprise that his sole passenger was able to secure lodging in a white area. Things were changing rapidly in South Africa, but the cab driver still could not believe that a hotel in Sandton had taken the booking of a black person. Behind the driver, in the rear passenger seat, John smiled smugly. *Money talks and could jump colour barriers.*

Days later, he would find out that in the fully booked hotel, he was one of three non-white guests, and the only one who was actually black. Two years earlier, a person with his racial appearance would not have been able to stay in any kind of lodging inside Sandton. The Group Areas Act (1966) enacted by the parliament of the apartheid regime prohibited non-whites from living in areas reserved for white inhabitants.

Moving in and around Sandton had been an interesting education for the Nigerian conman. Several yards, beyond the glass doors of his hotel, was Sandton City, a twenty-one-storey concrete shopping mall built in the brutalist architectural tradition. As John checked out the retail stores and restaurants within the concrete high-rise building, many of the white shoppers and customer services personnel looked at him with some curiosity. Although he felt uncomfortable with the incredulous stares, John smiled at all times. Right there and then, he recalled a memory from his childhood in Eastern Nigeria, and finally understood how those British archaeologists, working an excavation site in his hometown, back in the late 1950s, must have felt with a sea of black faces constantly staring at them.

One wrinkled old man with steely blue eyes, leaning on a walking stick, doffed his fedora to John, who reciprocated with a smile and nod. Later on, as he toured Sandton's Central Business District, the swindler reflected on the political situation in South Africa, which was undergoing a rapid transformation. Nelson Mandela had been free for three years; many exiled ANC stalwarts and their families had returned home from various parts of Europe and Africa, including those who had been living in Lagos at the expense of the Nigerian government. The apartheid regime in Pretoria was still firmly in charge of the country, but its long cherished segregationist policies were in full retreat.

Group Areas Act (1966), which imposed residential segregation by force of law, was gone. And so were the plethora of complementary land ownership laws that had reserved 87 percent of the total South African landmass for the exclusive use of whites. With the revocation of the Separate Amenities Act (1953), municipal officials stopped enforcing racial segregation of swimming pools, beaches, public toilets, parks, vehicles and public services.

The repeal of the Population Registration Act (1950) ended the forty-three-year-old practice of classifying and registering every inhabitant of South Africa according to the cast of his or her racial features. Under the abolished law, each inhabitant was allocated to one of four officially recognized racial categories: white, black, coloured (i.e. mixed) and Asian (i.e. Indian). The ability to live in certain areas; own property; access certain public services and local amenities; exercise political rights; gain educational opportunities; and improve one's economic situation were largely determined by the racial category to which an individual had been allocated.

As John walked out of the indoor shopping centre and into the large forecourt, with several pairs of eyes watching, he wondered what racial category he would have fallen under, given his light skin: *black* or *coloured?* The Office of Racial Classification (ORC), during its existence, would have been responsible for allocating a racial category to a person like John whose golden caramel skin tone and slim nose had failed to meet the "Bantu stereotype". This would usually happen at the conclusion of a gamut of pseudo-scientific racial identity tests, all of which elevated subjectivity, arbitrariness and shoddiness to an art form. Classification as "coloured" allowed a person more rights than one considered "black", but fewer rights than a person considered "white".

The authority to determine the race of individuals whose phenotypic traits did not match established stereotypes made gods out of ORC officials. In the exercise of that semi-divine power— backed up by "identity tests"— a person previously classified as "white" could suddenly be reclassified as "coloured". A person deemed "coloured" since birth could suddenly be hauled before ORC officials for tests that might result in a downgrade to "black" status. Since people of different races were compelled by law to live apart in different areas designated by government, a person who was previously of a different race before "reclassification" would find himself or herself facing eviction, loss of property, and loss of spouse and family members who were now in another racial category.

After an hour of sightseeing, John trekked back to his lodgement. As he was making his way to the staircase at the far end of the hotel lobby, he spotted an A-Frame display stand in front of the reception desk. The display stand contained a multi-coloured A3-sized poster within its plexiglass signage holder. He halted and made a beeline towards it.

The young auburn-haired female receptionist lowered the handset of the phone and shifted her gaze to the light-skinned black man approaching. Before she could speak, John pointed to the A-Frame. She smiled and turned her attention back to the telephone.

As she spoke Afrikaans into the mouthpiece of the handset, John bent over the brass display stand, his eyes focused on a picture of an old, white-haired

Nelson Mandela staring out of the garish poster. Next to the picture of the smiling Mandela were uppercase cream-coloured letters printed on beige background that read: LILIESLEAF FARM, RIVONIA. Below the capitalized heading, John read the short article written in blue colour. It described Liliesleaf Farm as a hideaway, a secret base for anti-apartheid activists of the African National Congress (ANC), located in Rivonia, a suburb of Johannesburg.

From 1961 to 1963, the farm—situated in the middle of a "whites-only" area— hosted clandestine meetings between anti-apartheid activists of different races. To fool government authorities, ANC activist Arthur Goldreich posed as the white "owner" of the farm, and the non-white activists— including a disguised Nelson Mandela—posed as cooks, handymen and servants on the property. The ruse ended with a police raid on the property on 11th July 1963. The arrest of Mandela and his colleagues resulted in the infamous Rivonia Treason Trial that concluded on 12th June 1964 with a verdict of life imprisonment. The convicted activists would spend many years behind bars before being reprieved. In the case of Mandela, the reprieve took twenty-seven years to arrive.

John shook his head slowly after reading the blue-coloured text and then shifted his gaze further down to two pictures, side by side. One was a picture of single-room house with a thatched roof, which the caption said was one of the original buildings in Liliesleaf Farm. The other picture was the cropped image of a road map showing that Liliesleaf Farm was six miles north of the Sandton Traveller Hotel. Below the pictures, near the bottom of the poster, was a message, in bold blue lowercase lettering, inviting hotel guests to sign up for the tour bus, which would be arriving over the weekend to ferry people to the famous farm in Rivonia. John stared at the tour fee with a derisive smile on his face. There was no way he was going to spend 350 Rand to view thatched houses set inside a bloody farm.

As if reading his mind, the receptionist, spoke. 'The trip is totally worth the cost,' she remarked with a thick accent.

John stared into the green eyes of the smiling woman for a moment. 'Sorry, I will be quite busy over the weekend. Can't go,' he replied, quickly heading off in the direction of the staircase at the far end of the lobby.

'Next time, then!' the receptionist called out as John disappeared into the stairwell.

Back in his hotel room, John went to the minibar and fixed himself a glass of Scotch whisky. He had heard the receptionist call after him, and his unspoken reply was simple: *there would never be a next time.* There was no way he was going to waste the equivalent of almost a hundred and ten dollars on a frivolous tour bus. He had already spent a fortune on the costliest and most daring swindle operation that his gang had ever embarked on, and that was only for the first two stages of Tunde's operational plan. A lot more cash was still waiting to be burnt through on the remaining stages of the plan.

John sauntered across the room to the glass window overlooking the large forecourt of Sandton City Mall. He took a sip of the liquor and reflected on the soaring expenditures. His gang was very rich and yet he hated to spend so much. Between himself in South Africa and Eugene in The Netherlands, he had spent approximately ₦450,000 ($26,471) on travelling and living expenses with eighty percent of the expenditure consumed by his Europe-based subordinate. And that did not include the initial expenses on research resources Tunde had used to trace the family tree of Harel Suzmann from Germany to London, and then from London to South Africa. The end product of Tunde's research work had been an impressive forty-page report that was then whittled down and whipped into a three-page operational plan divided into five stages, of which the first two had been completed.

With the third stage in the process of implementation, John was not terribly pleased with the soaring costs, a lot of it unforseen. The gang leader held no one responsible for unanticipated expenses, but he did hold his brilliant acolyte responsible for abrupt changes in plan that contributed to the ongoing depletion of the budget allocated to the operation—a case in point being Tunde's sudden insistence that the South African end of the operation be moved from Johannesburg city to Sandton.

Weeks earlier, the *Financial Times* and *Wall Street Journal* had reported that many South African business corporations— and several corporate law firms that serve them— in the city of Johannesburg were beginning to shift the centre of their operations further north. Tunde had no doubt that Harel, an ardent reader of the *Financial Times*, would have read all about it. So, for the wily conman, it was a no-brainer— the fictional Heintz & Sharmann would also have to announce its own move.

Already enjoying the sights and sounds of Johannesburg, John was loath to move, doubted the necessity of the relocation, and shuddered at the thought of burning through more cash. But Tunde had argued that Harel's confidence in the genuineness of the "Robert Suzmann Inheritance" would heighten if he thought Heintz & Sharmann was among the unnamed South African law firms said by the media to have relocated to a posher locale.

John remained dubious, but deferred to his genius. After all, it wasn't the first time that the he had reluctantly approved a risky and expensive strategy by Tunde, which, in the end, turned out to be magnificent.

The bedside telephone began to ring, startling John. He instinctively placed the glass of whisky on the sill of the window and walked briskly towards the upholstered headboard of his double bed. Sitting at the edge of the mattress, he picked up the handset from the bedside table.

'Hello,' he said as he held the curved plastic against the side of his head.

'It's me, boss. I'm back in Amsterdam,' replied the voice on the other end.

'How did the meeting go?' John asked, leaning against the padded velvet headboard. Over the phone, Eugene briefed his boss about his first meeting with Harel Suzmann in the terrace of a London café.

Following the agreed script, Eugene Igolo— posing as "Matthew Molozi"— had reiterated to Harel Suzmann over coffee that Heintz & Sharmann would not charge for its services, but the law firm was going to pass all expenses incurred while pursuing the inheritance claim to him. Matthew explained to the Briton that his law firm would expect to be reimbursed each time it spent above 500 Rand, an equivalent of about hundred pounds sterling. Harel had agreed to the arrangement without hesitation.

The cautious enthusiasm of the Briton had given way to outright delight when Matthew showed him authentic-looking bank documents. Harel was told that the documents were for an escrow account, which had been set up in the Royal Bank of Montreal in Canada. The anticipated inheritance money was going to be deposited into the account in ten equal installments as soon as Heintz & Sharmann were able to get Volkstar Diamond Limited to start paying.

Placing the documents back into his briefcase, Matthew had warned the excited Briton that wrenching the inheritance money from Volkstar might not go down so easily. The Cape Town-based diamond company might decide to take their chances with the law courts, citing the fact that Robert Suzmann had died intestate. Of course, Heintz & Sharmann would pick up the gauntlet and fight to get Harel his inheritance—Matthew had said with a reassuring smile— but the costs of hiring extra paralegals to help out in the lawsuit and other miscellaneous expenses would have to be reimbursed.

Already daydreaming about rolling in millions of unearned pounds, Harel reiterated his willingness to cover all overhead costs incurred in the pursuit of his South African inheritance. After coffee, both men swapped phone numbers and promised to keep in touch. Harel returned to his house in Maresfield Gardens, Hampstead while Eugene retired to a B&B lodging in Hayes, West London. The next morning he flew back to his base in Amsterdam.

John was pleased with Eugene's report and congratulated him on the success of his first meeting with the target. 'You will need to inform Mister Suzmann that Heintz & Sharmann is now based in Sandton,' John said, sitting up on the bed.

Eugene replied that he had already telephoned Harel to inform him about the development.

'Good, very good,' John said and then began to brief his subordinate about the next stage of the operation.

CHAPTER **31**

NOVEMBER 1993

LAGOS, WESTERN NIGERIA

That hot afternoon, on 24th November 1993, Chief Inspector Nduka Ikwunne told his uniformed police orderly, Corporal Emeka Umenyi, that he was going for a jog to exercise his legs. He instructed Emeka to refer anyone looking for him to his deputy in the APCS, Inspector Daoud Mamman.

The message struck Emeka as odd. In his four years as an orderly, he had never seen Nduka do anything but work. Although, the APCS leader was largely fit, the police corporal had never ever seen him engaging in any physical activity that could qualify as exercise; unless one counted the occasional pacing up and down the APCS squad briefing room as a form of exercise. And even if one accepted that the Chief Inspector had discovered a newfound love for physical activity, why the sudden urge to go for a jog while still on the clock and still in police uniform?

But then Corporal Emeka Umenyi was not particularly surprised by the latest set of weird vibes he was picking up from his superior. For the past three weeks, he had witnessed his normally jocular boss fall into an inexplicable state of despondency. He would often come into the Chief Inspector's office and find him stooped in his swivel chair, deep in thought. On many occasions, when they were alone in the squad car, he would ask his superior if anything was wrong. And with a weak smile, the melancholic APCS leader would always claim that everything was fine; there was nothing to worry about. The skeptical orderly would then nod silently and wait a few days before posing the same question again.

Initially, Emeka's meddlesomeness was taken in stride, but after a while, it became annoying and intolerable to his boss. The last time Emeka asked, Nduka snapped and berated him for suspecting trouble in places where there were none. After that outburst, the police orderly withdrew into himself and started keeping mum about his sincerely felt concern for his boss' well-being.

'Yes, sir, I will pass on the message to Inspector Mamman,' Emeka replied and saluted. A few questions popped into his mind, but he did not ask any of them. There was no need to stir up the hornet's nest, no need to endure a round of stinging rebuke.

On his part, Chief Inspector Ikwunne could clearly see the skepticism in his orderly's eyes, but he did not care. He had more important things to worry about. 'Good. I will see you when I am back in the office,' he smiled and tapped his orderly gently on the shoulder.

Corporal Umenyi watched in stunned silence as the APCS boss swung around and began to sprint down the street like a man under pursuit. After a few seconds of thoughtful observation, the police orderly shrugged, turned around, and began to walk back towards the entrance of Ikeja CID.

Nduka Ikwunne stopped running as soon as he disappeared around a corner. He leaned against a wall to catch his breath before entering an alley. He walked down the sloped narrow pavement inside the alley until he reached the arched exit. Stepping out of the alley and into the sidewalk of a major thoroughfare, he hailed a passing taxicab. The cab driver applied the brakes and the taxi pulled up a few inches ahead of the policeman. Nduka hurried towards the kerb where the yellow-coloured Peugeot 504 with battered outer door panels was waiting. The policeman bent over and peered into the driver's side window. 'Take me to Surulere,' he said.

The taxi driver, wearing a green T-shirt, a checkered cloth cap and dark eye glasses, nodded without looking sideways at the cop. '*Oga sir*, the fare is seventy naira,' he announced as the policeman opened the rear passenger door.

Nduka slid into the rear seat behind the empty front passenger seat. 'No problem, my dear driver,' he replied, slamming the battered rear door shut.

The driver pulled the Peugeot 504 from the kerb and propelled it into the main road. Ten minutes later, the cab ran into a traffic gridlock at Allen Avenue. The afternoon sun got brighter and Ikeja flagged under the intense heat.

'We gonna be stuck here for a while,' the driver announced with a sigh of resignation. He began to work a mechanical crank attached to the inner door panel, causing the adjacent car window to slide downwards. Nduka gazed through windscreen at the traffic chaos ahead, one that was very typical of Lagos. He observed the orange-uniformed traffic cop frantically trying to direct columns of vehicles on the road. Feeling the searing heat, the APCS boss began to rotate the crank sticking out of the door next to him. The cracked glass window slid down, letting in a wave of warm air. 'Don't you have air conditioner in this car?' he asked irritated.

The driver laughed contemptuously. 'How much do I make from this job? It is expensive to maintain an air conditioner. As a car owner, you must surely know this. Even if I made enough money, I would rather spend it on fixing all the cracked windows and paying a panel beater to deal with the battered bodywork of this car. Air conditioner is a damn luxury.'

Nduka smirked at the thought of a millionaire fraudster complaining about a luxury he could afford, several times over. The wealthy criminal behind the steering wheel was clearly enjoying his role-play as a taxi driver. Adamu Esan — the faux taxi driver— saw the distant traffic policeman gesturing to the line of vehicles in front of his cab. He promptly shifted the gear lever and lifted his left foot, releasing the clutch pedal. The vehicles in the queue began to move forward in a slow procession. After a few yards, the traffic policeman raised the palm of his gloved hand, indicating that the vehicles should halt. Adamu sighed heavily before disengaging the clutch and returning the gear lever to its neutral position.

Nduka thought it was now time to talk business. He had observed the two columns of queued vehicles far ahead, facing each other on the jammed dual carriageway, struggling to get through the traffic bottleneck, and it seemed to him that his taxicab might never get to Surulere in time for that *business chat* with Tunde. The crazy Lagos city traffic had an annoying way of disrupting even the best-laid plans.

'I thought I told you guys not to call my office,' Nduka huffed, recalling the recorded message left on the answering machine of his telephone, forty minutes earlier. In the audio message, Tunde had demanded a meeting at DePauls Bar & Restaurant and instructed the rogue cop on where to go and wait for a "special taxi ride" to the rendezvous in Surulere.

'You have not communicated in almost a month,' Adamu replied calmly as he watched the distant traffic cop gesturing in his direction again. 'We are worried. We want to know what's going on,' he continued, shifting the gear lever into the first gear and letting go the clutch pedal.

In the rear passenger seat, the Chief Inspector frowned as the Peugeot 504 began to follow the long procession of vehicles in front. 'What do you mean by that?' he asked as the taxicab manoeuvred around a couple of potholes on the tarmac.

'C'mon, you should know what I mean,' Adamu replied as his eyes flicked upwards from the centre of the windscreen to the rear-view mirror. 'We want to make sure we don't have a *Mike Otunba situation* on our hands.'

The mention of the dead cop's name sent a chill down Nduka's spine. A hundred frantic thoughts raced through his mind at once. Did the paranoid fraudsters think he was about to betray them? Was Tunde inviting him to a genuine meeting or was this a ruse to lure him to his death?

The Chief Inspector recalled the first ever meeting he had with Adamu and Tunde back in May 1993. The gangsters had welcomed him warmly into the Mushin head office of ELAJ Enterprises, thanked him for agreeing to spy for them, and then proceeded to tell him a cautionary tale about the late DI Michael Otunba. At the end of the two-hour conversation, which was conducted in a jovial atmosphere, with lots of drinks flowing, Chief Inspector Nduka Ikwunne learnt a couple of things. He would be rewarded handsomely if he cooperated with the gang. As he had long suspected, the men smiling at him from across the desk murdered Mike Otunba. Mike was dispatched because the gangsters believed he was about to sell them out. From that conversation, Nduka also realized that the smiling swindlers were a bunch of paranoiacs who saw failure to communicate regularly, without good reason, as a prelude to treachery. The APCS leader had been gripped by fear back then just as he was right now inside the searingly hot taxicab. The only difference being that the encounter of six months earlier had taken place inside an air-conditioned office, and he had left Mushin with a heavy laundry bag, measuring 2 feet long, 1⅔ feet wide and 1 feet high, that was filled with bundles of cash, all of which amounted to three hundred and fifty thousand naira.

'I thought I made it clear that I want to lie low and observe the situation before getting back to you,' he replied indignantly. He suppressed the urge to confront the driver about the implied threat in his earlier remark. The Chief Inspector did not want to give Adamu the satisfaction of knowing that he was terrified by the mention of murdered detective. But the gangster saw through the facade.

'Hey, calm yourself,' Adamu said with a mischievous grin. In the rear-view mirror, he had observed the look of terror flash across the face of his passenger. 'I understand your situation. Nonetheless, you must find a way to keep in touch or my boss may start getting the wrong idea, may think you are about to flip on us.'

Nduka suppressed a sigh. He had met John Nwosu—Adamu's boss—only once and was struggling to remember what he looked like. He focussed his thoughts, exerted himself, and his mind began to summon the mental images. Finally, he experienced a flashback. It was suddenly May 1993 again, and the Chief Inspector was in the middle of an animated discussion with Adamu and Tunde in the air-conditioned office in Mushin. Tunde was shovelling thick bundles of crisp twenty-naira bills from a tall stainless steel safe into a large laundry bag when the office door suddenly opened and a man entered. Nduka sized the man up. The Chief Inspector was himself fair-skinned and average-built. But man that just entered the office was a shade lighter in complexion and slightly taller. The newcomer was dressed in an expensive, well-cut navy blue suit and had an afro hair-do, which made him look like a character out of a 1970s American blaxploitation movie. It was only when Tunde and Adamu referred to the besuited man as "boss" that Nduka finally realized who he was staring at.

The boss, John, did not stay long. He shook Nduka's hand and then walked to the far end of the office where a kneeling Tunde was busy filling up the laundry bag. The gang boss jokingly warned Tunde not to steal all the money in the safe. Then he walked back across the deep-pile carpet, collected a manilla file from Adamu's mahogany desk, bid the Chief Inspector goodbye, and walked out of the office. John's cameo appearance in that office, six months earlier, had only lasted five minutes, which was why Nduka had problems recalling what he looked like.

'Why won't I be calm?' the Chief Inspector retorted as he leaned forward in the rear passenger seat of the car. 'I haven't done anything wrong. I have kept you guys well informed all these months. If there are any problems, then it is from your own side. It was you lot that bungled the assassination of that bastard, Ikenna. How difficult can it be to dispatch a single person?'

The rhetorical question lingered in the thick silence that followed. The taxicab was only two yards away from the traffic bottleneck, when the orange-clad traffic cop raised his gloved hand again. The vehicular procession halted again. Adamu stepped on the brake pedal and then on the clutch pedal before shifting the gear lever to its neutral position.

'Yes, we screwed up,' the taxi driver admitted in a grave voice, breaking the silence in the cab. 'Moses thought that the detective had perished in the blast along with his companions. Seems the detective, your bastard, went to the toilet for a pee. That saved his life.'

'Well, you guys have created a mess. That is why I have to lie low in the case if somebody at Ikeja CID suspects the involvement of an insider in the assassination attempt,' Nduka expostulated. Uneasy silence followed.

The traffic cop ahead began to gesture with both hands, and vehicular column was on the move again. The cause of the bottleneck suddenly came into view. Nduka saw the overturned light brown Datsun 510 sedan and broken shards of glass. Inches away, the traffic cop was using hand signals to direct motorists to manoeuvre around the wreckage. The vehicular column containing Nduka's taxicab swerved to avoid the overturned car and then snaked through the short stretch of road strewn with glass shards. Finally clear of the traffic jam, Adamu stepped on the accelerator pedal, darted out of his lane and overtook a couple of lumbering buses and lorries. 'Looks like we might get to Surulere, after all,' he said, swerving the taxicab back into the lane. Nduka grunted and glanced at his watch.

'It depends on how fast your jalopy can get there and if there isn't another traffic jam waiting for us ahead,' Nduka scoffed. 'By the way, where did you get this shitty car?'

Adamu pictured the driveway of his Victoria Island residence resplendent with exquisite sedans: a platinum-coloured Rolls Royce, a sleek black BMW and a cream-coloured Lexus. The vision was a far cry from the battered yellow Peugeot 504 SR taxicab he had hired for a day from its owner, an actual taxi driver. The aged taxi driver had just dropped off a passenger in Victoria Island and was preparing to steer the car from the kerb to the main road, when he spotted an image on his side-view mirror. He turned around and saw a dark-skinned man dressed in green T-shirt, jeans trousers and a checkered cloth cap jogging towards his cab. The taxi driver waited until the prospective passenger was abreast of his car. Leaning out of the car window, the old man told the much younger man in dark glasses to hop in and asked where he wanted to go. The response he received stunned him. The prospective customer was not interested in going anywhere with the taxi driver. In fact, he wanted to borrow the taxicab for the day and asked the old man to name his price.

Bemused, the old man pondered the bizarre request for a while. Business has not been that great in last few weeks. Jalopies such as his were facing tough competition from the newer and faster motorcycle-taxis, which could easily cut through dense traffic and arrive at destinations much quicker. After much thinking, the old taxi driver named ₦2,500 as his price. To his shock, the putative customer handed over a red polythene bag containing thick bundles of cash money worth ₦ 6,000. The old man laughed excitedly at his good fortune and hailed his patron as an angel sent by God. The "angel" adjusted his dark glasses and smiled. He jotted down the old man's Festac Town address on a small notepad and promised to return the rickety taxicab within eight hours. The aged taxi driver did not bother to ask what mission his borrowed vehicle was intended for. He was too busy praising God and whooping with laughter— such was the mesmerising effect of the eye-watering sums of money unexpectedly dropped on his laps.

'This shitty car cost me six thousand naira,' Adamu said as the taxicab circled a roundabout. 'And I can only have it for eight hours,' he added archly.

'You can't be serious. I always thought you guys were savvy. How can you let yourself be ripped off like that?' Nduka asked with a frown on his face.

'Actually, the old man who owns the car asked for much less. I decided to give him a lot,' Adamu replied.

Nduka shrugged in the rear seat. 'Well, it's your money, spend it however you wish.' There was momentary silence before he spoke again. 'You know what... if you are still feeling generous, then it wont be such a bad idea to shower me with some of your loose cash.'

'We pay you a lot, don't we?' Adamu asked rhetorically. Nduka agreed, but stated that he was not above receiving some extra cash, a generous bonus for his steadfast loyalty to the gang.

Adamu slowed down and swerved the car to avoid a pothole in the middle of the lane. 'We are always generous. And to prove it, this is for you!'

The conman pulled out a fat brown envelope from under the driver's seat without taking his eyes off the road. Then he tossed it over his head, towards the back of the car. In the rear seat, Nduka instinctively raised his hands above his head and caught the rectangular object in mid-flight. He ripped open the A4-sized envelope excitedly like a child anxious to know what gift lay inside a Christmas parcel. Five thick bundles of fifty-naira notes fell on to his laps from the upside-down envelope.

Adamu's eyes shifted intermittently between the rear-view mirror and the road ahead. In the mirror, he could see the excitement on Nduka's face as he flicked through a cash bundle with his fingers. 'That's twenty-five thousand naira on top of your standard hundred thousand naira fee. We need to know where Ikenna Kodilinye is with his investigations.'

'Can't you guys just order another hit on the bastard?' Nduka asked, playing with another thick bundle. The taxicab slowed down and made way for a speeding commuter bus to overtake it.

'Nah, we are done with all of that. No more assassination attempts. From now on, we'll just keep an eye on the detective,' Adamu replied as he drove past Gbagada General Hospital, a sprawling multi-storey healthcare centre set in the middle-class neighbourhood of Gbagada, ten miles from Ikeja.

'Not a very good idea,' Adamu remarked as he watched his sole passenger in the rear-view mirror attempting to stuff his pockets with cash from the thick bundles. 'For one, your pockets aren't big enough. For another, you don't want to be spotted returning from your "afternoon jog" with bulging pockets and bundles of cash in your hand. Use the envelope or better still look under your seat for something even larger.'

Nduka arched his brows, bent over and stuck his left hand in the space underneath the rear passenger seat. He groped around the space until his fingers felt a ridged fabric. Seconds later, he pulled out a brown corduroy tote bag and began to transfer the cash bundles into it.

'The bag belongs to Tunde, but you can keep it if you like,' Adamu remarked, his gaze shifting intermittently between the mirror and the windscreen. 'If any of your men are curious, you can always claim that you retrieved your wife's bag from the cobbler fixing it.'

Both men laughed heartily.

'Very funny, Adamu,' Nduka said as he transferred the last ill-fitting bundle of cash from his trouser pocket to the tote bag.

A few miles beyond Gbagada General Hospital, two columns of queued vehicles came into view. The rickety Peugeot 504 SR decelerated as it approached the new traffic gridlock.

'*Haba!* We are never going to get to Surulere at this rate!' Adamu exclaimed in frustration, staring at the long line of buses, lorries, vans and saloon cars ahead.

'Hey Adamu,' Nduka began as he zipped the bag shut. 'Tell Tunde not to call me. I feel I am being watched. If anything new pops up on the CID investigation, I'll call you guys from a secure line.'

'Fine, I'll tell him,' Adamu replied, feeling slightly flustered and annoyed at the same time. Then he paused when the import of Nduka's remark dawned on him. 'Wait a minute... we are on our way to meet the man in Surulere. You can tell him yourself.'

'Damn, it is so hot in here,' Nduka cursed and removed his black police beret and began to fan himself with it.

'It's your uniform. It is black and thick. Black materials absorb heat more effectively,' Adamu remarked as he watched the traffic chaos ahead with a growing feeling of resignation.

'Are you a scientist now?' Nduka asked sarcastically before glancing at his Seiko wristwatch.

'I have always been good in the sciences,' Adamu replied with a chuckle. 'I could have gone to university and studied to become a physicist, an engineer or even a medical doctor.'

'And yet, here you are, a common thief,' Nduka retorted with a derisive smile.

Adamu turned around and glared silently at the rear passenger for a full minute. He was about to say something rude when the queue of motorists behind his taxicab started yelling, howling, gesticulating wildly with arms sticking out of car windows and tooting their horns. For brief moment, the gangster was confused by what has happening, then it suddenly dawned on him—the motorists in the rear were angry with him for holding up traffic flow.

Turning back to face the windscreen, Adamu discovered, in the road ahead, that there was now a very wide gap between his taxicab and the column of vehicles further ahead. He quickly shifted the gear lever and released the clutch pedal. The taxicab bowled forward and within seconds, it had closed the gap in front and opened another gap in the rear. As if on cue, the tooting of car horns stopped, and the yelling, howling and gesticulation of arms quietened down. Almost in unison, the motorists engaged transmission gears and stepped on accelerator pedals, causing their queued vehicles to surge forward to close the gap behind Adamu's taxicab.

'Oh, sorry, I was just pulling your legs. I meant no offence,' Nduka said in a contrite voice. Changing the topic, the policeman continued, 'seeing the way the traffic is today, I don't think it is possible for me to make that meeting. You will have to apologize to Tunde on my behalf.'

'Be patient. The traffic holdup is just beginning to ease. Surulere is not too far from here.'

'No, it is too late for today, thanks to traffic delays. Besides, I told my orderly that I would be back soon,' Nduka said with a tone of finality. Awkward silence followed.

'Okay then,' Adamu replied, 'let me find somewhere to make a U-turn.'

Nduka was relieved that Adamu did not fight his decision. He never wanted the impromptu meeting called by Tunde in the first place, never wanted to be stuck in traffic under the scorching afternoon sun, and yearned to return to the comfort of his air-conditioned office in Ikeja.

Taking advantage of the easing traffic congestion, Adamu accelerated. His eyes flicked briefly to the mirror above. 'We want you to be happy because a happy informer provides quality information,' he remarked sonorously as the taxicab approached a roundabout.

'If Ikenna's investigation comes up with something new, you will know about it long before the Police Commissioner is briefed,' Nduka reassured Adamu.

The fraudster nodded slowly. Of course, he expected the Chief Inspector to deliver top level information, preferably in real time. The gang had done so much for the rogue policeman. Without them, the money in Nduka Ikwunne's secret bank account wouldn't have tripled within the space of three months and Mrs Chiamaka Ikwunne would not have opened an upscale boutique shop in Lagos Island.

'Okay then. I believe you,' Adamu said as he circled the roundabout for a U-turn. Moments later, the taxicab exited the rotunda, and the journey back to Ikeja began in earnest. Adamu's eyes flicked briefly to the mirror overhead. Nduka was holding the tote bag close to his chest as if he was expecting a thief to jump in through the window and snatch it.

Adamu saw that and shook his head from side to side. Lucky bastard, he thought, enjoy the cash while it lasts. He knew sooner or later the policeman would have to be dispatched. Ambitious rogue cops, like the Chief Inspector, would at some point in the future have to choose between the gang's pay packet and advancing their career, choose between maintaining loyalty to a gang that had been so generous to him and turning said gang over to the law to wide acclaim.

Adamu had a strong feeling that Nduka was secretly grappling with those choices much in the same way that Mike Otunba had done while alive.

John and the rest of the gang also had that same feeling. Nevertheless, the gangsters were in unanimity that Nduka was still useful and there were no signs that a betrayal was yet in the offing. That consensus began to breakdown when the Chief Inspector abruptly ended all contact with his handler, Tunde, and would not take calls from any member of the gang. That was three weeks ago.

It would take a blatant message left on an answering machine— the threat to cancel monthly payments— to bring Nduka back to his senses. It was the prospect of losing such a generous pay packet that compelled the crooked cop to agree to a meeting in Surulere.

However, long before that threat was communicated, there had been sharp disagreements within the gang over the reason for Nduka's behaviour. John and Moses were in five-alarm-fire panic mode; both believed that the cop was about to sell out the gang. The others, especially Adamu and Tunde, were more relaxed, believing that the rogue cop had been spooked by Ikenna's botched assassination. They speculated that Nduka was probably keeping a low profile, waiting for the uproar over the bungled affair of the Onitsha bombing to blow over before resuming contact. It was they who advocated that the rogue cop be given the benefit of the doubt. They also rejected Moses' call for Nduka's murder, and proposed the threat of pay cancellation as a means of forcing the policeman to resume communication.

John had gone along with the proposal to threaten a payment freeze, and when Nduka finally agreed to a meeting in Surulere, the gang leader issued another instruction: Adamu was to pump a bullet into the crooked cop if he detected any treachery in the offing. This was to be done in a secluded place, before or after the meeting had taken place.

Adamu had accepted to carry out the order, but only to humour his boss. The gangster was not a man given to rashness. On the contrary, he saw himself as a rather deliberative sort of fellow, and having thought deeply about the whole thing, it was his firm belief that there was no betrayal in the horizon. So, even before the Chief Inspector stepped into that borrowed taxicab, Adamu had already decided that he would not fire the SIG Sauer P226 concealed under his shirt. Of course, he was not averse to getting his hands dirty with the pistol. He was fully cognisant of his potential role as an executioner in a possible future that sees Nduka biting the generous hand feeding him. But in the present moment, inside the taxicab, the policeman was still more of an asset than a liability.

'What is "Da Silva"...is it some kind of codename... or is it a place?' Nduka asked as he put the black beret back on his head with his left hand. The corduroy tote bag was in the firm grip of the right hand.

'What on earth are you talking about?' Adamu asked, arching his eyebrows in confusion. His eyes shifted momentarily to the mirror to glance at the image of the passenger in the back seat.

'Oh, nevermind,' the rogue cop replied, 'it was something I once saw in Mike Otunba's diary. It's nothing that important. I was just curious.'

Adamu's confusion continued for a bit. Then he suddenly realized what Nduka was talking about. 'Oh yes, I remember now. It was a discreet call sign used by Otunba to request an emergency meeting with us. If my memory serves me right, he used that call sign sparingly.'

Nduka laughed. 'I knew it! I knew it was some kind of code. The other guys in the CID, including that bastard Ikenna, thought it was the name of a person or a place. But it was always clear to me.'

The Chief Inspector recalled the entry— *Da Silva at 1850 hours*— in Mike Otunba's paperback diary, which had intrigued his ad hoc team of homicide and APCS detectives conducting the preliminary murder investigation. Although Nduka had always suspected that "Da Silva" was code for something, he was not certain of it, and he never got a chance to probe further because Cyrus Udeh disbanded the ad hoc team and transferred the Otunba murder case to Ikenna's anti-scam squad.

'Well, what can I say? You are a smart guy,' Adamu said in a sarcastic tone, which Nduka failed to notice as he was busy congratulating himself for having all the right instincts needed for police work.

Arriving back at Allen Avenue—a busy thoroughfare in Ikeja— the Peugeot 504 taxicab was forced to decelerate. Adamu sighed heavily as he applied the brakes, stuck the gear lever in the neutral position, and lifted his foot from the clutch pedal. He had just run into the same traffic hold-up that he and his passenger had emerged from three-quarters of an hour earlier. The same bottleneck—the overturned Datsun 510 sedan—was still blocking parts of the dual carriageway. The orange-clad traffic cop who had earlier directed traffic flow had disappeared. In his place were three civilian traffic controllers wearing fluorescent green vests. There was also a tow truck, which wasn't there earlier. It was moving slowly towards the overturned saloon car.

Amidst the traffic gridlock, a small army of streetside hawkers—many of them teenagers— meandered in oblong spaces between long columns of queued vehicles, offering their wares to motorists and passengers trapped in saloon cars, buses, vans and lorries. The peddling business was performing quite well that sweltering afternoon. The hawkers had managed to sell off their crates of bottled water. Demand had been high for the chilled water, which the itinerant traders had ingeniously preserved in plastic crates filled with ice cubes.

'Damn Lagos traffic!' Adamu snarled, slapping the centre of the steering wheel repeatedly with his left hand. The the car horn tooted in response to each of his slaps. The hawkers heard the blaring car horn and began to move briskly towards the taxicab with their wares. A motorist had honked a summons, they all thought as they darted between lines of stationary vehicles in the gridlock.

Adamu and his sole passenger, Nduka, were surprised when a swarm of noisy hawkers, bearing trays of bananas and boiled groundnuts, and cartons containing tubs of yoghurt and ice cream, surrounded their taxicab.

Adamu glared at those clustering in front of his side window. The hawkers took no notice of his facial expression. They spoke simultaneously, talked over each other, each peddler struggling to raise his or her voice above the din, each making a sales pitch.

One hawker, a teenage boy in a dirty T-shirt and tattered shorts, pushed away another child-hawker and thrust a bunch of fresh bananas at Adamu's face. 'Please sir, buy my nice bananas,' he pleaded wearing his best fake smile.

Adamu opened his mouth for the umpteenth time to tell the noisy mob of itinerant traders that he was not interested in buying anything from them, but none was listening. So he decided to get physical. A clenched fist came out of the car window and struck the teenage banana hawker on the jaw, causing him to reel backwards. The stainless steel tray on his head fell and banana bunches scattered all over the asphalted tarmac. The other hawkers took no notice of the teenager's misfortune; they surged forward with their own wares, screaming their sale pitches at the top of their lungs.

Adamu turned to face Nduka with an expression of helplessness. The Chief Inspector barked an order above the din. The noisy mob paid no attention to him until the words "police" and "arrest" was heard. At that point, the hawkers froze and the noise died down. Several pairs of eyes flicked to the man in the back seat of the car dressed in a black uniform.

'If you don't back off, I will arrest all of you for public nuisance,' Nduka repeated angrily. He was bluffing, but the small crowd outside the taxicab did not know that.

The hawkers smiled apologetically and excused themselves. The teenage banana seller on the ground sprang to his feet, gathered his dusty banana bunches into his tray and fled. The itinerant traders knew what police officers were capable of. None of them wanted to be arrested for "public nuisance"—that would mean spending a couple of hours in a tiny police cell until one was ready to hand over their hard-earned money in exchange for freedom.

Adamu watched as the hawkers cowered and then ambled away. He felt a twinge of shame at his behaviour. As a teenager back in Benin City of the late 1950s, he had spent many weekends helping a school friend who had to hawk items to support his poor family. Despite coming from a middle-class household that lacked for nothing, Adamu was able to empathise with his poverty-stricken classmate, and partake in the deep frustration that all hawkers experience sometimes after spending a whole day making sales pitches that fail to get potential customers interested in buying something. Adamu knew perfectly well that some of the hawkers shooed away by Nduka would spend the entire afternoon under the scorching sun without making a single dime. It was a tough life that he was glad never to have lived, but was grateful to have witnessed through the struggling eyes of a less privileged classmate.

The Peugeot 504 taxicab and other vehicles in the traffic queue moved intermittently in a slow procession. Within ten minutes, Adamu came close enough to see the words—FRSC SPECIAL MARSHALS—emblazoned on the back of each fluorescent green vest worn by the civilian traffic controllers.

The *Special Marshal* designations indicated that all three civilian men were trained volunteers operating under the auspices of the Federal Road Safety Commission (FRSC), a uniformed traffic law enforcement agency established in 1988. The FRSC often deployed its volunteer civilian Special Marshals to direct road traffic inside cities while its regular uniformed officers patrolled the busy inter-state highways.

As the taxicab neared the site of the traffic bottleneck, Nduka spotted the emblazoned words on those fluorescent green vests and sighed heavily. It was another reminder that the Nigerian Police Force would never be allowed to catch a break. The Force would always have to contend with the pincer movement of the NDLEA and the FRSC. The former does all it can to strip the police of its right to participate in narcotic law enforcement while the latter gently erodes the authority of the police to enforce traffic rules on the nation's road networks.

'Not too long now,' Adamu remarked as he watched one Special Marshal direct traffic while the remaining two Marshals—plus the tow truck driver—were pushing against one side of the overturned Datsun 510 sedan. Moments later, they succeeded in getting a car lying on its roof to turn on its side and then onto its wheels. Shortly after, an electric steel cable winch, mounted in the back of a tow truck, was lifting the front end of the wrecked car.

'We should be moving anytime from now,' Adamu announced, expecting Nduka to say something positive. But the policeman was too preoccupied to respond. The gangster's weary eyes shifted to the mirror overhead. In that mirror, Adamu saw that the tote bag was open, that Nduka was no longer content with just flipping through each cash bundle. The cop was quietly counting individual banknotes in each bundle to confirm that the full amount was all there.

With traffic flow halted in either direction, while the winching operation was underway, Adamu killed the engine of his taxicab to save on fuel. Five minutes later, the tow truck propelled the wrecked Datsun away from the scene and in the direction of an auto-mechanic garage located three miles way.

With the bottleneck gone, traffic began to flow freely. Adamu heaved a sigh of relief and twisted the ignition key in the steering column. The engine roared to life, and soon the taxicab was weaving through the light traffic. As the taxicab approached the same spot from where it had earlier picked the cop, Adamu began to decelerate. His eyes stole a glance at the mirror overhead. Inside that mirror, the rear seat passenger was seen placing counted cash bundles back into the tote bag and fishing out other bundles for counting. Adamu smiled. Nduka Ikwunne was obviously having a nice day despite being stuck in traffic for over an hour in the sweltering heat.

'We are finally here,' Adamu said loudly as he steered the vehicle to the kerb. There, he pulled up and killed the engine. Ikeja CID complex was just one street away.

Nduka halted the counting process. He transferred the few cash bundles on his laps back into the tote bag and zipped it shut. Then he alighted with the bag slung over his right shoulder. He walked over to the driver's side window and bent over. 'Your taxi-driver disguise was brilliant. Here, take this,' he said, thrusting a fifty-naira note through the window.

'I thought we agreed on seventy naira,' Adamu said, laughing.

The policeman smirked and shook his head.

The cab driver snatched the banknote from the policeman. 'Thank you sir for the generosity,' he said sarcastically as he started the car engine.

Nduka waited for the taxi to disappear from view before walking briskly into the narrow alley. Ten minutes later, he was inside the foyer of Ikeja CID complex. When he finally made it back to his air-conditioned office on the third floor, he transferred the cash bundles to his reddish-brown portmanteau and tossed the tote bag into the waste paper bin. Then he turned his attention to the pile of manila files deposited on his desk by Inspector Daoud Mamman.

CHAPTER 32

While Nduka was surveying the pile of manilla folders on his desk, another policeman was busy doing something else in a smaller office, two floors above.

Detective-Sergeant (DS) Martin Okoye had just concluded the preliminary report on his clandestine operation against the Chief Inspector. The dossier was the product of a lucky break caught after twelve days of surveillance, during which Martin listened to ninety-six hours' worth of audio recordings captured by two transmitting bugs hidden inside Nduka's office.

For the first eleven days of the one-man surveillance operation, the audio recordings had failed to pick up anything suspicious. Then came the twelfth day, and everything changed. The day had started like any other. Martin came to work at 8.30 AM and began to attend to his main duties as a narcotics detective. He reviewed the case files of several suspects the Lagos Directorate of Public Prosecutions (DPP) were preparing to take to court on drug charges. At 2.30 PM, he turned his attention to the other task—the secret one that Gbolahan had given to him—and readied the cassette deck and his headphones to listen to a batch of five audio tapes.

The first and second tapes covered phone conversations of the previous evening. Like many others before them, the audio recordings turned out to be mundane and innocuous, and therefore useless. Martin put them away and moved on to the remaining three tapes containing audio recordings of that day, covering the period between 7.00 AM and 2.30 PM.

The third tape in the batch covered an early morning office meeting intercepted by the bug hidden underneath Nduka's desk. Martin chuckled as he listened to the audio of the Chief Inspector berating APCS detectives for lagging behind in their assignments, dismissing their complaints about the heavy workload as "worthless excuses". Although the recording was useless, as it contained nothing incriminating against Nduka, Martin was grateful for the window into the opaque inner workings of the largely secretive APCS. He was pleased to learn that those snobbish, overpaid detectives under the Chief Inspector's thumb got a tongue-lashing from time to time.

The fourth tape was a recording of three intercepted phone conversations, all related to each other. One was an early morning phone discussion between Nduka and the mechanic fixing his wife's car. The remaining two, separated by an interval of an hour, were phone conversations between the Chief Inspector and his wife about the progress the mechanic was making with the car. Martin placed the tape in the useless category.

The fifth tape, which was also the last in the batch, covered an afternoon phone conversation. Martin listened to the peculiar recording and realised that he had achieved a breakthrough. He rewound that tape in the cassette deck and adjusted his headphones. When he hit the relevant button on the deck, the audio played back as he transcribed on his typewriter:

Chief Inspector: 'Hello, Nduka Ikwunne speaking'
Unknown Voice (speaking Yoruba): 'E karo Oga Nduka'
Chief Inspector (in agitated tone): 'Shit! I told you not to call this office'
Unknown voice (speaking English): 'We have not heard from you in weeks. What's wrong?'
Chief Inspector: 'I got your message. Or should I say... your threat.'
Unknown voice (laughs): 'You left us no choice. Surely, you don't expect us to hold up our own end of the bargain in exchange for nothing. By the way, is your bug detector not working?'
Chief Inspector: 'I had to change a blown fuse in its plug. It now works well.'
Unknown voice: 'If it is effective and your phone line is secure, then why are you agitated?'
Chief Inspector: 'Well, no piece of equipment is perfect. It pays to be cautious. '
Unknown voice (laughs again): 'You are paranoid. If you don't want to talk over the phone, then we must meet in person. Now, listen, go downstairs, and catch a taxi to the usual place in Surulere. I'll be waiting.'
Chief Inspector: 'Okay, okay ...I'm coming.'
[*The phone conversation ends abruptly*]

Based on the transcript, Martin began to prepare a preliminary report. He wrote up a profile of the unknown voice, which he thought belonged to a Yoruba man between the ages of 30 and 45 years, most likely a native of Ondo State because of his accent. Midway, through typing the report, he pressed a button on his intercom and summoned the desk sergeant downstairs, at the reception area, for a quick chat.

Martin waited patiently for the portly policeman, who had run up four flights of stairs, to catch his breath before he began to question him. The sergeant noted that Nduka, accompanied by his orderly, Emeka Umenyi, had looked agitated when he walked past the reception area on his way out of the building. When the Chief Inspector returned to Ikeja CID over an hour later, he seemed to be in good spirits, smiling and bantering with constables in the reception area. The sergeant also could not help, but notice that Nduka was carrying a strange-looking corduroy tote bag, which he did not have on him earlier.

When Martin asked what was strange about the bag, the sergeant tittered before saying that corduroy was normally used for making clothes not bags. The detective smiled and thanked the sergeant for his cooperation. As the sergeant made his way downstairs back to his duty post, Martin resumed work on the typewriter. Two hours later, the preliminary report was ready for the eyes of his direct superior. It contained his own analysis of the revealing audio recording, a word-for-word transcript of that recording, and the desk sergeant's replies to his questions.

As Martin rose from his desk to go to Gbolahan's office, he felt a wave of confidence that he had secured the circumstantial evidence needed to persuade

CSP Cyrus Udeh to sanction a full-blown 24-hour surveillance of Nduka Ikwunne.

*****

Martin knocked on the door twice and a voice behind it asked him to come in. Gbolahan was placing the handset of the telephone back on its cradle when his second-in-command entered the office.

Gbolahan eyed the buff folder in Martin's hand. 'What do we have here?' he asked anxiously, waving his deputy to the empty chair across his mahogany desk.

'The preliminary report, sir,' the deputy narcotics squad leader replied as he handed the manilla folder to his boss. Sinking into the chair, Martin watched silently as Detective-Inspector Gbolahan Akinola opened the folder eagerly and began to read.

Halfway through the three-page report, Martin observed Gbolahan's eyes widen in excitement. Clearly, the narcotics squad leader thought he had found the "smoking gun" he needed to move formally against his enemy, Nduka.

Gbolahan was on the final page of the report, the transcript of the intercepted phone call, when Martin cleared his throat. The impressed narcotics squad leader paused and shifted his gaze to his second-in-command.

Martin asked his superior not to forward the report to Cyrus yet, as he still had one last task to complete to seal the circumstantial case against Nduka.

'Why? We already have what we need,' Gbolahan replied with a frown. He was already planning to drop by the Cyrus' office that evening to report on a surveillance operation, which the Ikeja CID boss did not authorize, and would probably never have authorized unless there was overwhelming evidence that the politically untouchable Nduka was indeed corrupt. Gbolahan was certain that whatever misgivings and anger felt by Cyrus about the unsanctioned operation, he would come to see the necessity of a fuller investigation of Nduka's activities. Gbolahan reckoned that he would get an earful from the DPO, but he would be quickly forgiven, and there would be grudging acceptance that he was right to ask Martin to plant listening devices in the APCS leader's office.

'There is no need to waste any more time,' Gbolahan added.

'Trust me, sir. I need to do one more thing,' Martin replied and then told a skeptical Gbolahan why he wanted a short delay before the report went to Cyrus.

'Okay then' Gbolahan sighed, placing the manilla folder in his bottom drawer. 'You have from now until tomorrow evening. After that, I will need to report to the DPO.'

Martin stood up, saluted, and left the office.

*****

At 9.00 PM that same day, the desk sergeant was behind the quadrangle-shaped reception counter, as usual, monitoring the dispatches streaming in via the police

radio from patrol cars on the beat. But for the intermittent static coming from the radio equipment, Ikeja CID complex was as silent as a tomb. Messages coming through from the patrol cars had been consistent for the last two hours: *the streets were calm, no problems so far.*
Bored out of his mind and feeling thirsty, Sergeant Uthman Bagudu decided he needed a short break. After all, there was no reason to believe that the message stream would change within the next hour.

He lifted his bulky frame from his high stool, straightened the shirt of his uniform, and walked across the marble floor to opposite end of the cavernous foyer where a bank of steel lockers were leaning against a wall. He jabbed a key into middle locker and turned it. The locker door sprang open. As he reached inside the darkened locker compartment for his favourite bottle of *Ogogoro*— a gin distilled from fermented palm wine—he heard the adjacent double doors creak open. Instinctively, he withdrew his hand from the compartment and slammed the locker door shut. He spun around and his heart nearly leapt into his mouth when he recognized the entrant clad in a blue T-shirt and matching jeans trousers. He stood at attention and threw his hand to his forehead in salutation. 'Good evening, sir.'

Martin smiled knowingly. 'Sarge, how many times have I told you that drinking on the job is forbidden?'

The rotund sergeant scratched his head and remained silent. He wanted to deny what he was about to do, but he knew it was useless. The detective could easily confirm the existence of alcohol by opening the locker compartment, which still had a small key sticking out of its door.

Martin looked into the pleading eyes of the sergeant and softened his tone. 'Look sergeant, this is the very last time I'll pretend that I did not see anything. Seek help for your drinking problem.'

The desk sergeant's head bobbed up and down as he made promises upon promises to quit drinking on duty.

'It is okay, Sarge,' the detective interrupted, holding up his right palm to halt the loud effusion of remorse and gratitude. 'I forgot an important case file in my office. I'm going upstairs to get it.'

Martin glanced at his watch and disappeared upstairs while the relieved sergeant shrugged and returned to his high stool behind the counter.

On the third floor, Martin produced the spare key he had lifted from the wooden racks in the cleaners' storage room. He inserted it into the keyhole on the door to Nduka's office. Moments later, he was inside the dark room, retrieving the corduroy tote bag that the Chief Inspector had carelessly tossed into a large waste paper bin earlier in the day.

The detective focussed the bright narrow beam of his pen torch on the tote bag. He smiled in satisfaction as he examined it. He had guessed correctly that the bag was still in the office. Earlier that day, the desk sergeant had observed a distraught Nduka leave the building empty-handed, only to return later, in high spirits, with the strange bag, and then leave again, at the end of office hours, without it.

Martin had mentioned the need to examine the bag when he asked Gbolahan to hold off on meeting Cyrus with the preliminary report. While doubting that a shrewd cop like Nduka would make the mistake of keeping the bag around, Gbolahan had agreed to the request for a delay.

Guided by halogen penlight, Martin searched the interior of the tote bag and found nothing. Then he redirected the narrow beam of penlight towards the only patch pocket on the bag. He pulled its zipper back, reached inside and fished out a business card. Surprised and excited at the same time, he shone his pen torch on the card and read the print. Then he spent a few more minutes going through the office before deciding there was nothing new to discover. With the sole exception of the business card, now in the back pocket of his trousers, he returned everything he had touched to the exact position they were in before his entry to the office...

Downstairs in the foyer, Uthman was sitting behind the reception counter, hunched over the police radio. He was so absorbed by the loud message dispatches streaming in from patrol cars prowling the streets that he had not sense a movement in front of his desk.

A hand suddenly nudged the sergeant in the shoulder, startling him. He looked up from the police radio and saw Martin standing in front of the counter. Turning down the volume of the radio, Uthman saluted. Martin bid him goodbye, then walked across the foyer, past the double doors at the entrance and out into the forecourt from where he melted into the silent night.

*****

Chief Superintendent Cyrus Udeh did not live inside Ikeja, the Lagos State capital. But his house was close enough for easy commute. Shogunle was located just outside Ikeja. Unlike places such as Victoria Island, Lekki, Ikoyi and Ikeja, the district of Shogunle was neither affluent nor well organized.

Housing in the district was a chaotic sprawl of duplex homes, bungalows and apartment complexes, a jarring patchwork of well-maintained and terribly rundown buildings, which reflected the variegated income demographics of the area— middle-class residents occupied houses in much better shape than those inhabited by their working-class neighbours living next door.

Cyrus and his wife shared a respectable middle-class dwelling in the heart of Shogunle. It was a long green bungalow inside a spacious compound surrounded on three sides by high concrete walls, each topped with a roll of barbed wire to discourage burglars. The fourth wall facing the street had a large gap in the middle, which was closed off with a tall solid iron gate topped with metal spikes.

Flanking the senior policeman's well-kept residence were two dilapidated low-income buildings. To the left of Cyrus' property was a two-storey rooming house with a dirty facade. On the right-hand side was a six-storey apartment

295

complex with several broken windows and paint peeling from its exterior walls. Cyrus hated their towering presence near his home. He had long perceived both poor dwellings as a security problem ever since four burglars who were tenants there attempted to break into his house. Consequently, he had planned to electrify the barbed wires to electrocute any burglar who repeated the idiocy of the last four, but his wife dissuaded him. She was all for arrest and prosecution of thieves, but extra-judicial killing was a step too far.

The police chief had bitten his lower lip before accepting his wife's advice. He would not attach a live electric cable to the barbed wires. But that did not mean he would not be on the lookout, especially at night, for intruders who might, against all the odds, make it over the the razor-sharp barbed wires and metal pikes. He wanted to be out there when that happened to congratulate such plucky intruders with smashing blows to both kneecaps before making an official arrest. His wife, the university academic, would undoubtedly disapprove of it and rant for thirty minutes about human rights, and he would certainly listen meekly while secretly relishing the fact that the crippled burglar had been put out to grass permanently. His kneecapping tool of choice was a large pipe wrench that he normally used for plumbing work around the house. At nights, he always had it underneath the sofa in the living room, where it was easy to reach, in case he needed to dart into the driveway and smash some limbs.

The night of 25th November was no different. The pipe wrench was in its usual location in the living room and the man who would wield it, if necessary, was reclining on the sofa, watching NTA News on the television.

Five minutes into the news broadcast, his concentration was broken by the sharp sound of a ceramic vase crashing outside. He bent over, reached for the wrench, and made for the front door. He turned the door handle and stepped down into the moonlit tarmacked driveway. He looked around and found the source of the noise. A stray cat had toppled one of his wife's flower vases. Cyrus sighed at the broken vase and the loamy soil spilled from it. He glared at the cat for a few seconds and started shooing it away. The furry creature jumped on top of the gate, easing itself into the vertical space between two metal spikes. Then it dived down onto the street below and disappeared. The house owner turned around and went back to his living room.

Cyrus returned the wrench to its previous position and reclined on the sofa. His eyes followed the female journalist on TV who was reporting a student riot that had taken place in the University of Jos in Plateau State. The news network televised video footage of the havoc wreaked by irate students during the disturbance. A camera shot of the wreckage panned across the TV screen, accompanied by a male voice-over. There were burnt-out cars belonging academic staff, broken chairs, smashed up windows in classrooms, and the smouldering ruins of what was once the University Vice Chancellor's Lodge. The campus was empty save for a few armed policemen patrolling the former war zone to keep the expelled students from sneaking back.

The video footage switched to a scene outside the university gates and the previously unseen male journalist doing the voice-over appeared on the TV screen. In front of the gates, he introduced the student union leader standing next to him before starting an interview. The student leader explained that the students were protesting the federal government's decision to increase school fees by 200 percent. The male reporter asked the student leader whether violence was the best way to protest against government policy. The student leader stated indignantly that the protest had been peaceful until the anti-riot police started firing live ammunition into crowds of demonstrators without provocation.

The televised footage then moved to another scene. The same male reporter, in a different location, was interviewing the spokesman for the Plateau State Police Command. The police spokesman rejected the student leader's claim that the protest was initially peaceful, explaining that the demonstrators were vandalizing and looting school property when his men arrived on the scene. The interviewer then asked him whether it was justified to fire live bullets at unarmed students.

'They were armed with stones and clubs!' the angry policeman snapped.

The unfazed reporter rephrased his question. 'Inspector, why use live ammunition? What about tear gas? Rubber bullets? Pepper spray? You know…the standard anti-riot equipment.'

The Inspector smiled contemptuously and walked out on the interviewer. The male reporter faced the camera, concluding gravely that the university would be shut down for at least a month while a federal government inquiry is held into the disturbance.

The telecast switched from the video footage back to the live studios of the Nigerian Television Authority (NTA). The female presenter sitting behind a studio news desk reported the reaction of Plateau State government and was in the middle of covering the reaction of a federal government spokeswoman when Cyrus heard the electric bell above the front door ringing

The DPO instinctively reached again for the pipe wrench under the sofa and then paused. Burglars did not politely ring the bell in properties they had come to rob. He released the unseen plumbing tool and withdrew his hand from under the sofa. He picked up the black remote control on the upholstered armrest of the sofa and reduced the TV volume. The bell rang again.

'I'll get it!' his wife called out loudly from the kitchen.

The DPO glanced at his watch. The time was 11.35 PM. He wondered who was paying him a visit at that time of the day. He rose from the sofa and started towards the front door, but his wife of twenty-seven years, suddenly entered the living room and brushed past him on her way to the front door handle. By the time he appeared at the doorway, she had crossed to the far end of the moonlit driveway and was talking to someone through a hatch on the solid iron gate facing the street.

At the doorway of the house, the DPO strained in vain to hear, over a distance of nine feet, what the male voice, speaking in low tones, was saying to his wife. Three minutes later, he stepped down into driveway and began to move unseeingly towards the gate under the glare of moonlight. Halfway there, he began to make out the male voice speaking English with a strong Yoruba accent. The police chief felt weird when he heard it. There was something familiar about that voice talking to his wife. He fetched his pair of glasses from the left side pocket of his pyjamas trouser and walked faster.

On reaching the gate, his wife shifted to one side to make room for him. He put on the eyeglasses and peered out of the square aperture on the gate. On the other side of the gate were two men dressed in identical black T-shirts and matching black chinos trousers.

Cyrus recognized both of them and frowned. 'What the devil are you guys doing here at this time of the night dressed like burglars?'

Gbolahan and Martin saluted the police chief. 'Sir, may we come in?' the narcotics squad leader asked with an apologetic smile.

Through the aperture, Dr. Ugonwa Udeh glared at the visitors and then turned to her husband. It was obvious to everyone that she wanted Cyrus to refuse the request.

Cyrus brushed aside his wife's unspoken demand. 'Yes, come in. But your reason for being here at this time of the night had better be good,' he hissed.

Ugonwa said something in Igbo language, which Gbolahan did not comprehend, and then stormed off. Next to Gbolahan, Martin was smiling ruefully. He understood perfectly well what the madam of the house had said.

'Sir, we apologise for disturbing you at this time. We wouldn't have done so if it were not important,' Gbolahan said.

The DPO nodded impatiently and closed the metal shutter on the square hatch. The detectives heard the rasping sound of giant bolts being pulled on the other side before the solid metal gate swung open.

Gbolahan apologised for angering the madam of the house. Cyrus told him not to worry about her as he led them past two saloon cars in the driveway and into bungalow. In the living room, the police chief paused to switch off the TV with the remote control before continuing to the study room.

Martin felt like a homebuyer being shown around. He was clearly impressed by the tastefully furnished living room, especially the chandelier lights hanging from the ceiling. Cream wallpaper, with a flower motif, on the four walls of the study room seemed to blend well with the light brown upholstery and cream-coloured Persian rug. Leaning against a wall at one end of the study room was an impressive floor-to-ceiling bookcase stacked with books on police technology, literature, law, politics, history and religion.

At the opposite end of the room, Cyrus sat down behind a lacquered desk facing the enormous bookcase. A few inches behind his padded chair was a wall from which hung a framed black-and-white picture of a much younger version of himself dressed in a black graduation gown receiving a long plastic canister from a much older man wearing a Tudor hat and the black-and-red robes of an academic. A small legend under the picture read: "Faculty of Law, University of Nigeria, Enugu Campus, 1964".

'Gentlemen, don't just stand there, please sit down,' the DPO said to the men enchanted by the room. 'My wife is an expert in interior decoration, if you guys need tips, she is the one,' he added as the detectives sat in two of the three chairs positioned across the mahogany desk.

'Okay sir, let me start from the beginning,' Gbolahan began.

'You had better do that,' the DPO said with a thin smile. 'And before that, explain to me why this could not wait until office hours, tomorrow.'

'Today, during office hours, we wanted to see you about an urgent matter, but your orderly said you were not coming to work today...'

'Yes, I had a bad headache. If it was so urgent why not call?' Cyrus interjected.

Gbolahan smiled weakly. 'Sir, in the afternoon, we rang your home telephone twice. Nobody picked up. Then we came here to the house, but still no luck.'

Cyrus Udeh grimaced. What the hell was Gbolahan talking about? he thought to himself. He was home all day. He had woken up in the morning with a throbbing head, a migraine. He had taken some paracetamol and called his trusted aide, Constable Dixon Nkwamkpa, in Ikeja CID to say he was taking the day off. So what was the detective sitting across the desk talking about? Then it finally hit him.

'What time did you come here?' he asked Gbolahan.

'We rang your home phone at twelve noon and again at one o'clock. Then we came here at two-thirty and rang the electric bell a few times. Nobody came to the gate, so we left.'

'I think I know what happened,' Cyrus began rubbing his chin. 'You guys probably came when I was having a nap. Like I said before, I was suffering from a headache and had to lie down a bit. But that does not explain why you guys had to come at night and this late. This could not wait till tomorrow?'

'No sir, it could not wait' Martin replied.

'Okay then, nevermind. Just tell me what it is all about.' Cyrus said irritated.

Gbolahan started from the beginning, telling his boss how he had defied his orders to leave Chief Inspector Nduka Ikwunne alone, how he had put Martin up to the task of surveilling Nduka.

Cyrus' facial expression revealed surprise for brief moment, and then his eyes flashed with anger. The police chief's hands clenched and unclenched. Though furious, Cyrus waited patiently for Gbolahan to conclude his story.

Martin looked into the eyes of the Ikeja CID boss and saw the storm clouds gathering. The chief of detectives was revving to erupt like a volcano as soon as Gbolahan shut his mouth. So he quickly fetched the mini-tape recorder from his pocket.

'Detective-Inspector Gbolahan Akinola, I warned you! I ordered you not to....'

Martin placed the tape recorder on the desk and hit the "play" button.

Cyrus froze and shook his head and began to listen attentively to the audio recording of the one-day-old phone conversation between Nduka and an unknown voice. As the audio recording played back, Cyrus' mood began to mellow. He nodded at intervals as if he was physically absorbing the sounds emanating from the tape recorder.

At the end of the playback, Gbolahan opened the brown satchel that he had brought with him and extracted a manilla folder, which he handed over to Cyrus. 'Sir, here is the preliminary report prepared by Martin on Nduka's nefarious activities.'

Cyrus put on his spectacles and read the report. When he was done, he removed his spectacles and gazed at the detectives. 'Detectives, under normal circumstances, I would have suspended you for doing this without authorisation from me,' he paused, inhaled deeply and continued. 'But under the circumstances, I won't resort to that line of action. The information you have brought to light is quite serious, and we must act quickly and firmly.'

Then a sudden enigmatic smile appeared on his face. The detectives heaved a collective sigh of relief. The police chief was back in a good mood even if they weren't exactly sure what he had in mind. They were not exactly at the stage at which they could arrest Nduka. The recording was only circumstantial evidence. More digging would be required to get something tangible on the corrupt cop.

Staring at Gbolahan, Cyrus remarked, 'I guess you have been somewhat vindicated.'

Gbolahan nodded in acknowledgement, but said nothing.

'I'm taking over your surveillance operation and expanding it to include some of the APCS detectives. Everybody knows that I loathe that ad hoc monstrosity called APCS, but its personnel are experts in surveilling corrupt policemen. Perhaps, we can use the help of a few good detectives on the third floor. These APCS guys know that bastard, Nduka, very well. Right now, we can...'

'Sorry sir, I strongly disagree. Those APCS detectives are too loyal to the Chief Inspector,' Martin cut in. 'Without exception, every single one of them will tip off the Chief Inspector and sabotage the investigation.'

Cyrus paused to consider his omission for a few seconds and then asked Gbolahan to disregard his instructions to involve the APCS. The police chief informed them that he would be asking for assistance from his counterpart in the neighbouring Ogun State Police Command. He was sure that his old friend, Ganiyu Onasanya, the Ogun State CID head, would not refuse to loan out four of his most experienced watchers for three weeks.

Cyrus revealed his plan for the covert investigation of Nduka to the detectives. The out-of-state watchers would be organised into an ad hoc surveillance team to be led by Martin who would then report to Gbolahan, who in turn, would report to the DPO. Martin would be quietly freed from his duties in the narcotics squad to lead the planned ad hoc team in watching Nduka and his patrons, day and night.

Cyrus, the DPO, concluded by reiterating the secret nature of the operation, hence the necessity of importing unknown cops from another police command. Then he rose from his desk to escort the men out of the study room.

DS Martin Okoye rose from the chair and suddenly remembered what he had forgotten. He slowly removed the business card from the back pocket of his trousers and passed it to the Ikeja CID boss. 'Sorry sir I forgot to mention it to you. Found it in the Chief Inspector's office.'

Cyrus scrutinized the card. It read:

TUNDE OLUKEMI
GENERAL MANAGER
ELAJ ENTERPRISES
EXPERTS IN THE BUSINESS OF VEHICLES

'Do you know this enterprise?' Cyrus asked, still examining the card.

'Yes, the company sells car spareparts to retailers. It is mainly a wholesale business,' Gbolahan replied.

'Where in Lagos is it based?' the DPO asked as he turned over the card. The answer he was looking for was printed on the back of the card, but he still listened patiently to Gbolahan's reply.

'Head office is in Mushin, but the company has a branch office in Ikeja. It also has warehouses all over Lagos State namely Idumota, Surulere, Lagos Island, Agege, and so on.'

Cyrus nodded and said, 'I'm impressed, detective. You seem to know a lot about this company.'

Gbolahan surprised the other men in the room by revealing that his cousin worked there.

'So you know this Tunde Olukemi?' the DPO asked, arching his eyebrows.

Gbolahan shook his head. 'Not personally, but my cousin, Shade, has mentioned him as one of the managers of ELAJ.'

'Shall I tap his phones?' Martin asked.

Cyrus gazed at the ceiling as he pondered the request. A minute later, he replied, 'no, it's too risky, if this Tunde is working with Nduka, he may already know what you and your colleagues look like. For that reason, I don't want anyone resembling a Lagos detective anywhere near our potential suspects. Ogun State CID men will do that job when they arrive.'

Martin nodded and the house owner guided them out of the study towards the front door in the living room.

'One more thing,' the Ikeja CID boss began as they walked along the tarmacked driveway towards the iron gates. 'This meeting did not take place. This remains a secret. I trust that you guys would be discreet. Gbolahan, I trust you won't breathe a word of this to your cousin. It is tempting to want to use her help, but she is not a police officer and that might put her life in danger.'

Gbolahan had intended to use his cousin to spy on her employers, but had not thought of the danger that could put her in. A ruthless gang guilty of a series of murders, including those of four police officers, would not hesitate to dispatch a mere office secretary.

'What about DI Ikenna Kodilinye? Are we keeping this from him?' Martin asked as he stepped out of the gates to join Gbolahan in the street.

The DPO rubbed his chin thoughtfully for a few seconds and replied, 'Leave Ikenna to me.'

The detectives interpreted the enigmatic remark as an order not to discuss the planned surveillance operation with Ikenna until authorized to do so.

'Good work, guys. I'll see you tomorrow in the office,' Cyrus said and started to close the gates when Dr. Ugonwa Udeh sudden appeared behind him. She spoke coolly in Igbo to her husband and then stalked back across the driveway and into the house.

Cyrus grinned in embarrassment. 'Good night, detectives,' he said and shut the gate. The rasping sounds of gate bolts slamming into place were heard again.

Outside the gate, on the moonlit street, Martin chuckled as his bewildered superior looked on.

'What did the Missus say?' Gbolahan asked his deputy who understood and spoke Igbo fluently.

Martin translated what Dr. Udeh had said into English. 'She told the boss to sleep on the sofa tonight.'

CHAPTER **33**

NOVEMBER 1993

HAMPSTEAD, NORTHWEST LONDON, UK

On 26th November 1993, the second meeting took place at the outdoor café overlooking the light traffic flow on Hampstead High Street.

Harel Suzmann sat behind a round, stainless steel table, scrutinizing a bank statement and smiling. Sitting across the table from him was his new business associate, the man he knew as Matthew Molozi. The man, with an unsincere smile on his face, was studying the Briton's reaction to the paperwork.

The document in Harel's hands indicated that the escrow account, opened for his benefit in Canada, had received its first deposit from Volkstar Diamond— the sum of ninety-six thousand five hundred Canadian dollars, which translated to fifty thousand pounds sterling.

Matthew told his pleased interlocutor that Heintz & Sharmann had started squeezing Volkstar Diamond Limited for the £25.5 million inheritance, bit by bit. However, there was still a long way to go. Executives of the Cape Town-based diamond company were caught between their refusal to pay out the full inheritance and their reluctance to take their chances in court.

Harel was told that Heintz & Sharmann lawyers had played hardball with the executive officers of Volkstar during their first meeting to discuss the inheritance. The lawyers had succeeded in bullying the recalcitrant company into agreeing to open an escrow account in a reputable bank outside South Africa. The account would hold the money the company was going to pay Harel once a final agreement had been reached.

'In our third meeting with them,' Matthew said, 'we accepted a proposal for an interim payment of five hundred thousand pounds in ten equal installments.'

Harel frowned. 'Only five hundred thousand?'

Matthew moved quickly to mollify his associate. 'This is only an interim agreement. We are still seeking more. It is going to take time, but we are squeezing them. We will eventually get the whole twenty-five million five hundred thousand pounds that you are owed.'

The fraudster picked the croissant on the saucer and took a bite.

Harel's face brightened. He held up the bank statement with his right hand and tapped the portion of the paper that had C$96,500 printed on it. 'I guess this is my first installment, fifty thousand pounds.'

Matthew nodded, chomping a mouthful of croissant. After the pastry had been masticated and swallowed, the fraudster said, 'I hope you understand that this is an escrow account. That means that we, the lawyers, working on your behalf, will hold the account in trust until a final settlement is reached. In other words, we control the account until Volkstar pays the entire inheritance. Once the full amount has been recovered from the company, we will transfer everything into your personal bank account. Of course, the entire process will take some time to conclude.'

Harel put on a brave face to conceal his disappointment, but he was not opposed to the escrow arrangement. Although, he had an inkling of how long it could take the inheritance to reach his personal account in Barclays Bank, he still asked his associate the question.

Matthew shrugged. 'I'm not sure. Could take anywhere from a month to a full year, depending on the level of progress being made in our negotiations with the company. The good news here is that they prefer to negotiate rather than fight it out in the courts. This gives us an advantage, which are using to turn the screws on them. At the moment, my colleagues in South Africa are recruiting extra paralegals. We are also seeking assistance from another law firm, a corporate legal practice, which specialises in cases such as these...just in case we need to go to court.'

Harel sipped his coffee, completely impressed with his associate. So far so good, he thought. Any doubts he had in the past about the credibility of the South African firm had long vanished. He trusted the Heintz & Sharmann with all his heart. After all, these lawyers had forced the delivery of the first tranche of a large sum of money that he had not earned. Money that belonged to a dead relative whose existence he had discovered only recently.

Once again, he began daydreaming about spending his South African inheritance on revigorating his business; on a holiday home in the Bahamas; on a new luxury car, a Maserati or Lambourghini, he could not decide. Then a still image of his estranged wife flashed across his mind. Oh yes, the damned bitch, he thought. No doubt, she would come crawling back to profess her undying love for him. He would pretend to believe her, accept her back for a few days, and then kick her out again. That would be his revenge on the cheating bitch, a humiliation worth relishing...

Matthew surveyed the dreamy smile on the face of the absent-minded Briton and realized that the time was ripe for the next stage, the fourth in Tunde's five-stage plan. He drank tea slowly from the cup while he gathered his thoughts together. By the time he had placed the teacup back on the saucer, the necessary talking points were ready and waiting to be pitched.

'The specialist, corporate law firm we have hired to assist us with your case, Russell Wilcox and Associates, is charging eight thousand pounds,' he said and paused to gauge Harel's reaction. Seeing no change yet in the countenance of the Briton, he continued in a rueful tone. 'We did complain about the steep fees, but our friends in Russell Wilcox were adamant. And they are the best in the business. Only lost three out of a total of eighty cases they had brought to court.'

Harel nodded gravely and gazed beyond the shoulder of Matthew at the street traffic, his brain busy analyzing what the faux South African lawyer had just said. He recalled the first meeting during which he learnt that Heintz & Sharmann would not charge a dime for services rendered, but would pass all extra expenses incurred in pursuit of the inheritance claim to him. In other words, the cost of engaging Russell Wilcox & Associates to assist in the case was being passed on to him. He would have to reimburse Matthew to the tune of £8000.

'You have paid the legal fees, eight thousand?' Harel asked, although he knew the answer.

'Yes,' Matthew replied, sipped some tea and smacked his lips. 'According to our agreement, all expenditure will be passed...'

'Yeah, yeah, yeah,' Harel cut in airily. 'Why not use the money in escrow?' he asked and then realized it was a stupid question.

Matthew set down his teacup on the table and shook his head gravely. 'Under our escrow agreement with Volkstar, the money cannot be touched until the final settlement is reached. The whole idea of having the escrow account is to allow the company to retrieve their deposit if no permanent agreement can be reached between them and us. I am sorry, but we cannot pay Russell & Associates from the escrow.'

Harel nodded and reached for his waist below the table and unhooked the bumbag round it. He placed it on the table. He unzipped it and fished out his new Barclays Bank cheque book.

'Do you normally carry your cheque book wherever you go?' Matthew asked, mildly surprised and delighted. He had not expected to get the money right away.

Harel smiled wrily and pointed at the bank across the street. 'I was there earlier today to see the bank manager. I got myself a new cheque book as well.'

He flipped open the blue booklet and started writing on it. 'I did not think I'll be spending this much so soon,' he grumbled as he appended his signature on a cheque.

'It's for good cause,' Matthew said, smiling broadly.

The British businessman ripped the cheque from the booklet and offered it to the man sitting across the table from him.

'Thank you. You will get a receipt by post from my firm in South Africa within a fortnight.'

The meeting ended five minutes later. Harel got into his Audi Quattro and drove home while Matthew travelled by train from London to Dover and from there took the ferry to the French city of Calais. He spent the next two days in Paris before returning to The Netherlands by road.

Back in Amsterdam, he deleted a copy of the forged bank statement he had given to Harel from the hard drive of his IBM Thinkpad 700C laptop. However, he retained the digital image of the Canadian bank's letterhead. He had scanned the image from an old bank statement issued to ELAJ Enterprises when the front company still held an account in the Royal Bank of Montreal. The bank account, opened in Canada in January 1991, had functioned as one of the receptacles for dirty money laundered through ELAJ Enterprises until February 1993, when it was closed and the money deposited there transferred to a more secure bank in Zurich, Switzerland.

When Tunde first suggested the use of fake bank statements, Eugene was worried that the British businessman might discover the forgery. But Tunde was confident that nothing of the sort would happen and reassured Eugene over the phone. Men with struggling business ventures, like Harel, were desperate and therefore vulnerable to "get-rich-quick" schemes.

'Mister Suzmann desperately wants to believe that our scheme is true. Boldly wave that bank statement with the five-figure sum of Canadian money in his face and tell him that this is only the first installment, that this is only the beginning of our strategy to extract every penny of his multi-million-pound inheritance from the penny-pinching Volkstar. Tell him that in a confident voice and he will believe you instantly. Just do it. There is nothing to worry about,' Tunde had said before ending the long-distance phone call.

Despite his misgivings, Eugene Igolo alias "Matthew Molozi" had done exactly as Tunde instructed, and as predicted, Harel Suzmann had fallen for the scam—hook, line and sinker.

*****

A week later, Harel Suzmann returned, sweating and panting, from his regular morning jog, the physical activity that normally took him from Maresfield Gardens to Hampstead Heath and back. His white T-shirt was soaked in sweat and the matching pair of white shorts had small brown spots where muddy water from a puddle had splashed on him during the trot.

He checked the newly installed letterbox on his gate for letters. There was only one letter there and, to his delight, it had South African stamps. He entered his house, dropped the letter on the coffee table in the living room, and went to the toilet for a pee. When he finally got around to slitting the envelope open, he discovered three folded documents. One was a handwritten cover letter signed by Eli Sharmann (Esq) informing him that the second installment of C$96,500 (£50,000) had been deposited into the escrow account as negotiations for a final settlement continues in earnest.

The second document had the familiar letterhead of Heintz & Sharmann. It was a receipt proving that the South African law firm had received his £8000 reimbursement.

Harel glanced at it before moving on to the third document. His face brightened when he saw that it had the letterhead of the Royal Bank of Montreal. It was apparently an original copy of a bank statement. He began to study it. The document showed two equal installments of C$96,500, the first of which he was already aware, as Matthew had shown him the preceding bank statement. The knowledge of the second deposit was new and gladdened his heart because it meant that there was now a total sum of C$193,000 (£100,000) in the escrow account.

306

Harel scrutinized the dates on the statement, noting that the first installment entered the escrow account on 15th November, eleven days before his last meeting with Matthew. The second installment was deposited on 29th November, just three days after that meeting. That was proof enough for him that the South African-based lawyers were serious about wrenching his inheritance from the devious executives of Volkstar Diamond. He smiled and put away the documents. As he rose to leave the living room, the telephone on the coffee table began to ring, causing him to pause. He picked up the handset from its cradle.

The caller was the assistant manager of a small company he had floated nine months earlier in an attempt to reverse his fortunes. The company, which specialized in surveillance equipment like closed circuit camera and its accessories, had not been doing well for sometime, and that worried Harel greatly.

'Yes, Derrick, what is it now?' he asked, half-expecting to hear more bad news, but he was wrong

'Oh, nothing bad, we made quite a bit of money, today,' Derrick Goldstein replied.

'Really? What did we make today?'

'A private security firm bought equipment worth a hundred and fifty thousand pounds'

'Wow! That is good news man!' Harel exclaimed and dropped into a sofa. 'You know, I was beginning to lose hope...you know the problems...' his voice trailed off. A few moments of awkward silence passed before Derrick spoke.

'Well, I think this is a good sign, sir. We mustn't be too hasty in writing off the business.'

Another moment of silence followed before Derrick broke it again. 'Sir, is there anything wrong? You haven't been to the office in a week.'

'Nothing is wrong, Derrick. I wasn't feeling well. Migraine, you know. I am now okay. I'll see you when I come in tomorrow.'

It was true that Harel was coming to office the next day, but he had been lying about the migraine. He had avoided the office for the past seven days to escape the pain and misery the place brought him. He was just fed up with watching his new enterprise slowly treading the same path to insolvency as his previous business ventures. The sale of equipment worth over a hundred thousand pounds had just boosted his morale, and he resolved to be in the office to attend personally to potential customers, should they come around.

'Sir...sir... are you still there?'

'Yes, Derrick, yes,' Harel answered, snapping out of his thoughts.

'Eh sir, just a gentle reminder that my son's Barmitzvah is on Sunday.'

'Oh really, I thought it was on fifth December.'

'Yes sir, it's the day after tomorrow.'

'Of course,' Harel said, embarrassed that he had already forgotten about it. He didn't particularly care for religious ceremonies, but he wanted to keep Derrick happy. Happy employees were productive employees.

'Of course, I won't miss such an important ceremony for...eh...what's your boy's name again?'

'It's Solomon, sir.'

'Yes, yes, I will definitely be there for Solomon's Barmitzvah.'

Derrick laughed heartily and the topic of the conversation shifted back to business. Five minutes later, the phone call was over. Harel dropped the handset and headed to the bathroom to take a shower.

CHAPTER 34

DECEMBER 1993

ABEOKUTA, WESTERN NIGERIA

The cold, dry and foggy trade winds of Harmattan were blowing that early morning, on the first day of December, when Cyrus and his men departed Lagos for Ogun State. The entire journey across state lines, from Ikeja to Abeokuta, should not have taken more than ninety minutes. But once the unmarked saloon car driven by DS Martin Okoye sped past the inter-state border, the smooth tarmacked roads of Lagos State were suddenly replaced by Ogun State's alternating chain of pothole-ridden asphalt roads and dirt tracks. A few yards beyond the border, the car began to shake violently as the tyres bumped against uneven road surfaces and the vehicle suspension system struggled to cushion the ride. Martin was forced to decelerate and, from then onwards, proceed in a slow and steady speed until he reached Abeokuta town, the state capital.

Martin arrived at the Abeokuta headquarters of the Ogun State Police Command at exactly 10.00 AM, two hours after he and his passengers set off on the journey. As soon as he pulled up on the unpaved forecourt, the adjacent building disgorged five uniformed police constables. They approached the car with their Mark IV bolt-action rifles dangling leisurely from straps slung over their shoulders.

The rear passenger door of the Peugeot 505 flung open and Cyrus Udeh alighted, dressed in the starched black uniform and beret of a Chief Superintendent of Police.

The policemen stood at attention and saluted. 'You are welcome sir,' they chorused.

Cyrus returned the salute. It was the first time he had been to the town since transferring from Ogun State CID to Lagos State CID, almost two decades earlier. On the first leg of every nine-hour-long car journey from Lagos to his native Enugu, Cyrus had always driven through the outlying districts of Ogun State along the Lagos-Ibadan expressway. And not once had he felt the urge to make a stopover at Abeokuta, not once did he veer-off the smooth asphalted expressway, to trundle along narrow pothole-ridden roads into the hinterlands of Western Nigeria, to visit his former place of work where his friend and former colleague now held sway. He had always promised to visit Abeokuta whenever he was on the phone with his friend, the Ogun State CID head; but he never did, because he was reluctant to squeeze out time from his extremely busy schedule to make the trip, unless it was absolutely vital...

'Is your boss in?' Cyrus asked as two doors opened in the Peugeot 505 behind him.

'Yes sir, he is expecting you,' a constable said, staring over the DPO's shoulder at the two men in plain clothes sliding out the saloon car.

'Okay, let's go,' Cyrus said as Gbolahan and Martin appeared behind him.

The welcoming party of five constables swung around and started towards the large police station with the visitors following. A few inches from the foot of the concrete steps, Cyrus halted, his eyes panning up and down the untidy facade of the three-storey police station with peeling paint. The last time he had seen the station, built in the Afro-Brazilian architectural style, its frontage was pristine and the painting fresh. That was back in August 1977. Many memories, both pleasant and unpleasant, had been formed in that building...

*****

Cyrus Udeh had joined the Nigerian Police Force almost straight out of the detention centre where he had done a four-month stretch for the crime of being a detective in the defunct Biafran Police. At the end of the war in January 1970, he was one of many middle-ranking police officers who had been rounded up and detained by the victorious Nigerian Army. Mirroring offers made by the Nigerian Armed Forces to ex-Biafran military officers, the Nigerian Police Force dangled career opportunities before the soon-to-be released Biafran Police detainees. Most detainees, upon release, opted to go home to their families and lead purely civilian lives. Cyrus was among the few that agreed to join the Nigerian Police Force.

Nine months of "retraining" in Lagos followed and then he started his new career as a uniformed police constable in Abeokuta. For the first two years, he was a patrolman driving through the dusty streets of the old town, sending radio dispatches to his police station at intervals. As a law degree holder who had once been a detective, Cyrus felt degraded by the lowly patrol work assigned to him.

Two requests for a transfer to Criminal Investigation Division (CID), citing his academic qualifications and previous work experience, were rebuffed. When he put in his first request, the Deputy Inspector-General of Police (DIG) in charge of petitions, promotions and complaints had coolly told him that he should be grateful that he had a job in the Nigerian Police Force. Several months later, he attempted again to rectify his anomalous situation and got an earful from the incensed DIG.

'Traitors like you and your kinsmen, the rebels against the country, should have been hanged after the war!' the senior policeman had screamed at him before ending the phone call abruptly.

The diatribe had shaken Cyrus, shocked him by its sheer brazenness, and yet he took it all in stride once he understood that a segment of the Nigerian population were determined to humiliate ex-Biafrans in general and ethnic Igbos in particular. After that incident, he resolved to send no more requests, electing to bide his time as a patrolman, vowing not to give bigots like the DIG the pleasure of seeing him sweat under the weight of humiliation.

By mid-1972, the anti-Igbo sentiment sweeping the country was beginning to wear away slowly, and there was a reshuffle within the top echelons of the Nigerian Police. A new DIG took over the office of petitions, promotions and complaints. While going through the contents of a steel filing cabinet that his retired predecessor had left behind, the new DIG stumbled upon a file languishing at the bottom drawer. He opened the file and found two written requests from a patrolman based in Abeokuta. After reading and digesting the contents of both documents, he reversed the decision made by his predecessor.

Days later, Cyrus unexpectedly got a letter from the office of the new DIG saying that his two-year-old request for a transfer had been approved. Shortly after, Cyrus received an accelerated promotion from constable to Inspector. Then he was sent to Lagos to take some refresher courses to update his knowledge in detective work.

The following year, he returned to Abeokuta not as a patrolman, but as a detective of the State CID. His partner in the CID for the next four years was a young native called Ganiyu Onasanya. As detectives of the Rapid Response Anti-Robbery Squad (RRARS), they joined the fight against a relatively new kind of crime called *armed robbery*, which first appeared in the immediate aftermath of the civil war.

Armed robbery, which had not existed in pre-war Nigeria, was birthed by the federal government's failure to collect all small arms from demobilised personnel of the Nigerian Army and elements of the defunct Biafran Army when hostilities ended. In the absence of new employment, a couple of these military veterans, on both sides of the doused conflict, began to use their Kalashnikovs, Madsens, CETMEs, Berettas and Sterlings to make a living by robbing banks or citizens travelling on highways.

From 1973 to 1977, Cyrus and Ganiyu were at the centre of RRARS operations that broke up several armed robbery gangs in Abeokuta and assisted the neighbouring Lagos Police Command in their own fight against the violent thieves. In that four-year period, the partnership between the two men blossomed into a friendship. Cyrus learnt that Ganiyu's ancestors were part of the original group of refugees that had fled the disintegrating Oyo Empire and founded Abeokuta in 1830. Ganiyu's great-great-grand father had been the head of an army of warriors that defended the town successfully, twice, against the invading army of King Gezu of Dahomey (now Bénin Republic) in 1851 and 1864.

Cyrus was genuinely surprised when his Yoruba friend told him that the twice-defeated Dahomeyian Army had many female warriors in its ranks and would probably have overrun Abeokuta if the British had not supplied superior arms to the local defenders. According to Ganiyu's historical narrative, the Kingdom of Dahomey was not the only entity seeking to conquer his hometown. There was also Ibadan, the powerful city-state, which had risen from the smouldering heap of the nearly dead Oyo Empire. With the threat of subjugation from both Ibadan and Dahomey successfully beaten back, Abeokuta would go on to exist as a de facto sovereign state until its British "allies and protectors" annexed it to their newly created colony of Nigeria in 1914.

Cyrus and Ganiyu remained partners until their promotions to Detective-Inspectors at the beginning of 1977. Few months later, Cyrus received paperwork transferring him to the CID headquarters of Lagos State Police Command in Ikeja. Apparently, the higher-ups in the Lagos police hierarchy were impressed by his armed robbery-bursting skills and had decided to poach him from Ogun State...

*****

'Sir is there anything wrong?' Martin asked the DPO who was standing, transfixed at the arched doorway of the building.

Cyrus slipped out of his reverie. 'Ah, there is nothing wrong, just a couple of fond memories from years ago. Let's go in.'

The constables ushered the visitors through the open doorway. Soon they were walking past a large room with a big white board mounted on the wall facing a row of wooden chairs. Despite the peeling paint and discoloured terrazzo floor, Cyrus instantly recognized it as the squad room where he used to hold briefing meetings with members of his old squad before each mission to storm the robbers' hideouts. In his mind, he could still visualize the enthusiastic faces of the squad members, both uniformed officers and plain-clothes detectives, who watched as he projected pictures of wanted criminals on the white screen with the aid of a slide projector.

Once they were past the squad room, three constables excused themselves from the entourage to return to their previous duties at the reception area while the remaining two carried on, leading the visitors down a dimly lit corridor, up a flight of stairs and then down another dimly lit corridor. The two constables halted upon reaching an open office door from which an oblong of bright light was leaking into the corridor.

Inside the spacious office, Chief Superintendent Ganiyu "Gani" Onasanya was reclining on his swivel chair, laughing into the phone handset pressed against his right ear. 'Yes sir...no problems...excuse me for a moment, sir.' He cupped the mouthpiece and gestured the visitors to three upholstered chairs positioned across his desk.

The two police guides withdrew from the doorway and shut the office door gently. Cyrus sat in the centre. Gbolahan and Martin sat on his left and right respectively.

Gani said his good byes to his unseen interlocutor on the phone and put down the handset. 'It's good to see you CY!' he said excitedly. Both Chief Superintendents rose and embraced across the width of the desk to the mild amusement of the plain-clothes detectives still seated. It wasn't everyday that they saw two senior black uniforms exhibiting such tenderness towards each other.

When the senior policemen sank back into their chairs, Cyrus introduced his detectives to his friend. The two police chiefs exchanged banters and reminisced

312

about the good old days when they were much younger and fitter. Then Cyrus cleared his throat to discuss why he had requested the meeting. Gani was anxious to hear in person what his friend had refused to say over the phone three days earlier.

'I would have called you a fortnight ago, but you were then on vacation,' Cyrus started as the intrigued Abeokuta man nodded slowly.

Cyrus turned to Martin who promptly passed the folder containing the preliminary report of his espionage work to CSP Gani Onasanya. The bemused Ogun State CID boss placed the folder on the desk and opened it.

'One of our men might be a mole for a group of fraudsters we have been trying to apprehend for the past two years,' Cyrus paused as Gani squinted at the first page of the report.

'You know the Logan–Grams–Otunba cases, the fraud plus homicide cases?'

'Yeah,' Gani replied and flipped to the second page. He had heard the about the peculiar fraud cases coming out of Lagos, which targeted foreigners, some of whom had later turned up dead or missing. He also knew about the extraordinary pressure that the police top brass in Abuja was exerting on Cyrus to deliver results. His Lagos-based friend was in an unenviable position.

The Ogun State CID head refocused his mind on the open folder before him. He went through the second page quickly and flipped to the transcribed phone conversation attached to the report.

'We have good reason to believe that the unknown voice chatting with our man, Nduka Ikwunne, is one Tunde Olukemi, the general manager of ELAJ, a successful car spare parts distributorship.'

'Could be a front,' Gani interjected, closing the folder.

The Ikeja CID boss nodded. 'I thought so. By mere stroke of luck, DI Gbolahan's cousin is the personal secretary of the company's distribution manger. A man named Adamu Esan.'

Gani's eyes flicked to Gbolahan for some few seconds and then returned to Cyrus. 'The girl could be useful in a sting operation,' the Ogun State CID head suggested, reclining on his chair.

Cyrus shook his head and explained the risks involved, why he didn't want her involved. 'They would not hesitate to kill her if they found out,' he told Ganiyu, 'I can't bear that on my conscience.'

The Abeokuta native considered this for a moment and smiled wrily. 'You haven't changed that much, always the good old bleeding heart. With the secretary out of the picture, you have no insider. This means you will need an expanded surveillance team to watch the suspected criminals and that ghastly Chief Inspector, arguably the most politically connected middle-level policeman in this country.'

'True,' Cyrus replied, 'quite true...let me run by you the information that we have so far.'

Gani sat up on his chair, rested his elbows on the desk and steepled his fingers in anticipation.

'We have established that the company has three executives. Tunde Olukemi is the general manager, Adamu Esan is the distribution manager and John Nwosu is the managing director. A quick enquiry by Martin here, posing as a customer, revealed that John is on a long vacation.'

Gani picked a pen from his desk and started toying with it. He suddenly stopped and asked, 'where did he go?'

Shaking his head, Cyrus informed him that none of the secretaries in ELAJ Enterprises knew where the director was holidaying. 'As you already know, the policeman we want to put under surveillance is shrewd. He is in charge of our APCS unit,' the Ikeja CID chief paused to let Gani discern where the conversation was heading.

Gani understood that the stakes were high. Nduka Ikwunne was in charge of a squad that routinely used electronic and human surveillance as a means of uncovering corrupt cops. It wouldn't take much for the crooked cop to realize he was being watched; so extra care would be required in handling an operation so delicate and fraught with risks.

Gani knew of Nduka's extraordinary ability to pull the strings of powerful politicians feared by police top brass in Abuja. No high-ranking officer in Force Headquarters would stick out his neck to save Cyrus, if the surveillance operation turned into a fiasco— that is, if Nduka discovered and scuppered the operation before evidence of his perfidy could be collected. In such a scenario, the cowards in Force Headquarters would run for the hills to avoid losing their heads, and Cyrus would face the prospect of immediate sack and loss of pension. And he, Gani, would face some punishment for helping his friend—perhaps, the loss of his current position as the chief of detectives in Ogun State or worse, a demotion in police rank.

'You don't want to use a lot of manpower under your command for this sensitive operation for fear of leaks. Would be very unfortunate if leaked information got back to this Chief Inspector Ikwunne before any wrongdoing could be proven,' Gani said, smiling to signal that he now understood why his friend had come to Abeokuta. 'The APCS detectives attached to Ogun State CID are nothing like their corrupt counterparts in Lagos. I could loan you some of them. Just how many would you need?'

Cyrus shook his head impatiently. 'I don't want any APCS detectives even if they are coming from heaven. I cannot trust anybody coming from that ad hoc monstrosity, which is subject to the whims of the politicians, a disgraceful and cancerous monstrosity that violates the chain of command, an alien entity whose members are not answerable to the police hierarchy. No way, I will not deal with any policeman attached to APCS regardless of where he comes from.'

Gani laughed heartily as he listened to his old friend ranting and raving. 'My dear CY... you really haven't changed in all these years...it is alright then. I would loan you detectives from our narcotics squad. How many men would you require?'

'Four men, you can spare, to join Martin, Gbolahan and another detective, Ikenna, in watching Nduka Ikwunne and the suspected fraudsters.'

'Four is not enough. I'll give you more,' Gani declared peremptorily as he slid the closed folder across the table towards Martin. 'I'll support your operation with six of my men. Two should watch and eavesdrop on your rogue cop and four should help keep an eye on the fraudsters.'

Cyrus was delighted. 'Thank you. Think you could loan them out for at least twenty-one days?'

'Sure,' Gani said, wishing that he had granted only four men as his Lagos counterpart had originally requested. In his enthusiasm to help, he had not considered the cost of loaning out his best undercover men for what may turn out to be the best part of a full month. Ogun State CID needed all the detectives it has got to combat the surge in crime.

As if reading his mind, the other Chief Superintendent apologised for having to take way his men. Gani smiled wrily and replied that the sacrifice was for a good cause. 'All six of them are currently on assignment. They will report to Lagos in two days time,' he added.

Cyrus pulled out a complimentary card and wrote on its back for a few seconds as Gani watched. 'Please let them report to this private address,' he said, handing the card to the Abeokuta native.

Gani gazed at the sprawling handwriting. He was about to ask why his men should not report directly to Cyrus' office when the answer suddenly came to him. Half a dozen out-of-state detectives marching into Ikeja CID complex, where the target of the surveillance worked, might set some tongues wagging.

'Your home address?' the Ogun State CID chief asked without taking his eyes off the card.

'Yes,' Cyrus replied. 'It's discreet. I'll expect the men by seven o'clock in the night. My wife prepares excellent dinner.'

Everyone in the room laughed. Gbolahan and Martin exchanged glances. Both detectives wondered whether their boss had informed his missus that she would be playing host to six visitors in forty-eight hours.

*****

Seven hours later, at 7.00 PM, Cyrus was relaxing at home in Lagos, watching his favourite sport, football, on the television. Enugu Rangers, the top Eastern Nigerian team, was leading Julius Berger team of Lagos by two goals to one.

Cyrus screamed at the television, urging the Rangers to score another goal to bury the arrogant Lagos team. But the footballers on the TV screen failed to listen. The score was still at two goals to one, in favour of the Rangers, when the referee blew the whistle for the half-time break.

Cyrus grunted in frustration and picked up the remote control as advertisements started flashing across the screen. He reduced the volume of the TV, rose from the sofa, and started towards the kitchen.

Inside the kitchen, Dr. Ugonwa Udeh was stirring a pot of tomato stew on a gas stove; a chore she found refreshingly simple and less tasking than her daytime job as a senior lecturer in the Political Science Department of the University of Lagos. Moreover, in her kitchen, she was in total control. There was no Head of Department or Faculty Dean to report to, and her husband respected her sovereignty over that part of the house.

'Hi, honey,' Cyrus said as he opened the door.

Ugonwa turned a knob on the gas stove and the blue flames on the burner vanished instantly. She turned around to face her husband standing in the doorway and smiled. 'CY, dinner would soon be ready.'

Cyrus smiled back. 'Honey...eh... you remember the six visitors...actually eight visitors, don't you?' he asked, suddenly remembering that Ikenna and Gbolahan had been invited too. 'They are coming for dinner in two days.'

The smile vanished from Ugonwa's face. 'CY, I am not cooking for eight people,' she said quietly, but firmly.

Cyrus grinned, 'Oh yes, you will. These are important police officers from out of town.'

'No, I won't.'

'Yes, you will.'

Ugonwa inspected the pot of boiling white rice and decided that it was nearly ready. The silence between husband and wife was tense.

Cyrus ventured a few inches beyond the doorway. 'Look, I have already invited them,' he began in a conciliatory tone. 'I told them that you are very good cook. The best I have ever seen.'

Flattery seemed to soothe the madam of the house and she smiled. 'CY, I will do this only once. Next time, you will have to take your guests to the restaurant. Okay?'

'Yeah darling, thank you very much.' Cyrus agreed immediately. He was about to say something else when he heard the announcement on the TV back in the living room. The second half of the football match was about to begin. 'Honey, many thanks, got to get back to the game,' he said and quickly left for the living room.

Ugonwa was transferring some tomato stew from the pot to a ceramic dish when she suddenly heard her husband scream, 'goal to Enugu Rangers, alleluia!' from the front room.

*****

Two days later, at midday, in the industrial estate of Mushin, a Toyota Cressida sedan pulled up in the tarmacked forecourt of a five-storey concrete and glass building. Above the veranda of the third floor, hung a long wooden signboard with the bold capital letters on it screaming, ELAJ ENTERPRISES.

The door on the driver's side of the car swung open and a forty-five-year-old man of fair complexion, emerged. He walked across ten feet of tarmac to reach

316

the solid wrought-iron front door of the building. He opened the door and began to ascend the staircase, reaching the landing for the third floor in three minutes.

The three secretaries were at the reception area gossiping when he entered. They paused and greeted him. He smiled knowingly. It was 4th December and the ladies had been tattling about their boyfriends and discussing their plans for the upcoming Christmas holidays.

One by one, the embarassed secretaries returned to their duty posts behind their electric typewriters. The fair-skinned black man walked past the reception area and entered a narrow corridor. He passed two doors and then stopped at the third one. He rapped gently on it and waited. A loud voice behind it asked him in. He opened the door and entered the room.

Tunde Olukemi was sitting behind his desk with his back to the window. On the other side of the table was Adamu Esan. Both seated men were dressed in impeccable black suits, both worked in the building. By contrast, the fair-skinned man, who had just entered the office, was casually dressed in a long sleeve shirt and denim trousers. Although a frequently seen face in and around the building, he did not work there, as he was not an employee of ELAJ Enterprises. In fact, he was the manager of another private business, Dixon Job Agency, which operated out of a prefabricated bungalow, a few yards down the road. Dixon Job Agency was hardly a real business organization. It had never turned a profit since its founding in 1990, and the main function of the light-skinned man managing it was simply to cook the books to conceal the fact that it survived solely on regular injections of cash laundered from the gang's ill-gotten gains.

'Moses, you are late as usual!' Tunde snapped to the man who had just entered the room. 'This is very bad, my friend.'

'Oh, I'm sorry for being late. You know the traffic chaos in Lagos,' Moses Adrika replied as he sat on the empty chair next to Adamu.

Tunde nodded impatiently. He had heard that excuse several times and did not believe that Lagos city traffic always ceased to flow whenever Moses was on the road. But he let that dubious explanation pass because he wanted to get on with the meeting he had called.

'The reason why I called you guys here is to give an update on the Harel Suzmann operation.'

The glazed eyes of Adamu suddenly lit up and focussed on Tunde's lips.

Moses sat up in his chair, anxious to hear what Tunde had to say. It had been a while since they last heard from their buddies in South Africa and The Netherlands.

'They have started milking him,' Tunde announced, smiling. He was referring to Harel Suzmann's cheque to Eugene Igolo.

'How much so far?' Adamu asked, pushing himself forward on his chair.

Tunde grimaced and replied, 'Not much, just eight grand. We cannot afford to move too fast or our British friend will smell a rat.'

Adamu frowned, 'What? We did not spend a fortune to send John and Eugene overseas in order to extract such pittance...eight thousand pounds...come on!'

Moses nodded in agreement. There was no point in waiting. The Briton would need to be persuaded to part with more cash or the operation was not worth his while.

Tunde's smile remained unfaltering. 'Eugene is currently cooking up another scheme to extricate no less than four thousand pounds. Like I said before, we will have to go slow and steady on this one.'

Moses nodded and reconsidered his earlier assessment. 'Okay then. Slow and steady...how did Eugene convince the man, how did he pull that one off?' Moses asked.

'Yesterday night, Eugene phoned from Amsterdam to tell me that the target, Mister Harel Suzmann, is now under our spell. Eugene had rung Harel three days ago and told him about some unforeseen overhead costs the law firm was struggling to overcome.' Tunde paused, but his associates, including the clearly unimpressed Adamu, urged him to continue.

'Apparently, our friend, the Briton, had been taken in by the growing amount of money in the bogus escrow account. We have given him bank statements showing two equal installments of ninety-six thousand five hundred dollars each. Both amount to one hundred and ninety-three thousand dollars, Canadian. That translates to a hundred thousand pounds sterling, if you were wondering. Contrary to my fears, Mister Suzmann did not see through the ruse. In fact, he was delighted to see the financial documents presented to him. This, of course, is a tribute to Eugene's excellent forgery skills. Very soon, he will be travelling from Amsterdam to London again with another set of documents to discuss soaring miscellaneous costs, all unforseen, and he is confident that this British man can be persuaded to hand over another cheque.'

Moses laughed mirthlessly and then began to share his doubts about the whole scheme. 'It's going well so far, but for how long can we use this "overhead costs" storyline to keep the cash coming? How many times can we use this schtick before our British friend sees through it? Correct me if I am wrong, but our objective is to extract at least five hundred thousand pounds from this man before he realises that anything is amiss, right?'

Tunde smiled because he loved challenging questions, because he had a ready answer. 'In our line of business, it is all about psychology. It's all about being bullish and making the correct impression on the person being scammed. It is all about speaking to the targeted individual in a soothing tone, calming fears and dousing the fires of doubt. To give credit where it is due, I'll say that Eugene is in top form. He is playing mind games with our quarry. He issues receipts for all the money that Harel is passing to us. These receipts bear a genuine-looking logo of our dummy law firm in Sandton, South Africa. For every receipt we post to London, we enclose an accompanying bank statement delivering good news about more money being paid in escrow. These bogus documents, the artifacts of our trade, have always had a profound effect on our targets, and Harel Suzmann is no different. He looks at the bank statements and sees money in the escrow account growing in geometric progressions. Then he compares the statements to the receipts and gets the idea that paying relatively small reimbursements is worthwhile. The more money he gives us, the more invested he would be in what we are selling him. Eugene is confident that our quarry now trusts Heintz and Sharmann completely. Mister Suzmann really believes that he has a multi-million-pound inheritance out there. He really thinks that we are going to get it for him. This is very good for us. Everything is going according to the plan I devised.'

Adamu smiled for the first time. He still had his misgivings, but who could doubt the sagacious mind of a genius like Tunde.

Staring straight at skeptical Moses, Tunde declared, 'there is nothing to be worried about. The trickle of money rolling in from our quarry will eventually turn into a flood, but we must bide our time. Eugene is now preparing the next bank statement and that will show a bigger deposit, three hundred and eighty-six thousand Canadian dollars in escrow.'

'What explanation is Eugene going to give for the sudden jump in the size of the deposit? Three hundred and eighty-six grand is four installments rolled into one.'

Tunde smirked, 'The explanation is quite simple. The diamond mining company suddenly decided to deposit larger chunks of money into the escrow account to accelerate the payment of the agreed interim settlement of five hundred thousand pounds. They want to get it out of the way in order to get on with the bigger issue of negotiating a final settlement.'

'How much are we requesting this time as fees for our extra paralegals?' Moses asked archly.

'Eugene will ask for ten thousand pounds, and a receipt would be issued as usual.'

'That's too much man. Our British friend will suspect something,' Adamu protested. He had finally come round to Tunde's reasoning. He now thought it was prudent to proceed slowly.

Tunde smiled smugly. 'Eugene will explain to Mister Suzmann that more experienced paralegals are to be borrowed on an ad hoc basis from another law firm. The paralegals need to be paid and the law firm has to be compensated for some lost earnings due to the absence of the loaned staff.'

Moses appeared doubtful. 'Do you think he is going to buy that crap?'

'Trust me my good friend. That guy, Harel Suzmann, trusts our Eugene a hundred percent. He will pay up. There is nothing to worry about.'

There was a knock on the office door. Tunde asked the secretary to come in. She came into the office, carrying a tray containing three cold bottles of Star Beer. When she was gone, Tunde lifted a bottle from the tray and said, 'guys, it's a hot afternoon. Let's drink to our success so far.'

CHAPTER **35**

DECEMBER 1993

LAGOS, WESTERN NIGERIA

The two-bedroom flat sequestering the six detectives from Ogun State CID was one-and-a-half miles away from Ikeja CID complex. It belonged to an old retired police sergeant who was currently on vacation in his hometown up in Northern Nigeria.

Until he retired in December 1990, the sixty-two-year-old pensioner was an officer attached to the records department of Ikeja CID. Cyrus had called him personally to ask for a favour— to allow his flat to be used for a police operation of great importance. Although he was not told what the operation was all about, the widower was happy to oblige. He even extended his intended two-week holiday to three weeks to give Ikeja CID more time to finish whatever it was planning to do with his apartment.

There was a knock on the front door of the flat and the six detectives jumped to their feet, pistols drawn. Their leader, Detective-Sergeant (DS) Theophilus Wey, walked slowly towards the entrance with his revolver aimed at the mid-section of the door. 'Who is it?' he growled.

'The day is bright. Come outdoors, Wey,' the voice of an unseen man replied from behind the closed door.

Theophilus relaxed; it was the agreed signal. He slotted the gun back into the waist holster and unbolted the door. The other detectives reholstered their weapons as well.

The door swung open and DS Martin Okoye entered the room, carrying an A4-sized manilla envelope. He quickly surveyed the living room illuminated by a long fluorescent tube on the ceiling. Standing before him were six anxious men— Detective-Constables Deji Balogun, Timothy Egbe, Kanayo Okeke, Zachary Botmang, Titus Ozekhome, and of course, their leader DS Theophilus Wey.

'How una dey?' Martin asked in Pidgin English, stepping forward to shake hands with the men he was meeting for the first time.

'We dey kampe. No shakings,' Theophilus replied smiling. Eyeing the A4-sized envelope, he asked, *'Wetin you bring for us?* What did you bring for us?'

Martin responded by tossing the envelope over to him. Theophilus caught it in mid-flight. He ripped open the envelope, scrutinized its contents at length, and then passed it on to Kanayo.

'Dat food wey Madam cook last night, e sweet well, well. Best food wey I don chop since birth.' Theophilus was referring to the delicious meal that Dr Ugonwa Udeh served them the night before.

Martin feigned a smile. He wasn't there that night. Nevertheless, he could not shake that feeling that the detective-sergeant from Ogun State CID was exaggerating about the culinary skills of the DPO's wife. Native Lagosians, Martin thought, were good in bragging and exaggerating things.

Theophilus Idongesit Wey was of mixed parentage. His father, who died when he was a toddler, was from the minority Efik/Ibibio ethnic group of Eastern Nigeria. His mother and maternal grandparents, who raised him, were Awori-Yorubas, the aboriginal people who founded the pre-colonial era Kingdom of Lagos on the Atlantic coast. The coastal kingdom's unabashed slave trading provided the pro-abolitionist British Empire with a perfect excuse for its subjugation in 1851 and conversion to a client state in 1852.

Formal British annexation in 1861 opened up Lagos to immigration. So that, by turn of the century, the Aworis found themselves being displaced by other Yorubas migrating from the hinterlands of Western Nigeria, and later on, by people of other ethnicities coming from faraway Eastern, Midwestern and Northern Nigeria. The end result is a present-day Lagos State with a cosmopolitan populace representative of the ethnic mix of the country. An ethnically diverse state where Yorubas of non-Awori stock have managed to retain a slim majority while the indigenous Awori-Yorubas themselves have become an insignificant minority.

Despite his mixed parentage and Efik/Ibibio surname, Theophilus considered himself a full-blooded Awori-Yoruba man and therefore a native Lagosian. While some who knew him perceived his choices to be disrespectful to his late father, given the highly patrilineal nature of the society, Theophilus did not see it that way. In addition to Yoruba language, he was also fluent in the radically different Efik/Ibibio language and still corresponded with the paternal side of his family. But the fact still remained that he identified more with his maternal relatives who raised him in the former slave-trading coastal town of Badagry in Lagos State. And right now, he was thrilled to be working in his home state for the first time since he joined the police force twelve years earlier.

Kanayo extracted the black-and-white glossy photos from the envelope and laid them out on the long dining table in the centre of the room. The other detectives quickly joined him there.

Theophilus bent over the table and glanced at an enlarged passport photo of a very dark-skinned man who seemed to be in his mid-forties. 'Who is he? ' he asked, turning to Martin who was standing beside him at the table.

Martin told him that the dark-skinned man was Tunde Olukemi; the same individual identified in the preliminary report as the owner of the business card recovered from Nduka's corduroy tote bag.

'Is this one Chief Inspector Nduka Ikwunne?' Titus asked, holding up another photograph so that Martin could see it from the other side of the table.

The narcotics detective nodded to confirm that it was indeed an enlarged version of Nduka's passport photo, which he had surreptitiously copied from a personnel file in the records department of Ikeja CID, twenty-four hours earlier.

'And who is this?' Theo asked, pointing to a different photograph. Martin glanced at the blurred picture of a light-skinned man emerging from a Toyota Cressida.

'Not sure,' Martin replied. 'I was staking out ELAJ Enterprises in Mushin this afternoon. From across the street, I saw him drive into the premises and pull up in one of the parking spaces marked as reserved for company staff. Two hours later, he emerged. I took a spur-of-the-moment decision to snap his picture.'

'Could be a customer buying spare parts,' Zachary remarked.

'Or one of the fraudsters,' Kanayo interjected

'Well for the purposes of our mission,' Theophilus said, 'we are assuming that he is one of them until proven otherwise. Martin, did you get the car registration number?'

'Yes I did. I checked with the licensing office. The car belongs to a Moses Adrika. He lives in Victoria Island.'

Minutes later, Kanayo scooped up the photographs and stuffed them back into the envelope. Theophilus placed an attaché case on the table and manipulated the combination locks at its base. When its lid sprang open, he reached into the velvet-lined compartment of the case and began to furnish Martin with the sophisticated bugs he had brought from Ogun State. The German-made listening devices had been borrowed from the lavishly funded APCS unit of Ogun State CID— a move that Cyrus Udeh would have disapproved of, if he had known. Theophilus and his men were under strict instructions from their boss, Ganiyu Onasanya, never to divulge to anybody at Ikeja CID how they got their hands on the sophisticated electronic devices.

'My secrecy order is for the good of Ikeja CID,' Ganiyu had said to his men before they left for Lagos, adding that Cyrus would reject their help if he knew the provenance of the bugs.

Surprised by the sophistication of the bugs, Martin asked the Ogun State CID men where they had obtained them.

Theophilus cleared his throat and narrated the concocted tale about the Kaduna-based Defence Intelligence Agency (DIA) donating some of their surplus equipment.

Martin digested the story with a healthy dose of skepticism. He really did not care where the listening devices came from. The exciting new reality was that the sophisticated bugs would be replacing the crude ones that the Lagos detective had planted earlier in Nduka's office. Unlike his home-made bugs, these new devices could transmit radio signals over a longer distance, well beyond Ikeja CID complex.

Martin placed the bugs from Ogun State CID in a bumbag he had brought to the apartment. For the next thirty minutes, he gave a general outline of his plan. First, he would return to Nduka's office and swap the old bugs for the new ones. Second, once those new bugs were up and running, an Ogun State detective would remotely monitor the Chief Inspector's ingoing and outgoing phone calls from the two-bedroom flat. Third, whenever Nduka was outside Ikeja CID, another Ogun

State detective would follow and watch him discreetly. Fourth, the rest of the out-of-state detectives would join Martin in Mushin district to monitor the suspected swindlers working out of ELAJ Enterprises.

Theophilus nodded, remarking that the plan was a good one. Then he turned and addressed his detectives. 'Okay boys, this is what we are going to do,' he began. Seconds later, he was allocating specific tasks to each of his men while Martin observed in silence.

*****

After seven days of tailing Tunde Olukemi all over Lagos, Kanayo and Zachary were tired and bored. They found nothing suspicious about the man they had been following. Tunde went to work every morning, came home at night and did mundane things that any other person would do. The only thing both out-of-state detectives found odd was that their quarry had no woman in his life. There was no wife, no mistress, and no girlfriend. The detectives thought it weird and shrugged: *to each his own.*

A professional break-in at the Mushin head office of ELAJ Enterprises, in the middle of the night, did not yield anything incriminating. The documents that Titus and Theophilus found related to day-to-day transactions conducted by the company. All appeared to be legitimate.

They later checked with the Federal Inland Revenue Service (FIRS). The records showed that ELAJ Enterprises had no tax problems. The company had two known bank accounts in the country, one in Union Bank and the other in United Bank of Africa (UBA). Both accounts had the combined sum of ₦90,000,000 ($5,294,118).

But unknown to both the police and the national tax agency—FIRS—the company also had offshore bank accounts in Seychelles and The Cayman Islands containing several more millions of dollars in undeclared profits. And that did not even include the other millions of dollars hidden in Switzerland— the money made by the owners of ELAJ Enterprises in their true form as criminals who swindle gullible rich foreigners.

On 12th December, the eighth day of surveillance, Zachary surreptitiously took pictures of Tunde meeting a fair-skinned individual whom he quickly identified as Moses Adrika— the man in the blurred photograph taken by Martin. Both suspected swindlers were meeting for lunch at a bar and restaurant in Surulere called DePauls.

As the suspects were having lunch in Surulere under the discreet watch of Zachary, eleven miles to the south in Victoria Island, Deji, Timothy and Theophilus were scaling the high walls fencing Tunde's mansion. Thankfully, there were no dogs or security guards, and the afternoon weather was clement.

Timothy picked the front door locks expertly. Minutes later, the intruders were inside the big house. The trio spent the next hour, going room to room,

323

carefully looking for any anything—especially documents— that could prove that the house owner was linked to advance fee fraud.

The dog-eared box folder they found inside a cupboard in the master bedroom contained interesting items. There were newspaper cuttings about the disappearance of David Steinberg and the unsolved murder of Pastor Michael Grams. Interestingly, there was a faxed copy of a police statement signed by the late American preacher and co-signed by the Nigerian Consul-General in Atlanta, Georgia, USA.

Detective-Constable Deji Balogun arranged the documents on a table and took pictures of each with his Japanese-made Yashika camera. When the intruders were satisfied that there was nothing else of importance left to see, they arranged everything the way they had found them earlier and left the mansion.

Ten minutes later, the police radio inside Zachary's Nissan saloon car crackled to life. He picked up the receiver and listened to it while Kanayo, behind the steering wheel, observed Tunde and Moses leaving DePauls bar and restaurant across the street.

'They got hold of a folder in the mansion and took a couple of photographs,' Zachary announced as he placed the receiver back on its catch below the dashboard.

Kanayo started the car engine. 'They recover anything useful?' he asked, as he got ready to tail the Peugeot 505 SR sedan bearing Tunde and Moses.

Zachary shrugged. 'I don't know. They will tell us later tonight.'

The Peugeot 505 SR bowled out from the bar and restaurant's driveway and joined the main road. Kanayo engaged the first gear and released the clutch pedal. The Nissan eased out of the kerb and onto the road. Soon the unmarked police car was hurtling after the Peugeot...

*****

That same day, around 9.00 PM, there was a meeting of six policemen around the dining table of the two-bedroom flat in Ikeja. At the head of the rectangular table was Chief Superintendent Cyrus Udeh. At the opposite end of the table, directly facing him was Theophilus Wey.

Ikenna, Martin, Gbolahan and Deji sat on opposite sides of the table, facing each other. Four detectives were not present at the meeting in the apartment because they were still out in the streets doing surveillance work.

Seventeen miles from the venue of the meeting, Kanayo and Zachary were sitting inside the Nissan saloon car, across the moonlit street from Tunde's walled mansion in Victoria Island. The cool and dry breeze from the Atlantic Ocean wafted in through the open window in their car.

Titus and Timothy were also in Victoria Island, but two streets away. From the confines of their Volkswagen Passat, they watched over Moses Adrika's palatial home. Both surveillance teams were in radio contact with the Ikeja flat, awaiting orders from the Chief Superintendent.

Back in the dining room, Cyrus asked Theophilus to report on the progress of the operation. Theophilus stood up dramatically, and walked over to the DPO.

'Sir, I think we have enough grounds to arrest all of them,' he said, dropping five enlarged colour photographs in front of the police chief.

Cyrus picked up two and studied them closely while the other men looked on.

'Timothy and Deji found a box folder containing newspaper cuttings and this document,' Theophilus paused and pointed to the enlarged photo of the faxed police statement signed by Pastor Grams and countersigned by the Nigerian Consul-General based in Atlanta, Georgia.

'That is the faxed police statement that Mister Michael Grams sent to Detective-Inspector Michael Otunba through our Consulate in Atlanta. It disappeared shortly after the death of Otunba,' Ikenna remarked excitedly. 'Sir, I think we have finally gotten our breakthrough in the case.'

Cyrus remained impassive. He dropped the photographs of the newspaper cuttings he was studying. Seconds later, he was holding the A4-sized photograph of the fax document. He scrutinized the two signatures at the bottom of the photograph and sighed in relief. Finally, there was indeed a breakthrough in the case threatening to ruin his career. Although, he was excited, he showed no outward signs of it. 'How soon can we get a warrant from the magistrate?' he asked phlegmatically.

Gbolahan told the Ikeja CID boss that it could be done first thing in the morning. Cyrus smiled broadly. He could no longer hold back his feelings.

'Yes we got them finally!' he said loudly, clenching both fists. Martin and Gbolahan started clapping, prompting Ikenna and Deji to join in.

Theophilus did not clap. There was a troubled look on his face when he interrupted the celebration. 'There is something else we are missing,' he said as room grew silent and all eyes focussed on him. 'From the information we were given by Martin, ELAJ Enterprises has three directors: John Nwosu, Adamu Esan and Tunde Olukemi. We only saw Tunde.'

Martin glanced up from the photographs in front of him. 'Yes, Mister John Nwosu is on vacation from what we have heard. The whereabouts of Mister Adamu Esan is unknown. I called his office posing as a prospective customer. His secretary has no idea where he had gone. The man just called the office one day, cancelled all his appointments, and disappeared.'

'When was this?' Cyrus asked, raising his eyebrows.

'The day after Theophilus and his men came to Lagos. The same day I photographed the man we have since identified as Moses Adrika,' Martin replied.

'You think he smelt a rat and bolted?' Cyrus asked, clearly perturbed.

Theophilus shook his head. 'I don't think so, sir. If that were the case then Tunde would have bolted too. Most likely Mister Esan travelled somewhere and would be back at some point.'

'He travelled without telling his own secretary where he is going?'

'Yes, it is not unheard of. After all, you don't always tell other people what you are up to. Do you, sir?'

Cyrus shook his head. The explanation offered by the Ogun State detective was plausible.

'Sir, I think we should wait for him and Mister Nwosu to return, so that we can arrest all of them at the same time,' Martin suggested.

Cyrus shook his head. The answer was 'no'. He was not going to risk waiting any longer; what if Tunde somehow found out about the police operation and slipped away. That would be a monumental disaster, an unacceptable scenario.

'We are not waiting. We will arrest Tunde and the other man... what's his name?'

'Moses Adrika,' Martin filled in.

'We don't have enough proof that Mister Adrika is one of the fraudsters,' Theophilus explained. 'We checked out his house, sir. We found nothing of particular interest. But he lives close to Tunde and they seem to hang out together a lot.'

'What does this Moses do?' Cyrus asked, staring intently at Martin.

'He co-owns an outfit called Dixon Job Agency. He has a partner called Eugene Igolo.'

'And where is this Eugene Igolo?'

'While searching Moses Adrika's house, we recovered a document with the letterhead of Dixon Job Agency. We found two names, two office phone numbers and a Mushin office address on it. One name on the letterhead was that of Mister Adrika. The other name belonged to this unknown Eugene Igolo. We dialled the office phone number printed under his name and got the recorded message of an answering machine. The message said Mister Igolo was on a business trip abroad and that all enquiries should be directed to his partner, Moses.'

The DPO digested and pondered what he had just heard while the others waited anxiously for his directives. After spending what seemed like an eternity in a trance-like state, he suddenly came back to life and started issuing orders while snapping his fingers. 'Gbolahan, please get that warrant tonight. I don't care if the magistrate is already in bed. Theophilus, Timothy and Deji join the other men in Victoria Island. I want you to bring in the suspects, both of them...'

'What if the magistrate refuses to be disturbed at this unholy hour?' Gbolahan interjected.

'I want both suspects brought into our custody; warrant or no warrant,' Cyrus blurted out.

Martin shifted uneasily on his seat. 'Sir, what about the men still at large?' he asked, unhappy with the instructions to make arrests straightaway. He wanted the surveillance to continue until the missing men returned from wherever they had gone. In that way, all five suspects would be apprehended at the same time. A piecemeal arrest would simply tip-off those still at large.

'Martin, we haven't a clue where the others have gone,' Cyrus replied. 'We cannot afford to wait. After all, we don't even know when they are coming back.

Could be a week, a month or a year's time. Further delay is dangerous. There are two suspects within our reach and we cannot risk them slipping away. We will arrest them and then worry later about the ones still at large.'

Martin nodded grimly. He still thought the DPO's gambit was wrongheaded, but he was not going to argue with the police chief.

Moments later, the detectives rose from the table and made for the door. Cyrus grabbed Ikenna's arm and asked him to sit down. The bemused Detective-Inspector retook his seat as the rest of the men left the two-bedroom flat for Victoria Island.

When the front door snapped shut, the DPO smiled broadly and leaned toward Ikenna. 'Let's go and get that bastard, Nduka.' he whispered and rose from the chair. He unholstered his Beretta semi-automatic and checked its magazine. Satisfied, he slammed the magazine back into the pistol, reholstered the gun, and headed for the front door.

Ten minutes later, Ikenna's car was heading in the direction of Ebute Metta. 'You have the address, sir?' the Detective-Inspector asked, swerving to avoid a pothole in the middle of the lane.

He had deep misgivings about arresting the APCS leader. The evidence gathered so far was thin and largely circumstantial. Nduka could always argue that he was a customer seeking to buy spare parts for his car from Tunde. Hence, the intercepted phone conversation recorded by Martin. Ikenna had aired his qualms on the matter as they headed out of the flat, but the DPO dismissed them. There was sufficient evidence to show Tunde was one of the elusive swindlers, Cyrus had countered. Therefore, Nduka's association with one of the suspected swindlers was enough grounds for an arrest.

'Yes, of course. I have the address that Martin lifted from the bastard's personnel file,' replied Cyrus from the front passenger seat. He turned on the courtesy lights to illuminate the car's interior. Then he began to read out the address that Martin had copied out for him on a piece of paper. When he was done, he pocketed the piece of paper and switched off the courtesy lights, throwing the car back into relative darkness.

*****

At 10.05 PM, there was a rude knock on the front door of a bungalow in Ebute Metta. Nduka Ikwunne stopped the Christmas film that was playing on the videocassette recorder while his wife made for the entrance.

Mrs Chiamaka Ikwunne opened the door and came face to face with two men in plain clothes. The older man in a khaki Safari suit greeted her in Igbo. '*Oriaku Ndeewo,* Hello Madam.'

With a wary look in her eyes, the lady asked, '*Ndeewo. Kedu onye unu na-acho?* Hello, who are you looking for?'

'*Anyi bu ndi uwe ojii.* We are policemen,' replied Ikenna.

Before Chiamaka could say another word, Nduka appeared beside her at the doorway. 'What is the meaning of this?' he asked Cyrus in an aggressive tone.

Ikenna quickly pushed the wife aside and stepped into the house. Nduka froze when he felt the cold muzzle of a revolver pressed against his abdomen. The friendly look on the DPO's face disappeared.

Chiamaka started screaming hysterically. Cyrus put his forefinger across his lips to indicate that the lady should keep quiet. Chiamaka covered her mouth with her right hand, her terror-stricken eyes pleaded for mercy.

Cyrus detached the pair of handcuffs dangling from the belt around his waist and entered the house. He walked past the whimpering woman and moved to the rear of the dumbfounded Chief Inspector.

'Mister Nduka Ikwunne, you are under arrest for aiding and abetting criminals wanted by the Lagos State authorities,' the DPO announced as he clamped the handcuffs on Nduka's wrists.

'No, no, no, that is not true!' Chiamaka cried out and grabbed the DPO's arm.

Cyrus glared at her and told her not to interfere or she would be arrested for obstruction.

She promptly retracted her hand and stood aside as Ikenna shoved her husband out of the house, across the driveway, and then onto the moonlit street where the unmarked police car was waiting by the kerb.

'Don't worry,' the stunned Nduka managed to say to his crying wife. 'Call my brother. He knows what to do.' The subdued man was about to speak again when Ikenna shoved him against the side of the car and conducted a humiliating body search.

Satisfied that the disgraced cop had no concealed weapon on him, Ikenna opened the rear passenger door and Nduka got in with his hands secured behind his back. Cyrus, armed with his Beretta semi-automatic, fell in beside the arrested man on the rear seat. Ikenna reholstered his revolver and got into the driver's seat.

As the car sped away, Chiamaka Ikwunne ran into the house, forgetting to close the front door. In the bedroom, she grabbed the handset of the phone with trembling hands and dialled the number of Barrister Obinna Ikwunne, her husband's brother. Seconds later, she was crying and babbling into the handset's mouthpiece.

CHAPTER **36**

DECEMBER 1993

BENIN CITY, MIDWESTERN NIGERIA

On the morning of 15th December 1993, a few minutes before midday, Adamu Esan climbed down from an aluminium step ladder in the living room of his grandmother's duplex house in Benin City— the current capital of Edo State and historic capital of the sovereign Kingdom of Benin, which existed from 1201 to 1897.

Standing beside the ladder, with folded arms, the gangster surveyed the Christmas decorations he had fitted all around. Suspended a few inches from the ceiling, and running across the living room, were glittering buntings. A Christmas tree festooned with flashing LED lights was standing in a corner of the room. On the opposite corner, a painting of the nativity of Jesus was hanging high up on the wall.

Adamu allowed himself a smile of accomplishment. He was sure that his ailing grandmother, currently resting in her bedroom, would be very happy to see the partial transformation of her living room. It would surely be a perfect tonic for her, he thought as he folded up the step ladder and made for the front door.

After stowing the ladder in the spacious garage, he returned to the living room and settled down on a sofa to relish the taste of a cold beer. He had no idea that his decision to leave Lagos State, ten days earlier, had saved him from coming under the watchful eyes of the police. More importantly, he was still unaware of the terrible events of the previous seventy-two hours in Lagos, the dreadful misfortune that had befallen his two comrades back in Victoria Island.

Ten days before, early in the morning, he was at home in Victoria Island preparing for work, when the telephone suddenly rang. His maternal uncle, Reverend Father Bonachristus Ighodalo, sounded grave over the phone. His spry granny, who still drove her Morris Minor sedan at the age of eighty, had just suffered a stroke, and it might be a good idea if he came back to be by her bedside, just in case.

Ten minutes later, Adamu, in a state of frenzy, rang the Mushin head office of ELAJ Enterprises. When his office secretary picked up the handset, he instructed her to cancel all his appointments and ended the phone call before the puzzled woman could ask any questions. An hour later, he was on a domestic flight to his home city, two hundred miles east of Lagos.

In a private ward, at the University of Benin Teaching Hospital, Professor Abel Osagie, was examining Beatrice Ighodalo when her anxious grandson breezed in. The cardiologist reassured him. Mama Beatrice had suffered only a minor stroke and was going to make a full recovery.

Seven days later, the old lady was back at home, convalescing with a hospital-assigned nurse and a grandson for company. His uncle, the Catholic priest, popped in every other day for a visit. He always made sure he had the holy oil ready in the boot of the car in case he needed to perform the sacrament of *extreme unction* on his devout mother. He also prayed with her and sprinkled holy water before leaving. Adamu always participated.

Though raised a Muslim, Adamu had never ceased to admire the tenacity with which his late mother and maternal grandmother practised their Catholic faith despite pressure from his father's side of the family to convert to Islam. As a teenager, his mother had occasionally taken him to church where he enjoyed listening to the Gregorian melodies of the choir. Based on this joyful experience, he had wanted to convert to Catholicism, but his relatively liberal Muslim father had forbidden it. He was free to continue attending Catholic Mass as much as he liked, but there would be no formal conversion to the Christian faith. That was the edict his deceased father, Bello Esan, had imposed on him. Many years later, as an adult, he would come to understand the significance of that fatherly diktat, which had sounded contradictory to his teenage mind.

The edict had been the best compromise that Bello could come up with to satisfy his natural liberal instincts and yet keep the tenuous relationship with his parents—Adamu's paternal grandparents—from breaking down completely. They still had not forgiven him for marrying a woman who did not belong to the small Igarra Muslim community of Benin City. The news of their grandson's conversion would have been the last straw.

'The decorations are beautiful,' Mama Beatrice remarked as she entered the living room, dressed in a silk blouse and brocade wrapper. She sank down into a sofa opposite her grandson and began to flip through her leather-bound diary.

'What's that, mama?' Adamu asked, gazing curiously at the diary.

The wrinkled woman paused and stared at him over the top of her spectacles and then laughed. 'It's my diary, what else would it be?'

'Of course, it is a diary,' Adamu said with a smile. 'I meant to ask what you are doing with it.'

'I may be old, my dear Addy, but I still have responsibilities.'

'You should be resting, not thinking of anything else.'

'Well, you are right. You have already taken care of the decorations for Christmas, so I will strike them from my list of things to do,' she said, flipping to the diary entry for 15th December 1993. Using a black fountain pen, she crossed out seven of the eight items she had scribbled down on the page.

'There is one more thing,' she said, looking up from the diary. 'Scented candles, I need them for my prayers.'

'Mama, don't worry, I will get them for you. Just relax,' Adamu replied.

The doorbell rang and Adamu rose from his seat and made for the front door. Moments later, Reverend Father Bonachristus was ushered into the living room by his nephew.

'My car is in the mechanic's garage for repairs. It broke down this morning. Otherwise, I would have been here earlier,' the priest said as he walked towards his mother.

Sitting next to her on the sofa, he asked softly, 'mama, how are you doing?'

'I feel better, my son,' she said, holding the priest's hand. 'Addy has just beautified this place for Christmas.'

The priest suddenly became aware of the changed appearance of the living room. His eyes quickly panned around the room, taking in the nativity painting, the overhead buntings and the electrified Christmas tree. 'Yes, it is wonderful. Well done, Addy,' he said.

'Thanks, uncle. It was the least I could do,' Adamu said as he sank back into the sofa facing his grandmother and uncle.

After thirty minutes of family conversation, the Catholic priest glanced at his watch and announced that he would be going within five minutes. Mama Beatrice and Adamu got down on their knees and he prayed over them. Holy water was sprinkled at intervals until the prayer session was over.

'I came here by taxi, but calling one is not an option right now. That will take too much time. Can you give me a lift back at the Cathedral?' the priest asked as he rose from the sofa.

'Of course,' Adamu replied, feeling slighted that his uncle would even make such a request. 'Even if you had plenty of time on your hands, there is no way I would have agreed to let you hire a taxi when I have a car that can take you anywhere you want to go.'

Shortly after, Adamu's rented BMW E36 coupé hit the road to Holy Cross Cathedral where Bonachristus performed the dual role of a parish priest and a secretary to the Catholic Archbishop of Benin.

The first seven minutes of the drive was great for Adamu. The priest, who had no idea of his nephew's criminal activities, had asked about ELAJ Enterprises.

Adamu was only too happy to discuss how the company was growing from strength to strength, the number of branches the company had opened across the country, and the future plans to acquire land in Benin City for the construction of new offices and warehouses.

Then the conversation segued into his personal life and the atmosphere inside the car rapidly became uncomfortable for the con artist. His uncle wanted to know when he was getting married; and more importantly, the state of his spiritual life. The priest also reminded him that his dad and paternal grandparents were all deceased. So there was nothing stopping him now from converting to Catholicism.

Adamu's grip on the steering wheel became firmer. He smiled politely and said nothing. Once upon a time, he had felt deeply spiritual and close to God, but that was long ago. Right now, he was indifferent to religion, and the only god he worshipped was money.

After a monologue that lasted fifteen minutes, Bonachristus finally realized that his silent nephew was not in the mood for a conversation about religious faith. So he said, 'don't worry Addy, I will pray for you.'

A visibly relieved Adamu nodded slowly and a thick silence descended until the rented BMW pulled up in driveway of the large church. The priest thanked his nephew profusely, collected his plastic bottle of holy water and alighted from the car.

Adamu waited for his uncle to pass through the doorway of the huge Art Deco-style cathedral before reversing the hired car out of the church compound. With some time to kill, Adamu decided to drive to certain parts of the city he had not seen since he arrived ten days earlier.

Every landmark he drove past brought back memories. There was the ultra-modern collection of buildings that housed the civil service of Edo State. Not too far away was the government house where the state governor himself lived and held court. Driving past the State Prisons caused him to flash back to his past...

*****

The date was 9th August 1967. The Biafran Army's expeditionary forces had surprised the world by launching a cross-border invasion designed to shift the theatre of war from Biafra to Nigeria. The expeditionary forces had stormed across the 4,606-foot long River Niger Bridge that connected the Biafran Republic to Midwestern Nigeria and quickly began to seize territory after territory. Within days, the Biafrans had captured and occupied Benin City, the largest urban centre in Midwestern Nigeria.

The Nigerian Military High Command, reeling from the surprise attack, withdrew large portions of its forces occupying Biafran territory and sent them to rescue Nigerian territories that the Biafrans had captured.

Meanwhile, the Biafran Army halted their advance to savour their first major victory since the war began the month before. To consolidate their hold on occupied Midwestern Nigeria, the Biafrans were planning to set up new administrative bodies and raise a local garrison militia to keep law and order.

The native peoples of Midwestern Nigeria were ethnically diverse and divided in their attitude to the Biafran occupation forces. The ethnic Bini majority held a rather dim view of the Biafran occupiers, seeing them as invaders. Ethnic minority groups such as the Urhobos, Itsekiris and Ijaws shared that point of view.

Unsurprisingly, the Midwestern Igbo minorities autochthonous to the outlying districts of the occupied Nigerian region saw things differently. They were happy with the presence of the Biafran troops—who were mostly Eastern Igbos from the other side of the River Niger—and were prepared to collaborate with them. So when the Biafran occupation authorities began to recruit for the local garrison militia, the vast majority of young volunteers who assembled at the State Prisons in Benin City to enlist were Midwestern Igbos.

Among the small numbers of youngsters who were not Midwestern Igbo, but had come to the State Prisons to volunteer for the garrison militia, was nineteen-year-old Adamu Esan. He had no ethnic, religious or ideological affinity with the Biafran occupiers, nor was he taken in by their exhortation to the local youths to join the militia in order to protect their "liberated" home region from the "vandals" of the Nigerian Army. He had joined the militia because he was bored at home, because he thought he would look smart in a uniform, because he would get to hold and fire a rifle.

For a while, things were calm and he was able to patrol Benin City in his smart militia uniform. Then things began to fall apart very fast. The occupation had unravelled because of Biafra's failure to capitalize on its initial military victories by quickly embarking on its planned three hundred-mile long march to Lagos city—then the seat of the Nigerian Federal Government. Weeks of delay and slow movement cost Biafra dearly for it gave the Nigerian Military High Command sufficient time to recover from the surprise invasion, to reorganize their troops, and finally mount an effective counter-offensive.

In September 1967— a month into the expedition— the Biafran government converted the occupied Nigerian territory into a puppet statelet named "Republic of Benin" (not to be confused with the francophone country, which changed its name from Dahomey to Bénin Republic).

Adamu's local garrison militia also got a makeover. It became a special paramilitary unit called the Republic of Benin (R.O.B) Brigade. Shortly after the creation of R.O.B, the reorganized Nigerian army counter-attacked. Adamu participated in the ferocious fighting that pushed the Biafran expeditionary forces back across the River Niger Bridge into Onitsha, the largest commercial city in Biafra.

The entity known as "Republic of Benin" collapsed and its territory reverted to being Nigeria's midwestern region. Surviving elements of the R.O.B Brigade fled to Onitsha to join up with the Biafran Army.

Shortly after their flight, the bridge was destroyed with high explosives to thwart the Nigerians who were in hot pursuit. Adamu and his fellow R.O.B Brigade paramilitaries, which included Eugene Igolo, would spend the remainder of the war fighting alongside regular Biafran soldiers within the territorial confines of the secessionist republic...

*****

Half a mile beyond the State Prisons, Adamu wound down the car window to let in fresh breeze. He slowed down to allow a semi-trailer truck to overtake his rented BMW. Once the heavy-duty vehicle was ahead, it slowed down. Its driver suddenly revved the engine, causing the truck's upright exhaust pipe to puff out thick clouds of black smoke, which drifted backwards towards the saloon car. A disoriented Adamu coughed and cursed as the dense clouds of smoke and oily soot engulfed the front portion of his BMW, fouling the air wafting into the car's interior and reducing visibility through the windscreen.

Recovering his bearings, the con artist swerved the car into the fast lane of the dual carriageway. He floored the accelerator and car lurched forward. Moments later, his car was abreast of the semi-trailer truck in the adjacent lane. He turned and glared at the scruffy, teenage-looking driver of the big vehicle. The truck driver was topless, wearing nothing besides a pair of shorts and a gaudy chain around his neck. He smiled knowingly at the angry BMW driver.

'Get that scrap metal off the road if you cannot get its foul engine fixed!' Adamu barked. The topless driver grinned and squeezed the accelerator pedal, causing the vehicle to move faster and ahead, belching more dense clouds of black smoke into the space behind it.

Adamu coughed and increased the speed of his car. His car overtook the smoke-belching semi-trailer truck. He swore and cursed. His mind conjured up the image of the SIG Sauer P226 pistol hidden inside the closed glove compartment and he toyed with the idea of blocking the road ahead and gunning down the impertinent truck driver, but he let it pass. The BMW picked up more speed.

By the time the rented car slowed down again, the truck was far behind, out of sight, and Adamu's anger had dissipated, freeing his mind to refocus on the leisurely drive. Soon, he was slowly driving past the gates leading to the palace of the *Omo n'Oba*, whose ancestors once presided over an independent kingdom that ceased to exist after it was conquered and its territory annexed by the British Empire.

A few yards beyond the palace, Adamu switched on the car radio. *Edo State Radio* was presenting the local news in Bini language. The con artist turned up the volume and listened. The female newscaster was reporting a courtesy visit by the state military governor to *Omo n'Oba* (King) Obanosa IV, who was previously known as Prince Alfred Izevbokun Eresonye until he ascended the throne and took a regnal name. The radio newscaster reminded its audience that two months earlier, the then newly-appointed military governor had snubbed the *Omo n'Oba*, refusing to pay homage to a man whom many ethnic Binis still revere as their spiritual and traditional leader.

Like all his predecessors after the British conquest of 1897, Obanosa's kingship was ceremonial. In other words, he was a king without a real kingdom, a monarch living in a city where he exercised a lot of moral authority and influence, but had no politico-administrative powers.

The new governor, a native of Northern Nigeria, imposed by the Abuja-based Federal Military Government, had little or no understanding of the local customs of the region. Upon his arrival in Benin City, the state capital, he cancelled the first courtesy visit his civilian staff had arranged for him, finding the idea of ingratiating himself to a ceremonial ruler ridiculous. Despite entreaties of his staff, he refused to pay homage to a man whose regnal title he considered a mere honorific.

But Obanosa IV was having none of it. He retaliated by summoning all his moral authority to call on the ethnic Bini-dominated state civil service to refuse to cooperate with the insolent governor. Some heeded the call, but most ignored it. The minority of civil servants who refused to work with the governor were sacked and the state exploded into violent protests. The Mobile Police (MOPOL)—the militarized wing of the Nigerian Police Force—was unleashed on the rioters. And true to their nature, MOPOL personnel fired live bullets into the mob and a lot of people were killed.

The governor called a meeting of his cabinet officials and told them that he was mulling over the idea of arresting the *Omo n'Oba* for "inciting the riots". The cabinet officials, mostly ethnic Bini civilians, were horrified and the plan was leaked to the local press. The next day, every newspaper had the leaked plan as banner headlines. All local radio stations and TV channels, both private and government-owned, were reporting it, outraging most citizens of the state. The riots quickly spread beyond the city to the outlying areas, rendering Edo State ungovernable.

Alarmed by the civil strife rocking one of the states in the country's Midwest, the Federal Military Government in Abuja threatened to sack the governor and declare a local state of emergency. At that point, the governor swallowed his pride. He not only reinstated the sacked civil servants, he went to pay homage to the ceremonial ruler that he had previously derided. Subsequently, Obanosa IV made a televised speech to citizens of Edo State that quietened things down...

The female state radio announcer concluded her news bulletin with a bold remark:

The last fifteen days have been quite peaceful in our state. Things have been returning to normal ever since our new governor, Colonel Osman Jallo, visited the palace of our spiritual father, the Omo n' Oba, to pay his respects. It seems the governor has learnt the hard way who wields real power in Edo State.

Adamu swerved the BMW coupé into a lay-by and pulled up. He glanced at the imposing building across the street. It was a museum celebrating ancient carvers and sculptors of the defunct Benin Kingdom who had recorded their history and traditions visually for four centuries through wood-ivory carvings and castings in bronze, brass and iron. As a young teenager, before the civil war, Adamu had visited that museum almost as many times as his favourite nature park, the Ogba Zoo. His father had insisted on it. A visit to the museum was more valuable than history lessons taught in the classroom, Bello Esan would often tell his son while showing him around the repository of artifacts, many of which were just replicas of the ancient carvings and sculptures. The original artifacts—over 2,500 ancient works of art, many dating back to the 13th century— were looted by the British colonial soldiers as they razed Benin City to the ground in February 1897.

Adamu got bored of the native language news service and began to rotate the tuning knob on the car radio. He switched to the federal government-owned *Radio Nigeria*. Sir Victor Uwaifo's 1965 Highlife song "*Joromi*" burst out from the concealed loudspeakers. Adamu listened appreciatively to the melodious voice of the award-winning Bini musician. After the song ended, the voice of a male newsreader came on and began to present the evening news in English.

Adamu listened and heard the usual mundane stuff— the military junta in Abuja had awarded several contracts for the building of new federal highways and bridges; the federal minister of education, a token civilian member of the junta, was negotiating with academics of federal-owned universities for a pay rise; certain state governors were under pressure from the teaching staff of state-owned universities who wanted bigger salaries; the new federal minister of power was reassuring citizens across the country, for the umpteenth time, that national power stations would keep up the supply of electricity throughout the Christmas period. Therefore, rumours peddled by mass media outlets about the possibility of widespread power outages were unfounded and irresponsible...

Adamu grew bored quickly. His hand was already on the tuning knob of the car radio when he heard something that startled him. The radio announcer had begun another news bulletin focussed on crime-fighting in the country's most populous state, Lagos. The events of the previous seventy-two hours were being broadcast. The newscaster mentioned the arrest of a well-known policeman, the leader of the anti-police corruption squad (APCS) attached to the Lagos State Criminal Investigation Division. Ironically, the APCS leader had been nabbed over charges of corruption, the same crime he was supposed to be rooting out within the ranks of the police.

Adamu retracted his hand from the tuning knob and leaned forward in the driver's seat. His heart began to thump like a jackhammer as he listened to the rest of the bulletin with great trepidation. Then the newsreader dropped the bombshell:

Two criminal suspects wanted by the police for fraud and murder were shot dead in Victoria Island while resisting arrest. Lagos State CID has confirmed that both men were criminal associates of Chief Inspector Nduka Ikwunne who is now in the custody of FIIB officers at Alagbon Close, Ikoyi.

Adamu started the car engine and slid out of the lay-by. He drove for another twenty minutes before a roundabout came into view. He circled it for a U-turn. Moments later, he was speeding in the opposite direction. He knew he had to get out of town, but he had to bid goodbye to his granny first. She would be confused and sad to see him go so suddenly, and in such haste. But he already had a good excuse. Some urgent business matters relating to his fledgling company had come up, he thought of telling the old lady. His granny would be very understanding of his need to return quickly to Lagos.

The gangster turned up the volume of the car radio and decelerated as the BMW approached the entry point of the side road leading to his granny's duplex house. He was about to swerve into the side road when he heard the newsreader say:

Lagos police are currently looking for three criminal suspects still at large. Yesterday, during a press conference, the Lagos State Police Commissioner floated the possibility that all three men may already be abroad. Neither the names of the suspects killed in the shoot-out nor those currently sought by the police have been released to the public.

Adamu changed his mind and continued driving straight. The police might think he was already abroad, but how long would it take for detectives hunting him to realize their mistake? he reasoned as he shifted the gear lever and stamped down on the accelerator pedal. He spared a thought for the deceased suspects. *Could Moses and Tunde really be dead?*

Running on survival instincts, his mind quickly conjured up the image of a road map leading him eastwards across four state lines, an international border and then to the neighbouring country, Republic of Cameroon. It was a getaway plan that echoed back to the escape route he and his criminal associates had used twenty-three years earlier.

Adamu began to gird himself for what was going to be an extremely long day on the road. His location in Benin City meant that he was hundreds of miles farther from the international border than he was on 16th January 1970. He was in the middle of estimating how long it would take him to reach the mountainous Nigeria-Cameroon border area when he suddenly realized that his journey would have to include a stopover at a financial institution. 'Good Lord, eight and half hours,' he said to himself after completing the mental calculation...

*****

After an hour-long drive on the four-lane Benin-Asaba expressway, Adamu crossed the first state line, entering Delta State through Agbor, a large town inhabited by Midwestern Igbos. He stopped at a petrol station, filled up the tank of the BMW coupé, and carried on. Forty-five miles later, he was in Asaba city, the capital of Delta State. The small city, also native to Midwestern Igbos, was situated on the western bank of the River Niger. Across the great river, on the eastern bank, was Onitsha, the largest city in Anambra State and unofficial commercial capital of Eastern Nigeria. Like the natives of Asaba in Delta State, the inhabitants of Onitsha were also Igbos. Eighty percent of the citizenry of the defunct Biafran Republic had been Igbos living on territories east of the River Niger.

Adamu entered Onitsha from Asaba by driving across the 4,606-foot-long River Niger Bridge. It was not the same bridge he had fled across as a nineteen-year-old. That one was demolished amidst heavy fighting in which nearly a hundred members of his paramilitary force perished. The box girder bridge he had just driven across was a replica, which looked even sturdier and nicer than the original.

As the BMW joined the light traffic stream on the roadways of Onitsha city, he shuddered as he recalled his close shaves with death twenty-six years earlier. He recalled the growling coastal artillery batteries firing high-explosive shells at Nigerian ships trying to land troops on the shorelines of Onitsha after the demolition of the bridge. The Nigerians would ultimately succeed after three attempts, but at the cost of heavy casualties and several sunken vessels.

Five minutes later, the rented BMW pushed into the centre of the city. He saw many familiar landmarks and a lot of surprising improvements. The famous Anglican-owned secondary school, Dennis Memorial Grammar School, was still there with its buildings of red bricks and Doric columns. Twenty-five years earlier, it had been the scene of a ferocious battle for the control of Onitsha between the Nigerian invaders and the Biafran defenders. When the city finally fell, Adamu and the rest of his R.O.B paramilitary buddies, stranded behind enemy lines, had to shoot their way out of the ring of advancing Nigerian troops in order to rejoin the retreating Biafran Army. During the battle, a bullet grazed his temple as he was taking cover. Had the flying bullet shifted a little to the right, he would have joined the extremely long list of combatants who never made it home after the war.

As he drove past the famous secondary school, he marvelled at the extraordinary post-war transformation of the city. The razed buildings, excavated roads, caved-in roofs, burnt metallic carcasses of blown-up vehicles, pockmarked buildings and desolate streets full of ruin were long gone. In their place were an energetic population going about their daily lives. There were people moving in and out of several tall buildings and low-rise supermarket blocks dotting the rebuilt landscape, pedestrians walking up and down the sidewalks of paved roads that were lively with crisscrossing traffic. In fact, it almost looked as if the city had never experienced the devastation of the war. Those scenes of post-war recovery would be a recurring theme throughout his journey across the East. After Onitsha, he would later see Owerri, Aba and parts of Enugu along the route to the international border and would never cease to be amazed at the relative speed with which the Igbos had managed to rebuild their post-war region almost singlehandedly. But that entire marvel was for later. While inside Onitsha, he had an important stopover to make, a business that needed attending to.

On the slightly sloped thoroughfare known as Upper New Market Road, the rented BMW decelerated and joined the chaotic, slow-moving traffic stream heading down towards Onitsha Main Market. In the absence of traffic cops, all sorts of vehicles were in a disorderly competition to reach the bottom of the busy road where the largest open-air market in West Africa was situated. Exquisite saloon cars, battered taxicabs, rickety city buses and garishly painted heavy haulage trucks were moving without any regard for the rules of traffic. Speeding motorcycles weaved dangerously through the chaos by darting through tight spaces between cars and tighter spaces between multiple convoys of semi-trailer trucks overloaded with merchandise from the distant farms of Northern Nigeria. The merchandise inside the long trailers included fresh tomatoes, yam tubers, vegetables, plantains, potatoes and other perishable food destined for the marketplace.

The cacophonous sounds of blaring vehicle horns rented the air above as irate motorists honked to warn off the daredevil motorcyclists who were moving so close to the saloon cars that their owners feared a broadside collision. Adamu was one of such motorists. He slammed his left hand multiple times on the centre of the steering wheel, causing the concealed horns to toot loud warnings to the swarms of buzzing motorcyclists wheezing past his side windows. As he operated the horns, a wave of disgust washed over him, and he swore and mumbled something about hanging motorcyclists for their outrageous behaviour.

About halfway through the sloped thoroughfare, Adamu began to scan the side of the road for high-rise building with the signage he was looking for. He vaguely recalled that a branch of UBA (United Bank of Africa) was located somewhere along the road. But the year 1968 was a long time ago; the bank branch might not be there anymore. After all, everybody knew about the vandalism, the scorched earth policy of the Nigerian Army, he thought. But then again, if the locals of Onitsha had managed the herculean feat of reconstructing their city, there was no reason to doubt that the bank building—if it was indeed razed down all those years ago—would have been rebuilt.

He searched hopefully for another three minutes, and smiled when he finally spotted what he was looking for. It was a brown-coloured four-storey concrete building with a giant signboard on its roof reading: UNITED BANK OF AFRICA (UBA). He swung the car towards its tall solid iron gates manned by two azure-uniformed security guards in front. The uniforms raised their rifles apprehensively. They had good reason to be scared.

Eight days earlier, two minibuses bearing twenty armed robbers, firing hot lead from M16 assault rifles, had screeched to halt in front of the gates. The outgunned guards fled. Inside the bank, the manager died in a hail of bullets as he reached for the phone to call the police. The robbers then forced the terrified staff to open the vaults. One staff member, at great risk to her life, escaped through the back door and ran to the nearest police station.

The desk sergeant, in keeping with Onitsha city police tradition, casually asked the hysterical lady to describe the bank robbers. When the lady described the kind of weapons at the criminals' disposal, the sergeant just knew that it was not a job for officers of the Onitsha Area Command. Policemen armed with antiquated Mark IV bolt action rifles were never going to face twenty M16 rifles blazing away with automatic fire. But, of course, the desk sergeant was not going to communicate that harsh reality to the visibly shaken bank clerk. So he affected a frown and said plainly, 'Madam, there is no petrol in any of our vehicles right now. You will have to wait for a while. Just calm yourself and have a seat in the corner.'

By the time the police finally made it to the bank, the robbers had been gone for an hour with the princely sum of ₦15 million, thus saving the city police the humiliation of having to fight and flee from superior firepower. More than a week later, the robbers were still at large; and probably would remain so, forever...

'Stop!' one of the uniformed security guards barked, swinging the barrel of his long gun, as he approached the BMW E36 coupé.

Adamu applied the brakes, wound down the side window, and put on a polite smile. He glanced at the menacing weapon and identified it as a CETME-58 rifle. The other guard standing by the gate was holding an identical rifle.

Adamu hesitated when he was asked to identify himself. Being a man wanted by the police, he had to be cautious. As he fumbled for his ID card, he suddenly remembered the radio announcer had said the police believed him to be outside the country. He let out a sigh of relief and smiled broadly, as he handed the laminated card to the anxious security guard standing over the car window.

The man scrutinised the passport photograph and printed words under the plastic laminate, and gazed at the BMW driver as if something was wrong. Adamu thought of reversing the car and making a run for it, but he was greatly discouraged by the rifle pointing menacingly at the outer panel of the car door shielding most of his torso from view. Adamu was still pondering what next to do when he noticed a change in the countenance of the security guard.

With a look of embarrassment on his face, the guard turned to his colleague and called out, 'Danjuma, open the gates. He is bonafide.'

Danjuma slung his rifle over his shoulder and started pulling the solid iron gates apart. The guard standing over the car window turned back to the driver. 'Sorry, sir,' he said softly before handing back the laminated identity card. 'We are only doing our job.'

'Oh that's fine,' Adamu said, smiling with relief. He held out a two ₦50 notes. 'These are for you and your colleague. When you get off work, go buy yourselves some bottles of beer and keep the change.'

The security guard accepted the naira notes with a smile on his face. He held them up for his colleague to see. Danjuma, standing by the open gates, smiled back and called out to the driver, '*Oga sir*, thank you!'

Moments later, the BMW swept past the open gates and pulled up inside the sprawling premises of the commercial bank. Adamu alighted from the car and entered the four-storey, high-rise building, which he thought was eerily quiet for a working day.

The view that confronted him when he stepped onto the shiny marble floor of the banking hall surprised him. He had expected the hall to be busy, to be teeming with customers. But no, it was empty. The cashier's counter was empty as well. Yet, the air conditioner mounted high up on the wall behind that counter was humming, suggesting that the bank cashier's absence was temporary.

While waiting for the return of the cashier, Adamu began to survey his environment. It didn't take him long to find a small table positioned in a corner at one end of the vast banking hall. The surface of the table was covered with a purple table spread. A glass-fronted photo frame of a young man was placed on the centre of the table flanked by two burning candles. At the foot of the photo frame was a large open notebook, which served as a condolence register.

The con artist bent over the table to sign the register. He glanced at the thirty-five-year-old smiling brightly from the photo frame, urging him to sign the immortal book. Adamu sighed and read the small note stuck to the base of the photo frame. It said that the bank manager, beloved by his staff, was murdered while trying to call the police. The note also said that the manager was in heaven because of his heroic attempt to thwart the bank robbers.

Adamu sneered at the picture. The man was a fool, he thought. *Why should a man lose his life over money that wasn't his? Money already insured by the Nigeria Deposit Insurance Corporation?*

The swindler shrugged and wrote some sweet words about God giving the hero's widow and three children the fortitude to bear the loss. Just as he was writing a fake name under his condolence message, he heard something move behind him.

'Hello sir, are you waiting to be served?' a female voice asked from behind. He turned and saw an attractive, fair-skinned lady standing behind the counter at the centre of the hall.

'Yes, please,' Adamu smiled and began to walk across the marble floor towards her.

The bank cashier apologised for delay in attending to him. 'Normally, there are at least ten cashiers here to serve,' she explained, 'but as you can see, it's just me today. Most of the cashiers are too upset...they are on a short leave because of what happened.'

Adamu understood what she meant. 'I am sorry for your loss,' he said, feigning concern.

The cashier dabbed her wet eyes with a blue handkerchief and forced a smile. 'It's okay. You are lucky, the bank was going to close in thirty minutes time and re-open to customers in seven days to give the staff some time to mourn him and attend the burial.'

'Once again, I'm really sorry for your loss,' Adamu said, grateful for the timing of his visit.

The lady nodded and turned to business. 'What can I do for you sir?'

Adamu told her that he was the manager of ELAJ Enterprises. He gave her the company's twelve-digit account number. The cashier tapped an unseen keyboard below the top of the counter and gazed at the computer monitor, which was partly visible to Adamu on the side of the counter.

A thick silence descended, occasionally punctuated by the clicking sounds of individual keys being tapped on the unseen keyboard. In the meantime, Adamu's heart pounded. What if the police had frozen the company's bank account? What if any attempt to access the account raises a red flag alert?

The longer it took the bank cashier to locate whatever she was looking for on the computer screen, the higher the tide of panic rose within the con artist's mind. He was struggling to maintain his composure when the cashier suddenly glanced up at him.

'Yes, I can see the account. What do you want us to do?'

'I will like to close the account.'

The lady was clearly surprised. 'Why sir? There is forty million naira in this account. Are you sure?'

Adamu read her mind and searched quickly for a good excuse. 'My company has two bank accounts, one here, and the other in Union Bank. Our enterprise is expanding into the Caribbean,' the fraudster paused to observe her reaction. Her face evinced sadness, but there was a willingness to understand.

'So we need to move the funds to our bank in The Cayman Islands,' he concluded with an apologetic smile. She asked him to wait and disappeared through a side door behind the counter.

She returned, a few minutes later, with a middle-aged man with a bushy mustache and a potbelly. He was dressed in the standard white-collar attire— a light blue long-sleeve shirt, a silk red necktie and a pair of black trousers. Adamu reckoned that the man's suit jacket was probably draped around a chair back in his unseen office.

The cashier introduced the man to Adamu as the acting bank manager. Both men exchanged smiles and shook hands across the top of the counter. Once again, Adamu offered his condolences on the death of the substantive bank manager. The acting manger, Mr. Callixtus Onyeka, smiled ruefully and said something about the deceased being a nice man who didn't deserve what came to him. But Adamu could sense that while Callixtus may be sad about the loss of innocent life, he was certainly not sad that he had been bumped up to bank manager, even if it was in an acting capacity.

With a straight face, the acting bank manager asked Adamu to produce a piece of identification to prove that he was who he said he was. The bank customer handed over his laminated ID card.

Upon ascertaining the customer's identity, Onyeka phoned the regional headquarters of his bank in Enugu city to obtain clearance for his branch to do a wire transfer. It took seven minutes of being put on hold for the call to be passed to his boss in the Enugu head office. Fifteen minutes later, he concluded the long-distance conversation with his superior and placed the handset back on its cradle. Then he gazed at the customer. 'Sir, are you sure you want to do this?' he asked evenly.

Adamu nodded solemnly in response.

'Very well sir,' the manager said, 'we will retain twenty thousand naira as service charge, and the rest will be wired to The Cayman Islands. Is that okay with you?'

The bank manager stared intently at Adamu. The fraudster smirked. He figured that the bank could not bear to lose all that money without charging steeply. Adamu told the man that he was fine with the deduction.

'Okay, please provide me with your bank details in the Caymans.'

Adamu gave the name of the bank and the account number to the acting manager, who was now sitting behind the computer terminal. The manager tapped furiously on the keyboard as the lady cashier stared impassively at her manager's busy fingers.

Mr. Onyeka suddenly paused and glanced at Adamu. 'Sir, this will take about forty minutes to do.'

The fraudster told the manager that he was a patient man. Turning to the cashier, the manager ordered, 'Adaora go to the fridge in my office and get our customer a bottle of Pepsi.'

Adaora opened the side door and disappeared through it. The manager gestured from the counter at Adamu. 'Please take a seat, sir.'

The swindler looked over his shoulder and saw the padded bench leaning against the wall opposite the counter. He thanked the manager and walked towards the bench. Shortly after, Adaora appeared with the chilled bottle of Pepsi.

Thirty-five minutes later, as he sipped the last contents of the bottle, Adamu heard the rasping sound of chair legs scraping against the floor. He gazed at counter and caught sight of the manager rising from the wooden chair behind the computer terminal. Although there was still five minutes remaining, the manager made a loud and cheerful announcement. The wire transfer had been successfully completed. With accomplished pride on his face, Mr. Onyeka emerged from the counter and swept across the marble floor of the banking hall to shake hands with the man who had just removed almost forty million naira from his bank. Moments later, the acting bank manager was escorting the happy customer to his BMW E36 coupé in the driveway.

Two hours later, with Onitsha several miles behind him, Adamu entered Owerri town, the capital of Imo State. Adamu knew the southeast territory very well. It was the scene of one of the heaviest fighting during the war, as the town changed hands alternately between Biafran and Nigerian forces. Ultimately, it was the last major population centre held by the Biafran Republic before its last provisional president, Major-General Philip Effiong took the fateful decision to surrender to Nigerian troops under the command of Colonel (later General) Olusegun Obasanjo on 15th January 1970.

Three and half hours later, Adamu entered Akwa Ibom State—incidentally, the home state of Effiong and his Efik/Ibibio co-ethnics. As darkness fell, he drove through the final state line into neighbouring Cross River State—also inhabited by Efik/Ibibios—and continued eastwards to the mountainous areas of the state. The swindler felt the weather getting colder and foggier as the BMW snaked through winding stretches of smooth tarmacked roadway carved into the side of a mountain.

By 7.30 PM, the car unceremoniously crossed the international border into English-speaking Southern Cameroon, which was once an appendage of the Nigerian Federation until its local population voted in a 1961 UN referendum to secede and then merge with French-speaking Republiqué du Cameroun.

Adamu drove for another three hours and ended up in Bamenda, a large city in Southern Cameroon, which once served as a fort for the German colonial army back in 1912. The city was also one that the con artist was quite familiar with. Back in the late 1950s, when Bamenda was under the suzerainty of Nigeria, Adamu was a frequent visitor to the city as his paternal uncle lived there and made a living as a secondary school teacher. That was until the Southern Cameroon referendum suddenly converted the teacher into a foreigner without right of abode in Bamenda. Distraught, this uncle would return home to Midwestern Nigeria to start life afresh.

By 10.45 PM, Adamu checked into a small hotel, paying cash for two nights. The Cameroonian receptionist in the shabby hotel happily accepted payment in naira notes since Nigerian currency had far more value than his own country's CFA Francs. Moments later, while perching on the edge of the bed in his cockroach-infested hotel room in Bamenda, he phoned his grandmother in Benin City.

Beatrice Ighodalo had only harsh words for her grandson for leaving Benin without even saying goodbye. The grandson apologized profusely, repeatedly stating that he had to leave in a hurry for Lagos to attend an emergency business meeting. 'Don't worry mama. I'll visit as soon as I clear my business concerns,' he promised her. 'Please forgive me for this.'

Somewhat mollified, Mama Beatrice said that she understood and all was now forgiven. Adamu asked his grandmother about the hospital nurse who was supposed to check on her regularly. The old lady informed him that the nurse was taking good care of her. Then she added that Reverend Father Bonachristus was still coming around to conduct the usual prayer sessions, and he was quite aghast that his nephew had left without telling anyone. Adamu apologised to his grandmother once again and promised to visit as soon as his 'business in Lagos was done.'

The second phone call he made was to a nicer hotel in Sandton, South Africa. This time he didn't have to pretend as if he was calling from Lagos State. It took him twenty minutes to inform John fully about the situation back in Nigeria. When he was done, John was too stunned to speak.

The gang leader had just been told that two of his men were dead, one of which was his precious, his gifted master planner, Tunde Olukemi. When the shock wore off, John complimented his subordinate for deftly transferring the money in UBA to The Cayman Islands. He also expressed regret that Adamu had not had the time to close the company's account in Union Bank, which contained fifty million naira.

'That money in Union Bank is now lost to us,' he remarked bitterly over the phone.

Adamu did not share the gang leader's bitter feelings; while on the run from the authorities, he had managed to salvage a little over 44 percent of the total amount of money that ELAJ Enterprises held in Nigerian banks. Besides, the lost fifty million naira was chicken feed compared to the millions of dollars held in numbered bank accounts in Zurich, Switzerland.

'Boss, I did all I could. I was only able to create time to visit UBA. Going over to Union Bank would have kept me in Onitsha for a longer amount of time. I had to get out as quickly as I could.'

'Oh, come on, Adamu, just stop... stop sweating over it,' the admonishing voice of the boss boomed down the phone line from South Africa.

'Okay boss, what's next? I don't have a lot of money on me.'

'Hmm...eh...let me think for a minute... okay, here is what we will do. You stay put in Bamenda while I get you an airline ticket to Seychelles. I will send it to you by DHL as soon as I collect it from my hotel's travel agency. If all goes according to plan, you should get it within forty-eight hours. Now, give me your address...'

Adamu recited the address of his shabby hotel from a large promotional sticker pasted on the headboard of his bed.

'Okay, Adamu, just stay put. Expect a DHL package within forty-eight hours, *ceteris paribus*,' John replied and ended the phone call.

The package arrived at Bamenda twenty-four hours later, and Adamu went to see the receptionist. He asked for half of his money back. 'I am not staying a second night here. So give me half of the money I paid you.'

The middle-aged Cameroonian receptionist shook his head. 'Sorry, it is non-refundable.'

'Listen, my friend, I am running low on cash. And I really don't want to argue,' Adamu said and lifted his shirt to reveal the handgrip of his SIG Sauer P226 pistol jutting out of his waistband.

The receptionist's defiant expression disappeared instantly. In its place was just raw fear. 'Sorry sir...eh...you can have the money...in fact, all the money in the cash register, if you like.'

'Don't be silly. Just give me half of the money that I paid you last night. Nigerian currency not your CFA Francs,' Adamu demanded as he let go of his shirt.

The receptionist watched the front of the shirt drop downwards, shielding the handgun from view. Then he opened the cash register and began to quickly cherry-pick naira notes from the neat rows of CFA Francs.

Ten minutes later, Adamu was on the road again. This time he was driving to Douala in the French-speaking part of Cameroon. The entire southerly journey from Bamenda to Douala took seven hours, not including three stopovers either to buy food or fill up the car's petrol tank.

Apart from being the biggest city in all of Cameroon, Douala had a rich history. From 1884 to 1902, it served as the capital of the German colony of Kamerun. In 1918, as part of its war reparations, the defeated German Empire was forced to surrender all its African colonies to the victors of the First World War. Kamerun was split into French and British sectors. British Cameroon—which included the Southern Cameroon subregion—was appended to the larger colony of Nigeria. In contrast, French Cameroon stood apart, with Douala serving once again as a capital city from 1940 until 1946 when the seat of the colonial regime shifted further east to Yaoundé city.

Adamu stayed overnight in Douala. His room in the two-star hotel was clean and decent. The following morning, he drove the BMW E36 coupé into the enormous car park of *Aéroport International de Douala*, the busiest of several airports scattered across Cameroon. He left the car key in the ignition switch. He had no more need for it. An international frontier and a road distance of 508 miles now separated him from the car rental agency back in Midwestern Nigeria.

The poor sods in Benin City were never going to see their fancy BMW coupé again, he thought as he alighted from the vehicle. He had no doubt in his mind that car rental people would file a report of theft with the Nigerian police as soon as they realise that the car won't be returning to their pool of vehicles. But Adamu had no worries at all. He had rented the coupé using a false name and a fake address, and he was no longer in Nigeria.

Minutes later, the con artist walked out of the car park and then into the one-storey concrete building that was the departures terminal of the international airport. Four hours later, he confirmed his ticket and boarded an Air France plane to Seychelles.

CHAPTER **37**

DECEMBER 1993

HAMPSTEAD, NORTHWEST LONDON, UK

On Christmas Eve 1993, there was a rattle on the gates barring the driveway of the residence on 1200 Maresfield Gardens.

In response to the noise, the black door in front of the detached red brick house opened, and Harel hurried unseeingly across the interlocking stone tiles of the driveway. Halfway through, he focussed his gaze on the gaps between the vertical bars of the grill gates. Through the December morning fog, he saw a dark-skinned man shuddering in the cold. The house owner paused and frowned. Then he suddenly recognized the figure and brightened up. 'Ah, my dear Mister Molozi, what are you doing here at this time of the day? Shouldn't you have called first?'

'Good morning, sir. May I come in?' Matthew Molozi said, pulling his navy blue wintercoat over his exposed neck.

'Yes, of course,' Harel replied and unbolted the gates. 'It is indeed cold. Six degrees centigrade, the last time I checked.'

The British businessman swung one of the gates open and Matthew stepped into the driveway.

'How do you manage with your attire in this cold?' he asked staring at Harel's white housecoat.

'Ah, well, I guess I'm used to the chilly weather. You being African, I can understand your plight,' Harel replied as he bolted the gate again. Seconds later, a shivering Matthew was walking across the driveway, behind the house owner.

Inside the warm foyer of the house, Harel turned around and smiled. 'Please make yourself at home,' he said and disappeared down a short corridor.

Matthew peeled off his winter coat and hung it on the brass hook mounted behind the front door. He walked a couple of brisk steps into the corridor and it suddenly opened up into a well-furnished living room.

As stepped on the thick pile rug, he couldn't help but admire the picturesqueness of the sitting room. There were the armchairs arranged in a semi-circle formation with the open end facing the fireplace. It had wood burning in it. Positioned between the fireplace and the chairs was a coffee table bedecked with newspapers and magazines. Matthew stood before the warm fireplace and glanced at the painting hanging on the wall above it. It was the portrait of an old man with a large white beard. The smirking white beard was dressed in dark suit with a black fedora hat to match.

Matthew wondered if it was the legendary Hapel Suzmann, the father of the house owner. His thoughts were interrupted by a bellow from a place that was out of sight, somewhere behind the living room.

'You are having coffee, right?' the loud question came again from behind a side door at the far end of the living room.

'Oh, yes, please,' Matthew called out as he walked across the rug to the side door. He opened the door and was suddenly eleven feet behind Harel and the coffee maker in a large room that was obviously the kitchen. He threaded across the terrazzo floor, past the kitchen stove, past a couple of dining chairs, and then around the edges of the long dining table. He stopped beside Harel who was now decanting a steamy hot brown liquid from the coffee maker into a porcelain jug.

'So what brings you to my humble abode, without warning, and so early?' Harel asked as he passed a steaming mug of coffee to his visitor.

'I have good news that couldn't wait. I wanted to deliver it in person,' Matthew beamed.

Harel appeared confused. 'You could have still called,' he said and sipped from his coffee mug.

Matthew ignored the remark and plunged into the narrative he had rehearsed in his mind on the early morning flight from Amsterdam to London. 'Volkstar has finally agreed to settle for the full amount!'

Harel's steel grey eyes lit up and his face broke into a smile and then laughter. 'My goodness!' he exclaimed. 'That is indeed great news, very surprising. How did that happen?'

Matthew unslung the satchel hanging from the side of his dining chair and placed it on the tabletop next to his coffee mug. He withdrew a couple of official-looking documents and began to explain what had transpired between Volkstar and Heintz & Sharmann lawyers, a few days earlier.

Harel leaned forward eagerly as Matthew began to slide the documents across the table to him. The story the African was telling him was as fascinating as it was surreal, and yet he believed every word of it. After all, he was gazing at the documents proving the truthfulness of it all.

According to Matthew, a couple of days earlier, Heintz & Sharmann lawyers began legal proceedings against Volkstar Diamond Limited. Forty-eight hours after a visit from a court bailiff, the recalcitrant executives of the diamond company threw in the towel and finally agreed to pay the entire £25.5 million.

'Our lawyers called their bluff. They knew they stood no chance in court. So they agreed to pay up,' Matthew said gleefully.

'Is that so? Seems to me they surrendered so quickly,' Harel remarked with his eyes fixed on the document in his hand.

Matthew did not know what to make of the remark, but he pressed on. 'Like I said, they stood no chance. If they had pursued the case in court, they will certainly lose and pay a lot more than the twenty-five-point-five million pounds. I'll say their decision to settle now was a wise one, given the circumstances.' Matthew paused when he noticed he was not getting a reaction from the Briton.

A thick silence descended as Matthew watched the expressionless Briton perusing a document. He observed a white streak in the middle of Harel's hair, which was usually jet-black. Was it the onset of old age or just stress? Matthew thought, recalling that the businessman was forty-five years old.

After what seemed like an eternity in silent contemplation, the pale face broke into a smile and those steel grey eyes shifted from the document to Matthew's face. 'Mister Molozi, I can see from the document here that our Volkstar friends have agreed to deposit the remainder of the five hundred thousand pounds into the escrow account. What happens next? Oh, please do continue with this delightful story.'

Matthew smiled and resumed the narrative. A new signed agreement stipulated that the remainder of the £500,000 interim settlement be paid off. This meant that C$ 772000 (£400,000) would be credited to the escrow account already holding C$193,000 (£100,000).

With the terms of the interim settlement implemented, the next step was for Volkstar to get on with paying the rest of Harel Suzmann's inheritance. The balance of the £25 million would be deposited in five equal installments of £5 million each. Once the entire inheritance had been collected, the escrow agreement will be terminated and all the funds moved to Harel's personal account in Barclays Bank.

'The documents in your possession were faxed to me three days ago,' Matthew said, pointing to the stack of documents on the table front of the Briton. 'But I want you to see an original copy of the final settlement that Volkstar executives signed with our lawyers. It was delivered to me in Amsterdam by DHL courier, two days ago.'

Harel quickly went through a faxed copy of Volkstar's letter to Heintz & Sharmann pledging to conclude the transfer of £500,000 to the escrow account, as per interim agreement, by 10th January 1994.

After he was done, he placed it on the neat stack of papers on the table and accepted the stapled five-page document that Matthew was offering. Moments later, he was slowly reading the original copy of the final settlement as his relaxed visitor sipped coffee intermittently.

It took the British businessman about ten minutes to finish reading the stapled document. He was somewhat disappointed when he came upon a paragraph in the second page of the document, which stipulated a period of four to six months for the diamond mining company to complete the transfer of the outstanding inheritance to the escrow account. In other words, it would be quite a while before he would gain access to the money.

The last sheet of the stapled document was the signature page. It contained four signatures. There was the signature of a company executive on behalf of Volkstar and another on behalf of Heintz & Sharmann. The remaining signatures were from the two witnesses to the final agreement—one from a lawyer representing Volkstar and the other from Russell Wilcox & Associates, which had assisted Heintz and Sharmann in the legal case.

'Everything seems to be in order,' Harel said flatly, as he put aside the document.

'Oh yes...is there a problem?' Matthew asked; a bit by the sudden shift in tone, a bit worried that Harel might not be receptive to what he was going to talk about later.

'When exactly will the inheritance reach me? Half a year, that's too long.'

Matthew gulped down some hot coffee and began to marshal his talking points. 'Mister Suzmann, you must have patience. Time runs very fast. Before you know it, we would be in April of next year. Then you will get the inheritance, every single dime.'

'Six months from now is June next year,' Harel pointed out before sipping his coffee.

'Yes, but the inheritance is likely to come sooner, four months from now, which is April, nineteen-nighty-four. Twenty-five-point-five million pounds; just think about that,' Matthew said with a smile.

Harel rubbed his chin thoughtfully for a full minute and then the smile was back. 'You are absolutely right. Don't mind me. I am just an impatient old man.'

Matthew laughed mirthlessly. 'You are not old yet. You still have a lot of years ahead, a lot of exciting years ahead once you get on your cousin's inheritance.'

'Shame, I never got to meet this cousin in his lifetime, he may have just saved mine,' Harel remarked and drank from the coffee mug.

'The late Robert Suzmann was a good man, one of our best clients. Everyone at Heintz and Sharmann was devasted when he died,' Matthew said as he wondered whether it was the right time to segue into what he really came to London to talk about.

'But I wonder though,' Harel began earnestly, placing the mug on the tabletop, a few inches from the neat pile of papers. 'What is in it for you guys? You are not charging anything for this service. Very strange, I would think.'

Matthew smiled. This was his cue to shift the conversation to the place he wanted it to go. 'Like I said earlier, Robert Suzmann was a great client. He would have wanted his next-of-kin to enjoy the fruits of his labour. Heintz and Sharmann felt obliged to get the money from Volkstar and transfer it to you, the nearest blood relative to Robert that we could find. But that is not all. There are some outstanding expenses, which you will have to cover, as per our agreement.'

Harel leaned forward. 'Yes, I am supposed to reimburse you guys. How much are we looking at here? A hundred pounds? Five hundred pounds? A thousand pounds?'

Harel was startled by Matthew's response. His face instantly took on a crimson complexion. 'The hell you say! Good Lord!'

Matthew calmly explained himself. Russell Wilcox & Associates, the corporate law firm contracted to help Heintz & Sharmann, asked for an initial engagement fee of £8,000. The senior law partners, Eli Sharmann and James Heintz, promptly paid the fee, which was later reimbursed by Harel. After weeks of negotiations with the executives of Volkstar, it became clear that legal proceedings might be the only way to force the diamond company to pay out the inheritance. Heintz & Sharmann then dipped into their coffers, paying a total sum of £10,000 to extra paralegals hired to help prepare the case and £4000 on miscellaneous overheads. Three highly experienced lawyers from Russell Wilcox & Associates were asked to spearhead the case brought in the High Court of Cape Town. Although legal action was scrapped following Volkstar's decision to settle out of court, Heintz & Sharmann still had to pay another £36,000 to Russell Wilcox & Associates. Therefore, Harel would have to reimburse Heintz & Sharmann's total expenses to the tune of £50,000.

'Among the documents that I passed to you, there is a faxed copy of our invoice breaking down the expenses,' Matthew said pointing at the neat stack of papers.

Harel frowned. He did not know what invoice Matthew was referring to. Perhaps, it was among the documents he had not studied. Apart from the stapled five-page "final settlement", there were eight single-sheet documents, of which he had managed to read six. He picked up the pile of papers and flipped through them until he found the fax copy of the invoice. He studied it for a few minutes and grimaced. 'I don't understand this...when I paid eight thousand pounds, I thought that was it. Now I am saddled with a fifty thousand pounds bill that I never asked for... I have a company that sells various security gadgets. It isn't doing very well at the moment. So, I am loath to take away money from my struggling business...' Harel shook his head indignantly as he spoke.

Matthew observed this and knew that he would have to bring all his powers of persuasion to bear on the backsliding Briton. Adopting a soothing tone, he began to make his pitch to the troubled man.

'Mister Suzmann, I completely understand that fifty thousand pounds is a lot,' he began. 'But you have to look on the bright side. With over twenty-five million pounds in your bank account, you can do a lot better than your small business enterprise. C'mon, think about it. What is fifty thousand pounds compared to twenty-five-point-five million pounds sterling?'

Harel Suzmann nodded thoughtfully. 'I suppose you are right.'

An inwardly relieved Matthew smiled and sipped from his coffee mug. He felt his confidence rising again. He was buoyed by the certainty that he would be leaving London with the cheque he had come for. It had to be that day or he would have to leave without it. He could not afford the luxury of lingering around in Europe for a few more days to convince Harel Suzmann. Not after the earth-shattering events of the week before.

Seven days earlier, on 17th December, he had received a phone call in his Amsterdam hotel room, which shocked him. Adamu had called from Seychelles to tell him that Tunde and Moses were dead, and John had already fled South Africa for the Cayman Islands.

Before Matthew could absorb the terrible news, he was informed that the Nigerian Police Force was seeking the help of the Interpol in Europe to apprehend him. There wasn't much time left, Adamu had said to him. The only option left was to visit Harel Suzmann at home, cajole as much money as possible from the unsuspecting Briton, and then make a run for it. Matthew agreed, but he had many questions and Adamu answered each of them carefully, relying heavily on the information he had gleaned from various Nigerian newspapers.

According to *The Vanguard* and *The Daily Times of Nigeria*, on the night of 12th December, the police had scaled the tall gates of Tunde's mansion and banged loudly on his front door. Nobody answered the door so detectives from both Lagos State CID and Ogun State CID took a hatchet to the wooden panel of the door. It took them eight minutes to hack the door from its hinges.

Apparently in that time period, Tunde had lifted the ceiling board above his bedroom and retrieved important dossiers he had on all the gang's victims. He succeeded in shredding the files on Gary Logan, Roy Seed, Alhaji Gamji, Mike Grams and David Steinberg, and was in the process of shredding the dossier on Harel Suzmann when the police smashed through the front door.

According to *The Punch*, Tunde had armed himself with two Browning pistols, one in each hand, and left the bedroom to confront the police raiders in his living room. At the end of a ten-minute gun battle, he was dead, and so was a detective called Zachary Botmang from Ogun State CID.

Over at Moses' house, two streets away, the police was still attempting to break down the door when they came under sustained submachine gun fire. The ensuing gun duel lasted thirty minutes. At the end of it, there were six casualties. Moses Adrika and three constables died, and two detectives sustained serious gunshot wounds.

Before ending the long distance phone call, Adamu said that the police had recovered the unshredded parts of the dossier on Harel Suzmann. From it, they were able to deduce that John had been in South Africa and Eugene was somewhere between Netherlands and London. The police also knew that both swindlers abroad were using false names.

After the phone call from Seychelles ended, Matthew's first thought was to abandon everything and flee Europe altogether. But he restrained himself, suppressed his fear, and spent the next six days thinking of a way to persuade his London-based quarry to part with £50,000. He hit on an idea on the second day. By the fifth day, he had finetuned the plan and prepared all the official-looking documents he would require to persuade Harel Suzmann. In the afternoon of sixth day, he booked a one-way early morning flight scheduled to run the next day from Amsterdam Schiphol to London Heathrow. For his return journey, he planned to use a circuitous route, just in case Interpol was tracking his movements.

'Mister Molozi, are you okay?' Harel asked with a concerned look on his face.

'Of course, I am,' Matthew said, blinking out of his thoughts.

'Alright, Mister Molozi, I have to admit that you are quite right,' Harel said brightly, and then the gloom returned. 'Nonetheless, before I part with such a steep amount of money, I need some more convincing, and I am sure you will do a good job of it.'

Matthew studied the glum face staring intently at him for a few seconds before speaking. 'Sir, you must realise that you are a lucky man. Usually, law firms in South Africa take five percent of the money their client has inherited. If the client's inheritance is in the form of fixed assets not liquid cash, then they will demand five percent of the monetary value of the assets as legal fees. And yet, Heintz and Sharmann had undertaken to get you your inheritance without charging a dime for its services. We are happy for you to keep the entire inheritance for yourself, save for our expenses.' Matthew paused and studied Harel's face for a few seconds. It was expressionless.

'Go on,' Harel urged him. 'And while you are at it, please kindly explain the Russell Wilcox angle. I don't really understand the need for these extra lawyers. They are the reason why this whole thing is costing me a fortune. First, it was eight thousand quid. Now, It is fifty thousand quid.'

Matthew's smile remained unfaltering as Harel huffed about the money he had been asked to pay. The conman already knew that, in spite of the bluster, Harel wanted to believe, was desperate believe that everything was on the level, and would eventually pay up. The Briton just needed some more soothing words to convince himself that he was doing the right thing.

'Yes, we hired Russell Wilcox and Associates because they are the best law firm in South Africa as far as inheritance cases are concerned. Their lawyers have tried eighty cases involving persons who died intestate and won all, except three. If there were any group of lawyers that Volkstar would be prepared to take seriously, it would be those from Russell Wilcox and Associates, present at the negotiation table. We were charged only eight thousand because the senior partners of Russell Wilcox had assumed that their role in the case would be ancilliary. Their seasoned lawyers didn't have to do anything beyond looking tough on negotiating table, putting the fear of God on the Volkstar executives. But then...'

Harel interrupted, 'I think I am beginning to get it, but please, do carry on.'

'Well, our gambit did not work out as we had anticipated. The Volkstar executives turned out to be tough negotiators unwilling to yield ground beyond the interim agreement for five hundred thousand pounds in escrow. They left us no choice than to initiate legal proceedings against their mining company. We chose Russell Wilcox and Associates as our chief litigator, vastly expanding its role in our legal case. Consequently, we had to pay thirty-six thousand pounds to the law firm. The rest of our money went to paralegals and other disparate expenses. These costs would have been much higher had Volkstar not agreed to settle the case out of court. Like I said before, the terms of the final settlement reached between us and the company is the completion of the transfer of the five hundred thousand pounds to the escrow account; and after that, the remaining twenty-five million pounds. So in conclusion, you are getting a multi-million pound inheritance and all we are asking is for you to offset the costs we have incurred in compelling Volkstar to settle.'

Matthew stopped, drank coffee, and watched for a change of countenance in the other man. There was none.

Harel sipped coffee, and then asked another question. 'Would it not have been better if I had hired the Russell Wilcox lawyers myself and cut out the middlemen?'

Matthew laughed mirthlessly. 'Russell Wilcox and Associates is a gold-star law firm. If you had hired its lawyers directly, you would be paying in the neighbourhood of two hundred thousand to five hundred thousand pounds for their services. And when you eventually win the inheritance from Volkstar, you will still be obliged to give them the standard five percent cut.'

Harel whistled softly, causing Matthew to pause momentarily.

'Oh yes, Mister Suzmann. They will charge you a fortune because they are the best in what they do. We are equally good in what we do. I am talking about divorce law, real estate law, bankruptcy law, and so on and so forth. In total, our friends at Russell Wilcox charged us a mere two hundred and ninety thousand rand, which is very cheap by their standards, because they were rendering a service to a fellow law firm...'

'Two hundred and ninety thousand rand? How much does that come to?' Harel cut in.

'That is fifty-eight thousand in pounds sterling, sir.'

'Oh yes, of course,' Harel said with a smile of embarrassment on his face.

'So you should really count your lucky stars, Mister Suzmann. You are getting more than twenty-five million pounds on the cheap.'

Harel thought about what his visitor had said. His brain worked out the arithmetic calculations. If another South African law firm were handling his case, he would have to agree to hand over five percent of £25.5 million. He would have to pay £1.25 million as part of his legal fees!

Matthew watched as Harel politely excused himself and left for his bedroom. Five minutes later, the British businessman reappeared with the familiar blue cover cheque book in his left hand.

When Harel settled back on his chair behind the dining table, Matthew waited expectantly for the booklet to be flipped open and a blank cheque filled out. He was mildly surprised when the Briton opened the booklet, detached a prefilled cheque, and handed it over. Matthew scrutinized the cheque for £50,000 with a smile on his face.

'So what happens next?' Harel asked.

'As it says in the final agreement, it will take four to six months for the entire money to be deposited. Like I said earlier, it would be done in installments. After each installment is deposited into the escrow account, you will receive a bank statement to show proof of it. Once the transaction is complete and we have your full inheritance, the escrow arrangement will terminate and the money will be moved to your Barclays account. Depending on how fast Volkstar is in transferring the funds, you will either get access to your money sometime between twenty-fifth April and sixth June, nineteen-ninety-four.'

Harel nodded at intervals as his visitor spoke and then cut in, venting his frustrations about the dawdling tactics of the diamond mining company. 'They can pay that entire money as a lump sum; instead they choose this piecemeal approach. Why is that?'

Matthew shrugged. 'Well, that is the way the Volkstar chaps want to play it. In the end, it doesn't really matter because by morning of sixth June, the money should all be there in escrow, ready to be transferred to you in the afternoon.'

Harel leaned back on his chair and thought of the prospect. He brightened up as his mind conjured images of a very healthy bank balance, fresh funds for new business ideas, a summer house in the Caribbean and a yacht.

'There is one more thing,' Matthew began. 'We won't be meeting again any time soon, not for the next three months.'

Harel looked worried.

'I have concluded the work I came to do for our European clients in Amsterdam. I also used part of the time to meet and keep you up to date on our dealings with Volkstar. So I am returning home to South Africa.'

Harel drank the remaining contents of his coffee mug. 'Can I keep these?' he asked, pointing at the neat stack of documents on the dining table.

'Of course,' Matthew said cheerfully. 'I'll be back in London sometime in middle of June next year. By then, you should be several millions of pounds richer. I'll bring a few documents for you to sign. That would conclude the business between you and my law firm. After that, you can buy me a drink down at the pub.'

'It will be an honour to buy you that drink,' Harel said, standing up.

Matthew quickly drained his coffee mug of its warm contents and sprang to his feet. He extended his right arm for handshake.

The Briton pumped the hand and then unexpectedly, to Matthew's surprise, went for a bear hug. 'Thank you very much, Matthew. It's a pleasure to have met you.'

'Likewise, Mister Suzmann,' Matthew replied and unlocked himself from the embrace.

'Oh, none of this "Mister Suzmann" business. Just call me Harel,' the house owner said waving a self-deprecatory hand in the air.

'Between January and mid-June next year, you will receive a series of bank statements, each one confirming the deposit of an installment into the escrow account. If you find anything confusing or need clarification, please do not hesitate to call our office in Sandton.'

'I will definitely do that.'

'Okay, Harel, I wish you a Merry Christmas...eh...sorry...I wish you a happy holiday season.'

Harel saw the look of embarrassment on Matthew's face and laughed. 'I'm not really observant. Not been to a synagogue in decades. Not that it matters. Have a Merry Christmas and a jolly good time, my friend.'

Matthew laughed in relief and then made his exit through the gates. Harel bolted the gates as the conman began to trudge along the snow-encrusted sidewalk of Maresfield Gardens towards Finchley Road. The time was 11.45 AM.

An hour later, he was on a train bound for Dover. Arriving at Dover at 2.33 PM, he took a P&Q Ferry to the French city of Calais. From Calais, he took a taxi further east to *Aéroport de Calais-Dunkerque* in the farming town of Marck. There, he boarded a plane bound for Amsterdam.

By late evening, he was back in his hotel room, erasing the hard disk drive of his IBM laptop, cleansing it of all the electronic templates he had used to forge all the worthless documents in the possession of Mr. Suzmann.

Before going to bed, he packed his travelling bag and checked his airline tickets for the flight out of Netherlands. The last thought on his mind before he drifted off to sleep was one hoping that the festive season of Christmas would prevent Interpol from immediately putting out a Red Alert Notice on Nigeria's request.

On the morning of 27th December, he checked out of the hotel and took a taxi to the Amsterdam branch of a well-known bank with headquarters in Zurich, Switzerland. Tunde had chosen the bank because of its obsessive secrecy in dealing with its prized customers.

The branch, a small one tucked discreetly at one end of an Amsterdam street corner, had only one visible staff, a male cashier sitting behind a large reception desk with glittering Christmas decorations stuck to its front and side panels.The cashier smiled and Matthew gave him two cheques signed by Harel, which amounted to a princely sum of £58,000.

The cashier turned sideways on his swivel chair to face a desktop computer. He tapped on the keyboard for some seconds, and then turned the monitor to shield its screen from the prying eyes of the customer. After a few minutes, the cashier glanced up and smiled politely.

Matthew told him what he wanted him to do with the cheques. The cashier nodded and asked for identification. This was provided immediately. Then the cashier asked him for a multi-digit number and a code name. Matthew revealed them. Then he asked some security clearance questions. Matthew answered them accurately. The cashier tapped on the keyboard again. A dot matrix printer beside the computer hummed as it printed on a slip of paper.

Still smiling, the cashier gave the paper slip to the highly satisfied customer before informing him that both cheques would clear in three days, and as requested, the £58,000 would be transferred to his account in the Zurich branch of the bank.

By afternoon of the same day, Eugene Igolo alias "Matthew Molozi" was safely onboard a KLM plane bound for the Caribbean.

PART FOUR

CHAPTER **38**

MARCH 1994

GEORGE TOWN, THE CAYMAN ISLANDS

On the beachfront, illuminated by the harsh glare of moonlight, was the silhouette of a condominium standing next to a grove of coconut trees. At the ungodly hour of two o'clock in the morning, most of the rooms in the high-rise building were dark. Among the few, with incandescent bulbs illuminating windows facing the Caribbean Sea, was the living room of a ground-floor apartment rented by three heavily bearded black men, who at that particular hour, were sitting around a circular coffee table playing a game of cards.

'Any news on what happened to Nduka?' John asked as he placed a spade card on top of the pile of cards already on the table.

'Not much beyond the fact that he was arrested,' Adamu answered, scratching the three-month-old beard that he began to grow upon his arrival in Grand Cayman, the largest of three islands that constitute the British overseas territory known as The Cayman Islands. Just like his colleagues, who had also grown beards to alter their appearance, he wasn't a great fan of facial hair, which he found uncomfortably itchy, but it was a necessary evil, a way of concealing their true identity from any law enforcement agency on the lookout for them.

'Do you think he will talk?' Eugene asked, contributing a card to the growing stack of cards.

John swigged beer from the bottle. 'I am sure he has already talked, but I won't lose any sleep over it. The man doesn't know much about us.'

'Nduka has met us before. He has seen our faces,' Eugene quietly reminded his boss.

'It won't make any difference. The police raided the homes of Tunde and Moses. Lot of pictures we took together were in their houses. In any case, I'll be surprised if the police have not searched our own houses by now. There are loads of photographs there too.'

Adamu yawned suddenly and glanced at his watch. It indicated that the time was 2.15 AM. 'Guys, I think I'll call it a day, go to sleep. Eugene, stop worrying. Nigerian police cannot even apprehend people hiding inside the country, not to mention people living thousands of miles away. Relax. We are safe here with all our money.' He yawned again and shared his playing cards equally between Eugene and John, and rose to leave.

John asked him a question. 'Talking about money, how much do we have exactly at the moment?'

Adamu, who doubled as the gang's bookkeeper, rubbed his eyes and rattled off the requested information. 'Well, we have twelve million dollars in Zurich;

four-point-six million dollars here in The Cayman Islands; and one-point-five million dollars in Seychelles. In total, we have eighteen-point-one million dollars, American.'

John and Eugene grinned. They enjoyed the histrionic manner in which Adamu recited the breakdown of their finances without reference to any written notes.

'We need to split the money three ways. What do you say boss?' Eugene asked, staring intently at John.

'Not yet, one last operation to net us at least another million, then we can retire for good and indeed share the proceeds,' John said and then dropped all his cards on top of the pile on the table.

'You ruined the game. I was going to win!' Eugene protested.

John waved him off. 'The game was boring,' he said wearily.

Adamu yawned again. 'Boss, it is one thing to carry out an operation when the police have no clue about your identity. It is another to do it when you are known and hunted by the Nigerian Police.'

John nodded and smiled enigmatically.

A bit irritated by John's smugness, Adamu continued, 'so what is the plan for making the extra million? Boss, you know that we are the subject of a possible international manhunt coordinated by Interpol. Any false moves and we will be caught.'

'All in good time, I will reveal all to you at the right time. You will have trust me, guys.' With that cryptic comment, the gang leader rose from the sofa and stretched. He glanced at Eugene and then at Adamu, and added, 'for now, we should only spend money from the Caymans account. Okay?'

The other men nodded hesitantly. They disliked being kept in the dark about plans for the future, but John was the boss, and they always deferred to his authority.

John patted Adamu on the back. 'Once again, I'll like to thank you, Adamu, for salvaging over forty-four percent of our company's money in the Nigerian banks. I got information that our personal and business accounts have all been frozen after the police found out that you removed huge chunks from UBA. You are truly the best, our new genius, now that Tunde is no more...oh...our beloved and saintly Tunde.'

Adamu smiled ruefully. He wasn't sure who was doing the talking—John himself or the large quantities of beer that John had consumed whilst playing cards for hours.

'Guys I'm going to bed,' the gang leader said and walked away.

Adamu glanced at Eugene. Eugene grimaced and then started packing up the cards. Adamu started towards the adjoining room, his bedroom.

*****

The following day, 4,800 miles away in Northwest London, a middle-aged man was up very early. The sleep of the night before had been restless. That cold Saturday morning, before the sun had fully cleared the horizon, that man, Harel Suzmann, was pacing up and down his study room, deeply agitated. By chance, he had discovered something that shocked him, disoriented him, and had him hopping mad.

It all started two days earlier, which was Thursday, 24th March 1994. That date was significant because it was three months to the day since his last meeting with Matthew Molozi on Christmas Eve, 1993. Once the New Year Festivities were over, the Briton had expected to hear from Heintz & Sharmann, but nothing of the sort happened. He did not received any of the promised letters and bank statements that were supposed to keep him informed of Volkstar's periodic payments into the escrow account set up in the Royal Bank of Montreal.

At first, he thought it was a delay in the post. Perhaps, it was taking time to arrive because of inefficiency either on the South African or British end of the postal system. He remained relaxed. January 1994 ran its full course and February came around. Still he kept calm, believing that the elusive bank statements and letters will eventually come, or at least his South African friend, Matthew, would call to apologise for the postal delays and update him on the current state of affairs. But nothing postmarked South Africa ever came to his address, and Matthew did not phone to apologise and explain.

The month of March rolled into place and Harel became a deeply worried man. He waited until the 24th day of that month to take action. He picked up the handset from the cradle of the telephone and opened his diary. Then, to his chagrin, he suddenly remembered that he had not added Heintz & Sharmann's phone number to his diary. That glaring omission had occurred because up until then he had never had cause to ring the South African-based lawyers. Eli Sharmann, one of two senior partners in Heintz & Sharmann, always rang him from South Africa and never the other way round. Besides, Matthew, a representative of the law firm, stayed in Amsterdam for three months and, during that time, visited London regularly for meet-ups. And when Matthew was unable to leave The Netherlands, he was always made it a point of duty to ring the Maresfields Gardens residence in northwest London to deliver information to Harel. For that reason, Harel never felt any impetus to make a note of the South African telephone number until he found himself desperately wishing he had done so.

After spending a minute or two denouncing his own complacency, he began to rummage through stacks of old letters in a shelf in his spacious living room. Moments later, he found a crumpled Heintz & Sharmann letter bearing the office telephone number plus extention. He quickly returned to the sofa, picked up the handset again, and started dialling the number on the letterhead of the crumpled sheet. He pressed the receiver of the handset against his right ear and waited with bated breath for somebody on the South African end to pick up the phone. The phone was picked up on the sixth ring.

He relaxed a bit when he heard a male voice, but that quickly changed to shock and dismay when the heavily accented voice informed him that he had just called Room 209 of the Sandton Traveller Hotel. Harel felt himself relax again. Surely, it was a joke, he thought. In a polite tone, he asked the voice on the South African end of the line to stop joking around and pass the call to Mr. Eli Sharmann as he had important business to discuss with him.

There was momentary silence on the South African end, and then the heavily accented Afrikaner voice returned with a boom. 'Hey Mister, if you don't believe me, then call the same number without the extension.'

Before Harel could reply, there was a click and the sound of the dial tone filled his ears. The owner of the voice had hung up. In a state of panic attack, Harel acted on the suggestion of the voice. He dialled the number again, but without the extension. The phone call was picked up again in South Africa. A female voice with a deep Afrikaner accent welcomed the Briton to the reception desk of the Sandton Traveller Hotel.

Harel was completely dumbfounded. He felt himself inside a surreal movie. After a few seconds of silent contemplation, he explained his predicament to the female hotel receptionist and asked if she could do him a favour. The receptionist was cautious but wanted to hear what he wanted. Harel requested that she should check the local city phone book for a certain law firm called Heintz & Sharmann, whose phone number he had lost due to carelessness.

'I am not supposed to do that,' she replied politely.

'Please it's a matter of life and death, the law firm is yet to authorize the release of essential funds required to treat my son's cancer,' Harel pleaded over the phone.

The receptionist hesitated, but the story of the boy afflicted by cancer who needed funds for treatment touched her. So she decided to break the rule of her hotel: *only deal with hotel guests and potential guests making booking enquiries.*

'Okay, hold on, sir.' She put Harel on hold and went for the Greater Johannesburg Area Phone Book. Four minutes later, she returned to the phone and delivered the bombshell. 'I am sorry, sir. The law firm, Heintz and Sharmann, is not in the phone book. '

'Are you sure?' the Briton asked fearfully as his adrenaline surged through the roof.

The lady sighed and said, 'may be they are not listed; some people don't like to be listed. I am sorry sir.'

Harel thanked her and hung up. He didn't believe for one minute that this was a simple case of a law firm not listing itself in a telephone directory nor did he believe that the phone number on the letterhead,which turned out to be that of a hotel, was a printing accident. There was something else, but he just couldn't accept what he thought had happened. Matthew Molozi was too much of a gentleman to be a mere con artist, he thought. 'No, no, it's not possible. We had tea together and he showed me all the papers. They are authentic,' he mumbled to himself. Although, at that point, he was no longer sure they were authentic even though they looked genuine.

An idea suddenly came to him. He rose from the sofa and walked across the green thick pile rug to the shelf to rummage for another document. Soon he was back on the sofa, dialling the telephone number printed on the letterhead of a bank statement bearing the logo of the Royal Bank of Montreal.

Thousands of miles away, in Saskatoon, Canada, a desk telephone trilled twice inside a bank and a man picked up the receiver. The male voice confirmed that Harel had indeed called the right place. The Briton drew a sigh of relief and began his enquiries in earnest.

'I'll like inquire about about an escrow account set up by Volkstar Diamond Limited and a law firm called Heintz and Sharmann. They are both South African.'

'We treat our clients' affairs confidentially and...'

Harel interrupted the Canadian bank manager. He let the manager know that Heintz & Sharmann were acting on his behalf.

The manager fell silent for a moment, and then he asked, 'okay sir, what is the account number?' Suzmann read out the number from the bank statement lying on the side stool next to the base of the telephone. Harel heard the clicking sounds of an unseen computer keyboard being tapped on the Canadian end of the line. The clicking sounds lasted for three minutes and then there was uneasy silence.

The bank manager broke the silence to ask the Briton to repeat the account number. Harel obliged, reading it out again as sounds of the unseen keyboard crackled on the other end of the phone line. Suddenly the sound stopped and the voice asked, 'are you sure that this is the account number?'

'Of course it is,' Harel retorted. Then his heart sank for he finally confirmed to himself what he had been thinking since he spoke to the South African hotel receptionist. It was now clear to him why he had not received any correspondence from South Africa since his last meeting with Matthew Molozi.

'I'm afraid. We don't have any bank account with that number,' the bank manager replied.

Harel slammed down the handset. He was furious. 'Bastards!' he screamed and collapsed on the floor crying. Twenty minutes later, he dried his tears and regained his composure. He picked up the handset again and placed his fourth call.

The telephone rang at the reception area of Hampstead Police Station and the desk sergeant picked the receiver. He listened carefully to the agitated voice of Mr. Suzmann. The sergeant asked him to wait and put the call from Maresfield Gardens on hold. Then he called the extension of Chief Inspector Thompson Baccus, the officer in charge of the station.

Thompson was busy in his office, typing up a report, which had to be submitted to his superior, Chief Superintendent David Westley, Commander of the Camden Borough Police Command. He was not happy when his intercom started buzzing. Reluctantly, he pressed a blinking green light. He wanted to shout 'sod off arsehole' down into the microphone pickup, but he restrained himself.

'What is it, sarge?' he growled into the intercom. The sergeant told him. Thompson ordered him to transfer Suzmann's call to the intercom immediately.

A day later, on 25th March 1994, three detectives from the Economic & Specialist Crime Command (SCD6) of the Metropolitan Police pressed the bell switch next to the wrought-iron grill gates in front a detached red brick house in Maresfield Gardens.

Harel emerged from that house and came to face to face with the visitors—two men and a woman—as he unbolted the gates. That Friday afternoon was overcast and depressing.

The wiry, ginger-haired policeman in plain clothes shook hands with Harel, introducing himself as Detective-Superintedent Victor Gardener. He introduced the rest of his companions, Detective-Inspector Alex Parsons and Detective-Sergeant Anna O'Brien. Both were also in plain clothes.

Harel nodded and shook hands with the woman and the other man. He stood aside and let them through the gates. Moments later, the visitors were in the foyer of his house, peeling off their overcoats. Harel collected them and took them to the small cloakroom next to the short corridor leading down to his tastefully furnished sitting room. After ushering them into the parlour he announced, 'I am making myself some coffee, do want some?'

The detectives answered in the affirmative and he walked across the thick pile rug towards a door at the far end of the large living room. He opened the door and disappeared into it, while his guests settled into the comfy armchairs near the fireplace. He returned five minutes later with a tray containing a porcelain jug, a cup of granular sugar, five teaspoons and four mugs.

As the Metropolitan Police detectives sipped hot coffee, Harel began to narrate his story starting from the first letter from Johannesburg to his meetings with Matthew Molozi. The captivated Detective-Superintendent asked questions at intervals, while the other detectives scribbled into notepads. At the end of the story, Victor Gardener was suprised by the meticulous execution of the scam by the Africa-based fraudsters. He requested for all the letters and the forged bank statements, those mailed directly from South Africa and those Matthew had delivered by hand.

Harel handed over some of the items requested by the Detective-Superintendent, apologising for misplacing some of the letters and fake documents.

Victor Gardener spoke for the others when he thanked Harel for his co-operation and promised that the detectives would apprehend the fraudsters. Victor said this boldly, although deep down, he doubted whether anything could be done to catch the swindlers. He had been in SCD6 for twelve years, and never in his career had he come across anything resembling the cross-continental scam that Mr. Suzmann had just described.

Unlike counterfeiters and other swindlers he had helped put away, these unknown fraudsters were foreigners operating from abroad. There was no evidence to indicate that they were really South Africans despite the fact that letters posted to London carried South African stamps. Victor reckoned that "Matthew Molozi" was likely a false name used by a fraudster who would be a fool if he were still in The Netherlands. The only consolation was that the police had a physical description of what "Matthew" looked like. But that was offset by the fact that they had nothing on the "partners" of the fictional Heintz & Sharmann law firm, except that "Eli Sharmann" had an American accent, which was allegedly acquired during his student days in USA.

"James Heintz" probably did not exist beyond the ink that was used to write the name on paper. Despite never seeing "James Heintz" or hearing his voice over the telephone, Harel had insisted that there was a separate individual going by that alias. That individual had authored the first letter he had received from South Africa, a letter he had since misplaced, and therefore, couldn't show to the visiting detectives.

Victor and his detectives believed Eli Sharmann and James Heintz were one and the same person. At the very least, the scam involved two con artists— the individual claiming to be Matthew Molozi and the person pretending to be two separate individuals named Eli Sharmann and James Heintz.

With so little information to go on, Victor expressed his doubts to his squad detectives as they walked to his car across the road from the gates of Harel's house. 'The only thing we can do is to file Mister Suzmann's statement and get the sketch artist to make a drawing of this Molozi guy,' he said as the others got into the rear seats of his Vauxhall Omega sedan. 'Those African blokes are long gone, probably thousand miles away from here. I don't think there is much we can do about this case.'

Twenty-fours later, Victor was proven wrong. That Saturday morning, while Harel was in his Northwest London home, pacing up and down, kicking himself for falling for the scam, Victor was in his office in South London catching up on some work.

At 9.00 AM, the fax machine on the edge of his long desk began to hum. Moments later, it started printing on paper. The Detective-Superintendent jumped out of his padded swivel chair and reached for the two printed papers ejected by the machine. The first printout was the fax cover sheet, which he set aside. The second printout, the actual fax, was a note from Interpol requesting assistance of the Metropolitan Police in apprehending three fraudsters wanted by the Nigerian Police Force.

The excited Metropolitan Police detective quickly went through the rest of the fax. It contained a physical description of each wanted men, one of which matched the description given by Harel Suzmann. Victor was about to sit back on his chair, when the fax machine started humming again. Another fax was on the way. He waited anxiously. The fax paper he retrieved from the machine had three colour photographs printed on it. He glanced at the photos and buzzed Detective-

Sergeant Anna O'Brien in her office further down the corridor. Anna, in turn, paged Alex Parsons who was out in the car park. Forty minutes later, the unmarked Vauxhall Omega stopped next to the kerb across the road from 1200 Maresfield Gardens, Hampstead.

Harel Suzmann had exhausted himself, pacing up and down for hours. He was slumped against the upholstered chair behind his study desk, steam billowing from the seventh cup of coffee he had made himself that morning. Then he heard the chiming of the electronic bell and knew that there was a visitor at the gate.

Who could it be? he wondered. He was not expecting any visitor that day. He doubted the unseen visitor was Derrick Goldstein, who helped run his business concerns, or his lawyer, Benny Sachs, who helped him navigate the perilous oceans of UK tax law, and helped fix his divorce settlement with *that cheating bitch.* Either man would have phoned first before coming over to the house.

The bell chimed again and he rose reluctantly from his chair and walked out of the study. He slouched across the thick pile rug to the door. Moments later, he was unbolting the grill gates with a quizzical look on his face.

Anna, Alex and Victor passed through the gates and were standing on the interlocking stone tiles of the driveway when Harel brusquely asked them to state their business. He doubted that the detectives had already caught the devils who swindled him. And he was not in the mood for another round of questioning. But the detectives surprised him.

'Do you recognize any of these men?' Anna asked, holding up a sheet of paper. Harel squinted at it. It was a printout containing three colour photographs. He did not recognize the fair-skinned black man on the righthand side corner of the paper and the dark-skinned man next to him, but he recognized the third picture, the face of the man who was the darkest of them all.

'That's the bastard that nicked my money! That is Matthew Molozi!' he growled, jabbing the picture with his forefinger.

Victor took the sheet of paper from Anna and glanced at the photograph that Harel had pointed out. After a few seconds, he looked up from the paper. 'Well, Mister Suzmann, your bastard is neither Matthew Molozi nor South African. He is really Eugene Igolo, formerly based in Lagos, Nigeria. The International Criminal Police Organization, Interpol, faxed those photos to me fifty minutes ago.'

Suzmann began to wring his hands. 'I will crush that scum of the earth! When I get my hands on him, I will crush him!'

Victor smiled scornfully. He thought Harel Suzmann was a fool that ought to be ashamed that he was conned in such a pathetic way. Without warning, he swung around and started walking across the driveway towards the gates. Anna and Alex exchanged puzzled glances and followed briskly behind their squad leader who was already past the gates.

'Hey! Hey! Detectives, when do I get my money back?' Harel shouted behind them.

Victor turned and said, 'oh, don't you worry, my dear Mister Suzmann. You will get your money back, eventually. It might take a while. Because the suspected swindlers are outside Britain, we will need the cooperation of various foreign police forces. My detectives will get to work as soon as we leave here. You will be kept up to date on the progress of the investigation.'

Harel nodded as he bolted the gates. As he turned to return to his house, the detectives crossed the road to the Vaxhaull Omega.

Anna watched Harel enter his house and shut the front door. 'He is an arse,' she remarked as she got into the rear passenger seat next to Alex.

'Yes, he is,' Victor grinned and turned the key in the ignition switch, starting the car engine. He was pleased. A little over twenty-four hours earlier, he had written off the possibility of ever solving the crime. But the information supplied by Interpol had given him and his subordinates something to work with. He made a mental note to make enquiries about how to get in touch with his counterparts in Nigeria who were also on the trail of the same criminals.

CHAPTER **39**

APRIL 1994

LAGOS, WESTERN NIGERIA

That Monday morning, on 11th April 1994, a police chief was inside his car, trapped in the traffic gridlock. It was a scene typical during rush hour periods in the city-state of over twelve million residents; a scene that had frustrated motorists yelling abuse at each other and at traffic cops, if they were present.

The police chief scanned the scene beyond his windscreen for signs of an authority figure directing traffic. There was not a single orange-clad traffic policeman within eyesight, which meant it was going to be a tough day on the road. But perhaps, time was on his side, he thought as he casually glanced at his wristwatch.

Thirty minutes later, he glanced again at the watch and his stoicism dissolved. Raw panic racked his body. He was facing the prospect of being late for his "special day" in the office. He yelled at the driver of the heavy-duty lorry in front of his Peugeot 505 GR sedan, and honked his horn repeatedly, but it was of no use.

The lorry driver could neither see the police chief at the rear nor hear his loud vituperations above the din of the noisy traffic. Even if the senior lawman's tirade were clearly audible, the lorry driver would still not have heard it as his attention was completely focussed on the vehicular manoeuvres he was making. His unrealistic attempt to perform a U-turn in the middle of the gridlock ended with the lorry hitting the bumper of a Volkswagen Beetle in the adjacent traffic lane.

The door of the battered VW Beetle opened and its driver emerged with a frown on his face. Moments later, the driver of the Beetle was standing in the space between two lanes of queued vehicles, facing the side window of the lorry, screaming and wagging his finger.

The lorry driver leaned out of that side window and screamed back at the lean man wagging an accusatory finger at him.

Cyrus was furious. He glanced at his watch again. He had just twenty-five minutes left to make it to the office before the interrogation of the high-profile suspect would begin with or without him. The police chief grimaced. No way, he thought. He had spent months waiting for the chance to participate in the interrogation of the crime suspect, the same one that he had long resented and deeply despised. He had to be present from the very beginning of the questioning session.

The blare of a car horn snapped him out of his thoughts and he quickly looked around him. A small crowd of motorists and motorcyclists had left their vehicles and gathered near the scene of the collision to watch the commotion. The lorry driver had jumped down from his haulage vehicle and was getting ready to trade blows with the driver of the Volkswagen Beetle. Some of the motorists in the small crowd stepped forward to restrain the road ragers.

The police chief had seen enough. He left the engine running when he emerged from the car. Despite the starched black uniform—the peaked cap was in the car—nobody took notice of the middle-aged man of average height pushing through the small crowd of bystanders that had encircled the bellicose drivers. He pulled out his service pistol with his left hand and flashed his police identity card with the other.

The motorists and bystanders suddenly became aware of his presence and scattered instantly. The pugnacious drivers calmed down immediately. None of them needed to see the ID card, the gun and the crisp black uniform was enough.

'What is wrong with you people?' the police chief yelled at the formerly bellicose drivers who were now smiling sheepishly at him.

'*Oga* police, I'm sorry,' the Volkswagen Beetle driver began. 'But he started it!' he said loudly, pointing an accusatory finger at the other driver.

'That's a lie!' the lorry driver snapped.

Cyrus ordered both men to shut up. Glaring at the lorry driver, he said, 'my car is just behind your lorry. I saw everything. So stop lying or I'll take you down to the station.'

The lorry driver's countenance changed from defiance to fear. He knelt down silently before the the police chief and raised his hands in supplication.

Many policemen enjoyed seeing scared civilians on their knees, begging for forgiveness. But Cyrus was not like many policemen. The grovelling of frightened civilians before uniformed personnel disgusted him. In any case, he was bluffing. It was not his job to deal with traffic violations. And even if he had wanted to do the job of a traffic cop, he had not the time to take the driver down to the police station. There was something far more important at hand, something due to unfold at Ikeja CID. He had to be there before the questioning session kicked off.

The police chief asked the kneeling lorry driver to stop embarrassing himself and get his knees off the asphalted tarmac. The lorry driver sprang to his feet and began to praise Cyrus for his kindness. The police chief nodded awkwardly to acknowledge the praise before ordering both drivers to hop back into their vehicles and bicker no more.

The VW Beetle driver would have loved to discuss damage compensation with the lorry driver, but the look on the face of the police chief made him drop the matter and scurry back to his small car.

The police chief waited for both drivers to return to their vehicles before he got back into his. Five minutes later, the traffic started flowing, but slowly. After the Peugeot 505 GR trundled two and half miles down the road, the scene of the traffic bottleneck came into view. Cyrus looked on with horror at the scene of the accidental collision between a Honda motorcycle and a Subaru 1300G saloon car. There were three orange-uniformed traffic policemen attending to a bloodied man by the side of road, which was strewn with shards of glass and blood splatter. As the Peugeot 505 moved slowly towards the diversion created to bypass the accident scene, Cyrus considered driving into the layby and getting out of the car to talk to the traffic cops, but he quickly decided against it. There was no time to intervene; he had less than fifteen minutes to be at the interrogation room in Ikeja CID.

He manoeuvred the car around the red traffic cones cordoning off the portion of the road occupied by the twisted vehicle carcasses and shards of glass and entered the narrow strip of road used as a bypass. Once the car was past the bottleneck, the road opened up and the police chief changed to the second gear and stepped on the accelerator pedal. Soon, the car was hurtling along the thoroughfare in the direction of Allen Avenue. He glanced at his watch again. There was nine minutes still left. He switched to a higher gear and the accelerator pedal under his foot moved a little closer to the floor mat.

Cyrus began to relax a bit. At the current speed of the car, he was confident that he would make it to the station with some seconds to spare. He had flashbacks to the time when the crime suspect was still a powerful policeman unaccountable to superior police officers in the chain of command. Back then, the suspect could afford to thumb his nose at his seniors in rank. Now, he was at the mercy of the police hierarchy that he had treated with disdain for years. And this time around, his powerful civilian friends in Abuja would not be able to save him.

Coincidentally, two days after the arrest of the suspect, Nduka Ikwunne, the powerful Federal Police Committee was dissolved and most of its civilian members arrested on allegations of misappropriating two hundred million naira meant for the upkeep of over three thousand APCS personnel scattered across the country.

As Cyrus swerved into the car park reserved for Ikeja CID staff, he recalled the prediction of Stanislaus Zikora about the short lifespan of ad hoc monstrosities such as the defunct Federal Police Commitee and the APCS units under its direct supervision. Cyrus was glad that he had taken the advice of the Lagos State Police Commissioner all those months ago. He had bided his time, waiting patiently for that insubordinate bastard, Nduka, to fall from grace.

The police chief smiled as he emerged from the car and headed towards the entrance of the five-storey building. Just then, his stomach rumbled and he felt a dull pain in his gut. He leaned against the wall adjacent to the double doors and massaged his belly at length. When rumbling stopped and the pain subsided, he grabbed his briefcase from the ground and made for the doors.

He had been suffering from diarrhoea for the past day and a half. He was not very sure how he caught the bacterial infection, but he had no doubt that it was sometime between the several plates of jollof rice he had eaten during his happiest day on earth—the *Igbankwu* of his only daughter, Chioma Udeh exactly two days before...

*****

On 1st April 1994, Cyrus Udeh and his wife took a week off from their respective jobs in Lagos to fly to Eastern Nigeria to prepare for the *Igbankwu* ceremony, which was set to take place in Agwu town, a rural settlement outside the city of Enugu, but well within the boundaries of Enugu State.

Upon arrival at their hometown, thirty-five miles from the city airport, they worked tirelessly to prepare for the upcoming ceremony in which their only child and her fiancé would be playing starring roles.

They hired a gardener to trim the overgrown grasses in the compound. Two painters were paid to give the facade of the house a face-lift. Several old women in the town were hired to prepare food for the large number of expected guests. The hired cooks were also paid to cook some extras for the inevitable gate-crashers who could not be shooed away without violating the Igbo tradition of offering hospitality to all who showed up at one's doorstep.

That Saturday afternoon, on 9th April 1994, the Igbo customs of marriage kicked off with Cyrus' prospective son-in-law arriving at the sprawling premises of the Udeh family's country home in Agwu town. The son-in-law did not come alone. He had with him a large entourage of his friends, his five female siblings, his parents and nearly every living member of his entire family tree. Every single person in the entourage was bearing a wrapped gift to be bestowed on the bride's family. Also accompanying the son-in-law's entourage was a live music band and a convoy of three refrigerated trucks stacked full with drinks and perishable food.

The Udeh family—consisting of Cyrus, his wife, his three brothers and several cousins—looked on with awe at the colourful cavalcade in the large forecourt of their house. Like many enlightened Igbo families, Cyrus had not asked his prospective in-laws for a bride price, but what the wealthy Obidi family had brought with them would have paid for the bride price six times over.

Watching the large entourage, Cyrus smiled with satisfaction. He had been right about the expansive forecourt being the right place for the *Igbankwu* to take place. As spacious as his country house was, it was never going to absorb the huge number of invited guests—and uninvited freeloaders—expected at the marriage ceremony.

Over a hundred people attended the outdoor event in the compound dotted with several canopy tents. The invited guests were seventy in total. They were split into groups and offered seats in the canopy tents. The remainder who could not be accommodated in the tents were mostly gatecrashers ambling up and down the forecourt, on the lookout for free food and drinks.

Also invited, but not counted among the seventy guests, were twenty-five uniformed constables from the Enugu State Police Command, provided as a courtesy to the Lagos police chief, to keep law and order at the event. With Mark IV rifles pointing downwards, the policemen sat together under a specially designated white canopy tent aptly positioned next to the wrought-iron gates of the Udeh family compound.

With the exception of the constables in their starched black uniforms and the gatecrashers in their faded and tattered western-style clothing, everybody else was dressed in colourful Igbo traditional attire. The men among the invited guests were each dressed in the Igbo male attire—the *Isiagu*—with a brimless red or black cap to match. The male members of the bride's and bridegroom's families were similarly dressed. The female members of both families were dressed in identical wrappers made of lace fabric. The style of dressing among female guests was diverse, ranging from colourful wrappers of satin fabric to batik-print cotton and cotton brocade. Nearly all of them wore traditional headgears with colours matching their wrapper.

Under their own canopy, in a corner of the forecourt, members of the live music band, also dressed in traditional attire, were busy setting up their equipment— a blend of European and traditional Igbo musical instruments.

With the guests seated in their canopies, the bridegroom and his entourage were formally ushered to the largest tent in the centre of the forecourt. In there, Cyrus and his wife, Ugonwa, were on hand to welcome them.

The band lived up to its billing. They played *Highlife*, a music genre blending American Jazz with traditional Igbo rhythm. Wine and food flowed freely. Despite Ugonwa's silent disapproval, Cyrus and the groom's father drank and ate until they dropped.

By the time, his daughter was ready to perform the most important part of Igbo custom—the presentation of a cup of palm wine to her chosen husband—Cyrus was mildly dazed. Surprisingly, his drinking partner, the industrialist, Evaristus Obidi, remained lucid. The alcohol did not seem to have any noticeable effect on the groom's father.

Through the daze, Cyrus had managed to perform his role as the bride's father, as ancient Igbo customs dictated, by filling a tall ivory cup with palm wine. With barely steady hands, he passed the cup to his daughter, the bride, and ordered, 'show us who your husband is.' Then he waited for her to perform her role in the ceremony.

The band suspended music and everybody waited anxiously with bated breath. Everybody at the gathering knew who her chosen husband was, but tradition was tradition. So she would have to wade through the seated crowd under canopies dotting the forecourt, scrutinizing different male faces, in a mock search for the "elusive" husband "hiding in plain sight".

During this dramatic aspect of the ceremony, it is common for male guests to tease the bride as she performs the mock search, asking her to hand them the tall cup of wine. If things go according to plan, the bride would ignore them with a polite smile and continue her "search" until she "finds" her soulmate. At this point, she kneels before him and offers the wine. By accepting and drinking the wine, the groom symbolically accepts her into his family and they become husband and wife. Alternatively, if the bride is being forced to marry against her will, this aspect of the *Igbankwu* provides her with an excellent opportunity to reap sweet revenge, wreak havoc, and embarrass her family before the guests. All she has to do to cause pandemonium and bring the event to a ghastly halt is give the palm wine to the wrong man— a guest or a male relative.

But that Saturday afternoon, nothing veered off course. Everything happened as it was supposed to. Arinze James Obidi, the bridegroom, was sitting on a long bench with eight male cousins. He watched his soon-to-be bride making a beeline towards his bench. The male cousins sitting next to him began to call out playfully to the bride to give them the cup of wine, claiming to be her rightful soulmate.

She stopped in front of the bench and looked around. The place would have been deathly silent, but for the mock pleas of the young men sitting next to her fiancé. As she knelt on the interlocking tiles on the forecourt, she could sense all human eyes in the gathering tracking her downward movement. In her kneeling position, she gazed into the eyes of her soulmate sitting on the bench. The cousins on the bench stopped talking and a thick silence descended. She sipped from the cup and then offered it to Arinze, a computer scientist in the employ of a commercial bank.

Arinze smiled broadly, accepted the cup, and sipped the wine. That elicited a thunderous roar from the crowd, followed by a round of applause. The live music resumed at a quicker tempo. Shortly after, the bare patch of ground, not occupied by canopies or parked refrigerated trucks, was soon filled with guests dancing frenetically. Attendees, eager to show off wealth, sprayed naira notes on the dancers. More cooked food flowed forth from the busy kitchen of the Udeh family mansion and chilled drinks in stacks of plastic crates came from the humming trucks.

Seven hours after the *Igbankwu* ceremony started, and after his fifteenth cup of palm wine, Cyrus felt a sharp pain in his lower tummy, followed by rumbling. He excused himself from the still lucid father of the bridegroom and dashed off into the family mansion. He spent thirty minutes in the toilet, passing out watery faeces. Upon realizing that he had diarrhoea, he regretted not listening to his wife.

The festive event that started at noon ended just before dusk. The gatecrashers were the first to depart unceremoniously as soon as the food and drinks stopped coming. The next group of people to leave the compound were the invited guests. However, the manner of their departure was different.

Before exiting the compound for their own homes, each guest first approached the long table behind which Cyrus, Ugonwa, Evaristus and his spouse were sitting. There, the guest exchanged brief pleasantries with the parents of the bride and bridegroom before handing over the parcelled gifts they had brought with them. This went on for quite a while. By the time all the seventy guests had left, the ground around the feet of the long table was filled with a garish pile of rectangular boxes, of various sizes, wrapped in paper of different colours.

Arinze Obidi, his parents and the rest of his huge entourage were the last to depart the compound for their own hometown, which was a mile from Agwu town. Now a member of the Obidi family, Chioma Udeh was in the motorcade that left her father's compound.

After the ceremony, Cyrus' tummy trouble became worse. He began visiting the toilet frequently. Ugonwa administered Oral Rehydration Therapy (ORT) to replenish lost body fluids. She tried unsuccessfully to persuade Cyrus to stay in

Agwu until he recovered, but he refused. There was no way he was going to miss the Monday morning interrogation of his arch-enemy in the presence of senior police brass and some visitors from UK and US law enforcement bodies.

By Sunday afternoon, he was on a plane flying back to Lagos. It was an unpleasant flight as he spent most of it in the claustrophobic toilet at the rear of the Boeing 727. When he got to his house in the Shogunle district of Lagos, his wife began to pester him again to take more time off work, to stay home and continue the ORT and a course of Imodium tablets. He had no problem with taking medication, but there was no way he was going to miss the interrogation of Chief Inspector Nduka Ikwunne.

The following day, Monday morning, he dressed in his smartest uniform and grabbed his peaked cap. He kissed his sulking wife goodbye and jumped into his car...

*****

Chief Superintendent Cyrus Udeh opened the double doors and walked into the expansive foyer of Ikeja CID complex. In far corner of the foyer, the desk sergeant, Uthman Bagudu, jumped out of his seat behind the reception desk and saluted. 'Good morning, sir!'

Cyrus smiled weakly and nodded in acknowledgement. 'Is everybody here?' he asked as his stomach began to rumble again, much to his embarassment. He removed his peaked cap and pressed it against his stomach. It seemed to relieve the dull pain in his gut.

The desk sergeant pretended as if he hadn't noticed anything. 'Everybody is waiting for you at the squad room,' he told the CID boss with a heavy Hausa accent.

'The squad room is the venue of the interrogation?'

'Yes sir.'

Cyrus was a bit suprised. Ikeja CID had bigger room on the ground (first) floor outfitted with a long table containing in-built microphones and speakers for use in questioning suspects. It was purposely called *The Interrogation Room*. The squad room on the floor above was smaller, was used for briefing sessions between CID squad leaders and detectives under them.

The DPO shrugged. May be the police commissioner or a higher-ranking officer had insisted on the squad room, he thought. He saluted the desk sergeant and walked across the marble floor towards the staircase. It took him two minutes to reach the landing of the second floor and enter a well-lit corridor. Walking along the corridor, he passed three doors and then stopped at the fourth one with a brass nameplate reading: SQUAD BRIEFING ROOM.

Behind the wooden panel of the closed door, he heard voices speaking English with a variety of accents. Some of the voices were familiar and others were not.

Cyrus placed his attaché case on the carpet and tucked the peaked cap under his right armpit. He took a moment to rub his stomach with his right hand. Then he grabbing the attaché case and used his left hand to open the door.

Inside the room, he came face to face with the people sitting behind a long mahogany desk with their backs to the wall. There were four white men, a white woman and three black men, all Nigerian police officers. Cyrus recognized Zonal Assistant Inspector-General (AIG) Stanley Idoko sitting at the centre of the table, flanked on either side by Detective-Inspectors Gbolahan Akinola and Ikenna Kodilinye.

AIG Stanley Ohimini Idoko was the most senior Nigerian police officer based in Lagos State. He had oversight of *Police-Zone-Two*, which consisted of Lagos and Ogun State Police Commands. In other words, he was the direct superior of both Lagos State Police Commissioner Stanislaus Zikora and his counterpart in neighbouring Ogun State, Commissioner Bernadette Omoruyi.

The foreign law enforcement officers sat on either flank of the three Nigerian police officers. The three-person Metropolitan Police team from London sat to the left of Gbolahan while two thickset white American men, wearing dark eyeglasses, sat to the right of Ikenna. There was only one empty seat behind the long table, and it was next to the blonde lady from the London team.

Cyrus glanced at the vaguely familiar object positioned on the table in front of the AIG. His eyes quickly scrutinized the large reels of magnetic tape fixed on it. He had not seen a reel-to-reel tape recorder in years. He wondered who had brought it into the building because the Ikeja CID squads only made use of compact cassette recorders for their work.

The Ikeja CID chief shifted his gaze from the table to the clock on the wall behind the police officers. It indicated that the time was 11.05 AM. Cyrus he was five minutes late. He smiled apologetically. 'Sorry I'm a bit late.'

The AIG nodded casually and Cyrus took the seat next to the lady. She turned and flashed a bright smile. Cyrus smiled back and nodded slightly.

The AIG waited a few seconds, and then cleared his throat. 'Cyrus, the three people sitting next you are from the London Metropolitan Police...'

Stanley introduced Detective-Superintendent Victor Gardener, Detective-Inspector Alexander Parsons and Detective-Sergeant Anna O'Brien.

Cyrus smiled and shook their hands one by one.

The AIG turned to the men in dark eyeglasses and dark suits and introduced them. They were Henry Kaplinsky and David Bateman Jr., both Special Agents of the Federal Bureau of Investigation (FBI).

Cyrus could not reach their end of the table to shake hands so he waved and the Americans nodded in unison. Cyrus could not help but notice the contrast between the two foreign police teams. The British team, dressed in casual clothes, were pleasant and friendly. The American team, dressed formally, were stiff-faced and hid their eyes under tinted glasses.

Addressing all of them, the AIG regretfully announced the unavailability of Commissioner Stanislaus Zikora. 'The Commissioner wanted to be here, but unfortunately he is suffering from a bout of flu,' Stanley explained.

A brief silence followed. Then the AIG glanced at his watch. 'Okay, we are about to start. The suspect should be with us in a couple of seconds.'

The pangs of pain hit Cyrus' belly again. His right hand discreetly reached under the table and rubbed the aching stomach. Unlike before, the pain did not subside with the stomach rub. In fact, pain increased in waves. Although the Ikeja CID boss maintained an outward appearance of calm, he really wanted to scream. And for the first time, he regretted his decision to come. The last thing he wanted to happen was to be disgraced out of the meeting. The thing that dreaded him the most was embarrassing himself. *What if that belly rumble and gut pains caused him to throw up or fart?*

There was a knock on the door and everyone gazed at it. 'Come in,' the AIG bellowed.

The door opened and Sergeant Uthman Bagudu led a shackled, haggard-looking, and gaunt Nduka Ikwunne into the squad room. The light-skinned suspect was dressed in a dirty grey T-shirt and a pair of faded jeans trousers. In handcuffs and leg manacles, he shuffled to the centre of the room.

Another policeman, a constable, walked into squad room, carrying a wooden chair. He positioned the chair two feet from the long mahogany desk and walked out of the squad room again.

Uthman stirred the suspect towards it. Nduka shuffled to the front of the chair and then sat down. The desk sergeant removed the handcuffs and the manacles from the suspect who mumbled 'thank you.' Seconds later, Uthman left the room, closing the door behind him.

Stanley leaned forward and depressed a red button on the tape recorder. The magnetic reels started rotating slowly. For the record, he announced the date, the time and the impending event. The small microphones on the recorder picked up his words and stored it on the magnetic tape.

Nduka's eyes quickly surveyed the people facing him on the table. 'Where is my lawyer?' he growled.

The AIG's countenance remained unchanged. 'You mean your brother, Barrister Obinna Ikwunne?'

'Yes!' Nduka snapped loudly.

'Your brother was not invited and never will,' the AIG stated evenly.

Nduka was outraged. He opened his mouth to say something foul, but the AIG quickly raised his right hand.

'Just for the record, before you speak again, let me make you a deal. See these gentlemen and lady at my sides,' he said, turning left and right to acknowledge the presence of the foreigners. 'They are here to listen to your interesting story about your patrons, the fraudsters. If you tell us all you know, I'll ask the prosecutor to push for a lenient sentence.'

Nduka took a moment to consider the offer. Then he asked, 'how lenient?'

The AIG turned to the Ikeja CID chief to provide the details of the offer.

A smile flashed across the Cyrus' face. His eyes mocked the suspect. 'You will get ten years in jail instead of twenty years or more. With good behaviour, you might be out of jail within four or five years. This is the deal, take it or leave it.'

Nduka rubbed his eyes and nodded to indicate that he was ready to cooperate.

Stanley smiled smugly. 'Good, a very wise decision...Now, I'm sure you know Chief Superintendent Cyrus Udeh, the Divisional Police Officer in-charge of Lagos State CID, and the owner of the building we are currently in.'

Everybody—except Nduka and the Americans—grinned at the joke. Stanley declared for the record that Cyrus Udeh would lead the interrogation. The foreign law enforcement officers were also free to ask questions too. 'Remember Mister Ikwunne, tell the truth for it shall set you free,' Stanley advised Nduka, paraphrasing a quote from the bible.

Anna squirmed in her seat. She wanted the AIG to dispense with the preamble and get on with the day's business. She had been in Lagos for the past 24 hours and was not enjoying any part of it.

One day earlier, at exactly 1.30 PM, the British Airways flight carrying Victor, Anna and Alex had landed on a runway in Murtala Mohammed International Airport, Ikeja. Upon clearing immigration and customs, the British police officers had loitered in the arrivals lounge of the airport for two hours before the driver of Nigerian Police car sent to pick them up finally appeared. The driver apologised profusely and blamed the notorious Lagos traffic for the delay. The weary visitors nodded that they understood.

On the way to their designated accomodation, Ikeja Airport Hotel, the car broke down. Anna and her colleagues were compelled to emerge from the car and stand on the side of the road under the glare and sweltering heat of the afternoon sun. They looked on as the driver opened the car bonnet and dived into the engine. After thirty minutes tinkering around the engine, the driver emerged and conveyed the good news to the flustered passengers. 'The car engine is fine now. Let us go.'

The red-faced foreigners clambered back onboard and the journey continued. To their dismay, the car ran into a traffic gridlock. The police driver turned and apologised once again. Despite all four side windows being open, the searing heat inside the car was almost unbearable. It would take another two hours before the tired passengers finally got to the hotel.

At the hotel, Victor and Alex shared a suite while Anna got a nearby single room. Later in the evening, Victor and Alex went on a tour of the city with the police driver acting as a guide. Anna had declined to join, still angry at what she saw as the tardiness of their host: *the Nigerian Police Force*.

Victor and Alex returned several hours later to regale her with stories of their visit to Lagos Island, the seaports at Apapa and Tincan Island, the numerous skyscrapers of the business districts and several other tourist attractions. They also toured the affluent Victoria Island and sat on the white sands of Lagos Bar beach. The Detective-Sergeant brightened up and wished she had gone along.

The next day, on morning of 11th April, the driver was late again in picking up the Metropolitan Police officers from the hotel. They would spend three hours in a traffic hold-up at Allen Avenue while en route to Ikeja CID. And Anna's dislike for the city of Lagos increased three-fold...

When she snapped out of her thoughts, Cyrus was standing next to her chair, throwing questions at the suspect while the rotating reels of magnetic tape recorded everything uttered.

'Mister Ikwunne, you have confirmed that you know who these men are,' Cyrus said, holding up a pink A3-size cardboard sheet with three enlarged passport photos glued to it. 'Would like to tell us where these men are?' The Ikeja CID chief was referring to the living fraudsters still at large.

Nduka Ikwunne glared at Cyrus and said nothing. The DPO gently dropped the cardboard on the desk near Anna's elbows and repeated the question to the suspect. The disgraced ex-policeman folded his arms across his chest and remained tight-lipped.

Before the lead interrogator could say another word, a sharp pain hit his stomach again. He wanted to grip his stomach, but restrained himself. He couldn't do that with all those people in the room watching. Nobody, except Nduka, seemed to have noticed what had transpired. The suspect's lips twitched as if he was suppressing a laugh.

Cyrus became worried that *the bastard* facing him had noticed his stomach ailment. He half-expected Nduka to come out with snide remarks alluding to his discomfort; remarks that would surely cause the AIG to observe him closely. Cyrus had no illusions what would happen if Stanley Idoko found out that he was ill. The AIG would order him to proceed on sick leave with immediate effect. The Ikeja CID chief envisioned the aftermath of such an order from the AIG. He pictured himself clutching his stomach on the way out of the squad room with Nduka laughing at him.

'Okay, I am going to pause briefly,' Stanley Idoko said calmly and pressed a white button on the tape recorder. The spinning reels of magnetic tape on the machine froze instantly. 'Mister Ikwunne, you agreed to cooperate with us. So you are going to answer the questions.'

Nduka's face broke into contemptuous smile. He locked eyes for a moment with the AIG.

'Look here, Mister Ikwunne! This is no laughing matter!' the AIG barked, startling everyone in the room.

The pangs gripping Cyrus's gut subsided and he suddenly felt better. He poised himself to resume the interrogation of the recalcitrant suspect.

Stanley pushed the white button again and the magnetic reels started spinning again atop the machine.

Nduka unfolded his arms and blurted out, 'I don't know where they are.'

Cyrus stared at him in disbelief.

Nduka added, 'do you honestly think those cynical gangsters would inform me of their movements?'

The DPO considered this for a while and decided to believe the former APCS boss. He picked up the cardboard again and held it up to Nduka. 'Tell us everything you know about these guys. Starting from the exact moment you started spying for them.'

The ex-policeman gazed into the mocking eyes of his interrogator. It was clear to him from the onset that Cyrus was enjoying every minute of his humiliation. He bit his lips regretfully as he reflected on his mistakes. If only he had trusted his instincts and fled the country with the money he had made from the swindlers...

*****

Since his arrest at home four months earlier, life had been hellish for Nduka Ikwunne. For the first seven days of his captivity, he was forced to share an overcrowded, smelly prison cell with hefty criminals in the ATW (Awaiting Trial Wing) of the state prison in Ikoyi district. Most of the criminals recognised him as cop and beat the daylights out of him. The prison warders knew about the abuse, but turned a blind eye. For those seven days, he was also denied the right to bathe.

On the eighth day, his arch-enemy came to visit, ostensibly to check the conditions in which the disgraced cop was being held. Chief Superintendent Udeh was appalled when he saw the once almighty APCS boss cowering in a corner of the cell with bullying cellmates standing over him, kicking and shouting abuses. This time the prison warders intervened. Two of them poised their antiquated shotguns at the bullies as the other warders opened the cell gates.

Upon seeing the gun barrels pointing their way, the bullies left Nduka alone and crossed to the opposite corner of the prison cell where they huddled together. Nduka was sitting on the ground, sobbing quietly. A warder helped him to his feet and stirred him out of the cell. As Nduka limped past the cell gates, Cyrus looked into his face and saw a thoroughly broken man. Nduka's face was bleeding from cuts on the cheeks and lips. There were dark bruises under his swollen eyes and he was suffering from an ankle sprain.

On Cyrus' insistence, the Prison Superintendent ordered his warders to transfer the disgraced policeman to a cleaner and bigger solitary cell. Shortly after, a prison doctor attended to Nduka's wounds and he was allowed to shower twice a day.

Four days later, Detective-Sergeant Martin Okoye questioned Nduka for the first time in the presence of his lawyer and elder brother, Barrister Obinna Ikwunne. That first interrogation was not a success because Obinna kept interrupting Martin, urging his brother not to answer certain key questions. 'He doesn't have to answer that' and 'brother, you should claim your right' were constant refrains coming from the combative lawyer throughout the questioning session.

Cyrus was furious when Martin later told him about the disruptive influence of the lawyer. Cyrus phoned Stanislaus Zikora, shortly after. With the blessing of the Lagos State Police Commissioner, the Ikeja CID chief called the Prison Superintendent and asked him to bar the lawyer from visiting Ikoyi Prison whenever the police were there to interrogate the suspect.

Obinna went to court the next day to file a challenge to the ban. When the Commissioner Zikora heard about it, he invited the lawyer to his office for a chat. The commissioner told him that Britain and America were interested in the case and that the police had a duty to interrogate his brother properly without undue interference. Knowing fully well about the intransigence of human rights lawyers like Obinna, the Police Commissioner stated, 'it is important for the image of our country that we extract information that will aid in the capture of the fugitives. Nothing will be allowed to stand in the way of us doing our jobs.'

Obinna asked him whether his statement meant that he would not obey court orders. Zikora did not respond, but the barrister already knew the answer. In his twelve-year career as a human rights lawyer, he had seen both the police and the military flout several court orders issued against them by the judges.

'Look Barrister, you are not doing your brother any good. It is more than clear to all that he is guilty,' Zikora told the lawyer. Then his voice softened and took on a conciliatory tone. 'I'm in a position to offer you a deal. I can lean on the Chief State Counsel to ask the judge for a lenient sentence. Your brother will serve only half of the minimum jail time. In return for this deal, you have to back off from our investigations.'

Obinna jumped out of his chair and barked at the Commissioner. 'No way! Let the court decide. You have no right to deny my brother his rights, his legal counsel.'

Stanislaus Zikora smiled ruefully. Wagging his finger at the stubborn lawyer, he warned, 'Barrister Ikwunne, you are not helping here. Like I said before, we are determined to trace the fugitives and we will not hesitate to beat the required information out of your brother, if it ever came to that.'

Obinna's countenance changed. He became visibly frightened. The courts were useless if the police did not intend to obey orders issued by judges. More importantly, the Commissioner had explicitly threatened to use torture to extract information from his brother. The prospect of that action being taken against his brother terrified him because he knew all too well what that often led to. Two years earlier, one of his clients, awaiting trial, was beaten to death in a holding cell inside Eleresun Police Station in the suburban district of Agege. The late victim had been a client whose case he had taken up under the auspicies of his human rights organisation, Civil Liberties Agency (CLA). The CLA offered free legal representation to people too poor to afford a lawyer of their own. The late victim was a nineteen-year-old suspect of burglary who had grown up in Ajegunle, a squalid slum in Lagos State.

A week before his extra-judicial murder, the badly beaten burglary suspect was visited in his cell by Obinna who had cheery news to share. He showed his semi-literate client the court injunction barring the police from further brutalizing him. Despite the suspect's skepticism, Obinna repeatedly assured him that the torture would stop now that the Orile Agege Magistrate Court has intervened.

The human rights lawyer was wrong. The police ignored the court order and continued to torture the suspect to "confess his crimes". One morning, after seeing the magistrate about the police refusal to obey the court order, Obinna received a phone call from the Superintendent of the Eleresun Police Station stating that the alleged burglar was dead and that he should come and collect his remains from the morgue...

'I'll take your deal,' Obinna said as he glared at Commissioner Zikora sitting across the table from him. 'What choice do I have? I won't let you thugs torture my only brother to death in your dungeons.'

Zikora sighed in relief. 'So you will drop the lawsuit against us? And leave us alone to do our jobs?'

'Yes, I will not only withdraw the lawsuit, I will even relinquish my right to represent him, but in exchange, I want full visitation rights, another lawyer to attend to his needs as soon it is convenient for you lot. Let me repeat again, I want full rights to visit my brother. And if a hair on his head is touched, our deal will be off. I hope I have made myself understood.'

'Yes, all understood,' Zikora said with a smile. 'Outside our interrogation hours, you will be allowed to visit him as much as you like. By the way, I was bluffing. Of course, I was never going to authorize the torture of Chief Inspector Ikwunne...actually...former Chief Inspector. Your brother has been sacked from the Nigerian Police Force. A disciplinary hearing was conducted a few days ago.'

'Is my brother not supposed to be present in such a hearing to defend himself against your allegations of corruption and misconduct?' Obinna asked, aghast at the short-circuiting of laid out procedures.

Zikora shook his head impatiently. 'There was no need for all that. We have your brother's bank account. We know that he took money from the murderous swindlers...the fugitives we are now trying to hunt down. That has earned him an automatic sack from the Force.'

Obinna swallowed. Saving Nduka's police career was at the bottom of his priorities. What was top priority to him was saving his brother's life. 'Okay, I am leaving, but I want everything in writing. You will not torture my brother and I will have full visitation rights.'

'It is all done, my friend. You'll get everything written down on pen and paper with the letterhead and rubber stamp of the Lagos State Police Command.'

Obinna got the Commissioner's promise in writing before withdrawing the lawsuit and relinquishing his right to represent his brother. For the next nine weeks, he was able to visit his brother frequently, until visitation rights were suddenly suspended. The barrister protested, but to no avail.

The Police Commisioner told Obinna that Nduka had refused to cooperate with the authorities despite being treated well in Ikoyi Prison. Therefore, tougher measures were required. Seeing the fear in the lawyer's eyes, Zikora moved to disabuse his mind. He assured Obinna that his brother would not be tortured. However, certain privileges would be withdrawn, and most likely, the ex-cop would have to be moved to a maximum security facility.

Obinna protested, waving the letter that Zikora had signed promising never to revoke his visitation rights. The Police Commissioner laughed and waved his hand dismissively. Three days later, Obinna learnt that Nduka had been transferred to Kirikiri Maximum Security Prison.

Two months after that, the ex-cop was still at the maximum security facility, awaiting trial, when a group of policemen unexpectedly came to whisk him off, in shackles, to Ikeja CID to be questioned by local and foreign law enforcement officers...

*****

Cyrus rubbed his stomach discreetly and spoke again. 'Mister Ikwunne, tell us how you came in contact with your criminal associates, the swindlers.'

Nduka glanced at the grim-faced AIG and opened up. He started from the arrest and escape of Moses Adrika from detention and the complicity of late Detective-Inspector Mike Otunba in that incident. He made sure to embarrass his interrogator, Cyrus, by addressing himself to the FBI agents and Metropolitan Police detectives, telling them that the Ikeja CID chief had been responsible for creating the utterly inept investigation panel that cleared Mike Otunba of involvement in the escape of the now dead swindler.

With an indignant look on his face, Nduka explained that as chairman of that panel he had wanted to get to the bottom of the incident, but Cyrus had frustrated all his efforts. Over Nduka's strong objections, the Ikeja CID chief had gotten the panel to exonerate the deceased detective.

Glaring and pointing a finger at Cyrus, the suspect added, 'I was accused of wanting to start a witch-hunt by that man interrogating me because I insisted Mike Otunba be subject to further investigation.'

A visibly irritated Stanley Idoko interrupted him. 'Mister Ikwunne, just drop the melodrama and get on with the story. We haven't got all day.'

Nduka withdrew the accusatory finger and continued the narrative. 'I never accepted that Mike had no involvement in the escape of Mister Moses Adrika. So after the ad hoc panel was dissolved, I carried on with the investigation, secretly, of course. I tapped his office phone and got my men to do professional break-ins. I didn't find anything incriminating, but I never stopped believing that he was a bent cop. So for nearly three years, December 1990 to April 1993, I kept an eye on Mike Otunba. I wanted to snoop on his personal bank accounts, to snoop around his house, but there was no way I could do it legally since a police investigative panel, which I supposedly chaired, had cleared the man. After Otunba's rotting corpse was discovered, I got a fresh opportunity to chair another panel charged with conducting a preliminary murder investigation. Now, this was one ad hoc panel I was proud to chair. It had a competent team of homicide and

382

APCS detectives. It had none of those idiots from the anti-scam squad or the narcotics squad loved by our Chief Superintendent here.'

'Please, go on,' AIG Stanley Idoko said, using a hand gesture to urge Nduka to continue.

'The excellent detectives from homicide and my own APCS began to connect the dots. This time I was able to get into the deceased's bank accounts. We produced an excellent preliminary report on our work so far and urged Chief Superintendent Cyrus Udeh, the DPO, to give us more time to get to the bottom of it, but the man bluntly refused. He shut down an active investigation because he hates my guts and transferred the case to his beloved anti-scam squad, the bunch of idiots led by the highly overrated Detective-Inspector Ikenna Kodilinye, who is sitting over there amongst you...'

Victor, Anna and Alex turned sideways to glance at Ikenna who remained composed and stone-faced as Nduka poured invectives on him.

'...these people, the anti-scam detectives, are useless. Look how long it took them to identify the scammers. If my ad hoc team of detectives were left in charge, we would have solved the case a long time ago. A month after my panel was disbanded, I finally found out who these scammers were. I found out who they were in May 1993. That was a clear seven months before the idiots sitting over there finally figured it out,' Nduka concluded while pointing at Ikenna and Gbolahan.

The ex-cop's last sentence hung heavy in the air like an invisible fog. A thick moment of silence followed before a clearly embarrassed AIG Stanley Idoko asked the foreigners if they had any questions for the suspect.

Anna cleared her throat and spoke for the first time. 'Why did they kill Mister Otunba?'

Cyrus smiled at her funny pronunciation of deceased cop's name. AIG Stanley's lips twitched briefly.

'He was going to betray them,' Nduka replied, eyeing the V-shaped neckline of her blouse.

Cyrus felt the pain in his gut subside as he asked the suspect to quit stalling and tell his story fully.

Nduka nodded and told the audience what happened after he found out the identities of swindlers.

'So you went into ELAJ Enterprises in Mushin hoping to blackmail these dangerous fraudsters,' Cyrus began with a look of incredulity on his face. 'Didn't you think it was a stupid thing to do? If they could kill Mike Otunba, what makes you think they would not hesitate to kill you?'

Nduka smiled smugly. 'Well, I did not go there to blackmail the scammers. I went there to offer them my services. They desperately needed somebody inside Ikeja CID. A person as highly placed as me was a massive boon to them. Having said that, I knew what I was doing was extremely risky. Those gangsters were paranoid and jittery, especially their leader. They had just disposed of a policeman who tried to double-cross them. So they were not above killing me if they suspected I had come to hoodwink them. I knew all this, and yet I took the calculated risk. I knew that if I left their Mushin head office alive then I would live to enjoy whatever they paid me. I was right. At end of my first meeting with them, I left their office with a laundry bag stuffed with money. It was three hundred and fifty thousand naira, cash. After that event, I became relaxed. From then onwards, all I had to do was supply them with information whenever they needed it, do not try to betray them, and then sit back and enjoy the money they were lavishing on me. The strategy paid off.'

There was momentary silence, and then Cyrus stated flatly, 'well, you lived long enough alright, but you will not be able to spend the money. We found all your hidden bank accounts. Every single one of them has been frozen.'

Nduka did not reply. He surveyed the faces sitting behind the long table opposite him. It became apparent to him that the Americans were bored. For the last fifteen minutes, the FBI agents had been toying with their pens. One of them kept glancing at his watch at intervals as if he had somewhere else to be and wanted the session to wrap up. The British, on the other hand, were busy scribbling words into their notepads. Nduka was sure that they were preparing some questions to ask later on.

Ikenna and Gbolahan also looked bored. Nduka was a bit surprised that none of them had responded to any of his vituperative outbursts. Why didn't they bother to defend themselves against his allegations that they were grossly incompetent? Didn't they care how the foreign visitors in the room might perceive them? And what was wrong with Cyrus? Was he sick or something?

Cyrus broke the silence in the room. 'Is that all, Mister Ikwunne?' he asked as his hand discreetly touched his stomach. He felt the pain and tremor of his bowels moving.

Nduka smiled knowingly. 'Is there something wrong with you, sir?'

Cyrus smiled back as his hand fell to his side. 'There is nothing wrong with me, Nduka. Shall we return to your story? How much did they pay you regularly?'

Nduka rubbed his chin and his eyes rolled upwards as if he was pondering over the question.

The AIG leaned forward with his elbows. He frowned at Nduka, 'Mister Ikwunne, please answer the question. How much were you paid monthly?'

'Why? You should know the answer. After all, you said, not that long ago, that you had found and frozen all my hidden bank accounts.'

'Yes, but we have visitors amongst us. So humour me...answer the question.'

'Well, like I said before, I received three hundred and fifty thousand naira at end of my first meeting with them. Subsequently, they began paying a standard monthly fee of one hundred thousand, but there was always more. I got extras...some of you will call them bonuses.'

Cyrus discreetly touched his tummy again. But this time, he felt the urge to visit the toilet. He suppressed the urge and asked the next question. 'How much did you get from these so-called bonuses?'

'It is hard to say,' Nduka said, rubbing his chin thoughtfully. 'Sometimes, I received a bonus of thirty thousand naira. Sometimes, it was twenty-five thousand or twenty-thousand or even less. There was no specific pattern for these extra payments. Sometimes, I got the bonus on top of my standard fee at the beginning of the month. Other times, these generous people, the scammers, would suddenly call me up and deliver an envelope stuffed with cash. I think they really appreciated my work and were willing to lavish money on me for it.'

Cyrus sneered at the suspect. 'Of course, they loved you for betraying your oath to enforce the law of the land. Okay, let us move on...Why did you decide to work for them? You uncovered their identities in May 1993. You could have arrested them, but you chose not to. Why work for them?'

Nduka seemed surprised. 'Why not? These chaps were wealthy, successful both in their legitimate car dealership business and in their murky criminal activities. There was no reason for me not to go for it.'

'But you were paid very well by the federal government. You and your men received special salaries well beyond your rank.'

Nduka laughed and started addressing the Americans and Britons again. 'Yes, that is true. The Chief Superintendent here deeply resented the fact that all of us in APCS were on special salaries. He didn't like the fact that I was paid higher than him. In fact...'

The AIG leaned forward. 'Mister Ikwunne, let us return to the matter at hand. Please answer the DPO's question. Why did you decide to work for the scammers despite your high take-home earnings?'

'I wanted more money. Besides, it was a great opportunity for me to throw a monkey spanner into the works. By keeping the scammers well informed, I ensured that they would always be many steps ahead of the clowns of the anti-scam squad. Detective-Inspector Ikenna Kodilinye would never be able to crack the case. And at some point, down the line, the frustrated Police Commissioner or even you, the Zonal AIG, would yank the case from Ikeja CID. The DPO would be forced to retire in disgrace and Ikenna would be humiliated and cut down to size.'

Cyrus shook his head slowly and then asked, 'did you steal the file relating to the Grams case? What about the items taken from the safe in Ikenna's office?'

Nduka arched his eyebrows in feigned amazement. 'What kind of question is that? If someone pays you handsomely, then you have got to deliver the goods and...'

'I take it that your answer is "Yes". You stole the items.'

Nduka seemed affronted by the interruption. Nevertheless, he confirmed what Cyrus had put to him. With a devious smile on his face, the disgraced ex-cop narrated how he had left his own office, gone down to the second floor and slipped into Ikenna's office to commit burglary during a brief toilet break called in the middle of a three-hour-long teleconference with a senior police officer based in Force Headquarters, Abuja.

Cyrus shook his head after listening to the ex-policeman's gloat. Then he pressed on with the interrogation. For another thirty minutes, Nduka answered questions about his knowledge of how the fraudsters operated. When Stanley Idoko finally switched off the tape recorder and declared a twenty-minute recess, Kaplinsky and Bateman collectively heaved a sigh of relief. Both of them rose immediately and left the room to stretch their legs and compile the questions they wanted to ask about the Logan scam, Gram's homicide, and the disappearance of Steinberg.

The British team huddled together in the room to compare notes. With the exception of the AIG and the suspect, all the Nigerians exited the room.

In the corridor, just outside the squad room, Cyrus excused himself from Ikenna and Gbolahan, and dashed into the men's room.

Twenty minutes later, everybody returned to his or her previous positions in the squad room and the interrogation resumed. The FBI agents took turns to throw questions at the suspect.

The suspect told them that he did not know much about Gary Logan, but he confirmed what the agents already knew about the murder of Pastor Michael Grams. About David Steinberg, the suspect said he knew little. 'The gangsters told me that they did it,' Nduka told them. 'But they refused to discuss any further. When I pressed them, they told me that the body was buried somewhere in Enugu. I was also told not to ask any more questions about things that I had no business knowing.'

Bateman nodded slowly; at least, he now knew for sure that David was dead, lying inside a covered shallow grave, somewhere remote, in that sun-kissed city-state. His previous assumption that Mr. Steinberg was simply hiding out in West Africa had finally been disabused.

The British detectives asked questions about the scam perpetrated against Harel Suzmann.

Nduka shook his head. He didn't know anything because his paymasters never divulged the details of their operations to him. But he had long suspected that the fraudsters were doing something big. He suspected an overseas criminal operation because the gang leader and one of his subordinates had been out of the country several months before the police raids in Victoria Island and Ebute Metta.

Cyrus asked Nduka if he was referring to John Nwosu and Eugene Igolo.

Nduka replied, 'John is the leader and Eugene is one of his loyal subordinates. But Tunde was the real brains behind all the gang's successful schemes.'

The interrogation ended fifteen minutes later. The entire event had been an hour long with a twenty-minute break in-between. But none of the foreign law enforcement officers was impressed. They had come to the country, expecting a detailed account from the suspect that would fill in the gaps that existed in their knowledge of the gangsters. Though both foreign teams had a general idea of how the swindlers operated, they wanted to know exactly how the gang gathered the information used in the meticulous planning of all their successful schemes. They also wanted to know more about the swindlers' offshore bank accounts; how fraudsters laundered and moved their ill-gotten gains from Nigeria to financial institutions overseas.

Both foreign teams left the police station for their hotel with the feeling that the Nigerian police had mislead them into believing that the suspect had all the answers when in fact he only knew slightly more than they did.

Later that evening, inside Ikeja Airport Hotel, Bateman Jr. and Kaplinsky left their rooms and went downstairs to the cocktail bar. Over drinks, they discussed what had transpired seven hours earlier at Ikeja CID complex.

'It's a pity that David Steinberg wound up dead in this god-forsaken country,' said Bateman in between sips of his red wine.

Kaplinsky smiled. 'At least that saved him the agony of a lengthy jail sentence in a federal pen for tax evasion.'

Bateman nodded in agreement and sipped his red wine. 'Well, we are back to square one. We now have an out-of-jurisdiction homicide to look into.'

'Damn, this wine is good. Made in Nigeria,' Kaplinsky remarked, smacking his lips as he read the label on the wine bottle.

David Bateman ignored his colleague's last remark and carried on with what was really bothering him. 'What can I say man...without any new information on the whereabouts of those criminals and their money, there isn't much for us to...' he trailed off.

At that point, Henry Kaplinsky leaned forward on the bar top fashioned from Iroko timber and gave a piece of his mind. 'Dave, I personally don't give a rat's ass whether or not these cases are solved. If a bunch of Africans can convince three Americans to come down here and surrender their entire life savings in exchange for silly promises of unlimited wealth, then I say they deserved what they got.'

Bateman smiled and said, 'I guess that makes the two of us, but I wouldn't put Pastor Grams in the same camp as the other two. He wasn't in it to make money. He was just a fucking bleeding heart.'

Inside the same bar, ten feet away from the FBI agents, the British team was sitting round a table. The mood among them was more sombre. Beyond the announcement of a five-hundred-pound reward for anyone with information leading to the capture of the three swindlers, they had nothing else to work with. They would have to shelve the case file until something new came up, perhaps from Interpol.

Victor Gardener ordered an extra bottle of Guinness Stout to soothe himself. He liked challenges and enjoyed overcoming them, but this case was something else. And he resented that.

'Sir, don't worry, we will get all those crooks,' Alex Parsons said, patting his superior in the shoulder.

Victor nodded in agreement, although both men knew that likelihood of catching the swindlers was low, at least for the time being. Nobody had a clue where in the world the fugitives were hiding.

Anna O'Brien sat there sipping her Heineken lager beer in silence, wondering what she was doing in West Africa. She had a forboding that the case might never be solved.

CHAPTER **40**

MAY 1994

GEORGE TOWN, THE CAYMAN ISLANDS

The sunny beach was teeming with scantily dressed tourists. Among the mostly European crowd were three bearded black African men dressed in nothing but identical khaki shorts. They sat next to each other in the damp white sand, their outstretched legs touching the water. John put on his dark eyeglasses and sipped his glass of fresh coconut juice. Eugene and Adamu watched a group of nubile bikini-clad ladies tossing a beach ball between them while their bare-chested male partners cheered. John gazed at what his associates were looking at and smiled. 'Aren't they lovely?'

'Oh yes, boss,' Eugene grinned, his eyes tracing the contours of the slim bodies in the bikinis.

Adamu scratched his bushy beard. He hated it for its itchiness and craved for a return to the days when he was clean-shaven. But he understood that it was still a long way off. That warm Sunday afternoon, 1st May 1994, marked his nineteenth week on the Caribbean island. So far, there hasn't been any hint that Interpol knew that he and his brothers-in-crime were hiding out there. Thankfully, none of the local newspapers had carried any story about the international manhunt. He and his fellow swindlers were very relaxed among the foreign tourists and the friendly natives of The Caymans.

But the confidence and certainty exuded by Adamu and the others about their safety on the island had not always been as rock solid as it was that Sunday afternoon on the beach. Long before their self-assuredness arrived and was set in stone, the swindlers' stay in the idyllic capital of the British overseas territory had been marred by a nagging fear of being caught by the long arm of Interpol. The first four weeks on the island had been an emotional rollercoaster for them as their fear kept waxing and waning with each passing hour and each passing day. Their nervousness was certainly not helped when a local man of the law suddenly showed up at the doorstep of their condominium in the third week of their stay...

*****

The first week on the sun-kissed island had been tense for the gangsters. But when the second week came around, and nothing bad happened, they began to relax slowly, believing that they were in no danger of being tracked down. They began to visit the beaches, the bars, the restaurants and shops of George Town. Although, they were clearly enjoying themselves at this point, flashes of nervousness kept cropping up whenever they encountered a uniformed policeman walking by. As the second week was ending, the men began to engage in some snorkelling activities in shallow waters not too far from their beachfront condominium.

On the second day of their third week on the island, the swindlers bought a speedboat on a whim. Twenty-fours later, a local policeman came to see them in their apartment.

It happened while the swindlers were preparing to go fishing in their new boat. John was in his room, picking up the fishing rods leaning against a wall when his eyes caught sight of something happening outside from his window. A wiry mixed-race man in a T-shirt and jeans trousers had materialized on the driveway and was walking slowly towards the front door of their condo apartment.

John gazed at the vaguely familiar figure through the window for a full minute. Then his eyes widened in alarm when he finally recognized the approaching man as Detective-Superintendent Warren Beatty of the Royal Cayman Islands Police Force (RCIPF).

The gang leader had seen Warren's picture in one of the local newspapers, *The Cayman News Observer*. The picture in the newspaper was accompanied by a bio profile, which, in part, said Warren had worked as a police officer in the Jamaican Constabulary Force (JCF) before emigrating to join the better paying, less violent and more respectable RCIPF.

The gang leader quickly shut the curtains on the window and rushed to the living room where his men were waiting for his instruction.

Eugene was convinced that the cop was there to arrest them. John thought that Eugene might be right. Adamu strongly disagreed, reasoning that if that were the case, the cop would not be alone. He would have come with dozens of armed police officers.

'May be the other cops are on the way,' countered Eugene.

They were still arguing amongst themselves when the doorbell started ringing. By then, John had come around to Adamu's way of thinking. He had agreed that the Caribbean policeman was not coming to arrest them. So there was no need to shoot their way out of the island, no need to jump into their speedboat and take their chances in the open sea, perhaps approach a vessel of the Cuban Revolutionary Navy in the guise of being "persecuted socialists" fleeing the "pro-imperialist regimes" of Nigeria and The Cayman Islands.

But Warren Beatty was no threat to the swindlers. He had no reason to suspect them of being criminal fugitives from Nigeria since their forged passports declared them to be citizens of Equatorial Guinea. Over a bottle of cold beer, he told the occupants of the condo's ground-floor apartment that the purpose of his visit was more or less a formality. As the head of General Criminal Investigations Department of the RCIPF, he was merely checking on new long-term foreign residents to make sure they were who they said they were.

In his lilting, sing-song Jamaican accent, the RCIPF detective politely asked the swindlers for their travel documents. After spending a few minutes scrutinizing passports and other paper documents, he apologised for the intrusion and asked them to be on the lookout and report any sightings of suspicious characters. As he turned on his heel to leave, the swindlers invited him to stay and have more beers with them.

Warren took a moment to consider the invitation. He had already violated RCIPF policy by downing one glass of cold beer while on official duty. And now, these chaps were inviting him to carry on with the violation. After a minute of gazing at the ceiling, Warren decided that it wasn't a big deal. In his previous life, as a JCF detective in central Kingston, the rules were not strictly followed. The problem here in The Cayman Islands wasn't him. It was the overly strict non-drinking policy of the RCIPF. Because the day was a hot and sunny, Warren thought he deserved to take something cold and soothing.

Ten minutes later, he was swigging from a perspiring beer bottle that was half-empty, its missing cold contents already down in his stomach.

As the RCIPF detective belched, Eugene smiled and passed him another sweaty bottle of beer. The policeman was then asked to expand on what he had said earlier in passing. What did he mean when he said that they should be on the lookout for suspicious characters? Were there dangerous criminals loose on Grand Cayman?

In between swigs of beer, the Jamaican explained that Interpol had indeed contacted the RCIPF and asked whether three fortyish-looking men on Nigerian passports had arrived on the island recently. The Joint Intelligence Unit of the RCIPF checked the entry records and found that no group of persons carrying such passports had entered any of the three islands that constitute the territory of The Cayman Islands. Smiling broadly, John asked the slightly inebriated detective if he had seen photographs of the wanted men.

'Yes, we received enlarged passport photos of the three men,' the detective replied flatly and swigged again from the bottle.

The swindlers were stunned. 'What did they look like?' Adamu asked, struggling to maintain his composure while John and Eugene watched the policeman carefully.

Warren shrugged. 'They looked normal; one was a light-skinned guy and the other two were dark-skinned. Nothing, you wouldn't find in any country that has a lot of black people. I looked at the photographs and thought these guys could well be from my country, Jamaica.'

Eugene was not satisfied by that vague answer. 'Did the suspects look like us?'

John glared at Eugene. Adamu was equally angry at Eugene's stupid question.

In response to Eugene's question, Warren gazed momentarily at the heavily bearded faces in front of him with mock seriousness and then laughed. 'I don't think so. You guys appear a bit older than those Nigerian suspects.'

John suppressed a sigh and sensed his men doing the same. Then, he passed another bottle to the detective who had just finished his second Budweiser.

'Well, I wish Interpol good luck at tracing those criminals,' Adamu said as he sipped from his beer glass.

Warren shook his head and began to talk again. The Red Alert Notice issued by Interpol doesn't seem to have led to the arrests of those fugitives anywhere in the world. In his own opinion, the Interpol had its hands full of cases, most of them more urgent than the search for the Nigerian scammers.

Adamu was relieved to hear the policeman boldly claim that Interpol would not waste limited resources on the search for the Nigerians. He passed the policeman a fourth bottle of cold Budweiser.

In the evening hours, when it was finally time to leave, the RCIPF detective was unable to stand on his own feet. He was in a state of drunken stupor.

Eugene and Adamu managed to get the detective to reveal his home address. Then, they propped him up by the arms and propelled him towards the front door.

Out in the driveway of the condominium, under the glare of moonlight, they threw the intoxicated policeman into the back seat of his own car. Adamu got behind the steering wheel, and moments later, the car was heading towards the detective's residence in the outskirts of George Town. Eugene followed in a rental car.

The detective's wife, a fat black woman, was not pleased to see her husband arriving back home almost comatose. Nevertheless, she thanked Adamu and Eugene as they laid Warren down on a sofa in the living room. And before the swindlers left together in the rental car, she implored them not tell anybody what had happened. Her husband could lose his job if his superiors in the RCIPF found out that he had been drinking...

*****

Eugene glanced at a German couple in bathing suits splashing about in the water, about five yards from where his feet were immersed, and then turned to John. 'You were going to tell us about your trip to London.'

John didn't respond. He kept his eyes on the bikinis playing beach ball. Adamu repeatedly scooped wet beach sand with his right hand and tossed it nonchalantly into the water. He only stopped when he noticed that the German couple had stopped splashing about and were now glaring at him. He smiled apologetically. After a few more seconds of glaring, the couple returned to where they had left off. Adamu sipped his coconut juice and learnt his voice of support to Eugene. 'Boss, we want to hear the story of your trip.'

John responded by springing to his feet. He dusted white grains of beach sand from his shorts and legs and donned his straw hat. 'Let's go to the condo. We have a lot to discuss,' he said quietly. Without waiting for the rest, he started jogging towards the second-hand Fiat Uno, he had purchased from a local tour guide. Adamu and Eugene exchanged a glance and sprang to their feet. The behaviour of their leader was becoming stranger by the day, they both thought as they walked towards the Italian-made hatchback.

392

Since both fraudsters arrived in the island, months earlier, they had witnessed their affable leader gradually withdraw into himself. He would pass at least half of each day just brooding. At first, his men couldn't understand why. But later they figured it out; the deaths of Tunde and Moses had hit the boss very hard. It was unbelievable to him that Tunde, his master planner, his genius, was no more. The surviving members, Adamu and Eugene, would talk several times to their grieving boss, trying to make him understand that it was time to move on. No amount of brooding will bring back the dead men. John seemed to have listened to them because, over the course of a few weeks, he slowly began to return to his old self. Although, as both subordinates noticed, the gang leader was never the same as before.

One day in mid-April, he announced to his astonished men that he was thinking of travelling to London to *"case a target"*—the same operational jargon used by the late Tunde to describe his study of the behaviour and activities of an individual marked down as a potential target of the gang's skulduggery.

Adamu's heart sank for he thought he had already succeeded in talking his boss out of such foolishness. As he had already done twice in the month of March, Adamu again reminded his boss that there was a warrant for their arrest in Nigeria and a Red Alert Notice from Interpol. In other words, John's chances of being apprehended if he set foot in the UK were very high, and so were his chances of extradition to Nigeria to stand trial. Agreeing with Adamu, Eugene urged his boss to reconsider. 'We have enough money here on the island, in Seychelles and in Switzerland. So why the unnecessary risk?' he wondered aloud.

The gang leader listened patiently. When Eugene and Adamu had had their say, he broke his silence, telling them calmly that he had made up his mind. Both men thought their boss was out of his mind, but they did not try to stop him. He left for Europe on 20th April 1994.

Ten days later, he returned to the Grand Cayman with extra luggage containing clothes he had bought for himself and his men in Oxford Street, London. His men were pleasantly surprised to have him back and anxious to know how his trip had gone. For the entire duration of his absence, they were afraid that he had been apprehended since he never bothered to communicate while he was overseas.

John smiled at his men, saying that he would reveal all at his own time. It had been a very long and tiring flight back to the Caribbean and so he needed some rest. Grateful for the new clothes and anxious to please, Adamu and Eugene didn't push. That day passed without John saying much about his journey to his men.

The following day, the morning of Sunday 1st May, John rose from bed, showered, and had breakfast with his men, still saying nothing to them about his overseas trip. At 12 noon, John looked out of the window of his bedroom and smiled at the sunny and warm weather. He met his subordinates in the sitting room and told them that he would like to go down to the beach in order to re-acclimatize himself to the tropical weather of the island. Adamu and Eugene did not particularly want to go out, but it was what the boss wanted. So they reluctantly tagged along. On their way to the beach, the gang leader promised to recount his London journey to them...

*****

At the bottom of the concrete driveway, John killed the engine of the Fiat Uno. He asked the others to stay behind and dashed into the condominium. His bemused lieutenants emerged from the car. Eugene looked askance at Adamu who shrugged. Three minutes later, they saw a smiling John trudging down the driveway towards them with three deck chairs between his hands. They rushed to relieve him of his heavy burden.

The three men, each carrying a deck chair, walked the thirty-two-yard distance between the bottom of the driveway and the beachfront. Adamu went back to the condo and came out with a small carton of canned beer. As soon as they settled into the comfy chairs facing the sheer vastness of the Caribbean Sea, John started narrating his interesting story...

It all started on the morning of 14th April. John was going through the local newspapers as usual, trying to see if there was any news article about a group of Nigerian fugitives hiding in the island. To his great relief, there was nothing of the sort in any of the four newspapers he had purchased. But he had stumbled on a mildly interesting news article while going through the arts section of *The Daily Caymanian*.

The news article was about the Christie's auction scheduled to take place on 25th April in South Kensington, London. A Pablo Picasso painting was up for sale and the auctioneers at Christie's were expecting to get £40 million or more for it.

John's interest on the subject matter evaporated halfway through the article. As he was preparing to skip to another page, his eyes caught the first sentence of an unread paragraph that caused him to change his mind. He relaxed and read on. The last three paragraphs of the news article was about an elderly British art collector and retired Royal Marines Officer— a Brigadier Maurice de Clovis— who had indicated interest in adding that painting to the private art gallery inside his mansion in the English countryside. *The Daily Caymanian* had predicted that Mr. de Clovis— a proud owner of several beachfront houses all over the Carribean— would offer more than £40 million to own that work of art...

Adamu interrupted John's narration. Something wasn't adding up for him. 'You say this Englishman is called Maurice de Clovis. Isn't that French?'

John smiled as if he expected the question. 'Yes, the name is French,' he replied smugly. For a fleeting moment, he felt himself channelling his deceased genius, Tunde Olukemi. Then he dived into ancient history. 'In the seventeenth century, a lot of French Protestants called *Huguenots* fled Catholic France to avoid persecution and death. Many of them fled to the safety of Protestant England.' John paused to let the information sink in. It was obvious that he was enjoying his new role as an eminent historian.

'So our man, de Clovis, is of that stock,' Eugene deduced.

'Yes, you are right. Just like Adamu, I was confused about the whole thing. An Englishman with a French surname did not make any sense to me. So I went to a public library in West London, posing as university student doing doctorate research, and read a couple of archived news articles about our man. An old magazine from 1986 contained an interview featuring Brigadier de Clovis. In it, the retired one-star general spoke about his French ancestors, the Calvinist preacher and his family, who managed to escape massacre in Paris and flee France. It was the first time I have heard of the *Huguenots*. So I broke away from the magazine and went to the library's reference section to learn more about these people, the *Huguenots*. It was an interesting read...the sort of thing that would have fascinated Tunde...' John's voice trailed off.

There was a moment of silence, and then Adamu said, 'we all miss him and Moses. I'm not a religious man, but wherever his spirit is, I'm sure it is at peace.'

In between gulps of canned beer, Eugene nodded his agreement with Adamu. It was now evening and the sun had begun its retreat. A cool breeze wafted towards them from the calm open sea. Adamu glanced at his Rolex watch. The time was 5.45 PM.

John smiled ruefully and resumed his narration. 'After spending forty-five minutes in the reference section with the encyclopaedia, I returned to the archive section to resume my reading of the old magazine. It turns out that in the year eighteen-seventy-five, another ancestor, Maurice's grandfather, Lawrence, migrated from England to Southern Africa as a seventeen-year-old. It was there, in the British Cape Colony, that Hugo de Clovis was born in nineteen-hundred. Lawrence, his wife and eight-year-old Hugo moved further north to Rhodesia. Hugo's own son, Maurice, was born in Rhodesia seventy-one years ago. Maurice grew up there, joined the Royal Marines, fought in World War Two, and retired eleven years ago to run his father's lucrative book publishing company from Southeast England.'

But John had not narrated the sequence of events linearly as they happened after he boarded the Airbus A321 jetliner at Grand Cayman's Owen Roberts International Airport in the early hours of 20th April. He had skipped six days worth of events in favour of talking up his work in the public library. He had done so because he wanted to prove to his skeptical subordinates that he was as good as Tunde when it came to researching the life history of a potential target. Once he was satisfied that his men were impressed by his research skills, the narrative jumped back in time to very beginning, starting with the series of events that preceded his visit to the public library in West London.

Adamu and Eugene leaned forward to listen to the captivating story...

*****

John had flown from The Cayman Islands to France on a passport that declared him Marcellus Severo Obiango, a native of the port city of Bata in Equatorial

Guinea. At a counter in the passport control area of *Aéroport de Paris-Charles-de-Gaulle*, an unsmiling, auburn-haired young man wearing the light blue shirt of the French Border Police took the passport and began to scrutinize it with his steel blue eyes.

John was slightly worried, but maintained his composure. Two minutes later, the steel blue eyes shifted from the passport to his face. John was asked a couple of questions and he answered them succinctly.

'Mister Obiango, what do you do for a living?'

'I am businessman.'

'What sort of business?'

'I import electrical appliances from Europe and Japan and sell them in Central and West Africa.'

'I see you have a multiple-entry short-stay visa. Are you staying for the entire permitted duration?'

'No. I intend to spend three nights here; that is April-twenty to April-twenty-three.'

'Is that not too short?'

'Well, I'll be visiting UK for a week. So the holiday trip is not that short. Besides, I will be back here for another visit, soon.'

The Frenchman in the glass-fronted booth smiled thinly, stamped the passport, and handed it back. After passing through a network of escalators, John finally got into the baggage reclaim hall where he waited for the spinning carousel to bring out his fibre suitcase. It was another fifteen minutes before he spotted and lifted his suitcase from the baggage carousel. He pulled on the bag's telescopic handle in order to extend it. Moments later, he began to wheel the bag towards the arrivals concourse where he intended to swap his Caymanian dollars for French Francs at the currency exchange booth.

Outside the airport building, with French banknotes in his pockets, he walked up to the taxi rank and soon he was on his way to Paris. By 10.00 PM, he was in his pre-booked bedroom in the three-star *Hôtel Bastille Bleu*, where he kicked off his shoes, peeled off his clothes and went to bed.

The next day, 21st April, he went on a tour of the city. Using his hotel's in-house tourist magazine as a guide, he visited the Eiffel Tower, Notre-Dame Cathedral, Louvre Museum, *Arc de Triomphe*, and *Avenue des Champs-Élysées* where he stopped to do some shopping. At nightfall, he enjoyed an expensive dinner in the waterfront terrace of a restaurant overlooking the Seine River.

When he woke up in his hotel room in the early morning of the 22nd April, he was in the best mood to get down to work. He took a quick shower and walked to a nearby shop, and bought a printing set. Back in his hotel room, he began to fabricate the ID card that will give him access to the gallery in one of Christe's busiest sales room in South Kensingston, London.

In the afternoon of 24th April, John flew into Gatwick Airport using his forged passport. Again, with bated breath, he waited as the UK immigration official at a passport control booth examined his travel documents. And again, he was relieved when the female official told him that his legally obtained visa was in order before stamping the false passport and handing it over.

Outside the South Terminal's arrivals hall, he stopped to pick up some pound sterling at the foreign exchange kiosk and then proceeded to the exit. He walked out of the terminal and entered the adjoining platform of the airport railway station. Five minutes later, he was on the Gatwick Express Train to London Victoria Station. At London Victoria Station, John disembarked, walked past the concourse and into the escalator moving underground. Several feet below ground level, he entered the Victoria line tube train, which whisked him to Green Park Station. There, he switched to another tube train, the Piccadilly line, and soon he was at South Kensington Station. Getting off the train, he ascended the escalators and a series of concrete steps to reach the street level part of the train station where the exit turnstiles were located.

Once he was outside the train station, it took him five minutes to get to the five-star hotel where he had a pre-booked room. It was quite expensive, but totally worth it in his mind. The five-storey terrace building on Old Brompton Road, whose picture he had first seen in *The Daily Caymanian*, was within walking distance of his hotel. Only a distance of 142 yards separated him from that building's busy ground floor where Christie's held 210 auctions yearly— putting on sale over 60,000 items— and produced an annual turnover of over £80 million.

By 8.45 AM, the following day, John dressed himself in a navy-blue two-piece suit and left his hotel for the venue of the auction. Upon reaching the terrace building, he stopped at the entrance of the ground floor sales room and proffered his homemade, but professional-looking ID card to the elderly doorman in a black overcoat.

The doorman scrutinized the print below the card's plastic laminate. It indicated that the bearer was an art journalist with a London-based Nigerian magazine, which he had never heard of. From the bold print, his gray eyes shifted to the small photograph on the right corner of the card, and then to the heavily bearded caramel-skinned face smiling at him. 'Mister...eh...Obiangow...you may proceed. Please, follow the signs for the press gallery,' he said, waving John through.

The auction began ten minutes after the con artist settled in the gallery alongside genuine journalists. But before that, he had pinned his fake press ID card to the breast pocket of his suit jacket after realizing that—unlike actual news reporters present— he had neglected to get himself a lanyard to tether his false credentials.

The auctioneer entered the sales room, mounted the rostrum, and introduced himself as Jeremy Wogan. The covered painting displayed next to the rostrum was unveiled. Jeremy spoke a bit about the painting to the people sitting in rows before him. Then he struck the gavel on a block. The bidding war had started.

From the gallery upstairs, John looked down on the rows of seated bidders. He counted twelve men and eight women. He estimated their average age to be sixty years. His eyes searched around for his potential victim and found him in less than two minutes. Maurice was sitting calmly in the middle row, surrounded by the frenzy of excited bidders bellowing out eight-digit sums of money. The retired Marine officer was silent, waiting patiently for the right moment to offer a price that no other bidder could match.

'Painting going for twenty million... Going, going...' Jeremy, the auctioneer, was interrupted by a woman sitting in front, close to the podium. She was offering £30 million for the painting.

'Baroness Mindsay is offering thirty million. Going, going...thirty million, going, going...'

'Thirty-five million pounds!' one old man cried.

'Thirty-five million from Mister Goodman... thirty-five million, going, going, going...'

Another woman wearing a big hat stood up and offered £40 million for the Picasso.

By this time, the press gallery, filled with excited reporters, was becoming noisy. Among the chattering journalists, the focus of attention and hot debate was on the retired Royal Marine officer who had not spoken yet. The argument was not over whether or not the old Brigadier would take the Picasso painting home. The bone of contention was how much the art collector would have to pay for it.

The noise eventually drew the intervention of the security team. The journalists were politely told to be quiet or be escorted out of the room. The rowdy gallery quietened down. Throughout the heated argument, John had observed in silence and when it was over, he turned his full attention back to the auctioneer downstairs.

Jeremy Wogan smiled. 'Forty-five million from Lord Bennet of Grimsby; forty-five million, going, going, going...'

'I'll offer fifty million,' a loud male voice cut in.

Everyone turned to the voice and it turned out to be Maurice de Clovis, the man of the moment. Jeremy wanted to laugh with joy, but didn't. Things were going well as expected. He was now hoping someone else would try to out-bid the retired military officer. Selling the painting for more than £50 million pounds wouldn't be a bad idea, he thought as he slammed his gavel on the block several times to squelch the noise coming from the reporters upstairs. The argument in the press gallery had not moved on from the ultimate sum the retired Brigadier would pay to have the expensive work of art.

'Fifty milion from Brigadier de Clovis... fifty million, going, going, going...'

A frail eighty-year old man raised his hand hesitantly and offered £55 million pounds.

An elated Jeremy cried, 'fifty-five million from Lord Winters...going, going...'

Maurice jumped to his feet. 'I'll offer sixty million for the painting,' the retired military man announced and turned to grin at Lord Nigel Winters of Cockfilgate

Jeremy's smile broadened. 'Sixty million, going, going, going, going...gone! The Picasso painting is hereby sold to retired Brigadier Maurice de Clovis.'

With this announcement, Jeremy Wogan banged the gavel on the wooden block. The painting was taken away from its display easel to be wrapped for its new owner as the failed bidders rose from their seats to depart.

As John descended the stairs and reached the auction floor, he could sense the feeling of defeat among the old people slowly exiting the sales room. He noticed that feeling particularly in Lord Winters who seemed to be taking the Brigadier's possession of the Picasso badly. The conman watched the aristocrat's face turn crimson as he glared at the Brigadier from the doorway of the sales room. The amused Brigadier winked at him. The Lord mumbled something to himself and disappeared along with his walking stick into the cold afternoon.

John came downstairs and shook hands with the new owner of a coveted painting. The retired Royal Marines officer seemed puzzled at the bearded black man shaking his hand. 'And who might you be, sir?' he asked with a wide smile.

John introduced himself as Marcellus Severo Obiango, a journalist with the *Nigerian Prime Observer Magazine.*

Maurice frowned, 'Never heard of the magazine. Where in Nigeria are you from?'

John shook his head. 'I work for a Nigerian publication, but I am from Equatorial Guinea.'

The Brigadier looked confused.

'Equatorial Guinea shares a border with Cameroon,' the conman added helpfully.

The art collector's smile returned. He had heard of Cameroon. 'Seems like you are the only coloured chap around here,' the old man remarked, his smile unfaltering.

John laughed and politely reminded the old man about the black security men standing next to the elderly doorman at the entrance.

'No, they don't count,' the Brigadier countered.

A petite brunette entered the room carrying a large flat object wrapped in brown paper that seemed too big for her. 'Here is your Picasso, sir,' she said holding it out to the Brigadier.

Maurice gripped the rectangular-shaped object with strong hands unaffected by arthritis. 'Thank you my dear,' he said with his upper-class English accent and then offered her a bank cheque that he had already completed.

The lady accepted the cheque, scrutinized it for a few seconds, and then she smiled. 'Thank you,' she said and walked away.

Turning back to John, the retired Brigadier said, 'okay, Mister Obiango, time for me to go and play with my hard-won painting. It was a pleasure to meet you.' Then he turned and walked away.

The next day, 26th April, John went to the Borough of Kensington & Chelsea Public Library to research the background of his intended target. He went through several newspapers and magazines, both old and new. The old papers were awash with information on the Brigadier's military career. The highest amount of newspaper and magazine articles on the retired Marine officer were focussed on the year 1982. That year, Maurice oversaw the amphibious landing of a Royal Marine contingent on the Falkland Islands to retake it from Argentine occupation forces.

Publications that were more recent focussed on his post-military life as an entrepreneur and art collector. One particular magazine, *The Spectator*, featured a 1986 interview in which the retired one-star general traced his family lineage from France to Britain to Zimbabwe and back.

John combined the library information with his own thoughts about the old man's behaviour during and after the auction, and used them to prepare a dossier.

For the next five days, John went sightseeing. He travelled up and down UK, visiting places he had never been to before in Wales, Northern England and Scotland...

*****

Ten cans of beer lay scattered on the sandy beach by the time John concluded his story. The reddish sun was on the horizon, half of it clearly visible above the glittering surface of the Caribbean Sea.

'Another beautiful day going,' Adamu remarked as he passed the last can of beer to Eugene.

John glanced at the dial of his watch. 'It will soon be dark. Let's go inside,' he said and rose, prompting his men to do the same.

'Wait a moment,' Eugene said before draining the beer can of its contents in a series of audible gulps.

'I hope you guys are sober enough to read my dossier on the Brigadier,' John remarked as they strode back towards the driveway of their condominium.

'Six cans of beer is nothing. I'm sober,' Eugene boasted as he adjusted his grip on the folded deck chair between his hands.

A minute-and-half later, the swindlers were back inside their ground floor apartment. Eugene and Adamu stacked the folded deck chairs against a wall in the corner of the sitting room while John disappeared through a side door. When he returned, both men were already on a long sofa waiting expectantly for him. He handed each man a manilla folder, which contained identical handwritten notes, British newspaper clippings and colour photographs of Maurice cut from a Caymanian magazine. As the men flipped open their folders, John sat on the wooden coffee table facing the sofa and waited patiently for them to finish reading.

It took eight minutes for Adamu and Eugene to digest everything in the dossiers handed to them. Adamu was the first to voice his misgivings. 'Boss, Tunde would never have approved this target.'

John stiffened, but said nothing.

Adamu continued. 'You stated in the dossier that this target, the Englishman, Clovis, was likely to be a bigot. That alone is already a huge impediment to our

400

ability to build rapport with him. Without rapport, we cannot get him to trust us. Without trust, we won't be able to persuade him to part with his money.'

Eugene nodded along to what Adamu was saying as if he was listening to music. He also voiced his concurrence. 'Boss, everything Adamu said is correct. Tunde always stressed the importance of going after desperate people; wealthy people who made bad business decisions and are feeling some financial pressure; the sort of people gullible enough to fall for our "get-rich-quick" schemes. From the story you have told us, and from what is inside this dossier, the old soldier, Clovis, does not fit the description of a desperate man at all. Boss, I have a bad feeling about this one. I think we should let it go.'

John was irritated by what he was hearing. He dismissed his men's misgivings with a wave of the hand. 'Tunde is dead. Please stop mentioning what he would or would not have done. I know what I am doing...'

'Boss, we are not questioning your wisdom,' Adamu cut in. 'We just think that this particular target is the wrong one. We should not waste our money and time on this man, Clovis. Besides, it is risky to be travelling to Europe when there is a Red Alert Notice for us, notwithstanding our altered facial appearance.'

'Well, you said it. Our hirsute faces have successfully kept us hidden in plain sight,' John replied quietly as he collected the two identical dossiers from the men. He placed them next to where he was sitting on the coffee table. His voice suddenly rose. And with an air of confidence, he said, 'We are going to offer the Brigadier an attractive deal, one that he won't refuse. All men are greedy. Maurice de Clovis is no different. We are going to bilk him just as we have done to the other targets. There is nothing to worry about, my good friends.'

Adamu and Eugene swallowed hard. They disagreed, but they knew their boss. Once his mind was made up, nothing could be done to change it. They would have to go along with his scheme and hope that this *final operation* would be as successful as the previous ones. They took solace in the fact that John had never failed to bilk a target before, and the fact that he had been able to pass through France and UK without being flagged as a person listed for extradition by Interpol.

'Okay, fill us in on the details of the operation, boss,' Eugene requested.

John was happy to oblige. He gave them a stage-by-stage account of how the swindle operation would unfold. 'By the time the old man realises what has hit him, a bunch of "darkies" will be holding at least five hundred grand of his money in their hands. Oh yes, I think he is prejudiced, but we can use that to our own advantage.'

Adamu was skeptical, but wanted his boss to elaborate.

'Maurice de Clovis looks like one of those guys who hold the stereotype that Africans are not bright enough to trick the white man. I think we can harness that. We will send him an introductory letter about our proposed deal. It is going to be written in such a way as to create the desired impression. He buys into our deal, thinking that we are not mentally capable, not intelligent enough to trick him...'

Adamu and Eugene were completely lost. They were not catching on to what their leader was saying.

John raised his arms in frustration. 'C'mon guys. It's all psychology. We sell him a scheme that will make him feel like he is in the driver's seat; allow him to wallow in the firm belief that the white man cannot be fooled by blacks. Before the complacent fool realizes what is truly happening, we will be long gone with his cash.'

The men nodded slowly. A vague picture of John's scheme had taken form in their minds, but they were still not sure how it could be implemented to gain the desired result.

'Gee, boss, it sounds good,' Eugene remarked. 'How can that be done?'

John stared at him momentarily and said, 'first, we write a letter with a couple of grammatical errors proposing a great deal. The letter would be carefully crafted to give him the impression that the deal on offer is lucrative and that the people he is dealing with are not very sophisticated. We would appear to be poorly educated.'

Adamu was not impressed at all. A sense of foreboding washed over him. But he had no wish to annoy the boss any further by raising concerns. So he joined Eugene in agreeing that the scheme would succeed in all its objectives.

'Good, very good,' John said in response to Adamu's grudging endorsement. 'I am glad that both of you are now onboard, in principle, with the plan, which I admit, is still a work in progress. While I flesh out the plan, you two will have to apply for British and French visas. I recommend you guys do it tomorrow as the application process may take a couple of weeks to conclude. We must be ready to action by the middle of next month.'

CHAPTER **41**

JUNE 1994

IPSWICH, SUFFOLK COUNTY, UK

The grandfather clock in a corner of the sitting room chimed at 12 midnight to herald the arrival of 10th June 1994. The sound of the clock's chime bounced around the mansion and finally woke Maurice de Clovis up from the restless sleep he had been struggling with for the past six hours.

The retired Marine officer sat up in bed, leaned towards the bedside lamp and thumbed on a switch, illuminating the room. His weary eyes shifted from the bedside lamp to the nightstand on which it was resting. He gripped a knob on the side of the nightstand and pulled out a small drawer, revealing a white plastic medicine bottle lying inside it. He gazed at the small bottle and then shut the drawer. 'No, I won't do it,' he said to himself, recalling his doctor's instruction to take one pill each night in order to have a good night's rest. He was not opposed to taking medicines per se. Indeed, he had taken many in the past—for headaches, for infections, for stomach aches, to reduce cold and flu symptoms. But he had never taken medicine for restless nights in bed and was reluctant to do so, even on the recommendation of a doctor that he generally trusted. As far as he was concerned, he did not have a medical problem. He had a crime problem, one that swirled around his subconscious mind at night, tormenting him whenever he tried to catch some sleep in his soft double bed.

The retired Brigadier blamed his one-month-old problem on a particular incident that occurred on the night of April Fools' Day. That night he was sound asleep when a loud noise downstairs awoke him. He had gone downstairs to investigate and found himself face to face with the scoundrel who had broken into his mansion. At knifepoint, the burglar asked him to hand over "madam's jewellery". The house owner calmly explained that he was a widower. There was no "madam's jewellery" as he had sold them off after his wife's death half a decade earlier. Keeping them around was such a painful reminder.

The burglar, a young man in his early twenties, had laughed in disbelief before stepping closer to prod the Brigadier's chest with the tip of his flick knife. 'I don't have time for jokes, old man. Just hand over the jewellery,' he hissed.

At that point, an enraged Maurice snapped and began to move quickly. He knocked the knife out of the intruder's hand and rammed both fists into the burglar's belly before delivering a flying kick. Before the stunned burglar could fully comprehend what was happening, he felt himself reeling and then crashing into a bookcase in a corner of the study room. Just before he blacked out, he saw the old man's shoe moving rapidly towards his head to deliver another kick. When he regained consciousness fifteen minutes later, he realised that his aching head was bruised, and the bones of his left hand and ribcage were broken. He screamed in pain, but Maurice de Clovis, gun in hand, asked him to be silent.

'I know I am all wrinkled now,' the ex-military man told the whimpering criminal, 'but that is no excuse to break into my castle.' To the relief of both the old man and the terrified burglar, the local police intervened shortly.

And ever since that day, the old man had trouble sleeping at night. This trouble was aggravated by widespread reports in the media that his house had a private gallery where he stored expensive art collections. Any of them would fetch a hefty price for any burglar brave enough to mount a home invasion. To safeguard his house, the Brigadier had spent a fortune on closed circuit television (CCTV) cameras, robust locks and tripwire alarms. Yet his mind remained troubled, would not let him sleep. His doctor had prescribed some sleeping pills, which the old man had reluctantly accepted, but had never consumed.

After the chiming clock woke Maurice at midnight, on 10th June, he rose from his bed and did what he had always done whenever he was woken up prematurely. He struggled into his night robe, picked up a bunch of keys from the nightstand and went down the stairs to the basement. There, he unlocked a door, stepped inside a dark underground room, which served as his private art gallery, and switched on the lights. Under the lens of three CCTV cameras pointing downwards from different corners of the ceiling, he walked across the room to the wall where his prized possessions were hanging. On that wall was his most recent acquisition, the Pablo Picasso. Hanging next to it were several paintings, including the Da Vinci painting he had purchased at an auction in Paris, three years earlier.

They are safe, thank God, he thought. With a smile on his face, he reached out to touch the gilded baroque frame of the Picasso painting. His fingertips were only inches away from the frame when he suddenly froze and sighed. He had almost forgotten that the paintings were hanging on cleverly disguised tripwires designed to trigger a concealed burglar alarm system if touched by an individual who had no business being in the underground art gallery. Alternatively, it could be triggered by a gallery owner who had forgotten to deactivate the alarm system before handling his paintings.

With a frown on his face, Maurice walked back across the room and stopped in front of a white rectangular box mounted on the wall next to the light switch. He gazed at the front panel of the box, which contained an array of green, red and blue LED lights; five rectangular buttons in a row; and a circle pin tumbler lock.

From the bunch of keys in his hand, the Brigadier selected a tubular key and slotted it into the lock. When he turned the key inside the lock, the green and red LED lamps went off, leaving the blue LED—the standby pilot lamp—as the only one still switched on. With the alarm finally deactivated, Maurice quickly walked across the room to spend some quality time with his art collection.

By 4.30 AM, Maurice, carrying a cup of hot tea, went outdoors to sit on a deck chair on the patio overlooking the large swatches of farmland that belonged to him. He had purchased it, along with the mansion, shortly after his retirement from military service.

Sunrise came at 4.47 AM and with it came the chirping of birds on treetops and crowing of roosters. The old man smiled when he saw a group of rabbits running across the farmland and frowned when he spotted a fox behind them. The fox stopped when it saw the frowning Brigadier. It studied the old man for a few seconds, then turned around and dashed off in the opposite direction. Maurice grinned and shook his head.

At 7.30 AM, he placed the now empty teacup gently on a side stool next to the deck chair. Five minutes later, he began to feel sleepy. He was about to drift off when he caught a glimmer of a figure in navy-blue suit and black peaked cap approaching from the far end of the farmland. His eyes widened as he sat up. It took him a moment to identify which postman was approaching the wooden gates positioned in the centre of the barbed wire perimeter fence surrounding his vast rural estate.

'Morning, Joe!' he called out, leaning forward on his chair. 'You got something for me?'

Joseph Cliveden, the postman, nodded and opened the wooden gates. 'I have a letter for you, sir,' the young man said as he crossed vast tracts of farmland on his way to the patio.

'Good, let me see,' Maurice said and put on his spectacles. In silence, he watched Joseph place the red mail bag on the floor of the patio and stooped over it for a rummage.

After a few seconds of fumbling inside the bag of envelopes and parcels, the postman found the white envelope addressed to "Brigadier M. de Clovis (rtd)" and proferred it to the old man.

The old man studied the envelope in his right hand closely and remarked, 'postmarked Paris.'

Joseph zipped up the red mailbag and sprang to his feet. He was slinging the bag over his shoulder when he heard the old man mumble something about not knowing anybody in Paris. 'Eh, it could be from an old military pal living or holidaying in France,' Joseph speculated.

'Doubt it,' the old man frowned as he reached for a letter opener on the stool next to the teacup.

Joe stood there watching as Maurice slit the envelope. He was curious to see who the letter was from. The Brigadier dipped his fingers inside the envelope, and then froze. He gazed enquiringly at the postman. Joe got the message instantly. The old man wanted privacy. He quickly said his goodbyes and scurried towards the gates.

The one-star general waited patiently for Joe to walk through the wooden gates and disappear from view before lifting the fingers clamping the folded letter from the envelope. He unfolded it quickly and started reading. Halfway through the body of the letter, he began to frown. The handwritten note was littered with grammatical errors.

The author of the letter began by praising the old man for his distinguished military career and his astute business skills as the director of a top publishing firm. In the second paragraph, the author introduced himself as Alhaji Tariq Gudana, personal assistant to Nigeria's Petroleum Minister.

Maurice de Clovis, the author claimed, was "destined to multiply his wealth" if he agreed to participate in a peculiar scheme devised by the Petroleum Minister. The Brigadier need not take on any "pro-active" role in the scheme. In fact, his role in the scheme would be "passively simple". All the old man had to do was agree to the gradual transfer of £250 million currently hidden in several Nigerian banks into his personal bank account in the UK. After nine months, seventy percent of the money would be moved to a Swisss bank to be nominated by the minister. The Brigadier would get to keep thirty percent—£75 million— for his troubles. The author declared the deal "a-once-in-a-lifetime" opportunity to make big money. Tariq Gudana concluded the letter by promising to reveal more details of the scheme in the coming weeks.

Maurice crumpled the letter in disgust and threw it on the grass before him. The nig-nog couldn't write good English to save his life, the old man thought. *Imagine the bloody cheek of that munt?*

But his disgust and anger had far more to do with the presumed physical features of the individual who wrote the letter. He would never entertain the idea of doing a business deal with a *munt* even if such an individual were fluent in English. Not after what those *munts* did to his brother and mother...

*****

Maurice de Clovis was born on 3rd January 1923 in the Rhodesian capital city of Salisbury to Sir and Lady Hugo de Clovis. His grandfather, Lawrence was the first member of the de Clovis family to settle on the African continent. As a plucky seventeen-year-old, Lawrence had emigrated alone from London to the Cape Colony in 1875. There wasn't much in the way of decent jobs going for someone like him so he joined the Cape Colonial Forces (CCF) commanded by British officers. Within the CCF, he learnt about the ghastly Dutch-Afrikaners, the ones who called themselves *Boers*, the ones who had fled Cape Colony after the British colonial regime violated their cherished tradition of *Baaskap* by abolishing slavery, freeing their 35,000 slaves in the process; by granting equal rights to the black African population of Cape Colony; and imposing English as the official language of the colony.

Through no fault of theirs, the Dutch-Afrikaner settlers had become British colonial subjects in 1814 after the British Empire formally annexed the Cape Colony it had earlier seized from The Netherlands. The Dutch settlers had resisted the sweeping social changes that the British were introducing. At first, they tried open revolt, but that was brutally put down by the British. Thereafter, they decided that their lot would improve if they could simply relocate to a territory beyond the boundaries of the British colonial enterprise. So they embarked on a six-month trek from the coast to the hinterlands of Southern Africa.

After finding fertile land and fighting off the local black Africans, the Dutch-Afrikaners founded two independent states—Republic of the Transvaal and Orange Free State—located over 400 miles from Cape Colony. The Boers thought they had outrun the British, but how wrong they were. The highly fluid boundaries of the British colonial regime did not stay restricted to areas around the Atlantic coast. Those boundaries moved slowly inland, in a northerly direction, and within a few years, they were abutting the independent Dutch-Afrikaner states.

Lawrence de Clovis was not really keen to fight the Boers as one-sixth of them were of French *Huguenot* ancestry, and he was sympathetic to their cause to build a life independent of British interference. Nevertheless, when the Boers declared war in December 1880 by firing on British colonial troops, Lawrence was ready to do his duty for Queen and Country. He would go on to fight both First and Second Boer Wars, which ultimately wiped out the Dutch-Afrikaner states, paving the way for their territories and citizenry to be absorbed into the now rapidly expanding British colony of South Africa.

After thirty-three years in the CCF, Lawrence had had enough of military life and applied for voluntary retirement in January 1908. Shortly after, he left South Africa for Southern Rhodesia with his Scottish wife and eight-year-old son, Hugo. He would go on to run a successful tobacco farm in the rural outskirts of the Rhodesian city named after Lord Salisbury, the British Prime Minister from 1885 to 1902.

The huge swathes of land on which Lawrence and other white British settlers had made their wealth had been expropriated from the native African population from the nineteenth century onwards. And so, there was always an ever-present unease about the ability to keep control of these possessions in the face of a deeply felt resentment from the bereft natives.

By the 1920s, the prosperous settler-colonists had begun to pay more attention to their minority status in the demographics of their tropical paradise. They started lobbying the British Colonial Office in London to merge their South Rhodesian colony with North Rhodesia and Nyasaland. The reasoning behind the campaign was quite simple— the combined population of the three colonies improved the size of the white population and the merger offered South Rhodesians access to the rich copper mines of Northern Rhodesia.

Sensitive to vehement black African opposition, the British Colonial Office rejected the colonists' request. Nevertheless, the tobacco farmers and industrialists in South Rhodesia continued promoting their cause. In the early 1930s, the promoters— known locally as the "cowboys"— appointed the septuagenarian Lawrence their leader. Buoyed by the steady flow of British immigrants into the colony, "the cowboys" intensified their lobbying of the Colonial Office for a merger of the three colonies. And again, in deference to African nationalists, the Colonial Office refused.

In 1940, Hugo took over as the leader of the cowboys following the death of his 82-year-old father. Under his leadership, "the cowboys" made progress in their quest. Post-war changes in the colony of South Rhodesia had brought about an increase in industrialisation and more British settlers. These developments helped Sir Hugo de Clovis argue that the amalgamation of the three colonies made economic sense. It would achieve larger markets and draw cheap African labour from Nyasaland. This time the Colonial Office agreed with "the cowboys" much to the chagrin of the African nationalists.

In 1953, the white settler-controlled South Rhodesia merged with North Rhodesia and Nyasaland to form the Central African Federation of Rhodesia and Nyasaland (CAFRN). The Africans violently resisted the creation of the super-colony in which they had token representation. In 1959, the federal government of CAFRN jailed many African nationalists and broke up demonstrations, but that did not quell the social unrest. The following year, it became clear to the British government that it would have to consider independence for the component units of the Federation at some point in the future.

In early 1963, the Colonial Office informed the irate Prime Minister of CAFRN, Sir Roy Welensky, that it was granting North Rhodesia and Nyasaland the right to secede from the Federation. Amidst howls of betrayal from the South Rhodesian settlers, the ten-year-old CAFRN dissolved in December 1963. Nyasaland and North Rhodesia gained independence in 1964 under the new names Malawi and Zambia respectively.

Hugo's "cowboys" were alarmed by British government's willingness to grant independence to its colonies, its willingness to turn over political power to the black African leaders in these former colonies over the strident objections of the white minority population. The idea of having to live in an independent South Rhodesia ruled by the black African majority horrified Hugo and his men as much as it did other white settlers. To forestall that, the cowboys bankrolled the hardline Rhodesia Front— the political party that had been administering the self-governing colony since 1962.

In 1965, the Rhodesian Front Prime Minister Ian Smith, declared the colony of South Rhodesia an independent state. The British government in London was appalled, but decided to confine its response to imposing sanctions on the rebel colony.

By 1970, a bitter war was raging between the African nationalist guerrillas and the Rhodesian Security Forces. Every able-bodied white man in Rhodesia was called up for military service. The war reached a military stalemate in the mid-seventies, during which both sides made out time to target the civilian population. Meanwhile, the trickle of whites fleeing the war in the unrecognized Rhodesian state turned into a flood.

In August 1976, Major Maurice de Clovis of the Royal Marines received a telegram from Southern Africa. It was from his father, Hugo. The telegram, which had arrived at Stonehouse Barracks in Southwest England, was bearing some bad news. Maurice's elder brother, Henri, a Colonel in the Rhodesian Light Infantry, had died in an ambush. According to Hugo, the commando unit was on its way to raid an alleged guerilla hideout in a forested area near the Zambian border when Joshua Nkomo's ZIPRA guerrillas suddenly emerged from a dense screen of shrubs. The Rhodesians made a doomed attempt to shoot their way out, but were slaughtered. Some of the Rhodesian soldiers died where they stood while others were thrown into the Zambezi River by the impact of the bullets and exploding grenades.

Although, his family would never know it, Colonel Henri de Clovis had survived the ambush, escaping by diving into the dense thickets. But two days inside the deep forest, bleeding from bullet wounds to the belly, with no medical help available, he died. His father organised a search party, but the body was never found. Three days later, his mother suffered a fatal stroke.

The news of both deaths devastated Maurice. He had not seen his brother, mother and father in over two years. Unlike the rest of his family, Maurice had decided as far back as 1940 that life as a farmer in the colony of South Rhodesia was not for him. He had joined the British Army in 1941, had fought in the North African and South European theatres of the Second World War. At the end of the war, he had returned briefly to South Rhodesia before moving to the UK where he resumed his military career, but this time, in the Corps of the Royal Marines.

His last visit to the unrecognized Republic of Rhodesia had been in November 1973 to visit his parents whom he tried and failed to convince to sell up and move to the UK. Maurice was no supporter of civil rights for Africans, but he could see the handwriting on the wall. With blacks outnumbering whites by a ratio of 22-to-1, the Royal Marines officer was convinced that Ian Smith's ramshackle republic had no chance of survival in the long term. His parents and brother had expressed their strong disagreements when he shared his views with them. Dismayed, he had returned to UK to face his military career and hope for the best. That was until the devastating telegram arrived at his barracks located near the port city of Plymouth.

By 1978, the shrinking population of white settlers, international ostracism, economic sanctions, and the financial costs of fighting the seemingly endless war had helped convince Ian Smith that the survival and recognition of his republic was now dependent on reaching an accomodation with the black African majority. In June 1979, Ian Smith stepped aside and allowed a proxy government to run his state, which had been renamed Zimbabwe-Rhodesia. The ceremonial President and the executive Prime Minister of Zimbabwe-Rhodesia were both black, but that did not pacify the African nationalist guerrillas. So the war continued until December 1979 when the Zimbabwe-Rhodesian authorities agreed to allow their territory to revert to its previous status as the British colony of South Rhodesia.

Once the territory was back under British colonial rule, a peacekeeping mission was deployed in preparation for the democratic elections that would precede an internationally recognized independence. Paradoxically, Major Maurice de Clovis was part of the peacekeeping mission sent to deal with the same African guerrillas that killed his brother and, in his opinion, caused his mother's death by stroke.

Following the democratic elections of 1980, South Rhodesia became the internationally recognized Republic of Zimbabwe, and many white settlers began to leave the black-ruled country for apartheid South Africa, Australia or the United Kingdom.

Before he relocated permanently to the UK, Hugo de Clovis wound down the family tobacco business and handed over his factories and farmland to the new Zimbabwean government. In accordance with the Lancaster House Agreement, he was paid compensation. With part of the compensation, Hugo purchased a bankrupt publishing firm in London and turned it into a viable enterprise.

After the Zimbabwe peacekeeping mission, Maurice did two separate stints as a military attaché in two British High Commissions—India and Malaysia—before returning to the UK to assume command of a Marine commando unit.

As a Royal Marines colonel, he participated in the Falklands War of June 1982. For bravery and saving the lives of his men, he was awarded a medal and promoted to Brigadier. Five months later, upon reaching the age of fifty-nine, he retired from military service and settled down with his wife in the vast country estate he had purchased in Ipswich.

When Hugo died in 1983, the day-to-day running of Clovis & Sons Publishing fell to Maurice and his wife. The art collecting came much later...

*****

Maurice picked up the letter he had dropped on the grass in front of the patio and read it again, shaking his head slowly as he did. These buffoons take me for a fool, he thought as his mind suddenly flashed back to a news article he had read recently in his favourite broadsheet newspaper, *The Daily Telegraph*. The article had described an elaborate scam sprung on a Jewish man from Northwest London by a gang of Nigerian fraudsters posing as South African lawyers. The fugitive fraudsters were currently sort by Interpol for the death of one American and the disappearance of another.

A mild chill of apprehension washed over the old man as he began to connect some dots. The scam described in the newspaper was not identical to the contents of the letter from Paris, which he had just read, but there were eerie similarities. The letter contains fantastic promises just like the scam described in the newspaper. The Nigerian scammers who defrauded the Jewish chap pretended to be South African lawyers. An individual claiming to be an agent of a Nigerian federal official wrote the letter from Paris...

At that point, the retired military officer knew what he had to do. He folded the letter, slotted it back into its envelope and trousered it. He picked up the teacup on the side stool and rose from the deck chair. Back inside his house, he rang the direct phone line of a high-ranking police officer based at the Martlesham headquarters of the Suffolk Constabulary.

At 11.00 AM, three hours after his phone call, there was a sharp knock on the front door of the mansion. Maurice looked over the top of his spectacles at the door. He dropped the broadsheet he was reading on the sofa and rose. Instead of making straight for the door, he walked up to the alcove between the grandfather clock and the front door. Set inside the alcove was an antique Georgian tambour desk. He pulled out a drawer in the desk, retrieved a Browning pistol from it, and moved to the door.

'Who goes there?' the old man growled with the gun in his right hand.

'Scotland Yard, we need to chat with Brigadier Maurice de Clovis,' a male voice replied from behind the closed door.

The puzzled Brigadier considered what he had heard for some seconds. The phone call to Suffolk Constabulary headquarters had ended with Deputy Chief Constable Bertie Capstick promising to have some detectives come down to the mansion the next day to take the old man's statement and pick up the letter from Paris.

Therefore, Maurice was not expecting any visit from the local Suffolk police that morning, not to mention one from the London Metropolitan Police.

'Okay, one moment, please!' He tucked the handgun into the waistband of his trouser and covered it with his shirt.

On the other side of the door, three plain-clothes detectives from London heard the click of a key turning inside the lock and the sound of two sets of bolts being pulled back. When the door opened, they came face to face with a spry, grey-haired man in a short sleeve shirt and khaki trousers.

Maurice surveyed the faces of his visitors in plain clothes, two men and a woman, all holding out their warrant cards.

The wiry ginger-haired man stepped forward. 'Sir, I'm Detective-Superintendent Victor Gardener and these are my colleagues, Detective-Inspector Alexander Parsons and Detective-Sergeant Anna O'Brien.'

Maurice reached out for the warrant card proffered by Victor. He spent a few seconds scrutinizing the insignia and the small full-face photograph on the card before returning it to the owner. 'It looks genuine,' the Brigadier remarked.

'It is genuine, sir,' Victor said softly, his eyes focussed nervously on the bulge in the old man's shirt near the waist. 'Do you have a license for that?' he asked finally.

The Brigadier smiled smugly, 'I am an ex-serviceman, young man. A true marine officer never gives up his side arm. Come in, please.' He stepped aside for his visitors to pass through the door into the foyer.

While the detectives waited patiently in the sitting room, the old man went into the alcove to lock the handgun inside the drawer of the tambour desk. After that, he announced, 'I am now going to put the kettle on in the kitchen. When I return, you will tell me what Scotland Yard detectives want with an old man in Ipswich.'

Twelve minutes later, as they sipped hot coffee around a long table in the dining room, Maurice de Clovis learnt that after his phone call to Martlesham,

Bertie Capstick had changed his mind about sending Suffolk police detectives to handle the matter. The Deputy Chief Constable had stumbled on the Interpol Red Alert Notice and decided to pass the old man's complaint to Scotland Yard, the headquarters of the London Metropolitan Police. From Scotland Yard, the word spread down to the small police station in South London where Victor, Anna and Alex had their offices.

'I know you haven't come in contact yet with any of these Nigerian fraudsters, but please have a look all the same,' Alex Parsons said, handing the ex-military man an A4-sized fax printout. 'Do you recognize any of these men in the photos?'

Maurice squinted at the colour pictures of three clean-shaven black men staring back at him from the sheet of paper. 'Nope, I have never seen any of them. But then, all of them look alike, don't they?'

An awkward moment of silence followed. Victor broke it. 'Well, you might want to keep an eye out. These Nigerian chaps are not just fraudsters; they are also vicious killers. They are responsible for the death of two Americans who had travelled to Nigeria. One death has been confirmed. The other is actually a missing person's case, but we have good reason to believe he was murdered, and then buried in a secret location. There was also the case of another American who committed suicide a couple of years ago. He was also defrauded by these fugitive criminals...'

'Always the Yanks...leave it to them to always eff things up,' Maurice cut in. 'How anybody can possibly fall for such nonsense, such "get-rich-quick" scams, is just beyond me.'

'Of course, this might be a tip of the iceberg,' Victor added cautiously, 'there could have been other scams that are unknown to us, the FBI and the Nigerian Police. Mister Suzmann may not be the only British victim of these criminals.'

'Ah, yes, the North London Jew...' Maurice stopped himself in time from expressing his inner thoughts on Harel Suzmann and his kind. Somehow, he had sensed that the detectives sitting across the table from him were not the right audience for his candid opinions. They were much younger and of a very different generation from him.

'Like I was saying,' Victor continued, 'there could be other victims that we don't know of. Their victims have nearly all been citizens of the United States and at least one Briton. We must stop them before they commit more crimes. We believe that they are behind the letter you received from Paris.'

'Good! The police in Paris can pick them up then,' Maurice remarked, passing the A4-sized sheet back to Alex Parsons.

'There is a Red Alert Notice for them. If they are seen anywhere in France, they will be picked up immediately. The problem is that they were able to enter Paris undetected and mail the letter to your address. How they got your home address is a mystery to everybody. These Nigerian chaps are clever. I don't think they will ever be casually picked up by any police force in Europe, and I dare say, the world. For all we know, they may have altered their appearance and travelling under false names and passports.'

'So what should we do? What do you want from me?' the ex-serviceman asked before sipping his black coffee.

His question was directed at Victor, but Alex provided the answer. Basically, the SCD6 detectives of the Metropolitan Police wanted to use him as bait to lure the Nigerian swindlers to London where they would be arrested. Maurice liked the idea and requested for a "battle plan". It was left to Anna' O Brien to give a detailed breakdown of the proposed sting operation.

The old man surprised everybody when he whipped out a notepad and started jotting down some of what Anna was explaining. At regular intervals, the ex-serviceman would interrupt Anna to point out certain flaws in the plan and suggest amendments. It was clear to the detectives that the old warrior was enjoying his newfound role as the ersatz commander of an imaginary Royal Marines commando unit.

By the time the meeting ended, Detective-Superintendent Victor Gardener was clearly impressed. The old man had not lost any of his military acumen.

CHAPTER **42**

JUNE 1994

PARIS, FRANCE

On the morning of 16th June, John Nwosu collected a blue envelope from the reception desk of *Hôtel Bastille Bleu*. Before he arrived to pick it up, the female receptionist had been wondering what to do with the envelope bearing an address block that read as follows:

ALHAJI TARIQ GUDANA
PERSONAL ASSISTANT
NIGERIAN PETROLEUM MINISTER
C/O: HOTEL BASTILLE BLEU
991 BLD RICHARD-LENOIR
75011 PARIS
FRANCE

Having gone through the computer records to confirm that no such foreign dignitary was a guest at the hotel or had booked a room for a future stay, the puzzled receptionist picked up the phone receiver to ring her supervisor for guidance. She was just in the process of dialling the number when the heavily bearded guest she knew as "Marcellus Obiango" came to the reception desk to ask if any letter had arrived from the UK for Alhaji Tariq Gudana.

She returned the phone receiver to its cradle and gazed warily at the guest. 'Yes sir, I have a letter addressed to a person by that name, but you are not him. How did...'

'Allow me to explain,' John cut in. 'I am a journalist with the *Nigerian Prime Observer Magazine*. The editor of the British-based magazine is the younger brother of Alhaji Tariq Gudana. He was the one who sent that letter from Ipswich in Southern England. I am supposed to pick it up here and hand-deliver it when I return to Nigeria.'

'Okay, but can I see some credentials,' the female receptionist said cautiously.

John smiled at the auburn-haired woman and proffered his fake press identity card. She scrutinized it for a few seconds and handed the letter over.

Back in his hotel room, he sank into the only available armchair while his men, sitting on the periphery of the double bed, looked on expectantly. Using the edge of a teaspoon handle as an improvised letter opener, he carefully slit the envelope open.

It took him three minutes to digest the contents of the handwritten letter from Ipswich. With a face beaming with smiles, he passed the letter to Adamu. 'He has agreed to meet me in the café near London Waterloo Station in a week's time. Guys, I told you this would work. We are on our way to making some good money from this old man.'

Adamu quickly went through the letter in stony silence. 'Boss, I have a bad feeling about this one,' he said, passing the letter to Eugene. 'A lot of things are wrong. He does not fit the profile of individuals we normally target. He is an old, wealthy, comfortable, ex-military man. There is nothing we can offer him that he doesn't already own. There is nothing for us to leverage. Doesn't seem like he is in debt or desperate for anything. Yes, he has responded to our letter, but that may well be a trap. What if he is trying to play us into the hands of the British police? I think we need to pause and consider if this whole thing is worth the risk.'

John waited patiently for Adamu to finish his expostulation before delivering a strident response. 'You have a bad feeling? Well, it is in your head. This senile old fool in England is no different from all the people we have conned. We are going ahead with this operation and that decision is final'— he paused to retrieve the letter from Eugene—'that old man is a piece of cake, trust me, guys.'

None of the men was impressed with their leader's bombast. Adamu made this clear to the gang leader while Eugene nodded gravely in agreement.

John sighed heavily. The men were still respectful in their disagreement with him, but that could quickly change to open mutiny, which would be a disaster. The plan would not work without their participation. He had to get them on his side.

Striking a conciliatory tone, he said, 'okay guys, I'll make you a deal'—he observed the men's facial expressions switch from skepticism to curiosity— 'you'll come to London with me and observe the meeting with the old man. If you are still unconvinced after our first meeting with him, then we will quit and go back to The Caymans. How about that?'

Adamu and Eugene paused to consider the proposition. John's inquiring eyes flicked from Adamu to Eugene and back. Moments later, both men nodded their agreement.

'Good, that is now settled,' the gang leader announced and went into the bathroom to take his morning shower. Adamu and Eugene rose to return to their own hotel rooms further down the corridor.

*****

When Detective-Inspector Ikenna Kodilinye landed at London Heathrow Airport in the afternoon of 21st June 1994, a wiry ginger-haired SCD6 detective, dressed in a black two-piece suit, was there to receive him.

It took forty-five minutes for the Nigerian detective to get through passport control, pick up his suitcase from baggage reclaim, pass customs, and enter the arrivals concourse where he was greeted by the besuited Victor Gardener.

'Nice to meet you again, Detective-Superintendent,' Ikenna said, shaking the hand proffered by the SCD6 detective.

'And you too. By the way, I'm now a D.C.S,' Victor said with a smile. The promotion from Superintendent to Chief Superintendent on the detective-ranking scale was already two months old.

Ikenna offered his belated congratulations. Moments later, he was outside the Terminal Four building of the airport, pulling his suitcase by its telescopic handle as Detective-Chief Superintendent (DCS) Victor Gardener led the way to the car park.

As Victor was out in the back, loading the suitcase into the boot of the unmarked police saloon car, Ikenna was busy peeling off the thick sweater he was wearing. He had forgotten that while UK was generally a cold place, warm to hot sunny weather did appear grudgingly for a few months each year. The month of June was one such month.

Victor's lips twitched knowingly when he saw Ikenna struggling out of the thick clothing. 'Nice weather, innit,' he remarked. 'If you stay in this country long enough, you will find that you need that piece of clothing and an overcoat.'

'Of course,' Ikenna blurted out with a look of mild embarrassment on his face as he walked behind the ginger-haired policeman.

'Okay, hop in, let's go,' Victor said as he opened the door to the driver's seat. He was about to get in when he noticed Ikenna standing behind him absent-mindedly. A look of bemusement appeared on his pale face for a brief moment then he suddenly realized the problem. 'In the UK, the passenger sits on the other side,' he explained with a smile.

'Oh yes, I nearly forgot,' Ikenna replied, suddenly remembering that he was in country where motorists drove vehicles from the front right-hand seat.

'So how is Nigeria?' Victor asked as soon as the car hit the motorway.

Ikenna adjusted himself on the front passenger seat and replied, 'fine, the weather here is even hotter than over there.'

'Really? Well, this weather is only here for a short while. After August, it is back to being chilly.'

'By the way, my boss, Chief Superintendent Cyrus Udeh sends his regards.'

Victor nodded and halted the car behind a long queue of vehicles. 'Shit!' he cursed under his breath. The traffic hold-up wasn't the only thing that piqued him. He resented the idea of having to drive to Heathrow to collect and babysit a copper from Africa. As far as he was concerned, only the Metropolitan Police should deal with the fraudsters as soon as they set foot in London. The criminals had defrauded a Briton on British soil. Therefore, they should be tried in English courts after arrest. There was no need for the Nigerian police to intervene in such a straightforward case.

That was exactly what Victor had said to his subordinate, Detective-Inspector Alex Parsons, who had opposed the idea of luring the fraudsters to the UK, preferring for Interpol and the French Judicial Police to be alerted to the presence of the criminals in *Hôtel Bastille Bleu.* Victor did not want Interpol or

French law enforcement authorities to get involved. Their involvement would mean the arrest and extradition of the swindlers from France to Nigeria, and therefore, no trial in the courts of the UK.

But Alex Parsons was not the only one who failed to see things Victor's way. Many senior police officers in the Metropolitan Police believed that the suspects, when arrested, should be sent to Nigeria for trial in Lagos. Forty-eight hours earlier, Deputy Assistant Commissioner (DAC) Peter Stanfields, head of the Economic & Specialist Crime Command (SCD6) had summoned Victor to his office for a meeting.

DAC Stanfields had allowed Victor to settle comfortably into a chair across the oak desk before telling him what he did not want to hear. The Nigerian Police Force had requested that one of their men be allowed to participate in the capture and extradition of the criminals.

'Extradition?' Victor had asked incredulously when his superior finished talking.

Stanfields nodded. 'Yes, the Nigerian authorities want those men home, to be tried in their courts in Lagos.'

'They committed the crime here in London. We should try them in our own courts!' Victor protested, upset that the opportunity to shine among his colleagues was about to be taken away from him, and given to the Nigerian clowns that called themselves a police force. 'They couldn't even catch a pickpocket to save their lives,' Victor would say much later to his subordinate, Anna O' Brien, after his meeting with Stanfields.

But during the meeting, Stanfields had tried in vain to explain to his subordinate why the extradition would happen. 'Well, my dear Victor, the criminals also killed two Americans, and in the case of the late Mister Steinberg, his diary indicates that part of the scam did take place in the United States. Yet, the American authorities are happy for these murderous fraudsters to be tried in Nigerian courts. In fact, senior FBI officials have actually communicated their wishes on this matter to me verbally by phone and in writing. They want those men transferred to Nigeria as soon as we have them.'

Stanfield's statement intensified DCS Victor Gardener's anger. He disliked the idea of Americans dictating to Scotland Yard. But it was no use arguing with a superior anxious to please the Yanks and the Nigerians.

'We are expecting Detective-Inspector Kodilinye of the Nigeria Police Force and you are going to pick him up from Heathrow on the twenty-first of this month, two days from now. And when he arrives, you must treat him with the utmost respect, if you please.'

The DCS wanted to protest, but Stanfields pre-empted him, 'that would be all, Victor.'

Victor nodded and left the office. After work, five hours later, he went straight to the pub across the street to pour out his heart to his subordinates, Anna and Alex, over a bottle of beer...

The black Vauxhall Omega sedan, bearing Ikenna Kodilinye as its sole passenger, manoeuvred past the traffic bottleneck and sped towards Acton Town, West London.

'We are expecting your folks to cross the English Channel from France in two days time. Once they set foot in the meeting location, we will seize them,' Victor announced.

Ikenna nodded. But then, the criminals were not his "folks". He asked the Vauxhall driver a question. 'Do you think they would suspect that we are unto them?'

Victor disliked the word, "we". The sting operation underway was solely a British affair. Though courteous, the SCD6 detective still considered the Nigerian policeman to be an interloper.

Victor shook his head in response to Ikenna's question and applied the brakes to avoid hitting a Labrador that had suddenly appeared on the road, three feet from the car. 'Crazy dog!' the driver hissed as the dog scurried across the road, tail behind its legs.

Ikenna suppressed a smile.

'Do you normally get a lot of stray dogs on your streets?' Victor asked at length, as the car gained speed once again.

'Oh yes, a good number of them.'

'What do you do about them?'

Ikenna shrugged. 'Nothing... sometimes, the environmental authorities shoot them to prevent rabies. But most times, they roam the street freely.'

'Fair enough,' Victor said without meaning it. A moment of silence followed.

'So where are they meeting?' Ikenna asked, changing the subject.

Victor made a left turn into a side street. 'This is a short cut to avoid the traffic,' he explained before responding to Ikenna's question. 'You asked about "they"?'

'Yes, the fraudsters. Where are they meeting?'

'Oh, in a café opposite Waterloo Station.'

'Waterloo Station?'

'Yes, it is a train station in South London.'

There was momentary silence. Then Victor spoke again. 'I'll take you to see my superior, DAC Peter Stanfields. After that, I'll take you to your hotel.'

Ikenna thanked him.

Victor flashed a smile and replied, 'it's a pleasure,' and he meant it.

*****

At about the same time Victor was driving his passenger to SCD6 headquarters in Southwest London, John and his associates were sitting around a table in a rooftop restaurant overlooking the Eiffel Tower, the greatest landmark in the city of Paris.

'Okay boys. We have two days left. I think we should ask for five million pounds as soon as we hook our man, Clovis,' John rattled out.

'Boss, there is no way that man will agree to give us five million pounds. The old man will simply walk away and the entire plan would collapse,' Adamu expostulated. 'We have never asked any of our previous targets for that much.'

'I think he will pay it if he believes that our proposal is real,' John replied confidently.

Eugene laughed. 'Boss, what makes you think the old man wouldn't suffer a heart attack once you quote that figure to him?'

John brushed aside Eugene's rhetorical question and repeated, 'I think he will pay the amount if he thinks our story is on the level. C'mon guys, that old man was willing to pay sixty million pounds for a grotesque painting by a long dead Spanish eccentric. Why would he not pay a mere five million in exchange for thirty percent cut of an oil deal worth two hundred and fifty million pounds?'

Adamu and Eugene thought about it for a few moments before conceding that their boss had made a good point.

John smiled triumphantly. The men were slowly coming around to his point of view. 'You guys are not going to observe. I want you to participate in the meeting. I'll tell the old man that you are my bodyguards.' John reached for the bottle of wine at the centre of the table.

Adamu laughed. 'Who have ever heard of a bodyguard participating in a confidential meeting?'

John noted his oversight. He wanted his men to join him at the table with Brigadier Maurice de Clovis so that they would see for themselves that swindling the ex-marine officer would be a cakewalk. But that would not be possible if they were mere bodyguards.

By convention, bodyguards stood guard some distance away from the protected boss whenever he was in a private meeting. They were not supposed to sit in on the meeting.

'Okay, you are right,' John said as he stroked the neck of the chilled bottle of wine. 'Eugene is Deputy Petroleum Minister and you, Adamu, would be introduced as the Accountant-General of the Federation. Clovis would learn your indispensable role as the man in charge of concealing our two hundred and fifty million pounds.'

'Boss, there is something else you are missing,' Eugene said with a grave look on his face. 'The old man had seen your face before. And when he saw it, you were Marcellus Obiango, an Equatorial Guinean journalist working for a Nigerian publication. Now, how are you going to say that you are a Nigerian citizen called Tariq Gudana working for the Nigerian Federal Minister of Petroleum?'

John waved a hand of dismissal. 'The Brigadier is an old man. I doubt he would remember our very brief encounter, which did not last more six minutes. Mind you, the Christie's auction happened two months ago. In any case, I doubt he will recognize me with the trimmed beard, haircut, and eye glasses.'

Adamu nodded to indicate that he agreed with John. Eugene did not argue.

'Boss, what about weapons? I think we should take them with us to London... just in case.'

John considered Adamu's suggestion for a few minutes. The gang had smuggled Browning pistols into France hidden under the false bottom of a metallic briefcase. At the customs area of *Aéroport de Paris-Charles-de-Gaulle*, a search of that briefcase by a French custom official had revealed only the equipment of a semi-professional photographer— one Canon EOS-5 camera, one 300mm-telephoto-zoom lens, four D-cell batteries and twelve canisters of unused 35mm-film rolls.

Throughout the perfunctory search, it never occurred to the Frenchman to check for the existence of a false bottom. After poking around for four minutes, he waved the men through to the arrivals concourse.

An hour before the swindlers left Grand Cayman for Europe, the same briefcase had set off the metal detector alarm at Owen Roberts International Airport, prompting airport security officers to conduct a check. The Cayman airport officials had failed to spot the existence of the false bottom.

Believing that only the aluminium skin of the briefcase and other metal bits within the camera equipment had set off the alarm, the airport security officers at Owen Roberts International had allowed the gangsters—posing as Equatorial Guinean photojournalists— to board the flight to France.

John had never been a fan of smuggling firearms into planes. The risk of being caught with such items during a security search at the airport was certainly not worth the effort, he thought.

Adamu and Eugene disagreed with their boss. If the long arm of the law began to approach, both men wanted the option of shooting their way to safety or die trying.

'Sure, we can take the weapons with us,' the gang leader replied with a thin smile. 'Hopefully, airport security people at Heathrow would be as relaxed as their French counterparts.'

The answer, even with its implicit sarcasm, was a great relief to Adamu who had anticipated the same opposition he had faced when he first suggested that pistols be brought clandestinely to Europe for purposes of self-protection.

John finally uncorked the bottle and wine foamed from its mouth. 'Okay then, with that settled, would you guys care to join me for a pre-celebratory drink?'

Eugene and Adamu responded by reaching for their wine glasses.

CHAPTER **43**

JUNE 1994

WATERLOO, SOUTHEAST LONDON, UK

On 23rd June, at exactly 3.30 PM, the retired Royal Marines officer stopped in front of the busy terrace of a café across the road from Waterloo Station. Luckily, he was able to find an unoccupied table and quickly took a seat behind it. A young lady wearing an apron, with the name of the café emblazoned on it, came to take his order. He asked for a jug of coffee, two mugs, and some croissants. When the young barista disappeared, he surveyed his surroundings.

Nearly all the tables on the terrace and inside the café were occupied by teeming numbers of white-collar people on lunch break from nearby places of work. Therefore, the mode of dressing all around Maurice de Clovis was predominantly formal.

The old man's eyes panned around the terrace, searching for any group of customers that looked out of place, trying to isolate the undercover police officers from the rest of the crowd. DCS Victor Gardener had promised that undercover policemen would be there in the café, ready to swoop on the criminals, when the time was right. The barista soon returned with the jug and the mugs and the old man gave up his vain attempt to spot the detectives hiding in plain sight.

'They are bloody good,' he murmured to himself before sipping the hot drink. None of the people he had seen in the café looked like a law enforcement officer to him. Before now, he had held the view that spotting plain-clothes police officers— including ones in the deepest cover— would be a piece of cake for a person of his calibre. However, five minutes of watching people come and go from the café had changed his mind.

He had just finished his first cup of coffee and was going to pour another from the jug, when he heard the shatter of chinaware behind him. He turned around. On the table behind him, were two men and two women dressed formally. They were staring sombrely at the ground between his chair and their table. Clovis gazed at what they were looking at. Pieces of porcelain that was once a teacup lay in a pool of spilled tea.

The young barista reappeared with a rag, a broom and a dustpan to clear the mess. As she settled to sweep the wet fragments into the dustpan, the pale-faced young lady responsible for the accident began an effusive apology.

The barista nodded impatiently, but said nothing. The fragments were swept up and discarded and the ground mopped. Then a new teacup was supplied to the table as replacement. The remorseful customers thanked the barista for her troubles.

Five minutes later, Maurice noticed three bespectacled black men enter the café terrace. They were lightly bearded. Their eyes darted round the room before zeroing on the old man. The Brigadier rose from his chair to receive them. He did not recognise the light-skinned black man he had spoken to after the Christie's auction eight weeks earlier. John's trimmed beard was a far cry from the heavy beard he wore in his previous trip to London.

'Hi, Brigadier de Clovis,' John smiled, extending his hand to the old man.

'Hello, Alhaji Tariq, I presume... I wasn't expecting your associates,' Maurice de Clovis replied, shaking the fraudster's hand. The old man was lying. Although the Paris letter did state that "Tariq" would be having a one-on-one meeting with the retired marine officer, Detective-Chief Superintendent (DCS) Victor Gardener had told the retiree to expect two more men to accompany the fraudster. 'They usually operate as a group,' the detective of the London Metropolitan Police had warned, the day before.

'Sorry. I didn't give you forewarning,' John said, smiling. 'These are my associates: Mallam Adamkus Challas, the Deputy Petroleum Minister and Alhaji Musdapher Abdullahi, the Accountant-General of the Nigerian Federation.'

The beared men behind John stepped forward and shook hands with the old man. At that point, two white men and a black man stepped into the terrace. They started walking slowly towards the backs of the criminals.

As he shook hands with Eugene, Maurice's eyes gazed beyond the shoulder of the criminal at the three men, dressed in T-shirts and jeans trousers, approaching. He recognized the white men as Victor and Alex. He did not recognize the Nigerian detective walking abreast of Victor and Alex.

John swung round and came face to face with the three detectives in T-shirts and jeans.

'You are all under arrest!' Victor barked.

The men and women, dressed in business suits, on the table behind Maurice de Clovis jumped to their feet, pulled out revolvers and poised them at the gangsters. The retired marine officer was mildly surprised when he realised it was the same group that had broken a teacup earlier.

Given their possession of firearms, the old man deduced that they were from the Specialist Firearms Command (SO19) of the Metropolitan Police. But why deploy firearm officers? he asked himself. Then the answer dawned on him. *The gangsters were probably armed and nobody thought to warn him in advance.*

The Brigadier was outraged. He thought of his trusty firearm, currently locked inside his antique tambour desk, miles away in Ipswich. Mister Gardener would get an earful for not giving an advance warning, Maurice thought; although, he understood why he never got the heads-up. Victor had not mentioned that the criminals might be armed because he was afraid the retired marine officer would bring his own gun to the meeting.

Maurice was violently yanked out of his angry thoughts when he felt two strong hands grab him by the scruff of his neck and drag him across the table, overturning the jug and a mug, spilling coffee all over the place. Seconds later, he saw himself been pulled towards "Tariq Gudana". The pulling only stopped when his crimson face was only inches away from the caramel-skinned face of his assailant.

The frightened old man gazed at that face and finally recognized it. 'I know you! It's you from the auction at Christie's, a few months ago... You black bastard... let me go now!'

While John was busy manhandling the old man, Adamu and Eugene threw themselves on the floor and rolled over, firing several rounds from their Browning pistols.

Three bullets hit Victor. One smashed into the shin of his left leg while the other two buried themselves on the thigh of his right leg. A bullet from the volley of gunshots fired by the criminals hit Alex in his left arm. One male undercover SO19 officer took a bullet to the chest. His Smith & Wesson revolver fell to the ground and discharged a round.

Pandemonium broke out in the terrace and inside the busy café. A stampede ensued inside the café as customers squeezed out onto the terrace, then to the road.

Ikenna, who was there to observe not to affect the arrest, snatched the undercover detective's gun from the ground. But he couldn't shoot back because screaming customers, running helter-skelter, blocked his line of fire.

The rest of the undercover cops were prevented from reaching their fallen colleague as they were surrounded by crowds of customers trampling over each other to flee the café. Amidst the chaos, the fraudsters and their hostage, Maurice de Clovis, disappeared from the terrace.

When the café cleared of people, Ikenna and the undercover SO19 officers attended to the wounded policemen. Police vans halted in front of the terrace and disgorged several uniformed police officers bearing long guns. Some of the uniforms secured the perimeter around the café while the other surged into the building.

Five minutes later, a wailing ambulance pulled up in front of the terrace. The siren went silent and six paramedics emerged to attend to the three wounded men.

Ikenna dropped into a squatting position next to the paramedic who was cutting through the legs of Victor's blood-soaked trousers.

The injured SCD6 detective—whose face had assumed a pallid complexion—smiled weakly when he saw Ikenna. Despite being in excruciating pain, he managed to say, 'you have no power of arrest here, no right to bear firearms in the UK.'

A rueful smile broke out on Ikenna's face. His eyes flicked to the paramedic attending to Victor's legs. 'Take good care of him,' he instructed the paramedic and rose to his feet to leave.

Victor looked up at the Nigerian detective. In a strained voice, he said, 'those vicious bastards are from your country. So I guess we can bend the rules a bit. Just bring back the gun in one piece.'

Ikenna nodded, turned around, and began to make his way from the terrace into the café building. As he slithered through overturned tables, broken chairs and shards of smashed porcelain on the floor inside the café, he heard a commotion somewhere in the building followed by four gunshots. He crashed through a door leading to the café's kitchen and came face to face with a bloodied corpse surrounded by three policemen bearing Heckler & Koch MP5 carbines. Under filtered light, Ikenna moved closer to the corpse and identified it moments later as that of Adamu Esan. 'What happened?' he asked without taking his eyes off the dead body.

'He fired at us so we put him down,' one policeman said as he held a bloodstained white handkerchief to the side of his head that had been grazed by a bullet.

Three baristas cowering behind a cupboard emerged and fled the scene.

'Where are the others?'

'They went that way,' a police constable replied, pointing to a metal door, four feet. The Lagos detective asked the wounded policeman to seek treatment from the paramedics in the terrace. The wounded man removed the walkie-talkie clipped to his belt, pressed a button and started speaking into it quickly.

Inside the dimly lit storage room filled with empty cartons and jute sacks of coffee beans, Maurice de Clovis felt the cold muzzle of a pistol being held against his lower abdomen. Any false move, Eugene had warned, would result in his being shot immediately. For the first time in his life, the Brigadier felt helpless. A bunch of crooks were holding him hostage and there was nothing he could do about it.

The door at the far end of the storage room suddenly burst open and the moving silhouette of man materialized in the doorway for brief moment.

John Nwosu fired his semi-automatic. But by then, the silhouette had disappeared. There was a sudden movement near a floor-to-ceiling shelving unit filled with crockery. John fired again. A bullet hit a jute sack, puncturing it. Coffee beans started pouring out from the clean hole in that sack.

'Don't make a sound,' John hissed at Maurice. Eugene poked the the old man's ribcage with the handgun to drive home the message. Moments later, John rose from his crouching position next to Eugene and the retired Brigadier. With his Browning pistol poised, he began to move slowly towards the centre of the dimly lit room.

As the gang leader reached the centre of the room, the silhouette reappeared from behind the shelving unit and fired two bullets. The gang leader felt a burning sensation on his stomach and left arm as hot lead tore into his skin. He screamed in pain and fell on the floor.

The silhouette stepped forward and fired one more bullet into the screaming swindler and the room fell silent.

Two more silhouettes ran through the doorway and into the dark room. One of the entrants pressed a button on the wall switch and the flourescent tubes fixed to the ceiling came on, flooding the room in bright white light. The silhouette standing over John's inert body turned into Ikenna. The other silhouettes were Metropolitan Police officers.

They glanced at the body sprawled on the floor and then started towards the Nigerian detective, eyeing him suspiciously.

He read their thoughts and said calmly, 'he fired at me first. It was self-defence.'

The constables stopped some inches from him, their eyes darting about the large room. 'Where is the hostage and remaining suspect?' one of them asked Ikenna.

Before Ikenna could answer, Maurice de Clovis rose from behind a tall pile of jute bags. The muzzle of a handgun was poised at his head. Behind that handgun, Eugene was shaking and growling. 'Back off or I'll blow out his brains. I swear to God, I'll do it,' he snarled, jabbing the old man's head with the semi-automatic.

The two constables dropped their carbines and raised their hands in the air. 'Calm down. We are willing to cooperate with you, just let Brigadier de Clovis go,' they requested.

Eugene's eyes flicked from the British policemen to Ikenna.

The Lagos detective was glaring at him with his revolver still pointing downwards at John's corpse.

'What are you waiting for?' Eugene asked, alarmed. 'Drop your gun or I will waste the old man.'

Ikenna remained unmoved. The British policemen turned furiously to the detective. 'What the devil do you think you are doing? Do as he says, drop the gun,' one constable shouted at him.

But Ikenna did not budge. At that point, five more constables, armed with Heckler & Koch MP5 carbines, were seen approaching the doorway from a distance. They were wearing bulletproof vests with the words "Metropolitan Police" emblazoned on them.

Eugene panicked and was about to squeeze the trigger of his pistol, when three gunshots rang out in quick succession.

Maurice de Clovis was splattered with blood, brain matter and cerebro-spinal fluid. He screamed as Eugene's hand at the scruff of his neck slackened.

Ikenna stepped forward with the revolver as Eugene's lifeless body hit the ground with a dull thud.

Maurice rushed towards one of the constables while Ikenna stood over the twitching body. The back of the fraudster's head was open. A mixture of brain matter and blood seeped out of the gaping hole and into the carpet. The lifeless eyes and the frozen expression on Eugene's face conveyed the shock he was in when the first bullet hit his forehead. He was already dead when the other bullet went through the palm of his right hand.

'Are you mad? You could have gotten the old man killed!' a voice shouted behind Ikenna.

Ikenna spurn round to face the constable that had urged him to obey Eugene's instruction by dropping the gun. The Nigerian's lips twitched.

'Oh, you find that funny!' the constable exclaimed. 'We don't do things like that in a hostage situation!'

'My way is much better. The hostage-taker was going to pull the trigger. I saved the life of the Brigadier,' Ikenna retorted and walked past the constable, heading towards the tumultuous atmosphere forming at the doorway of the storage room.

A wall of policemen stood in front of the doorway, barring a small crowd of reporters and photographers from getting to the scene of the swindlers' last stand. When the policemen saw Ikenna, they made way for him to emerge from the room.

A sizeable number of the reporters and photographers broke away from rest of the crowd and went after him, throwing all sorts of questions in his way.

'Are you a policeman?' one blonde female reporter asked.

Ikenna remained silent.

'We heard you are with the Nigeria Police Force. Can you confirm that?' a man holding out a minitape recorder asked.

Silence.

'You fired a gun at a suspect on British soil. Don't you know that it is illegal? Please comment.'

'No comment. All of you should go away!'

The reporters kept throwing questions at Ikenna, none of which was answered, as he moved silently into the spacious kitchen area, where a police cordon had been set up around Adamu's body.

The journalists followed him out to the terrace and then gave up. At that point, it had become clear that the Nigerian policeman could not be persuaded to talk. So they turned around and began making their way back to the narrow corridor to rejoin the press crowd adjacent the doorway of the storage room.

Ikenna found Alex Parsons amidst the broken chairs, overturned tables, smashed chinaware and spilt coffee and tea in the terrace of café.

With his heavily bandaged left arm in a sling round his neck, the SCD6 detective was leaning against an overturned table. He smiled at the approaching Nigerian. 'How are you doing mate? I heard you finally got your men. And you used one of our own revolvers to do it, which is a bit of a problem.'

A male paramedic emerged from the ambulance parked next to the terrace and began to walk towards the policemen.

'Yes,' Ikenna replied wearily. 'I have been told that it is illegal to do so... although, an innocent life was saved.'

'That is not the point,' Alex snapped. 'We have rules and procedures. You can't just...'

'We have to go now,' the male paramedic cut in. 'Your wound requires further attention at the hospital.'

Alex waved him off and turned back to Ikenna. 'I heard the shots. So I presume they are dead, right?'

Ikenna nodded and asked a question he knew the answer to. 'Where is D.C.S Gardener?'

Alex winced and touched the bandaged arm. 'He is in the hospital,' he replied in a strained voice.

The paramedic examined the bloodstained wrap of bandages. 'Mister Parsons, we have to go to the hospital straightaway. These stitches won't hold for much longer.'

Alex threw his good right arm over the neck of the paramedic and they plodded towards the ambulance.

'Good bye mate, I'm sure the higher-ups in Scotland Yard will be in touch about that revolver,' Alex called out without turning around to see Ikenna's reaction. Moments later, the ambulance driver waved at the Nigerian through the window and drove way.

*****

Twenty-five minutes after the three swindlers were killed, the uniformed personnel of the London Metropolitan Police finally managed to expel all the reporters from the crime scene and secure the perimeter around the terrace and the café building with white-and-blue barrier tape.

It was now 4.10 PM in the evening and the warm winds that blew in the afternoon had been supplanted by a cool breeze. Outside the crime scene and several feet from the white-and-blue police tape, the Nigerian detective watched as groups of Metropolice police investigators dressed in white forensic suits went through the police cordon. He was still trying to guess how long it would take the Nigerian Police Force to catch up to the level of their UK counterparts when his thoughts were interrupted by a sound. He turned around and suddenly he was facing a tall blue-eyed man in the uniform of the London Metropolitan Police.

'You are alright?' DAC Peter Stanfields asked the Nigerian policeman.

Ikenna replied that he was okay, though he was feeling tired. He asked Stanfields about Victor. The senior Metropolitan Police officer replied that the Detective-Chief Superintendent would live to use his legs again. The bullets had missed the bones of his leg, only passing through flesh.

Within minutes, a swarm of reporters and photographers surrounded Stanfields and Ikenna. They fired questions at them as camera bulbs flashed intermittently.

A group of constables broke through the small crowd to rescue the senior police officer and the visiting Nigerian detective. Stanfields and Ikenna were hurriedly guided into a patrol car.

Once the Vauxhall Astra, painted in the liveries of the Metropolitan Police, was in motion, the head of SCD6 turned to the Nigerian cop and said, 'my dear detective, I was briefed on what happened thirty minutes ago. I must say that

some of the details were quite troubling. First, you picked up a revolver belonging
to one of our firearms officer and used it in the café multiple times. Secondly, I
got a disturbing report about the way you handled one of the hoodlums, the one
called John. I must say...'

'It was self-defence,' Ikenna interjected defensively.

The blue eyes staring back regarded him for a few seconds and then smiled
knowingly. 'It's quite difficult to claim self-defence, my dear detective. You shot
him again when he was lying on the ground, already incapacitated by the two
bullets you had fired earlier.'

Ikenna was about to speak again, but Stanfields quickly cut him off. 'I know
that is how you do things back in your country, but here we do things differently.
In any case, that is your cup of tea not ours. The most important thing is that you
finally got your fugitives, albeit in body bags.'

The Nigerian detective heaved a sigh of relief. The senior Metropolitan
Police officer had just signalled that the matter would not be pursued any further.

'A sordid affair, I must say... but one that must now be put behind us. I guess
that saves the Nigerian taxpayers the cost of a lengthy trial.'

Ikenna agreed with Stanfields completely. He did not care about the fuss
over the police code of conduct. He was relieved that the men that had made his
job a nightmare for fourteen months were finally gone forever. He knew there
were accolades waiting for him back home in Nigeria. That alone pleased him.

THE END

IKENNA KODILINYE WILL RETURN IN "THE
SECTION BREAKERS"

BOOKS PENDING RELEASE

OUR MAN IN SOVIET EAST BERLIN

A collection of five novellas featuring African spy, political and crime stories, some of which are loosely based on real-life events that occurred in the cold war era of the 1970s and 1980s. The themes of espionage, criminality and political conflict running through these stories involving Africans are set in countries that no longer exist such as East Germany, Rhodesia and Biafra as well as in countries that still exist, namely Nigeria, Ghana, United Kingdom and Poland.

THE SECTION BREAKERS

It is the early 2000s. Democracy has since supplanted military dictatorship as the system of government in Nigeria. More importantly, the internet, which made its first appearance in the country in 1995, is also thriving. With it comes a gale of internet-based scams, which has the non-tech savvy Nigeria Police Force scrambling to keep up. Detective Ikenna Kodilinye is put in charge of a special taskforce set up to deal with this unfamiliar wave of electronic crimes. This novel is a direct sequel to **The Grifter's Razor**.

A THANK YOU NOTE

Thank you for reading this novel. I hope you enjoyed it. Please do not forget to leave a review on the website of the retailer from which you purchased **The Grifter's Razor**. If you would like to be notified when new books are released, please follow the sign-up instructions on my **Stay-Up-To-Date** page.